RED AND BLACK

A NEW TRANSLATION
BACKGROUNDS AND SOURCES
CRITICISM

➤➤ A NORTON CRITICAL EDITION ➤➤

STENDHAL

RED AND BLACK

A NEW TRANSLATION
BACKGROUNDS AND SOURCES
CRITICISM

➤➤➤◀◀◀

Translated and Edited by

ROBERT M. ADAMS

UNIVERSITY OF CALIFORNIA AT LOS ANGELES

W · W · NORTON & COMPANY · INC · New York

ISBN 0 393 04251 0 Cloth Edition

ISBN 0 393 09821 4 Paper Edition

COPYRIGHT © 1969 BY W. W. NORTON & COMPANY, INC.

Library of Congress Catalog Card No. 67–16619

PRINTED IN THE UNITED STATES OF AMERICA

9 0

Contents

v

Foreword

Fascination with Stendhal needn't be explained, and perhaps can't be. Yet one probably ought to mistrust it. Stendhal survived splendidly his years of neglect; whether he can make it through the snowstorms of modern criticism and scholarship is still a moot question. The Happy Few are now so many, so industrious (and, if they try to keep up with the thundering flood of scholarship, so bowed-down) that they may soon be known as the Miserable Innumerable.

The cure for this ancient complaint is of course just to bypass the scholarship and go back to renew one's friendship with the author in his text. There may be writers who demand to be read in variorum editions, under the shadow of the bibliographies, with serried admonitory critics staring over one's shoulder—but *ce cher Stendhal* is not one of them. He is best encountered, I should think, in a well-heated flat overlooking the Luxembourg, as late winter gives way to early spring, with an occasional interlude of music by Rossini and/or Cimarosa, and a glass of dry white wine at the end of each session. But of course we must all settle for something less than perfection. This translation has been prepared in Ithaca, New York, and South Chicago, Illinois.

Feeling, though, that the way to make the reader really free of apparatus is to answer his questions, not ignore them, I have exercised some deliberate pedantry on the footnotes. Stendhal was fond of *petits faits vrais*, a good reader of Stendhal is fond of them too, and it may be that of all secondary materials they provide most help for a reader at the cost of least distraction. So I have been profuse at the foot of the page. Thus even the reader ideally situated in his Luxembourg flat should not be haunted as he reads by too many unanswered questions of detail. But if the notes, instead of moving the novel forward, threaten to interfere with its action, the reader is implored to forget about them. Most of them aim only to put the modern Anglo-Saxon in possession of information that was commonplace to a Parisian reader of 1831. As for the critical texts in the back of the book, I don't think I deprecate them, or say anything of which their authors would not vigorously approve, in suggesting that they be saved till one has savored the full text of the novel. The novel does not need them; only, after it has produced its own effects, they may serve to enrich and diversify the pleasant process of meditation, reflection, and retrospective rearrangement.

For preliminary translations of the critical selections by Prévost, Poulet, Richard, Lampedusa, and the *Gazette des Tribunaux,* the editor is indebted to Mr. Robert Richardson; final responsibility for the translations, however, is his own. The editorial staff at W. W. Norton have been, as usual, cooperation personified.

ROBERT M. ADAMS

The Text of
Red and Black

A Note on the Text

The present translation was made from the 1960 edition prepared for Classiques Garnier by the late, great Henri Martineau. Only one edition of the *Rouge* was published during Stendhal's life (by Levavasseur, 1831), and no manuscript survives; M. Martineau was editing the text for the fourth time (previous editions for Bossard, 1925; Le Divan, 1927; and La Pléiade, 1932). All this should make for a relatively straightforward text. Still, a modest problem remains. Before his death Stendhal made marginal annotations in a published copy of the novel, known as the Bucci copy, from its owner, Signor Clodoveo Bucci of Civitavecchia. In addition, two posthumous editions of the *Rouge* (that published by Hetzel in 1846 and that of Lévy in 1854) were supervised by Stendhal's good friend and literary executor Romain Colomb. They contain various additions to, and modifications of, the 1831 text. The problem raised by all these variants is exacerbated by the fact that they cannot be accepted or rejected wholesale; it is a matter of the editor's individual judgment with regard to each individual change. Some of the Bucci corrections really and patently are Stendhal's afterthoughts and improvements. Some, however, are the author's idle comments and scribblings on his own fiction; they may indicate, for example, a general wish that he had done thus or so in a particular passage, but they offer no basis for emending the text. Similarly with the Hetzel and Lévy editions; Colomb made on his own initiative a great many moderate changes, mostly of verb tenses and pronoun references, in order to present his friend's work in what he considered its best light; but he made here and there a few other changes, for which it is evident he had some manuscript authority. According to his lights, and those of the day, he was a responsible editor and would not have revamped text or altered epigraphs (as in II, 6) without some sort of warrant from his author. So here too the editor must pick and choose.

As all these variants are recorded at large in the footnotes of the 1960 Martineau (Classiques Garnier) edition, I have not encumbered my text or apparatus by reproducing them *in extenso*. Where minor changes seemed both authentic and of literary advantage, I incorporated them silently, sometimes using an alternative reading merely to color the English equivalent. (For example, when Julien after long pleading triumphs over Mme. de Rênal's renascent virtue, in Book I, Chapter 30, the text says his reward, obtained thus by art, *"ne fut plus qu'un plaisir."* The Bucci copy substitutes for *plaisir* the word *triomphe*. Running the two notions of "pleasure" and "complacency" together, one gets an English equivalent like "gratification.") Where the variants were more extensive (these instances are all from the Bucci copy), I supplied them within the identifying boundaries of square brackets.

Contents of *Red and Black*

Book I

Book II

Red and Black:[1]
Chronicle of 1830

Editor's Note[2]

This work was about to appear when the great events of July came along to give all our thoughts a turn away from the free play of imagination. We have reason to suppose the following pages were written in 1827.

Book I

Truth, bitter truth.
—Danton[3]

Chapter 1

A SMALL TOWN

Put thousands together
Less bad,
But the cage less gay.
—Hobbes[4]

The little town of Verrières must be one of the prettiest in the Franche-Comté. Its white houses with their steep, red tile roofs spread across a hillside, the folds of which are outlined by clumps of thrifty chestnut trees. The Doubs flows a couple of hundred feet below the town's fortifications, built long ago by the Spaniards and now fallen into ruins.[5]

---

1. "Chronicle" implies a historical document; 1830 is the year of the great bourgeois revolution (the July days) during which the Bourbon regime (which since the Restoration of 1815 had comprised two brief kings, Louis XVIII and Charles X) was expelled and replaced by the bourgeois monarchy of Louis-Philippe. Stendhal's novels are carefully placed in time; *Armance,* for instance, is a novel of the early reaction; the *Rouge* (as our present novel will be called in these notes) of the moment of insurrectional imbalance; while *Lucien Leuwen* deals with the doldrum days after the liberal "triumph."

2. This little disclaimer, like the more elaborate ones prefixed to the *Life of Henry Brulard* (henceforth, in these notes, simply *Brulard*), is pure piffle; the novel was written in 1829–30, as Stendhal explicitly said on several occasions.

3. Danton was a revolutionary leader of rude and turbulent energy, guillotined by Robespierre in 1794; the epigraph is in his spirit but has not been located among his writings.

4. The quotation from Hobbes is imaginary, but the attribution invokes a hard-minded cynic.

5. The Franche-Comté is a province in eastern France bounded on the north by

1

Verrières is flanked on the north by a lofty mountain, one of the spurs of the Jura. As soon as it grows cold in October, the ragged peaks of Verra are covered with snow. A brook which drops from the mountain-passes through Verrières before falling into the Doubs provides power for a number of sawmills; it is a simple industry and yields a certain prosperity for a fair number of the inhabitants, who are peasants rather than bourgeois. Still, the sawmills are not what has made this little town rich. The manufacture of so-called Mulhouse cotton prints is responsible for the general affluence that, since the fall of Napoleon, has resulted in new façades for almost all the houses of Verrières.

Scarcely inside the town, one is stunned by the racket of a roaring machine, frightful in its appearance. Twenty ponderous hammers, falling with a crash which makes the street shudder, are lifted for each new stroke by the power of a water wheel. Every one of these hammers makes, every day, I don't know how many thousand nails. The workmen are pretty, fresh-faced girls; they slip little slivers of iron into place beneath the sledge hammers, which promptly transform them into nails. A primitive factory like this provides one of those sights that most surprise the traveler as he enters for the first time the mountains separating France from Switzerland. If, when he gets into Verrières, the traveler asks who owns that handsome nail factory which deafens everyone on the main street, he will be told, in drawling tones: *Oh, that? It's the mayor's.*

And now let the traveler pause a few minutes in this main street of Verrières which rises from the bank of the Doubs to the peak of the hill; it's a hundred to one that he will see somewhere along it a big man looking busy and important.

The minute he appears, every hat is lifted. His hair is gray, and he is dressed in gray. He wears the ribbons of several orders; his features are impressive, his nose aquiline, and, all in all, his appearance does not fail of a certain regularity: at first glance one even finds that it combines, with the dignity of the town mayor, that sort of ingratiation still possible in a man of forty-eight or fifty years. But shortly the visiting Parisian is struck with a certain air of self-satisfaction, perhaps of sufficiency, combined with something limited and unimaginative. One feels in the end that the talent of

---

Lorraine and on the south by Switzerland. After a turbulent medieval career as a semi-independent faction of the duchy of Burgundy, it became, early in the sixteenth century, tributary to Spain, but was captured for France by Louis XIV about two hundred years later. There are several little towns called Verrières in the valley of the Doubs (pronounced Dou), a river running close to the northern border of the Franche-Comté; but Stendhal took nothing from their various realities. Verrières has a few marks of a diminished Grenoble, Stendhal's native town (he said it was for him like the memory of a violent indigestion), but in reality Grenoble is 150 miles to the south of the Doubs, and Verrières is largely imaginary.

this man is confined to exacting every penny owing to him, and paying his own debts at the last possible minute.

Such is the mayor of Verrières, M. de Rênal. Having walked solemnly down the street, he enters the town hall and disappears from the view of the traveler. But, a hundred feet further on, if our traveler continues his stroll, he will see a fine house and, through an iron grating next to the house, magnificent gardens. Beyond, the broken horizon formed by the Burgundian hills seems outlined on purpose to give delight to the eye. This view makes the traveler forget the pestilent atmosphere of petty financial worries in which he has been close to stifling.

He learns that the house belongs to M. de Rênal. Thanks to the profits from his great nail factory, the mayor of Verrières now owns this fine mansion of cut stone, which has just been completed. They say that his family is Spanish, ancient, and (at least, this is how the report runs) was established in the land long before the conquest of Louis XIV.

Since 1815 he has been ashamed of being in trade: 1815 made him mayor of Verrières.[6] The terrace walls holding up various parts of that magnificent garden which descends in stages to the Doubs are also the reward of M. de Rênal's dexterity in the iron trade.

Never expect to find in France those picturesque gardens that surround the handicraft towns of Germany, such as Leipzig, Frankfurt, and Nuremberg. In the Franche-Comté, the more walls one builds, the more one covers the land with rocks placed atop each other, the more one is entitled to the neighbors' respect. M. de Rênal's gardens, encumbered with walls, are still admired because he purchased, for their weight in gold, certain minute scraps of land which they cover. For example, that sawmill, so singularly situated on the bank of the Doubs, which struck you as you entered Verrières, and on which you read the name SOREL, written in gigantic letters on a board nailed to the rooftree—six years ago, it stood precisely where the wall for the fourth terrace of M. de Rênal's gardens is going up.

For all his pride, the mayor had a hard time with old Sorel, a tough, stubborn peasant; he had to pay over plenty of good gold louis to get the old man to move his sawmill elsewhere. As for the *public* sluice which powered the saw, M. de Rênal, by means of his special influence at Paris, got it turned aside.[7] This favor came his way after the elections of 182__.

6. 1815, the date of Napoleon's defeat at Waterloo, marks a decisive victory, in Stendhal's mind, for reaction over rationality.

7. The intimate connection between money and politics, in Verrières as on a larger scale, is one of Stendhal's major points; he never loses an opportunity to emphasize it.

He gave Sorel four acres further down the Doubs, for one. And though the new position was much better for his trade in pine planks, old Papa Sorel (as they call him since he has been rich) had the shrewdness to extract from his neighbor's impatience and *land owning mania* the sum of six thousand francs.

It is true that this deal was criticized by the local wiseacres. One Sunday about four years ago, M. de Rênal was returning from church in his official uniform when he saw in the distance old Sorel, surrounded by his three sons, and smiling upon him. That smile marked a fatal moment in the mayor's mind; ever since, he has been sure he could have got the land for less.

To stand well in Verrières the essential thing is to build plenty of walls, but not to adopt any of those plans brought from Italy by masons who each spring pass through the gorges of the Jura on their way to Paris.[8] Any such innovation would gain for the rash builder a permanent reputation as a *hothead*, and he would be lost forever in the judgment of those wise and moderate folk who make public opinion in the Franche-Comté.

As a matter of fact, these folk wield the most wearisome *despotism*: and this is why, for anyone who has lived in the great republic called Paris, life in the provinces is insupportable. The tyranny of public opinion—and what an opinion!—is as *stupid* in the small towns of France as it is in the United States of America.[9]

Chapter 2

A MAYOR

Importance! Well, sir, is it worth nothing at all? Respect from fools, awe from children, envy from the rich, and disdain from the wise.
—Barnave[1]

Happily for M. de Rênal's reputation as an administrator, an immense *containing wall* was required by the public terrace that runs along the hillside a hundred or so feet above the Doubs. This admirable site gives the town one of the finest views in France. But every springtime, rains used to silt up the promenade, cut little gullies into it, and render it impassable. This difficulty, which was felt by all, put M. de Rênal under the happy necessity of immortal-

---

8. Stendhal as a freemason and a lover of Italy alludes here underhandedly to an international traffic in liberal ideas.
9. For Stendhal, as for many Europeans, America represented a shopkeeper's civilization, the last word in mean and petty values. His opinions of the New World were reinforced by perusal of Mrs. Fanny Trollope's *Do-*

mestic Manners of the Americans (1832), a translation of which he read and annotated.
1. Antoine Barnave (1761–93) was, with Mirabeau, one of the great orators of the French Revolution; he came from Grenoble and had been known to members of Stendhal's family (see *Brulard*, Chap. 5).

izing his administration with a wall twenty feet high and thirty or forty rods long.[2]

The parapet of this wall, for which M. de Rênal had to make three special trips to Paris, since the previous minister of the interior was a declared enemy of the terrace at Verrières—this parapet now rises four feet above ground level. And, as if in defiance of all ministers past and present, it is even now being capped with a layer of cut stone.

How many times, my mind still dwelling on the balls of Paris which I left the night before, have I leaned on these great blocks of bluish-gray granite, gazing deep into the valley of the Doubs! Over yonder, on the left bank, wind five or six valleys, at the bottom of which the eye distinguishes little brooks. They leap from falls to falls and disappear into the Doubs. The sun is hot in these mountains; when it stands overhead, the meditative traveler is shaded on this terrace by magnificent plane trees. Their rapid growth and greenish-blue foliage are due to the fill the mayor has poured in behind his immense containing wall, for, in spite of opposition from the municipal counsel, he has widened the terrace by more than six feet (though he's a conservative and I'm a liberal, I give him credit); and this is why, in his opinion, and in the opinion of M. Valenod, fortunate director of the Verrières poorhouse, this terrace can fairly be compared with that of Saint-Germain-en-Laye.[3]

For my part, I can find only one thing to criticize on LOYALTY SQUARE; this official name is to be seen in fifteen or twenty places on marble plaques which earned an extra cross for M. de Rênal. What I would criticize on Loyalty Square is the barbaric way the administration clips and snips these vigorous plane trees back to the very quick. They stand there, with heads held low, shaved and flattened like the most vulgar of domestic vegetables, when they would like nothing better than to assume those splendid shapes they are free to take in England.[4] But the mayor's will is supreme, and twice a year all the trees belonging to the town are pitilessly pruned back. The liberals of the district claim, but they exaggerate, that the official gardener wields a heavier hand since Vicar Maslon has started to engross for himself the products of the shearing.

2. The irrationality of wall-building and of walls in general is a major theme of the novel. Julien is continually climbing, hiding, or escaping from behind walls, while society (as here) puts inordinate and irrational efforts into erecting and guarding them.
3. The poorhouses, established by Louis XVI and abolished by Napoleon, were reintroduced by the Bourbons in 1815; a clever, unscrupulous man could make a good deal of money running one, both from the labor of the inmates and on public contracts for their maintenance. The terrace of St. Germain-en-Laye, a few miles from Paris, was built in the late seventeenth century; as it is a hundred feet wide and a mile and a half long, comparison with that at Verrières is a bit generous.
4. Stendhal's love of trees, which he hated to see clipped and trimmed, comes out in *Brulard*, Chap. 41, and here in Chap. 24, when the sight of free trees comforts Julien in the seminary.

This young ecclesiastic was sent down from Besançon some years ago to keep an eye on Abbé Chélan[5] and several other priests of the district. An old surgeon-major from the army of Italy, retired at Verrières, and who, according to the mayor, had been both a Jacobin and a Bonapartist, had the audacity one day to complain about the periodic mutilation of these fine trees.

—I'm very fond of shade, replied M. de Rênal, with that touch of disdain which is so appropriate when one is talking to a surgeon and a member of the Legion of Honor; I'm very fond indeed of the shade; I have *my* trees trimmed in order to give shade; I don't suppose a tree is really good for anything else, unless, like the useful walnut, *it yields a return.*

There now is the grand phrase that decides everything at Verrières: YIELD A RETURN. That phrase alone represents the mental life of three quarters of the townspeople.

Yielding a return decides everything in this little town which at first seemed so attractive to you. The stranger, as he arrives, is so entranced by the beauty of the cool, deep valleys that he imagines the natives are themselves responsive to beauty. It is true they talk, even to excess, of how beautiful their town is; they make a great to-do over it. But the reason is simply that the scenery attracts various outsiders, whose money enriches the hotel keepers and thus, through the tax-collecting machinery, *yields a return to the town.*

One fine autumn day M. de Rênal was strolling on Loyalty Square, with his wife by his side. Even as she listened to the grave discourse of her husband, Mme. de Rênal was watching anxiously the gyrations of three little boys. The eldest, who might be as much as eleven, kept wandering over to the parapet and seemed about to climb on top of it. A gentle voice then called the name of Adolphe, and the youngster turned back. Mme. de Rênal seemed a woman in her thirties, but still quite handsome.

—Oh, he'll regret it, this fine Paris gentleman, said M. de Rênal with indignation, his cheek a little paler than usual. I'm not without a certain number of friends at the castle. . . .[6]

5. *Abbé:* This term is used loosely on the Continent, especially in France, for almost any clergyman, whether beneficed or not. François I, by agreement with Pope Leo X, first got the right to appoint abbots *in commendam* (that is, provisionally, and without duties) to most of the abbeys in France. Many young gentlemen of very secular tastes (for example, the author of *Manon Lescaut*, Abbé Prévost) took a short course in theology, assumed a modified tonsure, wore a special violet coat, practiced a sort of celibacy, and were known as abbés. These completely secularized abbés are not to be found in the nineteenth century; but the word continued to be used loosely of anyone who had a sort of connection with the church (a tutor, a theological student), as well as of regular clergymen. The name and perhaps some of the character of Abbé Chélan come from a historical personage, described in *Brulard*, Chap. 5.

6. Charles X and his court lived at the Château de St. Cloud, and were thus referred to familiarly as the castle.

But though I intend to speak of provincial life for two hundred pages, I shall not be so cruel as to inflict on you the full dimensions, and all the *clever turns,* of a provincial dialogue.

This fine Paris gentleman, so distressing to the mayor of Verrières, was no other than M. Appert, who two days before had found means to get into the prison and the poorhouse of Verrières, and even into the free hospital run by the mayor and the principal gentry of the district.[7]

—But after all, said Mme. de Rênal timidly, what harm can this Paris gentleman do, since you look after the welfare of the poor with the most scrupulous honesty?

—He comes only to find fault, and afterward he'll have articles in all the liberal newspapers.

—But you never read them, my dear.

—People will talk to us about these Jacobin articles; the whole business distracts us, and *prevents us from doing good.*[8] Personally, I'll never forgive that priest.

Chapter 3

THE WELFARE OF THE POOR

A priest who is virtuous and no intriguer is a blessing upon his village.
—Fleury[9]

Though eighty years old, the priest of Verrières, thanks to the sharp air of these mountains, had a character and a constitution of iron; he also had the right to visit, at any time of day, the prison, the hospital, and even the poorhouse. M. Appert, who had been commended to the priest from Paris, had been prudent enough to arrive in a small town eaten up with curiosity at six in the morning. He went directly to the presbytery.

As he looked over the letter written to him by the Marquis de La Mole, peer of France and the richest landowner of the province, the priest, M. Chélan, grew pensive.

—I have grown old here, and am well loved, he murmured at last; they would never dare! And he turned abruptly on the gentleman from Paris, with eyes in which, despite old age, there glittered that sacred fire which accompanies the pleasure of performing a fine deed that is at the same time a bit dangerous.

7. Benjamin Appert was an actual philanthropist and prison reformer of the day. He visited Antoine Berthet (whose story provided one of the models for Julien Sorel's) during his trial at Besançon, to make sure he was properly defended.
8. Historic [Stendhal's note].

9. Fleury was an early eighteenth-century cardinal and statesman, whom Stendhal uses here as a type of the authentic, old, uncorrupted clergy. His *Ecclesiastical History* was placed on the Index as tainted with Gallicanism, that is, the doctrine that would limit papal authority (see *Brulard,* Chap. 10).

—Come with me, sir, and remember, in the presence of the jailer and above all of the poorhouse wardens, you must express no opinion about the things we shall see. M. Appert understood that he had to do with a man of feeling: he accompanied the old priest, visited the prison, the clinic, the poorhouse, asked plenty of questions, and in spite of some very strange answers, gave not the slightest sign of disapproval.

The visit lasted for several hours. The priest asked M. Appert to dinner, but he claimed to have letters to write; he did not want to compromise any further his generous friend. About three o'clock, they returned to complete their inspection of the poorhouse, and then went on to the prison. In the doorway there they found the jailer, a kind of giant six feet tall and bowlegged; his coarse features had become hideous with terror.

—Ah, sir, said he to the priest as soon as he saw him, this gentleman with you here, isn't he M. Appert?

—Why do you ask? said the priest.

—Because I received just yesterday the most precise orders, sent by a police officer from the prefect himself, and he had to gallop all night long, *not* to let M. Appert into the jail.

—Well, Monsieur Noiroud, said the priest, I can assure you that this visitor with me is in fact M. Appert. Now do you remember that I am free to enter the jail at any hour of the day or night, and to bring with me anyone I want?

—Yes, your reverence, grumbled the jailer, lowering his head like a bulldog yielding reluctantly to the menace of a club. Only, your reverence, I've got a wife and children; if there's a complaint, I'm out; and I've got nothing to live on but this job.

—I should be just as unhappy to lose my own, said the priest, with feeling.

—What a difference! the jailer replied quickly; you, your reverence, everyone knows you've got eight hundred florins a year of your own, free and clear. . . .

Such were the events that, embroidered and distorted in twenty different ways, had been stirring up over the past two days all the hateful passions of the little town of Verrières. At this very moment, they were serving as the theme of M. de Rênal's conversation with his wife. He had gone that morning, accompanied by M. Valenod, director of the poorhouse, to call on the priest and express furious disapproval of what he had done. M. Chélan had no protector; he bore by himself the full brunt of their words.

—Well, gentlemen! I shall be the third eighty-year-old priest in this district to be deprived of my position. I've been here for fifty-six years; I have baptized nearly every person in this town, which was nothing but a crossroads when I came here. Every day I marry young people whose grandparents I married in the old days. Verrières is my family; but [fear of having to leave it will never make me traffic with my conscience or grant another person authority over my actions;] when I saw that visitor, I said to myself: "This man from Paris may really be a liberal, there are only too many of them; but what harm can he do our paupers and prisoners?"

The outcries of M. de Rênal, and especially of M. de Valenod, the poorhouse director, became even louder:

—All right, gentlemen, cried the old priest in a quavering voice, go on, have me thrown out. I'll live here just the same. Forty-eight years ago, it's well known, I inherited an estate that brings in 800 florins; I'll live on that. I haven't used my position to graft, gentlemen, and maybe that's why I'm not terrified at the prospect of losing it.

Though M. de Rênal was extremely considerate of his wife [who had a very rich aunt], he did not know how to answer her timidly repeated question, "But what harm could that man from Paris possibly do the prisoners?" and was on the point of losing his temper when she suddenly cried aloud. The second of her sons had just climbed up on the parapet and was running along it, though the drop to a vineyard on the other side was more than twenty feet. Fear of startling her son and making him fall kept Mme. de Rênal from calling out to him. Finally the boy, laughing at his own adroitness and looking to his mother, saw her pallor, leaped to the ground, and ran to her. He was thoroughly scolded.

This little episode changed the course of the conversation.

—I've really decided to take on young Sorel, the carpenter's son, said M. de Rênal; he will look after the children, who are starting to be too much for us. He's a young priest, or just as good as, he's clever at Latin and will keep the children at their lessons, for the priest says he's strong willed. I'll let him have three hundred francs and his board. On the score of morality I had some doubts; for he was the protégé of that old surgeon, member of the Legion of Honor, who came to live with the Sorels, under pretext of being their cousin. Down deep that man may very well have been nothing but a secret agent of the liberals; of course, he said the mountain air was good for his asthma, but there's no proving that. He was with *Buonaparté*[1] on all his Italian campaigns and, they even say, once, long ago, signed something against the empire. This liberal taught Latin to young Sorel and left him some of his books. Ordinarily, I would never consider putting a carpenter's son in charge of our children. But the priest told me, just the night before that last quarrel of ours, that young Sorel has been studying theology for the

1. In giving Napoleon his Corsican, semi-Italian name, M. de Rênal is trying to repudiate him as a foreigner.

last three years, hoping to enter the seminary; so he isn't a liberal, and he does know Latin.

—This arrangement works out in several different ways, M. de Rênal went on, glancing at his wife with the air of a diplomat; that fellow Valenod is proud of the two Norman horses he's just bought for his carriage. But he doesn't have a tutor for his children.

—He might very well get this one away from us.

—Then you approve of my plans? said M. de Rênal, thanking his wife with a quick smile for the excellent insight she had just had. Fine, then it's all decided.

—Good Lord, my dear! you're so sudden in your decisions!

—That's because I have a bit of character, I do, and I let that priest see the edge of it. Let's not fool ourselves, we're surrounded by liberals here. All these cotton merchants are envious of me, I'm certain of it; two or three of them are getting really rich. All right, I want them to see the children of M. de Rênal passing by, going for a walk *with their tutor*. That will make an impression. My grandfather often told us that in his youth he had a tutor. He may very well cost me a hundred crowns, but it's simply one of those expenses that are necessary to keep up a social position.

This sudden decision left Mme. de Rênal quite pensive. She was a tall woman, and well proportioned, who had been the beauty of the countryside, as they say in this mountainous district. She had a certain air of simplicity, and the spring of youth in her step. In the mind of a Parisian, this simple elegance, full of innocence and liveliness, might even have roused notions of sensual pleasure. If she had realized that she was attractive in this way, Mme. de Rênal would have been deeply ashamed. Neither coquetry nor affectation had ever touched her heart. M. Valenod, the rich poorhouse director, was reputed to have sighed for her, but without success, a story that lent particular luster to her virtue; for this M. Valenod was a bluff young man, strongly built, highly colored, with big black whiskers—one of those gross, bold, loud fellows who in the provinces are known as handsome men.

Mme. de Rênal, who was quite timid and apparently of retiring character, was particularly distressed by M. Valenod's continual abrupt motion and bursts of noise. Her dislike of everything that in Verrières is considered fun had caused her to be thought a snob. She never gave the matter a thought, but was very glad to find the townspeople calling upon her less often. We shall not hide the fact that *those* ladies thought her a fool because she often overlooked occasions to get herself fancy hats from Paris or Besançon. Provided people left her free to wander alone in her fine garden, she never thought herself ill used.

She was an innocent soul who had never risen even to the point of passing judgment on her husband and admitting that she was bored. Without saying so directly, she supposed things were always about this way between husbands and wives. She was particularly fond of M. de Rênal when he talked about his plans for their children, one of whom was to be a soldier, the second a magistrate, and the third a churchman. In a word, she found M. de Rênal a good deal less boring than most men of her acquaintance.

This conjugal opinion was perfectly sensible. The mayor of Verrières owed his reputation for wit and social poise to a half dozen jokes he had inherited from an uncle [and brought out on state occasions]. Old Captain de Rênal had served before the Revolution in the Duc d'Orleans' infantry regiment, and when he visited Paris used to be admitted to the salons of the prince. There he had observed Mme. de Montesson, the famous Mme. de Genlis, and M. Ducrest, the redesigner of the Palais Royal.[2] These figures turned up, all too often, in the anecdotes of M. de Rênal. But gradually the recollection of things so hard to put into exact words had become a chore for him, and for some time now it was only for special events that he trotted out his anecdotes concerning the House of Orleans. As he was generally a very polite man, except when the talk turned to money, he passed with good reason for the most aristocratic personage in Verrières.

Chapter 4

FATHER AND SON

And is it my fault
If that's how things are?
—Machiavelli[3]

—My wife is really pretty shrewd, said the mayor of Verrières to himself, about six o'clock the next morning, as he strolled down to old Sorel's sawmill. Though I saw it was important to keep up our social position, I hadn't really considered that if I don't pick up this little Abbé Sorel—they say he knows Latin like an angel—the director of the poorhouse, who's always up to something, might get the same idea and snatch him away from me. And wouldn't he be complacent, talking to me about his children's tutor! . . . Once he's in my house, will this tutor wear a cassock, I wonder?

M. de Rênal was working over this question when he saw in the distance a peasant, nearly six feet tall, who seemed to have been busy since the first light of dawn measuring some tree trunks which

2. These names from the court society before the Revolution serve simply to suggest a splendid, worldly, but now remote elegance.

3. The quotation is not word-for-word anywhere in Machiavelli, but the spirit behind it is authentic.

had been laid alongside the Doubs on the towpath. The peasant was not particularly pleased to see the mayor approach; for his tree trunks blocked the path, and were laid there illegally.

Old Sorel, for it was he, was much surprised and even more pleased with the unusual proposal M. de Rênal made regarding his son Julien. But all the same he listened to it with that air of peevish discontent and indifference which these mountaineers know so well how to cast over their shrewdness.[4] Slaves in the days of the Spanish dominion, they still retain in their features this trait of the Egyptian fellah.

At first Sorel replied by reciting at length all the formulas of polite conversation he knew by heart. While he was repeating these empty phrases with an awkward smile which emphasized the air of falsity and almost of trickery natural to his features, the old peasant's quick wit was trying to imagine why such an important man would want to take into his house that good-for-nothing son. He had no use for Julien, yet it was for him that M. de Rênal was offering the unexpected salary of 300 francs a year, plus board and even a clothing allowance. This last request, which old Sorel had had the genius to put forward at the very beginning, had been granted at once by M. de Rênal.

This demand put M. de Rênal on the alert. He thought: Since Sorel is not overwhelmed with joy at my proposal, as he ought to be, it's clear that he has been receiving offers from some other quarter; and where could they come from, if not from Valenod? In vain did the mayor press old Sorel to reach a decision then and there; the peasant refused shrewdly and stubbornly, saying he had to talk it over with his son—as if, in the provinces, a rich father ever consulted a poor son except for form's sake.

A sawmill consists of a shed beside a stream. The roof rests on a frame, supported by four heavy wooden columns. In the middle of the shed, rising to the height of eight or ten feet, is the saw, going steadily up and down, while a simple mechanism pushes against it a piece of wood. A water wheel turned by the stream powers this double mechanism—the saw that goes up and down, the carriage that moves the wood gradually against the saw, so that it can be split into planks.

Approaching his mill, old Sorel bellowed for Julien; nobody answered. He saw only his elder sons, a couple of giants who were working with heavy axes, squaring off some pine trunks they were preparing for the saw. They were intent on following exactly the black lines drawn on the wood; at every blow of their axes huge chips flew through the air. They did not hear their father's voice.

4. In *Brulard*, Chap. 7, Stendhal attributes much the same expression and character to his own father.

He turned toward the shed, entered, and looked vainly for Julien at the station where he should have been, beside the saw. At last he saw him, five or six feet higher, astraddle one of the roof beams. Instead of keeping close watch on the working of the machine, Julien was reading a book. Nothing could have been more disagreeable to old Sorel; he might perhaps have pardoned Julien his slender figure, unsuited to hard labor and unlike his elder brothers'; but this passion for reading was hateful to him, as he didn't know how to read himself.

He called Julien, vainly, two or three times. The young man's absorption in his book, much more than the roar of the saw, prevented him from hearing his father's terrible voice. Finally, despite his age, the old man jumped lightly onto the tree trunk which was being sawed and from there to the crossbeam which helped support the roof. A violent blow sent Julien's book flying into the stream; a second cuff, just as heavy, fell on his head and caused him to lose his balance. He was about to fall a distance of ten or fifteen feet into the middle of the machinery, which would have ground him up, but his father caught him, with his left hand, just as he was falling:

—All right, loafer! still reading your damn books while you're supposed to be watching the saw? Read them after work, when you're wasting your time with the priest, why don't you?

Julien, though stunned by the force of the blow and bleeding slightly, went to his proper station alongside the saw. His eyes were full of tears, less from physical pain than for the loss of his book, which he worshipped.

—Get down from there, animal, I want to talk to you.

The roar of the machinery still prevented Julien from hearing this order. His father, who had returned to the floor and didn't want to bother climbing up on the machinery again, took a long pole used for knocking down nuts and struck him across the shoulder with it. Scarcely was Julien on the ground when his father, driving his son before him, set out for the house. God knows what he's going to do to me! thought the young man. As they passed the stream into which his book had fallen, he glanced sadly aside; it had been his favorite book, the *Mémorial de Sainte-Hélène*.[5]

He walked on, with flushed face and lowered eyes. He was a slightly built young man, eighteen or nineteen years old, feeble in appearance, with irregular but delicate features, and an aquiline nose. Big dark eyes, which in repose expressed fire and reflection, were filled at this moment with the most ferocious hatred. Dark

5. The chivalric Emanuel Las Cases, who had a clear affinity for lost causes, had been an émigré in the early years of the Revolution but joined Napoleon just in time to accompany him in his final exile on St. Helena. He wrote there the long and richly rhetorical *Mémorial*, which is a keystone of the Napoleonic legend.

brown hair growing low over his forehead gave him, in moments of anger, an ugly look. Among the innumerable varieties of human expression, there is perhaps no other that is so striking. A slender and finely molded figure suggested a man or more nerve than strength. The pensive air and extreme pallor which had marked him from early youth convinced his father that he would not live long, or would prove merely a drag on the household. An object of scorn to the entire family, he hated his brothers and his father; and in the Sunday games on the public square he was invariably beaten.

About a year ago his handsome features had started to give him a few friendly voices among the girls. Scorned by everyone as a weakling, Julien had worshipped that old surgeon-major who one day dared to address the mayor on the subject of the plane trees.

This surgeon sometimes paid old Sorel a day's wages for his son's time, and then taught him Latin and history, that is, all the history he knew, the Italian campaign of 1796.[6] When he died he left Julien his cross of the Legion of Honor, the arrears of his half pension, and thirty or forty volumes, the most precious of which had just been pitched into the *public water supply*, diverted by the mayor's influence.

Scarcely was he in the house when Julien felt his shoulder gripped by his father's powerful hand; he shuddered, expecting more blows.

—Answer me now, and no lies! The old peasant's voice grated in his ears, while his heavy hand spun Julien about like a child playing with a tin soldier. Raising his great black eyes filled with tears, Julien stared into the little, gray, suspicious eyes of the old sawyer, who seemed intent on reading the very depths of his soul.

Chapter 5

HAGGLING

Cunctando restituit rem.
(By stalling he gained his point.)
—Ennius[7]

—Answer me now, and no lies, if you can manage that, you little hound; how do you know Mme. de Rênal, when did you talk with her?

—I've never talked with her, said Julien, the only time I've seen the lady is at church.

—But you've ogled her there, you shameless scoundrel?

6. Napoleon's Italian campaign of 1796 was for Stendhal the classic tale of military glory: a ragged, heroic, youthful army overcoming, in a sequence of smashing engagements, the troops of an ancient tyranny, and receiving an ec-static welcome from swarms of beautiful, operatic women.
7. Cato the Elder quotes these lines from the ancient Roman poet Ennius, whose work survives largely in quoted snippets like this.

—Never! You know that at church I see only God, said Julien with a little hypocritical look which he thought quite the best way to prevent another cuff.

—Just the same, there's something behind all this, said the surly peasant, and paused a moment; but I'll never get anything out of you, you confounded hypocrite. The fact is, I'm going to get rid of you, and my saw will run all the better for it. You've worked the priest, or somebody else, into fixing you up with a soft job. Go get your things together, and I'll take you to M. de Rênal's house, where you will be a tutor for his children.

—And what will I be paid?

—Food, clothing, and three hundred francs wages.

—I don't want to be a servant.

—Stupid animal, who's talking about being a servant? You suppose I'd want my son to be a servant?

—Well then, whom will I eat with?

This question upset old Sorel; he felt that if he said anything he might compromise himself; so he got angry with Julien, poured insults on him, accused him of softness, and left him to go talk it over with his other sons.

Julien saw them soon after, leaning on their axes, and holding a family council. He watched them for a long time, but then, seeing he could not guess what was going on, went around to the other side of the saw, so that they shouldn't come on him unexpectedly. He wanted to think over this unforeseen news, which was about to change his destiny, but found himself incapable of prudence; his imagination was wholly occupied in picturing what he would find in M. de Rênal's fine house.

Still, I must give it all up, said he to himself, rather than sink to eating with the household servants. My father will try to push me into it; I'd sooner die. I've saved fifteen francs and eight sous, I can run away tonight; in two days, using the back roads where I won't meet with policemen, I'll be at Besançon; there I'll enlist, and if necessary, I'll cross over into Switzerland. But no future there, no more rising in the world, no more of this fine priesting it, that leads to all good things.

This horror of eating with servants was by no means natural to Julien; in order to make his fortune he would have done other things much more painful in themselves. He had picked up this notion from Rousseau's *Confessions*. It was the only book his imagination had made use of in constructing a picture of the social world. A collection of bulletins from the Grande Armée and the *Mémorial de Sainte-Hélène* filled out his Koran.[8] He would have

8. The Koran, used to suggest a pagan creed. Stendhal himself used to sharpen his style for the *Rouge* by reading the Code Napoleon. His admirations for

gone to the stake for these three works. He never believed in any other. Taking his hint from the old surgeon-major, he looked upon all the other books in the world as lies written by rascals to gain advancement.

With a fiery spirit Julien united one of those astounding memories which are so often joined to complete stupidity. Seeing that his future depended on the old priest Chélan, he had won him over by learning the whole New Testament verbatim in Latin; he also knew M. de Maistre's book *On the Pope*,[9] and believed as little of one as of the other.

As if by common consent, Sorel and his son avoided talking to one another for the rest of the day. When evening fell, Julien went off to take his lessons in theology from the priest, but he thought best to tell him nothing at all of the strange proposal made to his father. Perhaps it's a trap, said he to himself; I'd better pretend to have forgotten it.

Early next morning, M. de Rênal sent for old Sorel, who, after delaying an hour or two, finally arrived and immediately started to make a hundred different excuses all mixed up with as many compliments. After working his way through all sorts of objections, Sorel was given to understand that his son would eat with the master and mistress of the house, and that when there was company, he would eat alone in a separate room with the children. The more he observed the mayor's impatience, the more Sorel was disposed to raise difficulties, and besides he was mistrustful and surprised; he asked to see the room where his son would sleep. It was a large room, finely furnished, into which men were already carrying the beds of the three children.

This incident was a gleam of light for the old peasant; at once he asked boldly to see the suit of clothes that would be his son's. M. de Rênal opened his desk drawer and took out a hundred francs.

—With this sum your son can go to M. Durand the tailor and get a complete black suit.

—And even if I take him home again, said the peasant, who had suddenly forgotten all his obsequious expressions, he'll still keep the black suit?

the laconic precision of an army bulletin, for the psychological subtlety and truth-at-the expense-of-meanness of Rousseau, and for the noble resignation of Las Cases' *Mémorial*, make up for Julien a literary trinity.

9. Joseph de Maistre, most brilliant of the anti-philosophical Catholic reactionaries generated by opposition to Napoleon, published his two-volume treatise *On the Pope* in 1819; it took the highest conceivable view of papal absolutism. Stendhal's own early education (described in *Brulard*, Chap. 10) consisted in good part of memorizing certain Latin texts without any real understanding of what they said or even of the language in which they were written. Among other things, he tells us he learned the Latin New Testament by heart (*Brulard*, Chap. 20).

—Of course.

—All right, said Sorel, in drawling tones, then there's only one thing left to settle between us: how much money will you give him?

—What's this? cried M. de Rênal in a rage, we agreed on that yesterday. I'm giving three hundred francs. In my opinion, it's a great deal of money, and maybe even too much.

—That was your offer, I won't deny it at all, said old Sorel, talking still more slowly; and then, by a stroke of genius which will astonish those who do not know the peasants of the Franche-Comté, he looked straight at M. de Rênal and said: *We can do better elsewhere.*

At these words the mayor appeared stunned. But he recovered, and after a masterly conversation of two long hours, during which not a word was said without its purpose, peasant shrewdness won out over rich-man's shrewdness, which is not needed for survival. All the various clauses that would control Julien's future existence were settled; not only was his pay set at four hundred francs but he was to receive it in advance, on the first of each month.

—All right, I'll send him thirty-five francs, said M. de Rênal.

—Just to make a round figure, a rich and generous gentleman like our mayor, said the peasant in a coaxing tone, will surely make it thirty-six francs.[1]

—Yes, said M. de Rênal, but that's the end.

At that moment his rage gave him the tone of a decisive man. The peasant saw there was no more progress to be made; and then M. de Rênal, in his turn, began to forge ahead. He absolutely refused to give the first month's thirty-six francs to old Sorel, who was very anxious to bring them to his son. It occurred to M. de Rênal that he might have to describe to his wife the part he had played in all this bargaining.

—Give me back those hundred francs I gave you, he said crossly. M. Durand owes me some money. I'll go with your son to pick up the black suit.

After this vigorous gesture old Sorel wisely fell back upon his formulas of respect; they took up a good quarter of an hour. Finally, seeing that there was really nothing more to be gained, he took his leave. His final compliment finished with these words:

—I shall send my son up to the manor house.

This was the term the mayor's subordinates applied to his house when they wanted to flatter him.

When he got back to his mill, Sorel looked about vainly for his son. Uneasy about what might happen, Julien had slipped out in

---

1. If one paid in *écus* (crowns) worth six francs apiece, thirty-six francs would make a round sum.

the middle of the night to find a safe place for his books and his cross of the Legion of Honor. He had taken everything to a young lumberman, his friend, a man named Fouqué[2] who lived up on the big mountain that stands over Verrières.

After his return: —God knows, said his father, if a lazy loafer like you will ever have the grace to repay me all the money I've been laying out for your food all these years. Pack up your rubbish and get over to the mayor's.

Surprised that he hadn't been beaten, Julien hastened to leave. But scarcely out of sight of his terrible father, he slackened his pace. He thought it might be useful to his hypocrisy to stop off in the church.

The word surprises you? Before reaching this horrible expression, the soul of the young peasant had passed through a long development.

When he was a mere child he had seen certain dragoons of the 6th, with their long white cloaks and helmets decked with long black horsehair, on their way back from Italy. Julien watched them tie their horses to the grilled windows of his father's house, and grew wild to be a soldier. Later, he listened with passionate excitement to those stories about the battles at the bridge of Lodi, of Arcola and Rivoli, which he heard from the old surgeon-major.[3] He noted the pride and enthusiasm with which the old man kept glancing at his cross.

But when Julien was just fourteen, they began to build at Verrières a church which could fairly be called magnificent for such a small town. There were four columns of marble, in particular, the sight of which struck Julien; they became famous throughout the countryside, by reason of the deadly feud they caused between the justice of the peace and the young vicar, sent from Besançon, who was thought to be a spy for the congregation.[4] The justice of the peace was sure to lose his post, or such at least was the general impression. Hadn't he dared to quarrel with a priest who every two weeks went to Besançon, where, people said, he visited the bishop himself?

2. The original of Fouqué was an acquaintance of Stendhal's youth, François Bigillion, who was generous and open-hearted but killed himself when his wife deceived him.
3. Stendhal's Italian service had been with the Sixth Dragoons. Lodi (May 10, 1796), Arcola (November 15–17, 1796), and Rivoli (June 14, 1797) were classic battles of Napoleonic strategy.
4. A congregation is any of a variety of pious, voluntary organizations that existed after the seventeenth century in France. They might include laymen as well as ecclesiastics, and they had to have the approval of the diocesan bishop and sometimes of the pope. They ordinarily grew up around a religious figure (the Virgin), symbol (the Sacred Heart), or order (the Jesuits). Stendhal's special black imagination regarding clerics may have attributed to them a sinister power they did not always possess; yet there can be no doubt that in small provincial towns they wielded great influence.

Meanwhile, the justice of the peace, who was father of a numerous family, rendered a number of decisions that seemed unjust; they all seemed to bear against townspeople who read the *Constitutionnel*.[5] The party of virtue was triumphant. The fines never amounted, it's true, to more than three or five francs; but one of these petty mulcts fell on a nailmaker, Julien's godfather. In his rage this man declared: —What a change! And to think that for twenty years and more everybody thought that justice was an honest man! The surgeon-major, Julien's friend, was dead.[6]

Quite suddenly Julien stopped talking of Napoleon; he declared that he wanted to become a priest, and he was constantly observed about his father's sawmill, memorizing a Latin Bible the priest had loaned him. That good old man, amazed at his progress, devoted whole evenings to teaching him theology. Julien never displayed before him any but pious sentiments. Who could have guessed that that girlish face, so pale and soft, concealed an unshakable resolution to die a thousand deaths rather than fail to make his fortune!

For Julien, making his fortune meant, first of all, getting out of Verrières; he loathed his home town. Everything he saw there chilled his imagination.

Ever since he was a boy, he had had moments of secret exultation. He dreamed with joy of one day being introduced to the pretty women of Paris; he would, of course, attract their admiration with some brilliant action. Why should he not win the love of one of them, just as Bonaparte, when still young, had been loved by the brilliant Mme. de Beauharnais?[7] Over the past several years, Julien had scarcely passed an hour without reminding himself that Bonaparte, starting as a poor and obscure lieutenant, had made himself master of the world, with his sword alone. This idea consoled him amid his sorrows, which he considered great, and multiplied his joys when he had any.

The building of the church and the sentences imposed by the justice of the peace illuminated him, as by a flash; an idea that came to him rendered him for several weeks almost mad, and finally took possession of him with the irresistible power which his first-born idea exercises over every passionate soul.

—When Bonaparte made his name, France was in danger of invasion; the soldier's trade was necessary and fashionable. Nowadays, there are forty-year-old priests who draw salaries of a hundred

5. Though not avowedly liberal itself, the *Constitutionnel* became a rallying point after the Restoration for whatever liberal opinion the Bourbons permitted.
6. The abrupt and unexplained combination of ideas in this paragraph is one of the triumphs of Stendhal's art. Julien puts bare, brief sentences beside one another, and they fall into a pattern with an almost audible click.
7. Mme. de Beauharnais later became the Empress Josephine; it would seem she was not at first much impressed with the scrawny, penniless, provincial young man who was destined to make himself emperor—and her an empress.

thousand francs, three times as much as the famous division commanders of Napoleon. They need subordinates. Think of that justice of the peace, once a good judge and an honest man, and now grown old, who covers himself with disgrace, for fear of displeasing a young vicar thirty years old. The thing to be is a priest.

Once, in the midst of his new piety, when Julien had been studying theology for two years, he was betrayed by a sudden outburst of the passion that was devouring him inwardly. It was at M. Chélan's, at a dinner of clerics to whom the old priest had presented him as a prodigious scholar: he found himself babbling frantic praises of Napoleon. He strapped his right arm to his chest, pretended that he had dislocated it while shifting a tree trunk, and carried it in this painful position for two months. After this judicial penalty, he pardoned himself. Such was the young man, nineteen years old, but so frail that he would never have been thought more than seventeen, who entered the splendid church of Verrières with a little parcel under his arm.

He found the church dark and deserted. Because of a festival, all the windows of the building had been covered with scarlet cloth. As a result, the sun struck through in shafts of brilliant light, creating an impressive and religious atmosphere. Julien shivered. All alone in the church, he took a seat in the finest pew. It bore M. de Rênal's coat of arms.

On the lectern, Julien noted a scrap of printed paper, set out there as if for him to read. He glanced at it and saw:

> *Details of the execution and last moments of Louis Jenrel,*[8] *executed at Besançon, on the* ——

The paper was torn. On the other side were the first words of a line: *The first step. . . .*

Who could have left this paper here? thought Julien. Poor fellow, he added with a sigh, his name has the same ending as mine. . . . He crumpled up the paper.

As he went out, Julien imagined he saw a pool of blood by the baptismal font; it was merely some holy water which had been spilled; the red curtains covering the windows made it look like blood.

At last, Julien grew ashamed of his secret terrors.

—Am I going to be a coward? he said. *To arms!*

This phrase, so often recurring in the battle stories of the old surgeon, was a heroic word for Julien. He rose and walked swiftly toward the house of M. de Rênal.

In spite of his fine resolutions, as soon as he was within twenty feet of it he was overcome by an access of timidity. The iron gate

8. Louis Jenrel is an anagram of Julien Sorel.

was open, it seemed magnificent to him, and he had to go inside it. Julien was not the only person deeply disturbed by his arrival in this house. Mme. de Rênal's modesty was much distressed by the idea of this outsider, whose work would continually bring him between her and her children. She was used to having her children sleep in the same room with her. That morning tears had flowed freely when she saw their little beds carried off into the room set aside for the new tutor. She had implored her husband in vain that the bed of Stanislas-Xavier, her youngest, might be returned to her room.

Feminine delicacy was carried to an extreme in Mme. de Rênal. She had formed in her mind a most disagreeable picture of a gross and slovenly creature, whose duty it would be to scold her children simply because he knew Latin, a barbarous language on account of which her children would be whipped.[9]

Chapter 6

BOREDOM

What I am I no longer know,
Nor what I'm doing.
—Mozart (*Figaro*)[1]

With the swift grace that was natural to her when unconstrained by the sight of men, Mme. de Rênal was going out the living room door that gave onto the garden when she noticed by the main entry a young peasant, scarcely more than a child, very pale and showing traces of recent tears. He wore a white shirt and was carrying under his arm a cotton jacket of violet color, neatly folded.[2]

The complexion of this little peasant was so pale, his eyes so soft, that Mme. de Rênal's somewhat romantic disposition took him at first for a girl in disguise who might have come to beg some favor of the mayor. She felt an impulse of pity for this poor creature, hesitating in the doorway, and apparently fearful of lifting her hand to ring the bell. Diverted a moment from her own bitter distress over the arrival of the tutor, Mme. de Rênal came closer. Julien, his eyes fixed on the door, did not notice her approach; he started when a gentle voice, speaking close beside his ear, said:

—What do you want here, my child?

Julien turned suddenly, and was so struck by the kind glance of Mme de Rênal that he forgot part of his timidity. Then, astonished

9. Stendhal had had a tutor, Abbé Raillane, whom he represented as just such an ignorant and brutal tyrant as Mme. de Rênal instinctively fears. See *Brulard*, Chaps. 7–9.
1. The phrase is from Cherubino's aria in Act I and describes young Cherubino's intense erotic fantasies.
2. This scene, if not imitated from, at least parallels that in Rousseau's *Confessions* (Book II) where he first makes the acquaintance of Mme. de Warens.

by her beauty, he forgot everything else, including his purpose in coming. Mme. de Rênal had repeated her question.

—I've come to be the tutor, madame, he said at last, covered with shame for the tears he was trying his best to efface.

Mme. de Rênal was overcome with surprise; they stood quite close and looked at one another. Julien had never seen anyone so well dressed, nor a woman with so fine a complexion, who spoke to him so gently. Mme. de Rênal looked at the great tears standing on the cheeks, once so pale and now so pink, of the young peasant. Then she began to laugh, with all the absurd gaiety of a young girl, laughing at herself and yet unable to think why she felt so happy. So this was the tutor whom she had imagined as an unwashed, slovenly priest who would scold her children and whip them!

—Well, sir, she said at last, so you know Latin?

This word "sir" surprised Julien so much that he hesitated for an instant.

—Yes, madame, he said timidly.

Mme. de Rênal was so happy, she dared to say to Julien:

—You won't scold the poor children too much?

—Scold them? said Julien, in astonishment. I scold them? Why should I?

—Then, sir, she added after a short silence, and in a voice that grew every instant more emotional, then you will be kind with them, you promise it?

Hearing himself called "sir" again, in perfect seriousness, and by a finely dressed lady, was altogether beyond Julien's expectations; in none of the splendid fantasies of his youth had he ever imagined that a lady of fashion would deign to say a word to him before he had a fancy uniform. Mme. de Rênal, for her part, was completely deceived by the fresh complexion, the great dark eyes of Julien, and his fine head of hair which curled a little more than usual, because, in order to cool off, he had just ducked his head in the public fountain. To her great joy, she discovered the timid manner of a young girl in this terrible tutor whose fierce look and surly manners had seemed to threaten such terrors for her children. For Mme. de Rênal's placid disposition, the contrast between her fears and what she actually saw was a great event. At last she recovered from her surprise. She was astonished to find herself at the doorstep of her own house, with this young man, almost in his shirt, and standing so close to him.

—Come in, sir, said she, in some embarrassment.

In her whole lifetime a completely pleasant experience had never struck Mme. de Rênal so profoundly; never had such a gracious event succeeded such disturbing fears. So her pretty little children, over whom she had watched so carefully, were not to pass into the

dirty hands of a grumbling old priest. Scarcely were they in the hallway when she turned back toward Julien, who was following her
timidly. His look of astonishment at such a beautiful house was one
more charm in the eyes of Mme. de Rênal. She could hardly believe
her eyes; it seemed to her particularly strange that the tutor was not
dressed in black.

—But is it true, sir, she said, stopping again and mortally afraid
of having made a mistake, for she was so happy in her illusions, is
it true that you know Latin?

These words struck at Julien's pride, and dispelled the charm in
which he had been floating for the past quarter hour.

—Yes, indeed, madame, said he, seeking to assume a chilly tone;
I know Latin as well as the priest does, and, as he is occasionally
kind enough to say himself, perhaps even better.

Mme. de Rênal noted that Julien had a particularly cruel expression; he had stopped two paces from her. She moved toward him
and said softly:

—But these first days, you will promise not to beat my children,
even if they don't know their lessons?

This gentle, almost supplicating tone on the part of a fine lady
suddenly caused Julien to forget his reputation as a Latinist. Mme.
de Rênal stood very close to him; he breathed the perfumed scent
of a woman in light summer clothing—an astonishing thing for a
young peasant. Julien blushed deeply, sighed, and said faintly:

—Have no fear, madame, you shall be obeyed in everything.

Only at this moment, when her fears on behalf of her children
were completely relieved, did Mme. de Rênal notice that Julien was
extremely handsome. The almost feminine delicacy of his features
and his awkward air seemed in no way ridiculous to a woman who
was herself extremely timid. The blunt, masculine air commonly
considered necessary to male beauty would have frightened her.

—How old are you, sir? she asked Julien.

—Nearly nineteen.

—My oldest son is eleven, said Mme. de Rênal, quite at her ease;
he will be almost like a friend for you, you can reason with him.
Once his father had occasion to whip him and the boy was sick
for a whole week, yet he was not hit hard at all.

How different from me, thought Julien. Only yesterday my father
beat me up. Don't these rich people have it easy!

Mme. de Rênal was already reaching after the slightest subtleties
of reaction within the tutor's soul; she took his look of grief for
further timidity, and tried to encourage him.

—What is your name, sir? she asked, in a tone and with an expression whose full charm Julien experienced without being able to
explain it.

—I am Julien Sorel, madame; I am terrified at entering a strange household for the first time in my life; I shall need your protection and your pardon for many faults during the first days. I have never gone to college, I was too poor; I have never talked with other men except for my cousin, the surgeon-major, who was a member of the Legion of Honor, and M. Chélan, the priest. He can give you a good account of me. My brothers have always beaten me up; you must not believe them if they say evil things about me; pardon my faults and errors, madame, I shall never mean any harm.

Julien gained in confidence during this long speech, and he examined Mme. de Rênal. Grace is perfect when it is natural and unself-conscious; Julien, who had distinct ideas about feminine beauty, would have sworn at that moment that she was only twenty years old. All of a sudden the wild idea occurred to him of kissing her hand. At first he was afraid of his own idea; an instant later he said to himself: It will be cowardice on my part not to carry out a scheme that may be useful to me, and cut down this fine lady's contempt for a laborer just liberated from his sawmill. Perhaps Julien was somewhat encouraged by that phrase, *good-looking boy*, he had been hearing every Sunday for the past six months or so from several girls. While these inner debates were going on, Mme. de Rênal gave him a few words of advice on the way to win the confidence of the children. The violence of Julien's inner struggles rendered him pale again; he said, with an air of constraint:

—Never, madame, shall I lift a hand against your children; I swear it before heaven.

And as he said these words, he had the audacity to take Mme. de Rênal's hand and carry it to his lips. She was astonished at this action, and on thinking it over, shocked. As it was quite hot, her arm was completely bare beneath her shawl, and Julien's action of raising the hand to his lips uncovered it entirely. A few moments later she scolded herself for not having grown indignant quickly enough.

M. de Rênal, who had heard their talk, emerged from his study; with the same majestic and paternal air he assumed when he married people at the mayor's office, he said to Julien:

—It is imperative that I have a word with you before the children see you.

He invited Julien into a room and brought his wife along, though she wanted to leave them alone together. When the door was closed, M. de Rênal seated himself and put on a solemn expression.

—The priest has assured me that you are a worthy person; everyone here will treat you with respect, and if I am satisfied, I may well help you toward a modest but respectable position. I desire that you see no more of your parents or your friends, their tone can scarcely be suitable for my children. Here are thirty-six francs for your first month's pay; but I require your word of honor that not a single sou of it shall go to your father.

M. de Rênal was furious with the old man, who in this bargain had got the better of him.

—Now, *sir*, for by my orders everyone here will address you as "sir," and you will find the advantages of living in a well-ordered household; now, sir, it is by no means suitable that the children see you in a workman's jacket. Did any of the servants see him? M. de Rênal asked his wife.

—No, my dear, she replied, as if deep in thought.

—So much the better. Put on this, said he to the surprised young man, handing over one of his own coats. Now let us pay a visit to M. Durand, the tailor.

An hour later, when M. de Rênal returned with the new tutor all dressed in black, he found his wife still sitting in the same room. She felt calmer in the presence of Julien, and as she watched him she forgot to be afraid. Julien gave her not a thought; for all his lofty views of destiny and human kind, his soul at that moment was a child's; he felt he had lived for years in the three hours since he stood trembling in the church. He took note of Mme. de Rênal's chilly attitude and understood that she was angry at his boldness in kissing her hand. But the sense of pride he felt at wearing clothes so different from his usual garb distracted him, and he was so hard put to repress his delight that all his gestures became abrupt, almost wild. Mme. de Rênal looked upon him with astonished eyes.

—A little gravity, sir, M. de Rênal said to him, if you wish to be respected by my children and my servants.

—Sir, Julien replied, I feel ill at ease in these new clothes. I am a poor peasant and have never worn anything but a jacket. With your permission, I shall retire to my room.

—What do you think of our new acquisition? M. de Rênal asked his wife.

By an instinctive reflex, the meaning of which she never declared to herself, Mme. de Rênal masked the truth from her husband.

—I am by no means as delighted as you are with this little peasant, she said; your kindness will make him impertinent, and then you'll have to turn him off within a month.

—So be it, then! I'll turn him off; we may be out a hundred francs or so, and Verrières will be in the habit of seeing a tutor with M. de Rênal's children. We would not have gained that point if I had left Julien in a workman's blouse. If I turn him off, naturally I'll keep the black suit I just got at the tailor's. He will keep only what I picked up for him off the ready-made rack.

The hour during which Julien kept to his room seemed an instant to Mme. de Rênal. The children, who had heard of their new tutor's arrival, overwhelmed their mother with questions. At last

Julien came forth. He was an entirely new man. To say that he was grave would be absurd; he was gravity incarnate. He was introduced to the children and spoke to them with an air that astonished M. de Rênal himself.

—I am here, young gentlemen, said he at the end of his allocution, to teach you Latin. You know what it means to recite your lessons. Well, here is the Holy Bible, said he, showing them a little black-bound duodecimo. It is, specifically, the story of our Lord Jesus Christ, the part known as the New Testament. I shall often ask you to recite your lessons; now I want you to make me recite mine.

Adolphe, the eldest of the children, had taken the book in his hand.

—Open it at random, said Julien, and read off the first three words of a verse. I shall repeat from memory the sacred book, guide of conduct for us all, until you stop me.

Adolphe opened the book and read a couple of words; Julien recited the entire page as fluently as if he had been speaking French. M. de Rênal cast toward his wife a look of triumph. The children, seeing that their parents were astonished, opened their own eyes wide. A servant came through the doorway; Julien continued to recite Latin. The servant stopped still for a moment, then disappeared. Soon madame's maid and the cook appeared in the doorway and stood there; by then Adolphe had opened the book in eight different places, and Julien was still reciting as glibly as ever.

—Oh, good Lord, what a pretty little priest! the cook said aloud; she was a good girl and very devout.

M. de Rênal's self-esteem was aroused; far from dreaming of examining the tutor, he was busy rummaging through his memory for a few Latin tags; at last he succeeded in repeating a verse of Horace. Julien knew no Latin outside the Bible. He answered with a frown:

—The holy ministry for which I am destined precludes my reading so profane an author.

M. de Rênal cited a pretty liberal number of pretended verses from Horace. He explained to his children who and what Horace was; but the children, struck with admiration, paid scarcely any attention to what he was saying. They were watching Julien.

As the servants were still crowding into the doorway, Julien felt he had to prolong the test:

—And now, said he to the youngest child, I should like M. Stanislas-Xavier[3] to select for me a passage of holy writ.

3. The names of Mme. de Rênal's children are not wholly arbitrary. Adolphe is probably named after the romantic hero of Benjamin Constant's novel (1815); Stanislas-Xavier were the given names of Louis XVIII. One notes that since the first couple of chapters, Mme. de Rênal's three children have quietly been reduced in number to two.

Little Stanislas, flushed with pride, read as well as he could the first word of a verse, and Julien recited the whole page. That nothing should be lacking to M. de Rênal's triumph, as Julien was reciting there entered M. Valenod, owner of those fine Norman horses, and M. Charcot de Maugiron, subprefect of the district. This scene earned Julien the title of "sir"; henceforth not even the servants dared refuse it.

That evening all Verrières poured in upon M. de Rênal to witness the marvel. Julien replied to everyone with an air of gloom that kept them at a distance. His glory spread through the town so rapidly that, a few days later, M. de Rênal, who feared that somebody might woo him away, proposed that he sign a contract for two years.

—No, sir, Julien replied coldly, should you decide to dismiss me, I would be obliged to leave. A contract that binds me but commits you to nothing is altogether unfair; I must decline it.

Julien managed so cleverly that within a month of his arrival M. de Rênal himself respected him. Since the priest had quarreled with Messieurs de Rênal and Valenod and nobody could reveal Julien's former admiration for Napoleon, he never spoke of him without horror.

Chapter 7

ELECTIVE AFFINITIES[4]

They can touch the heart only by bruising it.
—A Modern

The children worshipped him, he liked them not at all; his thoughts were elsewhere. What the little ones did had no power even to make him impatient. Cool, judicial, impassive and yet beloved, because his coming had in some degree relieved the boredom of the household, he was a good tutor. On his own account, he felt only hatred and horror for the high society to which he was now admitted, if only at the foot of the table—a circumstance which may explain his hate and horror. At certain formal dinners he could hardly contain his hatred of everything that surrounded him. One day in particular of the festival of St. Louis,[5] when M. Valenod was dining with M. de Rênal, Julien almost gave himself away; he fled into the garden, on the pretext of looking after the children. What harangues about honesty, he cried; you'd think it was the only virtue there is; and yet, what consideration, what fawning respect, for a man who's obviously doubled and tripled his estate since he's been in charge of the poorhouse! I'll bet he even makes a profit out of

4. The chapter title is the name of a fine novel by Goethe which Stendhal had read many years before.
5. The festival of St. Louis falls on August 25; this date makes some trouble for the chronologist of the novel, since according to indications it should be later in the year at this point.

the orphans, paupers whose misery is specially sacred. Ah, monsters, they're all monsters! And I'm a sort of orphan myself, hated by my father, my brothers, my whole family.

A few days before the festival of Saint Louis, Julien had been walking alone and saying his breviary in a little park called the Belvedere, which stands above Loyalty Square, when he saw his two brothers approaching along a deserted path. His first impulse was to avoid them. These clumsy oafs were so provoked by the fine black suit of their brother, by his look of extreme cleanliness, and by the sincere contempt he felt for them that they beat him up and left him on the ground bloody and unconscious. Mme. de Rênal, strolling with M. Valenod and the subprefect, arrived by accident in the little park; she saw Julien stretched on the ground and supposed him dead. Her anguish was such as to rouse M. Valenod's jealousy.

His alarm was premature. Julien thought Mme. de Rênal very lovely, but he hated her for her beauty; it was the first reef on which his career had almost run aground. He talked to her as little as possible, hoping to make her forget the folly that had led him, the first day, to kiss her hand.

Elisa, Mme. de Rênal's maid, had not failed to fall in love with the young tutor, and often talked of him with her mistress. Mlle. Elisa's affection earned Julien the hatred of one of the valets. One day he heard this man saying to Elisa: You never talk to me any more since that greasy tutor's been in the house. Julien deserved no such epithet; but with the instincts of a good-looking young fellow he paid extra attention to his appearance. M. Valenod's dislike of him redoubled as well. He said publicly that such elegance was unbecoming in a young abbé. Except for the cassock, that was the dress that Julien wore.

Mme. de Rênal noted that he talked frequently with Mlle. Elisa; she learned that these talks were occasioned by the extreme meagerness of Julien's wardrobe. He had so little linen that he was often obliged to have it laundered outside the house, and it was in these little arrangements that Elisa served him. Such extreme poverty, of which she had never had a suspicion, touched Mme. de Rênal; she would have liked to give him a present, but did not dare; this inner resistance was the first painful sensation that Julien caused her. Until then, his name and the sense of a pure and spiritual joy had been synonymous for her. Tormented by the thought of Julien's poverty, Mme. de Rênal spoke to her husband about making him a present of some linen:

—What foolishness! he told her. That's some idea, giving presents to a man who's serving us perfectly well already. We might do it if he were slacking off and we wanted to rouse his eagerness again.

Mme. de Rênal was humiliated by this way of looking at things; before Julien came she would never have noticed it. She never saw his costume, very neat but very simple, like that of a young abbé, without thinking to herself: poor boy, how can he possibly manage?

Gradually she came to feel pity instead of shock at all the things Julien lacked.

Mme. de Rênal was one of those provincial women whom you might very well take for fools the first two weeks of your acquaintance. She had no experience of life and made no effort at small talk. Since she was gifted with a delicate and lofty soul, her instinct for happiness which is natural to all living creatures provided that mostly she paid no attention to the behavior of the gross creatures amid whom fortune had thrust her.

She would have been noted for the instinctive quickness of her wit if she had received the least education. But as an heiress she had been raised among devotional nuns with a passion for the *Sacred Heart of Jesus* and a violent hatred for those Frenchmen who were assumed to be enemies of the Jesuits. Mme. de Rênal had the good sense to forget immediately, as ridiculous, whatever she had been taught in the convent; but she put nothing in its place, and ended by knowing nothing. The premature flatteries to which she had been subjected as heiress to a great fortune, and a distinct leaning toward passionate devotion, had given her a whole inner life of her own. With the most perfect air of condescension and a self-sacrificing manner which all the Verrières husbands cited to their wives as exemplary and which was M. de Rênal's chief pride, she still managed her existence on the principle of the most lofty disdain. Any princess distinguished for her pride pays infinitely more attention to what her attendants do than did this lady, so gentle and modest in appearance, to the words or deeds of her husband. Until Julien came she had really paid no attention to anyone except her children. Their little ailments and pains, their little pleasures, had occupied the entire consciousness of this soul who in her whole life had never adored anyone but God when she was in the *Sacred Heart* of Besançon.

Though she would not have ventured to say a word to anyone, a feverish spell on the part of one of her children could reduce her almost to the same condition as if the child had died. A burst of crude laughter and a shrug of the shoulders accompanied by some trivial proverb about the folly of women were the only sort of welcome she ever got when the need to open her heart led her, in the first years of her marriage, to discuss troubles of this sort with her husband. His variety of humor, especially when it concerned the illnesses of her children, twisted the knife in Mme. de Rênal's heart. And it was for this that she had exchanged the obsequious and honeyed flatteries of the Jesuit convent where she had passed her youth. She achieved her education through grief. Too proud to talk openly about troubles of this sort, even to her friend Mme. Derville, she supposed that all men were like her husband, like M. Valenod, like the subprefect de Maugiron. Coarseness and brutal indifference to everything that was not money, promotion, or a cross; a blind hatred for any sort of thought that went against their interests—these qualities seemed to her as natural to the sex as wearing boots and felt hats.

After many years Mme. de Rênal was not yet accustomed to these money men among whom it was her fate to live.

Hence the success of the young peasant, Julien. She found many sorts of pleasure, all bright with the charm of novelty, in the sympathy accorded by his proud and noble spirit. Mme. de Rênal quickly forgave him his extreme ignorance, which was only one grace more in her eyes, and the rudeness of his manners, which she succeeded in correcting. She found that he was worth listening to, even when the talk ran on the most ordinary topics, even in the matter of a wretched dog, crushed as it was crossing the street by the cart of a peasant going by at a trot. The sight of such suffering provoked her husband to his coarse laughter, whereas she noted that Julien's dark, finely arched eyebrows contracted in a frown. Gradually, it seemed to her generosity, nobility of spirit, and humanity existed only in the person of this young abbé. She felt for him all the sympathy, and even worship, that these virtues arouse in well-born natures.

In Paris, Julien's position with regard to Mme. de Rênal would quickly have been simplified; but in Paris, love is the child of novels. The young tutor and his timid mistress would have found in three or four novels, or even in the couplets of the Gymnase, a clarification of their position.[6] The novels would have outlined for them the roles to be played, provided them with a model to imitate; and this model, sooner or later, though without the least pleasure and perhaps even reluctantly, vanity would have forced Julien to follow.

In a little village of the Aveyron or the Pyrenees, the slightest incident would have been rendered decisive by the heat of the climate. Under our darker skies, a poor young man who is ambitious only because the delicacy of his heart makes absolutely necessary for him some of those pleasures that money bestows can see every day a woman of thirty, sincerely virtuous, devoted to her children, and who never thinks of looking in novels for examples of conduct. Everything progresses slowly, things are done gradually in the provinces, behavior is more natural.

6. The Gymnase Dramatique, a theater erected in 1820, was largely given over to vaudeville comedies in couplets.

Often, as she thought of the young tutor's poverty, Mme. de Rênal was moved almost to weep. Julien came upon her one day when she was actually in tears.

—Ah, madame, have you had some misfortune?

—No, my friend, she answered; call the children, we'll go for a walk.

She took his arm, and leaned on it in a way that seemed extraordinary to Julien. This was the first time she had called him "my friend."

Toward the end of the stroll Julien noted that she was blushing deeply. She slowed her steps.

—You will perhaps have heard, she said, without looking at him, that I am the only heiress of a rich aunt who lives near Besançon. She loads me down with presents. . . . My boys are making such progress . . . such amazing progress . . . that I would very much like to ask you to accept a little present as a token of my gratitude. It is only a matter of a few louis so you can get some linen. But . . . she added, blushing even more deeply, and she fell silent.

—What, madame? asked Julien.

—It would be unnecessary, she continued, lowering her head, to speak of this to my husband.

—I may be humble, madame, but I am not base, Julien replied, stopping and drawing himself up to his full stature, while his eyes sparkled with anger; perhaps you have not thought about that enough. I should be worse than a menial if I put myself in the position of concealing from M. de Rênal anything having to do *with my money.*

Mme. de Rênal was crushed.

—His honor the mayor, Julien went on, has made five payments of my thirty-six franc salary since I have been in his household. I am ready to display my account book to M. de Rênal, or to anybody else, even to M. Valenod, who hates me.

After this outburst, Mme. de Rênal remained pale and trembling, and the walk ended without either one of them finding any pretext for renewing the discussion. Love for Mme. de Rênal became more and more impossible in Julien's haughty heart; on her side, she admired, she respected him; she had been scolded by him. Under pretext of atoning for the humiliation she had unintentionally caused him, she allowed herself to pay him the most delicate attentions. The novelty of these maneuvers provided a week's happiness for Mme. de Rênal. They had the further effect of partially soothing Julien's anger; he was far from seeing in them anything that could resemble personal affection.

That's how rich people are, he told himself; they humiliate you and then think they can set things right with a few monkey tricks!

Mme. de Rênal's heart was so full, and still so innocent, that in spite of her resolutions on this point she told her husband about the offer she had made to Julien and the way in which he had rejected it.

—How in the world, said M. de Rênal in great indignation, could you endure a refusal on the part of a *servant?*

And when Mme. de Rênal exclaimed against this term:

—I speak, madame, as the late Prince of Condé did when introducing his courtiers to his new wife: "*All these people,* said he, *are our servants.*" I read you the passage from Besenval's *Memoirs,*[7] it's important in these matters of precedence. Anyone who isn't a gentleman, who lives in your house and receives a salary, is your servant. I'll have a few words with this M. Julien, and give him a hundred francs.

—Ah, my dear, said Mme. de Rênal, trembling, at least you must not do it in front of the other servants!

—You are right, they might be jealous, and rightly so, said her husband, and he took himself off, much impressed by the vastness of the sum.

Mme. de Rênal dropped into a chair, almost fainting with grief. He is going to humiliate Julien, and it will be my fault! She felt a horror of her husband, and buried her face in her hands. She swore then never to confide in him again.

When she saw Julien again, she was all atremble, her throat so choked that she could hardly manage to say the least word. In her embarrassment, she took his hands and wrung them.

—Well, my friend, she managed to say at last, are you pleased with my husband?

—Why not? said Julien, with a bitter smile; he just gave me a hundred francs.

Mme. de Rênal looked hesitantly at him.

—Give me your arm, she said to him, finally, with an accent of decision Julien had never noted in her before.

She ventured to go to the bookseller of Verrières, in spite of his frightful reputation for liberalism.[8] There she selected books to the value of ten louis which she presented to her sons. But the books were just those that she knew Julien wanted. She demanded that each of her sons write his name in the books that had been selected for him, and do it immediately, in the bookseller's shop. While

7. Besenval, a Swiss officer in service of the French king during the eighteenth century, left behind some (unreliable) memoirs and a novel which Stendhal prized as representations of life under the old regime. The point here is M. de Rênal's effort to copy aristocratic manners at very long range indeed.

8. The only bookstore in Stendhal's Grenoble was a center of liberal thought, hence bookstores in the Stendhalian fiction are generally centers of leftist influence, despised by good society.

Mme. de Rênal was happy in making this sort of audacious repara-
tion to Julien, he was lost in amazement at the number of books to
be seen in a bookstore. Never had he dared to set foot in such a
profane place; his heart was thumping. Far from even trying to
think what was going on in Mme. de Rênal's heart, he was lost in
thought about how it would be possible for a young theological
student to get hold of some of these books. The idea occurred to
him at last that with some cleverness one might persuade M. de
Rênal that it would be good for his sons to write themes based on
the lives of celebrated gentlemen born in the district. After a month
of managing, Julien got this idea across, and to such effect that
shortly afterward he ventured, in a conversation with M. de Rênal,
to propose an action that would otherwise have been very painful
for the noble mayor; it was a matter of contributing to the prosperity
of a liberal by taking out a subscription to the lending library. M. de
Rênal agreed, indeed, that it would be wise to give his elder son
a visual impression of various books he might hear mentioned when
he went off to the military academy; but Julien saw that his honor
refused stubbornly to go a step farther. He suspected a secret motive,
but could not guess at it.

—I was thinking, sir, he remarked one day, that it would be
highly inappropriate for the name of a gentlemen, a name like
Rênal, to appear in the dirty ledgers of a bookseller.

M. de Rênal's brow cleared.

—It would also be a very bad business, Julien continued in even
humbler tones, for a poor student of theology, if someone some day
should find that his name had been in the accounts of a bookseller
who keeps a lending library. The liberals could accuse me of having
asked for the most infamous books; who knows, they might go so
far as to write in after my name the titles of these perverse volumes.

But Julien was off the track. He saw the mayor's face resume its
expression of embarrassment and ill temper. Julien fell silent. I
have him on the hook, said he to himself.

A few days later the elder boy asked Julien about a book that had
been advertised in the *Quotidienne*;[9] M. de Rênal was present.

—In order to avoid all occasions for triumph by the Jacobin party,
and yet to provide me with a way to answer M. Adolphe, said the
young tutor, it might be possible to take out a subscription at the
library in the name of the lowest of your servants.

—Not a bad idea at all, said M. de Rênal, in great good humor.

—Yet it must be specified, Julien added, with that grave and
almost unhappy expression which suits certain people so admirably
when they see that something they have desired for a long time is

9. The legitimist, that is, the royalist *Quotidienne* stood in diametrical op-
and authoritarian newspaper. The position to the *Constitutionnel*.

about to come true, it must be specified that the servant shall not withdraw any novel. Once in the house, these dangerous books may corrupt madame's maids and the very servant himself.

—You are forgetting to ban political pamphlets as well, added M. de Rênal with a haughty air. He was trying to conceal his admiration for the shrewd middle course discovered by his children's tutor.

Julien's life was composed of a series of such petty negotiations; and his success in them counted much more, with him, than the sentiment of marked personal preference which he could have seen, if he had only looked, in the heart of Mme. de Rênal.

The moral position he had occupied all his life repeated itself in the household of the mayor of Verrières. As in his father's saw-mill, he despised in his heart the people among whom he lived, and they hated him. Every day he observed, from the stories told by the subprefect, by M. Valenod, by the other acquaintances of the family, when they talked about things that had just taken place beneath their very eyes, how little their ideas corresponded with reality. If an action seemed admirable to him, that was precisely the deed which called forth blame from the people around him. His inward comment on them was always: What monsters, or what fools! The joke is that with all his pride, he often did not understand the first thing of what was being talked about.

In his whole life he had spoken sincerely with only one person, the old surgeon-major; the few ideas he had all bore on Bonaparte's campaigns in Italy or the practice of surgery. His youthful courage was fired by detailed accounts of extremely painful operations; he used to tell himself: I wouldn't have flinched.

The first time that Mme. de Rênal tried to talk with him on some topic other than the education of children, he began to talk about surgical operations; she turned pale, and begged him to stop.[1]

Julien knew nothing else. And so, as he spent much time in the company of Mme. de Rênal, the most extraordinary silence sprang up between them as soon as they were alone together. In the drawing room, though his deportment was always humble, she noted in his eyes an air of intellectual superiority over whatever company came to the house. Finding herself alone with him for a minute, she saw him grow visibly embarrassed. She was disturbed by it, for her woman's instinct warned her that this embarrassment was in no way sentimental.

As a result of an odd idea picked up from some tale of good

1. The mechanical association of ideas within Julien's mind controls his behavior rigidly, even at the expense of his intentions; see a similar story in Rousseau of how, because he liked her, he was compelled to accuse the serving girl Marion of theft (*Confessions,* Book II, toward the end).

society told by the old surgeon-major, Julien felt humiliated as soon as there was a moment's silence anytime he was in the company of a woman, as if this silence were bound to be his personal fault. When they were alone together, the sensation was a hundred times more painful. His imagination was full of the most exaggerated, the most Spanish,[2] ideas about what a man should say when he is alone with a woman; it offered him, in his difficulties, only unacceptable ideas. His soul might be in the clouds, but he could not break out of this humiliating silence. Thus the severe air he assumed during his long walks with Mme. de Rênal and the children was intensified by the most cruel sufferings. He despised himself horribly. If, unhappily, he forced himself to talk, he always managed to say the most ridiculous things conceivable. To complete his misery, he saw and exaggerated his own absurdity; but what he did not see was the expression of his eyes; they were so fine and expressed so ardent a spirit that sometimes, like good actors, they gave meaning to words which in themselves had none. Mme. de Rênal noticed that when he was alone with her he never succeeded in saying anything good except when he was distracted by some unforeseen event and forgot about turning a neat compliment. As the friends of the family did not spoil her with an excess of new and brilliant ideas, she took great pleasure in the flashes of Julien's wit.

Since Napoleon fell, every semblance of gallantry has been strictly banished from the manners of the provinces. People are afraid for their jobs. Rascals seek support from the congregation; and hypocrisy has made splendid headway even among the liberal classes. Boredom is thicker than ever. The only pleasures left are reading and farming.

Mme. de Rênal, rich heiress of a pious aunt, married at sixteen to a respectable gentleman, had never in her life seen or experienced anything that resembled in any way whatever the passion of love. Her confessor, the good Curé Chélan, was almost the only man who had ever mentioned the topic to her, in connection with M. Valenod's advances, and he had given her such a disgusting picture of it that the word represented nothing, in her mind, but the most depraved libertinage. She regarded as wholly exceptional, and perhaps even as unnatural, love as it had been presented to her in the very moderate number of novels that had chanced to meet her eyes. Thanks to this ignorance, Mme. de Rênal, in perfect happiness, occupied herself continually with Julien, and was far from blaming herself in any way.

2. Via a train of association leading through a favorite great aunt, Elisabeth Gagnon, Pierre Corneille, and his play *Le Cid*, Stendhal always associated a magnanimous heroism touched by grandiloquence with *espagnolisme*, Spanish ideas and style.

Chapter 8

SMALL HAPPENINGS

Then there were sighs, the deeper for suppression,
And stolen glances, sweeter for the theft,
And burning blushes, though for no transgression.
—*Don Juan*, Canto I, stanza 74

Mme. de Rênal's angelic temper, which was due to her character and her present happiness, was disturbed a little only when she came to think of her maid, Elisa. The girl came into a legacy, made her confession to Abbé Chélan, and told him she wanted to marry Julien. The priest was really delighted at his friend's good fortune; but he was greatly surprised when Julien told him, in a decisive tone, that Mlle. Elisa's offer was by no means acceptable to him.

—Keep watch, my son, said the priest with a frown, over this disposition of yours. You are turning down a very adequate fortune; if it is simply because of your priestly vocation, let me congratulate you. For fifty-six years I have been priest of Verrières, yet now, it seems, I am going to be turned out. Even though I have an income of eight hundred florins, I find this distressing. I remind you of this detail simply so you will have no illusions about your future as a priest. If you expect to make your way with the men of power, the fate of your soul is sealed. Perhaps you can make a fortune, but you will have to trample on the wretched while flattering the subprefect, the mayor—the important man, whoever he is—by playing on his passions. Such conduct, known in the world as shrewd policy, may not, in the case of a layman, be absolutely destructive of every hope of salvation; but in our condition, we must choose to flourish in this world or the next one; there is no middle course. Go along with you now, my dear boy, think it over, and three days from now come back with a final answer. At the root of your character, I seem to see (and I am sorry for it) a sort of gloomy energy which does not suggest the moderation and perfect indifference to earthly advantage that is proper to a priest. I expect great things of your intellect; but let me tell you (added the good man, with tears in his eyes) that if you are a priest, I shall fear for your salvation.

Julien was ashamed of his emotion; for the first time in his life he saw that someone loved him; he wept with joy, and went off to hide his tears in the deep woods above Verrières.

—Why am I in this state? he said to himself at last; I feel I would give my life a hundred times over for this good priest Chélan, and yet he's just demonstrated to me that I'm a fool. He is the man above all others that I must deceive, and he's seen through me. That secret energy which he talks about is my plan to get ahead in the world. He thinks me unworthy of the priesthood, and just at the moment when I thought my rejecting a fifty louis income would give him the grandest impression of my pious vocation.

—From now on, Julien continued, I must rely only on those parts of my character that I've thoroughly tested. Who would have supposed that I would find pleasure in tears, that I would love the man who proves to me that I'm only a fool!

Three days later Julien had discovered the pretext he should have had ready from the beginning; it happened to be a slander, but what matter? He made known to the priest, with many hesitations, that a certain reason, which he could not explain because it would implicate a third party, had set his mind against the proposed marriage. It amounted to an accusation against Elisa. M. Chélan noted in his behavior a certain worldly passion quite different from that which ought to inspire a young levite.

—My boy, he said again, be a respectable tradesman in the provinces, well liked and well educated, rather than a priest without conviction.

Julien replied to these new warnings rather well, as far as words went; he found just the expressions that an ardent young seminarian would have used, but the tone in which he pronounced them, the ill-concealed fire that glittered in his eyes, alarmed M. Chélan.

Let us not think too poorly of Julien's future; he was inventing, with perfect correctness, the language of a sly and prudent hypocrisy. At his age, that's not bad. In the matter of tone and gestures, he lived among yokels, and so had never studied the great models. Later, circumstances permitted him to approach closer to fine gentlemen; no sooner had he done so than he was as skillful with gestures as with words.

Mme. de Rênal was surprised that her maid's stroke of good fortune didn't make her any happier; every day the girl went off to the priest and returned in tears; finally Elisa spoke to her of her marriage.

Mme. de Rênal thought herself ill; a sort of fever kept her from sleeping; she was alive only when she had either Julien or her maid under surveillance. They were all she could think of, and she dreamed of the happiness they would find together. That meager little house where they would have to live on fifty louis a year seemed altogether heavenly to her. Julien might very well become a lawyer at Bray, the subprefecture a couple of leagues from Verrières; in that case, she might possibly see him from time to time.

Mme. de Rênal really thought she was going mad; she said so to her husband, and at last actually fell ill. That evening, as her maid was serving her, she noticed that the girl was weeping. She was feeling angry with Elisa, and had just spoken sharply to her; now she begged her pardon. Elisa's tears flowed afresh; with her mistress' permission, she said, she would tell the whole story.

—Speak up, said Mme. de Rênal.

—Well, madame, he has refused me; people have told him nasty tales about me, and he believes them.

—Who has refused you? said Mme. de Rênal, scarcely able to breathe.

—Who else, madame, who else but M. Julien? the maid replied, through her tears. The priest can't talk him out of it; for the priest doesn't think it's right for him to turn down a good girl just because she was a chambermaid. After all, M. Julien's father is nothing but a carpenter; and how did he himself earn his living before he came here?

Mme. de Rênal was no longer listening; overcome by joy, she was almost out of her mind. She insisted on hearing, several times over, that Julien had refused in a most positive manner which absolutely precluded a more sensible reconsideration.

—I will make a last effort, she said to her maid, I will talk to M. Julien myself.

The next day after lunch Mme. de Rênal indulged in the delicious pleasure of pleading her rival's cause, and of seeing Elisa's hand and fortune turned down, again and again, for an entire hour.

Gradually Julien passed beyond merely shrewd responses, and ended by answering Mme. de Rênal's prudent suggestions with wit and intelligence. She could not support the torrent of joy that flooded her soul after so many days of despair, and became really unwell. When she was revived and taken to her room she sent everyone away.

—Can I be in love with Julien? she said to herself at last.

This discovery, which at any other time would have plunged her in remorse and deep distress, was at the moment merely an unusual spectacle to which she remained quite indifferent. Her soul, worn out by all it had endured, could no longer respond to her feelings.

Mme. de Rênal tried to work but fell into a deep sleep; when she awoke she was not as much afraid as she should have been. She was too happy to suspect the turn of events. Simple and innocent, this good provincial lady had never plagued her mind to work up a new response for each new shade of passion or of grief. Before Julien came she had been wholly absorbed in that mass of work which, outside of Paris, falls to every good mother of a family; Mme. de Rênal thought of the passions as we think of the lottery— inevitable delusion, a path to happiness taken only by madmen.

The dinner bell sounded; Mme. de Rênal blushed deeply as she heard the voice of Julien, bringing in the children. Being a little cleverer since she fell in love, she explained her flushed features by pleading a frightful headache.

—That's women for you, M. de Rênal struck in with a guffaw; there's always something out of order in those machines!

Though she was used to this sort of wit, the tone of voice shocked Mme. de Rênal. To divert her mind, she looked toward Julien; had he been the ugliest man in the world, at that moment he would have been pleasing to her.

Always intent on copying court manners, M. de Rênal moved out to the country during the first fine days of spring, to Vergy; it is the little town rendered famous by the tragic story of Gabrielle.[3] A few hundred feet from the picturesque ruins of the old Gothic church, M. de Rênal owned an old country house, with its four corner towers and a garden designed like that of the Tuileries, with plenty of box hedges and rows of chestnut trees which were clipped twice a year. Eight or ten magnificent walnut trees marked the edge of the orchard; their immense masses of foliage rose to a height of nearly eighty feet.

—Every one of those damn walnut trees, said M. de Rênal to his wife when she admired them, costs me the yield of a quarter acre of ground; wheat won't grow in the shade.

To Mme. de Rênal, the countryside seemed altogether fresh and new; her admiration reached almost to transports. Her enthusiasms gave her new spirit and resolution. The day of their arrival at Vergy, when M. de Rênal had returned to town on official business, Mme. de Rênal hired some workmen. Julien had given her the idea of a little gravel path that would pass through the orchard and under the walnut trees, on which the children could walk during the early morning without getting their shoes soaked in the dew. The idea was given shape less than twenty-four hours after being conceived. Mme. de Rênal passed a merry day with Julien supervising the workers.

When the mayor of Verrières returned from town, great was his surprise to find the path already completed. His return was a sur-

3. Gabrielle de Vergy is the heroine of a late-thirteenth-century romance popular in the Renaissance and since translated to the tragic and operatic stage. Briefly, it tells how the Duchess of Burgundy falls in love with a man who is already in love with Gabrielle, chatelaine of the castle of Vergy; the duchess, enraged by his rejection, complains to the duke that he has assaulted her. He exculpates himself without difficulty, but in the process reveals his love for Gabrielle. The duke betrays this confidence, and the duchess is furious with Gabrielle. As a result, Gabrielle commits suicide, and her lover, remorseful, stabs himself over her dead body. This is a high-minded, almost parodically chivalric intrigue; but in the young man torn between a high-born destructive mistress and a provincial, sensitive one appear certain thematic parallels with the *Rouge*. Vergy itself is in the right general area for Stendhal's story, not far from Dijon, but his picture of the countryside is founded on memories of a country house near Grenoble which his sister Pauline occupied during the second decade of the nineteenth century. A recent operatic version of Gabrielle's story, by Mercadante, had had its premier on August 8, 1828.

prise for Mme. de Rênal as well; she had quite forgotten his existence. During the next two months he never ceased talking sulkily about the boldness of some people who, without consulting him, had executed such an important piece of *repair work;* but as Mme. de Rênal had done it at her own expense, that consoled him a bit.

She passed the days playing with her children in the garden and chasing butterflies. They made themselves great nets of gauze with which to capture the poor *Lepidoptera*—that was the barbarous name that Julien taught Mme. de Rênal. For she had ordered from Besançon the handsome treatise of M. Godart;[4] and Julien read to her from it accounts of these insects and their remarkable habits.

They pinned them pitilessly to a mounting board of stiff paper, also designed by Julien. And thus at last there came to be, between Mme. de Rênal and Julien, a subject of conversation; he was no longer exposed to the frightful sufferings imposed upon him by moments of silence.

They talked continually, and with great animation, though always of perfectly innocent matters. This active, bustling, cheerful life was much to the taste of everyone except Mlle. Elisa, who found herself badly overworked. Even during carnival time, said she, when there are dances at Verrières, madame never takes such pains over her toilette; here she changes dresses two or three times a day.

As we have no intention of flattering anyone, we shall not deny that Mme. de Rênal, who had a splendid complexion, took pains to wear dresses that liberally exposed her arms and throat. She had an admirable figure, and this manner of dress suited her to perfection.

—You've *never been so young,* my dear, said all her friends from Verrières when they came out to dine at Vergy. (It's an idiom of the country.)

A remarkable fact, which very few of us will believe, is that Mme. de Rênal took all these pains without any real conscious purpose. It pleased her to do so; and without thinking about it, whenever she was not chasing butterflies with the children and Julien, she worked with Elisa on her wardrobe. Her one trip to Verrières was made in order to buy new summer dresses just arrived from Mulhouse.

She brought back with her to Vergy a young lady to whom she was distantly related. Since her marriage, Mme. de Rênal had gradually grown attached to Mme. Derville, with whom she had formerly attended the Convent of the Sacred Heart.[5]

Mme. Derville laughed a great deal at what she called the crazy notions of her cousin: by myself, she said, I'd never think such

4. J. B. Godart wrote a standard account of French butterflies early in the nineteenth century.

5. Cool, sensible, and unparticularized in the fiction, Mme. Derville nonetheless enshrines an early flame of Sten-

thoughts at all. When she was with her husband, Mme. de Rênal was ashamed of these odd notions, which in Paris are called sallies of wit, as if they were something stupid; but in the presence of Mme. Derville she took courage. At first she expressed her thoughts only timidly; but when the ladies had been alone together for a while, Mme. de Rênal grew more spirited, and a long, solitary morning passed in an instant, leaving the two friends perfectly merry. On this particular trip, reasonable Mme. Derville found her cousin much less witty and much more happy.

Julien, for his part, had lived like a perfect child ever since they moved to the country, as happy to run after butterflies as his pupils. After all that constraint and crafty managing, now that he was alone, far from the sight of men and instinctively unafraid of Mme. de Rênal, he yielded to the sheer pleasure of existing, which is so vital at his age, and to the pleasures of the most beautiful mountains in the world.

When Mme. Derville arrived Julien was at once convinced that she was his friend; he hastened to show her the panorama that opens up at the end of the new walk under the walnut trees. It's really equal, if not superior, to the finest landscapes of Switzerland and the Italian lake country. If one climbs the steep slope which begins a few paces further on, one comes suddenly on a series of great precipices crowned with oak trees which fall away almost to the river. Atop these tumbled rocks, Julien, happy, free, and, moreover, king of the household, guided the two ladies and delighted in their admiration of the magnificent view.

—There's something about it that reminds me of Mozart's music, said Mme. Derville.

The jealousy of his brothers, the continual presence of his despotic, angry father, had spoiled the countryside around Verrières for Julien. At Vergy, he had no such bitter thoughts; for the first time in his life, when he looked about him he saw no enemy. When M. de Rênal was in town, as frequently happened, he was free to read; soon, instead of reading at night (and taking pains to hide his lamp under an overturned flowerpot), he could go to sleep; for during the day, between the children's lessons, he could come to these rocks with the one book which served as the rule of his conduct and the object of his passion. At different times he found in it happiness, ecstasy, and consolation for momentary discouragement.

Certain things that Napoleon says on the topic of women and various discussions on the merits of novels fashionable during his

---

dhal's; her name in real life was Sophie Boulon. She came from Grenoble and Stendhal's private pseudonym for her, a quarter century before the *Rouge* was written, was Mme. Derville.

reign now gave Julien for the first time certain ideas which any other young man of his age would have had years ago.

The dog days came; they got in the habit of spending the evening under an immense linden tree a few feet from the house. It was very dark there. One evening Julien was talking animatedly and enjoying the very real pleasures of talking well, and to young women, when, in the course of a gesture he touched the hand of Mme. de Rênal, which was lying on the back of a painted wooden garden chair.

The hand was swiftly withdrawn; but Julien thought it was his *duty* to make sure that the hand was not withdrawn when he touched it. The idea of an obligation to fulfill, and of ridicule, or at least a sense of inferiority, to be endured if one did not succeed, immediately drove the last trace of pleasure from his heart.

Chapter 9

AN EVENING IN THE COUNTRY

The Dido of M. Guerin, a charming sketch!
—Strombeck[6]

His glances the next morning, when he saw Mme. de Rênal, were remarkable; he looked her over like an enemy with whom he was bound to fight. These glances, so different from those of the evening before, drove Mme. de Rênal to distraction; she had been kind to him, and he seemed annoyed. She could not turn her eyes from his.

Mme. Derville's presence permitted Julien to talk less and think more about his preoccupation. The only thing he did all day was to strengthen himself by reading the inspired book in which his soul was to be tempered.

He cut short the children's lessons, and then when reminded of his need for glory by the presence of Mme. de Rênal, he decided it was absolutely necessary that his hand should remain in hers that very evening.

As the sun sank slowly and the decisive moment approached, Julien's heart began to beat furiously. Night fell. With a joy that seemed to lift an immense weight from his heart he saw that it would be very dark. The sky, heavy with thick clouds driven forward by a hot wind, seemed to promise a storm. The two ladies strolled about for a long time. Everything they did that evening seemed peculiar to Julien. They were enjoying that time of day which, for

6. A German friend whom Stendhal met at Brunswick when he was there on military assignment in 1806–08 and whom he kept in touch with thereafter. Pierre Guerin was a popular painter of the Napoleonic era; his "Aeneas Relating to Dido the Disasters of Troy" was a great success in 1817 and now hangs in the Louvre.

certain delicate souls, seems to augment the pleasure of loving.

At last they sat down, Mme. de Rênal next to Julien, Mme. Derville on the other side of her friend. Preoccupied with his great attempt, Julien found nothing to say, and the conversation languished.

Will I be cringing and miserable like this at the first duel that befalls me? Julien asked himself—for he was too suspicious, of himself and others, not to be aware of his own state.

In his anguish of soul any danger would have seemed preferable. How often did he pray that some little piece of business would come up which would oblige Mme. de Rênal to go back into the house and leave the garden! The violence of his inner struggle had its effect on his voice; soon the voice of Mme. de Rênal began to tremble too, though Julien was unable to notice it. The frightful struggle between his sense of duty and his timidity was too absorbing for him to notice anything outside himself. Quarter of ten had just struck on the house clock, and still he had not dared to make a move. Furious at his own cowardice, Julien said to himself: At the stroke of ten either I will do what I have been promising myself to do all day or I'll go upstairs and blow out my brains.

After a final moment of anxious waiting, during which his excess of emotion nearly drove Julien out of his mind, the hour of ten began to sound on the clock above his head. Every stroke of that fatal gong reverberated through his body, causing something like a convulsion.

Then, as the last stroke of ten was still sounding, he reached forth his hand and grasped that of Mme. de Rênal, who immediately withdrew it. Julien, without knowing very clearly what he was doing, grasped it again. Though deeply agitated himself, he was struck by the icy chill of the hand he held; he wrung it with convulsive force; a last effort was made to withdraw it, but at last it remained in his possession.

His soul was flooded with joy, not because he loved Mme. de Rênal but because an atrocious torment had ceased. To prevent Mme. Derville from noticing anything, he supposed himself obliged to talk; his voice was now strong and resonant. Mme. de Rênal's, on the other hand, was so full of emotion that her friend supposed she was ill and suggested that they go in. Julien sensed the danger: if Mme. de Rênal goes back to that drawing room, I fall back on the frightful posture in which I passed the entire day. I haven't held onto the hand long enough to count it a definite conquest.

As Mme. Derville renewed her suggestion that they go in, Julien pressed vigorously the hand that had been abandoned to him.

Mme. de Rênal was already getting up, but sat down again, saying in a languid voice:

—I really do feel a little ill, but the fresh air is doing me good.

These words confirmed Julien's happiness, which in that instant was at its peak: he talked, he forgot to pretend, he seemed, to the two listening ladies, the world's most amiable man. And yet there was a little cowardice behind this eloquence which suddenly came flooding over him. He was in mortal terror that Mme. Derville, wearied by the wind which was starting to blow as a prelude to the storm, might go indoors by herself. Then he would be left alone with Mme. de Rênal. He had found, almost by accident, enough blind courage to take a single action; but he felt utterly incapable of saying the simplest word to Mme. de Rênal. However mild her reproaches, he would be beaten down by them and his newly gained advantages canceled.

Happily for him, that evening his earnest, eager speeches found favor with Mme. Derville, who often considered him childishly awkward and rather dull. As for Mme. de Rênal, with her hand in Julien's, she thought of nothing at all; she allowed herself to live. The moments passed under that great linden tree, which local tradition says was planted by Charles the Bold,[7] were for her a whole age of happiness. She listened with delight to the sighs of the wind in the thick foliage, and the noise of a few scattered rain-drops which were starting to fall on its lower leaves. Julien failed to notice one circumstance which would have much relieved him; Mme. de Rênal, who had been obliged to take back her hand in order to help her cousin right a flowerpot overturned at their feet by the wind, as soon as she sat down again returned her hand to his almost without difficulty, as if the whole matter were now settled between them.

Midnight had long struck; it was time to go in, and the little group at last broke up. Mme. de Rênal, overwhelmed with the sensation of being in love, was so ignorant as scarcely to reproach herself at all. Her happiness kept her awake. But Julien slept like a log; he was exhausted by the struggles which pride and timidity had been waging all day in his heart.

Next morning he was awakened at five; and it would have been a bitter blow for Mme. de Rênal if she had known that he scarcely gave her a thought. He had carried out *his duty, and a heroic duty*. Overjoyed at this thought, he locked himself into his room and surrendered himself with a new sort of pleasure entirely to reading of the exploits of his hero.

When the bell sounded for lunch he had forgotten, in the course of reading bulletins of the Grande Armée, all his advantages of the night before. He said to himself blithely, as he descended the staircase: I've got to tell this woman I love her.

7. Charles the Bold, a fifteenth-century duke of Burgundy, is several times men- tioned opportunely when Julien is called upon to be audacious.

Instead of glances charged with affection, which he was expecting, he found the stern features of M. de Rênal, who had arrived two hours ago from Verrières, and made no effort to hide his displeasure that Julien had spent an entire morning without paying any attention to the children. Nothing could have been uglier than this important man in an angry mood and feeling free to express his anger.

Every sharp word her husband uttered pierced the heart of Mme. de Rênal. Julien, on the other hand, was so deeply plunged in reverie, still so preoccupied by the mighty events that had been passing before his eyes during the last hours, that he could scarcely bring his mind down to the harsh words being addressed to him by M. de Rênal. At last he said brusquely:

—I was sick.

The tone of this phrase would have wounded a man much less touchy than the mayor of Verrières; for a moment he thought of answering Julien by dismissing him on the spot. He was restrained only by the maxim he had set for himself, never to act hastily in business.

This young fool, he said to himself, has picked up a sort of reputation in my house; either Valenod will take him in or else he can marry Elisa; in either case, he can afford to make light of me.

For all the wisdom of his thoughts, M. de Rênal's ill humor did not subside without a series of grumbles and insults which gradually infuriated Julien. Mme. de Rênal was on the point of bursting into tears. When lunch was over she asked Julien to lend her his arm for a stroll; and she leaned closely upon him. To everything she said Julien replied only by murmuring:

—*That's how rich people are!*

M. de Rênal walked beside them; his presence added to Julien's wrath. Suddenly he noticed that Mme. de Rênal was leaning markedly upon his arm; under an impulse of horror he shook her violently off and freed his arm.

Happily, M. de Rênal did not observe this fresh impertinence; only Mme. Derville noted it; her friend burst into tears. Meanwhile M. de Rênal rushed off, throwing stones at a little peasant girl who in taking a short cut had passed through a corner of his orchard.

—Monsieur Julien, be a little calmer, if you will, Mme. Derville said rapidly, remember we all have moments of ill humor.

Julien glanced at her coldly, with eyes in which appeared the most sovereign contempt.

This glance astonished Mme. Derville, and would have surprised her even more if she could have guessed its true meaning; she would then have seen in it a still-vague hope of the most atrocious vengeance. No doubt it is moments of humiliation like this one that are responsible for figures like Robespierre.

—Your Julien has a violent temper, he frightens me, Mme. Derville murmured to her friend.

—He is right to be angry, replied the other; after the extraordinary progress the children have made with him, what matter if he takes off a morning? Men are very strict about these things, we must agree.

For the first time in her life Mme. de Rênal felt a sort of desire for vengeance upon her husband. Julien's furious hatred of the rich was about to break out openly; but happily M. de Rênal called for the gardener and busied himself with the latter in building a barrier of thorny sticks across the short cut at the corner of the orchard. During the rest of the walk, Julien answered not a word to the various advances that were made in his direction. Scarcely had M. de Rênal disappeared when the two ladies, pleading fatigue, both demanded the support of his arm.

Standing between these two women, whose cheeks were flushed with distress and embarrassment, Julien, with his lofty pallor, his gloomy and determined air, provided a strange contrast. He despised these women and all their sensitive feelings.

What! he exclaimed mutely, not even five hundred francs with which to finish my courses! Ah, how I'd love to tell him off!

Absorbed as he was in these bitter thoughts, the little he deigned to hear of the ladies' kind words displeased him as foolish, inane, feeble, in a word, *feminine.*

As she continued to chatter, merely to keep the conversation alive, Mme. de Rênal chanced to say that her husband had come from Verrières because he had bought some wheat straw from one of his farmers. (In this district they use wheat straw to fill the mattresses.)

—My husband won't be back, added Mme. de Rênal; he'll be busy with the gardener and his valet; they're changing all the mattresses in the house. This morning they put new straw in all the beds on the first floor, this afternoon they'll do the second.

Julien grew pale; he glanced at Mme. de Rênal with a singular expression, and shortly took her a little aside by stepping out somewhat faster. Mme. Derville let them go.

—Save my life, Julien said to Mme. de Rênal; only you can do it; for you know that valet is my mortal enemy. I must confess to you, madame, that I have a portrait, and I have hidden it in my mattress.

At this word Mme. de Rênal became pale in her turn.

—Only you, madame, only you can go to my room at this moment; look, but without leaving any traces, in the corner of the mattress closest to the window; you'll find there a little box of black cardboard, quite smooth.

—It contains a portrait, said Mme. de Rênal, scarcely able to hold herself erect.

Her air of discouragement was apparent to Julien, who promptly took advantage of it.

—I have a second favor to beg of you, madame; I beg you not to look at the portrait, it is my secret.

—It is a secret! repeated Mme. de Rênal in a suffocated voice.

But though she had been raised among people proud of their fortune and with a single-minded interest in money, love had already introduced some generosity into her soul. Cruelly wounded though she was, Mme. de Rênal questioned Julien with an air of the purest devotion about the things she must know to fulfill her mission.

—And so, she said as she left him, it is a little round box, of black cardboard and rather smooth.

—Yes, madame, said Julien with that hard, abrupt tone that men assume in the presence of danger.

She climbed to the second floor of the house, pale as if she were going to her death. To heighten her misery, she felt that she was about to faint; but the need to help Julien restored her strength.

—I must have that box, she said, hastening forward.

She heard her husband talking to the valet in Julien's very room. Happily, they passed on into the children's. She snatched the mattress and plunged her hand into the straw so violently that she scratched her fingers. But though generally sensitive to minor griefs of this nature, she was not even aware of the pain, for just at this moment she felt the cardboard box. She grasped it and fled.

Scarcely was she delivered from the fear of being surprised by her husband when the sense of horror which this box caused her was on the point of really making her faint.

Julien then is in love, and I have here the portrait of the woman he loves!

Seated on a chair in the antechamber of the upstairs apartment, Mme. de Rênal fell prey to all the horrors of jealousy. Her remarkable ignorance was particularly useful to her at this point, since astonishment tempered her grief. Julien appeared, snatched the box without a word of thanks or a word of any sort, and ran to his room where he lit a fire and burned it on the spot. He was pale and haggard; he exaggerated the extent of the danger he had just run.

The portrait of Napoleon, he said to himself, shaking his head; and found on a man who professes such hatred for the usurper! Found by M. de Rênal, a black reactionary and in a bad humor! And to top it all, on the cardboard mounting of the portrait, phrases written in my hand which leave no doubt of the depth of my admiration! Each one of these transports was dated, too, and the last one just yesterday!

My whole reputation would have fallen, blasted in a minute! said Julien as he watched the box burn; and my reputation is my fortune, it's all I have to live by—and, good God, what a way to live!

An hour later weariness and self-pity disposed him to more tender sentiments. Meeting Mme. de Rênal, he took her hand and kissed it with more sincerity than he had ever showed her before. She blushed with happiness, and almost at the same instant pushed Julien away with a gesture of anger and jealousy. Julien's pride, so recently wounded, made a fool of him at that moment. He saw nothing in Mme. de Rênal but a rich woman, dropped her hand with disdain, and walked away. After strolling pensively in the garden for a few minutes, he began to smile bitterly.

Here I am walking about like a man whose time is his own! I'm not busy with his children! I'll have more harsh words from M. de Rênal, and he will be right. He ran at once to the children's room. The caresses of the younger, of whom he was fond, did something to calm his black mood.

This little one doesn't despise me yet, Julien thought. But shortly he felt that this comfort was merely a new weakness. These children are fond of me just as they're fond of that new puppy who was bought yesterday.

Chapter 10

LOFTY HEART AND LITTLE FORTUNE

> But passion most dissembles, yet betrays,
> Even by its darkness; as the blackest sky
> Foretells the heaviest tempest.
> —*Don Juan*, Canto 1, stanza 73

M. de Rênal, who was going through all the rooms of the house, returned to the children's room with the servants who were bringing back the mattresses. The sudden appearance of this man was for Julien the last straw.

Paler than usual, and more gloomy, he strode toward him. M. de Rênal stopped and glanced toward his servants.

—Sir, Julien said to him, do you suppose that with any other tutor your children would have learned as much as they have with me? If you suppose not, Julien continued, without allowing M. de Rênal a single word, then how do you dare to accuse me of neglecting them?

M. de Rênal, scarcely recovered from his first fear, concluded that the strange tone being taken by this little peasant came from his having in hand another offer, and that he was going to resign. As Julien continued to talk, his wrath increased:

—I can live without you, sir, he added.

—I am very sorry to see you so upset, replied M. de Rênal, stammering slightly. The servants were a few feet apart, busily rearranging the beds.

—This isn't my style, sir, Julien went on, beside himself; just think of the abominable things you said to me, and in the presence of ladies, too!

M. de Rênal understood only too clearly what Julien was demanding, and a painful struggle took place in his heart. Finally, Julien, in an access of rage, cried:

—I know where to go, sir, when I leave your house.

At that moment, M. de Rênal had a vision of Julien in the service of M. Valenod.

—Well, sir, he finally said, with a sigh and the sort of expression he would have put on when asking the surgeon to perform a hideous operation, I grant your request. After tomorrow, which is the first of the month, your salary will be fifty francs a month.

Julien felt an impulse to laugh and then stood stupefied; all his anger disappeared.

I didn't despise this animal sufficiently, he said to himself. No doubt he's just made the best apology of which his degraded mind is capable.

The children, who had been listening open-mouthed to this conversation, dashed off to the garden to tell their mother that M. Julien was furious but that he was going to have fifty francs a month.

Julien followed them mechanically, without even glancing at M. de Rênal, whom he left in a state of profound irritation.

That's a hundred and sixty-eight francs, muttered the mayor to himself, that M. Valenod has cost me. I really will have to say a few firm words to him about his scheme for the foundlings.

An instant later Julien again confronted M. de Rênal:

—I must consult with M. Chélan on a matter of conscience; I should like to advise you that I shall be absent for several hours.

—Eh, my dear Julien! said M. de Rênal, with a hollow laugh, all day if you wish, all day tomorrow too, my dear fellow. Take the gardener's horse for the trip to Verrières.

Now there he goes, said M. de Rênal to himself, off to give his answer to Valenod; he didn't promise anything—but we'll have to let that hot young head cool off.

Julien departed at once, climbing along the forest trails that lead from Vergy to Verrières. He had no wish to arrive too soon at M.

Chélan's. Far from wanting to undertake another scene of hypocrisy, he had a need to see more clearly into his own soul, and to give audience to the crowd of feelings agitating him.

I've won a battle, he said to himself, as soon as he was into the woods and away from people; so I've won a battle!

The phrase described his position clearly enough, and restored to his mind some of its tranquillity.

Here I have a salary of fifty francs a month; so M. de Rênal must have been thoroughly frightened. But of what?

What could have frightened that contented and powerful man against whom, an hour before, he had been boiling with rage? Thinking about this problem restored Julien's calm. For a moment he was almost aware of the amazing beauty of the forests through which he was passing. Enormous bare boulders of rock had once fallen from the mountainside into the middle of this forest. Beside these great rocks, and almost as tall, rose beech trees whose shade kept the path deliciously cool three feet from spots where the heat of the sun would have made it impossible to stop.

Julien paused to catch his breath for a moment in the shadow of the great rocks, then resumed his climb. Soon, by a narrow pathway, almost unmarked and used chiefly by goatherds, he found himself poised on an immense rocky crag, where he could be sure of standing apart from everyone. This physical stance made him smile, it indicated so clearly the position he wanted to attain in morality. The pure mountain air filled his soul with serenity and even joy. The mayor of Verrières was, and always would be, in his eyes, the representative of the rich and insolent of this earth; but Julien sensed that his hatred for this man, despite its recent violence, was in no way personal. If he had stopped seeing M. de Rênal, in a week he would have forgotten him, his house, his dogs, his children, and his whole family. Without knowing quite how, I've forced him into the greatest sacrifice of which he is capable. What! more than fifty crowns a year! And yet just an instant before, I had barely escaped the gravest dangers. There are two victories in one day. The second was undeserved; I'll have to figure out the reason for it. But I'll go into that dreary business tomorrow.

Julien, standing atop his great rock, looked up into the sky, heated by an August sun. Locusts were chirring in the field below the rock; when they paused, all was silence around him. At his feet lay twenty leagues of countryside. A solitary eagle,[8] risen from the rocks over his head, appeared from time to time, cutting immense silent circles in the sky. Julien's eye followed mechanically the bird

---

8. The eagle, bird of augury and empire, becomes in this scene something like an emblem of Julien's own exalted spirit.

of prey. Its calm, powerful movements struck him; he envied this power, he envied this isolation.

Such had been the destiny of Napoleon; would it some day be his?

Chapter 11

AN EVENING

> Yet Julia's very coldness still was kind
> And tremulously gentle her small hand
> Withdrew itself from his, but left behind
> A little pressure, thrilling, and so bland
> And slight, so very slight that to the mind
> 'Twas but a doubt.
> —*Don Juan,* Canto I, stanza 71

But he had to put in an appearance at Verrières. As he left the presbytery a lucky accident brought Julien into the presence of M. Valenod, whom he hastened to inform of his new raise in pay.

Once back at Vergy, Julien did not descend into the garden until night was falling. His spirit was weary from the many powerful passions that had stirred it in the course of the day. What shall I say to them? he asked uneasily, as he thought of the ladies. He was quite unable to see that his soul was precisely on the level of those petty circumstances that generally absorb the full interest of women. Julien had often been incomprehensible to Mme. Derville and even to her friend; and he himself often only half understood what they said to him. This resulted from the force, and, if I may say so, grandeur of the passions in this ambitious young man. For this extraordinary being, almost every day was bound to be stormy.

As he entered the garden that evening Julien was quite prepared to concern himself with the ideas of the attractive cousins. They were awaiting him impatiently. He took his regular seat beside Mme. de Rênal. Soon the darkness deepened. He sought to grasp a white hand which had for some time been in view, resting on the back of a chair. There was a moment of hesitation, but the hand was then withdrawn, not without some indications of ill humor. Julien was disposed to consider the matter closed and continue with a pleasant conversation when he heard M. de Rênal approaching.

Julien still heard, ringing in his ears, the insulting words of the morning. Now, said he to himself, wouldn't it be a good way of mocking this creature, who has all the advantages of fortune, if I should take possession of his wife's hand, right in his presence? Yes, I'll do it, the very person he treated with so much contempt.

M. de Rênal talked angrily of politics: two or three Verrières manufacturers were becoming noticeably richer than he and were

preparing to stand against him in the next elections. Mme. Derville
was listening to him. Julien, irked by the harangue, shifted his own
chair closer to Mme. de Rênal's. The darkness hid all his gestures.
He had the boldness to put his hand close to that pretty arm half
concealed under drapery. His head was in a whirl, he could no
longer control himself; he bent over the pretty arm and brushed it
with his lips.

Mme. de Rênal shuddered. Her husband was four paces away;
she hastened to give her hand to Julien and at the same time to
push him away slightly. As M. de Rênal continued to denounce the
upstarts and rich radicals, Julien covered the hand that had been
granted him with passionate kisses, or at least they seemed such to
Mme. de Rênal. And yet in the course of that tragic day the poor
woman had had proof that the man she adored (without admitting
it to herself) loved somebody else! Throughout the period of Julien's
absence she had been subject to a profound depression, which
caused her to reflect on her situation.

Good Lord, she said to herself, it seems I'm in love! A married
woman and yet I'm in love! Well, she said, but I never felt anything
for my husband like this morbid folly which keeps me from thinking
of anything but Julien. He's only a child, of course, and feels nothing
but respect for me! I'll get over it. How can it matter to my husband
that I have feelings for this young man? M. de Rênal would be
bored by the topics I discuss with Julien; they're only things of the
imagination. He's got his business to think about. I'm not taking
anything from him to give to Julien.

No hypocrisy clouded the purity of this innocent spirit, haunted
by a passion it had never known before. She was deceived but un-
knowingly, and yet an instinct of virtue had been terrified. These
were the torments that racked her when Julien made his appearance
in the garden. She heard him speak; almost at the same instant she
saw him sitting by her side. Her soul was carried away by that charming sense of delight that for the past two weeks had been surprising
her more even than it enchanted her. Everything for her was unexpected. Yet after a few moments she said to herself, Well! so all
Julien has to do is appear for a few minutes and all his faults are
forgotten? She was struck with terror; and that was the moment
when she withdrew her hand.

The passionate kisses, such as she had never received before, made
her forget suddenly that he might possibly love another woman.
The end of her agony born of suspicion, the presence of a joy such
as she had never dreamed of, inspired in her transports of affection
and wild gaiety. The evening was delightful for everybody except
the mayor of Verrières, who was incapable of forgetting his upstart
manufacturers. Julien gave no further thought to his black ambition

or to his projects, so difficult to realize. For the first time in his life he was carried away by the power of beauty. Lost in a vague delightful dream, wholly foreign to his character, gently pressing that hand which seemed to him perfectly beautiful, he only half heard the rustling of the linden tree in the light night wind and the distant barking of dogs by the mill on the Doubs.

But this emotion was a pleasure, not a passion. Returning to his room, he thought only of one happiness, of getting back to his favorite book; at the age of twenty, the idea of the world and the effect to be produced there is more important than anything else.

Soon, however, he set aside the book. In thinking over the victories of Napoleon, he had learned something about his own. Yes, I've won a battle, he told himself, but I must press my advantage and crush the pride of this fine gentleman while I have him on the defensive. That's Napoleon, that's his style. [He charges me with neglecting his children.] I'll ask for a leave of three days in order to visit my friend Fouqué. If he refuses, I'll threaten to leave, but he won't refuse.

Mme. de Rênal could hardly sleep a wink. She felt that until this moment she had never really been alive; and she could not stop thinking about the pleasure of feeling Julien covering her hand with hot kisses.

Suddenly the frightful word *adultery* came to her mind. All the most disgusting images that vile debauchery can attach to sensual love came thronging into her imagination. All these ideas sought to blacken the tender and sacred image she was forming of Julien and the joy of loving him. The future drew itself up before her in horrible colors. She saw herself the object of contempt.

It was a terrible moment; her soul was moving toward unknown lands. During the evening she had experienced delights never known before; now she found herself plunged unexpectedly into atrocious suffering. She had had no conception of such misery; it attacked her very reason. For an instant the thought crossed her mind of telling her husband that she was afraid she loved Julien. It would have been, at least, an occasion to talk about him. Happily she recalled a precept once given her by an aunt on the day before her wedding; it warned of the dangers of confiding in a husband, who after all is a master. In the agony of her distress, she could only wring her hands.

She was dragged this way and that by contradictory images, all painful. At one moment her fear was that he did not love her; the next moment she was tortured by the frightful thought of her crime, as if on the morrow she was to be exposed in the pillory, on the public square of Verrières, with a placard explaining her adultery to the populace.

Mme. de Rênal had no experience of life; even in broad daylight and when completely rational she would have seen no difference between being guilty in the sight of God and being publicly covered with all the most humiliating marks of general contempt.

When the terrible idea of adultery and the life of shame which she considered its necessary consequence had ceased to torture her and she began to dream of living with Julien in perfect innocence, just as before, she was seized by the horrible idea that Julien loved another woman. She recalled his sudden pallor when he thought he might lose her portrait, or might compromise her by letting it be seen. For the first time then she had surprised a trace of fear on that lofty, emotionless face. Never had he showed himself in such distress for her or for her children. This excess of misery attained the absolute limit of anguish which the human soul can endure. Without being aware of what she was doing, Mme. de Rênal gave a shriek that awakened her maid. Suddenly she saw the glow of a lamp approaching her bed and recognized Elisa.

—So it's you he loves? she cried out, in her madness.

The maid, wholly astonished to find her mistress in such a distracted state, fortunately paid no attention to this extraordinary expression. Mme. de Rênal became aware of her imprudence: "I feel feverish," she said, "and perhaps I have a touch of delirium; stay with me." Being now quite awakened by the necessity for concealment, she found herself less miserable; reason resumed the sway her drowsiness had canceled. To escape the maid's attentive eye she asked her to read aloud from the newspaper, and it was to the monotonous accompaniment of the girl's voice, reading a long article from the *Quotidienne,* that Mme. de Rênal finally reached the virtuous resolution that when she next saw Julien she would treat him with chilly correctness.

Chapter 12

TRAVEL

At Paris you will find elegant folk, in the provinces there may be people with character.   —Siéyès[9]

Next morning, when it was barely five o'clock, before Mme. de Rênal was about, Julien had obtained from her husband permission to be gone for three days. Unexpectedly, Julien found himself want-

9. Shrewd, lean, and subtle, Abbé Siéyès rose to be a vicar general in the church before abjuring his faith, during the Revolution, and becoming a diplomat, politician, and all-purpose conniver. His sentiments here are perfectly commonplace, but his name is that of a clever, selfish man whom nobody trusted.

ing to see her again; he was dreaming of her pretty hand. Though he waited in the garden, Mme. de Rênal was slow in appearing. But if Julien had been in love with her, he would have seen her behind the half-drawn shutters of an upstairs window, her brow resting against the glass. She was watching him. Finally, in spite of her resolutions, she determined to go into the garden. Her customary pallor was replaced by a rosy coloring. This innocent woman was evidently distressed: a sense of constraint, and even of anger, had replaced her expression of profound serenity and of superiority to the vulgar interests of life, an expression that gave added charm to her heavenly features.

Julien approached her hastily; he was admiring those beautiful arms which could be seen beneath a hastily thrown-on shawl. The fresh morning air seemed to heighten further the brilliance of a complexion rendered sensitive by the agitations of the night. This modest and appealing beauty, which was nonetheless full of thoughts never found among the lower orders, seemed to reveal to Julien an aspect of his own soul of which he had never been aware. Completely absorbed in admiring the charms uncovered to his avid glance, Julien never doubted of the friendly greeting he was expecting to receive. All the more, then, was he shocked at the glacial chill with which he was met, and behind which he even seemed to sense an intention of putting him in his place.

The smile of pleasure faded on his lips; he thought of the rank he really occupied in society, especially in the eyes of a rich and noble heiress. Instantly there appeared on his face only arrogance and self-contempt. He felt an access of scorn for himself at having delayed his departure more than an hour for a humiliation like this.

Only a fool, said he to himself, would be angry with other people: a stone falls because it's heavy. Am I going to be a child forever? When did I get into the habit of giving these people my soul in exchange for their money? If I want to be respected by them, and by myself, I have to show them that it's my poverty that trades with their wealth, but that my heart is a thousand leagues from their insolence, and in a sphere too lofty to be touched by their petty marks of favor or disdain.

While these thoughts were crowding through the mind of the young tutor, his features took on an expression of angry pride and ferocity. Mme. de Rênal was distressed by it. The look of chilly virtue she had sought to impose on her greeting gave place to an expression of interest, an interest motivated by surprise at the sudden change she had just seen. The empty words that are usually exchanged in the morning on such topics as one's state of health and the lovely weather perished on both their lips. Julien, whose judg-

ment was clouded by no passion whatever, quickly hit upon a way
of showing Mme. de Rênal how little he supposed himself on terms
of friendship with her: he neglected to tell her anything of the little
trip he was taking, bowed, and departed.

As she watched him going, thunderstruck at the gloomy arrogance
of his glance, so amiable the night before, her elder son came running up from the end of the garden, kissed her, and said:

—We have a vacation, Julien is going on a trip.

At these words Mme. de Rênal felt herself seized by a mortal
chill; she was wretched in her virtue and even more so in her weakness.

This new incident quickly took possession of her whole imagination; she was carried far beyond the virtuous resolutions derived
from her terrible midnight meditations. Her problem was not how
to resist this agreeable lover, it was the peril of losing him forever.

She had to go in to breakfast. To climax her misery, M. de Rênal
and Mme. Derville chose to talk of nothing but Julien's departure.
The mayor of Verrières had noted something unusual in the firm
tone with which the leave had been demanded.

—No doubt this little peasant has in pocket an offer from somebody else. But this somebody, even if it's M. Valenod, is going to
be a bit discouraged by the sum of 600 francs, which is what the
annual expense is going to be now. Yesterday, at Verrières, he must
have asked for three days to think over the offer; and now, this
morning, in order to avoid giving me a straight answer, our little
gentleman takes off for the mountains. Having to haggle with a
miserable workman who plays hard to get—that's what we've come
to nowadays!

Mme. de Rênal said to herself: Since my husband, who doesn't
understand how deeply he's insulted Julien, thinks he's going to
leave, what hope can I have myself? Ah, it's all finished now!

So that she could at least weep freely and evade the questions of
Mme. Derville, she pleaded a frightful headache and went to bed.

—That's a woman for you, M. de Rênal repeated, there's always
something wrong with their complicated machinery. And he went
off in rare good humor.

While Mme. de Rênal was suffering the cruelest pangs of the
terrible passion in which misfortune had entrapped her, Julien followed cheerfully along his path amid the most beautiful scenery
our mountains can afford. He had to cross the great chain lying
to the north of Vergy. The path he followed, rising gradually
through great forests of beech trees, scribes an infinity of zigzags
along the slope of the lofty mountain that outlines on the north the
valley of the Doubs. Soon the glances of the traveler, rising above

the lower hills which hedge in the Doubs to the west, extended over
the fertile plains of Burgundy and Beaujolais. However insensitive
this ambitious young man naturally was to this sort of beauty, he
could not help stopping from time to time in order to survey a
panorama so vast and so impressive.

At last he rose to the crest of the great ridge he had to cross in
order to reach, by this cross-country path, the lonely valley where
lived his friend Fouqué, the young dealer in wood. Julien was in
no hurry to see him, nor for that matter any other human being.
Lurking like a bird of prey among the naked rocks which cap the
great mountain, he could watch the distant ascent of any man who
tried to come near him. In the almost vertical face of one of the
cliffs he discovered a little grotto, clambered up to it, and was soon
established in his retreat. Here, said he—his eyes shining with
pleasure—here people will never be able to get at me. He had
the notion of indulging himself by writing down those ideas
which, everywhere else, were so dangerous for him. A square block
of stone served as a desk. His pen flew; he forgot his surroundings
entirely. At last he noted that the sun was setting behind the distant mountains of Beaujolais.

Why not spend the night here? he asked himself; I have a bit
of bread, and *I am free!* His soul exulted in this grand phrase, his
hypocrisy prevented his feeling free even with Fouqué. Cradling his
head in his hands [and looking out over the plain], Julien sat still
in his cave, happier than he had ever been in his life, stirred only
by his dreams and the delight of feeling free. Idly he watched the
last rays of the sunset fade one by one from the heavens. In the
midst of an immense darkness his soul wandered, lost in the contemplation of what awaited him some day in Paris. It would be,
first of all, a woman, far more beautiful and of a more exalted genius
than any he had ever been able to see in the provinces. He adored
her; he was beloved in return. If he left her for only a few moments
it was to cover himself with glory and thus merit even more of her
devotion.

Even if possessed of Julien's imagination, a young man raised
amid the sad actuality of Paris society would have been awakened
at this point in his daydream by a touch of chilly irony; heroic
actions, and the hope of performing them, would have been sup-
planted by the familiar maxim: Leave your mistress alone and
you'll be betrayed, alas, two or three times a day. This young peasant saw no gap between himself and the most heroic achievements
except the want of opportunity.

Meanwhile thick darkness had fallen, and he still had two leagues
to cover before reaching the little hamlet where Fouqué lived. Be-

fore leaving his grotto Julien struck a light and carefully burned everything he had written.

He rather startled his friend by rapping on his door at one o'clock in the morning. Fouqué was busy over his ledgers. He was a tall young man, ungainly and rather hard faced, with an immense nose and a warm supply of good humor hidden beneath this rather repellent exterior.

—I suppose you've had a fight with M. de Rênal, the way you drop in on me without any notice?

Julien recounted to him, but with due discretion, the events of the day before.

—Stay with me, Fouqué told him, I see you know M. de Rênal, M. Valenod, the subprefect Maugiron, and Abbé Chélan; you understand the fine points of character in gentry like these; that makes you very fit to negotiate contracts with them. Your mathematics is better than mine; you can keep my accounts. I make good money in this trade. But I can't do everything myself, and if I take in a partner I'm afraid of getting a rascal; so every day I'm forced to pass up some excellent deal. Not a month ago I put Michaud de Saint-Amand in the way of making six thousand francs—I hadn't seen him for six years, and I met him only by accident at the auction in Pontarlier. Why shouldn't you have made those six thousand francs, or at least three thousand of them? For if I'd had you with me that day I'd have put in my own bid for that stand of wood, and I'd have got it too. So be my partner.

This offer disturbed Julien; it interfered with his crazy dreams. Throughout the supper which the two friends prepared for themselves like Homeric heroes (for Fouqué lived all alone), he went over his books with Julien and showed him the advantages of his trade in wood. Fouqué had the loftiest notion of Julien's character and intelligence.

When Julien was at last alone in his little pine-paneled bedroom, he took stock. It is true, he told himself, I can make a couple of thousand francs here, and then be in a good position to take up the soldier's trade, or the priest's, depending on which is then fashionable in France.[1] The little bit of money I can save up here will smooth the way in either line of work. Even though living alone in the mountains, I can do something to dissipate my frightful ignorance of the things that occupy society people. But Fouqué, though he's decided not to marry, keeps telling me that loneliness makes him wretched. It's obvious that if he takes in a partner who has no capital to put into the business he hopes to find a friend who will never leave him.

1. Julien's cool indifference between these alternatives is a notable feature of his character, rendered here with perfect absence of emphasis.

And shall I betray my friend? Julien said angrily to himself. This creature, for whom hypocrisy and cold calculation were the ordinary means of refuge, could not on this occasion endure the idea of even the slightest dishonorable act toward a man who was fond of him.

But suddenly Julien was happy; he had a reason for his refusal. What! to squander in base pursuits seven or eight years! In that way I should reach the age of twenty-eight; and by that age Bonaparte had already performed his finest actions. Even if I make a little devious money by running around to wood auctions and currying the favor of some subordinate scoundrels, how can I suppose I'll still have the sacred fire with which one makes oneself a name?

Next morning Julien spoke to the good Fouqué, who was already taking the partnership for granted, and told him, with the greatest coolness, that his sacred vocation would not allow him to accept the other's offer. Fouqué was thunderstruck.

—But just think, he kept repeating, I put you in the way of four thousand francs a year, or if you prefer it this way, I give them to you. Yet you want to go back to M. de Rênal, who despises you like the dirt on his shoes! After you've piled up a couple of hundred louis of your own, what prevents you from entering a seminary? I'll tell you something else; I can guarantee to get you the best vicarage in the countryside. For, listen here (Fouqué added, lowering his voice), I supply firewood to M. le _____, M. le _____, and M. _____. What I give them is first-quality oak wood, what I charge them for is ordinary pine, but money was never better invested.

No arguments could overcome that of Julien's vocation. Fouqué finally decided he was a little crazy. Early on the morning of the third day Julien left his friend, to spend the day among the rocks of the high mountains. He sought out his little grotto again, but peace of mind had left him, driven away by his friend's offers. Like Hercules, he found himself faced with a choice, not between vice and virtue but between comfortable mediocrity and the heroic dreams of youth.[2] Well, he said to himself, I don't really have a firm character after all—and this was the thought that caused him deepest pain. I'm not made of the stuff that goes into great men, since I'm afraid that eight years spent in money making will rob me of the sublime energy that goes into the doing of extraordinary deeds.

2. The theme of Hercules forced to choose between painful virtue and contemptible ease is a frequent one in Renaissance painting. Stendhal in his youth had actually entered the wholesale grocery business in Marseilles, hoping to make enough money in a few years to devote the rest of his life to art. See Paul Arbelet, *Stendhal épicier*.

Chapter 13

NET STOCKINGS

A novel: it's a mirror being carried along a highway.
—Saint-Réal[3]

When Julien caught sight of the picturesque ruins of the old church of Vergy, he reflected that not once in the last two days had he given a thought to Mme. de Rênal. The other day as we said goodbye that woman reminded me of the distance that divides us; she treated me like the child of a workman. No doubt she wanted to show me her regret at having granted me her hand the previous evening. . . . Still, that's a very pretty hand! And what charm, what nobility in the glances of that woman!

His chance of getting ahead in the world with Fouqué gave a certain fluency to Julien's speculations; they were not now spoiled so often by irritation and a bitter sense of poverty and contempt in the eyes of the world. Placed as it were on a lofty promontory, he could judge and exercise dominion, so to speak, over the alternatives of extreme poverty and the comparative comfort he called wealth. He was far from taking stock of his position like a philosopher, but he had enough insight to feel that he was *different* after his brief trip through the mountains.

He was struck by the air of deep anxiety with which Mme. de Rênal listened to the little story of his trip which she asked him to tell her.

Fouqué had had various projects of marrying, but his love affairs had been unhappy;[4] long exchanges on this topic had filled the conversations of the two friends. Having found happiness too quickly, Fouqué had discovered that he was not without rivals. All his stories had astonished Julien; he learned a great deal that was new to him. His solitary life compounded of imagination and mistrust had distanced him from everyone who could enlighten him.

While he was away life had been nothing for Mme. de Rênal but a succession of different torments, all intolerable; she was really ill.

—Above all, said Mme. Derville when she saw Julien returning, sick as you are, you won't sit out in the garden this evening; the night air will make you worse than ever.

Mme. Derville noted with amazement that her friend, who was always being scolded by M. de Rênal for the excessive simplicity of

---

3. César de Saint-Réal, seventeenth-century French historian, probably never made this statement about novels —a statement that is less true of Stendhal's own novels than of most others.

4. The biographical original of Fouqué, François Bigillion, had in fact committed suicide out of humiliation at being cuckolded.

her dress, had put on net stockings and a pair of charming little
slippers direct from Paris. For the past three days Mme. de Rênal's
only amusement had been in having Elisa make for her, as quickly
as possible, a summer dress; it was of a very pretty material, quite
in the latest style. The dress was finished only a few minutes after
Julien's return; Mme. de Rênal put it on at once. Her friend had
no further doubts. She's in love, poor thing! said Mme. Derville
to herself. She now understood all the symptoms of her friend's
malady.

She watched her talking with Julien. Pallor alternated with
blushes. Her anxious eyes were fastened on those of the young
tutor. Mme. de Rênal expected that at any moment he would
explain his position and announce that he was leaving the house,
or would stay. Julien was far from saying any such thing; he never
gave this matter a thought. After frightful inner struggles Mme.
de Rênal finally brought herself to say to him, in a voice that
trembled and revealed all her feeling:

—Will you be leaving your pupils and taking a position somewhere else?

Julien was struck by Mme. de Rênal's quavering voice and glance.
This woman is in love with me, he said to himself; but after this
moment of weakness, which her pride is already ashamed of, as
soon as she no longer fears my leaving, she'll turn arrogant again.
This survey of his position took place, in Julien's mind, with the
speed of light; he replied cautiously:

—I should be much distressed to leave children who are so attractive and *so well born*, but perhaps I will have to. One has duties
toward oneself, as well.

As he pronounced the words *so well born* (it was one of those
aristocratic phrases Julien had recently picked up), he was stirred
with a deep sense of hostility.

In the eyes of this woman, he reflected, I myself am not well
born.

Mme. de Rênal as she listened to him admired his spirit, his
charm; her heart was lacerated at the thought of the separation
he was forcing her to contemplate. All her friends from Verrières,
who during Julien's absence had come to dinner at Vergy, had
complimented her lavishly on this astonishing man whom her husband had been lucky enough to discover. It wasn't that anyone
knew whether the children were learning anything. The fact that
he knew the Bible by heart, and actually in Latin, had inspired in
the people of Verrières an admiration that will probably last a
hundred years.

Julien, who talked to nobody, was unaware of all this. If Mme.
de Rênal had had the least self-composure, she would have compli-

mented him on the reputation he had earned, and when Julien's pride had been set at rest, he would have been gentle and agreeable to her, especially since the new dress seemed delightful to him. Mme. de Rênal, who was also pleased with her pretty dress, and with the things Julien said about it, wanted to stroll in the garden; soon, however, she had to confess that she could go no further. She seized his arm, and far from restoring her strength, contact with his arm took away her last remaining energy.

It was evening; scarcely were they seated when Julien, resuming his former privilege, ventured to bring his lips close to the arm of his pretty neighbor and to grasp her hand. He was thinking of the boldness Fouqué had demonstrated in his love affairs and not at all of Mme. de Rênal; the phrase *well born* still weighed heavily on his spirit. His hand was grasped warmly, but it gave him no pleasure. Far from being proud of or even grateful for the feelings that Mme. de Rênal revealed all too openly that evening, her beauty, elegance, and freshness left him completely cold. There can be no doubt that purity of spirit and freedom from hateful passions prolong one's youth. With most pretty women it's the features that first harden into age.

Julien was sullen all evening; hitherto, he had been angry only with his destiny and with society, but since Fouqué had offered him a vulgar way to wealth, he was angry with himself as well. Absorbed in his own thoughts, though from time to time he spoke a few words to the ladies, Julien ended by thoughtlessly releasing the hand of Mme. de Rênal. The poor woman was devastated by this act; she saw in it a foreshadowing of her own fate.

Had she been confident of Julien's affection, perhaps her virtue might have found strength against him. But she was fearful of losing him forever, and her passion drove her to the point of reaching out for Julien's hand, which in his distraction he had rested momentarily on the back of a chair. Her action reawoke the ambition in Julien: he would have liked to be seen by all those arrogant gentry who, at dinner when he sat at the foot of the table with the children, looked upon him with complacent smiles. This woman can't despise me any more: very well, in that case, said he to himself, I ought to be aware of her beauty; indeed, I owe it to myself to become her lover. Such an idea would never have occurred to him before he had heard the naïve confessions of his friend.

The abrupt decision he had just reached provided an agreeable distraction. He said to himself: I must have one of these two women; and then he was aware that he would much have preferred to make his advances to Mme. Derville—not that she was more attractive, but she had always seen him as a tutor honored for his learning, not as a journeyman carpenter, with his rough vest folded under his arm, as he had appeared before Mme. de Rênal.

It was precisely as a young workman, blushing to the whites of his eyes, pausing before the house door and not daring to ring, that Mme. de Rênal remembered him most fondly. [This woman, whom the shopkeepers of the district considered so arrogant, rarely thought of social status at all, and the slightest assurance in a man's character impressed her more than all the promises held out by his rank. A cart driver who had showed some real bravery would have stood higher, in her eyes, than a fearful captain of hussars, complete with moustache and pipe. She thought Julien's soul nobler than those of all her relatives, though they were all gentlemen of the blood and several of them titled.]

As he continued the summary of his position, Julien saw that he must not dream of the conquest of Mme. Derville, who was no doubt aware of Mme. de Rênal's attraction to him. Forced, then, to consider the latter, Julien asked himself: What do I really know about the character of this woman? Only one thing: before I went away I took her hand and she withdrew it, now I withdraw my hand and she reaches after it. A fine chance to pay her back for all her contempt of me. God only knows how many lovers she's had! She's probably interested in me only because the arrangements are so easy.

Such, alas, is the unhappy effect of too much civilization! At the age of twenty a young man's spirit, if he has any education at all, is a thousand miles from that ease without which love is often only the most laborious of obligations.

I'm all the more duty bound to succeed with this woman, Julien's petty vanity pursued, since if ever I make my fortune and someone throws up at me that I held the low post of a tutor, I can let it be understood that love alone induced me to accept such a position.

Once again Julien let fall the hand of Mme. de Rênal, then took it up and clasped it warmly. As they were returning to the drawing room about midnight, Mme. de Rênal said to him in an undertone:

—Are you going to leave us, will you go away?

Julien answered with a sigh:

—I must go, indeed, for I love you passionately, and that is a crime . . . what a crime for a young priest!

Mme. de Rênal leaned upon his arm, and with so little constraint that her cheek felt the warmth of Julien's.

These two beings passed very different nights. Mme. de Rênal was exalted by transports of the most exalted moral pleasure. A flighty young girl who learns the ways of love early gets accustomed to its troubles; when she reaches the age of real passion the charm of novelty is altogether missing. As Mme. de Rênal had never read any novels, all the subtleties of her happiness were new to her. No gloomy truths could freeze her spirit, not even the specter of the future. She looked forward to being as happy ten years hence as she was at that moment. Even the notion of her virtue, and the fidelity she had pledged to M. de Rênal, which had so much disturbed her several days before, knocked vainly on her consciousness; it was sent away like an unwanted guest. Never will I accord any favor to Julien, Mme. de Rênal told herself, we will live in the future exactly as we have lived the past month. He will be a friend.

Chapter 14

ENGLISH SCISSORS

A girl of sixteen had a rose-petal complexion and wore rouge.
—Polidori[5]

In effect, Fouqué's offer had robbed Julien of all happiness; he couldn't settle on any line of action. Alas! perhaps I'm lacking in character; I would have made a poor soldier for Napoleon. At least, he added, my little intrigue with the lady of the house will distract me for a while.

Happily for him, even in this minor episode the depths of his soul bore little relation to his crude language. He was afraid of Mme. de Rênal because her dress was so pretty. In his eyes this dress constituted the advance guard of Paris itself. His pride would not allow him to leave anything to chance or to the inspiration of the instant. Relying on the confidences made him by Fouqué and the little he had read about love in the Bible, he drew up a highly detailed plan of campaign. And as he was much worried, though unable to admit it, he wrote down this plan.[6]

Next morning in the drawing room Mme. de Rênal was for an instant alone with him.

—Don't you have any other name besides Julien? she asked him.

The question was flattering, but our hero knew not what to answer; there was no room for this episode in his plan. If he had

5. John W. Polidori was Lord Byron's physician and secretary. Stendhal met them both in Milan in October, 1816. The epigraph reappears in different forms, as part of the text of Book I, Chap. 15, and as the epigraph to Book II, where it is attributed to Sainte-Beuve. Chances are it was neither Polidori's nor Sainte-Beuve's remark, but an invention of Stendhal's.

6. The idea of a prearranged plan of conquest in a love affair was ancient with Stendhal; he drew up just such a program for the siege of Mme. Daru. See the "Consultation pour Banti," in *Mélanges Intimes* (Divan ed.) XVI, pp. 57–96.

not been so stupid as to make up a strategy beforehand, Julien's quick wit would have served him very well; his surprise would only have added to the brilliance of his phrases.

He was awkward, and exaggerated his awkwardness. Mme. de Rênal pardoned him quickly enough; she saw in his clumsiness the effect of a delightful simplicity. And the only thing she had found lacking in this man, to whom everyone else attributed a great genius, was precisely an air of candor.

—I don't trust your little tutor, Mme. Derville sometimes said to her. He always seems to be calculating and to act only out of craft. He's a sly one.

Julien remained deeply humiliated by his failure to find an answer for Mme. de Rênal.

A man like me must redeem a failure like that, he thought; and seizing the moment when they were passing from one room to another, he felt it his duty to try to give Mme. de Rênal a kiss.

Nothing could have been less suave, nothing less agreeable for either of them, and nothing more imprudent. They were nearly overseen. Mme. de Rênal thought him mad. She was frightened and above all shocked. This crudity reminded her of M. Valenod.

What would happen to me, she asked herself, if I were left alone with him? All her virtue returned, because her love was in eclipse.

She arranged things so one of her children would always be at her side.

The day was a complete bore for Julien; he spent it carrying clumsily forward his scheme of seduction. He never once glanced at Mme. de Rênal without a question in his eyes. Still, his folly did not prevent him from seeing that he had succeeded in being neither agreeable nor, far less, seductive.

Mme. de Rênal could not get over her astonishment at finding him both so bashful and so bold. It is the timidity of first love in a man of wit! she finally told herself, with immense delight. Is it possible that he was never loved by my rival!

After lunch Mme. de Rênal returned to the drawing room to receive a visit from M. Charcot de Maugiron, the subprefect of Bray. She was working on a little raised tapestry loom, with Mme. Derville by her side. It was under these circumstances, and in full daylight, that our hero found it appropriate to reach forth his foot and press it against the pretty foot of Mme. de Rênal, whose net stockings and pretty Paris slippers were actually drawing admiring glances from the gallant subprefect.

Mme. de Rênal was terrified; she dropped her scissors, her ball of yarn, and her needles; thus Julien's gesture could pass as an awkward effort to prevent the scissors from falling—as if he had seen them slipping. Happily these little scissors of English steel were broken in their fall, and Mme. de Rênal was lavish in deploring the fact that Julien had not been nearer to her.

—You saw them falling before I did, you might have caught them; as it is, your eagerness has brought me nothing but a kick on the ankle.

All this business deceived the subprefect, but not Mme. Derville. This pretty boy has awfully crude manners, she thought to herself; even in a provincial capital this sort of clumsiness won't pass. Mme. de Rênal found occasion to say to Julien:

—Be more careful, I command you.

Julien was aware of his own clumsiness and grew angry. He spent a long time debating inwardly whether he ought to be angry over that expression: *I command you.* He was stupid enough to think: she might very well say *I command* if it was a question involving her children's education, but in a love affair we presuppose equality. Without *equality* love is impossible . . . ; and his mind lost itself in the recitation of commonplaces about equality. Wrathfully he repeated to himself a verse of Corneille that Mme. Derville had taught him a couple of days before:

> . . . Love
> Makes its equalities, it does not seek them out.

Since Julien persisted in playing the role of a Don Juan, he who had never in his life had a mistress, he was paralyzingly dull all day. He had only one sensible idea; bored with himself and Mme. de Rênal, he was terrified at the approach of evening and the prospect of sitting beside her in the garden and the gathering dusk. So he told M. de Rênal that he was going to Verrières to see the priest, left after dinner, and came back only late at night.

At Verrières Julien found M. Chélan busy moving out; he had in fact been removed from his position; Vicar Maslon was replacing him. Julien helped the good curé with his things, and even got the idea of writing to Fouqué that his irresistible impulse toward a sacred calling had recently kept him from accepting certain kind offers, but now he had just seen such a shocking example of injustice that perhaps it would be safer for his salvation not to enter holy orders.

Julien was much pleased with his own cleverness in using the dismissal of the curé to provide himself with an easy retreat to the world of commerce just in case melancholy prudence should win out in his soul over heroism.

Chapter 15

COCKCROW

Love in Latin is *amor*,
And in this love we find the source
Of danger, death, and biting cares,
Tears, sorrows, traps, grief, and remorse.
—Love's Heraldry

If Julien had had a bit of the shrewdness he so liberally ascribed to himself, he might have been able to congratulate himself the next morning on the effect produced by his visit to Verrières. His absence had caused his clumsiness to be forgotten. Even on this next day, however, he was still fairly sullen; but in the evening a ridiculous idea occurred to him, and he communicated it to Mme. de Rênal with a singular boldness.

Scarcely were they seated in the garden when Julien, without even waiting for dusk to fall, leaned toward the ear of Mme. de Rênal, and at the risk of compromising her terribly, whispered:

—Madame, tonight at two o'clock I must come to your room; I have something to tell you.

Julien was in an agony of fear lest his demand be granted; his role of seducer weighed on him so horribly that if he had been free to follow his own instincts, he would have retired to his own room for a few days and seen no more of these ladies. He understood that by his masterful policy yesterday he had spoiled all the prospects that seemed so fine the day before, and he no longer knew which way to turn.

Mme. de Rênal replied to Julien's impudent proposal with genuine indignation, which was in no way exaggerated. He thought he caught a note of scorn in her curt response. It's beyond question that in this answer, which was only whispered, the expression *for shame* appeared. Pretending that he had something to tell the children, Julien went to their room, and when he came back placed himself beside Mme. Derville and at a distance from Mme. de Rênal. He thus eliminated all possibility of grasping her hand. The discussion was serious, and Julien came off very well, apart from several moments of silence during which he groped desperately for a phrase. Why can't I invent some fine maneuver, he asked himself, that would force her to repeat those signs of tender feeling that convinced me, a few days ago, that she was mine for the taking!

Julien was greatly distressed by the almost desperate posture into which he had guided his affairs. And yet nothing would have embarrassed him more than success.

When the party broke up at midnight, his pessimism convinced him that Mme. Derville despised him, and that probably he was no better off with Mme. de Rênal.

Badly out of humor, and much disgruntled, Julien was unable to sleep. He was not far from giving up on all his efforts,[7] all his schemes, and living from day to day with Mme. de Rênal in the childish happiness each hour would bring him.

He exhausted his mind in inventing elaborate strategies that, an instant later, he found absurd; in a word, he was most unhappy when two o'clock struck on the farmhouse clock.

The sound roused him as the cockcrow roused Saint Peter.[8] He saw himself on the verge of a terrifying venture. Since the moment when he made it, he had not given another thought to his impertinent proposal: it had been so unfavorably received!

I told her that I would come to her room at two o'clock, he said to himself as he got up; I may be inexperienced and boorish like the son of a peasant—Mme. Derville has made that perfectly clear to me. But at least I shan't be a weakling.

Julien was perfectly right in admiring his own courage; never had he undertaken a more disagreeable task. As he opened the door he trembled so violently that his legs gave way beneath him, and he had to lean against the wall.

He was barefoot. For a moment he paused outside the bedroom of M. de Rênal, who could be heard snoring away. Julien was distressed to hear it; he had no other pretext to prevent him from going to her. But good God! what would he ever do there? He had no strategy worked out, and even if he had, he felt himself too distressed ever to carry it out.

At last, suffering a thousand times worse than if he had been marching to his execution, he crept into the little corridor leading to Mme. de Rênal's room. With trembling hands he opened the door; it made a frightful noise.

The room was lit; a night lamp was burning on the mantle. He had not expected this particular misfortune. As she saw him come in Mme. de Rênal flung herself angrily out of bed. Wretch! she cried. There was a moment of confusion. Julien forgot all his empty projects and recovered his natural self; to fail of pleasing such an attractive woman seemed to him the blackest of misfortunes. He answered her scoldings only by falling at her feet and catching her about the knees. As she talked to him extremely harshly, he burst into tears.

Several hours later, when Julien left Mme. de Rênal's room, one

7. Stendhal's sentence actually says, "He was a thousand leagues [i.e., very far indeed] from giving up," etc. One might read the sentence as saying, then, "He rejected with horror an idea which he yearned for instinctively"—if that weren't a little too cute. Accordingly, I have rationalized the sentence to conform with its major element.
8. See Mark 14. Stendhal repeatedly uses the story as an emblem of spiritual awakening.

might have said, after the fashion of novelists, that he had nothing
further to desire. Actually, he owed to the love he had previously
inspired, and to the unexpected impression produced on him by
feminine charms, a victory to which all of his clumsy subtleties
would never have conducted him.

But in the moments of supreme delight, victim of his own strange
pride, he insisted on playing the role of a man accustomed to triumph over women: he made incredible efforts to spoil the effect of
all his own charm. Instead of paying attention to the transports of
delight he aroused and to the remorse that sharpened them, he
focused his attention entirely on the idea of *duty*. He feared that
he would be the victim of a fearful disgrace and of perpetual ridicule
if he departed from the ideal of behavior he had set himself. In a
word, what made Julien a superior being was precisely the quality
that prevented him from seizing a pleasure that lay directly in his
path. He was like a young girl of sixteen with a charming complexion, who, when she's going to a dance, is foolish enough to
cover her cheeks with rouge.

Mortally terrified when Julien actually appeared, Mme. de Rênal
was quickly overwhelmed with other griefs. Julien's tears and unhappiness distressed her deeply.

Even when she had nothing further to refuse, she spurned Julien
from her presence with genuine indignation, and the next instant
flung herself into his arms. There was no policy behind this conduct.
She saw herself damned without pardon and sought to hide her
vision of hell by covering Julien with the most ardent caresses. In a
word, nothing was lacking to our hero's happiness, not even a
passionate sensitivity on the part of his beloved, if he had only
known how to enjoy it. Not even Julien's departure put a stop to
her transports of uncontrollable joy and to the attacks of bitter remorse that tore at her conscience.

Good Lord! being happy, being in love, is that all it is?[9] This was
the first thought of Julien as he regained his bedroom. He was in
that condition of astonishment and uneasy discontent which generally overtakes the soul that has just obtained its heart's desire.
Such a soul is accustomed to yearning, no longer has anything to
yearn after, and has no memories as yet. Like a soldier just back
from review, Julien was intent on examining all the details of his
conduct.

—Did I fail in any of my responsibilities to myself? Did I play
my role well?

And what role was that? The role of a man accustomed to shine
before women.

9. *N'est-ce que ça?* is the eternal cry
of the romantic confronted with the
disappointing reality of his heart's
desire. See *Brulard*, Chap. 46, and
Fabrizio's disappointed retrospect on
the experience of Waterloo, *Chartreuse*,
Chap. 5.

Chapter 16

THE MORNING AFTER

He turned his lip to hers, and with his hand
Call'd back the tangles of her wandering hair.
　　　　　—*Don Juan*, Canto 1, stanza 170

Fortunately for Julien's glory, Mme. de Rênal had been too disturbed and too astonished to observe the stupidity of this man who in an instant had become the whole world to her.

As she was begging him to leave her, just as day was beginning to break:

—Oh, Lord! she said, if my husband has overheard anything, I'm ruined forever.

Julien, who had time to make fine phrases, thought of this one:

—Should you regret losing your life?

—Ah, terribly, just now; but I should never regret having known you.

Julien found it accorded with his dignity to return deliberately to his room in broad daylight and with the greatest indiscretion.

The minute care with which he studied his own behavior, in the foolish expectation of appearing a man of experience, had only one good result; when he saw Mme. de Rênal at lunch his comportment was a masterpiece of prudence.

As for her, she could hardly look at him without blushing furiously, and she looked at him all the time. Becoming aware of her own distress, she made extra efforts to conceal it. Julien raised his eyes to hers only once. At first Mme. de Rênal admired his discretion. But then, seeing that single glance was not repeated, she grew alarmed: "Perhaps he no longer loves me," she told herself; "alas, I'm much too old for him, I must be ten years older."

As they strolled from the dining room out into the garden she clasped Julien's hand. In the moment of surprise caused by such an open mark of affection he glanced at her with passion, for she had in fact seemed beautiful to him at lunch, and even as he lowered his eyes he had passed the time by thinking of her charms. This glance brought some comfort to Mme. de Rênal; it did not relieve all her disquiet, but then her disquiet served to efface almost entirely any remorse she might have felt concerning her husband.

At lunch the husband noticed nothing; neither did Mme. Derville, who thought Mme. de Rênal was simply in danger. Throughout the day her bold and incisive friendship took the form of hints and allusions designed to paint in the most hideous colors the danger her friend was running.

Mme. de Rênal was furiously impatient for a moment alone with Julien; she wanted to ask if he still loved her. Despite the unshakable sweetness of her character, she was several times on the point of letting her friend understand how troublesome she was being.

In the garden that evening, Mme. Derville arranged matters so well that she got herself stationed between Mme. de Rênal and Julien. Mme. de Rênal, who had built up a delicious expectation of holding Julien's hand and raising it to her lips, was unable even to address a word to him.

This maneuvering increased her distress. She was haunted by one regret in particular. She had reproached Julien so bitterly for his audacity in visiting her the night before that now she was in terror he might not come again. She left the garden early, and retired to her bedchamber. But, unable to control her impatience, she came and pressed her ear against Julien's door. In spite of the uncertainty and violent passions that were devouring her, she dared not enter. Such an action seemed to her the last word in crude behavior, simply because it provides the text of a provincial proverb.

The servants were not yet all abed; discretion finally forced her to retire to her own room. Two hours of waiting were two centuries of torment.

But Julien was too faithful to what he called *his duty* to fail of executing, point by point, the program he had laid down for himself.

As the clock tolled one he slipped silently from his room, made sure that the master of the house was fast asleep, and appeared before Mme. de Rênal. That night he experienced more real pleasure with his mistress, for he thought less continually about the role he was playing. He had eyes to see and ears to hear. What Mme. de Rênal told him of her age helped to give him some assurance.

—Alas, I'm ten years older than you! How can you possibly love me? She repeated these words without ulterior motive, simply because the idea oppressed her.

Julien could form no idea of her grief, but he saw that it was real, and he forgot almost all his fears of seeming ridiculous.

The silly notion that he might be regarded as a hired lover, because of his low birth, disappeared as well. As gradually Julien's transports gave new confidence to his timid mistress, she recovered both a little happiness and the power of judging her lover. Fortunately that night he had little of that artificial manner that had made the previous night's encounter a victory but not a pleasure. If she had become aware of his efforts to play a part, the discovery would have destroyed her happiness forever. She could have seen in it only a bitter consequence of the difference in their ages.

Although Mme. de Rênal had never reflected on the theories of love, disparity of age is, after disparity of fortune, one of the great commonplaces of provincial humor whenever love is mentioned.

Within a few days Julien, quite restored to the natural ardor of his age, was desperately in love.

No one can deny, said he to himself, the angelic beauty of her soul, and they don't come any prettier.

He had almost entirely dismissed the idea of a role to be played. In a moment of self-abandon, he even told her of his anxieties. This confession lifted even higher the passion he inspired. So I never had a successful rival, Mme. de Rênal told herself joyously. She ventured to ask him about the portrait by which he placed such store; Julien swore to her that it was the portrait of a man.

When Mme. de Rênal had enough self-possession to meditate, she could not get over her astonishment that such happiness should exist and that she should never have suspected it.

Ah! she told herself, if only I had known Julien ten years ago, when I could still pass for pretty!

Julien was far from sharing these thoughts. His love was still a form of ambition; it was his joy in possessing—he, a wretched and despised creature—such a noble and beautiful woman. His acts of adoration, his transports of delight at the attractions of his mistress, succeeded at last in reassuring her slightly about the disparity in their ages. If she had had a touch of that worldly wisdom which, in the more civilized nations, women of thirty normally have, she would have shuddered for the future of a love that seemed to depend altogether on novelty and the flattery of self-esteem.

At times when his ambition was forgotten, Julien admired with ecstasy Mme. de Rênal's very hats and dresses. He never tired of their perfume. He opened her mirrored closet and spent hours on end wondering at the beauty and order of everything he found there. His mistress, leaning against him, watched his face while he admired all the jewels and frippery which on the occasion of a marriage fill a hope chest.

And I might have married such a man! Mme. de Rênal sometimes reflected; what a fiery spirit! what a marvelous life with him!

As for Julien, he had never found himself so close to these terrible weapons of feminine artillery. It's impossible, said he to himself, that even in Paris there should be anything more beautiful! And at that point he found nothing to object to in being happy. Frequently his mistress' sincere admiration and transports of pleasure caused him to forget the empty theory that had made him so affected and almost absurd in the first moments of their affair. There were even instants when, in spite of his habitual hypocrisy, he found great joy in admitting to this great lady who so admired him his unfamiliarity with a whole mass of little forms. The rank of his mistress seemed to lift him out of his own. For her part, Mme. de Rênal found it the most delicate of moral pleasures to instruct in the niceties of behavior a young man of genius who, as everyone agreed, would some day go far. Even the subprefect and M. Valenod could hardly refrain from admiring him; because they did so, she thought them less stupid. As for Mme. Derville, she was far from sharing these feelings. Desperate over the things she guessed, and seeing that her good advice was odious to a woman who had, in fact, lost control of herself, Mme. Derville left Vergy without offering any explanation and without being asked for one. Mme. de Rênal shed a few tears over her departure and soon felt twice as happy without her. In her friend's absence she could be alone almost every day with her lover.

Julien abandoned himself all the more fully to the sweet society of his mistress because, whenever he was too long by himself, the fatal proposal of Fouqué returned to disturb him. In the first days of this new life there were moments when he, who had never loved or been loved by anybody, found such delicious pleasures in sincerity that he was on the point of confessing to Mme. de Rênal the ambition that had been, up to this point, the secret essence of his existence. He would have liked to consult her on the strange attractiveness of Fouqué's offer, but a little episode occurred that blocked all thoughts of frankness.

Chapter 17

THE FIRST DEPUTY

> O, how this spring of love resembleth
> The uncertain glory of an April day;
> Which now shows all the beauty of the sun
> And by and by a cloud takes all away!
> —*Two Gentlemen of Verona*

One evening at sunset he was sitting by his mistress at the foot of the orchard, far from any intruder, sunk in deep reverie. Can such delectable moments, he asked himself, possibly last forever? His thoughts were caught up with the difficult necessity of finding a position; he lamented that sudden burden of unhappiness which puts an end to childhood and spoils the young manhood of anyone born poor.

—Ah, he exclaimed, Napoleon was really the man sent by God to the youth of France! Who can take his place? What will those wretches do who are even richer than me, who have just the meager sum needed to get a good education, but not enough money to buy a man and get started in a career at twenty![1] Whatever becomes of us, he added with a sigh, this fatal memory will prevent our ever being really happy!

Suddenly he noted that Mme. de Rênal was frowning, had assumed a cold and disdainful air; this way of thinking seemed to her suitable only to a servant. Brought up in the consciousness of wealth, she took it for granted that Julien was too. She loved him more than life itself [She would have loved him had he proved unkind or betrayed her], and money was a matter of no moment to her.

Julien was far from guessing what was in her mind. Her frown brought him back to earth. He had enough presence of mind to modify his terms and convey to this noble lady seated beside him on a grassy bank that the speech he had just delivered was one he had overheard on his recent visit to the wood dealer; that was how wicked worldlings talked.

—All right, just don't get yourself mixed up with that lot, said Mme. de Rênal, still with that glacial air that had abruptly replaced a manner of melting [and intimate] tenderness.

This frown of hers, or rather regret at his own imprudence, was the first setback for the illusion that was carrying Julien away. He said to himself: She is good, she is sweet, she is fond of me, but she has been raised in the enemy camp. They are bound to be afraid of spirited men, well educated, who don't have enough money to take up a career. What would happen to these noblemen if ever we were matched with them in even fight? If I, for example, were mayor of Verrières, honest and well meaning as I suppose M. de Rênal is at bottom! Wouldn't I get rid of the vicar, of M. Valenod, and their whole bag of tricks! Justice would really triumph in Verrières! It's not talents like theirs that would know how to stop me. They're born bumblers.

Julien's happiness that day was on the verge of becoming lasting. Our hero simply lacked the audacity to be sincere. It required boldness to give battle, and on the spot; Mme. de Rênal had been surprised by Julien's words because the men she knew always said a Robespierre might arise any minute precisely from among those well-educated, ambitious young men of the lower orders. Her severe expression lasted a long time, and to Julien seemed particularly marked. But the reason was that her first dislike of the idea was followed by regrets at having said something indirectly disagreeable to him. Unhappiness made itself quickly apparent on those features, which were so pure and innocent when she was happy and unworried.

1. "Buying a man" seems to envisage career bribing an official or purchasing as normal procedure for a commercial someone's favor.

Julien no longer dared meditate openly. Growing more calm and less passionate, he found that it was impractical to continue meeting Mme. de Rênal in her bedroom. It was better that she should come to his; if a servant saw her wandering about the house, there were twenty different pretexts at hand to explain it.

But this arrangement too had its inconvenient side. Julien had received from Fouqué various books which he himself, as a student of theology, could never have requested in a bookstore. The only time he dared open them was at night. Very often he would have been glad enough not to be interrupted by a visit; before the little scene in the orchard, mere expectation of such a visit would have rendered him incapable of reading.

Because of Mme. de Rênal, he now understood books after a wholly new fashion. He had ventured to ask her about a whole throng of little matters, ignorance of which stops short the understanding of a young man brought up outside society, however intelligent we suppose him to be.

This education in love, conducted by an extremely ignorant woman, was sheer delight. Julian moved directly to an understanding of society as it really is today. His intelligence was not clouded by recitals of what it used to be two thousand years ago, or just sixty years ago in the era of Voltaire and Louis XV. To his indescribable joy, the scales fell from his eyes and he understood at last what was going on in Verrières.

In the foreground, various complicated intrigues had been in process for some two years now around the prefect of Besançon. They were supported by letters written from Paris and signed by all the most distinguished names in the land. And the purpose of all this was to make M. de Moirod, the most devout man in the countryside, first rather than second deputy of the mayor of Verrières.

His rival was a rich manufacturer whom it was of the utmost importance to push down into the position of second deputy.

At last Julien understood the allusions he had overheard when good company came to dine at M. de Rênal's. This privileged group was profoundly involved in the selection of the first deputy—a process of which the rest of the town, and above all the liberals,[2] were wholly unaware. What made it all so important was that, as is well known, the main street of Verrières had to be widened, on its eastern side, by more than nine feet, since the street was declared a royal road.

2. The role of the liberals, and especially of the true or sincere liberals, is a constant comic subtheme in Stendhal's novels; see especially the cuts taken at them in Chaps. 18 and 22.

But, if M. de Moirod, who had three houses in the way of the new improvement, should become first deputy and thus mayor in the event of M. de Rênal's being named representative, he would look in the other direction and people could make imperceptible repairs on houses that were blocking the new road, and by this means they would last another hundred years. In spite of M. de Moirod's lofty piety and recognized probity, everyone was sure he would be *understanding*, for he had several children. Of the houses that had to be moved back, nine belonged to the top circles of Verrières society.

In Julien's eyes this intrigue was far more important than the historic battle of Fontenoy,[3] the name of which he had just seen for the first time in one of the books sent him by Fouqué. There were some things that had puzzled Julien for five years, ever since he started to study evenings with the curé. But discretion and spiritual humility are the chief qualities of a theological student, so it had been impossible for him to make inquiries.

One day Mme. de Rênal gave an order to her husband's valet, who was Julien's enemy.

—But, madame, this is the last Friday of the month, replied the man, putting on a peculiar expression.

—Off with you, said Mme. de Rênal.

—So that's it! said Julien, he's going to that hay warehouse that used to be a church and was recently restored to the uses of religion. But what do they do there? That's one of the mysteries I never could solve.

—It's a very useful institution, but also a very odd one, replied Mme. de Rênal; women aren't admitted. All I can learn is that all the people who go there are on very familiar terms. For example, this servant will meet M. Valenod there, and that arrogant, stupid fellow will not be at all distressed when Saint-Jean talks to him as an equal; he'll answer in the same tone. If you really want to know what they do there, I'll ask M. de Maugiron and M. Valenod.[4] We pay twenty francs for every servant, to prevent them from cutting our throats some day [in case the Terror of '93 returns].

Time fled by. Thinking of his mistress' charms distracted Julien from his black ambition. His inability to talk with her about gloomy, reasonable things, because they were of opposite parties, increased (though he never suspected it) the happiness she gave him and her power over him.

3. At the classic battle of Fontenoy (May 11, 1745) the French, aided by a brigade of Irish exiles, defeated a British and allied army.
4. The congregations, which began as voluntary devotional organizations, were particularly apt to be transformed, during times of social stress, into vigilante and espionage groups. Stendhal's contempt for the fraternizing of servants and masters in these groups contrasts with his fitfully egalitarian sentiments elsewhere.

At times, when the presence of too-understanding children reduced them to talking the language of cold reason, Julien sat with perfect docility, watching her with eyes in which love glittered, while she explained to him the way of the world. Often in the midst of telling about some clever bit of rascality in connection with a road or a purchasing order Mme. de Rênal grew ecstatic with joy; Julien had to warn her, she was allowing herself to use with him the same intimate gestures she used with her children [she ran her hand through his hair]. There were in fact days when she had the illusion of loving him like her own child. Didn't she have to reply constantly to his simple-minded questions about a thousand elementary things a well-born child knows by the age of fifteen? A moment later, she worshipped him as her master. His genius came close to terrifying her; she could see more clearly every day, so she thought, the future great man in this young cleric. She saw him as the pope, she saw him as a great minister, like Richelieu.[5]

—Will I live to see you in your glory? she said to Julien; the time is ripe for a great man; church and monarchy are in need of one. [Our gentlemen say every day: if some Richelieu doesn't cut off the torrent of personal judgment, all will be lost.]

Chapter 18

A KING AT VERRIÈRES

Are you good for nothing but to lie there like a corpse of a people, inanimate and bloodless?
— Speech of the bishop, in St. Clement's.

On the third of September at ten o'clock at night a police officer roused all Verrières by charging up the main street at a gallop; he brought news that his majesty the king of ____ would arrive the following Sunday, and here it was already Tuesday. The prefect authorized, that is to say, ordered, formation of a guard of honor; the show must be as big as possible. A courier was dispatched to Vergy; M. de Rênal arrived that same night and found the town in turmoil. Every man had his pretensions; the least important people were renting balconies from which to view the king's entry.

Who will command the guard of honor? M. de Rênal saw instantly how important it was, in view of those houses that might have to be moved back, that M. de Moirod should be in command. That might open his way to the office of first deputy. There was nothing to be said against M. de Moirod's devotion, it was quite

5. Cardinal Richelieu served, through the early seventeenth century, as the supreme architect of French royal power. He was an implacable, calculating, and brilliant statesman.

unparalleled, but he had never sat upon a horse. He was thirty-six years old, timid in every way, fearful alike of falling off his horse and of making himself ridiculous.[6]

The mayor summoned him at five o'clock in the morning.

—Look here, sir, I'm asking your advice today as if you already held the post for which all right-thinking men support you. Now, in this unfortunate town industry is flourishing, the liberals are all becoming millionaires, their group aspires to power and will make a weapon of anything. Let us safeguard the interests of the king, of the monarchy, and above all of our holy religion. Now who do you think, my dear sir, should be entrusted with command of the guard of honor?

Despite his horrible fear of horses, M. de Moirod finally accepted this distinction like a martyr. "I shall be able to give the occasion a proper style," he told the mayor. There was barely time to get ready the uniforms that seven years before had served for the arrival of a royal prince.

At seven Mme. de Rênal arrived from Vergy with Julien and the children. She found her drawing room filled with liberal ladies, all preaching the reconciliation of parties and all come to beg from her husband a place for their husbands among the guard of honor. One of them suggested that if her husband was not chosen, out of sheer humiliation he would go bankrupt. Mme. de Rênal quickly sent this crowd packing. She seemed very thoughtful.

Julien was surprised and angry that she kept from him the reason for her concern. Just as I thought, he said bitterly to himself, her love is eclipsed by the joy of having a king in her house. This whole uproar has overwhelmed her. Perhaps she'll love me again when the ideas of her caste no longer disturb her mind.

An astonishing thing: he loved her all the more for this behavior.

Upholsterers were starting to flood through the house; he sought long and vainly for an occasion to have a word with her. Finally he found her, coming out of his room, Julien's own room, carrying one of his suits. They were alone. He tried to speak with her. She turned away, and refused to listen to him. —I'm a fool to be in love with such a woman; ambition has driven her just as crazy as her husband.

But she was even crazier; one of her great desires, which she had never admitted to Julien for fear of shocking him, was to see him put off, if only for a day, his gloomy black suit. With a subtlety really to be admired in a woman who was so natural, she obtained, first from M. de Moirod, and then from the subprefect de Maugiron, the nomination of Julien for the guard of honor, in preference to

6. Falling off a horse is a standard Stendhalian gesture of disgrace, almost a test of character. Lucien Leuwen falls sentimentally from a horse in front of Mme. de Chasteller, and Julien (see Chap. 33) has his troubles in Paris.

five or six young men, sons of wealthy manufacturers, of whom two
at least were distinguished for their piety. M. Valenod, who had
expected to make his carriage available to the town's prettiest
women and to have his fine stallions admired, agreed to lend one
of his horses to Julien, whom he hated above all other beings. But
all the guards of honor either owned or had borrowed one of those
sky-blue uniforms with the two silver stars of a colonel which had
glittered so splendidly seven years before. Mme. de Rênal wanted
a new uniform altogether, and she had only four days in which to
send to Besançon and get back the uniform, side arms, cocked hat,
and so forth—everything that makes an honor guard. What is most
amusing is that she thought it imprudent to have Julien's outfit
made at Verrières. She wanted to surprise him, him and the town.

His duty having been done with respect to the honor guard and
the expressions of public joy, the mayor had now to concern himself
with a great religious ceremony; the king of _____ did not want to
pass Verrières without seeing the great relic of Saint Clement,
which is preserved at Bray-le-Haut, only one short league from the
town.[7] The clergy must be well represented; this was the hardest
matter of all to arrange, since M. Maslon, the new priest, wanted
above all to avoid the presence of M. Chélan. In vain did M. de
Rênal object to him the rashness of this procedure. The Marquis
de La Mole, whose ancestors had been for many years governors of
the district, had been appointed to accompany the king of _____.
For at least thirty years he had been acquainted with Abbé Chélan.
He would certainly ask for news of him, immediately upon reaching
Verrières, and if he found him disgraced would be capable of going,
with all the dignitaries he could summon, to look him up in the
humble cottage to which he had retired. What an insult!

—I am disgraced, both here and in Besançon, replied Abbé
Maslon, if he makes an appearance among my clergy. A Jansenist,
Good God![8]

—Whatever you say, my dear abbé, replied M. de Rênal, I shall
not expose the whole administration of Verrières to an affront from

7. Not far from Grenoble are the
church and convent of St. Marie d'en
Haut, on which Stendhal may have
modeled the abbey of Bray-le-Haut.
St. Clement, who is the subject of
many myths, was an early bishop of
Rome, where some of his alleged relics
are in fact to be found in the ancient
church of St. Clement's. Stendhal gives
him here the double characters of a
soldier and a saint, a waxy image and
a rotten relic, to emphasize various
parallels with Julien.
8. In the middle of the seventeenth
century the French church divided between factions calling themselves Jansenists (after Cornelis Jansen, whose
book on St. Augustine, posthumously
published in 1640, was deeply influential) and anti-Jansenists, the leaders
of whom were generally Jesuits. Tem-
peramentally and by conviction the
Jansenists tended to be austere, rigorous, inflexible types who emphasized
the soul's intimate and personal relation to God; thus they were often
accused of sympathy with Protestantism, and especially Calvinism. The
Jesuits, on the other hand, were popu-
larly supposed to be supple intriguers
whose failings tended to be in the
direction of worldliness.

M. de La Mole. You don't know him, he's a sound man at court, but down here in the provinces he has a wicked satiric wit; he's a mocker who tries only to embarrass people. Simply to amuse himself, he's capable of covering us with ridicule in the eyes of the liberals.

It was only in the course of the night between Saturday and Sunday, after three days of negotiation, that the pride of Abbé Maslon yielded before the mayor's fears as they gradually changed to courage. It was necessary to write a honeyed letter to Abbé Chélan, begging him to attend the ceremony of the relic at Bray-le-Haut, if indeed his advanced years and infirmities allowed him to do so. M. Chélan requested and obtained a letter of invitation for Julien, who was to accompany him as subdeacon.

Sunday morning thousands of peasants arriving from the mountains flooded through the streets of Verrières. The sun shone brilliantly. Finally, about three o'clock, the whole crowd was stirred by the sight of a great beacon fire atop a peak two leagues from Verrières. This signal made known that the king had entered upon the territory of the district. At once the sound of all the bells pealing and repeated shots from an old Spanish cannon belonging to the town gave evidence of the population's joy at this great event. Half the people climbed to the roof tops. All the women crowded onto balconies. The honor guard stirred itself. There was admiration for the brilliant uniforms; everyone recognized a relative or a friend. There was laughter at the timidity of M. de Moirod, who kept a prudent hand ready at every instant to clutch the saddle bow. But one spectacle caused all the others to be forgotten: the first horseman of the ninth file was a handsome boy, very slender, whom at first nobody recognized. Shortly a cry of indignation from some, and an astonished silence from others, bore witness to a general sensation. This young man, astride one of M. Valenod's Norman horses, was recognized as young Sorel, the carpenter's boy. With one voice everyone cried out against the mayor, especially the liberals. So that was it, just because this little workman disguised as an abbé gave lessons to his brats, he had presumed to name him to the guard of honor, over the candidates of Messieurs So and So, wealthy manufacturers! All the other ones, said a lady banker, ought to throw out that little brat, born on a dunghill.—He's sneaky, and he has a saber, replied her neighbor; he'd be just crooked enough to give them a slash across the face.

The comments of the well born were more dangerous. The ladies asked one another if the mayor alone was responsible for this striking indecorum. In general, they did ample justice to his scorn for those of low birth.

While he was the center of all these comments, Julien was the happiest of men. Naturally bold, he sat a horse better than most young men in this mountain village. He saw from the glances of the women that he was the center of attention.

Because they were new, his epaulets were more brilliant than anyone else's. His horse reared at every moment; he was in his glory.

His joy exceeded all measure when, as they passed by the old rampart, the noise of the little cannon caused his horse to shy out of line. By great good luck, he did not fall off, and from that moment on he felt himself a hero. He was one of Napoleon's orderlies in the act of charging a battery.

One person was happier than he. She had seen him first from one of the windows of the town hall; getting into her coach then, and swiftly accomplishing a wide detour, she arrived in time to tremble for him when his horse shied out of the column. Then, her carriage galloping furiously out another one of the town's gates, she was able to regain the road along which the king would pass, and to follow the honor guard at a distance of twenty paces amid a noble cloud of dust. Ten thousand peasants cried: Long live the king! when the mayor had the honor to harangue his majesty. An hour later, all the speeches being finished, the king was about to enter the town and the little cannon began to fire hasty shots. But an accident occurred, not to the artillerymen who had served their guns at Leipzig and Montmirail[9] but to the future first deputy, M. de Moirod. His horse lowered him gently into the only mud puddle on the broad highway, and this made for some disorder, since he had to be pulled out before the king's carriage could pass.

His majesty alighted at the fine new church, which that day was arrayed in all its crimson draperies. The king was to dine and then shortly return to his carriage in order to go and worship at the famous relic of St. Clement. Scarcely was the king at the church when Julien was galloping toward the house of M. de Rênal. There, he put off with a sigh his fine sky-blue uniform, his saber and epaulets to resume his seedy little black outfit. Once more he took to horse, and in a few moments was at Bray-le-Haut, which occupies the summit of a very pretty hill. Enthusiasm brings out these peasants in swarms, Julien thought. There's scarcely room to turn around in Verrières, and here are ten thousand more of them around the old abbey. Half ruined by vandalism during the Revolution, it had been magnificently rebuilt since the Restoration, and people were starting to talk of miracles. Julien sought out Abbé Chélan, who scolded him sharply and gave him a cassock and surplice. He

9. Leipzig (October, 1813) and Montmirail (February, 1814) were Napoleonic battles of the last days of the First Empire.

dressed at once, and followed M. Chélan, who was to wait upon the young bishop of Agde. This was a nephew of M. de La Mole, recently named to the post, and now charged with displaying the relic to the king. But the bishop could not be discovered.

The clergy grew impatient. They were waiting for their leader in the dark gothic cloister of the old abbey. Eighty curés had been assembled to represent the former chapter of Bray-le-Haut, composed before 1789 of eighty canons.[1] Having deplored for three quarters of an hour the extreme youth of the bishop, the curés thought fit that their dean should seek out monsignor and advise him that the king was approaching and it was time to enter the choir. M. Chélan's great age had made him dean; despite his crossness with Julien, he made a sign for him to follow. Julien wore his surplice very gracefully. By some sort of ecclesiastical toiletry he had flattened out his fine head of hair; but, by an oversight which irked M. Chélan even further, under the long folds of his cassock appeared the spurs of an honor guard.

When they reached the bishop's apartment various lace-covered lackeys barely deigned to explain to the old curé that monsignor was not to be seen. They disregarded him when he tried to explain that as dean of the noble chapter of Bray-le-Haut he was entitled at all times to be admitted to the presence of the officiating bishop.

Julien's lofty mood was shocked by the insolence of these lackeys. He began to run through the dormitories of the ancient abbey, opening every door he saw. A particularly little one opened to his efforts, and he found himself in a room full of the bishop's valets, all dressed in black with gold chains about their necks. Supposing from his anxious expression that he was on an errand for the bishop, these gentry let him pass. He took a few steps and found himself in an immense and very dark gothic hall, paneled in dark oak; all the pointed windows, except for one, had been bricked up. Nothing concealed the crudity of this masonry, and it formed a melancholy contrast with the magnificence of the wood paneling. The two long sides of this room, famous among scholars of Burgundian antiquities and built by Charles the Bold about 1470 in expiation of some sin or other, were lined with wooden stalls, richly carved. In varicolored woods were to be seen there all the mysteries of the Apocalypse.

This gloomy magnificence, degraded by the presence of raw bricks and naked plaster, stirred Julien's heart. He stopped and stood silent. At the other end of the hall, near the only window that admitted light, he saw a portable mirror framed in mahogany. A young man

1. Eighty canons, before the Revolution, would have involved eighty ceremonial posts of great magnificence, eighty sinecures probably held by younger sons of important families.

Like so many things in Stendhal's world, the chapter of Bray-le-Haut is a makeshift restoration created by rounding up eighty random clergymen of the district.

in violet robes and lacy surplice, but bareheaded, was standing a
few feet from the mirror. It seemed a strange piece of furniture for
such surroundings; doubtless it had been brought from town.
Julien thought the young man seemed irritated; with his right hand
he kept bestowing benedictions in the direction of the mirror.

What's all this about? thought Julien. Is there some sort of preliminary ceremony that this young priest is performing? Perhaps
it's the bishop's secretary . . . he'll be arrogant like the lackeys . . .
well, never mind, let's give it a try.

He stepped forward and walked slowly the length of the room,
always looking toward the single window and the young man, who
continued to mime benedictions, slow but numerous and executed
without a moment's pause.

As he approached he was better able to distinguish the angry
look of the other. The richness of his lace-lined surplice stopped
Julien involuntarily a few paces from the splendid mirror.

It's my duty to speak first, he said to himself at last; but the
beauty of the hall had touched him, and in anticipation he was
already wounded at the harsh words that he expected.

The young man saw him in the glass, turned, and abruptly putting off his angry air, said to him in the gentlest of tones:

—Very well, my dear sir, has it finally been set to rights?

Julien was thunderstruck. As the young man turned toward him,
Julien saw the pectoral cross about his neck; it was the bishop of
Agde. So young, thought Julien; at most, six or eight years older
than me!

And he was ashamed of his spurs.

—Monsignor, he replied timidly, I am sent by the dean of the
chapter, M. Chélan.

—Ah, he's been warmly recommended to me, said the bishop in
a polite tone that completed Julien's enchantment. But I beg your
pardon, sir, I mistook you for the person who is supposed to bring
back my miter. They packed it so clumsily in Paris that the silver
star on top has been horribly twisted. That will make a very ugly
impression, the young bishop added gloomily, and I'm still waiting
for it to come back.

—Monsignor, I will go look for the miter, if your eminence
permits.

Julien's fine eyes had their effect.

—Please do so, my dear sir, the bishop replied, with charming
courtesy, I really need it right away. I am deeply distressed to keep
the gentlemen of the chapter waiting.

When Julien was in the middle of the hall, he glanced back toward the bishop and saw that he had begun to deliver his benedictions again. What can that possibly be? Julien asked himself; no

doubt it's some sort of ecclesiastical preparation required by the ceremony which is going to take place. As he reached the anteroom where the valets were gathered, he saw the miter among them. Yielding involuntarily to Julien's imperious glance, these gentlemen placed monsignor's miter in his hands.

He felt proud to be carrying it. As he crossed the long hall he walked slowly; he held it with respect. He found the bishop seated before the mirror; from time to time his right hand still gestured, though wearily, a benediction. Julien helped him to put on the miter. The bishop shook his head.

—Ah, that will do, he said to Julien contentedly. Would you be good enough to step away a few feet?

The bishop strode swiftly to the center of the room, then walked very slowly toward the mirror, resumed his cross expression, and made a series of solemn benedictions.

Julien stood motionless with surprise; he was tempted to understand, but did not dare. The bishop paused, and glancing at him with an expression from which gravity rapidly faded, asked:

—What do you think of my miter, sir, does it fit me properly?

—Very well indeed, monsignor.

—It's not too far back? That would look pretty silly; but then you can't wear it down over your eyes, either, like an officer's shako.

—It seems to me exactly right.

—The king of _____ is used to a venerable and no doubt extremely grave clergy. Particularly because of my age, I shouldn't like to give too casual an impression.

And the bishop began to walk about again, bestowing benedictions.

It's perfectly clear, thought Julien, daring at last to understand, he's practicing his benedictions.

After a few more minutes, the bishop said: —I'm ready now. Would you go, sir, and give notice to the dean and the gentlemen of the chapter.

Shortly M. Chélan, followed by the two senior curés, entered through a vast and magnificently sculptured doorway, which Julien had not noticed before. But this time he remained in his proper position, in the last rank of all, and could see the bishop only over the shoulders of the ecclesiastics as they crowded through the doorway.

Slowly the bishop walked down the hall; as he reached the threshold, the curés formed a line of march behind him. After an instant of disorder the procession moved forward, intoning a psalm. The bishop walked last between M. Chélan and another very elderly cleric. Julien, as an adjunct of Abbé Chélan, managed to get quite close to monsignor. They walked down the long corridors of the abbey of Bray-le-Haut; despite the brilliant sunshine outside, the walls were dark and dank. At last they reached the gate of the cloister. Julien was overcome with admiration for such a splendid ceremony. Ambition, stirred by the youth of the bishop, disputed in his heart with admiration for his sensitivity and exquisite courtesy. His politeness was quite another thing from that of M. de Rênal, even on one of his good days. The higher one rises in society, Julien thought to himself, the more one finds these charming good manners.

They entered the church by a side portal. Suddenly a frightful noise caused the ancient vaults to reverberate; Julien thought they would fall down. It was that little cannon again; it had just arrived, drawn at a full gallop by eight horses; and no sooner arrived than it went into action, with the cannoneers of Leipzig firing five shots a minute just as if they had the Prussians in their sights.

But this glorious racket made no impression on Julien; he had no more dreams of Napoleon and military glory. So young, he thought, to be bishop of Agde! But where is Agde? And how much does it bring in? Two or three hundred thousand francs, probably.[2]

Monsignor's lackeys appeared with a magnificent canopy; M. Chélan grasped one of the poles, but in fact Julien supported it. The bishop took his place beneath it. He had actually succeeded in giving himself the appearance of an old man; our hero's admiration knew no bounds. What can't be done with a little cunning! he thought.

The king appeared. Julien had the privilege of seeing him from quite close. The bishop harangued him with great unction, not forgetting to add a little touch of extremely polite reproof to his majesty.

We shall not describe at length the ceremonies of Bray-le-Haut; for two weeks they filled all the columns of all the newspapers in the district. Julien learned from the bishop's speech that the king was a descendant of Charles the Bold.

Later it became part of Julien's duties to check over the accounts detailing what this ceremony had cost. M. de La Mole, who had made his nephew a bishop, undertook the additional gesture of paying for the whole show. The ceremony of Bray-le-Haut alone cost three thousand eight hundred francs.

After the bishop's speech and the king's response, his majesty placed himself beneath the canopy, where he kneeled very devoutly on a cushion placed by the altar. The choir was lined with stalls

2. Cardinal de Retz, toward the end of the first part of his *Mémoires*, tells how he was named Bishop of Agde when barely twenty-five years old. The post in those days (two hundred years before Julien's time) was worth thirty thousand livres a year. But de Retz declined it because he had his eye on a Paris position.

and the stalls were raised two steps above the floor. On the upper of these two steps sat Julien at the feet of M. Chélan, almost like a train bearer with his cardinal, in the Sistine Chapel at Rome. There was a *Te Deum*, clouds of incense, infinite volleys of musketry and artillery; the peasants were delirious with joy and piety. One such day undoes the work of a hundred issues of Jacobin newspapers.

Julien was six feet from the king, who was in fact praying earnestly. For the first time he noticed a short man with a sharp glance wearing a perfectly plain suit. But on this very simple costume he wore a sky-blue ribbon. He was a good deal closer to the king than numerous other gentlemen, whose costumes were so covered with gold braid that, as Julien said to himself, one could hardly see the basic material. A few moments later he learned that this was M. de La Mole. He seemed to have a lofty, even insolent, manner.

This marquis wouldn't be courteous like my fine bishop, thought he. Ah, doesn't a job in the church render a man bland and good! But the king came here to worship the relic, and I don't see any relic. Now where can St. Clement be?

A little cleric beside him made known that the venerable relic was in an upper part of the building in a *chapelle ardente*.

What's a *chapelle ardente*? Julien asked himself.[3]

But he did not want to ask for an explanation of the phrase. He watched more closely than ever.

When a reigning prince visits, etiquette requires that the canons not accompany the bishop. But as he set out for the *chapelle ardente*, the bishop of Agde asked Abbé Chélan to accompany him, and Julien ventured to follow.

Having mounted a long staircase, they reached an extremely narrow doorway, the frame of which was splendidly gilded. This work seemed to have been done yesterday.

Before the door was kneeling a group of twenty-four girls belonging to the most distinguished families of Verrières. Before opening the door, the bishop kneeled for a moment among the girls, all of them pretty. While he was praying loudly they were lost in admiration of his fine laces, his graceful gestures, his youthful, sensitive face. This spectacle deprived our hero of what remained of his reason. At that moment he would have fought for the Inquisition, and with full conviction. Abruptly the door opened and the chapel appeared, glowing with light. On the altar were visible more than a thousand candles divided into eight tiers, with bouquets of flowers in between. The strong odor of fine incense rose in clouds from the doorway of the sanctuary. The newly gilded chapel was narrow but lofty. Julien observed that on the altar there were some candles

3. Actually, a *chapelle ardente* (for which English has no brief equivalent) is a chapel lit with candles where, ordinarily, a corpse is laid out before burial. The candles are what make it *ardente*, a "burning" chapel.

more than fifteen feet high. The girls could not repress a cry of admiration. No one had been admitted into the little vestibule of the chapel except the twenty-four girls, the two curés, and Julien.

Shortly the king arrived, followed by M. de La Mole and by his grand chamberlain. The guards themselves remained outside, kneeling and presenting arms.

His majesty flung himself, rather than placing himself, on a low stool. Only then did Julien, drawn back against the gilded door, perceive, under the bare arm of a girl, the enchanting statue of St. Clement. He was concealed beneath the altar, wearing the costume of a young Roman soldier. A wide wound appeared on his neck, from which blood seemed to flow. The artist had quite outdone himself; the Saint's dying eyes, still full of grace, were half closed. A budding moustache adorned that charming mouth, which, though half closed, still seemed to be praying. Seeing this, the girl beside Julien wept bitterly; one of her tears fell warm on Julien's hand.

After a moment of silent prayer, broken only by the distant sound of bells tolling in all the villages for ten leagues around, the bishop of Agde begged permission of the king to speak. He concluded his short but very moving talk with these words, the more effective for their simplicity.

—Never forget, young Christians, that you have seen one of the greatest kings on earth kneeling before the servants of an omnipotent and terrible God. These servants, though weak, persecuted, and done to death on earth, as you see from the still-bleeding wounds of St. Clement, have their triumph in heaven. Do you promise, young Christians, to hold this day in remembrance? You must hate impiety, then. Forever you must remain true to a God who is great, who is terrible, and who is also good.

At these words the bishop rose with an air of authority.

—You promise me? said he, holding up his arms like one inspired.

—We promise, cried the girls, melting into tears.

—I receive your promise in the name of almighty God! said the bishop in a voice of thunder. And that was the end of the ceremony.

The king himself was weeping. Only much later did Julien regain enough coolness to ask where were the saint's bones, sent from Rome to Philip the Good, Duke of Burgundy. He was told that they were hidden inside the charming wax figurine.[4]

His majesty graciously permitted the young ladies who had been with him in the chapel to wear a red ribbon on which were em-

4. Philip the Good was a fifteenth-century Duke of Burgundy. The interplay of Charles the Bold and Philip the Good is only one of the lovely red-black duplicities of this chapter.

The conversion of St. Clement, who was both soldier and saint, into a whited sepulcher, a charming wax figurine over old bones, is a climactic irony.

broidered these words: DOWN WITH IMPIETY, ADORATION FOREVER.

M. de La Mole ordered a distribution among the peasantry of ten thousand bottles of wine. That night, at Verrières, the liberals found it appropriate to light up their houses a hundred times brighter than the royalists. Before he left, the king paid a call upon M. de Moirod.

Chapter 19

TO THINK IS TO SUFFER

The grotesque quality of everyday life conceals from you a real misery of the passions.   —Barnave[5]

As he was replacing the everyday furniture in the room which had been occupied by M. de La Mole, Julien came across a sheet of heavy paper folded in four. At the foot of the sheet he read:

To His Excellency, M. le Marquis de La Mole, peer of France, knight of the orders of the king, etc.

It was a petition, in the clumsy handwriting of a cook.

Monsieur le marquis,
I have had good religious principles all my life. I was in Lyons exposed to bombs during the siege of '93 of detestable memory. I take communion. I go Sundays to mass at the parish church. I never missed my Easter duty, not even in '93 of detestable memory. My cook, before the Revolution I had servants, my cook has orders that we fast on Friday. I have an excellent reputation in Verrières, and make bold to say I deserve it. I walk under the canopy in the processions beside his honor the priest and his honor the mayor. I carry at big festivals a fat candle bought at my own expense. Concerning which matters certificates are at Paris at the ministry of finance. I request of M. le marquis the lottery office at Verrières,[6] which cannot fail to be available soon, one way or another, the incumbent being very sick and besides voting badly in the elections, etc.
                                      De Cholin.

In the margin of this petition was an endorsement signed *De Moirod*, which began with this line:

I had the honor to speak *yessturday* of the good subject who makes this request, etc.

So even that imbecile de Cholin shows me the path to be taken, said Julien to himself.

A week after the king of _____ passed through Verrières, the one topic of discussion that survived innumerable lies, stupid explanations, ridiculous opinions, etc., etc., which fastened successively on

5. See p. 4, note 1.
6. A national lottery was operated in France during the last quarter of the eighteenth and the first quarter of the nineteenth century.

the king, the bishop of Agde, the Marquis de La Mole, the ten thousand bottles of wine and poor tumble-down de Moirod, who, in hopes of a cross,[7] left his house only a month after his fall—the one topic was the frightful impropriety of having *hoisted* into the honor guard Julien Sorel, the carpenter's son. You should have heard on this topic the rich manufacturers of figured cloth who night and day bawled themselves hoarse in the cafés on the subject of equality. That snob Mme. de Rênal was responsible for the abomination. And why? The bright eyes and fine complexion of little Abbé Sorel were reason enough.

Scarcely were they back in Vergy when Stanislas-Xavier, the youngest of the boys, came down with a fever; Mme. de Rênal fell victim at once to a frightful remorse. For the first time she looked upon her love affair in a coherent, consecutive way; she seemed to understand, as by a miracle, the enormity of the fault into which she had let herself be carried. Though profoundly religious by nature, she had never until this moment thought of her crime as it must appear in the eyes of God.

Years ago, in the Convent of the Sacred Heart, she had loved God passionately; in her present circumstances she feared him equally. The conflicts that ravaged her spirit were all the worse because there was nothing reasonable about her terror. Julien soon found that the least trace of logic infuriated rather than calmed her; she saw in it the language of hell. So that, as Julien was himself very fond of little Stanislas, it seemed better to talk to her about his sickness; then she quickly assumed a grave calm. But continual remorse prevented Mme. de Rênal from sleeping; she never broke her somber silence; if she had opened her mouth, it would have been to proclaim her guilt to God and man.

—I implore you, Julien told her, let me be the only one to whom you tell your troubles. If you still love me, don't talk to anyone else; your words can never relieve our Stanislas of his fever.

But his consolations were fruitless; he did not know Mme. de Rênal had got it into her head that her jealous God would be satisfied only if she hated Julien or suffered the loss of her son. It was because she knew she could never hate her lover that she was so wretched.

—Go away, she said one day to Julien; in the name of God, leave the house; it's your being here that's killing my son.

God is punishing me, she added in a whisper, he is a just God, I worship his justice; my crime was horrible and I felt no remorse! It's the first sign that God has given me up; I shall be doubly punished, and I deserve it.

Julien was deeply moved. He saw neither hypocrisy nor exaggeration in her remorse. She thinks that in loving me she is killing her

---

7. "Cross" stands for the ribbon and medal of an honorary order.

boy, and yet the poor woman loves me better than her own son. No doubt about it, that's the grief which is killing her; and that's real magnificence of feeling. But how could I give rise to such a passion, poor as I am, ill taught, ignorant, sometimes crude in my manners?

One night the child was in crisis. About two in the morning M. de Rênal came to see him. Flushed with fever, the boy could not recognize his father. Suddenly Mme. de Rênal threw herself at the feet of her husband: Julien saw she was going to tell everything and ruin herself forever.

Fortunately, her dramatic gesture irked M. de Rênal.

—Goodbye, goodbye! he cried, and turned to go.

—No, no, listen to me, cried his wife, kneeling before him and trying to hold him back. Here is the whole truth. I am killing my own son. I gave him life and I'm taking it away from him. Heaven is punishing me, in the eyes of God I am guilty of murder. I must destroy and abase myself; perhaps that sacrifice will appease the Lord.

If M. de Rênal had been a man of imagination, he would have understood everything.

—Romantic ideas, he cried, pushing away his wife as she tried to clutch his knees. All romantic notions, that stuff! Julien, call the doctor as soon as it's morning.

And he went back to bed. Mme. de Rênal fell to her knees, half fainting, and repelling Julien with a convulsive gesture as he offered to come to her aid.

Julien stood amazed.

So this is adultery, he said to himself. . . . Is it possible that those knavish priests . . . . could be right? Can they, who commit so many sins themselves, have the special privilege of understanding the real principle of sin? What a fantastic thought!

For twenty minutes after M. de Rênal left, Julien watched the woman he loved resting her head on the child's little bed, motionless and almost unconscious. Here is a woman of superior spirit reduced to the pit of misery because she has known me, he said to himself.

Hours passed swiftly. What can I do for her? I must decide. There's no question of my interests here. What do I care about men and their stupid shows? What can I do for her? . . . leave her? But I leave her alone, in prey to the most atrocious griefs. That automaton husband of hers does more harm than good. He'll say something crude to her, out of sheer clumsiness; she may go mad, throw herself out of a window.

If I leave her, if I no longer watch over her, she'll tell him everything. And who knows, maybe, in spite of the fortune she must have brought him, he'll make a scandal. She might tell everything, Good God! to that b____ Abbé Maslon who's been using the illness of a six-year-old as a pretext for sticking close to this house, and not without his own purposes. In her grief, and with her fear of God, she will forget everything she knows about this man; she'll see in him only a priest.

—Go away, Mme. de Rênal said to him, suddenly opening her eyes.

—I would give my life a thousand times over to know how to serve you best, Julien replied; never have I loved you so much, my darling, or rather, it's only at this moment that I've begun to love you as you deserve. What would become of me far from you, and knowing that you are unhappy because of me! But let's not talk of my troubles. I'll go, indeed I will, my love. But if I leave you, if I cease to watch over you, to be between you and your husband, you'll tell him everything, you'll ruin yourself. Only think, he'll drive you out of his house in disgrace; all Verrières, all Besançon, will be buzzing with the scandal. They'll put all the blame on you; you'll never be able to live it down . . .

—That's just what I want, she cried, leaping up. I'll suffer; so much the better.

—But this horrible scandal will make him miserable too!

—But I humiliate myself, I drag myself in the mud; and perhaps in that way I'll save my son. This humiliation before the whole town may be a form of public penance. As far as I can judge, and I'm a weak woman, isn't this the greatest sacrifice I can make to God? Perhaps He in his mercy will accept my humiliation, and leave me my son! Tell me of a more painful sacrifice and I'll perform it.

—Let me punish myself, as well. I too am guilty. Shall I enter a Trappist monastery? The austerity of that life may appease your God. . . . Ah, God, why can't I take on myself the sickness of Stanislas. . . .

—Ah! you love him too, cried Mme. de Rênal, rising and throwing herself into his arms.

At the same time she pushed him away with horror.

—I believe you! I believe you! she continued, once more back on her knees; oh, my only friend, oh, why aren't you the father of Stanislas? Then it would not be a horrible sin to love you better than your son.

—Will you let me stay if in the future I love you only as a brother? It's the only sensible form of expiation, perhaps that will appease God's anger.

—And how about me? she cried, rising, taking Julien's head between her two hands, and holding it before her eyes at a little distance; how about me? Shall I love you as a brother? Do you think it's in my power to love you like a brother?

Julien broke into sobs.

—I obey you, he said, falling at her feet, I obey you in every-thing you decree; it's all that's left for me to do. My mind is blinded; I see no way out. If I leave, you'll tell everything to your husband, destroy yourself and him with you. After such a scandal, he'll never be named deputy. If I stay, you'll think me responsible for your son's death, and you'll die of grief. Shall we try the consequences of my leaving? If you wish, I'll punish myself for our sin by leaving you for a week. I'll spend it in some retreat, wherever you say. At the abbey of Bray-le-Haut, for example; but you must swear that while I'm away you won't say anything to your husband. Remember, I'll never be able to return if you talk.

She promised; he left, but two days later she called him back.

—Without you I'll never be able to keep my vow. I'll tell my husband if you're not continually here to silence me with your glances. Every hour of this horrible existence seems to last a whole day.

At last the clouds lifted for the wretched woman. Little by little Stanislas began to recover. But the glass was cracked; her reason had measured the extent of her sin, and she could no longer regain her balance. Remorse remained, and became what it should be in a deeply sincere heart. Her life was heaven and hell: hell when Julien was out of her sight, heaven when she was at his feet. I'll never delude myself again, she said to him, even at the moments when her love was at its highest pitch: I am damned, damned without hope of pardon. You are young, you yielded to my seductions, you may be pardoned; but for me, it is damnation. I know it, beyond any question. I'm afraid; who wouldn't be terrified at the prospect of hell? But really, I have no regrets. I would sin again, if my sin were still before me. Let God simply forbear to punish me in this world, and through my children, and I'll have more than I deserve. But you, at least, Julien, she cried at other moments, are you happy? Do you think I love you enough?

Julien's suspicion and anxious pride, which required above all a love built on sacrifice, could not hold out against a sacrifice so vast, so unquestionable, so continual. He adored Mme. de Rênal. What matter if she is noble, and I the son of a workman, she loves me. . . . In her eyes, I am no valet employed on the side as a lover. Once this fear was destroyed, Julien fell into all the madness of love, all its mortal uncertainties.

—At least, she said, seeing his doubts about her love, at least let me make you happy during the few days we have together! We must hurry; tomorrow, perhaps, I can no longer be yours. If God strikes at me through my children, it will be useless for me to try to live only in your love, to forget that my crime killed them. I shall never survive them. Even if I wanted to, I wouldn't be able; I should go mad.

—Oh, if only I could take on myself the blame for your crime, as you in your generosity wanted to assume the fever of Stanislas!

This great moral crisis changed entirely the nature of the bond that united Julien to his mistress. His love was no longer simply an admiration for her beauty compounded with pride of possession.

Henceforth, their happiness was of a finer grain; the passion that devoured them was more intense. They underwent transports of total folly. In the eyes of the world, perhaps, their happiness would have seemed greater than it was before. But they never could recover that delicious serenity, that cloudless felicity, that easy joy of their first falling in love, when Mme. de Rênal's only fear was that Julien might not love her enough. Their happiness now wore sometimes the expression of a crime.

In their moments of greatest happiness, when things seemed on the surface most tranquil: —Oh, great God, I see hell before me! Mme. de Rênal would cry suddenly, clutching Julien's hand convulsively. What horrible torments! yet I've deserved them all! She drew him to her, as ivy clutches a wall.

Julien tried vainly to calm this tormented spirit. She grasped his hand, covered it with kisses. Then, falling into a gloomy reverie, she said: Hell, now, real hell, would be a relief to me; on earth I would still have some time to spend with him, but to have hell in this world as well, the death of my children. . . . Yet, after all that suffering, perhaps my crime would be pardoned. . . . Oh, almighty God, don't pardon me at that price. My poor children have done you no harm; I'm the guilty one, I alone; I love a man who is not my husband.

Then it seemed to Julien that Mme. de Rênal had reached a stage of calm. She was striving to gain control of herself because she did not want to embitter the life of the man she loved.

Amid these alternatives, the remorse and pleasure of love, time passed for them with the speed of light. Julien lost the habit of reflection.

Mlle. Elisa went to Verrières, where she had a little legal business to attend to. There she found M. Valenod much irritated with Julien. She hated the young tutor, and often talked of him with his enemy.

—You would be scandalized at me, sir, if I told you the truth! . . . she said one day to M. Valenod. When it's anything important, the masters all see eye to eye. . . . There are certain things they'll never pardon a poor servant for mentioning. . . .

After these routine phrases, which the impatience and curiosity of M. Valenod found ways of shortening, he managed to learn certain things most distressing to his self-esteem.

This woman, the most distinguished of the district, whom for six years he had been assiduously plying with attentions, and unhappily in the sight of the whole world; this proud woman, whose lofty disdain had so often put him to the blush, had just accepted as her lover a little workman disguised as a tutor. And to add the crowning touch to the indignity of the poorhouse director, Mme. de Rênal adored this lover.

—And, what's more, the maid added with a sigh, M. Julien made no special effort to achieve this conquest; he never even altered for madame his usual coldness.

Elisa had been convinced only by events in the country, but she suspected the intrigue had been going on longer than that.

—I'm sure that was the reason, she said angrily, that he refused to marry me that time. And I, like a fool, I went to Mme. de Rênal; I begged her to talk to that little tutor.

That very evening M. de Rênal received from town, along with his newspaper, a long anonymous letter that informed him in the very greatest detail of what was happening in his house. Julien saw him grow pale as he read this letter, written on bluish paper; and he noted several surly glances. For the rest of the evening the mayor remained in distress; Julien tried vainly to flatter him by inquiring about the genealogies of all the best families of Burgundy.

Chapter 20

ANONYMOUS LETTERS

> Do not give dalliance
> Too much the rein: the strongest oaths are straw
> To the fire i' the blood.
> —*The Tempest*

As they left the drawing room about midnight, Julien found an instant to tell his mistress:

—Let's not meet this evening, your husband is suspicious; I'm sure that letter he was grumbling over tonight was a denunciation.

By good fortune Julien was in the habit of locking his bedroom door from within. Mme. de Rênal had the crazy notion that this warning was only a pretext not to see her; she lost her head completely, and at the regular hour came to his room. Julien, who heard noises in the hallway, put out his light at once. Efforts were made to open his door; was it Mme. de Rênal or was it a jealous husband?

Next morning quite early the cook, who was fond of Julien,

brought him a book, on the cover of which he read these words in Italian: *Guardate alla pagina 130.*

Julien shuddered at such indiscretion, turned to page 130, and found pinned to it the following letter, written in haste, stained with tears, and full of misspellings. Ordinarily Mme. de Rênal wrote very correctly; he was touched by this detail, and forgot for a moment her terrifying rashness.

You wouldn't let me in last night? There are times when I'm sure I don't know you at all. Your looks terrify me. I'm afraid of you. Good God, perhaps you never even loved me! In that case, I hope my husband discovers everything and shuts me away forever in some solitary place deep in the country and far from my children. Perhaps that is what God wishes. I shall die soon. But you will be a monster.

Don't you love me any more? Are you tired of my folly, of my remorse, wretch that you are? Would you like to ruin me? I'll give you an easy weapon. Go, show this letter throughout Verrières, or instead just show it to M. Valenod. Tell him I love you; but no, that's blasphemy, don't say that, tell him I adore you, that life only began for me the day I saw you, that in my craziest childish dreams I never imagined such happiness as I've had with you, that I sacrifice my life to you, my soul. And you know that I've sacrificed even more than that.

But what does he know about sacrifices, that man? Tell him, tell him just for spite that I defy all evil tongues, that there's only one sorrow left in my world, when I see a change of heart in the only man for whom I want to live. What happiness for me to give up my life, to offer it as a sacrifice, and have nothing further to fear for my children!

Never doubt it, my dearest, if there is an anonymous letter it comes from that odious man who for six long years has been persecuting me with his loud mouth, his great deeds as a horseman, his fatuity, his endless enumeration of his own advantages.

Is there an anonymous letter? Wretch, that's what I wanted to talk about with you; but no, you were right. If I held you in my arms, perhaps for the last time, I would never have been able to talk cold policy with you, as I can when alone. From now on, our happiness will not come so easily. Will that distress you? Yes, probably on the days when you haven't received some amusing book from M. Fouqué. But the die is cast; tomorrow, whether there's an anonymous letter or not, I'm going to tell my husband that I myself have received such a letter, and that he must immediately pay you off lavishly, find some decent pretext, and send you back at once to your own people.

Alas, my darling, we shall be separated for a couple of weeks, perhaps even a month! Go, then, I'm sure you will be as unhappy

over this as I am. But after all, this is the only way to ward off
the effect of that anonymous letter; it's not the first one my
husband has received, and on my account too. Alas! How I
laughed at the others!

The whole point of my acting is to make my husband think
the letter comes from M. Valenod, as I don't doubt it does. If
you have to leave this house, don't fail to settle yourself in Verrières somewhere. I'll arrange for my husband to get the idea of
spending a couple of weeks there in order to show the fools that
there's no estrangement between him and me. Once at Verrières,
make yourself the friend of everyone, even the liberals. I know
you'll be a favorite with all the ladies.

Don't quarrel with M. Valenod or slice his ears as you threatened to do once; on the contrary, court his favor. The big thing
is to make everyone in Verrières think you are going to enter
his household, or some other such, as tutor to the children.

That's what my husband will never endure. Even if he brings
himself to allow it, well, at any rate, you'll still be in Verrières
and I'll be able to see you. My children, who love you so much,
will go to see you. My God, it seems to me I love my children
more because they love you. What unhappiness! Where will it
all end? . . . I'm bewildered. . . . Well, you see how to act; be
courteous, be polite, don't be in any way lofty with these clods,
I beg of you on bended knee: they are going to be the masters
of our fate. Never suppose for a minute that my husband won't
conform, in every detail concerning you, to the program that
public opinion will prescribe for him.

Now you must furnish me with my anonymous letter; you'll
need patience and a pair of scissors. Cut out of a book the words
with which I'll furnish you; then glue them on the sheet of blue
notepaper enclosed here; it was sent me by M. Valenod. Anticipate that your room will be searched; burn the remaining pages
of the book you've cut up. If you don't find the exact words, take
time to form them letter by letter. To ease your task, I've cut the
letter short. Alas, if you don't love me any more, as I fear, how
long my own letter will seem to you.

Madame,
All your little tricks are known; but the people who will want
to prevent them have been told. In the name of our old friendship, I implore you to get rid of the little peasant for good. If
you can manage that, your husband will think the note he has
received was false, and he can be left to think it. Keep in mind,
I have your secret; tremble for your guilt; from this moment on,
you must *walk the straight and narrow* under my eyes.

As soon as you have finished piecing this letter together (do
you recognize the director's habits of speech in it?), leave the
house, and I'll meet you.

I'll go to town and return looking troubled—as in fact I will be. My God, what risks I'm running, and all because you *thought you suspected* an anonymous letter. Finally, with an incredulous look, I'll give my husband this letter, which will have been handed to me by an unknown man. You, meanwhile, will walk out along the forest road with the children, and come back only at dinnertime.

From the rocky part of that road you can easily see the dovecote. If our business succeeds, I'll put a white handkerchief in the window, otherwise nothing.

Perhaps your thoughtless heart will find a means of telling me that you love me before you leave on your walk? Whatever happens, you may be sure of one thing: I shall never survive our final separation, not for a day. Ah, what a wicked mother! Two empty words I have written there, dear Julien. They have no meaning for me; at this moment I can think only of you, and I wrote them only to forestall your blame. Now that I see myself about to lose you, why pretend? Let my soul seem horrible in your eyes, all right, but I don't want to lie to the man I adore! My life has been too full of lies. Go now. I forgive you if you no longer love me. I have no time to reread this letter. It's no great matter, I think, if I have to pay with my life for the days of joy I've spent in your arms. You know they will cost me more than that.

Chapter 21

DIALOGUE WITH THE MASTER OF THE HOUSE

> Alas, our frailty is the cause, not we:
> For such as we are made of, such we be.
> —*Twelfth Night*

With childish pleasure Julien spent an hour assembling words. As he left his room, he met his pupils and their mother; she took the letter with a simplicity and courage so unruffled that he was terrified by it.

—Is the paste dry enough? she asked him.

And is this the woman whom remorse was almost driving to distraction? he thought. What is she planning to do now? He was too proud to ask her; but never before, perhaps, had she pleased him more.

—If this turns out badly, she added, as coolly as ever, I lose everything. Hide these things out on the mountain somewhere; they may one day be all I have.

She handed him a red morocco case with a glass top, filled with gold and some diamonds.

—Now go, she said.

She kissed her children, the younger twice. Julien stood still. She walked swiftly away without looking back.

From the moment when he opened the anonymous letter M. de Rênal had led a frightful existence. He had not been so upset since a duel he nearly had in 1816,[8] and to do him justice, the prospect of getting shot on that occasion had made him less unhappy than now. He went over the letter from every point of view: Isn't it a woman's hand? he asked himself. In that case, what woman could have written it? He reviewed mentally all the women he knew in Verrières without being able to settle his suspicions. Could a man have dictated the letter? Then what man? The same uncertainty here; he was envied, and no doubt hated, by most of the men he knew. I'll have to ask my wife, he said out of sheer habit, rising from the chair in which he had sunk.

But scarcely was he up—Great God! he cried, striking his brow, she's the person I have to mistrust more than anyone; from now on, she's the enemy. And tears of sheer rage came to his eyes.

It was due retribution for that dryness of heart that is known in the provinces as practical wisdom that the two men whom M. de Rênal suspected most, at this moment, were his two most intimate friends.

After that pair, I have maybe ten friends, and he numbered them over, estimating for each one how much consolation might be had from him. Every one of them, every last one, he cried in a rage, would be delighted at my trouble! Fortunately, he thought himself envied by one and all—not wholly without reason. Apart from his superb town house, which the king of ＿＿＿ had just distinguished forever by sleeping in it, he had made a fine thing out of his country house at Vergy. The front was painted white, the windows furnished with fine green shutters. For an instant he was consoled by the thought of this magnificence. The fact is that his house was visible at a distance of three or four leagues, much to the discredit of all the other country houses or so-called *chateaux* of the district, which had been allowed to fade into the humble gray tones imposed by time.

M. de Rênal could indeed count on the tears and sympathy of one friend, the church warden of the parish; but this man was an imbecile who had sympathy for everyone. Yet he was the mayor's only recourse.

What misery like mine! he cried, furiously; what loneliness!

Can it possibly be, this really wretched man asked himself, is it actually possible that in my misfortunes I don't have a single friend to talk to? My reason is giving way, I'm sure of it. Ah, Falcoz!

8. Most of M. de Rênal's troubles and anxieties date back to the early days of the Restoration, when a lot of tables were turned; see p. 106, note 4.

ah, Ducros![9] he cried bitterly. They were two childhood friends whom he had estranged by his arrogance in 1814. They were not noble, and he had tried to change the terms of equality on which they had lived since childhood.

One of them, Falcoz, a man of spirit and feeling who sold paper in Verrières, had bought a print shop in the district capital and undertaken a daily newspaper. The congregation set out to ruin him: his paper had been condemned and his license to print withdrawn. In these bitter circumstances he undertook to write to M. de Rênal for the first time in ten years. The mayor of Verrières felt obliged to reply like an ancient Roman: "If the king's minister did me the honor to ask my advice, I should tell him: Ruin without mercy every printer in the province, and make printing a government monopoly like tobacco." Such a letter to an intimate friend, which all Verrières had admired at the time, now caused M. de Rênal to shrink in horror. Who would have thought that with my rank, my fortune, and my decorations I should some day regret it? It was in transports of rage like these, directed now against himself, now against his surroundings, that he passed a night of torture; but, by good fortune, he did not get the idea of spying on his wife.

I am used to Louise, he said to himself, she knows all my business; if I were free to remarry tomorrow, I wouldn't find anyone to replace her. And then he consoled himself with the idea that his wife might be innocent; seeing things in this light saved him from the necessity of displaying some character, and pleased him much better; after all, everyone knows women are often subjected to calumny!

But then, he exclaimed suddenly, walking convulsively about, why do I have to act like an ordinary nobody, a ragamuffin, while she makes game of me with her lover! Do I have to see all Verrières sniggering over my complacency? What haven't they said about Charmier (he was a notoriously deceived husband of the district)? Anytime his name is spoken, there's a grin. He's a good lawyer, but who ever talks about his professional qualities? Ah, Charmier, they say, Bernard's Charmier; they call him by the name of the man who brought about his disgrace.

Thanks be to God, said M. de Rênal at other moments, I have no daughter, and the way in which I shall punish the mother won't hold back my sons in their careers. I can catch the little peasant with my wife and kill them both; that way the tragic ending of the story will soften the absurdity of it. This idea pleased him; he worked it out in all its details. The penal code is on my side, and,

---

9. Falcoz the Grenoble bookseller and Ducros the librarian whom Stendhal knew as a boy are here recalled with sympathy (compare *Brulard*, Chaps. 16 and 20).

whatever happens, our congregation and my friends in the jury will protect me. He examined his hunting knife, and it was very sharp; but the idea of blood terrified him.

I can have this insolent tutor beaten up and driven out of the house; but what a scandal in Verrières and throughout the department! After we smashed Falcoz's paper, when his editor-in-chief got out of prison, I helped to have him fired from a job worth six hundred francs. They say that scribbler has had the boldness to turn up again in Besançon; he can lampoon me from there, and so cleverly that I'll never get him into a court. Get him before a court! The scoundrel will suggest in a thousand ways that he's told nothing but the truth. A man of good birth who upholds his rank as I do gets hated by all the common ruck. I'll see my story in those horrible Paris newspapers. Oh, good God! what a sewer! to see the ancient name of Rênal[1] dragged in the mud of derision. . . . If ever I take a trip, I'll have to use another name, yes, abandon this name which makes up my strength and my glory. What a ghastly thought!

If I don't kill my wife, just drive her out in disgrace, she has her aunt at Besançon, who will hand over her whole fortune. My wife will go to Paris where she'll live with Julien; everyone will know it at Verrières, and once again I'll be thought a dupe. At this point the miserable man noted by the paling of his lamp that dawn was starting to break; he decided to go out into the garden for a bit of fresh air. He had almost decided not to make a scandal, largely as a result of the idea that a scandal would overjoy his good friends in Verrières.

A stroll in the garden calmed him somewhat more. No, he exclaimed, I shall not break with my wife, she's too useful to me. He imagined with horror what his house would be like without his wife; his only female relative was the Marquise de R———, old, imbecilic, and mean.

An extremely sensible idea occurred to him, but carrying it out required force of character far greater than the poor man possessed. If I keep my wife, he said, I know my own character; one day when I'm impatient with her I'll accuse her. She's proud, we'll quarrel, and all that is bound to happen before she's inherited from her aunt. Then what fun they'll make of me! My wife loves her children; her whole fortune will end up going to them. While I, I will be the laughing stock of Verrières. Some man, they'll say, he didn't even know how to get back at his own wife! Wouldn't it be better to sit on my suspicions and not try for certainty? Then I tie my own hands; I can never reproach her again.

1. The ancient name of Rênal might have for a Frenchman overtones of kidneys (the adjectival form of *rein* is *rénal*) or of foxes (*renard*), but aristocratic dignity it doesn't particularly have.

An instant later M. de Rênal, still in the grip of his wounded vanity, was laboriously repeating to himself all the terms used in the billiard parlor of the *Casino* or the *Noble Circle*[2] in Verrières, when some fine talker interrupted a round of pool to divert himself at the expense of a betrayed husband. How cruel, at this moment, such raillery seemed to him!

Good God! Why isn't my wife dead? Then I would be safe from ridicule. I wish I was a widower! I could go and spend six months at Paris in the best society. After this moment of happiness at the idea of being a bereaved husband, his imagination returned to the question of finding out the truth. At midnight, when everyone was abed, he might sprinkle a thin layer of bran before the door of Julien's bedroom; the next morning, when day broke, he could look for footprints.

But this scheme is no good, he exclaimed with sudden anger, that bitch Elisa would notice, and it would be all over the house that I'm jealous.

In another story told around the *Casino* a husband had verified his sad state by using a bit of wax to fasten a hair that closed, as with a seal, his wife's door and that of the gallant.

After so many hours of uncertainty this method of gaining certainty seemed to him by all odds the best, and he was thinking of how to put it in practice when, at the intersection of a path, he encountered the very woman he wanted to see dead.

She was on her way back from town. She had gone to hear mass in the church of Vergy. A tradition, very dubious in the eyes of a cold historian, but which she believed, had it that the little church in use today was once a chapel attached to the castle of the lord of Vergy. This idea obsessed Mme. de Rênal all the while she had spent trying to pray in the church. She continually imagined her husband killing Julien while out hunting, killing him as if by accident and then that evening forcing her to eat his heart.[3]

My fate, she told herself, will depend on what he thinks when he hears me. After that fatal fifteen minutes, I may never again have a chance to speak with him. He is not a wise or reasonable man. If he were, I might with my own feeble reason foresee what he's likely to do or say. He will decide both our fates; he has the power to do it. But really that fate lies in my hands, in my skill at directing the ideas of this harebrain, who's blinded by his own anger and incapable of seeing half of what's happening. My God, I need skill, I need coolness, and where to find them?

2. Social clubs in French provincial towns were, of course, engines of social snobbery. Stendhal's uncle Romain Gagnon had belonged to the extreme right-wing club in Grenoble, known as the *Casino*.

3. This ancient folklore motif actually got attached to the story of Gabrielle de Vergy in a 1777 version for the stage by Dormont de Belloy.

Calm possessed her as if by magic as she entered the garden and saw her husband in the distance. His rumpled hair and disordered dress showed that he had not slept all night.

She handed him a letter which had been unsealed but folded up again. Without opening it, he stared wild-eyed at his wife.

—Here is an abominable thing, she said, which was given to me behind the notary's garden by an ugly man who pretended to know you and to owe you some gratitude. I demand just one thing of you, that you send this Julien back to his own people without an instant's delay. Mme. de Rênal hastened to make this speech, getting to the point perhaps a little prematurely, in order to escape the hideous prospect of having to say it.

She was overwhelmed with joy at seeing the pleasure it caused her husband. From the fixed gaze he bent upon her, she grasped that Julien had guessed right. Instead of being disturbed by her present troubles, she thought of him: What genius! What perfect tact! And in a young man still without experience of the world! What won't he accomplish in the future? But then, alas, his successes will cause him to forget me.

This instant of admiration for the man she adored relieved her distress entirely.

She applauded her own policy. I have not been unworthy of Julien, she told herself, with a sweet and intimate pleasure.

Not saying a word, for fear of committing himself, M. de Rênal examined the second anonymous letter, composed, if the reader recalls, of printed words pasted on a piece of bluish paper. They're taunting me on all sides, said M. de Rênal to himself, overcome with fatigue.

New insults to look into, and always on account of my wife! He was on the point of assailing her with gross abuse, but the prospect of the Besançon inheritance barely restrained him. Feeling obliged to vent his rage on something, he ripped the paper of this second anonymous letter to shreds and began to stride off; he absolutely had to get away from his wife. A few minutes later he returned to her side, somewhat calmed.

—We have to take immediate steps and send Julien away, she said to him at once; after all, he's nothing but a workman's son. You will pay him off with a few crowns, and besides, he's clever and will easily find a place, for example, with M. Valenod or the sub-prefect de Maugiron, both of whom have children. Thus you won't be harming him. . . .

—Now you're talking like the fool you really are, shouted M. de Rênal in a bellow. What good sense ever comes out of a woman? You pay no attention to what's reasonable; how do you expect to know anything? You're sloppy, you're lazy, you're good for nothing but chasing butterflies—feeble creatures, who bring misfortune with you when you enter our families! . . .

Mme. de Rênal let him talk, and he talked on for a long time; he was *passing his anger*, as they say in the country.

—Sir, she answered him at last, I speak as a woman outraged in her honor, that is, in her most precious possession on earth.

Mme. de Rênal preserved a cool, fixed calm throughout this disagreeable conversation, on which depended all her chances of ever living again under the same roof with Julien. She sought out all the ideas she considered most suitable to guide her husband's blind rage. She had been unmoved by all the insults he hurled at her; she never heard them; she was thinking of Julien. Will he be pleased with me?

—This little peasant whom we have covered with kindness and showered with gifts may be innocent, she said at last, but nonetheless he is the occasion of the first affront I ever received. . . . Sir, when I read that abominable letter, I vowed that either he or I must leave your house.

—Do you want to make a scandal, to dishonor me and yourself as well? You'll gratify every scandal-monger in Verrières.

—It's true, they're all envious of the prosperity your wise management has created for yourself, your family, and the town. . . . All right! I shall require Julien to ask a month's leave of you, which he will spend with that mountaineer wood-seller of his, fit companion for this little mechanic.

—Restrain yourself, said M. de Rênal, speaking with a fair measure of calm. What I require of you, mainly, is not to talk with him. You'd lose your temper and involve me in a quarrel with him; you know how touchy this little gentleman is.

—He's a young man altogether without tact, replied Mme. de Rênal; maybe he's learned, you know about that, but at bottom he's nothing but a peasant. For my part, I've never thought well of him since he refused to marry Elisa, who was a proper fortune ready-made for him; and all on the pretext that sometimes she makes secret visits to M. Valenod.

—Aha! said M. de Rênal, lifting an exaggerated eyebrow, is that it, did Julien tell you that?

—No, not exactly; he always talked about his calling to the holy ministry; but, believe me, the real calling for all these little people is always filling their bellies. He gave me to understand that he was not in the dark about these secret visits.

—And I was, I was! cried M. de Rênal, returning to rage and emphasizing every word. Things go on in my house that I don't know about. . . . What's this now, something going on between Elisa and Valenod?

—Pooh! that's ancient history, my dear, said Mme. de Rênal with a laugh, and perhaps there's no harm in it after all. It began at a time when your good friend Valenod would not have been unhappy to have it said in Verrières that he and I enjoyed a little, perfectly platonic, relationship.

—I once had that idea myself, cried M. de Rênal, smiting his brow and striding furiously from discovery to discovery; but you never said a word to me.

—And was I to stir up trouble between two friends on account of a little puff of vanity in our dear director? Where is there a woman of society to whom he hasn't addressed a few letters, very witty indeed and maybe even a bit gallant?

—Has he written to you?

—He writes a great deal.

—Show me those letters at once, I command you; and M. de Rênal drew himself up six feet taller than usual.

—I certainly will not, she told him with a gentleness that verged almost on indifference; I'll show them to you some other day when you are less distressed.

—This very instant, damn it! shouted M. de Rênal, drunk with rage, yet happier than he had been any time in the last twelve hours.

—Will you give me your word, Mme. de Rênal said gravely, never to quarrel with the director of the poorhouse over the matter of these letters?

—Quarrel or no, I can put him out of the orphan business; but, he went on furiously, I want those letters this very minute; where are they?

—In a drawer of my desk; but I certainly shan't give you the key.

—I can break it, he shouted, rushing off toward his wife's room.

And, in fact, he broke with an iron bar a precious desk of fine-grained mahogany, brought from Paris, which formerly he used to polish with his coat tails whenever he thought there was a spot on it.

Mme. de Rênal climbed at a run the hundred twenty steps to the dovecote and tied a white handkerchief by its corner to one of the iron bars of the little window. She was the happiest of women. Tears in her eyes, she looked out toward the great forests of the mountainside. No doubt, she said to herself, Julien can see this happy signal from his post under one of those spreading beeches. For a long time she listened, cursing the monotonous song of the cicadas and the chatter of the birds. Without their irksome noise, a cry of joy, rising from the steep rocks, might have been audible. Her eye moved greedily across that immense slope of dark verdure, thick and solid as a meadow, formed by the tree tops. Why doesn't he think, she asked in a mood of sudden tenderness, of making some signal to show that his joy is equal to mine? She came down from the dovecote only when she began to fear that her husband would come looking for her there.

She found him in a rage. He was running through the insipid phrases of M. Valenod, never before perused with so much emotion.

Seizing a moment when her husband's exclamations had subsided enough for her to be heard:

—I still think my first idea is best, said Mme. de Rênal; Julien had better take a trip. He may know Latin, but he's no better than a peasant; he's often clumsy and lacking in tact; every day, thinking that he's being polite, he offers me exaggerated compliments in very bad taste, which he's learned by heart out of some novel. . . .

—He never reads novels, exclaimed M. de Rênal; I'm sure of that. Do you think I'm a blind master who knows nothing of what goes on under his own roof?

—All right, if he doesn't read these ridiculous compliments in a book, he makes them up, and that's no better for him. He must have talked about me in this vein around Verrières . . . ; and even if he didn't go that far, said Mme. de Rênal with the air of making a discovery, he must have talked this way before Elisa, which is all one as if he had talked to M. Valenod.

—Aha! roared M. de Rênal, shaking the table and the whole room with a mighty blow of his fist, the printed anonymous letter and these other letters of Valenod are written on the same paper!

—At last! thought Mme. de Rênal; she appeared stunned by this conclusion, and without having courage to add a single word took a seat on the sofa at the far end of the room.

The battle had now been gained; but she had some trouble in keeping M. de Rênal from going to confront the supposed author of the anonymous letter.

—How can you fail to see that provoking a scene with M. Valenod, without having sufficient proof on your side, is the greatest blunder in the world? You are the victim of envy, my dear; whose fault is it? It's because of your talents: your wise policies, your handsome properties, the fortune I brought you, and then there's the very considerable inheritance that we can expect from my good aunt, an inheritance that has, of course, been immensely exaggerated—all these things have made you the most important person in Verrières.

—You didn't mention my noble birth, said M. de Rênal with a small smile.

—You are one of the most distinguished gentlemen in the district, Mme. de Rênal said with fresh enthusiasm; if the king was free and could do justice to distinguished birth, you would doubtless sit in the house of peers, . . . and so forth, and so on. And now, given your splendid position, do you want to give envy an incident to work on?

Accusing M. Valenod of his anonymous letter is like proclaiming to all Verrières, or rather to Besançon, to the whole district, that this petty bourgeois, once admitted (no doubt incautiously) to intimacy with *a Rênal*, has found a way to offend him. Suppose these letters you have just discovered contained proof that I had responded to M. Valenod's proffered love; then you should kill me. I would have deserved it a hundred times over, but you should not show anger toward him. Keep in mind that all your neighbors are only looking for a pretext to be revenged for your superiority; remember that in 1816 you had a hand in various arrests. That man who took refuge on the roof of your house. . . .[4]

—What's clear is that you have neither respect nor kindness for me, cried M. de Rênal in the full bitterness of these memories; and what's more, I haven't been made a peer! . . .

—My own opinion, dear friend, said Mme. de Rênal with a smile, is that I shall be richer than you, that I have been your associate for twelve years, and that on both these scores I should have a voice in your decisions, especially in today's business. If you prefer someone like M. Julien to me, she added, with ill-concealed scorn, I am quite prepared to go and spend a winter with my aunt.

This phrase was *happily* turned. Though cloaked in polite forms, it had a latent firmness that settled M. de Rênal's judgment. But after the provincial fashion, he continued to talk for a long time, going back over his arguments; his wife let him talk; there was still anger in his expression. At last, two hours of useless babble exhausted the energies of a man who had been in spasms of rage all night long. He settled the lines of policy to be followed with regard to M. Valenod, Julien, and even Elisa.

Once or twice in the course of this great scene, Mme. de Rênal was on the verge of feeling some sympathy for the very real sufferings of this man who for twelve years had been her husband. But real passions are selfish. And besides, she kept expecting that at any minute he would say something about the anonymous letter received the day before, and this he never did. Mme. de Rênal could not have been sure of her position without knowing what ideas had been suggested to the man on whom her whole fate depended. In the provinces husbands are the masters of public opinion. A husband who complains against his wife covers himself with ridicule, a fate that is becoming less and less dangerous in France; but his wife, if he refuses to supply her with money, falls to the condition of a workingwoman at fifteen sous a day, and even at that price the respectable will make scruples of employing her.

4. A Grenoble scandal from the days of 1816 is glanced at here: a liberal named Tabaret took refuge from some infuriated conservatives on the roof of a neighbor's house and was shot to death there.

An odalisque in a harem had better love the sultan at all hazards; he is all powerful, she has no hope of diminishing his authority by a series of petty diplomacies. The master's punishment is terrible, bloody, but military, noble; a dagger stroke finishes everything. It is with blows of public contempt that a husband kills his wife in the nineteenth century; it is by closing all the drawing rooms to her.

The sense of her danger was sharply revived in Mme. de Rênal when she retired to her room; she was shocked at the disorderly state in which she found it. The locks of all her pretty little jewel chests had been smashed; several squares of the parquet floor had been ripped up. He would have had no mercy on me, she said. To ruin in this way an inlaid floor of which he was so proud! When one of the children stepped on it with dirty shoes, he used to be purple with rage. And now it's ruined forever! The spectacle of this violence dissipated at once the last regrets she felt for her too-easy victory.

A little before the bell sounded to dinner, Julien returned with the children. Over dessert, when the servants had withdrawn, Mme. de Rênal said to him in a very dry tone:

—You've indicated a desire to spend a couple of weeks at Verrières; M. de Rênal has kindly granted you a leave. You may depart when you choose. But, to be sure the children don't waste their time, we will send their themes to you every day, and you can correct them.

—I shall certainly not grant you more than a week, M. de Rênal added in his sourest tone.

Julien noted on his features the uneasiness of a man in profound torment.

—He has not yet settled on what he's going to do, said he to his mistress, during a moment when they were alone together in the drawing room.

Mme. de Rênal told him briefly what she had been doing since morning.

—The details tonight, she added with a smile.

Perversity of women! thought Julien. What pleasure, what instinct leads them to deceive us?

—It seems to me you're both inspired and blinded by your love, he told her with some coolness; your conduct today was admirable; but is it sensible for us to try to meet tonight? This house is swarming with enemies; think of Elisa's bitter hatred for me.

—That hatred is much like your own passionate indifference to me.

—Even if I were indifferent, I should be bound to save you from dangers in which I involved you. If by chance M. de Rênal talks to Elisa, a word from her may disclose everything to him. Why couldn't he hide himself near my room with a weapon. . . .

—What's this? Not even courage! said Mme. de Rênal, with all the disdain of a woman of quality.

—I shall never lower myself to talk about my courage, said Julien coldly, that's vulgar. Let the world judge from events. But, he added, taking her by the hand, you cannot imagine how deeply I'm attached to you and what a joy it will be to have a chance to take leave of you before this cruel separation.

Chapter 22

WAYS OF ACTING IN 1830

> Speech was given to man to conceal his thought.
> —R. P. Malagrida[5]

Scarcely had he reached Verrières when Julien began reproaching his injustice toward Mme. de Rênal. I would have despised her as a silly female if, through weakness, she had mishandled her scene with M. de Rênal! She carried it off like a diplomat, and now I sympathize with the loser, who is my enemy. There's something middle class about my attitude; my vanity is offended because M. de Rênal is a man! An immense and magnificent corporation, this, of which I happen to be a member! Really, I'm no better than a fool.

M. Chélan had refused various offers of lodging made him by the most eminent liberals of the district at the time when he was forced out of his presbytery. The two rooms he had rented were crowded with his books. Julien, wanting to show Verrières what it was to be a priest, went to his father for a dozen pine planks, which he carried on his own back the length of the main street. Then he borrowed tools of a former friend and had soon built a sort of bookcase, in which he arranged the books of M. Chélan.

—I thought you would be corrupted by the vanity of the world, said the old man, with tears of joy; but here's an action that fully redeems that childish business with the honor guard and the gaudy uniform, which made you so many enemies.

M. de Rênal had told Julien to stay in his house. Nobody suspected what had happened. The third day after his arrival Julien saw coming up to his room no less a personage than the subprefect, M. de Maugiron. It was only after two long hours of insipid gossip

5. R. P. (Révérend Père) Gabriel Malagrida was an Italian Jesuit who served nearly thirty years as a missionary in Brazil. He returned to Portugal in time to help the victims of the Lisbon earthquake (1755) but was accused of complicity in an attempt to assassinate the king and was burned alive on September 21, 1761. He did not make the statement about human speech attributed to him here: Talleyrand perhaps did, or at least abundantly exemplified it. Stendhal probably heard of Malagrida through Voltaire's *Siècle de Louis XV*.

and tedious jeremiads about the evil habits of men, the dishonesty of public officials, the perils confronting our poor France, etc., etc., that Julien finally caught a glimpse of the point of the visit. They were already at the head of the staircase, and the poor tutor half in disgrace was leading to the door with all appropriate respect the future prefect of some fortunate province, when the latter decided to concern himself with Julien's prospects, to praise his splendid moderation in matters affecting his own interests, etc., etc. At last M. de Maugiron, clasping him in his arms with the most paternal affection, suggested that he should leave M. de Rênal and take service with an official who had children to raise and who, like King Philip,[6] would thank God not so much for the children themselves but for being allowed to have them in due proximity to M. Julien. Their tutor would receive an income of eight hundred francs, payable not on a monthly basis (which is not noble, said M. de Maugiron), but quarterly, and what's more, in advance.

Now it became Julien's turn; for an hour and a half he had been waiting for the other to get to the point. His reply was perfect, and as long as an episcopal sermon; it let everything be understood, and yet said nothing clearly. There appeared in it, all at the same time, respect for M. de Rênal, veneration for the public of Verrières, and gratitude to the illustrious subprefect. The subprefect, astonished to find a bigger Jesuit than himself, struggled vainly to get out of him something clear. Julien in high glee seized the occasion to exercise his wits, and began his reply all over again, using other terms. Never did an eloquent minister, trying to talk his way through the last hours of a session when the house is threatening to wake up, use more words with less substance. Hardly was M. de Maugiron out the door when Julien began to laugh like a maniac. While his Jesuitical vein was flowing, he wrote a nine-page letter to M. de Rênal in which he described everything that had been said to him, and humbly begged his advice. And yet that scoundrel never told me the name of the person who's making the offer! Of course, it must be M. Valenod, who sees my exile to Verrières as the effect of his anonymous letter.

When his letter had been dispatched, Julien, as happy as a hunter who marches forth at six in the morning of a fine autumn day onto a plain teeming with game, set forth to seek counsel of M. Chélan. But before he reached the good curé's house, fate, which was being lavish in dispensing pleasures to him, threw into his path M. Valenod, from whom he did not conceal that his heart was sorely torn; a poor boy like himself should devote himself wholly to the vocation that heaven had written in his heart, but in this

6. King Philip of Macedon was glad not only to have a son (Alexander the Great) but to have a son whom Aristotle could educate.

fallen world one's vocation wasn't everything. To labor worthily in the Lord's vineyard, and not to disgrace one's many learned co-workers, instruction was necessary; one must spend two years in the seminary at Besançon, and very costly they would be; it was therefore indispensable [and one might even say, after a certain sort, one's duty] to save up a sum of money, which would be much easier to do on a salary of eight hundred francs paid quarterly than with six hundred francs paid from month to month. On the other hand, didn't heaven, when it placed him in charge of the Rênal children, and inspired him with a particular affection for them, show that it would not be fitting to abandon this task for another? . . .

Julien attained such perfect skill in this sort of eloquence, which has replaced the decisive action of the empire, that he ended by boring himself with the sound of his own words.

Back at the house he found a servant of M. Valenod's, in full livery, who had been looking for him throughout the town with an invitation to dinner that very day.

Julien had never been in this man's house; just a few days before he had been thinking only of how to give him a good cudgeling without risk from the police. Though dinner was announced for one o'clock, Julien thought it more respectful to present himself about twelve-thirty in the office of the director of the poorhouse. He found him exercising his importance in the midst of a pile of papers. His thick black whiskers, his enormous head of hair, his Phrygian cap cocked crossways on his head, his huge pipe, his embroidered slippers, the thick gold chains strung every which way across his chest, and all that apparatus of a provincial money man who thinks himself a lady-killer made no impression on Julien; he thought all the more of that cudgeling which was due him.

He requested the honor of meeting Mme. Valenod; she was in her dressing room and could not see him. By way of compensation, he was privileged to attend the poorhouse director in his dressing room. Then they met with Mme. Valenod, who introduced her children with tears in her eyes. This lady was one of the most respectable in Verrières; she had a broad, mannish face to which she had applied rouge for this great occasion. She displayed a good deal of maternal pathos.

Julien thought of Mme. de Rênal. His habitual suspicion scarcely left him susceptible to anything but those memories that are called up by contrasts, but then he could be touched to the point of tenderness. This mood was augmented now by the look of the poorhouse director's establishment. Everything in it was splendid and new, and he was told the price of each piece of furniture. But Julien found something ignoble about it, as if it stank of stolen money.

Everyone there, even the servants, had the look of hardening his features against contempt.

The tax collector, the assessor, the chief of police, and two or three other public officials arrived with their wives. They were followed by a number of rich liberals. Dinner was announced. Julien, already ill at ease, was struck with the idea that on the other side of the dining room wall were the poor prisoners, whose allotments of food had perhaps been *chiseled* in order to buy all this ostentatious luxury with which people were trying to astonish him.

Perhaps they are suffering from hunger at this very moment, said he to himself; his throat choked up, he found it impossible to eat and almost to talk. It was much worse a quarter of an hour later; in the distance there were heard various phrases of a popular song, rather vulgar it must be admitted, being sung by one of the inmates. M. Valenod cast a glance at one of his servants in full livery, who disappeared; shortly thereafter the song stopped. At that moment a valet offered Julien some Rhine wine in a green glass, and Mme. Valenod seized the occasion to observe that this wine cost nine francs a bottle direct from the grower. Julien, holding his green glass, said to M. Valenod:

—They're not singing that miserable song any more.

—Blast 'em, I should think not, replied the director in triumph, I've had the beggars shut up.

The phrase was too much for Julien; he had the manners, but not yet the feelings, of his social position. Despite all his much-practiced hypocrisy, he felt a tear flow down his cheek.

He tried to conceal it with his green glass, but found it absolutely impossible to do honor to the Rhine wine. *Stop the man from singing!* he murmured to himself, Oh my God! And you permit it!

Fortunately nobody noticed his moment of ungentlemanly emotion. The assessor had struck up a royalist song. During the uproar of the refrain, which was sung in chorus: There now, Julien's conscience said to him, that's the dirty fortune you're going to attain, and you'll enjoy it only under these circumstances and in this sort of company! Maybe you'll get a place worth twenty thousand francs, but while you gorge yourself on rich foods, you'll have to shut the mouth of a poor prisoner who's trying to sing. You'll give banquets with the money you've stolen from his miserable pittance, and while you're eating he'll be made more miserable than ever! Oh Napoleon! What a joy it was in your day to rise through the perils of the battlefield; but to feed like a coward on the misery of the helpless!

I confess that the weakness which Julien displays in this monologue gives me a poor opinion of him. He would be a worthy colleague of those conspirators in yellow gloves who pretend to change the whole way of life of a great nation but don't want to be responsible for inflicting the slightest scratch.[7]

Abruptly Julien was recalled to his role. It was not to dream and be silent that he had been invited to dinner in such good company.

A retired manufacturer of calico prints, corresponding member of one academy at Besançon and another at Uzès, called to him down the full length of the table to ask if it was true that he had made such astonishing progress as people were saying in his study of the New Testament.

At once complete silence was established; a Latin New Testament appeared, as if by magic, in the hands of the learned member of two academies. No sooner had Julien agreed than a half sentence of Latin, chosen at random, was read to him. He recited: his memory served, and this prodigous feat was admired with all the clamorous energy of an after-dinner performance. Julien noted the candlelit features of the ladies; several were not bad looking. He picked out the wife of the assessor who sang so loudly.

—But really I'm ashamed to talk Latin before these ladies for so long, he said with a glance at her. If M. Rubigneau (that was the member of the two academies) will be kind enough to read a Latin sentence at random, instead of repeating the Latin text that follows, I'll try to translate it impromptu.

This second display raised his glory to its peak.

There were in the group several rich liberals, fortunate fathers of children capable of winning scholarships, and as such suddenly converted since the last mission.[8] In spite of this neat political stroke, M. de Rênal had never been willing to receive them in his house. These fine gentry, who knew Julien only by reputation and from seeing him on horseback when the king of _____ came to town, were his most enthusiastic admirers. When will these fools get tired of listening to this Biblical style, which they can't understand at all? he thought. Quite the contrary, this style amused them because it was strange; they laughed at it. But Julien grew tired.

He rose with a serious expression as six o'clock struck and spoke of a chapter in the new theology of Ligorio[9] which he had to learn in order to repeat it on the morrow for M. Chélan. For it's my trade,

7. Conspirators in yellow gloves are in effect parlor liberals, a familiar breed.
8. Missions within France itself were essentially revivalist movements propagated after 1815 by Abbés Rauzon, Forbin-Janson, Fayet, and their ilk, with the approval of the parish priest and his bishop, in the hope of reviving the zeal of the faithful.

9. Stendhal is probably thinking of St. Alphonsus Maria Liguori, an eighteenth-century Neapolitan casuist who was beatified in 1816; but he may also be making a private pun on the name of Piero Ligorio, a sixteenth-century architect noted for his facades and an antiquarian renowned for his forgeries.

he added jovially, to make other people recite lessons and to recite them myself.

They laughed a good deal; they admired him; this is wit as they understand it in Verrières. Julien was already on his feet, and everyone else rose, regardless of decorum; such is the power of genius. Mme. Valenod kept him for another quarter hour; he simply must hear her children recite their catechism. They made the most comical errors, which he was the only one to notice. He made no effort to correct them. What ignorance of the first principles of religion! he thought. At last he said good night, and hoped to make his escape; but he had to undergo a fable of Lafontaine.

—This author is thoroughly immoral, said Julien to Mme. Valenod; one of his fables on Messire Jean Chouart[1] ventures to asperse with ridicule the most venerable matters in the world. He is sharply reproved for this by the best commentators.

Before he left, Julien had received four or five other invitations to dinner. This young man does great credit to our district, all the diners cried unanimously, in high good humor. They went so far as to discuss a pension, to be voted out of municipal funds, which would enable him to continue his studies in Paris.

While this rash idea was resounding through the dining room, Julien had made his way hastily to the carriage entry. Ah, the swine! the swine! he murmured three or four times over, drinking in the fresh air with pleasure.

At this moment he saw himself as a complete aristocrat, he who for so long had been irked by lofty smiles and arrogant airs which he sensed behind all the polite phrases addressed to him at M. de Rênal's. He could not fail to notice the extraordinary difference. I won't consider, said he to himself as he left, that all this money was stolen from the poor inmates, who are even forbidden to sing! But would M. de Rênal ever take it on himself to tell his guests the price of every bottle of wine he set before them? And this M. Valenod, when he counts up his belongings, as he's always doing, can never talk of his house, his grounds, and so on, when his wife is present without saying *your* house, *your* grounds, and so on.

This lady, who seemed so responsive to the pleasures of possession, had just made an abominable scene during dinner because one of the servants had broken a piece of stemware and *spoiled one of her sets*; and the servant had answered her back with supreme insolence.

What a crowd! said Julien to himself; they could give me half their haul and I still wouldn't want to live with them. One fine

1. La Fontaine's fable of the Curé and the Corpse (VII, 11) is a satire on clerical greed; Maître Jean Chouart is a name from Rabelais borrowed by Lafontaine for use in the fable. Stanislas, when he refers later in the chapter to the fable of the Crow and the Fox, also has Lafontaine in mind (I, 2).

day I'd give myself away; I couldn't keep from showing the scorn I feel for them.

He was required, however, on orders from Mme. de Rênal, to attend several dinners of the same sort; Julien was the fashion; people excused his donning the guard of honor uniform, or rather that act of folly was the real cause of his success. Before long the only question discussed in Verrières was who would win out in the struggle to obtain this learned young man, M. de Rênal or the director of the poorhouse. These gentlemen formed with M. Maslon a triumvirate which for some years now had been tyrannizing over the town. There was jealousy of the mayor, all the liberals complained of him; but after all, he was noble and trained for lofty positions, while M. Valenod's father had not left him an income of six hundred florins. He had had to rise from being pitied for the mean apple-green jacket in which everyone had seen him when he was young to the stage of being envied his Norman horses, golden chains, Paris suits, and all his present prosperity.

In the flood of this society, all new to Julien, he thought he had discovered an honest man; this was a geometer named Gros,[2] considered a Jacobin. Julien, who had sworn an oath never to say anything except what seemed false to him, was obliged to maintain suspicions with regard to M. Gros. Fat packets of themes kept arriving from Vergy. He was counseled to see his father frequently, and submitted to this sad necessity. In a word, he was patching up his reputation rather nicely when one morning he was startled to be wakened by a pair of hands held over his eyes.

It was Mme. de Rênal, who had come to town, climbed the stairs in great haste, leaving her children to bring along a favorite rabbit who had made the trip with them, and thus reached Julien's room an instant before they did. It was a delicious moment, but very short: Mme. de Rênal was out of sight when the children came in with the rabbit, which they wanted to show to their friend. Julien welcomed everyone warmly, even the rabbit. He seemed to be back with his own family; he felt that he loved these children, that he enjoyed chattering with them. He was struck by the gentleness of their voices, the simplicity and dignity of their little ways; his imagination had to be washed clean of all the vulgar manners and disagreeable thoughts he breathed in every day at Verrières. Everywhere was the fear of failure, everywhere luxury and misery were at one another's throat. The people with whom he dined, when they talked about the roast, made confidential statements humiliating for themselves and disgusting for anyone who listened.

2. Gros was the actual name of a man who tutored young Stendhal in geometry at Grenoble and thus enabled him to escape from his native town. Stendhal never ceased to hold him in grateful esteem.

—You others, who are noble, you have good reason to be proud, he told Mme. de Rênal. And he described the many dinners he had endured.

—So, then, you're all the rage! And she laughed heartily at the thought of all that rouge which Mme. Valenod felt obliged to use whenever Julien was coming. I daresay she has designs on your heart, she added.

Lunch was delightful. The presence of the children, though apparently a constraint, actually increased the general happiness. These poor children did not know how to express their joy at seeing Julien again. The servants had not failed to tell them that he was being offered two hundred francs more to *raise* the young Valenods.

In the midst of lunch Stanislas-Xavier, still pale from his terrible illness, suddenly asked his mother how much the silverware at his place and the goblet from which he was drinking were worth.

—Why do you want to know?

—I want to sell them and give the money to M. Julien, so he won't be a *dupe* for staying with us.

Julien kissed him, with tears in his eyes. His mother wept openly, while Julien, who had taken Stanislas on his knee, explained to him that he shouldn't use the word *dupe*, which, when used in this sense, is a vulgar expression for servants. Seeing the pleasure this gave to Mme. de Rênal, he tried to explain by means of picturesque examples that would amuse the children what a *dupe* really is.

—I understand, said Stanislas, it's the crow who's stupid and drops his cheese so the fox can take it, who's a flatterer.

Mme. de Rênal, delirious with happiness, covered her children with kisses, which she could scarcely do without leaning somewhat on Julien.

Suddenly the door opened; it was M. de Rênal. His severe, sour face made a strange contrast with the simple happiness which he drove from the room. Mme. de Rênal grew pale; she felt herself incapable of denying anything. Julien began to talk, and speaking loudly, repeated to his honor the mayor the story of the silver goblet that Stanislas wanted to sell. He was certain this story would be unwelcome. In the first place, M. de Rênal tended to frown out of sheer habit at the mention of silver.[3] The very name of that metal, said he, is always a prelude to some demand on my pocketbook.

But here there was more than a matter of money, there was an increase of suspicion. The happy atmosphere that surrounded his family in his absence did nothing to smooth things over, especially with a man whose vanity was so touchy. As his wife was describing to him the graceful, witty way in which Julien introduced his pupils to new ideas:

3. In French, of course, *argent* is the normal word for both silver and money.

—Sure, sure, I know; he makes me hateful to my own children. It's easy enough for him to be a hundred times more agreeable than I am, just because I'm the master. Everything in this century works to make *legitimate* authority odious. Ah, poor France!

Mme. de Rênal did not pause to examine the subtleties of her husband's attitude. She had just glimpsed the possibility of passing half a day with Julien. She had a long list of purchases to make in town and said she absolutely insisted on eating dinner in a tavern; whatever her husband might do or say, she stuck to that idea. The children were ecstatic at the very word *tavern*, which modern prudery pronounces with such pleasure.

M. de Rênal left his wife at the first notion shop she entered, saying he had some calls to make. He came back even gloomier than he had been in the morning; he was convinced that the whole town was talking of him and Julien. As a matter of fact, nobody had so much as insinuated to him the offensive part of the public gossip. What he had heard dealt simply with the question of whether Julien would stay with him at six hundred francs or would accept the eight hundred offered by the poorhouse director.

Said director, when he met M. de Rênal in society, was very much the *cold fish*. His comportment in this matter was not without its clever side; there's very little unconsidered behavior in the provinces; impulses are so rare that they're easily suppressed.

M. Valenod was what they call, at a hundred leagues from Paris, a boldfaced slob.[4] It's a species that is pompous and stupid by nature. His triumphant career, since 1815, had added emphasis to his natural gifts. At Verrières he reigned, so to speak, under the dispensation of M. de Rênal; but being much more active, ashamed of nothing, mixed up in everything, continually on the go, writing, talking, shaking off humiliations, and laying claim to no personal dignity, he ended up by seeming, at least to the ecclesiastical power, the mayor's[5] equal. M. Valenod had as good as said to the businessmen in town: give me your two biggest fools; to the lawyers he'd said, pick out a pair of your dumbest; and to the medical men, name me your two biggest charlatans. When he had assembled the most shameless members of every trade, he said to them, let's get together and make a government.

The manners of these people disturbed M. de Rênal. M. Valenod was too gross to be offended by anything, even when young Abbé Maslon called him a liar in public.

But in the midst of this prosperity M. Valenod had constantly to reassure himself by acts of petty insolence designed to ward off the

---

4. In the original, *faraud*.
5. The first-edition reading would be translated, "his master's equal"; some-one got confused between *maire* and *maître*.

hard truths that he very well knew everyone could cast up to him. He had been doubly active as a result of the fears inspired by M. Appert's visit; he had made three trips to Besançon; he wrote three letters by every post; he sent others off by unknown couriers who stopped by his house during the night. Perhaps he had been wrong in securing the dismissal of the old curé Chélan; for this vindictive step had earned him, among several pious ladies of good birth, a reputation as a wicked man. Besides, this favor received had made him absolutely dependent on the grand vicar de Frilair, from whom he received some rather odd instructions. His intrigues had reached this stage when he yielded to the pleasure of writing an anonymous letter. To add to his problems, his wife had declared that she must have Julien in her household; her vanity was intoxicated at the very thought.

Under these circumstances M. Valenod foresaw a decisive scene with his old colleague M. de Rênal. The latter might storm and bluster; no matter; but he might write to Besançon and even to Paris. The cousin of some minister might drop down upon Verrières all of a sudden and take the directorship of the poorhouse. M. Valenod thought of reaching an arrangement with the liberals: that was why several of them had been invited to the dinner at which Julien recited. He might, with their help, have held his own against the mayor. But elections might be called for, and it went without saying that a post in the poorhouse and a wrong vote were incompatible. These schemes, shrewdly reconstructed by Mme. de Rênal, had been sketched for Julien's benefit as he was escorting her from one shop to another, and had gradually led them to LOYALTY SQUARE, where they passed several hours almost as peacefully as at Vergy.

During this period M. Valenod was at work, stalling off a decisive break with his former chief by himself assuming a lofty tone. On this particular day the strategy worked, but it increased the mayor's ill humor.

Never did vanity at odds with mean and bitter cupidity reduce a man to a state more wretched than that of M. de Rênal as he entered the tavern. On the other hand, never had he seen his children more cheerful and joyous. The contrast completed his pique.

—So far as I can see, I'm not wanted in my own family! he said as he came in; he was trying to be impressive.

For her only answer, his wife took him aside and told him that Julien must be sent away. The hours of happiness she had just enjoyed gave her the strength and firmness of purpose necessary to carry out the plan she had been meditating for the last two weeks. What put the poor mayor of Verrières to the ultimate torture was the knowledge that people were making jokes throughout the town about his excessive fondness for *ready money*. M. Valenod had the generosity of a crook, but he, the mayor, had performed in a manner more prudent than brilliant in the last five or six collections for the Confraternity of Saint Joseph, the Congregation of the Virgin Mary, the Congregation of the Holy Sacrament, etc., etc.

Among the country gentry of Verrières and vicinity, neatly listed on the books of the collecting friars in order of generosity, it had more than once been noted that the name of M. de Rênal occupied the very last line. In vain did he protest that he *earned nothing*. The clergy allow no jokes on this score.

Chapter 23

SORROWS OF AN OFFICIAL

The pleasure of holding high one's head all year is amply repaid by certain quarter hours one must live through.
—Casti[6]

But let's leave this little man to his little fears; why did he take into his household a man of feeling when what he wanted was the spirit of a valet? Why doesn't he know how to choose his people? It's a general rule in the nineteenth century that when a man of power and position meets a man of feeling, he kills him, exiles him, imprisons him, or humiliates him until the other is stupid enough to die of grief from it. By good fortune, in the present instance it's not yet the man of feeling who is suffering. The great unhappiness of little French towns, and of elective governments like that in New York, is that there one can't forget the existence of creatures like M. de Rênal. In a town of twenty thousand inhabitants these people make public opinion, and public opinion has terrible power in a country with the charter.[7] A man with a noble, generous spirit, who might have been your friend but who lives a hundred leagues away, judges of you by the public opinion of your town, which is formed by fools whom fortune has created respectable, rich, and moderate. Woe to the man who distinguishes himself!

Shortly after dinner they left for Vergy; but on the second day after Julien saw the whole family return to Verrières.

An hour had not passed when, to his great surprise, he found that Mme. de Rênal was keeping something from him. As soon as he appeared she broke off conversations with her husband, and she almost seemed to wish him away. Julien asked for no second hint.

6. G. B. Casti was an eighteenth-century Italian poet of rather licentious tastes. It is reasonably certain that he never said anything like what the epigraph attributes to him.

7. A "country with a charter" is one with a constitution—and, by implication, a representative government. The opposite would be an absolute monarchy.

He became cold and withdrawn; Mme. de Rênal took note of the fact and sought no explanations. Is she going to supply me with a successor? Julien thought. Only the day before yesterday, so intimate with me! But they say this is how fine ladies are. It's like kings, who never show more kindness than to the minister who when he goes home finds his letter of dismissal.

Julien observed that in these conversations that faded suddenly at his approach there was frequent mention of a big house belonging to the commune of Verrières, old but vast and comfortable, which stood opposite the church in the best commercial section of the town. What's the connecting link between that house and the new lover! Julien asked. In his distress he repeated to himself those pretty verses of François I, which seemed new to him because it was only a month since Mme. de Rênal had taught them to him. At that time how many vows, how many caresses were ready to deny each one of these verses:

> *Souvent femme varie,*
> *Bien fol qui s'y fie.*
> [Woman's a constant deceiver,
> And men are great fools that believe her.][8]

M. de Rênal left by the mail coach for Besançon. The trip was taken on two hours' notice; he seemed much agitated. When he came back he flung onto the table a thick packet wrapped in gray paper.

—And so much for that stupid business, he said to his wife.

An hour later Julien saw the bill sticker take away the packet; he followed him eagerly. I'll know the secret at the first street corner.

He waited impatiently behind the bill sticker while the latter slathered paste on the back of the notice with his big brush. Scarcely was it stuck up when Julien, in his curiosity, was busy reading a detailed announcement of the sale, by public auction, of a lease to that big old house that was so often being discussed by M. de Rênal and his wife. The awarding of the lease was announced for the following day at two o'clock, in the town hall, at the extinction of the third light. Julien was much disappointed; he thought the notice given was rather short: how could all the possible bidders be notified in time? But for the rest, this notice, which was dated two weeks earlier, and which he read all the way through in three different places, told him nothing.

8. Brantôme tells us (in Discours IV of his *Vies des dames galantes*) that François wrote a phrase about female fickleness by the window in the château de Chambord; legend embroidered this rather plain statement into the present verses, which Victor Hugo incorporated in their most famous form in Act IV of *Le roi s'amuse* (1832).

He went to visit the house that was for sale. As he approached unobserved, the doorman was speaking mysteriously to a neighbor:

—Bah! Bah! It's a waste of time. M. Maslon has told him he'll have it for three hundred francs; and when the mayor kicked up a fuss, he was sent up to the bishop by the grand vicar de Frilair.

Julien's arrival seemed very distressing to the two friends, who cut short their conversation.

Julien did not fail to attend the auction. There was a crowd gathered in an ill-lit room; but people kept *eyeing one another* in an extraordinary way. Everyone was looking at a table where Julien saw three bits of candle end flickering in a tin plate. The bailiff cried aloud: *Three hundred francs, gentlemen!*

—Three hundred francs! That's going too far, one man murmured to his neighbor. And Julien was between the two of them. The house is worth more than eight hundred; I'm going to raise it.

—You're wasting your breath. What's the good of getting yourself in trouble with Maslon, Valenod, the bishop, and his terrible grand vicar de Frilair, and the whole crowd?

—Three hundred twenty francs, cried the other.

—Stubborn brute! said the other; and then he added, pointing to Julien, and here's the mayor's spy, right on the spot.

Julien swung around to answer this charge; but the two countrymen were no longer aware of him. Their cool indifference restored his. At that moment the last candle end flickered out, and the drawling voice of the bailiff awarded the house for nine years to M. de Saint-Giraud, section chief in the prefecture of _____, at a rental of three hundred and thirty francs.

As soon as the mayor left the room conversation opened up.

—There's thirty extra francs for the town because Grogeot spoke up, said one man.

—But M. de Saint-Giraud will get back at Grogeot, said another, he'll know how to pass it along.

—What a disgrace! said a fat man on Julien's left: there's a house for which I personally would have given eight hundred francs for my business, and at that I'd have had a good bargain.

—Bah! said a young manufacturer of the liberal party, isn't it clear that M. de Saint-Giraud is in the congregation? Aren't his four children a great expense? Poor fellow! The town of Verrières just has to pitch in and provide him with an extra five hundred francs, that's all.

—And to think that the mayor couldn't prevent it! remarked a third. For he may be a reactionary, if you like, but a thief he isn't.

—Not a thief? said another, no, of course not, it's the little birds that take everything. The whole thing goes into one big pile, and they divide it up at the end of the year. But here's young Sorel: let's get out of this place.

Julien returned home very much out of sorts; he found Mme. de Rênal in a melancholy mood.

—You're just back from the auction? she asked.

—Yes, madame, where I had the pleasure of being taken for the mayor's spy.

—If he'd followed my advice, he would have been out of town today.

At that moment M. de Rênal appeared; he too was gloomy. Dinner was eaten in complete silence. M. de Rênal ordered Julien to take the children to Vergy; the trip was somber. Mme. de Rênal comforted her husband:

—You must get used to these things, my dear.

That evening they were seated silently around the hearth; only the crackle of a burning beech log served to distract them. It was one of those moments of desolation that occur in the most closely knit families. One of the children cried joyfully:

—There's somebody at the door!

—By God! if that's M. de Saint-Giraud come to put me down by pretending to thank me, cried the mayor, I'll tell him what's what. He's gone too far. It's that Valenod he ought to be thanking, I'm just the one who gets the blame. What am I going to do if these damned Jacobin newspapers get hold of the story and try to turn me into a M. Nonante-cinq?[9]

An extremely handsome man with big black whiskers entered at this moment, behind the servant.

—Mr. Mayor, I am Signor Geronimo.[1] Here is a letter for you, given me when I left by M. le Chevalier de Beauvaisis, adjutant at the Neapolitan embassy; that was only nine days ago, added Signor Geronimo, glancing gaily at Mme. de Rênal. Signor de Beauvaisis, who is your cousin and my good friend, madame, tells me you know Italian.

The good humor of the Neapolitan changed a melancholy evening to a gay one. Mme. de Rênal insisted on his having a late supper. She set the whole household to bustling; she wanted to distract Julien at any cost from the insult of being called a spy, a word that had twice been applied to him that day. Signor Geronimo was a celebrated singer, a man used to good society and yet very cheerful himself, qualities that in France are hardly compatible any more. After supper he sang a little duet with Mme. de Rênal. He told a number of delightful anecdotes. At one o'clock in the morning the children protested when Julien told them it was bedtime.

9. A Marseilles magistrate, M. Mérindol, who hated liberals, used the phrase *nonante-cinq* for the number 95 (properly *quatre-vingt-quinze*) and was ridiculed for it by all the liberal journals.
1. Don Geronimo is a bass part in the *Matrimonio Segreto* of Cimarosa, of which Stendhal was passionately fond. The part was often taken by Luigi Lablache, famous basso, who was born in Naples, trained there in the Conservatorio, and made his London and Paris debuts precisely in 1830.

—Just this one story, said the eldest.

—It's my own personal story, young sir, replied Signor Geronimo. Eight years ago, I was like you, I was a young student in the conservatory of Naples; I mean, I was just your age, for I didn't have the honor of being the son of the illustrious mayor of the beautiful town of Verrières.

The phrase drew a sigh from M. de Rênal; he glanced at his wife.

—Now Signor Zingarelli, the young singer went on, exaggerating his accent in a way that made the children burst out laughing, Signor Zingarelli[2] is an excessively severe teacher. He is not well liked at the conservatory; but he insists on being treated as if he is very well liked indeed. I sneaked out as often as I could; I used to go to the little theater of San Carlino, where I heard music fit for the gods: but, oh, good heavens! how to scrape up the eight sous for a seat in the orchestra? An enormous sum, he said, goggling at the children until they laughed. Signor Giovannone,[3] director of the San Carlino, heard me sing. I was sixteen years old: This child is a treasure, says he.

—How would you like a job, my friend? he asks.

—What'll you pay?

—Forty ducats a month. (That, gentlemen, would be a hundred and sixty francs.) I thought the sky was falling down.

—But, said I to Giovannone, how am I going to arrange it so that tyrant Zingarelli lets me go?

—*Lascia fare a me.*

—Leave it to me! cried the older boy.

—Exactly, young man. Signor Giovannone says to me: First of all, dear boy, a little bit of a contract. I sign: he gives me three ducats. I'd never seen so much money in my life. Then he tells me what to do.

Next morning I ask to see the terrible Signor Zingarelli. His old servant brings me in.

—What do you want, you imp? says Zingarelli.

Maestro, say I, I'm sorry for all my faults. I'll never sneak out of the conservatory again by climbing over the iron railings. I'll work twice as hard as ever.

—If I wasn't afraid of spoiling the best bass voice I ever heard, I'd put you in jail on bread and water for two weeks, you little ruffian.

—Maestro, I said, I'm going to be a model pupil for the whole school, *credete a me.* But I want to ask one favor, if anyone comes to offer me a job singing outside, please tell them no. I beg of you, tell them it's impossible.

---

2. Zingarelli, an actual personage, was director of the Naples conservatory when Lablache studied there.

3. Giovanni Stile was director of the theater of San Carlino.

—And who the devil do you think is going to ask for a bad lot like you? Do you think I'll ever let you leave the conservatory? Are you trying to make fun of me? Out, out, get out of here! he shouted, trying to give me a kick in the pants, or it will be dry bread and close quarters for you.

An hour later Signor Giovannone appears in the director's office:

—I want you to help me be a rich man, says he; let me have Geronimo. If he sings in my theater, I'll be able to marry off my daughter this winter.

—What do you want with that trash? says Zingarelli. I won't consent; you shan't have him. And besides, even if I consented, he'll never leave the conservatory; he just told me so.

—If all we're worried about is his consent, says Giovannone solemnly, pulling my contract out of his pocket, well, *carta canta!*[4] here's his signature.

At that Zingarelli, in a rage, rushes to the bell pull: Throw Geronimo out of the conservatory, he roars, boiling with rage. So they threw me out, helpless with laughter, and that night I sang the aria *del Moltiplico.*[5] Pulchinello had his mind on an approaching marriage that evening and spent it counting up on his fingers all the different things he would need to set up housekeeping, and losing track at every count.

—Oh, won't you please sing us that aria, begged Mme. de Rênal.

Geronimo sang, and everyone laughed until the tears came. It was two in the morning before Signor Geronimo went off to bed, leaving the family enthralled with his good manners, his good nature, and his good humor.

Next morning, M. and Mme. de Rênal gave him various letters that would be useful to him at the court of France.

So it goes, dishonesty everywhere, said Julien. Signor Geronimo is going to London with engagements worth sixty thousand francs. If it hadn't been for the shrewdness of the director of San Carlino, very likely his wonderful voice would have been known and appreciated only ten years later. . . . My word, I'd rather be a Geronimo than a Rênal. He's not so much respected by society, but he doesn't have the shame of presiding over deals like that one yesterday, and his life is a merry one.

One thing surprised Julien; the weeks he had spent alone at Verrières in M. de Rênal's house had been a happy period for him. He had experienced melancholy thoughts and disgust only at the dinners that were given for him; but, alone in the house, he had

4. *carta canta:* paper talks (literally, sings).
5. None of the musicologists I have consulted have been able to direct me to a specific *aria del Moltiplico* which Geronimo might have sung; but Professor Anthony Caputi tells me that the *commedie dell'arte* contained frequent *lozzi* or comic turns, involving staircases, baggy pants, bottomless pockets—or tricks with the multiplication table. One of these turns might be converted to a comic aria.

been free to read, write, and think without disturbance. He was not being distracted from his glittering dreams at every instant by the need to study some low mind which then he would have to deceive by tricks or hypocritical words.

Is happiness really so near at hand? . . . There's no expense to such a life; I could, just as I please, marry Mlle. Elisa or become a partner with Fouqué. . . . But the man who's just climbed a mountain sits down at the top, and finds perfect satisfaction in resting there. Would he be just as happy if forced to rest all the time?

Mme. de Rênal's mind had reached a new stage of self-doubt. In spite of a resolve not to do so, she had told Julien the whole story of the crooked lease. In the same way, he'll make me forget all my resolutions, she thought.

She would have sacrificed her own life unhesitatingly to save that of her husband, if she had seen it endangered. She was one of those noble, romantic souls for whom a generous action unperformed gives rise to remorse as bitter as that for an actual crime. Yet there were dark days when she could not get out of her mind the thought of the joy that would be hers if she were suddenly widowed and could marry Julien.

He loved her children much more than their own father did; though his justice was strict, they adored him. She realized that if she married Julien they would have to leave Vergy, whose leafy shades were dear to her. But she would live at Paris, and continue to provide her children with that education which everyone so admired. Her children, she, Julien, everybody would be perfectly happy.

Strange effect of marriage, as the nineteenth century has created it! The boredom of married life is sure to destroy love, whenever love has preceded the marriage. Indeed, a philosopher would say, it even leads (where people are rich enough not to have to work) to a profound boredom with all tranquil satisfactions. Yet among women it is only the dried-up souls whom it does not predispose to love.

The philosopher's reflection makes me excuse Mme. de Rênal, but nobody excused her in Verrières, and without her suspecting it the whole town was occupied with nothing but the scandal of her affair. Because of this great scandal, people were less bored that fall than usual.

Autumn, and part of winter, passed quickly; it was time to leave the woods of Vergy. Respectable society in Verrières began to grow indignant that its anathemas had made so little impression on M. de Rênal. In less than a week various grave personages who atone for their habitual seriousness with the pleasure of running certain errands inspired in him the most cruel suspicions while still making use of the most circumspect language.

M. Valenod, who was playing it close to the vest, had placed Elisa in an aristocratic and well-considered family where there were five ladies. Elisa was afraid, she said, that she might not find a post for the winter, and so asked of this family only about two thirds of what she had received from the mayor. Of her own accord, this girl got the excellent notion of going to confess to the old curé, Chélan, and at the same time to the new curé, in order to inform them both of the latest details of Julien's love life.

The day after his return, at six o'clock in the morning, Abbé Chélan called Julien to him:

—I ask you no questions, he said; I beg of you and if necessary I order you to tell me nothing. I demand that within three days you leave, either for the seminary at Besançon or for the home of your friend Fouqué, who is still ready to provide a magnificent future for you. I have foreseen everything, arranged everything, but you must leave, and not come back to Verrières for at least a year.

Julien made no answer; he was wondering whether his honor shouldn't take offense at all the pains that M. Chélan, who after all wasn't his father, had lavished on him.

—Tomorrow at this same time I shall have the honor of calling on you again, he said at last.

M. Chélan, who had counted on carrying the day by main force over so young a man, talked a great deal. Drawn into the humblest possible posture and expression, Julien never opened his mouth.

At last he got away and ran to tell Mme. de Rênal, whom he found in despair. Her husband had just talked to her with a certain frankness. The natural weakness of his character, sustained by a prospect of the Besançon inheritance, had induced him to consider her perfectly innocent. He had just told her of the strange condition in which he found the public opinion of Verrières. This public was mistaken, misled by envious men, but what, after all, were they to do?

For a moment Mme. de Rênal had the illusion that Julien might accept the offers of M. Valenod and remain in Verrières. But she was no longer the simple, timid woman of the year before; her fatal passion, her attacks of remorse, had enlightened her. To her grief, she was soon convinced, as she listened to her husband, that a separation, at least for the moment, had become necessary. Far from me Julien will take up again those ambitious projects which are so natural when one is penniless. And as for me, good God, I'm so rich! And it's so useless for my happiness! He'll forget me. Admirable as he is, he will love and be loved. Ah, unhappy woman! . . . But what am I complaining about? God is just; I have not been able to forsake the crime, therefore he destroys my judgment. It was up to me to shut Elisa's mouth with money; nothing would have been easier. I didn't take enough trouble to think for a minute, those mad dreams of love absorbed all my time. And so I'm lost.

Julien was struck by one thing when he heard from Mme. de Rênal the terrible news of his departure; she raised no selfish objections. She seemed to be making great efforts not to weep.

—We must be strong, my friend.

She cut a lock of his hair.

—I don't know what will become of me, she said, but if I die, promise never to forget my children. Whether from far or near, you must try to make honest men of them. If there's a new revolution, the aristocrats will all have their throats cut, and their father will emigrate no doubt, because of that peasant who was killed on his rooftop. Watch over the family. . . . Give me your hand. Goodbye, my friend: These are our last moments together. Once this great sacrifice is made, I hope that in public I'll be brave enough to think only of my reputation.

Julien had been anticipating despair. The simplicity of these farewells affected him.

—No, I won't accept your goodbyes in this way. I'll go away; they want me to, and so do you yourself. But three days after I leave I'll come back to visit you at night.

Mme. de Rênal's existence was changed. Julien must love her since he had had, on his own, the idea of coming back! Her frightful grief changed into one of the sharpest impulses of joy she had ever experienced in her life. Everything became easy for her. The certainty of meeting her lover again took away from these last moments all their anguish. From this instant the conduct of Mme. de Rênal, like her expression, was noble, firm, and perfectly conventional.

Shortly M. de Rênal returned; he was beside himself. He finally talked to his wife of the anonymous letter he had received two months before.

—I'm going to take it to the Casino and show everyone it came from that villain Valenod, who was a beggar when I took him up and made him one of the richest men in Verrières. I'll shame him in public, and then challenge him to a duel. This has gone too far.

I could be a widow, great heavens! thought Mme. de Rênal. But almost at the same instant, she told herself: If I don't stop this duel, and it's certainly in my power to do so, I'll be my husband's murderer.

Never had she managed his vanity with so skilled a hand. In less than two hours she had made him understand, and always for reasons that he had discovered, that he must be more friendly than ever with M. Valenod, and even take back Elisa into his household. Mme. de Rênal needed great courage to call back this girl, cause of all her misfortunes. But the idea came from Julien.

At last, after being set back on the proper path three or four times, M. de Rênal arrived under his own power at the idea, extremely painful to him from a financial point of view, that the most disagreeable thing for him would be to have Julien staying amid the gossippy talkers of Verrières as tutor to M. Valenod's children. Julien's evident interest lay in accepting the offers of the director of the poorhouse: it served M. de Rênal's reputation much better that he should leave Verrières altogether and enter the seminary at Besançon or that at Dijon. But how to bring him to that decision, and after that how would he live there?

M. de Rênal, seeing that a financial sacrifice was imminent, suffered worse than his wife. For her part, after this conversation she was in the state of a man of feeling who has grown tired of life and taken a dose of stramonium;[6] he acts only automatically, so to speak, and takes no interest in anything. Thus it happened, when Louis XIV lay dying, that he said: *When I was king.* A wonderful expression!

Early next morning M. de Rênal received an anonymous letter. This one was in the most insulting style. The grossest words applicable to his position appeared in every line. It was the work of some envious inferior. This letter brought back to his mind the thought of a duel with M. Valenod. Soon his courage had reached the point where he was contemplating immediate action. He went out by himself and went to the gun shop to get some pistols, which he loaded.

After all, he said to himself, suppose the strict rule of the Emperor Napoleon is reinstated; I can't be blamed for a penny of actual theft. At most I've turned a blind eye now and then, but my desk is full of excellent letters authorizing me to do so.

Mme. de Rênal was terrified at her husband's cold rage; it reminded her of that possible widowhood which she had been at such pains to put out of her mind. She closeted herself with her husband. For several hours she talked to him in vain; the new anonymous letter had decided him. But finally she succeeded in transforming the courage to slap M. Valenod's face into the courage to offer Julien six hundred francs for a year's board in a seminary. M. de Rênal, cursing a thousand times over the day when he had the fatal notion of taking a tutor into his house, forgot the anonymous letter.

He was a little consoled by a notion he didn't mention to his wife: with a little clever management, and by playing on the young man's romantic notions, he hoped to dissuade him a little more cheaply from taking up M. Valenod's offer.

Mme. de Rênal had much trouble proving to Julien that, since he was setting her husband's mind at rest by giving up a post worth

6. stramonium: a poisonous narcotic derived from the Jimson weed.

eight hundred francs a year, a post that had been publicly offered him by the director of the poorhouse, he could accept a sum of money in compensation without loss of honor.

—But, Julien kept repeating, I never had for an instant any intention of accepting that offer. You've got me too used to an elegant life; the crudity of those folk would kill me.

Harsh necessity, with fist of steel, bent Julien's will. His pride allowed him to accept the sum offered by the mayor of Verrières, but only as a loan; he made out a note promising repayment in five years, and with interest.

Mme. de Rênal still had several thousand francs hidden out on the mountainside.

She offered them to him, trembling, and all too certain of meeting with an angry refusal.

—Are you trying to render the memory of our love abominable? Julien asked her.

At last Julien left Verrières. M. de Rênal was completely happy; at the fatal moment of taking his money, Julien found it was too great a sacrifice. He refused point blank. M. de Rênal fell on his neck, with tears in his eyes. Julien having asked for a certificate of good conduct, he was unable in his enthusiasm to find expressions magnificent enough to describe that conduct. Our hero had five louis in his savings account and anticipated being able to borrow a similar sum from Fouqué.

He was deeply moved. But when he had gone a league from Verrières, where he was leaving behind him so much love, he was no longer thinking of anything except the pleasure of seeing a capital city, a great military center like Besançon.

During this short absence of three days Mme. de Rênal fell victim to one of the cruelest deceptions of love. Her life was bearable; between her and ultimate grief stood always that final meeting with Julien. She counted the hours, the minutes, that separated them. At last, during the night of the third day, she heard in the distance the prearranged signal. After passing through a thousand dangers, Julien appeared before her.

From this moment forward she had only one thought, and that was, I am seeing him for the last time. Far from responding to her lover's ardors, she was like a barely animate corpse. If she forced herself to tell him she loved him, it was with an awkward air which came close to proving the contrary. Nothing could distract her from the bitter thought of their eternal separation. Julien, in his mistrust, thought for a while that he was already forgotten. The hints he cast forth of this possibility were met only with silent tears and almost convulsive handclasps.

—But, good God, what do you expect me to believe? Julien replied to his mistress' cold protestations; you would show a hundred times more sincere feeling for Mme. Derville, for a simple acquaintance.

Mme. de Rênal, petrified, had no answer but this:

—It's impossible to be more wretched . . . I hope I shall die . . . I feel my heart is frozen. . . .

These were the longest answers he could obtain from her.

When daybreak rendered it necessary for him to leave, Mme. de Rênal's tears ceased altogether. She watched him tie a knotted cord to the window without saying a word, without returning his kisses. In vain did Julien say to her:

—Here we are in the condition for which you've been longing. Henceforth you'll be able to live without remorse. When your children have a minor ailment, you'll no longer see them already in the grave.

—I am sorry you could not kiss Stanislas goodbye, she told him coldly.

In the end, Julien was deeply struck by the icy kisses of this living corpse; he could think of nothing else for several leagues. His soul was unstrung, and before passing over the mountain, as long as he could see the church steeple of Verrières, he kept turning to look back.

Chapter 24

A CAPITAL CITY

> What a racket, what a lot of busy people! what a lot of ideas for the future in a twenty-year-old head! what a lot of distractions from love!
> —Barnave

At length he saw on a distant mountain some dark walls; it was the fortress of Besançon. What a difference for me, said he with a sigh, if I were coming into this splendid military town in order to serve as a sublieutenant in one of the regiments charged with defending it!

Besançon is not only one of the prettiest towns in France, it's full of people of feeling and wit. But Julien was only a little peasant and he had no sort of access to distinguished men.

He had borrowed from Fouqué a shopkeeper's jacket, and it was in this guise that he passed over the drawbridges. Preoccupied with the story of the siege of 1674,[7] he wanted to see the ramparts and the fortress before shutting himself up in the seminary. Two or three times he was on the point of being arrested by sentinels; he was able to get into places which the military close to the public, so that they can sell the hay raised there for twelve or fifteen francs a year.

---

7. In the war to liberate the Franche-Comté from Spain, Besançon was twice besieged and captured by the French—in 1660 and then in 1674.

The high walls, deep moats, and terrible aspect of the cannon had preoccupied him for several hours when he passed by the main café on the boulevard. He stopped stock still in admiration; though he could read the word *café* in huge letters over the two immense doors, he could hardly believe his eyes. He tried to overcome his timidity; he ventured to go in, and found himself in a room thirty or forty feet long, with a ceiling at least twenty feet high. On that day everything seemed enchanting to him.

Two games of billiards were being played. The waiters called out the scores; the players moved about the tables through numerous onlookers. Clouds of tobacco smoke pouring from every mouth filled the room with a blue haze. The tall stature of these men, their round shoulders, heavy strides, enormous whiskers, and the long overcoats that enveloped them, all attracted Julien's attention. These noble offspring of ancient Bisontium conversed only in bellows; they acted the part of terrible warriors. Julien admired the furnishings; he was thinking of the immensity and magnificence of a capital city like Besançon. He felt himself absolutely devoid of the courage necessary to ask for a cup of coffee from one of those lofty gentlemen who were calling out the billiard scores.

But the young lady behind the bar had noted the charming features of this young countryman who had stopped three feet from the stove, and, still holding his little parcel under his arm, was studying a fine white plaster bust of the king. This young lady, a robust product of the Franche-Comté with an admirable figure and the sort of dress one needs to be noticed in a café, had already twice called in a modest voice intended only for Julien's ears: Monsieur! Monsieur! Julien glanced into a pair of big blue eyes with a gentle expression and understood that he was being addressed.

He stepped briskly up to the counter and the young lady, as if he were charging an enemy. As he executed this maneuver, his parcel fell to the floor.

What pity will be felt for our bumpkin by those Paris schoolboys who at fifteen already know how to enter a café in such distinguished style! But these children, so modish at fifteen, turn to the *common* at eighteen. The impassioned timidity one sees in the provinces occasionally transcends itself, and then becomes a pathway to will. As he approached this beautiful girl who was kind enough to speak a word to him, I must tell her the truth, thought Julien, whose courage was thriving on conquered timidity.

—Madame, for the first time in my life I've come to Besançon; I should like to have, to purchase for money, that is, a roll and a cup of coffee.

The girl smiled a little and then blushed; she feared this handsome young fellow would draw ironic commentary from the billiard players. He would be terrified by that and would never come back.

—Sit here beside me, she said, showing him to a marble table almost entirely concealed behind the enormous mahogany bar which stood out in the room.

The young lady leaned across this counter, an action that gave her occasion to display a superb figure. Julien took notice; all his ideas changed.[8] The pretty girl had just set before him a cup, a sugar bowl, and a roll. She paused before calling a waiter to bring coffee, because she foresaw that the coming of the waiter would put to an end her private conversation with Julien.

Julien, in thoughtful mood, was comparing this blond, gay beauty with certain memories that often disturbed him. The idea of the passion he had inspired drove away almost all his timidity. The pretty girl had only a minute; she read something in Julien's eyes.

—This tobacco smoke makes you cough; come for breakfast tomorrow before eight; at that time I'm almost alone.

—What's your name? Julien asked, with the caressing smile of timidity set at ease.

—Amanda Binet.

—Will you let me send you within an hour a little parcel about as big as this one?

The fair Amanda thought for a bit.

—I have to be careful of the boss; what you're asking may get me in trouble; but no matter, I'll write my address on a card, which you can put on your parcel. You can send it to me without fear.

—My name is Julien Sorel, said the young man; I have no relatives or friends in Besançon.

—Ah, so that's it! she said joyfully, you're coming to the law school?

—Alas, no, Julien replied, they're sending me to the seminary.

Darkest discouragement overspread Amanda's features and she called the waiter; she was decisive enough now. The waiter poured Julien's coffee without so much as seeing him.

Amanda took in money at the bar; Julien was proud of himself for having dared to speak up: a quarrel was in process at one of the billiard tables. The shouted charges and denials of the players echoed through the enormous room, making an uproar that almost stunned Julien. Amanda was dreamy and her eyes downcast.

—If you prefer, mademoiselle, he said to her suddenly with assurance, I can say that I'm your cousin.

This little air of authority pleased Amanda. This young man isn't a nobody, she thought. And she said to him very quickly, without looking at him, for she had to keep an eye out lest anybody come up to the counter:

—I come from Genlis near Dijon; say that you're from Genlis too, and my mother's cousin.

8. This sentence is famous for its brevity.

—I won't forget.

—Every Thursday at five o'clock during the summer all the young gentlemen from the seminary come past the café here.

—If you're thinking of me when I come past, have a bouquet of violets in your hand.

Amanda looked at him in amazement; this look converted Julien's courage to rashness; but he blushed deeply as he said to her:

—I feel that I love you with an overwhelming passion.

—Don't talk so loud then, she said with a frightened glance.

Julien had the idea of summoning up the phrases of a volume of the *Nouvelle Héloïse* which he had read at Vergy.[9] His memory served him well; for ten minutes he recited the *Nouvelle Héloïse* to Mlle. Amanda Binet, who was in ecstasies; and he was pleased with his own gallantry, when suddenly the fair Franc-Comtoise assumed an icy expression. One of her lovers had entered the doorway of the café.

He came up to the counter, whistling and swaggering; he stared at Julien. At once the imagination of the latter, always rushing to extremes, was filled with ideas of a duel. He grew very pale, pushed his cup aside, put on a confident expression, and stared steadily back at his rival. As this rival looked aside for a moment to pour himself a small glass of brandy at the bar, Amanda with a single glance ordered Julien to lower his eyes. He obeyed, and for two minutes sat motionless in his chair, pale, resolute, and thinking only of what was going to happen. The rival had been astonished at the look in Julien's eyes; having gulped down his brandy, he said a few words to Amanda, stuffed his hands in his overcoat pockets, and strode off to a billiard table, breathing heavily and staring at Julien. The latter sprang to his feet in an access of rage; but he did not know the procedures of insult. He put down his parcel, and in the most strutting gait he could manage, marched toward the billiard table.

It was in vain that prudence reminded him: Fight a duel the day you come to Besançon and your career in the church is over.

—What matter? no one will ever say I failed to resent an insult.

Amanda took note of his courage; it made a fine contrast with the simplicity of his manners; in an instant she preferred him before the big young man in the overcoat. She rose, and even as she seemed to be following with her eyes someone out in the street, moved swiftly to place herself between him and the billiard table.

—I don't want you to stare at that gentleman, he's my brother-in-law.

9. The *Nouvelle Héloïse*, Rousseau's passionate rhetorical novel, provided several generations of Frenchmen with their sentimental rhetoric.

—What do I care? He stared at me.

—Do you want to get me in trouble? No doubt he looked at you, perhaps he'll even come and talk to you. I told him you were related to my mother, that you'd just come from Genlis. He's from the Franche-Comté, and has never gone past Dôle on the Burgundy road; you can tell him anything you want, he'll never know the difference.

Julien still hesitated; she quickly added, as her barmaid's imagination furnished her with lies in abundance:

—All right, he stared at you; but that was when he was asking me who you were; he's a man who's rough with everybody; he didn't mean to insult you.

Julien's eye still followed the supposed brother-in-law; he watched him buy a number in the game getting underway at the farther of the two billiard tables. Julien heard his heavy voice blare out, in a threatening tone, *"All right, I'm in!"* He stepped swiftly around Mlle. Amanda and took a step toward the billiard table. Amanda caught him by the arm:

—Come and pay me first, she told him.

Quite right, thought Julien; she's afraid I'll go away without paying. Amanda was just as distressed as he, and very red; she returned his change as slowly as she could, meanwhile saying to him in an undertone:

—You must leave the café at once, otherwise I won't like you any more; and yet I do like you very much.

So Julien left, but slowly. Isn't it my duty, he kept saying to himself, to go over to that crude type and stare and snuffle at him? This question kept him pacing the boulevard in front of the café for an hour, waiting to see if his man would come out. He didn't, so Julien left.

He had been in Besançon only a few hours and already he had an experience to regret. The old surgeon-major had once, in spite of his gout, given him a few lessons in fencing; that was the only science Julien could summon to the service of his anger. But this ignorance would have been nothing if he had only known how to pick a quarrel in some other way than by striking his man; if it had come to a fist fight, his rival, an enormous oaf, would have beaten him up and left him for dead.

For a poor devil like me, Julien said to himself, a man without protectors or money, there won't be much difference between a seminary and a prison; I'll have to leave my layman's dress in some inn where I'll change to my black suit. If ever I can get out of the seminary for a few hours, I might very well, if I had layman's clothing, see Mlle. Amanda again. This was fine reasoning; but though he walked by all the inns he didn't dare enter any of them.

Finally, as he was passing by the Ambassadors Hotel for the second time, his restless glance encountered the eyes of a fat woman, still fairly young and ruddy of complexion, who seemed to have a cheerful disposition. He went up to her and told his tale.

—Certainly, my fine young abbé, said the hostess of the Ambassadors, I'll keep your lay clothes for you, and even brush them now and then. You can't just leave a good suit hanging without touching it. She took a key and led him into a room, advising him to make an inventory of what he was leaving.

—Lord now, don't you look good that way, M. l'Abbé Sorel, said the fat woman, when he came down to the kitchen, I'm going to fix you a good dinner now, and what's more (she added in an undertone) it'll cost you only twenty sous instead of the fifty everyone else pays; you've got to be careful of your little *stockpile.*

—I have ten louis, Julien replied with a certain lofty air.

—Oh, good Lord, said the hostess in alarm, don't talk so loud; there are plenty of crooks in Besançon. They could get that money away from you in less than a minute. Above all, keep out of the cafés, they're full of crooks.

—Really! said Julien; this last sentence gave him something to think about.

—Never go anywhere except here. I'll have coffee for you. Remember, you'll always have a good friend here and a good dinner at twenty sous; I guess that won't hurt, eh? Go sit down at the table, I'll serve you myself.

—I won't be able to eat, Julien told her, I'm too upset. When I leave your house, I'll be going to the seminary.

The good woman let him go only after filling his pockets with food. Finally Julien set out for his fearful destination; from her doorstep the hostess pointed out the direction.

Chapter 25

THE SEMINARY

> Three hundred thirty-six dinners at 83 centimes, three hundred thirty-six suppers at 38 centimes, chocolate for those entitled; how much is there to make on the contract?
> —The Valenod of Besançon

From a distance he saw the gilded iron cross on the door; he walked slowly forward; his legs seemed to give way beneath him. So this is the hell on earth from which I can never escape! Finally he decided to ring. The sound of the bell echoed as if in an abandoned house. After a wait of ten minutes a pale man dressed in black came to open the door for him. Julien glanced at him and abruptly lowered his eyes. It seemed to him that this doorman had an extraordinary face. The prominent, green pupils of his eyes expanded and contracted like those of a cat; the unblinking eyelids announced the impossibility of all sympathy; his thin lips were stretched tight over protruding teeth. Yet the face was not that of a criminal; rather, it suggested that complete insensibility which for young people is even more terrifying than crime. The only emotion Julien's rapid glance could discover on that long, pious face was a perfect contempt for every subject one might bring up that did not serve the interests of heaven.

With a great effort Julien looked up, and speaking in a voice that the pounding of his heart caused to tremble, declared that he wanted to speak with M. Pirard, the director of the seminary. Without uttering a word, the black man signaled him to follow. They climbed two flights of a wide stairway with a wooden baluster; the stairs sagged noticeably on the side away from the wall and seemed on the point of collapsing. A little doorway, over which hung a big wooden cemetery cross painted black, was opened with difficulty, and the porter brought him into a low, dark room, the whitewashed walls of which were adorned with two big paintings grown black with age. There Julien was left alone; he was terrified, his heart was beating furiously; he would have been happy to summon up the courage for tears. A deathly silence reigned through the whole building.

After a quarter of an hour, which seemed a whole day to him, the sinister porter reappeared in a doorway at the other end of the room, and without deigning a word made a sign for him to come along. He entered a room much larger than the other and very badly lit. Here too the walls were whitewashed; but there was no furniture at all. Only in a corner near the door Julien saw as he passed a bed of white wood, a pair of wicker chairs, and a little armchair of pine planks without a cushion. At the other end of the room, by a little window with yellowed panes and some very dirty flowerpots, he saw a man in a ragged cassock seated before a work table; he seemed angry, and was picking up, one after the other, a number of little squares of paper which he arranged on his desk after writing a few words on each. He did not take notice of Julien's presence. The latter stood motionless in the middle of the room, where he had been left by the porter, who shut the door as he went out.

Ten minutes passed; the badly dressed man kept writing. Julien's terror and distress were such that he felt ready to faint. A philosopher would have said, perhaps wrongly: this is the violent impression made by the ugly on a soul formed to love the beautiful.

The man looked up in the middle of his writing; Julien noticed him only after a moment, and even after seeing him, he still stood

motionless as if struck dead by the terrible glance that was turned
on him. Julien's misty eyes could barely make out a long face
covered with red spots except on the forehead, which was of a
deathly pallor. Between the scarlet cheeks and the white forehead
glittered two little black eyes, formed to strike terror in the bravest.
The vast expanse of his brow was defined by a mass of thick,
straight, jet-black hair.

—Will you come over here, yes or no? the man said at last,
impatiently.

Julien stepped forward uncertainly, and at last, ready to collapse,
and pale as he had never before been in his life, he stopped three
paces from the little wooden table covered with paper squares.

—Closer, said the man.

Julien stepped forward, holding out his hand as if trying to steady
himself on something.

—Your name?

—Julien Sorel.

—You're very late, he said, fixing him once more with a terrible
glance.

This look Julien could not sustain; holding out his hand as if to
catch himself, he fell full length to the floor.

The man rang his bell. Julien had lost only the power of sight
and of motion; he heard footsteps approach.

They picked him up and set him in the little wooden armchair.
He heard the terrible man say to the porter:

—He seems to be an epileptic; that's all we needed.

When Julien could open his eyes, he saw that the red-faced man
had resumed his writing and the porter had gone. I must take heart,
said our hero, and above all conceal what I feel: he felt a sharp pain
at his heart; if I show weakness, God knows what they'll think of me.
At last the man stopped writing, and looked askance at Julien:

—Are you well enough to answer my questions?

—Yes, sir, said Julien weakly.

—Well, that's lucky.

The black man had half risen and was looking impatiently for a
letter in the drawer of his pine table, which opened with a creak. He
found it, sat slowly down, and looked Julien over again with a
glance fit to wrench from him the little life still remaining:

—You are recommended to me by M. Chélan, the best priest in
the diocese, a virtuous man if one ever lived, and my friend for the
past thirty years.

—Ah, then it is M. Pirard himself whom I have the honor of
addressing, said Julien with a dying fall.

—So it seems, replied the director of the seminary, casting a surly
look at him.

The glitter in his little eyes brightened, and was followed by an involuntary motion of the muscles at the corners of his mouth. It was like the expression of a tiger anticipating the pleasure of devouring his prey.

—Chélan's letter is short, he said as if talking to himself. *Intelligenti pauca*,[1] as things go now a man can hardly write too little. He read aloud:

> I am sending to you Julien Sorel, of this parish, whom I baptized going on twenty years ago; son of a rich carpenter, who will give him nothing. Julien will be a remarkable laborer in the vineyard of the Lord. Memory and intelligence aplenty; he can think. Will his calling last? Is it sincere?

—*Sincere!* repeated Abbé Pirard with an air of astonishment, looking again at Julien; but already the abbé's glance was less devoid of humanity; *sincere!* he repeated, lowering his voice and resuming his reading:

> I ask of you a scholarship for Julien; he will earn it by undergoing the necessary examinations. I have showed him a bit of theology, that good old theology of people like Bossuet, Arnault, Fleury. If this young man doesn't please you, send him back to me; the director of the poorhouse, whom you know well, offers him eight hundred francs to act as tutor to his children. —My conscience is at rest, thanks be to God. I am growing used to the terrible blow. *Vale et me ama.*

Abbé Pirard, slowing his speech as he read the signature, pronounced with a sigh the word *Chélan.*

—He is at rest, said he; well, a man of his virtue deserves that reward, anyhow. May God grant it to me under the same circumstances.

He glanced upward and made a sign of the cross. At the sight of this holy symbol Julien felt a slight easing of the profound horror that had frozen him since he entered this house.

—I have here three hundred and twenty-one aspirants to the holiest of positions, said Abbé Pirard at last, speaking sternly but not angrily; only seven or eight are recommended to me by men like Abbé Chélan; thus among the three hundred and twenty-one, you will be number nine. But my protection is neither favor nor weakness; it is redoubled attention and severity against vice. Go lock that door.

Julien struggled to his feet and succeeded in not falling. He noted that a little window near the entryway opened onto the countryside. He looked out at the trees; the sight comforted him, as if he had seen old friends.

1. "To an understanding man, few words suffice."

—*Loquerisne linguam latinam?* (Do you speak Latin?) said Abbé Pirard as he returned.

—*Ita, pater optime* (Yes, most excellent father), replied Julien, regaining a bit of self-possession. Certainly no man in the world had ever seemed to him less excellent than M. Pirard during the last half hour.

The conversation continued in Latin. The abbé's eyes grew softer; Julien regained some poise. What a weakling I am, thought he, to let myself be impressed by these shows of virtue! This man is going to turn out to be simply another swindler like M. Maslon; and Julien congratulated himself on having hidden almost all his money in his shoes.

Abbé Pirard examined Julien in theology, and was surprised at the extent of his knowledge. His astonishment increased when he asked him some detailed questions on the Scriptures. But when he came to questions on the teachings of the Church Fathers, he saw that Julien knew nothing, hardly even the names, of Saints Jerome, Augustine, Bonaventura, Basil, etc., etc.

In fact, thought Abbé Pirard, here is that same fatal tendency to Protestantism which I've always rebuked in Chélan. A profound, a too profound, knowledge of the Scriptures.

(Julien had just been talking, and not in answer to a specific question, of the *actual date* when Genesis and the other books of the Pentateuch had been written.)

Where does it lead, this endless study of the Holy Scriptures, thought Abbé Pirard, if not to *personal questioning* that is, to the most frightful Protestantism? And alongside this unwise erudition, no patristic learning at all to act as a balance.

But the astonishment of the director knew no bounds at all when he interrogated Julien on the authority of the pope, and the young man, instead of repeating the maxims of the ancient Gallican church, recited to him the entire book of M. de Maistre.

A strange man, this Chélan, thought Abbé Pirard; can he have taught the boy this book in order to make him mock it?

In vain did he question Julien further, trying to find out if he believed seriously in the doctrine of M. de Maistre. The young man replied only with his memory.[2] From this point on, Julien was really in fine form, he felt master of himself. After a protracted examination it seemed to him that M. Pirard's severity toward him was no longer anything more than superficial. In fact, if it hadn't been for the principles of austere gravity which for fifteen years he had schooled himself to practice toward his pupils, the director of the seminary would have kissed Julien in the name of logic, such clarity, precision, and sharpness was manifest in his answers.

2. By using his memory Julien, like Fabrizio in the *Chartreuse* (Chap. 7), conceals his true self from a prying inquisitor.

A bold, strong spirit, said he, but *corpus debile* (the body is feeble).

—Do you often collapse as you did? he asked Julien in French, pointing at the floor.

—That was the first time in my life; the porter's face paralyzed me, Julien said, blushing like a child.

Abbé Pirard came close to smiling.

—Such are the effect of the world's vanities; you seem to be used to laughing faces, theaters for the display of falsehood. Truth is austere, sir. But our task in this world is austere too, is it not? You must take care to guard your conscience carefully from this weakness: *Excess of feeling for vain exterior charms.*

—If you were not recommended to me, said Abbé Pirard, resuming the Latin tongue with obvious pleasure, if you were not recommended to me by a man like Abbé Chélan, I would address you in the vain language of the world, to which it appears you are all too well accustomed. The full scholarship you request is the hardest thing in the world to obtain. But Abbé Chélan has merited very little by his fifty-six years of apostolic devotion if he cannot command a scholarship at the seminary.

After this speech Abbé Pirard advised Julien not to join any group or secret congregation without his permission.

—I give you my word of honor, said Julien with the heartfelt impulse of an honest man.

For the first time the director of the seminary smiled.

—That expression has no meaning here, said he, it suggests too much the vain honor of worldly men which leads them into so many errors and often into crimes. You owe me sacred obedience by virtue of paragraph seventeen of the bull *Unam Ecclesiam* of St. Pius V.[3] I am your ecclesiastical superior. In this house, my very dear son, to hear is to obey. How much money have you?

Here we are at the point, said Julien to himself; this was the reason for the *very dear son.*

—Thirty five francs, my father.

—Keep careful track of how you spend that money; you will have to account for it to me.

This painful interview had lasted three hours; Julien called the porter.

—Put Julien Sorel in cell number 103, Abbé Pirard told this man.

As a special mark of favor, Julien was given a room to himself.

—Take up his trunk, too, he added.

Julien looked down and noticed his trunk right in front of him; he had been looking straight at it for three hours and had not recognized it.

3. Pius V was a rigorous, disciplinarian pope of the sixteenth century, but the bull *Unam Ecclesiam* is a Stendhalian fiction.

When he reached number 103, a little room eight feet square on the top story of the house, Julien saw that it looked out on the ramparts, and beyond them on the fine fields that are separated by the Doubs from the town itself.

What a delightful view! Julien exclaimed; even as he said them, he did not feel anything of what the words expressed. The many violent sensations he had experienced during his short time at Besançon had completely exhausted his energies. He sat down by the window on the single wooden chair in the cell and promptly slipped into a deep slumber. He never heard the supper bell nor that for benediction; he had been forgotten.

When the first rays of the sun woke him the following morning he found himself stretched out on the floor.

Chapter 26

THE WORLD, OR WHAT A RICH MAN LACKS

I'm alone on the face of the earth, nobody bothers to think of me. All the men whom I see getting ahead have an outward boldness and an inward hardness of heart which is not in me. They hate me for my easy good will. Ah! before long I shall die, either of hunger or of unhappiness at seeing men so cruel.

—Young[4]

He hastened to brush off his clothes and go downstairs; he was late. An usher scolded him sharply; instead of trying to excuse himself, Julien crossed his arms over his chest:

—*Peccavi, pater optime* (I have sinned, I admit my fault, oh father), he said with a contrite expression.

This first step was a great success. The clever fellows among the seminarians saw they had to do with a man who didn't have to learn the rudiments of the game. When the recreation hour came, Julien was the object of general curiosity. But he replied only with reserve and silence. Following the maxims he had made for himself, he considered his three hundred and twenty-one comrades as so many enemies, and the most dangerous of all, in his eyes, was Abbé Pirard.

A few days later Julien had to select a confessor; they provided him with a list.

Well, good Lord, what do they take me for? said he; do they suppose I don't know what it's all about? and he chose Abbé Pirard.

Though he didn't suspect it, this step proved decisive. A little seminarian, almost a child, who came from Verrières and had

4. Young: the tone of this quotation, in French in the original novel, is intended to suggest Edward (*Night Thoughts*) Young; but nothing in Young's magniloquent blank verse directly parallels Stendhal's pathetic prose.

declared himself a friend from the first day, told him that if he had chosen M. Castanède, deputy director of the seminary, he might well have acted with greater prudence.

—Abbé Castanède is opposed to M. Pirard, who is suspected of Jansenism, added the little seminarian, bending toward Julien's ear.

All the first actions of our hero, who considered himself such a politician, were, like his choice of a confessor, acts of folly. Misled by the presumption natural to an imaginative man, he mistook his inward intentions for outward acts and considered himself a consummate hypocrite. His folly reached the height of blaming himself for his supposed success in this art of the weak.

Alas, it's my only weapon! In another age, said he, it would have been eloquent actions in the face of the enemy that enabled me to *earn my bread*.

Satisfied with his own conduct, Julien looked about him and found everywhere the appearance of the most spotless virtue.

Eight or ten seminarians lived in the odor of sanctity and experienced visions like St. Theresa and St. Francis when he received the stigmata atop Mount Verna in the Apennines. But it was a great secret; their friends concealed it. These poor fellows with the visions were almost always in the infirmary. A hundred others managed to combine robust faith with unwearying industry. They worked themselves almost sick, but without learning much. Two or three were distinguished by a real talent, among others a man named Chazel;[5] but Julien felt hostile to them and they to him.

The rest of the three hundred and twenty-one seminarians were gross creatures, never entirely sure they understood the Latin words they recited all day long. Almost all were the sons of peasants, who preferred to gain their daily bread by repeating a few Latin words instead of swinging a pickax. It was after surveying this field, during his first few days, that Julien promised himself quick success. In every line of work intelligent people are needed; after all, there's a job to be done, he told himself. Under Napoleon, I'd have been a sergeant; among these future priests, I can be grand vicar.

All these poor devils, he added, who were day laborers from birth, have lived until they came here on curds and black bread. In their native huts they ate meat maybe five or six times a year. Like Roman soldiers, who regarded warfare as a holiday from garrison duty, these cloddish peasants are enchanted with the pleasures of the seminary.

Julien never saw in their blank eyes anything but a sense of physical satisfaction after dinner and an expectation of physical pleasure before dinner. Such were the people among whom he must

5. Chazel is the name of a Grenoble classmate of Stendhal's (see *Brulard,* Chap. 8).

distinguish himself; but what Julien did not know, and what people took care not to tell him, was that gaining first place in the various courses given at the seminary in dogma, ecclesiastical history, etc., etc., was in their eyes nothing but a *sin of pride*. Since Voltaire's time, since government by two houses, which is nothing at bottom but *distrust of authority and personal examination*, which instills in the people the bad habit of *doubt*, the church in France seems to have understood that books themselves are its real enemy. In the eyes of the church, inward submission is all. Who can prevent the superior man from passing over to the other side like Siéyès or Grégoire![6] The terrified church clings to the pope as to its only hope of salvation. Only the pope can attempt to put an end to personal examination and, by the pious ceremonial pomp of his court, make an impression on the bored, sick spirits of modern worldlings.

Julien, half grasping these various truths, which nonetheless every word spoken in a seminary tends to deny, fell into a deep melancholy. He worked hard and rapidly succeeded in learning a number of things very useful to a priest, very false in his eyes, and which interested him not at all. He thought this was his only way out.

Am I then forgotten by the whole world? he asked himself. He did not know that M. Pirard had received, and flung into the fire, various letters postmarked from Dijon, in which, despite all the decorums of the most respectable style, the deepest ardor was apparent. Profound regret seemed to struggle, in these letters, against passion. So much the better, thought Abbé Pirard, at least it was not an impious woman with whom this young man was in love.

One day Abbé Pirard opened a letter that seemed half obliterated by tears; it was an eternal farewell. At last, the writer told Julien, it has been granted to me to hate, not the author of my fault, who will always be for me the dearest thing in the world, but my fault itself. The sacrifice is made, my darling. It was not made without tears, as you see. The welfare of those beings for whom I am wholly responsible and whom you loved so well has carried the day. No longer will a just but terrible God be able to revenge on them the crimes of their mother. Farewell, Julien, be just toward men.

The ending of this letter was almost entirely illegible. The writer gave an address at Dijon but hoped that Julien would never answer it or at least that he would use only words which a woman returned to virtue's path could read without blushing.

Julien's melancholy, helped along by the mediocre diet furnished to the seminary by a contractor at 83 centimes, was starting to have

6. For Siéyès, see p. 54, note 9. Abbé Gregoire became a liberal deputy for Grenoble and was regarded by the local ultras as a traitor.

an influence on his health, when one morning Fouqué turned up abruptly in his room.

—I finally got in. Five times I came to Besançon, it's not your fault, just to see you. Always old wooden face. I posted a watchman on the seminary gate; why the devil don't you ever go out?

—It's a test I've imposed on myself.

—You really have changed. Well, at last I'm here. Two fine six-franc crowns just taught me what a fool I was not to have offered them in the first place.

The conversation between the two friends was endless. Julien changed color when Fouqué said to him:

—By the way, have you heard? The mother of your pupils has turned religious.

And he talked on, in that offhand way that makes such a singular impression on the impassioned soul whose dearest interests are being, all unconsciously, tumbled about.

—Yes indeed, my friend, the highest strains of devotion. They say she's going on pilgrimages. But to the eternal disgrace of Abbé Maslon, who did all that spying on M. Chélan, Mme. de Rênal wants no part of him. She goes to confession at Dijon or Besançon.

—She comes to Besançon, said Julien, his brow suffused.

—Quite frequently, replied Fouqué in a questioning tone.

—Do you have any *Constitutionnels*[7] about you?

—What's that you say? replied Fouqué.

—I asked if you have any *Constitutionnels*, Julien repeated in a tone of perfect tranquillity. They sell here at thirty sous an issue.

—Really! even in the seminary we find liberals! cried Fouqué. Ah, poor France! he added, assuming the hypocritical voice and dulcet accent of Abbé Maslon.

This visit would have made a profound impression on our hero if next day a word addressed to him by that little seminarian from Verrières, who seemed to him so childish, had not led to an important discovery. Since he had been at the seminary Julien's conduct had been nothing but one false step after another. He laughed scornfully at himself.

Actually, the important actions in his life had been skillfully managed; but he was not clever at the details, and in the seminary clever fellows pay attention only to the details. Thus, he was already considered by his fellows a *free thinker*. He had been betrayed by a host of little actions.

In their eyes he was already guilty of one enormous vice: *he thought, he judged for himself*, instead of following blindly *authority* and precedent. Abbé Pirard had been of no help to him; outside

7. See p. 33, note 9. Julien's use of liberal politics as a red herring to distract his friend from a personal involvement is very clear here.

the confessional he had not said a single word to him, and even in the confessional he listened more than he talked. Things would certainly have been very different had he chosen Abbé Castanède.

The moment Julien became aware of his folly, his boredom disappeared. He wanted to know the full extent of the damage and to that end emerged slightly from the lofty, obstinate silence with which he had rebuffed his fellows. Then they got their own back. His advances were met with a scorn that reached the point of derision. He realized that since he entered the seminary there had not been a single hour, especially during the recess periods, which had not hurt or helped him, which had not augmented the number of his enemies or earned him the good will of some seminarian who was either sincerely virtuous or at least a little less gross than the others. The damage to be repaired was immense, the task difficult in the extreme. Henceforth Julien was constantly on the alert; his task was to create for himself a whole new character.

Managing his eyes, for example, gave him a great deal of trouble. It's not without good reason that in places of this sort they are always kept lowered. What presumption I showed at Verrières, Julien said to himself; I thought that was life; it was only a preparation for life; here I am at last, in the world as it is going to be for me until I play out my role, surrounded by real enemies. What immense difficulty, he added, in this minute-by-minute hypocrisy! It's worse than the labors of Hercules. The real Hercules of modern times is Sixtus V,[8] deceiving by his modesty for fifteen years on end forty cardinals who had seen him proud and vigorous in his youth.

So learning counts for nothing here! he said to himself with scorn; ability to learn dogma, sacred history, etc., counts only on the surface. Everything they say on this subject is only to make fools like me fall into their trap. Alas! my only merit was in my studies, my knack for reciting their humbug. Perhaps in their hearts they estimate that stuff at its true value? Perhaps they think of it just as I do? And I was fool enough to be proud of myself! All those first places I accumulated did nothing but accumulate mortal enemies for me. Chazel, who knows more than I do, always puts into his compositions some piece of idiocy which sets him down to fiftieth place; any time he's in first place, it's by mistake. Ah, how a word, just one word from M. Pirard, would have helped me!

As soon as the scales fell from Julien's eyes, the lengthy practices of ascetic piety, such as rosary drill five days a week, hymns to the Sacred Heart, etc., etc., all of which used to seem so mortally tedious, became occasions for his most interesting acting. Reflecting

8. Stendhal's notions about the Renaissance pope Sixtus V came from a rascally eighteenth-century biography published under the anagram Geltio Rogeri by a spoiled priest whose real name was Gregorio Leti. Stendhal's picture of Sixtus' massive hypocrisy does not vary much from Leti's.

critically on his behavior, and striving above all not to exaggerate his methods, Julien did not aspire, like the seminarians who served as models for the others, to perform at every moment a *significant* action, that is, one giving evidence of some Christian perfection. Not all at once. In the seminary there's a way of eating a boiled egg which declares how far one has progressed down the saintly path.

The reader, who no doubt is smiling, will be kind enough to recall all the mistakes in eating an egg made by Abbé Delille when invited to lunch by a great lady in the court of Louis XVI.[9]

Julien sought as his first stage to reach the *non culpa*, that is, the state of the young seminarian whose deportment, whose manner of moving his arms and eyes, etc., reveals nothing of the worldly spirit, it is true, but does not yet show the mind wholly absorbed in the idea of the other world and the *absolute nullity* of this one.

Everywhere Julien saw, scribbled with charcoal on the corridor walls, phrases like this: What are sixty years of trial compared with an eternity of joy or an eternity of boiling oil in hell? He did not despise these slogans; he understood it was necessary to have them constantly before one's eyes. What will I be doing all my life? he asked himself; I'll be selling the faithful a seat in heaven. How will that seat be made visible to them? by the difference between my exterior and that of a layman.

After several months of constant application, Julien still had the look of a *thinker*. His way of moving his eyes and opening his mouth did not declare a man of implicit faith, ready to believe everything and endure everything, even martyrdom. With rage Julien saw himself outdone in this respect by the most boorish of peasants. They had good reason not to look like thinkers.

How he taxed himself to achieve that [blissful, narrow look, that] expression of blind, fervent faith, ready to believe all and suffer all, which is so often found in Italian convents, and of which Guercino has left, for us laymen, such perfect examples in his ecclesiastical paintings.[1]

On high festival days the seminarians were given sausages with their cabbage. Julien's table companions had noted that he was indifferent to this delight; that was one of his first sins. His comrades saw it as a trait of the most odious hypocrisy; nothing made

9. Jacques Delille (1738–1813), illegitimate as well as provincial by birth, and forced to gain his livelihood by teaching elementary Latin, came abruptly to public attention with a translation of Virgil's *Georgics* in 1769; he was then taken up by Mme. Geoffrin, at the height of her reputation, and polished to such effect that toward the end of his life he wrote one of his best poems on the art of worldly conversation. No doubt his debut at Mme. Geoffrin's salon was the occasion of all his troubles with the egg; but I have not found a specific account of them. Sainte-Beuve consecrated to Delille a not very friendly *Portrait Littéraire* (Vol. II).

1. See in the Louvre n. 1130, François Duc d'Aquitaine laying aside his armor and putting on monastic robes. [Stendhal's note].

him more enemies. Look at that bourgeois, that snob, they said; look how he pretends to despise our best grub, sausages with kraut. What an ugly fellow! What an arrogant attitude! Damn him!

[He ought to have left part of it on his plate, sacrificed it, and then said to some friend, with a gesture at the kraut: What can man offer an all-powerful being if not *voluntary suffering?*

Julien did not have the experience which makes things of this sort so easy to see.]

It's my misfortune that the ignorance of these young peasants, who are my comrades, gives them an immense advantage over me, Julien exclaimed in his moments of discouragement. When they enter the seminary, the professor has no need to deliver them from the frightful quantity of worldly ideas which I bring with me, and which they can read in my face, no matter what I do.

Julien studied with an attention that approached envy the crudest of the young peasants who came to the seminary. At the moment when they were stripped of their nankeen jackets to put on the black habit their education was limited to an immense respect for *dry and liquid* money, as they say in the Franche-Comté.

It is their sacramental and heroic way of expressing the sublime idea of *cash on the line.*

Happiness for these seminarians, as for the heroes of Voltaire's stories, consisted primarily of a good dinner. Julien found that nearly all of them had an instinctive respect for the man who wore a suit of *good goods.* This sentiment of theirs values *distributive justice,* as our courts hand it down, at its proper price or even something less. What can be gained, they often asked one another, by pleading against a bigshot?

That's the expression used in the Jura valleys to describe a rich man. Imagine then what respect they have for the richest group of all: the government!

Not to smile respectfully at the very name of the prefect seems, to the peasants of the Franche-Comté, an act of folly; but folly on the part of poor people is quickly punished by loss of bread.

After having been almost suffocated at first by his sense of contempt, Julien ended by feeling some pity: it had often befallen the fathers of most of his comrades to come home on a winter night to their hovels and to find there neither bread nor chestnuts nor potatoes. So what's surprising, Julien asked himself, if they consider a happy man to be one who's just had a good dinner, and after that the man who has a good suit of clothes? My comrades have a sure vocation; that is, they see in their churchly functions a long spell of this happiness: having a good dinner and a warm suit of clothes in winter.

Julien happened to overhear a young seminarian endowed with imagination say to his companion:

—Why shouldn't I become Pope, like Sixtus V, who kept swine?

—Only Italians get made pope, replied his friend; but you can count on it, they'll draw lots among us for jobs as grand vicars, canons, and maybe even bishops. M. P——, bishop of Châlons, is the son of a tub maker; now that's my father's job.

One day, in the middle of dogma class, Abbé Pirard summoned Julien. The poor young man was delighted to be withdrawn from the moral and physical atmosphere into which he had been plunged.

Julien received from the director the same welcome that had so terrified him the day he entered the seminary.

—Explain to me what you see written on this playing card, he said, looking at Julien in a manner to make him sink through the floor.

Julien read:

"Amanda Binet, Café of the Giraffe, before eight o'clock. Say you're from Genlis and my mother's cousin."

Julien saw the immensity of the peril; Abbé Castanède's agents had stolen this address from him.[2]

—The day I enrolled here, he said, looking at Abbé Pirard's forehead, for he could not endure his terrible glance, I was in terror: M. Chélan had told me this would be a place full of informers and all sorts of malice; spying and tale bearing are encouraged here. Heaven will have it so, to show young priests life as it is, and to fill them with disgust for the world and its empty displays.

—And you have the audacity to make phrases like that to me, cried Abbé Pirard in a rage. You young scoundrel!

—At Verrières, Julien replied cooly, my brothers used to beat me up when they had occasion to be jealous of me. . . .

—Come to the point! the point! cried M. Pirard, almost beside himself.

Without being in any way intimidated, Julien resumed his tale.

—The day of my arrival in Besançon, toward midday, I was hungry and entered a café. My heart was filled with detestation of a place so profane; but I bethought me that my lunch would cost less there than at a hotel. A lady, who seemed to be in charge of the place, took pity on my innocent air. Besançon is full of crooks, she told me; I fear for you, sir. If you get into any sort of trouble, call on me, send a message to my house before eight o'clock. If the porters at the seminary refuse to carry your message, say that you are my cousin, and come from Genlis. . . .

—All this fiddle-faddle will have to be investigated, cried Abbé Pirard, who was unable to sit still and had begun striding back and forth in the room.

---

2. Abbé Castanède, who turns up in Part II of the book as a full-fledged officer of the secret police, is Stendhal's idea of a Jesuit politician.

—Back to your cell with you!

The abbé followed Julien and locked him in. The latter at once began to look into his trunk, at the bottom of which the fatal card had been carefully hidden. Nothing was missing from the trunk, but several things were out of order; yet the key had never been out of his hands. What a good thing, thought Julien, that during the time of my blindness I never accepted that permission to leave the seminary offered me so assiduously by M. Castanède with a kindness I now understand. I might perhaps have been weak enough to change my garments and go to see the fair Amanda; I would be ruined. When they saw they couldn't use their information that way, rather than waste it, they made a direct charge out of it.

Two hours later the director sent for him.

—You didn't lie, he said to him with a less forbidding glance; but to keep such an address is an act of folly the gravity of which you cannot possibly conceive. Wretched boy! In ten years, perhaps, it may rise to harm your career.

Chapter 27

FIRST EXPERIENCE OF LIFE

The present time, great God! is like the ark of the covenant. Unhappy the man who touches it!

—Diderot[3]

The reader will kindly allow us to provide very few clear, precise facts on this period of Julien's life. It's not that we lack them, quite the contrary; but perhaps the life he lived at the seminary is too black for the middling colors we have tried to use in these pages. Modern men who suffer from certain things cannot recall them without a horror that freezes every other pleasure, even that of reading a story.

Julien had little success in his efforts at a hypocrisy of gestures; he fell into moments of disgust and even of complete discouragement. He was unsuccessful, and in a degrading career, at that. The least help from outside would have heartened him again; the difficulty to be overcome was not so great, but he was alone like a boat abandoned in the midst of the ocean. And suppose I succeed, he told himself; to pass one's whole life in such bad company! Gluttons who dream only of the ham omelet they are going to wolf down at dinner, or men like Abbé Castanède, for whom no crime is too repulsive! They'll rise to the seats of power, all right; but at what a price, good God!

3. The quotation from Diderot is invented; several possible alternative sources have been proposed.

Man's will is powerful, I read it everywhere; but is it strong enough to surmount disgust like mine? The great men of history had it easy; however terrible their test, they thought it beautiful; and who but myself can understand the ugliness of everything that surrounds me?

This moment was the most trying in his whole life. It would have been so easy for him to enlist in one of the fine regiments garrisoned at Besançon! Or he could live by teaching Latin; he needed so little to live on! But then, no more career, no more future for his imagination: it was death to think of. Here is a detailed account of one of his bitter days.

How often I used to flatter myself on being different from other young peasants! Well, I've lived enough to see that *difference begets hatred*, he told himself one morning. This great truth had just been brought home to him by one of his most irksome failures. He had been working for a week to please a student who lived in the odor of sanctity. They were walking together in the courtyard listening submissively to some paralyzing drivel. Suddenly the weather turned stormy, the thunder grumbled, and the saintly student exclaimed, shoving Julien away with a rude gesture:

—Look here now, it's everyone for himself in this world; I don't want to be struck by lightning: God may blast you as an unbeliever, a Voltaire.

His teeth clenched in rage, his eyes glaring up at the lightning-streaked sky, Julien cried aloud:

—I'd deserve to be crushed if I went to sleep during the tempest. All right, I'll have to try working on some other fag.

It was time for the course in sacred history given by Abbé Castanède.

The young peasants, terrified of their fathers' drudgery and poverty, learned from Abbé Castanède that the government which seemed so terrible to them, the government itself, had no real and legitimate power except as this was delegated to it by God's vicar on earth.

Render yourselves worthy of the Pope's bounty by the sanctity of your life, by your obedience, *be as a rod in his hands*, he added, and you will obtain a marvelous position where you will command from on high, free of all control; a post from which you cannot be dismissed, in which the government will pay one third of your salary, and the faithful, guided by your preachings, the other two thirds.

As he left the classroom, Abbé Castanède paused in the hallway [among his pupils, who that day were especially attentive].

—It's certainly true of priests what they say in general: a man gets what he earns. As he spoke, the students formed a circle around him.

—I myself have known, as sure as I'm speaking to you here, little mountain parishes where the perquisites came to more than many town priests get. There was just as much money, not to speak of the fat capons, the eggs, the fresh butter, the innumerable little delicacies here and there; and out in the country, the priest is number one and no rivals: never a good feast to which he's not invited, where he's not fussed over, etc.

Scarcely had M. Castanède retired to his apartment when the students split into groups. Julien belonged to none; they drew away from him as from a sheep with the scab. In each group he saw one of the students tossing a coin in the air; his success in calling heads or tails was supposed to indicate to his fellows whether he would shortly have one of those fat livings.

Next came the anecdotes. Such and such a young priest, scarcely ordained for a year, gave a tame rabbit to the servant of an old curé, got made vicar by that means, and then a few months later, for the old priest died almost at once, succeeded him in a snug berth. Another fellow had succeeded in getting himself named successor to the priest of a wealthy country town by attending at all the meals of the old curé, who was paralyzed, and cutting up his chicken very dexterously indeed.

Seminarians, like young men in all professions, exaggerate the effect of these little tricks whenever they're out of the ordinary and strike the imagination.[4]

I must take part in these conversations, Julien thought. When they weren't talking of sausages and good livings, their talk ran much to the worldly side of ecclesiastical politics; they talked of quarrels between bishops and prefects, between priests and mayors. Julien saw at the back of their minds the idea of a second God, a God much more powerful and more to be feared than the other; this second God was the Pope. It was actually murmured, but in an undertone and when M. Pirard could not possibly overhear, that if the Pope doesn't choose to name all the prefects and mayors of France himself, it's simply because he's entrusted this duty to the king of France, by naming him elder son of the church.

About this time Julien thought he might turn a profit on his knowledge of the book *The Pope*, by M. de Maistre.[5] As a matter of fact, he astounded his comrades; but even this was a misfortune. He irked them by expressing their own opinions better than they could themselves. M. Chélan had been a foolish counselor for Julien, as he had been for himself. After accustoming him to good logic and teaching him to avoid empty verbiage, he neglected to tell

4. Stendhal never tires of describing devices by which base ingenuity makes its way in the world.
5. De Maistre's book does not come far short of the seminarians' fantasies in proposing the power of the pope to appoint and dismiss heads of government.

him that in a person of low rank these customs are criminal; for all good reasoning is irksome.

Julien's fine speech was therefore a fresh offense. His comrades, having been compelled to notice him, succeeded in expressing all their horror of him in a single phrase; they nicknamed him *Martin Luther*; mainly, they said, because of that infernal logic of which he is so proud.

Several of the seminarians had fresher complexions and could be thought better looking than Julien, but his hands were white and he could not conceal certain habits of personal cleanliness. His advantage in this respect was not one in the gloomy quarters where fate had cast him. The dirty peasants among whom he lived declared that his morals were miserably lax. We are afraid of tiring the reader by describing the thousand misfortunes which befell our hero. For instance, the more muscular of his comrades tried to make a habit of beating him up; he was obliged to arm himself with an iron compass and to make plain, but by gestures, that he was ready to use it.[6] Gestures cannot be represented, in a spy's report, as conveniently as words.

Chapter 28

A PROCESSION

> All hearts were stirred. The presence of God seemed to descend upon these narrow, Gothic streets, stretching out in every direction and carefully sanded by the solicitude of the faithful.
>
> —Young[7]

It was useless for Julien to make himself humble and stupid; he could not please, he was too different. And yet, he said to himself, all these professors are clever men, chosen from among thousands; how is it they aren't pleased with my humility? Only one of them all seemed ready to accept his complaisance in believing everything and seeming the dupe of everyone. This was Abbé Chas-Bernard, director of ceremonies in the cathedral, in which he had been hoping for the last fifteen years to receive a canonry; while waiting, he taught sacred eloquence in the seminary. During the period of his blindness, Julien had regularly found himself in first place in this class. Abbé Chas had taken this as grounds for showing him some friendship, and after class would gladly take his arm for a stroll around the garden.

6. Another trait from Leti's biography of Sixtus V; Sixtus is said to have used a bundle of heavy keys, when he was in the monastery, to brain an inimical brother in Christ.
7. As on p. 140, the quotation is in French. It does not, by its content, suggest any particular Young (neither Edward nor Arthur, among the better-known Youngs) and is probably, like the previous epigraph, an invention of Stendhal's.

What's he getting at? Julien asked himself. He saw with astonishment that for hours on end Abbé Chas would talk to him about the ornaments the cathedral possessed. It had seventeen gold-braided chasubles, quite apart from the special trappings of mourning. They had high hopes of old President de Rubempré's widow;[8] this lady, who was ninety years old, had been keeping for at least seventy of those years her wedding dress, of superb Lyons silk embroidered with gold. Just imagine, my friend, said Abbé Chas, stopping short and opening his eyes very wide, these dresses will stand up by themselves, that's how much gold there is in them. It's a very general opinion in Besançon that, under the old lady's will, the treasury of the cathedral will be enriched by more than ten chasubles, not to mention four or five capes for high holy days. Nay, I will go further, added Abbé Chas, lowering his voice, I have good reason to think the President's widow will leave us eight magnificent silver-gilt candlesticks, which are supposed to have been bought in Italy by the Duke of Burgundy, Charles the Bold, whose favorite minister was an ancestor of hers.

But what's this man getting at with all this flimflam? Julien thought. He's been a century building up to something, but nothing comes. He must really be afraid of me! He's cleverer than the rest; you can see to the bottom of them in a couple of weeks. But I understand, this fellow's ambition has been on the rack for fifteen years!

One evening in the midst of military drill,[9] Julien was summoned by Abbé Pirard, who told him:

—Tomorrow is the feast of Corpus Christi. Father Chas-Bernard needs you to help decorate the cathedral, go and obey him.

Abbé Pirard called him back, and added in a tone of compassion:

—It's up to you whether you want to take a ramble through the town.

—*Incedo per ignes*,[1] replied Julien—that is to say, I'll watch my step.

Next morning at sunrise Julien reported to the cathedral, walking with lowered eyes. The sight of the streets, and of the bustle just beginning in the town, was good for him. Everywhere the house fronts were being decorated for the procession. All the time he had spent in the seminary now seemed to him no more than an instant.

8. Alberte de Rubempré, a cousin of Delacroix, had been for several months Stendhal's mistress, till she replaced him with Mérimée, and then replaced Mérimée with the Baron de Mareste; there is more than a touch of malice in the fictional age attributed to her here.
9. The idea that theological students were being drilled in their seminaries by Jesuit officers seems, at best, mildly paranoid; but it is in an old Voltairean tradition to represent the Jesuits as committed to using, in every way possible, the secular arm (see *Candide*, Chap. 14).
1. *incedo per ignes:* from Horace *Odes* II, i.

His thoughts were in Vergy, and with that pretty Amanda Binet whom he might just meet, as her café was not far off. In the distance he noted Abbé Chas-Bernard at the gate of his beloved cathedral; he was a bulky man with a jovial face and an open expression. On this particular day he was in his glory:

—I was expecting you, my dear son, he cried as soon as he saw Julien, you are welcome. The day's work will be long and hard; let us strengthen ourselves with a first breakfast; our second one will come at ten o'clock during high mass.

—Sir, said Julien gravely, I beg of you not to leave me alone for an instant; and will you be good enough to note, he added, pointing at the clock above their heads, that I came here at one minute before five.

—Ah, so you're afraid of those young imps at the seminary! You are too generous in giving them a thought, said Abbé Chas; is a road less beautiful because there are thorns in the hedges alongside it? Travelers push forward and leave the nasty thistles standing in their places. But now to work, my dear friend, to work.

Abbé Chas was right in saying the day's work would be hard. The day before there had been a great funeral service in the cathedral; nothing had been got ready; thus it was necessary, in one single morning, to cover all the Gothic columns lining the nave and the two aisles with a sort of red damask that was to be no less than thirty feet high. The bishop had imported four upholsterers from Paris by mail coach, but these gentlemen could not do the whole job themselves, and far from correcting the clumsiness of their helpers from Besançon, they increased it by making fun of them.

Julien saw that he must climb the ladder himself; his agility served him well. He took command of the local upholsterers. Abbé Chas watched in enchantment as he vaulted from ladder to ladder. When all the columns were draped in damask, the problem arose of placing five enormous bunches of feathers atop the huge canopy over the high altar. A rich crown of gilt wood was supported by eight big twisted columns of Italian marble. But to reach the center of the canopy, above the sanctuary, it would be necessary to walk across an old wooden cornice, probably worm-eaten and forty feet high.

The prospect of this dangerous climb extinguished the gaiety, hitherto so brilliant, of the Paris upholsterers; they looked up from below, discussed the matter at length, and did no climbing. Julien grasped the bunches of feathers and ran up the ladder. He placed them very suitably on the ornament, in the form of a crown at the center of the canopy. As he was climbing down the ladder, Abbé Chas-Bernard caught him in his arms:

—*Optime!* cried the good priest, I shall tell monsignor of that exploit.

Ten o'clock breakfast was very merry. Never had Abbé Chas seen his church look so well.

—My dear disciple, he told Julien, my mother used to rent out chairs in this venerable structure, so that in a way I was actually brought up here. Robespierre's terror ruined us; but at the age of eight, which I then was, I was already serving at private masses, and on mass day I got fed.[2] Nobody could outdo me at folding a chasuble; the braid was never broken. Since Napoleon restored the faith, I have been fortunate enough to manage everything in this ancient cathedral. Five times a year my eyes behold it decked in these splendid ornaments. But never has it been so splendid as today, never have the damask curtains been so well attached or clung so close to the columns.

—At last he's going to tell me his secret, thought Julien; he's got to talking about himself, there's a kind of warmth. But nothing in the least revealing was ever said by this man, though he was evidently in an exalted state. And yet he has worked hard, he is happy, said Julien to himself; and what's more, the good wine has not been spared. What a man! What an example for me! This takes the cake! (The latter was a low expression he recalled from the old surgeon.)

When the sanctus bell tolled during high mass, Julien made as if to put on a surplice in order to follow the bishop in the grand procession.

—And the robbers, my friend, the robbers! cried Abbé Chas, you've forgotten about them. The procession will go out; the church will be left empty; we'll watch over it, you and I. We'll be very lucky if we don't lose more than a few yards of that fine gold braid which runs around the foot of the columns. That's another gift from Mme. de Rubempré; it comes from the famous count her great grandfather; and it's pure gold, my friend, added the abbé, whispering into his ear with an air of great excitement, nothing imitation about it! I want you to take charge of inspecting the north aisle, don't leave it. I'll take on the south aisle and the nave. Keep an eye on the confessionals; that's where the robbers' girl-friends hang out to spy on us the moment our backs are turned.

As he finished his instructions the clock struck quarter of twelve, and shortly the big bell's tolling made itself heard. It was sounding at full volume; these rich, solemn tollings stirred Julien. His imagination rose from the earth.

The odor of incense and rose petals cast before the Blessed Sacrament by little children dressed as St. Johns completed his exaltation.

2. When the churches were closed, under the Terror, private masses were said in houses. The youthful Stendhal in Grenoble had assisted at some of these.

The solemn tolling of the bell should have caused Julien to think only of the work being done by twenty men at fifty centimes apiece and assisted perhaps by fifteen or twenty of the faithful. He should have calculated the wear and tear on the ropes or on the beams, should have considered the dangers from the bell itself, which falls every two centuries, and should have worked out ways to lower the pay of the ringers, or to pay them with an indulgence, or some other favor that can be drawn from the church's stockpile without depleting her purse.

Instead of these sensible calculations, Julien's soul, exalted by virile and capacious sounds, was wandering through imaginary space. Never will he make a good priest or a great administrator. Souls that can be so stirred are good, at most, to produce an artist. Here Julien's presumption makes itself fully apparent. Perhaps fifty of his comrades in the seminary, who had been awakened to life's realities by public hatred and the Jacobinism they had learned to suspect of lying in wait behind every hedge, would have thought when they heard the great bell of the cathedral only of the money being given to the ringers. They would have estimated, with the genius of a Barême,[3] whether the degree of emotion aroused in the public was worth the money being expended for labor. If Julien had tried to think of the material interests of the church, his imagination, rushing far beyond its goal, would have thought of saving forty francs on the construction and lost a chance to get out of paying twenty-five centimes.

While the procession moved slowly through Besançon, under the most beautiful sky one could want, and halted at all the glittering stations raised by the various authorities in competition with one another, the church remained perfectly silent. In the half darkness an agreeable coolness prevailed; the church was still embalmed with the perfume of flowers and incense.

The silence, the perfect solitude, the coolness of the long nave rendered Julien's reverie all the sweeter. He had no fear of being disturbed by Abbé Chas, who was busy in another part of the edifice. His soul had almost escaped its mortal envelope, which continued to stroll slowly up the north aisle, over which it was to watch. He was all the more at ease because he had made sure there was nobody in the confessionals but a few pious women; his eye looked without seeing.

But his vacant mood was partly distracted by the sight of two well-dressed women on their knees, one in a confessional, the other, near the first, seated on a chair. He looked at them without seeing them; but, then, whether it was a vague sense of duty or admiration

3. Barême was a seventeenth-century mathematician, author of a little book on accounting which made his name a household word for an accurate calculator.

for the refined simplicity of the ladies' dress, he reflected that there was no priest in that confessional. It's curious, he thought, that these fine ladies aren't kneeling before an altar, if they're religious, or aren't sitting in the front row of a balcony if they're of the world. How well that dress suits her! What grace! He slowed his pace in an effort to see them.

The one who was kneeling in the confessional turned her head aside a bit when she heard the sound of Julien's footsteps in the midst of that great stillness. Suddenly she gave a little shriek and fainted.

As she lost consciousness this kneeling lady fell back; her friend, who was nearby, rushed forward to help. At the same moment Julien saw the shoulders of the stricken lady. A rope of large pearls, well known to him, caught his eye. What were his feelings when he recognized the hair of Mme. de Rênal; it was she. The lady who was holding her head, and trying to keep her from falling full length, was Mme. Derville. Julien, beside himself, sprang forward; Mme. de Rênal's collapse might have dragged down her friend if Julien had not held them up. He saw Mme. de Rênal's head, pale and absolutely unconscious, drooping on her shoulder. He helped Mme. Derville to prop that charming head on the back of a wicker chair; he was on his knees.

Mme. Derville looked back and recognized him:

—Leave us, sir, leave us! she said to him, in accents of the most passionate anger. She must not see you again, whatever happens. The sight of you ought to be horrible for her; she was so happy before you came! Your actions are atrocious. Leave us; go away, if you have any shame left in you.

This speech was delivered with such authority, and Julien was so weak at this moment, that he left. She has always hated me, said he, thinking of Mme. Derville.

At the same time the nasal chanting of the first priests in the procession resounded through the church; the procession was returning. Abbé Chas-Bernard called several times for Julien, who at first did not hear him; at last he came and plucked him by the arm from behind a pillar where Julien had taken refuge, nearly dead. He wanted to introduce him to the bishop.

—But you're not feeling well, my child, said the abbé when he saw him so pale and almost incapable of walking; you've overworked. The abbé lent him an arm. Come sit down here on this little sacristan's bench beside me; I won't let you be seen. They were then beside the main entry. Calm yourself; we still have twenty good minutes before the bishop appears. Try to get your strength back; when he passes, I'll give you a hand, for I'm still strong and vigorous, in spite of my age.

But when the bishop passed by, Julien was so shaky that Abbé Chas gave up on the idea of introducing him.

—Don't worry about it, said he, I'll find another occasion.

That evening he sent to the seminary chapel ten pounds of candles, saved, as he said, by Julien's industry and the promptness with which he had put them out. Nothing could have been less true. The poor boy was extinguished himself; he had not had a single idea since catching sight of Mme. de Rênal.

Chapter 29

A FIRST PROMOTION

He knew his century, he knew his district, and he is rich.
—*The Precursor*[4]

Julien had not yet emerged from the long reverie into which he had been plunged by events in the cathedral when one morning he was summoned by stern Abbé Pirard.

—Here is Abbé Chas-Bernard who writes me a letter in your favor. I'm pretty well pleased with your conduct as a whole. You are extremely rash and even scatterbrained, that's perfectly apparent; but so far your heart seems to be good, even generous; the mind is superior. All in all, I see in you a spark that must not be put out.

After fifteen years of labor, I am about to leave this establishment: my crime is having left the seminarians to their own free wills, to have neither protected nor harmed that secret society of which you told me in the confessional.[5] Before I leave, I want to do something for you; I might have acted two months sooner, for you deserve it, had it not been for that denunciation based on the address of Amanda Binet found in your possession. I create you tutor in the Old and New Testaments.

Julien, overwhelmed with gratitude, had the notion of falling to his knees and thanking God; but he yielded to a truer impulse. He went up to Abbé Pirard, took his hand, and carried it to his lips.

—What's this? exclaimed the director, with an angry look; but Julien's eyes were even more eloquent than his action.

Abbé Pirard looked at him in astonishment, like a man who for many long years has been out of the way of delicate feelings. This moment of thought betrayed the director; his voice changed.

4. *The Precursor* was a Lyons newspaper. But with a hero destined for decollation, Stendhal may have had special reasons for wanting to get its title into his book.
5. On the oblique angle at which this secret society and the military drill in the seminary (see p. 152) enter the narrative, see "France in 1830" in the "Backgrounds and Sources" section of this edition.

—Well, yes, my child, it's true, I'm fond of you. Heaven knows, it's not of my impulse. I must be just and bear neither hate nor love toward anyone. Your career will be a hard one. I see in you a quality that offends the vulgar mob. Jealousy and calumny will dog you. Wherever providence leads you, your comrades will never be able to look upon you without hatred; if they pretend to love you, it will be only to betray you more securely. Against all this there is just one remedy; put your trust only in God, who bestowed upon you, as a punishment for your presumption, this quality of making enemies. Let your conduct be pure; I see no other safety for you. If you hold to the truth with unshakable strength, sooner or later your enemies will be confounded.

It had been so long since Julien heard a friendly voice that he must be pardoned for a weakness; he burst into tears. Abbé Pirard opened his arms; the moment was precious for them both.

Julien was mad with joy; this promotion was his first; it brought him immense advantages. To imagine them, one must have been condemned to pass months on end without an instant of solitude and in the immediate presence of comrades who were irksome at best and mostly unbearable. Their guffaws alone would have been enough to disorder a delicate system. The exuberant spirits of these well-fed, well-dressed peasants could find relief, could fulfill themselves completely, only when they were shouting at the top of their lungs.

Now, Julien ate alone, or almost so, an hour later than the other seminarians. He had a key to the garden and could walk there whenever it was empty.

To his great astonishment, Julien found himself less hated; he had expected a storm of spite. His secret wish not to be talked to, which was all too apparent and had earned him so many enemies, was no longer a token of ridiculous arrogance. In the opinion of the gross boors around him, it evinced a proper sense of his own dignity. The hatred ebbed perceptibly, above all among his younger fellow-students, who now became his pupils and whom he treated with great politeness. Gradually he even gained some supporters; it was ill bred to call him Martin Luther.

But why enumerate his friends, his enemies? It's all ugly, and all the uglier because the picture is a true one. Yet these are the only teachers of morality that the populace has, and without them what would become of it? Can the daily newspaper ever replace the priest?

Since Julien's new dignity, the director of the seminary made a point of never talking to him except in the presence of a third party. This behavior showed prudence on the part of the master, as well as for the disciple; but, more than anything, it represented a *test*. The invariable principle of the severe Jansenist Pirard was this: Does a man have merit in your eyes? then put obstacles in the way of everything he wants, everything he undertakes. If his merit is real, he'll be able to overturn or get around the obstacles.

Hunting season came, and Fouqué had the notion of sending to the seminary a buck and a boar, as from Julien's relatives. The dead animals were laid in the passageway between the kitchen and the refectory. There all the seminarians saw them as they came to dinner. They aroused much comment. The boar, dead as he was, terrified the younger seminarians; they fingered his tusks. Nothing else was talked of for a week.

This gift, which classed Julien's family in the section of society that must be respected, put an end for good to envy. His superiority had been consecrated by fortune. Chazel and the most distinguished of the seminarians made approaches to him, and almost reproached him openly for not having told them his family was rich, since he had thereby exposed them to the crime of showing disrespect for money.

There was a conscription call from which Julien, as a seminarian, was exempt. This incident moved him deeply. Well then, there goes the moment at which, if I'd lived twenty years ago, a life of heroic action would have begun for me!

He was walking alone in the seminary garden and overheard a talk between two masons working on the cloister wall.

—Well, we'd better clear out, here's a new conscription come along.

—In the *other man's* time, well, that was more like it! a mason got to be officer, got to be general; that happened once.[6]

But look at it now! Nobody goes but the beggars. Anyone who's *anybody* stays home.

—If you're born poor, you stay poor, that's how it is.

—Hey, tell me now, is it true what they say, asked a third mason, is the other man really dead?

—That's what the bigshots tell us, get it? They were scared of that other one.

—What a difference, the way things got done in his day! And they say he was betrayed by his marshals. There's always a traitor somewhere!

This conversation brought Julien some comfort; as he walked away, he repeated with a sigh:

The only king whose memory the people cherish![7]

6. Among Napoleon's senior staff, Murat was the son of an innkeeper, Masséna of a wine merchant, and Ney (like the bishop of Châlons in Chapter XXVI) of a tub maker. These masons are, of course, not only casual workmen but also free masons.
7. A verse that was originally applied to Henri IV and used to be written on the base of his statue on the Pont-Neuf.

Examination time came around. Julien answered brilliantly; he saw that even Chazel was doing his utmost.

On the first day, the examiners appointed by the famous grand vicar de Frilair were distressed at having always to rank first, or at worst, second, on their lists that Julien Sorel who had been pointed out to them as the Benjamin of Abbé Pirard.[8] Bets were placed within the seminary that in the over-all classification Julien would rank first, an eminence that carried with it the honor of dining with the bishop. But at the end of one session where the questions had dealt with the church fathers, a clever examiner, after questioning Julien on St. Jerome and his passion for Cicero, began to talk of Horace, Virgil, and other pagan writers. Working in secret, Julien had learned by heart a number of passages by these authors. Carried away by his own success, he forgot his circumstances, and under urgent questioning by the examiner repeated and paraphrased enthusiastically several odes of Horace. Having let him dig his own grave for twenty minutes, the examiner abruptly changed his expression and bitterly reproached him for wasting his time on these profane studies which could do nothing but fill his head with useless or criminal notions.

—I am a fool, sir, and you are absolutely right, said Julien modestly, recognizing the clever trick which had been played on him.

The examiner's trap was considered unfair, even in the seminary, but this opinion did not prevent Abbé de Frilair, that clever man who had woven so skillfully the network of the congregation in Besançon, whose dispatches to Paris struck terror into judges, prefects, and general officers of the garrison, it did not prevent him from placing the number 198 alongside the name of Julien Sorel. He was overjoyed to humiliate in this way his old enemy, Abbé Pirard.

For the last ten years the main business of his life had been to remove Pirard from administration of the seminary. The latter, following in his own life the policies he had outlined to Julien, was sincere, pious, free of intrigue, attached to his duty. But fate, for his sins, had given him a bilious temperament, prone to resent bitterly insults and hatred. Not one of the affronts offered to him was ever overlooked by this ardent spirit. He would have resigned a hundred times over, except that he thought himself useful in the post that providence had assigned him. I'm holding up the advances of Jesuitism and idolatry, he told himself.

At the time of the examinations, it was perhaps two months since he had addressed a word to Julien, and yet he was sick for

8. Benjamin: child of the right hand, favorite son.

a week when upon receiving the official letter announcing the results he saw the number 198 placed by the name of that student whom he considered the glory of his house. The only consolation open to this stern man was to concentrate on Julien all his methods of surveillance. He was overjoyed to discover in him neither resentment nor any project of revenge, nor discouragement.

Several weeks later Julien shuddered at receiving a letter; it bore a Paris postmark. At last, he thought, Mme. de Rênal has remembered her promises. Someone signing himself Paul Sorel and claiming to be his relative sent him a bill of exchange for five hundred francs. There was a further note that if Julien continued his successful study of good Latin authors, a similar sum would be sent him each year.

It is she, that's her goodness, Julien said to himself with feeling, she wants to comfort me; but why not a single word of affection?

He was mistaken about this letter. Mme. de Rênal, under the influence of her friend Mme. Derville, was wholly given over to her deep regrets. In spite of herself, she thought frequently of the strange being whose passage through her life had so convulsed it, but she never considered writing to him.

If we were talking seminary language, we might call this gift of five hundred francs a miracle, and say that heaven was making use of M. de Frilair himself in order to bestow this bounty on Julien.

Twelve years before, Abbé Frilair had arrived in Besançon with a very slender carpetbag, which, as the story went, contained his entire fortune. He now found himself one of the richest landowners in the district. In the course of making all this money, he had bought half a property, the other half of which passed by inheritance to M. de La Mole. Hence a great lawsuit between these two figures.

In spite of his brilliant life in Paris and appointments at court, the Marquis de La Mole sensed that it might be dangerous to make war in Besançon upon a grand vicar who was reputed to be a maker and unmaker of prefects. Instead of arranging a little fifty-thousand-franc tip for himself, disguised under some word or other that would pass in the budget, and then abandoning to Abbé de Frilair his grubby fifty-thousand-franc action, the marquis took umbrage. He thought his case was good; as if that were a proper legal consideration!

For, if one may presume to ask: where is the judge who doesn't have a son, or at any rate a cousin, to push forward in the world?

As if to convince the blindest, a week after he won his first judgment, Abbé de Frilair took the bishop's own private carriage and went himself to bestow the cross of the Legion of Honor on his lawyer. M. de La Mole, taken aback by the boldness of his enemies and feeling his own lawyers weakening, took counsel with Abbé Chélan, who put him in touch with M. Pirard.

At the time of our story these relations had already lasted several years. Abbé Pirard brought to the business his naturally impulsive character. Consulting continually the lawyers of the marquis, he studied the whole case, found the marquis in the right, and openly became his partisan against the all-powerful grand vicar. The latter was infuriated by such insolence, and to have it coming from a little Jansenist was worse!

—You see what this court nobility amounts to, though it pretends to be so powerful, Abbé de Frilair used to say to his friends. M. de La Mole has not even sent one miserable cross to his agent at Besançon, and is going to let him be dismissed from his job without a murmur. And yet they tell me this noble peer never lets a week pass without going to display his blue ribbon in the drawing room of the keeper of the seals, for whatever that's worth.

In spite of Abbé Pirard's best efforts, and though M. de La Mole was on the best of terms with the minister of justice and particularly with his agents, the best he had been able to do after six years of effort was to keep from losing his case outright.

In continual correspondence with Abbé Pirard over matters both of them followed with passion, the marquis gradually came to appreciate the abbé's way of thinking. Little by little, despite the immense difference in their social positions, their correspondence took on the tones of friendship. Abbé Pirard told the marquis that he was being forced by repeated outrages to tender his resignation. Furious at the infamous stratagem he said had been employed against Julien, he described his pupil's story to the marquis.

Though extremely rich, this great lord was by no means miserly. He had never been able to prevail on Abbé Pirard to accept reimbursement even for the postal charges occasioned by the trial. He seized the occasion to send five hundred francs to his favorite pupil.

M. de La Mole took the trouble to write in his own hand the covering letter. This made him think of the abbé.

One day the latter received a little note requesting him to go at once, on a matter of urgent business, to an inn in the suburbs of Besançon. There he met M. de La Mole's steward.

—M. le Marquis has instructed me to bring you his carriage, said this man. He hopes that when you have read this letter it will suit your purposes to leave for Paris within four or five days. I will spend the time until you are ready in visiting the estates of M. le Marquis, here in the Franche-Comté. After which, on the day you see fit, we will leave for Paris.

The letter was brief:

—My dear sir, set aside all these provincial squabbles, come breathe a calmer air in Paris. I have sent you my carriage with orders to wait four days for your decision. I shall wait for you myself, in Paris, until Tuesday. All I need from you is one word, *yes*, to accept, in your name, one of the best livings in the neighborhood of Paris. The richest of your future parishioners has never laid eyes on you, but is more devoted to you than you can imagine; he is the Marquis de La Mole.

Without altogether realizing it, stern Abbé Pirard loved this seminary which was full of his enemies, and to which, for fifteen years on end, he had devoted all his thoughts. M. de La Mole's letter was for him the appearance of a surgeon charged with performing a painful and necessary operation. His dismissal was a certainty. He told the steward to return in three days.

For forty-eight hours he was in a fever of uncertainty. Then he wrote to M. de La Mole, and composed for the bishop a letter, a masterpiece of ecclesiastical style but a bit long. It would have been hard to find more impeccable expressions, or any which breathed a more sincere respect. And yet this letter, intended to give M. de Frilair an awkward hour with his patron, listed all the serious grounds of complaint and descended into all the little dirty tricks which now, after he had endured them with resignation for six years, had forced Abbé Pirard to leave the diocese.

They stole the wood out of his shed, they poisoned his dog, etc., etc.

His letter completed, he had Julien waked; at eight o'clock in the evening, he was already asleep, like all the other seminarians.

—You know where the bishop's palace is? he asked him, speaking classical Latin. Take this letter to Monsignor. I shall not conceal from you that you are entering the wolf pit. Be all eyes and all ears. No lies in any of your answers; but remember, the man who is questioning you would perhaps be overjoyed to do you harm. I am glad, my child, to give you this experience before leaving you, for I shan't conceal it, this letter is my resignation.

Julien stood stock still; he loved Abbé Pirard. It was useless for prudence to remind him:

After this honest man leaves, the party of the Sacred Heart will dismiss me from my post and perhaps drive me out of the seminary altogether.

He could not think of himself. What troubled him was a sentence he wanted to cast in an elegant form, but for which his mind refused to serve him.

—Well, young man, aren't you going?

—Well, sir, you see, they say, Julien said timidly, that during your long administration here you have never put anything aside. I have six hundred francs.

Tears prevented him from continuing.

—*That too will be observed,* said the ex-director of the seminary, coldly. Go to the palace, it is getting late.

As luck would have it, Abbé de Frilair was on duty that evening in the bishop's drawing room; Monsignor was dining at the prefecture. It was therefore M. de Frilair himself to whom Julien delivered the letter, though he did not realize this.

Julien saw with amazement that this abbé boldly opened the letter addressed to the bishop. The handsome features of the grand vicar soon showed surprise mingled with lively pleasure, then an access of gravity. As he read, Julien, struck by his handsome features, took time to inspect him. The face would have had more weight if it were not for the extreme subtlety that appeared in several expressions, and which might even have indicated dishonesty if the owner of that fine face had ceased for a moment to compose it. The prominent nose formed a single absolutely straight line and unfortunately gave to a countenance, perfectly distinguished in every other respect, an unalterable resemblance to a fox. For the rest, this abbé who seemed so concerned with the resignation of M. Pirard was dressed with an elegance that delighted Julien, and that he had never seen in any other priest.

Only later did Julien discover the special talent of M. de Frilair. He knew how to entertain his bishop, a kindly old man intended by nature to live in Paris, who regarded Besançon as a place of exile. This bishop had weak eyes and was passionately fond of fish. Abbé de Frilair boned the fish that was served to the bishop.

Julien was watching silently as the abbé reread the letter of resignation, when suddenly the door opened with a crash. A lackey in full finery passed swiftly through the room. Julien had scarcely time to turn toward the door; he saw a little old man wearing a pectoral cross. He fell on his knees; the bishop cast him a kindly smile and passed on. The handsome abbé followed him out, and Julien remained alone in the drawing room to admire its sacred magnificence at leisure.

The bishop of Besançon, a man whose character had been tested but not crushed by long years of trouble as an *emigré*, was more than seventy-five years old and cared very little indeed what would be happening ten years from now.

—Who is that clever-looking seminarian whom I seemed to see as I came in? asked the bishop. Shouldn't they all be in bed, as my rule is, at this hour?

—This one is wide awake, I assure you, Monsignor, and he brings great news; it's the resignation of the last Jansenist left in your diocese. At last that terrible Abbé Pirard has taken the hint.

—All right, said the bishop with a laugh, but I defy you to replace him with a man as good. And to show you the value of this man, I'm going to invite him to dinner tomorrow.

The grand vicar wanted to slip in a few words on the choice of a successor; but the bishop, feeling indisposed to talk business, said to him:

—Before we bring in a new man, let's learn a little about the old one. Bring in that seminarian; there's truth in the mouths of babes.

Julien was summoned: I'm going to be caught between two inquisitors, he thought. Never had he felt himself more courageous.

As he entered, two tall valets, better dressed than M. Valenod himself, were disrobing Monsignor. The prelate, before getting around to M. Pirard, thought it his duty to ask Julien about his studies. He asked a few questions about dogma and was astonished. Soon he turned to humanistic studies, Virgil, Horace, Cicero. Those are the names, Julien thought, that earned me my rank of 198. I have nothing to lose, I'll try to shine. He was successful; the prelate, an excellent humanist himself, was delighted.

At dinner in the prefecture a girl, whose fame was well deserved, had recited the poem "La Madeleine."[9] The bishop was in the vein of literary talk and quickly forgot M. Pirard and all business matters in order to discuss with the seminarian an important question, whether Horace was rich or poor. The prelate cited several odes, but sometimes his memory failed him and Julien would recite the whole poem with a modest air; what struck the bishop most was that Julien never departed from the tone of good conversation; he recited his twenty or thirty Latin verses as he would have described events in the seminary. They talked for a long time of Virgil, of Cicero. At last the prelate could not refrain from paying the young seminarian a compliment.

—It would be impossible to pursue one's studies more successfully.

—Monsignor, said Julien, your seminary can furnish you with a hundred ninety-seven subjects far less unworthy of your esteemed approbation.

—How's that? said the prelate, astounded at the figure.

—I can furnish official proof of what I have the honor of affirming before Monsignor.

9. Delphine Gay, who in 1831 would become Mme. de Girardin, wrote "La Madeleine"; Stendhal admired her poetic talents but did not wholly appreciate her habit of giving frequent recitations of her poetry.

At the annual examination of the seminary, when I answered precisely on the topics which at this moment earn me Monsignor's approbation, I received the rank of 198.

Ah, it's the Abbé Pirard's Benjamin, cried the bishop with a laugh and a glance at M. de Frilair; we ought to have expected this; but it's fair play. Tell me, young man, he added, turning to Julien, did they wake you up to send you here?

—Yes, Monsignor. I have left the seminary unaccompanied only once in my life, to help Abbé Chas-Bernard decorate the cathedral on the feast of Corpus Christi.

—*Optime*, said the bishop; then you were the one who showed so much courage in placing the bunches of feathers atop the canopy? Every year I'm terrified of that; I'm always afraid they'll cost the life of a man. My young friend, you will go far; but I don't want to cut short your brilliant career by making you die of hunger.

And, on the bishop's orders, servants brought in some biscuits and Malaga wine, to which Julien did justice, and the Abbé de Frilair did even more justice, since he knew his bishop liked to see people eat merrily and with good appetite.

The prelate, feeling more and more cheerful at the end of his evening, spoke a little on church history. He saw that Julien understood nothing of it. The prelate passed on to the moral condition of the Roman empire under the emperors of Constantine's age. The end of paganism was accompanied by a state of uneasiness and doubt such as brings desolation to gloomy and bored souls in the nineteenth century. Monsignor remarked that Julien seemed scarcely to know even the name of Tacitus.

Julien replied frankly, to the prelate's astonishment, that this author was not to be found in the seminary library.

—I'm happy to hear it, said the bishop cheerfully. You've relieved me of a difficulty: for the past ten minutes I've been thinking of a way to thank you for this pleasant evening you've provided for me, and in a most unexpected fashion. I didn't expect to find a man of learning in a student of my seminary. Though the gift may not be too canonical, I should like to present you with a complete Tacitus.

The prelate sent for the set of eight volumes, handsomely bound, and undertook to write himself, on the title page of the first, a compliment in Latin to Julien Sorel. The bishop prided himself on his Latinity; he ended by saying, in a serious tone quite different from that of the rest of the conversation:

—Young man, if you *behave yourself*, you shall one day have the best living in my diocese, and not a hundred leagues from the episcopal palace itself; but you must *behave*.

Weighed down by his volumes, Julien left the palace in a state of great astonishment, about midnight.

The bishop had not said a word to him about Abbé Pirard. Julien had been struck, above all else, by the bishop's extreme politeness. He had never before conceived of such urbanity in the social forms, combined with such natural dignity. Julien was particularly struck by the contrast when he saw somber Abbé Pirard, who was waiting for him in a state of high impatience.

—*Quid tibi dixerunt?* (What did they say to you?) he cried at the top of his voice, as soon as he caught sight of Julien.

Julien had a little trouble translating into Latin the conversation of the bishop:

—Speak French, and recite the bishop's actual words, without adding or omitting anything, said the ex-director in his harsh voice and inelegant manner.

—What a strange gift from a bishop to a young seminarian! said he, fingering through the superb Tacitus, the gilded spine of which seemed to fill him with horror.

Two o'clock had struck when, after a long and detailed report, he at last allowed his favorite pupil to return to his room.

—Leave with me the first volume of your Tacitus, in which the bishop's Latin compliment is inscribed, said he. That line of Latin will be your lightning rod in this house after I am gone.

Erit tibi, fili mi, successor meus tanquam leo quaerens quem devoret. (For to you, my son, the man who succeeds me will be like a hungry lion, seeking whom he may devour.)

Next morning Julien found something strange in the way his fellow-students spoke to him. This made him all the more withdrawn. Here now, said he, is an effect of M. Pirard's resignation. It's known throughout the house, and I'm considered his favorite. There must be an insult in these new manners; but he could not discover it. On the contrary, there seemed to be less hatred in the eyes of all those he met throughout the dormitories. What does this mean? A trap, no doubt; I'd better play it close. At last the little seminarian from Verrières said to him, laughingly: *Cornelii Taciti opera omnia* (Complete Works of Tacitus).

At this word, which was overheard, all the others vied with one another to compliment Julien, not only on the magnificent gift received from Monsignor but on the two-hour conversation with which he had been honored. They knew about it down to the smallest details. From that moment on there was no more envy; everyone paid court to him humbly: Abbé Castanède, who only the day before had behaved toward him with the utmost insolence, now came to take him by the arm and invite him to luncheon.

By a freak in Julien's character, the insolence of these boors had caused him great pain; their humility caused him disgust and no pleasure.

Toward midday Abbé Pirard left his pupils, not without addressing to them a severe lecture.

—Do you want the honors of the world, he asked them, social
advantages, the pleasures of authority, the pleasure of deriding the
laws and being insolent to all men with impunity? Or else do you
want eternal salvation? The least brilliant among you have only to
open their eyes to see the two paths.

Scarcely had he left the seminary when the devotees of the
Sacred Heart of Jesus went off to intone a *Te Deum* in the chapel.
No one in the seminary took seriously the ex-director's last lecture.
He is bitterly angry at being dismissed, they said on all sides; not a
single seminarian had the simplicity to believe he had voluntarily
resigned a post that put him in touch with so many big contractors.

Abbé Pirard took a room in the finest inn of Besançon; and
under pretext of some business, which really he did not have, proposed to spend a couple of days there.

The bishop had invited him to dinner; and by way of a joke on
his grand vicar de Frilair, undertook to make him shine. They were
in the midst of dessert when there arrived from Paris news that
Abbé Pirard was named to the magnificent living of N_____, just
four leagues from the capital. The good prelate congratulated him
sincerely. He saw in the whole business a well-played game which
put him in good spirits and gave him the highest opinion of the
abbé's talents. He presented him with a magnificent Latin certificate and imposed silence on Abbé de Frilair when he ventured to
complain.

That evening Monsignor expressed his admiration in the drawing
room of the Marquise de Rubempré. It was great news in the upper
circles of Besançon society; people bewildered themselves with con-
jectures about this extraordinary shift in favor. They saw Abbé
Pirard as a bishop already. The cleverest ones guessed that M. de
La Mole was now a minister, and for this one day permitted themselves to smile at the imperious airs which Abbé de Frilair assumed
in society.

Next morning Abbé Pirard was almost followed through the
streets, and merchants came to the doorways of their shops when
he went to confer with the judges in the marquis' case. For the first
time he was politely received. The stern Jansenist, indignant at
everything he saw, worked for a long time with the lawyers he had
chosen for the Marquis de La Mole and then left for Paris. He
was weak enough to tell two or three old friends, who accompanied
him to the carriage and stood there admiring the coat of arms, that
after administering the seminary for fifteen years he was leaving
Besançon with savings of five hundred twenty francs. The friends
bade him farewell with tears in their eyes, then said among them-

selves: really, the good abbé might have spared us that lie, it's much too ridiculous.

Vulgar men, blinded by cupidity, were unable to understand that his sincerity alone had given Abbé Pirard the strength to struggle singlehanded for six years against Marie Alacoque, the Sacred Heart of Jesus, the Jesuits, and his bishop.

Chapter 30

AMBITION

> There's only one really noble rank left, that's the title of *duke;* marquis
> is ridiculous, at the word *duke* heads turn round.
> —*Edinburgh Review*[1]

The abbé was surprised by the noble air and almost gay manners of the marquis. Yet this future minister received Abbé Pirard without any of those little lordly tricks so polite but so impertinent for a man who understands them. It would have been time wasted, and the marquis was deep enough in public business to have no time to waste.

For six months he had been scheming to make the king and the nation both accept a certain minister who, out of gratitude, would make him a duke.

The marquis had been vainly demanding from his Besançon lawyer for some years now a clear, exact accounting of his lawsuit in the Franche-Comté. How could the celebrated lawyer possibly have explained it, since he didn't understand it himself?

A little slip of paper which the abbé handed him, explained everything.

—My dear abbé, said the marquis, having dispatched in less than five minutes all the polite formulas and personal questions, my dear abbé, in the midst of all my surface prosperity, I have no time to concern myself with two little matters which for all that are pretty important: my family and my business affairs. I concern myself in a broad way with the interests of my house, I may carry it far; I concern myself with my own pleasures, and that's what should come first, at least in my opinion, he went on, noting some surprise in the glance of Abbé Pirard. Though a person of sense, the abbé was amazed to see an old man talking so frankly of his pleasures.

No doubt work gets done in Paris, the nobleman continued, but only in the garrets, and as soon as I come to terms with a man, he moves down to the second floor and his wife starts a *day;*[2] and then, no more work, no effort for anything except being or seeming a man

---

1. Another faked epigraph.
2. A social "day" appointed for callers, conversation, cards, scandal; a salon.

of the world. As soon as they have their daily bread, that's all they care for.

For my lawsuits, of course, and actually for each individual lawsuit, I have lawyers who work themselves to death; one of them had a stroke just the other day. But as for my general business, would you believe it, my dear sir, for the last three years I've been without hope of finding a man who, while he's writing something for me, will condescend to think a little seriously of what he's doing? But this is all a preface.

I think well of you, and I will venture to add, though this is our first meeting, I'm going to like you. Will you serve as my secretary, with a salary of eight thousand francs, or, if you like, twice that much? I shall be the gainer, I assure you; and I shall make it my business to hold onto your fine living, against the day when we no longer get on with one another.

The abbé declined, but toward the end of the conversation he saw the marquis was in genuine difficulties, and this suggested an idea to him.

—I left, back in my seminary, a poor young man who, unless I'm much mistaken, is going to be brutally persecuted. If he were only a simple religious, he would already be *in pace*.[3]

So far this young man knows nothing but Latin and the Holy Scriptures; but it's not impossible that one day he will give proof of great talents, either for preaching or for the cure of souls. I don't know which way he will go; but he has the sacred fire, and may go far. I was counting on sending him to our bishop if ever we had one with a little of your way of looking at men and business.

—Where does your young man come from? asked the marquis.

—They say he's the son of a carpenter in our mountains, but I rather suspect he's the natural son of some rich man.[4] I have seen him get an anonymous or pseudonymous letter containing a note of exchange for five hundred francs.

—Ah! it's Julien Sorel, said the marquis.

—How do you know his name? said the abbé in astonishment; and as he was blushing for that question:

—That is what I am not going to tell you, replied the marquis.

—Very well, said the abbé, you could try to make him your secretary; he has energy and good judgment; in a word, he's worth a try.

—Why not? said the marquis; but is he the sort of man to let his palm be greased by the prefect of police, or somebody else, to play the spy on me? That's my only objection.

3. *in pace:* in peace, that is, dead.
4. Julien's illegitimacy, never hinted at before, is merely a suspicion here but will grow to become almost an article of faith. Like Fabrizio, Julien is or may be a bastard because Stendhal wants to suggest how far "outside" society he stands.

Having received favorable assurances from Abbé Pirard, the marquis produced a thousand-franc note.

—Send this to Julien Sorel for traveling money; tell him to come.

—It's clear to see, Abbé Pirard told him, that you live in Paris. [Placed as you are in an elevated social position,] you don't appreciate the weight of tyranny that lies on us poor provincials, especially on priests who aren't friendly with the Jesuits. They won't want to let Julien Sorel go; they'll cover themselves with clever pretexts, they'll tell me he's sick, the post office will have mislaid letters, etc., etc.

—One of these days I shall carry a letter from the minister to that bishop of yours, said the marquis.

—I forgot one word of warning, added the abbé: this young man, though of low birth, has a high spirit; he will be of no use to you [in your business] if his pride is ruffled; you would only make him stupid.

—That rather pleases me, remarked the marquis, I shall make him my son's comrade; will that be good enough?

Shortly after, Julien received a letter written in an unknown hand and postmarked from Châlons; it contained a draft on a merchant in Besançon and instructions to proceed to Paris without delay. The letter was signed with an assumed name, but as he opened it, Julien trembled: a dried leaf had fallen at his feet; that was the sign he had arranged with Abbé Pirard.[5]

Less than an hour later Julien was called to the episcopal palace, where he was received with paternal warmth. Even as he cited verses of Horace, Monsignor referred to the lofty destinies awaiting him in Paris, making a series of extremely clever compliments which practically required, from the responder, some sort of explanation. Julien could say nothing, mainly because he knew nothing, and the bishop showed him many marks of high esteem. One of the little priests about the palace wrote to the mayor, who hastened to bring over, in his own person, a passport which had been signed but on which the name of the traveler had been left blank.

That night before twelve o'clock Julien was with Fouqué, whose wise judgment expressed more surprise than pleasure at the future that seemed to open before his friend.

—It'll all end for you, said this liberal voter, with a post in the government which will involve you in a deal for which you'll be libeled in all the papers. I'll get news of you when you're in disgrace. Remember, even in a financial sense, it's better to earn a hundred

5. The Bucci copy reads: " . . . Julien trembled. A great blot of ink had fallen in the middle of the thirteenth word; that was the sign. . . . " And Stendhal explained his change in a further note: "The spy who opened the letter might not replace the leaf."

louis selling wood honestly, and owning your own business, than to get four thousand francs from a government, even King Solomon's.

Julien saw in this nothing but the petty spirit of a country bourgeois. At last he was going to make his appearance in the theater of the world. The happiness of going to Paris, which he supposed to be full of witty people, very devious, very hypocritical, but all as polite as the bishop of Besançon and the bishop of Agde, closed his eyes to every other consideration. To his friend he explained [in all humility] that he was practically deprived of his own free choice by Abbé Pirard's letter.

Next day about noon he arrived in Verrières, the happiest of men; he expected to see Mme. de Rênal again. He went first to his old protector, Abbé Chélan, where he found a gruff reception.

—Do you recognize any obligation at all to me? asked M. Chélan, without answering his greeting. Then you will have lunch with me; while you are eating, another horse will be rented for you, and you will leave Verrières *without seeing anybody else*.

—To hear is to obey, Julien replied with the meek mien of a seminarian; and they talked of nothing else but theology and good Latin.

He mounted his horse and rode a league, after which, seeing a wood and nobody around to spy on him, he hid himself within it. At sunset he sent back the horse. Later he went to the house of a peasant, who agreed to sell him a ladder and to help him carry it as far as the little grove which stands above LOYALTY SQUARE in Verrières.

—I'm helping out a poor draft dodger . . . or a smuggler of some sort, said the peasant as he bade him farewell; but why should I worry? my ladder has been well paid for, and I've had to get through some awkward moments in life myself.

The night was very dark. About one o'clock in the morning, Julien, burdened with his ladder, entered Verrières. As soon as he could, he climbed down into the bed of the stream which passes through M. de Rênal's magnificent gardens, in a gorge about ten feet deep between two walls. With the ladder Julien easily climbed to ground level. What sort of welcome will I get from the watchdogs? he thought, that's the whole question. The dogs barked and rushed at him; but he whistled softly and they came fawning toward him.

Climbing thus from terrace to terrace, though all the gates were shut, he found it easy to get just under the window of Mme. de Rênal's bedroom, which on the garden side is only eight or ten feet above ground level.

There was in the shutters a little opening in the shape of a heart, which Julien knew well. To his great distress, this little opening was not lit by the glow of a night light.

—Good Lord! said he to himself, Mme. de Rênal is not sleeping in this room tonight [otherwise there would be a light.] Where can she be? The family is in Verrières, since the dogs are out; but in this unlit room I may find M. de Rênal himself, or a stranger, and then what a scandal!

The wisest step was to withdraw; but the thought of such a step horrified Julien. If it's a stranger, I'll run away as fast as I can, leaving the ladder behind; but if it is she, how will she greet me? She has turned to remorse and profound piety, I can't doubt it; but anyhow, she still remembers me a little, since she just wrote to me. This reason determined him.

His heart trembled within him, but he was resolved to see her or perish; he threw some pebbles against the shutters, but there was no response. He leaned his ladder against the wall beside the window and knocked on the shutter, gently at first, then more sharply. In all this darkness they may go after me with a gun, Julien thought. This idea reduced the whole insane undertaking to a matter of physical bravery.

The room is empty tonight, he thought; if anyone were sleeping there, they'd be up by now. No need to worry about an occupant then; I just have to try not to be heard by people sleeping in other rooms.

He climbed down, set his ladder against one of the shutters, climbed up again, reached through the heart-shaped opening, and was lucky enough to find almost at once the metal wire attached to the latch that closed the shutter. He pulled at it, and felt, with indescribable joy, that the shutter was no longer locked, but yielded under his hand. I must open it gradually, and let my voice be recognized. He opened the shutter enough to get his head in, saying meanwhile in an undertone: *It is a friend.*

He made certain, by applying his ear, that the deep silence within the room was unbroken. But definitely there was no night light, not even a darkened one, on the mantelpiece; that was a bad sign indeed.

Keep an eye out for guns! He thought for a bit; then, with his finger, he ventured to rap on the windowpane: no answer; he tapped harder. Even if I break the glass, I have to get in. As he was knocking very loudly, he seemed to half see in the pitchy darkness a sort of white shadow crossing the room. Then he could no longer doubt; he saw a shadow that seemed to come toward him very slowly. Suddenly he saw a cheek pressed against the pane of glass to which he had applied his eye.

He shuddered and drew back. But the night was so dark that, even at that distance, he could not tell whether it was Mme. de Rênal. He feared lest there be a cry of alarm; he could hear the dogs prowling and growling around the foot of his ladder. It is I, he repeated quite loudly, a friend. No answer; the white phantom had disappeared. Please open up, I must talk with you, I am too wretched! and he knocked as if to smash the window.

A little dry noise was heard; the catch of the window opened; he pushed up the casement and leaped easily into the room.

The white phantom drew back; he grasped its arms; it was a woman. All his courageous ideas vanished in a flash. If it is she, what will she say? What were his feelings when he knew, by a little cry she gave, that it was Mme. de Rênal!

He strained her in his arms; she shuddered, and had scarcely strength to repel him.

—Wretch! What are you doing?

Her choked voice could scarcely articulate the words. Julien saw that she was genuinely angry.

—I have come to see you after fourteen months of cruel separation.

—Go away, leave me, this very instant. Ah, M. Chélan, why did you prevent me from writing to him? I might have prevented this horrible scene. She flung him away with a strength that was really extraordinary. I repent of my crime; God was good enough to enlighten me, she repeated in a muffled voice. Go away! Leave me!

—After fourteen months of misery, I certainly shan't leave without speaking to you. I want to know everything you've been doing. Ah, I have loved you well enough to deserve this confidence. . . . I want to know everything.

Despite Mme. de Rênal, this tone of authority had power over her heart.

Julien, who had been holding her passionately in his arms and resisting all her efforts to break loose, relaxed his grasp. This gesture reassured Mme. de Rênal somewhat.

—I am going to pull up the ladder, he said, so we shall not be discovered if some servant, roused by the noise, makes a tour of inspection.

—Ah, leave me, leave me instead, she said to him, in genuine rage. What do I care about men? It is God who sees the frightful situation you have created, and He will punish me for it. You are taking mean advantage of feelings I once had for you, but which I don't have any more. Do you understand that, Master Julien?

He drew up the ladder very slowly, in order to make no noise.

—Your husband is in town? he asked her, not out of impudence, but carried away by force of habit.

—Don't talk to me that way, if you please, or I'll call my husband. Already I'm all too guilty, I should have driven you away, whatever happened. I pity you, she told him, trying to wound his pride, which she knew to be sensitive.

Her refusal of intimacy, her brusque way of breaking a bond of tenderness on which he had still counted, raised Julien's transports of love to delirium.

—What now? Is it possible you no longer love me, he said to her, in those heartfelt tones which are so hard to hear unmoved.

She answered nothing; for his part, he was weeping bitterly [she heard the sound of his sobs.]

As a matter of fact, he no longer had strength to speak.

—So I'm completely forgotten by the only creature who ever loved me! What good to live now? All his courage had left him as soon as he no longer had to fear meeting a man; everything had left his heart except love.

For a long time he wept in silence. He took her hand, she tried to withdraw it; but after a few almost convulsive movements, she let him keep it. It was extremely dark; they found themselves seated side by side on Mme. de Rênal's bed.

What a difference from things as they were fourteen months ago! thought Julien; and his tears flowed more freely. Thus absence is sure to destroy all human feelings!

—Please tell me what has happened to you, Julien said at last, in a voice choked with sobs.

—Beyond any doubt, Mme. de Rênal began, in a sharp voice, the tone of which seemed to bear within it something dry and reproachful of Julien, my follies were known throughout the town at the time of your departure. You had been so imprudent in your behavior! Some time later, when I was in despair, that good man M. Chélan came to see me. For a long time he tried vainly to obtain a confession. One day he had the idea of taking me to that church in Dijon where I made my first communion. There he ventured to speak with me. . . . Mme. de Rênal was interrupted by her tears. What a shameful moment! I confessed everything. The good old man did not overwhelm me with the weight of his indignation; he sympathized with my sorrow. In those days I used to write you letters every day, which I didn't dare to post; I hid them away, and when I was too miserable, I used to shut myself in my room and reread my own letters.

Finally M. Chélan persuaded me to let him have them. . . . Some of them, written with a little more prudence than the rest, had been mailed to you; but you never answered.

—Never, I swear it, never did I receive a single letter from you at the seminary.

—Good God, who can have intercepted them?

—Imagine my wretchedness; until the day I saw you in the cathedral, I didn't know if you were alive or dead.

—God in his mercy gave me to understand how deeply I had sinned toward Him, toward my children, toward my husband, Mme.

de Rênal resumed. He has never loved me as I thought then that you loved me. . . .

Julien flung himself into her arms, acting blindly and instinctively. But Mme. de Rênal pushed him aside and continued with a certain firmness:

—My respectable friend M. Chélan showed me that in marrying M. de Rênal I had promised him all my affections, even those of which I was not yet aware, and which I had never experienced before a certain fatal affair. . . . Since the great sacrifice of those letters, which were so precious to me, my life has passed, if not happily, at least with a fair amount of calm. Don't disturb it; be a friend to me, the best of my friends. Julien covered her hand with kisses; she sensed that he was still weeping. Don't weep, you make me so unhappy. . . . Tell me now, what you have been doing. Julien could not speak. I want to know how you lived in the seminary, she repeated, then you will go away.

Without thinking of what he was saying, Julien described the intrigues and innumerable jealousies he had met with at first, then of the quieter life he had led since being named tutor.

That was the period, he added, when after a long silence which was clearly intended to show me, as I can see only too clearly now, that you no longer loved me, and that I had become a figure of indifference to you. . . . Mme. de Rênal pressed his hands. That was the period when you sent me a gift of five hundred francs.

—Never, said Mme. de Rênal.

—It was a letter postmarked Paris, and signed Paul Sorel, in order to avoid suspicion.

A little discussion sprang up on the possible source of this letter. The moral position shifted. Without realizing it, Mme. de Rênal and Julien had dropped the tone of solemnity; they had returned to that of tender friendship. They could not see one another, the darkness was too thick, but the tone of voice told all. Julien passed his arm around his mistress' waist; it was a risky gesture. She tried to dislodge Julien's arm, but he rather cleverly distracted her attention for the moment with an interesting episode in his story. The arm was forgotten and remained where it lay.

After many speculations on the sender of the five-hundred franc letter, Julien resumed his tale; he was gaining more control over himself as he talked on about his past life, which, actually, by comparison with what was happening at the moment, interested him very little. His thoughts were entirely concentrated on the way in which his visit would end. You must get out of here, she kept telling him from time to time, in a curt accent.

What a disgrace for me, if I'm given the gate! It will be a humiliation to poison my whole life, he thought to himself; and she will never write to me. God knows when I will ever return to this district! From that moment, whatever heavenly joy there was in Julien's position disappeared completely from his heart. Seated beside a woman whom he adored, holding her almost in his arms, in this room where he had been so happy, plunged in profound darkness, yet well aware that for the last minute she had been weeping, sensing from the motion of her breast that she was shaken with sobs, he unfortunately became a cold politician, almost as chilly and calculating as when in the seminary courtyard he saw himself the butt of some nasty trick played by a schoolfellow stronger than he. Julien spun out his story and talked of the unhappy life he had led since he left Verrières. That's how it is, said Mme. de Rênal to herself, after a year of absence during which he had no sign that anyone remembered him, he still thought only of the happy days at Vergy, while I was forgetting him. Her tears flowed more freely. Julien noted the success his story was having. He understood it was time to play his last card: he came abruptly to the letter he had just received from Paris.

—I have taken leave of Monsignor the bishop.

—What, you're not going back to Besançon! You're leaving us for good?

—Yes, Julien answered in a resolute tone; yes, I am leaving a land where I am forgotten even by the person I loved best in my life, and I'm leaving it never to return. I am going to Paris. . . .

—You're going to Paris! Mme. de Rênal cried aloud.

Her voice was almost choked with tears, and showed the violence of her grief. Julien had need of this encouragement; he was about to take a step that might decide everything against him; and before this exclamation, being unable to see anything, he had no notion of what effect he might produce. Now he hesitated no longer; fear of future regrets gave him complete command over himself; he added coldly as he rose to his feet:

—Yes, Madame, I am leaving you forever, be happy; farewell.

He took several steps toward the window; he was in the act of opening it. Mme. de Rênal ran to him and flung herself into his arms. [He felt her head on his shoulder, her cheek pressed against his.]

Thus, after three hours of discussion, Julien obtained what he had desired so passionately during the first two. Had they come a little sooner, the return to tender sentiments and the eclipsing of Mme. de Rênal's remorse might have been the occasion of heavenly joy; but obtained as they were with art, they yielded nothing more than gratification. Julien absolutely insisted, against the pleas of his mistress, on lighting the night light.

—Would you prefer, he asked her, that I not have a single memory of having seen you? Is the love which doubtless fills those charming eyes to be lost to me forever? Will I never be able to see the whiteness of that lovely hand? Think that I may be leaving you for a very long time.

[What a disgrace! said Mme. de Rênal to herself; but she] had no objection to raise against this idea which caused her to dissolve in tears. Dawn was starting to outline the shapes of the pine trees on the mountain to the east of Verrières. Instead of leaving, Julien, drunk with pleasure, begged Mme. de Rênal to let him spend the whole day hidden in her room, and to leave only the following night.[6]

—Why not? she replied. This fatal relapse has destroyed all my self-respect and condemned me to lifelong misery, and she pressed him to her heart. My husband is no longer the same, he is getting suspicious; he thinks I managed him through this whole affair, and shows his resentments against me. If he hears the slightest noise, I am lost; he will drive me out of the house like the wretch I am.

—Ah, that's like a speech from M. Chélan, said Julien; you wouldn't have talked to me that way before I went to that cruel seminary; you used to love me then!

Julien was repaid for the coolness he put into this speech: he saw his mistress forget at once the danger she was running from her husband's presence in order to think of the much greater danger that Julien might doubt her love. Daylight came rapidly on, and lit up the whole room; Julien recaptured all the delights of pride when he saw in his arms and practically at his feet this charming woman, the only one he had ever loved, and who a few hours before had been wholly absorbed in her fear of a terrible God and in devotion to duty. Resolutions fortified by a year's constancy had not been able to withstand his courage.

Soon household stirrings began to be heard; a matter she had not previously considered arose to disturb Mme. de Rênal's mind.

—That nasty Elisa will be coming into the room; what shall we do with this enormous ladder? she asked her lover; where shall we hide it? I'll carry it up into the attic, she suddenly exclaimed, speaking almost playfully.

—But you have to go through the servant's room, said Julien in astonishment.

—I'll leave the ladder in the hallway, call for the servant, and send him on an errand.

—But you must have ready beforehand a word of explanation, in case the servant, when he passes by the ladder in the hallway, remarks upon it.

—Yes, my angel, said Mme. de Rênal, giving him a kiss. And for

6. In connection with this episode, it is customary to recall that Stendhal himself spent three days in July of 1824 being concealed by the Comtesse Curial in an empty room of her house at Monchy.

your part, get ready to hide yourself quickly under the bed in case Elisa comes in while I'm away.

Julien was amazed at this sudden gaiety. I see, thought he, physical danger when it approaches restores her gaiety instead of troubling her, because in it she can forget her remorse! What a wonderful woman! This is a heart in which it's glorious to reign! Julien was in ecstasies.

Mme. de Rênal took the ladder; it was obviously too heavy for her. Julien went to help her; he was admiring her elegant figure, which was far from giving evidence of physical strength, when suddenly she seized the ladder, lifted it without aid, and carried it off as she would have carried a chair. She took it swiftly down the third-floor hallway and laid it along the wall. Then she called the servant, and in order to give him time to dress, went up into the dovecote. Five minutes later, when she returned to the hall, the ladder was gone. What had become of it? If Julien had been out of the house, the problem would not have bothered her. But now, if her husband found the ladder here! there could be a nasty scene. Mme. de Rênal hunted everywhere. At last she discovered the ladder in the garret where the servant had carried it, and even concealed it. It was an odd circumstance; at another time it might have alarmed her.

Why should I worry, she thought, over what can happen twenty-four hours from now when Julien will be gone? Won't everything then be simply horror and remorse?

She had a vague sentiment that she would be able to live no longer, but what matter? After a separation she had supposed would last forever, he had returned to her, she could see him again, and what he had gone through to reach her showed so deep a love!

As she told Julien the story of the ladder:

—What shall I say to my husband, she asked him, if the servant tells him where that ladder was found? She thought for a moment; they will need at least twenty-four hours to find the peasant who sold it to you; and then, throwing herself into Julien's arms and clinging to him convulsively: Oh, to die, to die here and now! she cried, covering him with kisses; but we can't let you die of hunger, she said laughingly.

Come now; first I'll hide you in Mme. Derville's room, which is always locked. She stood guard at the end of the corridor, and Julien ran down it. Don't open even if someone knocks, she told him, as she turned the key on him; if it should happen, it will be only the children at one of their games.

—Bring them into the garden, under the window, said Julien, so that I can have the pleasure of seeing them; I want to hear their talk.

—Yes, oh yes, cried Mme. de Rênal, as she left him.

Soon she returned, carrying oranges, biscuits and a bottle of Malaga wine; she had found it impossible to steal any bread.

—What's your husband doing? Julien asked.

—He's writing up some market business with various peasants.

But eight o'clock had struck; the house was abustle. If Mme. de Rênal were not seen, people would come looking for her; she had to leave him. Soon she returned again, bringing him, against all prudence, a cup of coffee; she was afraid he would die of hunger. After lunch she succeeded in bringing her children under the window of Mme. Derville's room. He found them much taller, but they had picked up a common look, or else his ideas had changed.

Mme. de Rênal talked with them about Julien. The older one responded, expressing friendship and regret for his former tutor; but it seemed the younger ones had almost forgotten him.

M. de Rênal did not go out all morning long; he climbed up and down stairs, busy closing deals with peasants to whom he was selling his potato crop. Until dinnertime, Mme. de Rênal had not a free moment to devote to her prisoner. When dinner was served, the idea occurred to her of stealing a bowl of hot soup for him. As she was silently approaching the door of the room where he was hidden, carrying her bowl with great care, she found herself confronting the same servant who that morning had hidden the ladder. At the moment, he too was walking silently down the corridor, as if listening for something. Probably Julien had walked about too incautiously. The servant made off in some confusion. Mme. de Rênal entered boldly into Julien's room; her encounter made him shudder.

—You're afraid, she told him; as for me, I'll meet any trouble in the world without flinching. Only one thing terrifies me, the moment when I shall be left alone after you go; and she ran off again.

—Ah! said Julien to himself in a rapture, remorse is the only thing this sublime soul fears!

At last evening came. M. de Rênal went to the Casino.

His wife declared a frightful headache, withdrew to her room, sent Elisa away at once, and promptly got up to open the door for Julien.

In fact, he really was suffering from hunger. Mme. de Rênal went to the pantry to get him some bread. Julien heard a shriek. Mme. de Rênal returned and told him that as she entered the darkened pantry and approached a cupboard where there was bread she had reached out and touched a woman's arm. It was Elisa, who had uttered the shriek heard by Julien.

—What was she doing there?

—Either stealing sweets or else spying on us, said Mme. de Rênal with absolute indifference. Fortunately, I found a pie and a big loaf of bread.

—And what's that? asked Julien, pointing to the pockets of her apron.

Mme. de Rênal had forgotten that since dinner they had been stuffed with bread.

Julien strained her in his arms with the most passionate feeling; never before had she seemed to him so lovely. Even in Paris, he told himself confusedly, I shall never find a more splendid character. She had all the awkwardness of a woman little accustomed to this sort of intrigue and at the same time the true courage of a person who fears only dangers of a different, and far more terrible, order.

While Julien was eating avidly away, and his mistress was joking about the simplicity of his meal, for she had a horror of serious talk, the door of the room was suddenly shaken furiously. It was M. de Rênal.

—Why have you shut yourself in? he shouted.

Julien had just time to slip under the sofa.

—What's this? You're fully dressed, said M. de Rênal as he came in; you're eating and you've locked yourself in!

On ordinary days this question, put with the full crudity of a husband, would have upset Mme. de Rênal, but she realized that her husband had only to lower his glance a bit in order to catch sight of Julien; for M. de Rênal had flung himself down in the chair which Julien had occupied a moment before, just opposite the sofa.

The headache served as an excuse for everything. While her husband told her at length all the episodes of a game he had won in the billiard room of the Casino, a pot of nineteen francs, begad, he added, she noticed on a chair, not three feet away, Julien's hat. Cooler than ever, she began to disrobe, and at a certain moment, passing swiftly behind her husband, threw a dress across the back of the chair and on top of the hat.

At last M. de Rênal took his leave. She begged Julien to tell her again the story of his life at the seminary; I wasn't listening to you yesterday; all I could think of was where would I find the strength to send you away.

She was boldness personified. They talked very loudly; it must have been two o'clock in the morning when they were interrupted by a violent banging at the door. It was M. de Rênal again.

—Open up at once; there are thieves in the house! he cried; Saint-Jean found their ladder this morning.

—This is the end of everything, exclaimed Mme. de Rênal, throwing herself into Julien's arms. He will kill us both; the thieves are just a story; I shall die in your arms, happier in death than ever I was in life. She answered not a word to her husband, who grew furious; she was holding Julien in a passionate embrace.

—Save Stanislas' mother, he said to her, with a commanding glance. I shall jump down into the yard from the closet window and escape through the garden; the dogs know me. Make a bundle of my clothes and throw it into the garden as soon as you can. Meanwhile, let them break down the door. Above all, no confessions, I forbid them; it's better for him to be suspicious than certain.

—You will kill yourself with that jump! was her only reply and her only anxiety.

She went with him to the closet window; then she took time to hide his clothing. At last she opened the door to her husband, boiling with rage. He searched the room, searched the closet, without a word being said, and left. Julien's clothes were bundled out the window; he seized them and ran swiftly toward the lower end of the garden, beside the Doubs.

As he ran, he heard the whistle of a bullet and the report of a gun. That's not M. de Rênal, he thought; he's not that good a shot. The dogs were running silently beside him; a second shot apparently struck one of them in the paw, for he began to emit yelps of pain, Julien leaped down the wall of one terrace, ran fifty feet under its shelter, then began to flee in another direction. He heard the voices of men shouting to one another and clearly saw the servant, his enemy, fire another shot; a farmer came, too, and shot at him from the other end of the garden, but Julien had already reached the bank of the Doubs, where he dressed himself.

An hour later he was a league away from Verrières, on the road to Geneva; if they have any suspicions, Julien thought, it's on the road to Paris that they'll look for me.

Book II

She isn't pretty, she wears no rouge.
—Sainte-Beuve[7]

Chapter 1

COUNTRY PLEASURES

O rus quando ego te aspiciam!
—Virgil[8]

—No doubt the gentleman has come to catch the mail coach for Paris? said the landlord of an inn where he stopped for breakfast.

—Today's or tomorrow's, it doesn't matter which, Julien replied. The mail coach arrived as he was playing the indifferent. Two places were vacant.

—Well! so that's you, my old friend Falcoz, said the traveler just coming from Geneva to the one who climbed into the coach along with Julien.

—I thought you had settled down near Lyons, said Falcoz, in that delightful valley near the Rhone.

—Settled down, indeed! I'm in flight.

—What's this? in flight? you, Saint-Giraud, with that virtuous expression of yours, you've been committing crimes? said Falcoz with a laugh.

—On my word, I might as well have. I'm in flight from the abominable sort of life one leads in the provinces. As you know, I'm fond of green trees and quiet fields; you've often accused me of being a romantic. But I never could stand political talk, and it's politics that have driven me out.

—Why, what's your party?

—I have no party, that's the root of my misfortune. Here's the sum of my political views: I love music and painting; a good book is a big event in my life; I shall soon be forty-four years old. What's left of my life? Fifteen, twenty, maybe thirty years at the most? All right. I submit that in thirty years the ministers will be a little more clever but exactly as honest as the ones we have today. English history provides me with a mirror in which to see our future. There will always be a king anxious to enlarge his prerogative; always political ambition and the memory of Mirabeau[9] who gained glory along

7. Already used twice in Book I, as the epigraph to Chap. 14 and in the text of Chap. 15, this phrase about rouge is attributed here to Sainte-Beuve, probably out of sheer perversity.
8. The alleged quotation from Virgil is really from Horace, *Satires*, II, iv,

60. Though often cited in perfect seriousness, it is attributed by Horace to a usurer who indulges in sentimental dreams of the simple life while grabbing at his *cent per cent*.
9. Mirabeau (1749–91), an early, eloquent, and deeply corrupt leader of the

with several hundred thousand francs will keep our rich provincials awake nights: they will call it liberalism and love of the common people. Always our ultras will be eaten up by the passion to become peers or chamberlains. Aboard the ship of state everybody will want to stand at the helm, because the job pays well. But won't there ever be a meager little place for the ordinary passenger?

—Indeed, indeed, and it ought to be very amusing for a man of your quiet character. Is it these recent elections that are forcing you out of your district?

—My troubles date back before that. Four years ago I was forty years old and had five hundred thousand francs; today I'm four years older and probably fifty thousand francs poorer—that's about what I'll lose on the sale of my property at Monfleury, right by the Rhone in a magnificent location.

At Paris I was weary of that perpetual comedy in which nineteenth-century civilization, so-called, forces everyone to take a part. I yearned for friendship, for simplicity. So I bought a property among the mountains by the Rhone, nothing more beautiful under the sun.

For six months the vicar of the village and the local gentry paid court to me; I fed them dinners; I told them I had left Paris in order never again to hear, or be obliged to talk, about politics. You see, I told them, I don't subscribe to a newspaper; and the fewer letters the postman brings me, the better I like it.

But this wasn't the vicar's game; and before long I was subjected to a thousand different indiscreet requests and bits of chicanery. I want to give two or three hundred francs a year to the poor; they demand it of me for various pious associations, Saint Joseph's, the Virgin's, and so forth.[1] I refuse; then they load me with insults. I'm stupid enough to be irked. I can no longer go out in the morning to rejoice in the beauty of our mountains without discovering some irritation which drags me down from my reverie and reminds me disagreeably of men and their mean dispositions. During the Rogation processions, for example, in which I'm very fond of the singing (it's probably a Greek melody), they refuse to bless my fields because, says the vicar, they belong to a blasphemer. The cow of a pious old peasant woman dies, she says it's because of a nearby pond belonging to me, the blasphemer, the philosopher from Paris, and a week later I find all my fish floating belly up in the water, poisoned with lime. Intrigues surround me everywhere I turn. The justice of the peace, an honest man but afraid for his post, always rules against me. My rural peace becomes a hell. Once people see I've been abandoned by the vicar, head of the village congregation,

---

Revolution, was buried with national honors in the Pantheon and removed from it a year and a half later when his secret correspondence with Louis XVI was uncovered.

1. Various pious associations: see p.76.

and not taken up by the retired captain who's head of the liberals, they all fall on me, even the mason whom I've been supporting for a year, even the smith who tried to cheat me with the utmost impunity when I had my ploughs repaired there.

In order to get some support and win at least a few of my law cases, I turned liberal; but, as you were saying, these damned elections came along and they asked my support. . . .

—For an unknown?

—Not at all; for a fellow I know only too well. I refused: a frightful indiscretion! From that moment, I had the liberals on my hands, as well, and my position became intolerable. I think if it had occurred to the vicar to accuse me of having murdered my serving girl there would have been twenty witnesses, of both parties, to swear they had seen me commit the crime.

—You want to live in the country without flattering your neighbors' passions, without even listening to their chatter. What a mistake!

—I've corrected it now. Monfleury is for sale; I'll lose fifty thousand francs if necessary, but I'm overjoyed, I'll get out of this hell of hypocrisies and intrigues. I'm going to get my solitude and rural peace in the only place where they can be found in France, a fourth-floor apartment off the Champs Elysées. And even there, I'm wondering whether I hadn't better begin my political career in the district of Roule[2] by presenting the blessed bread in the parish church.

—None of that would have happened under Bonaparte, said Falcoz, his eyes glittering with anger and regret.

—Doubtless, doubtless, but why couldn't he manage to hold onto his position, your Bonaparte? Everything I'm suffering today is really his fault.

Here Julien became especially attentive. He had grasped, from the first words spoken, that the Bonapartist Falcoz was the former childhood friend of M. de Rênal, repudiated by him in 1816; and that the philosopher Saint-Giraud must be the brother of that head of the prefecture of _____, who knew how to have town property granted to him on easy terms.

—And all that is what your Bonaparte did, Saint-Giraud continued. An honest man, harmless as a man can be, forty years old and with five hundred thousand francs, cannot live in the country and find peace there; Bonaparte's priests and nobles will drive him out.

—Ah! don't speak ill of him, cried Falcoz, never did France stand so high among the nations as during the thirteen years of his rule. Then there was a sort of grandeur in everything that men did.

2. The district of Roule, formerly a little country village by this name, has for a long time now been a central district of Paris, between the Faubourg Saint-Honoré and the Champs Elysées.

—Your emperor, may the devil fly away with him, returned the man of forty-four, was great only on the battlefield, and when he reorganized the finances around 1802. What does his behavior since then amount to? With his chamberlains, his ceremonies, his receptions at the Tuileries, he simply offered a new version of all the old imbecilities of the monarchy. It was a corrected version, it might have got by for a century or two. The priests and nobles wanted to go back to the old version, but they don't have the iron hand needed to force public acceptance.

—There's the old printer talking now!

—Who drove me off my land? the printer went on, wrathfully. The priests, whom Napoleon recalled with his concordat, instead of treating them as the state treats doctors, lawyers, and astronomers, instead of recognizing them simply as citizens, without inquiring into the business by which they earn their bread. Would there be so many arrogant gentry today if your Bonaparte hadn't created barons and counts? No, that sort of thing was out of fashion. After the priests, it is these little country noblemen who bothered me most and forced me to turn liberal.

The discussion was endless; this subject will occupy France for another half century. As Saint-Giraud kept repeating that it was impossible to live in the provinces, Julien timidly put forward the example of M. de Rênal.

—Gad, young man, that's a good one! cried Falcoz. He's made himself into a hammer in order not to be an anvil, and a terrible hammer he is. But all the same, I see he's been outdone by Valenod. Do you know that rascal? He's the genuine article. What will your M. de Rênal say when he finds himself kicked out of office, one of these fine days, and that Valenod set in his place?

—He will be left alone to reflect on his crimes, said Saint-Giraud. So you know something about Verrières, then, young man? All right. Bonaparte, confound him, he and his ragbag monarchy made possible the rule of people like de Rênal and Chélan, which led in turn to the rule of Valenod and Maslon.

This gloomy political conversation astonished Julien and distracted him from voluptuous reverie.

He paid little attention to his first sight of Paris as he saw it in the distance. The castles in Spain which he was constructing on the basis of his future career had to struggle with the still-vivid memory of the twenty-four hours he had just spent in Verrières. He swore never to abandon the children of his beloved, and to leave everything in order to protect them, if ever priestly excesses lead us back to a republic and provoke persecutions of the nobility.

What would have happened the night he came back to Verrières if, when he placed his ladder against Mme. de Rênal's window, he had found the room occupied by a stranger, or by M. de Rênal?

But also, what bliss in those first two hours, when his mistress really wanted to dismiss him, and he pleaded his case, seated beside her in the darkness! A soul like Julien's is haunted by such memories for an entire lifetime. The rest of their meeting had already mingled indistinguishably in his mind with the first period of their love, fourteen months before.

Julien was awakened from his deep meditation when the coach stopped. They had just entered the courtyard of the post office in Rue J.-J. Rousseau. —I want to go to Malmaison, he told a cabman who approached him.

—At this hour, sir, and what for?

—None of your business. Let's go.

True passion never thinks of anything but itself. This, it seems to me, is why the passions are so absurd in Paris, where your neighbor always pretends that people are thinking about him all the time. I shall not try to describe Julien's transports at Malmaison. He was in tears. What, you say? In spite of those ugly white walls, just put up that year, which cut the park into little pieces? Yes, sir: for Julien, as for posterity, there was no line to be drawn between Arcola, St. Helena, and Malmaison.[3]

That evening Julien hesitated a long time before going to the theater; he had strange ideas about this sink of iniquity.

A deep-seated suspicion prevented him from admiring the Paris of today; he was moved only by the monuments left behind by his hero.

Here I am now in the center of intrigue and hypocrisy! This is the kingdom of those men who protect Abbé de Frilair.

On the evening of the third day his curiosity prevailed over his plan to see the entire city before reporting to Abbé Pirard. The abbé explained to him in a chilly tone the manner of life that would be expected of him at M. de La Mole's.

—If at the end of several months you haven't proved useful, you will go back to the seminary, but by the front door. You will live with the marquis, one of the most distinguished gentlemen in France. You will dress in black, but like a man in mourning, not an ecclesiastic. I insist that three times a week you continue your theological studies at a seminary where I shall introduce you. Every day at noon you will present yourself in the library of the marquis, who wants you to write letters for him, about his lawsuits and other business matters. The marquis will write in a couple of words, on the margin of each letter, the sort of answer it should get. I have

3. Arcola, scene of one of Napoleon's greatest military triumphs (November 17, 1796), St. Helena, where he was exiled (1815–21), and Malmaison, the property near Paris furnished and enlivened by Josephine as a sort of rural artistic court for the First Consul.

undertaken that within three months you will be able to write replies such that, out of every dozen you present for his signature, he will be able to sign eight or nine. In the evening, at eight o'clock, you will get your desk in order, and at ten you will be free.

It may be, continued Abbé Pirard, that some old lady or some soft-voiced man will propose certain immense advantages to you, or quite crudely will offer you some money in exchange for your letting him see some of the letters received by the Marquis. . . .

—Oh, sir! cried Julien, blushing.

—It is curious, said the abbé with a bitter smile, that poor as you are, and after a year in the seminary, you still retain a bit of virtuous indignation. You must have been blind to a lot.

Can it be his blood that tells? said the abbé in an undertone, as if talking to himself. What is really curious, he added, glancing at Julien, is that the marquis knows you. . . . I don't know how. As a starting salary he will give you a hundred louis. He is a man who acts only on impulse; that is his weakness; his childishness will be equal even to yours. If he is pleased with you, your salary may be raised in time to eight thousand francs.

But you understand, the abbé added, with an edge in his voice, he is not giving you all this money just to look pretty. You've got to be useful. If I were in your position, I would talk very little indeed, and never about matters of which I was ignorant.

Ah! added the abbé, I have looked into some other matters for you; I was forgetting about the family. There are two children, a daughter and a son of nineteen, as elegant as can be, a kind of lunatic who never knows at noon what he will be doing at two o'clock. He has wit, he is brave; he served in the Spanish campaign.[4] The marquis hopes, for some reason I don't understand, that you will be friends with young Comte Norbert. I have told him that you are a great Latinist; perhaps he hopes you will teach his son some readymade opinions about Cicero and Virgil.

In your place, I should never allow myself to be chaffed by this fine young man; and before answering his overtures, which will be perfectly polite but spoiled by a touch of irony, I should make him repeat them for me at least twice.

I shall not conceal from you that young Comte de La Mole is bound to despise you at first, because you are nothing but a little bourgeois. One of his own ancestors was at court, and had the honor of being beheaded in the Place de Grève, on the twenty-sixth

4. The efforts of Spanish liberals to establish a stable regime (1820–23) were crushed by a French invasion under the Duc d'Angoulême, and from then on the French did a good deal of intervening in Spanish political affairs. But as Norbert is only nineteen, we cannot suppose his soldiering amounted to much. Stendhal is not very exact about ages—we note that Mathilde is nineteen, like her brother.

of April, 1574, as a result of a political intrigue. As for you, you are the son of a Verrières carpenter, and what is more you are in the pay of his father. Weigh these differences properly, and study the history of this family in Moreri;[5] all the flatterers who come to dinner here make from time to time what they call delicate allusions to it.

Be careful how you reply to the jests of M. le Comte Norbert de La Mole, commander of a squadron of hussars and future peer of France, and do not come around to complain to me afterward.

—It seems to me, said Julien, blushing deeply, that I should not even answer a man who despises me.

—You have no notion of this form of contempt; it will find expression only in exaggerated compliments. If you were a fool, you might be taken in by them; if you want to make your fortune, you ought to let yourself be taken in by them.

—On the day when all this business no longer suits me, said Julien, will I be considered an ingrate if I return to my little cell, number 103?

—No doubt you will, said the abbé; all the fawners around the house will slander you, but then I will appear. *Adsum qui feci.* I will tell them that the decision stems from me.

Julien was dismayed by the bitter and almost malicious tone which he noted in M. Pirard; this tone altogether spoiled his last reply.

The fact is that the abbé felt a scruple of conscience over his fondness for Julien, and it was only with a sort of religious terror that he meddled so directly in the fate of another human being.

—You will also see, he added, with the same ill grace, and as if fulfilling a painful duty, you will see Mme. la Marquise de La Mole. She's a big blonde woman, pious, proud, perfectly polite, and wholly insignificant. She is the daughter of the old Duc de Chaulnes, well known for his aristocratic prejudices. This great lady is a sort of epitome, in high relief, of everything that makes up the basic character of women of her rank. She herself makes no secret that having had ancestors who went on the crusades is the only quality that interests her in a person. Money comes far behind that. Does that surprise you? We are no longer in the provinces, my friend.

In her salon you will find various fine gentlemen talking of our princes in a tone of singular levity. Mme. de La Mole herself lowers her voice out of respect every time she mentions a prince and above all a princess. I should not advise you to say in her presence that Philip II or Henry VIII were monsters. They were KINGS, and

5. Louis Moreri (1643–80), author of a *Historical* (actually biographical) *Dictionary*.

that gives them unquestionable right to respect from everyone, particularly creatures of no birth, like you and me. However, added M. Pirard, we are priests, for she will take you for such; on that basis, she considers us household servants necessary for her salvation.

—Sir, said Julien, it seems to me that I shan't be very long in Paris.

—Just as you say; but remember, there is no way to rise, for a man of our cloth, except through the fine lords. With that indefinable something, at least I can't define it, in your character, if you don't make your fortune, you will be persecuted; there is no middle state for you. Make no mistake. Men can see that they give you no pleasure by speaking to you; in a country as social as this one, you are doomed to misery if you don't earn peoples' respect.

What would have happened to you at Besançon, if it hadn't been for this whim of the Marquis de La Mole? One day you will understand what an extraordinary thing he did for you, and if you are not a monster, you will cherish an undying gratitude for him and his family. How many poverty-stricken abbés, more learned than you, have lived years and years in Paris on the fifteen sous for their masses and the ten sous for their classes in the Sorbonne! . . . Remember what I told you last winter about the first years of that wretched man, Cardinal Dubois.[6] Are you arrogant enough to suppose yourself more gifted, perhaps, than he was?

I myself, for example, though a placid and ungifted man, I was expecting to die in my seminary; I was childish enough to grow attached to it. All right. I was about to be fired when I submitted my resignation. Do you know what my fortune was? I had five hundred and twenty francs of capital, no more, no less; I had not a single friend, and scarcely two or three acquaintances. M. de La Mole, whom I had never seen, got me out of that jam; he had only to say a word, and I was given a post where all my parishioners are comfortable folk, far above the vulgar vices, and the income fills me with shame, it is so disproportionate to my work. I have spoken at such length only to get a bit of ballast into your head.

One word more: it is my misfortune to have a bad temper; it is possible that you and I may cease to be on speaking terms.

If the arrogance of the marquise or the sarcasms of her son make this house unbearable for you, I advise you to finish your studies in a seminary within thirty leagues of Paris, and better to the north than to the south. There is more civilization in the north,

6. Cardinal Guillaume Dubois (1656–1723) is better known for his debauched and dissolute old age than for his penurious youth, but he certainly sprang from humble origins.

and less injustice; and besides, he added, lowering his voice, I must admit that having the Paris newspapers near at hand makes the petty tyrants fearful.

If we continue to find pleasure in one another's company, but the house of the marquis doesn't suit you, I can offer you a post as my vicar, and will divide equally with you the income of my living. I owe you that and even more, he added, cutting off Julien's thanks, for the extraordinary offer you made me at Besançon. If instead of five hundred and twenty francs I had had nothing, you would have been my salvation.

The abbé had lost his harsh tone of voice. Much to his humiliaton, Julien felt tears come to his eyes; he yearned to throw himself into the arms of his friend: he could not keep from saying, in the most manly voice he could assume:

—My father hated me ever since I was in the cradle; it was one of my greatest griefs; but I shall no longer complain of fortune, I have found another father in you, sir.

—Very well, very well, said the abbé in some embarrassment; then he recalled a timely expression from his days as director of the seminary: you must never speak of fortune, my boy, he told Julien, say providence instead.

The cab stopped; the driver raised a bronze knocker on an immense door: it was the Hôtel DE LA MOLE; and, lest the passersby remain in any doubt, the same words were to be seen on a black marble slab over the door.

This affectation displeased Julien. They are so fearful of the Jacobins! They see a Robespierre and his cart behind every hedge; they're so worked up, it would make you die laughing, and they placard their house like this so the rabble will recognize it in a riot and be sure to sack it. He expressed his thoughts to Abbé Pirard.

—Ah, my poor boy, you'll be my vicar before long. What an appalling idea occurred to you there!

—I can think of nothing simpler, said Julien.

The solemnity of the porter and above all the cleanliness of the courtyard struck him with admiration. A bright sun was shining.

—What magnificent architecture! he said to his friend.

He was talking about one of those flat-faced façades in the Faubourg Saint-Germain, built around the time of Voltaire's death. Never have the stylish and the beautiful been so distant from one another.

Chapter 2

ENTERING THE WORLD

> Absurd and touching recollection: the first drawing room in which one appeared at the age of eighteen, alone and unsupported! the glance of a woman was enough to intimidate me. The harder I tried to please, the more awkward I became. I formed mistaken ideas about everything; either I surrendered without a reason, or I supposed a man was my enemy because he had looked gravely upon me. But then, amid the frightful torments of my timidity, a fine day could be *so* fine!
>
> —Kant[7]

Julien stopped in the middle of the courtyard, struck with wonder.

—Try to look like a reasonable man, said Abbé Pirard; you get these horrible ideas, yet you're nothing but a child! Where is the *nil admirari* of Horace? (Never show any enthusiasm.) Keep in mind that this rabble of lackeys, when they see you in place here, will try to ridicule you; they will see in you an equal, unjustly promoted over their heads. Under the guise of good nature, good advice, attempts to help you along, they'll try to push you into some stupid blunder.

—I dare them to try it, said Julien, biting his lip; and he resumed all his earlier distrust.

The rooms through which these gentlemen of ours passed before reaching the study of the marquis on the first floor would have seemed to you, oh my reader, as melancholy as they were magnificent. If anyone made you a present of them, just as they were, you would have refused to live in them; they were the natural habitat of yawns and gloomy disputes. They completed Julien's enchantment. How could one possibly be unhappy, he thought, when one lives amid such splendid surroundings!

At last our gentlemen arrived at the ugliest of all the rooms in this splendid dwelling: it received hardly any daylight at all; there was a little lean man, quick of eye, and wearing a light periwig. The abbé turned to Julien and introduced him. It was the marquis. Julien could scarcely recognize him, he was so polite. This was no longer the fine gentleman, with such lofty expressions, whom he had seen at the abbey of Bray-le-Haut. It seemed to Julien that his wig was much too hairy. Thanks to this impression, he was not in the least abashed. The descendant of the good friend of Henri III struck him as giving a rather mean impression. He was very spare of figure, and moved about a great deal. But he quickly remarked that the marquis had a style of politeness even more agreeable to

7. Needless to say, the writings of Kant do not yield any passage like this. Stendhal's epigraphs are often of his own invention and attributed at random to different likely, or unlikely, speakers.

his interlocutor than that of the bishop of Besançon himself. The conversation did not last three minutes. As they went out, the abbé said to Julien:

—You inspected the marquis as you would have done a painting. I am no authority on what these people call politeness, before long you will be better versed in it than I am, but the openness of your stare seemed to me hardly polite.

They returned to their cab; the driver stopped near the boulevard; the abbé brought Julien into an apartment of spacious rooms. Julien noted that they were largely unfurnished. He was looking at a magnificent gilt clock, representing a subject he considered indecent in the extreme, when a most elegant gentleman approached smilingly. Julien made him a slight bow.

The gentleman smiled back and placed his hand on his shoulder. Julien quivered and stepped back a pace. He was red with anger. In spite of his gravity, Abbé Pirard laughed until the tears came. The gentleman was a tailor.

—I grant you two days' leave, said the abbé as they went out; only after that time can you be presented to Mme. de La Mole. Anyone else would watch over you like a young girl in these first days of your stay in the new Babylon. Go ruin yourself at once if you're going to ruin yourself at all, and I shall be free to forget about you completely. On the day after tomorrow, in the morning, this tailor will bring you two suits; you may give five francs to the fitter. Otherwise, don't let these Parisians hear so much as the sound of your voice. If you say a single word, they will find a way of turning you to ridicule. That's their special talent. Day after tomorrow, come to my lodgings at noon. . . . Run along now, ruin yourself. . . . Oh, I was forgetting, go and order yourself boots, shirts, and a hat at the places listed here.

Julien noted the handwriting of the addresses.

—That's the marquis' hand, said the abbé; he is an active man, who foresees everything and who would rather do something himself than order it done. He is taking you into his household in order to save himself this sort of trouble. Will you be clever enough to carry out properly all the orders this quick-witted man will convey to you in half a word? That's what time will tell; meanwhile, take care of yourself!

Without uttering a single word, Julien made his way to the shops indicated on his list of addresses; he noted that he was received with great respect, and the bootmaker, when entering his name on the register, wrote M. Julien de Sorel.

At the cemetery of Père-Lachaise a gentleman who was extremely kind and particularly liberal in his opinions offered to show Julien

the tomb of Marshal Ney, which a prudent administration has left
without the honor of an epitaph.[8] But when he parted from this
liberal, who with tears in his eyes almost hugged him, Julien no
longer had a watch. It was with the riches of this experience in
mind that he presented himself, two days later, to Abbé Pirard,
who looked him over carefully.

—You are perhaps going to become a fop, the abbé told him with
a severe expression. Julien had the look of a very young man in
deep mourning; he did in fact look quite well dressed, but the good
abbé was too provincial himself to note that Julien still had that
swagger of the shoulders which in the provinces denotes elegance
and importance. The marquis, when he saw Julien, saw his social
graces in quite another light than the good abbé, to whom he said:

—Should you mind if M. Sorel took some dancing lessons?

The abbé was petrified.

—No, he said at last, I should not mind. Julien is not a priest.

The marquis, mounting two at a time the steps of a little hidden
staircase, went in person to establish our hero in a neat attic room
looking out on the immense garden behind the house. He asked
how many shirts he had ordered of the haberdasher.

—Two, replied Julien, abashed to see so great a gentleman descend to such petty details.

—Very good, said the marquis, speaking seriously and with a
certain imperious, curt tone to his voice which gave Julien to think;
very good! Now order twenty-two more shirts. Here is your salary
for the first quarter.

As they came down from the attic, the marquis called to an
elderly man: Arsène, said he, you will take care of M. Sorel. A few
minutes later, Julien found himself alone in a splendid library; it
was a delicious moment. Lest he be observed in his emotion, he hid
himself in a dark little corner, and from there he contemplated with
delight the glittering backs of the books. I could read all that, he
said to himself. And how could I be unhappy here? M. de Rênal
would have thought himself dishonored forever if he had done
for me a hundredth part of what the marquis de La Mole has just
done for me.

But let's see what letters there are to copy. When this work was
done, Julien ventured to approach the books; he nearly went mad
with joy on discovering an edition of Voltaire. He ran to open the
door of the library, lest he be taken by surprise. Then he gave himself the pleasure of opening each one of the eighty volumes. They
were magnificently bound; it was the masterpiece of the best book-

8. Marshal Ney, the "bravest of the
brave," rejoined Napoleon for the Hundred Days, was executed by a firing
squad at the instance of the Bourbons
and buried in an unmarked grave.

binder in London. Less would have served to raise Julien's admiration to a peak.

An hour later the marquis entered, glanced at the copies, and noted with amazement that Julien wrote *cela* with two l's, *cella*.[9] Everything the abbé told me about his learning is simply a story, then! Much discouraged, the marquis said gently to him:

—You are not sure of your spelling?

—That's true, said Julien, wholly unaware of the harm he was doing himself; he had been softened by the consideration of the marquis, which made him think of M. de Rênal's harsh tone.

It's a waste of time, this whole experiment with a little priest from the Franche-Comté, thought the marquis; but I did have such need of a dependable man!

—*Cela* is written with just one l, the marquis told him; when you have finished your copying, you must look up in the dictionary any words of which you're not sure.

At six o'clock the marquis summoned him; he looked with obvious dismay at Julien's boots:—I am at fault, I should have told you that every day at five-thirty you must dress.

Julien looked at him, uncomprehendingly.

—I mean, put on stockings. Arsène will remind you; for today, I will make your apologies.

As he spoke, M. de La Mole showed Julien into a room glittering with gilt. On similar occasions, M. de Rênal never failed to push forward quickly so he might have the gratification of passing first through the door. His former patron's petty vanity was thus the reason that Julien trod on the heels of the marquis and caused him considerable pain because of his gout. Ah, he's even more of a lout than the average run, said the marquis to himself. He presented him to a tall woman of imposing appearance. It was the marquise. Julien decided she had a pretentious air, rather like Mme. de Maugiron, wife of the subprefect of the Verrières district, when she attended the dinner on St. Charles's day. Being slightly embarrassed by the extraordinary magnificence of the room, Julien did not understand quite what M. de La Mole was saying. The marquise barely deigned to glance at him. Several men were present, among whom Julien recognized with indescribable pleasure the young bishop of Agde, who had condescended to talk to him several months before at the ceremony of Bray-le-Haut. This young prelate was doubtless alarmed by the tender glances which Julien, in his timidity, cast toward him, and gave no sign of recognizing this provincial.

The men gathered together in this drawing room seemed to Julien to have about them something melancholy and constrained; people

9. The error of spelling *cela* with two l's was Henri Beyle's when he came to the war office as a young man to clerk for Pierre Daru; see *Brulard*, Chap. 41.

talk in undertones at Paris and don't exaggerate small circumstances.

A handsome young man, very pale and tall, came in at about six-thirty; he had an extremely small head.

—You always keep us waiting, said the marquise, as he kissed her hand.

Julien understood that this was Comte de La Mole; he found him charming at first glance.

Is it possible, he asked himself, that this is the man whose offensive joking is going to drive me out of the house?

Having studied Comte Norbert's person, Julien noted that he wore boots and spurs; and I should be wearing shoes, as a social inferior, evidently. They went in to dinner. Julien heard the marquise utter a sharp remark, raising her voice slightly. Almost at the same moment, he noticed a young lady, very blonde and very shapely, who placed herself opposite him. She did not attract him at all; yet, on more careful inspection, he decided that he had never seen such beautiful eyes; but they expressed great coldness of spirit. Later, Julien thought they expressed a kind of watchful boredom which nonetheless always remembers the need to impress others. Mme. de Rênal had fine eyes, he told himself, people were always making compliments about them; but they had nothing in common with these. Julien did not have enough social experience to understand that it was the glitter of wit that shone from time to time in the eyes of Mlle. Mathilde, for so he heard her named. When Mme. de Rênal's eyes grew animated, it was with the fire of passion, or with generous indignation at the description of some wicked action. Toward the end of the meal Julien found a word to describe the sort of beauty he found in the eyes of Mlle. de La Mole: they scintillate, he told himself. In other respects she bore a cruel resemblance to her mother, whom he was disliking more and more, and he ceased to look at her. On the other hand, Comte Norbert seemed to him admirable in every respect. Julien was so carried away that the idea never occurred to him of feeling hatred and jealousy because this man was richer and better born than himself.

It seemed to Julien that the marquis was getting bored.

About the second course, he said to his son:

—Norbert, I must beg your good offices for M. Julien Sorel, whom I've just added to my staff, and propose to make a man of, if that (*cella*) can be done.

—It's my secretary, said the marquis to his neighbor, and he writes *cela* with two l's.

Everyone looked at Julien, who made a somewhat excessive bow in Norbert's direction; but in general, they were satisfied with his appearance.

The marquis must have said something about the sort of education Julien had received, for one of the diners tackled him on the topic of Horace: it was precisely by talking about Horace that I succeeded with the Bishop of Besançon, Julien said to himself; apparently this is the only author they know. From that moment on, he was perfectly in control of himself. This attitude was the easier for him to assume because he had just decided that Mlle. de La Mole would never be a woman in his eyes. Since his days in the seminary he expected the worst of men, and was not easily intimidated by them. He would have been perfectly at ease if the dining room had been less splendidly furnished. In fact, it was two enormous mirrors, each eight feet high, in which from time to time he caught sight of his interlocutor as he talked about Horace, which still daunted him. His sentences were not too long, for a provincial. His eyes were fine, and their timidity, either trembling or joyful when he had scored a good hit, enhanced his attractiveness. He was judged agreeable. This sort of trial added a bit of interest to an otherwise formal dinner. The marquis made a sign to Julien's adversary to push him harder. Can it be possible that he really does know something? was his thought.

Julien answered, and found new thoughts as he talked; he lost enough of his timidity to be able to display, not wit precisely, a thing impossible to anyone who does not know the special dialect of Paris, but new ideas, though presented without grace or ease of application; and it was clear that his Latinity was sound.

Julien's adversary was a member of the Academy of Inscriptions who, by accident, knew Latin himself; discovering in Julien an excellent humanist, he lost all fear of disgracing him, and really made an effort to test him. In the heat of combat, Julien finally forgot the splendid furnishings of the room and succeeded in expressing various ideas about the Latin poets which his opponent had never seen in print. As an honest man, he therefore gave credit for them to the young secretary. Fortunately, the discussion focused on the question whether Horace had been poor or rich; a pleasant, pleasure-loving careless man, making verses for his own amusement like Chapelle,[1] Molière's friend, and La Fontaine; or a poor devil of a poet laureate, following the court around and making odes for the king's birthday, like Southey the calumniator of Lord Byron. They talked of the state of society under Augustus and under George IV: in both ages, the aristocracy was all-powerful, but in Rome it saw the power snatched from it by Maecenas, a mere knight; while in England, it had reduced George IV to a position scarcely more influential than that of a Venetian doge. This discus-

1. Chapelle (Claude Emmanuel Luillier, illegitimate son of a great court functionary at the end of the seventeenth century) was very well off indeed and made his verses, like his *bons mots,* for fun.

sion seemed to draw the marquis out of the torpid state in which boredom had plunged him at the beginning of the dinner.

Julien understood nothing at all of the modern names, like Southey, Lord Byron, George IV, which he was just hearing for the first time. But no one could fail to see that when there was a question of incidents at Rome, of anything that could be learned from the works of Horace, Martial, Tacitus, etc., he held an unchallenged advantage. Julien made unscrupulous use of several ideas he had acquired from the bishop of Besançon in the course of his famous discussion with that prelate; and these were not the least acceptable.

When they were tired of talking about poets, the marquise, who made it a rule to admire everything that amused her husband, condescended to cast a glance upon Julien. The awkward manners of this young abbé may perhaps conceal a man of learning, said the academician to the marquise, who was sitting near him; and Julien partly overheard the words. Ready-made phrases were altogether pleasing to the lady of the house; she adopted this summary of Julien, and was pleased that she had asked the academician to dine. He amuses M. de La Mole, she thought.

Chapter 3

FIRST STEPS

> This immense valley filled with glittering lights and so many thousands of men dazzles my sight. Not one of them knows me, they are all my superiors. My thoughts fail me.
> —Poems of the advocate Reina[2]

Next morning very early Julien was copying letters in the library when Mlle. Mathilde entered by a little secret door carefully concealed as part of the shelving. While Julien was admiring this contrivance, Mlle. Mathilde seemed much astonished, and rather displeased, to find him there. Julien, seeing her in curl papers, decided she looked hard, arrogant, and almost masculine. Mlle. de La Mole had a little habit of taking books from her father's library without his knowledge. Julien's presence rendered this morning's visit fruitless, which irked her the more since she had come to get the second volume of Voltaire's *Princess of Babylon*, a book very suitable to complement an education that had been eminently monarchical and religious, an education that was the masterpiece of the Sacred Heart![3] The poor girl, at nineteen years of age, already required the spice of wit to be interested in a novel.

2. Francesco Reina (1772–1826), Milanese lawyer, critic, and minor poet.
3. Voltaire's *Princesse de Babylone*, a *conte* vaguely reputed to be scabrous; the Convent of the Sacred Heart was in 1830 as now a finishing school for daughters of the distinguished, conservative social set.

Comte Norbert appeared in the library about three o'clock; he came to study a newspaper in order to be able to talk politics that evening and was very pleased to find Julien, whose existence he had forgotten. He was perfectly charming; he offered to take him riding.

—My father leaves us free till dinnertime.

Julien understood that *us,* and was enchanted by it.

—Good Lord, Monsieur le comte, said Julien, if it were a matter of felling an eighty-foot tree, trimming it, and cutting it up into planks, I should do pretty well at it, I daresay; but getting on a horse is something I haven't done six times in my life.

—All right, this will be the seventh, said Norbert.

In the back of his mind, Julien recalled the entry of the king of _____ into Verrières, and thought himself an excellent horseman. But, as they were returning from the Bois de Boulogne, right in the middle of the rue du Bac, he fell, while trying to dodge a passing cab, and covered himself with mud. It was a good thing he had two suits. At dinner the marquis, trying to bring him into the conversation, asked about his ride; Norbert hastened to reply in general terms.

—Monsieur le comte is much too kind to me, said Julien; I thank him for it, and appreciate his generosity. He was good enough to give me the most docile and easy of his horses; but after all, he could not fasten me onto it, and, as a result, I fell off, right in the middle of that long street, near the bridge.

Mlle. Mathilde tried vainly to stifle a peal of laughter; then, carried away by her curiosity, demanded details. Julien carried it off with great simplicity; he had an unconscious air of grace.

—I look for good things from this little priest, said the marquis to the academician; a simple provincial in such a scrape! Such a thing was never seen before and never will be again; besides which, he tells about his disgrace before *ladies!*

Julien put his listeners so much at their ease over his mishap that after dinner when the general conversation had taken another turn Mlle. Mathilde began to ask her brother about the details of the accident. As her questioning continued, and Julien met her glances several times, he ventured to reply directly, though the question had not been addressed to him, and all three ended by laughing together, like three young country folk of a village hidden deep in a forest.

Next day Julien attended two classes in theology and then returned to transcribe a score of letters. He found established next to him in the library a young man, very carefully dressed, but of a mean appearance and an envious expression.

The marquis appeared.

—What are you doing here, Monsieur Tanbeau? he asked the newcomer with a severe expression.

—I thought . . . the young man started to reply, with an obsequious smile.

—No, sir, *you did not think*. This is an experiment, but it has not worked.

Young Tanbeau rose in a rage and left the room. He was a nephew of the academician, Mme. de La Mole's friend, who hoped for a career in literature. The academician had arranged for the marquis to take him on as a secretary. Tanbeau, who worked in a separate room, had heard of the special favors bestowed on Julien, wanted to partake of them, and had arrived that morning to set up his desk in the library.

At four o'clock Julien ventured, after a moment's hesitation, to seek out Comte Norbert. The latter was about to go riding, and was embarrassed, for his manners were perfect.

—I expect, he said to Julien, that shortly you will go to riding school; and after a few weeks' time I shall be absolutely delighted to go riding with you.

—I wished to take the occasion to thank you for all your kindness toward me; believe me, sir, Julien added with great seriousness, I am quite conscious of how much I owe you. If your horse has not been hurt as a result of my clumsiness yesterday, and if it's not spoken for, I should very much like to ride it today.

—Gad, my dear Sorel, on your own head be it! Will you suppose that I have made every objection that prudence herself would have? The fact is, it's four o'clock, and we have no time to lose.

Once he was mounted:

—What must one do not to fall off? Julien asked the young count.

—Plenty of things, replied Norbert, with a burst of laughter; for example, sit further back in the saddle.

Julien set off at a full trot. They were in the square of Louis XVI.

—Ah! you young daredevil, said Norbert, there are too many carriages, and all with reckless drivers too! Once you're down, their tilburys will roll right over you; they're not going to risk spoiling their horses' mouths by pulling up short.

Twenty times Norbert saw Julien on the verge of falling; but finally, the ride finished without mishap. As they came back, the young count said to his sister:

—Let me introduce a real rough-rider.

At dinnertime, talking to his father from the full length of the table, he did full justice to Julien's boldness; it was the only thing one could praise in his horsemanship. During the morning the young count had heard the grooms in the yard make Julien's fall a pretext for deriding him outrageously.

Despite all this kindness, Julien soon felt himself completely isolated in the midst of this family. All their customs seemed strange to him, and he could not live up to them. His social blunders were the delight of the footmen.

Abbé Pirard had left for his parish. If Julien is a weak reed, let him snap; if he is a man of courage, let him make his way alone, thought he.

Chapter 4

THE HOTEL DE LA MOLE

What's he doing here? pleasing himself?
trying to please himself?
—Ronsard

If everything seemed strange to Julien in the well-bred drawing room of the Hotel de La Mole, for his part this young man, pale of countenance and dressed in black, seemed quite remarkable to the people who deigned to notice him. Mme. de La Mole suggested to her husband that they might send him on errands whenever certain people came to dinner.

—I want to carry the experiment out to its end, replied the marquis. Abbé Pirard tells me we are wrong to destroy all the self-esteem of the people we take into our household. *You get no support except from what resists,* and so forth. This fellow is bothersome only because his face is unknown, for the rest he's a deaf mute.

In order to learn my way among these people, Julien told himself, I'll have to write down the names, and a word on the characters, of all the people I see appear in this drawing room.

He placed in the first rank five or six friends of the family, who wooed him urgently, supposing him to be protected by a caprice of the marquis. They were sorry wretches, more or less drab; but it must be said in behalf of this class of men, as they turn up nowadays in the drawing rooms of the aristocracy, that they were not all equally servile to everybody. Some of them allowed themselves be insulted by the marquis, though they would bitterly have resented a harsh word addressed to them by Mme. de La Mole.

Too much pride and too much boredom underlay the characters of the master and mistress of the house; they were too inclined to insult others for their own diversion to expect any genuine friendship. But, except for rainy days and moments of ferocious boredom, which were rare, they never failed to appear perfectly polite.

If the five or six trucklers who displayed such fatherly affection for Julien had abandoned the Hotel de La Mole, the marquise would have been subjected to long periods of solitude; and women of this rank consider solitude a frightful affliction: it is the mark of *disgrace.*

202 · Red and Black

The marquis was exactly suited to his wife; he made sure that her salon was properly filled; not, however, with peers, for he found his new colleagues were hardly noble enough to visit his house as friends, nor amusing enough to be invited as subordinates.

It was only later that Julien came to know these secrets. Questions of social policy, such as make up the main subject of conversation in bourgeois houses, are never mentioned by people of the marquis' class, except in moments of distress.

So powerful, even in this bored century, is the need for amusement that even on the days of dinner parties people fled from the room the instant the marquis left it himself. Provided one didn't joke about God, or the priests, or the king, or the men in power, or the artists protected by the court, or about any part of the establishment; provided one said nothing good about Béranger,[4] or the opposition newspapers, or Voltaire, or Rousseau, or of anything which involves the use of free speech; provided, above all, that one never talked politics, one could talk freely about anything whatever.

There is no income of a hundred thousand crowns, there is no blue ribbon, that can prevail against a salon so constituted. The smallest live idea seemed like a gross indiscretion. In spite of good breeding, perfect politeness, and a desire to please, boredom was written large on every countenance. The young people who attended out of duty were afraid to talk of anything which might arouse suspicion that they had been thinking, or reveal that they had read some prohibited book, so they fell silent after a few well-chosen words on Rossini and the weather.

Julien noted that the conversation was generally kept alive by two viscounts and five barons whom M. de La Mole had known during the emigration. These gentlemen rejoiced in incomes of eight to ten thousand florins; four of them were devoted to *La Quotidienne* and three to the *Gazette de France*. One of them was compelled to recite every day some new anecdote from the Castle,[5] in which the word *admirable* was used with some freedom. Julien took notice that he wore five crosses; the others generally had no more than three.

On the other hand, there were in the antechamber no fewer than ten liveried lackeys, and throughout the evening ices and tea were served every quarter of an hour, while at midnight there was a sort of supper with champagne.

That was the reason why Julien sometimes stayed to the end; otherwise, he failed to see how anyone could listen seriously to the ordinary conversation in this salon, with its magnificent gilded

4. Pierre Jean Béranger (1780–1857) was a songwriter of immense fluency and popularity. He went to jail for three months in 1821 and for nine months in 1828 as a result of sarcasms and ironies against the Bourbons. His "Le Vieux Drapeau" ("The Old Flag") was a powerful and popular rallying cry in July, 1830.
5. The Castle is the court of Charles IX at Saint Cloud.

walls. Sometimes he looked curiously at the speakers to see if they themselves weren't aware of the absurdity of what they were saying. M. de Maistre whom I know by heart, thought he to himself, has said all this a hundred times better, and even he is a great bore.

Julien was not the only one to be aware of moral asphyxiation. Some of the guests consoled themselves by eating a great many ices, others by the pleasure of saying for the rest of the evening: I've just come from the Hotel de La Mole, where I heard that Russia, etc.

Julien learned from one of the trucklers that less than six months ago Mme. de La Mole had rewarded more than twenty years of assiduous attendance by making a prefect out of poor Baron le Bourguigon, who had been a subprefect since the Restoration.

This great event had rekindled the zeal of all these gentry; before it, they would have been offended at any small slight; afterward they were offended at nothing. Rudeness here was rarely direct, but Julien had already overheard at the dinner table two or three curt dialogues between the marquis and his wife, painful to those who sat near them. These noble folk took no trouble to hide their sincere contempt for anyone not descended from people who *rode in the king's coaches.* Julien noted that the word *crusade* was the only one that brought to their faces a look of intent seriousness, mingled with respect. Their ordinary respect had always a shade of condescension.

Amid this splendor and this boredom, Julien took an interest only in M. de La Mole; he was pleased one day to hear him protest that he had had no hand in the promotion of poor le Bourguignon. It had been done out of regard for the marquise: Julien learned the truth from Abbé Pirard.

One morning while the abbé was working with Julien in the library of the marquis on that interminable lawsuit with de Frilair:

—Sir, said Julien abruptly, is dining every day with the marquise one of my duties, or are they doing me a favor?

—It's a great honor! said the abbé, scandalized. Why, M. N_____, the academician, who's been paying them court for fifteen years, has never been able to obtain such a favor for his nephew M. Tanbeau.

—For me, sir, it's the most painful part of my job. I was less bored in the seminary. Sometimes I see even Mlle. de La Mole yawning, though she ought to be used to these friends of the family and their nice manners. I'm afraid of falling asleep. For heaven's sake, get leave for me to go off and eat a forty-sou dinner in a second-class tavern.

The abbé, who was a real parvenu, had a great sense of the honor involved in dining with a member of the nobility. While he was trying to convey this thought to Julien, a slight noise made them turn their heads. Julien saw Mlle. de La Mole, who was listening. He blushed. She had come looking for a book, and had overheard everything; it gave her some respect for Julien. This fellow wasn't born on his knees, she thought, like that old abbé. Lord! isn't he ugly?

At dinner, Julien did not venture to glance toward Mlle. de La Mole, but she was good enough to talk to him. That day they were expecting a lot of company, and she begged him to stay for it. Girls in Paris are not very fond of persons of a certain age, particularly when they are carelessly dressed. Julien had not required much worldly wisdom to note that the colleagues of M. le Bourguignon who remained in the drawing room were generally the butts of Mlle. de La Mole's mockery. That day, whether from affectation or not, she was cruel in her treatment of the bores.

Mlle. de La Mole was the center of a little group that formed almost every evening behind the immense easy chair of the marquise. There one might find the Marquis de Croisenois, the Comte de Caylus, the Viscount de Luz, and two or three other young officers, friends of Norbert or of his sister. These gentlemen sat on a large blue sofa. At the other end of the sofa from that occupied by the brilliant Mathilde, Julien sat silently on a little low caned chair. This modest position was the envy of all the trucklers. Norbert gave countenance to his father's secretary in the possession of it by addressing him directly or mentioning his name every so often in the course of the evening. This particular day Mlle. de La Mole asked him how high was the hill on which the fortress of Besançon stands. Julien could not possibly have told whether this hill was higher or lower than Montmartre. He often laughed aloud at the things that were said in this little group; but he felt himself incapable of saying anything similar of his own. It was like a foreign language he could understand [and appreciate], but which he could not talk.

Mathilde's friends were in a state of open warfare that evening against the guests who kept arriving to fill the [magnificent] drawing room. The friends of the family attracted first attention, being better known, and Julien paid strict attention. Everything interested him, both the things that were talked about and the way they were ridiculed.

—Ah! here is M. Descoulis, said Mathilde, he's left his wig at home. Perhaps he expects to get a prefecture through his genius and is showing off that bald brow which he says is filled with lofty thoughts.

—He's a man who knows the whole world, said the Marquis de Croisenois; he visits my uncle the cardinal, as well. He is capable of cultivating a special lie with each one of his friends for years on end, and he has two or three hundred friends. He knows how to cultivate friendship, that's his special gift. Just as you see him here, he sometimes appears in the mud of the roadway before the house of one of his friends at seven o'clock of a winter morning.

From time to time he has a quarrel and writes seven or eight letters to keep it going. Then he is reconciled, and has seven or eight letters for the transports of friendship. But it is the frank, sincere openness of an honest man who has nothing whatever to conceal that offers him the most brilliant part to play. That's his style when he has something to ask for. One of my uncle's grand vicars is really splendid when he describes the life of M. Descoulis since the Restoration. I shall bring him to see you.

—Bah! I shouldn't believe those tales, said the Comte de Caylus; it's nothing but the professional jealousy of little people.

—M. Descoulis will have a name in history, replied the marquis; he made the Restoration, along with Abbé de Pradt, M. Talleyrand, and Pozzo di Borgo.[6]

—This man has played with his millions, said Norbert, and I can't imagine why he comes here to swallow my father's insults, which are often abominable. How many times have you betrayed your friends, my dear Descoulis? he shouted to him the other day, from one end of the table to the other.

—But is it true that he has betrayed people? said Mlle. de La Mole. After all, who hasn't?

—Who's this? said the Comte de Caylus to Norbert, you have here M. Sainclair, the great liberal; and what the devil is he doing here? I must go over, talk to him, and get him to talk; they say he's very witty.

—But how is your mother going to receive him? said M. de Croisenois. He has such extreme ideas, so generous, so independent. . . .

—Take a look, said Mlle. de La Mole, there's your independent man who's bowing to the floor before M. Descoulis and grasping his hand. I almost thought he was going to carry it to his lips.

—Descoulis must stand better with the powers that be than we thought, replied M. de Croisenois.

6. At the Congress of Vienna (1814–15), Talleyrand, representing France, and Pozzo di Borgo, representing Russia, did play major roles in working out the restoration of the Bourbons; the Abbé de Pradt, though associated with Talleyrand, was a relatively peripheral and uninfluential figure on this occasion. On the basis of relationships and similarities, M. Claude Liprandi has worked out an identification of M. Descoulis as an amalgam of le Comte Louis, i.e. Joseph Dominique, Baron Louis (who may very well be indicated in II, 4, as "le Baron L_____") and M. Antoine-Athanase de Laborie: see *Le Divan*, #290 (1954), pp. 362–70. Most of the people seen at M. de La Mole's assemblage seem to have been drawn from life, sometimes several lives. In particular, the sardonic portrait of M. Sainclair, the famous liberal who is so servile, was intended to represent Mérimée, who had just published (January, 1830) a story called "The Etruscan Vase," the hero of which was named Sainclair. Comte Chalvet may very well be Paul-Louis Courier, at least in part.

—Sainclair is here to get into the academy, said Norbert; look, Croisenois, at the way he greets Baron L____.

—It would be less vulgar if he got down on his knees, said M. de Luz.

—My dear Sorel, said Norbert, you're a man of spirit though just come down from your mountains; try never to greet people the way that great poet does, not even God the Father.

—Ah! here comes a man of spirit, the real article, M. le Baron Bâton, said Mlle. de La Mole, parodying the voice of the lackey who had just announced him.

—I think even your servants are making fun of him. What a name, Baron Bâton! said M. de Caylus.

—What's in a name? as he said to us himself, only the other day, remarked Mathilde. Imagine the Duc de Bouillon announced for the first time; all the public needs, in any case, is a little time to get used to it. . . .

Julien left the company around the sofa. He was not yet particularly fond of the delicate touches of light raillery; if he was to laugh at a joke he required that it be founded on reason. In the chatter of the young people he saw nothing but the sneering tone, and he was shocked by it. His prudery, which was provincial or perhaps English, went so far as to suspect the speakers of envy, in which he was assuredly mistaken.

Comte Norbert, said he to himself, whom I've seen making three rough drafts of a twenty-line letter to his colonel, would be very glad indeed to have written one page in his whole life like those of M. Sainclair.

Passing unnoticed because of his unimportance, Julien wandered from group to group; he was following at a distance Baron Bâton, and wanted to hear him talk. This clever man wore a look of some disquiet, and Julien saw that he regained his composure only when he had enunciated three or four well-turned sentences. It seemed to Julien that this sort of wit required open space.

The baron was incapable of epigrams; he needed at least four sentences of six lines each in order to shine.

—*That man lectures, he doesn't chat,* said someone behind Julien. He turned, and blushed with pleasure to hear the name of Comte Chalvet. This was the wittiest man of the day. Julien had often read his name in the *Mémorial de Sainte-Hélène* and the bits of history dictated by Napoleon. Comte Chalvet was curt in his speech; his phrases were flashes of light, accurate, swift, [often] penetrating. If he spoke on any topic, one immediately saw the conversation move forward to a new level. He had the facts at hand; it was a pleasure to listen to him. In politics, however, he was a shameless cynic.

—Personally, I'm an independent, he said to a man wearing three decorations, whom he was apparently mocking. Why should I try to have the same opinion today that I had six weeks ago? That would make me the slave of my own judgment.

Four solemn young men standing around him looked sour at this; such people never appreciate levity. The count saw he had overstepped himself. Fortunately he caught sight of honest M. Balland, the artist of honesty. The count began talking to him; a circle gathered, seeing that poor Balland was going to be flayed alive. By virtue of morals and morality, though he was horribly ugly and had got his start in life by some indescribable expedients, M. Balland had married an extremely rich woman, who died; then he married another woman, also very rich, who never appears in society. In all humility he now enjoys an income of sixty thousand florins and has his own toadies. Comte Chalvet discussed the whole business with him, mercilessly. They were soon surrounded by a circle of thirty persons. Everyone smiled, even those grave young men, the hope of the age.

Why does he call on M. de La Mole, where he's obviously a laughing stock? Julien thought. He crossed the room to ask Abbé Pirard.

M. Balland left the room.

—Good! said Norbert, there's one of my father's spies who's gone; there's nobody left now but little lame Napier.

—Is that the answer to the puzzle? thought Julien. But in that case, why does the marquis invite M. Balland at all?

Severe Abbé Pirard was making faces in a corner of the room every time he heard a new name called out by the footmen.

—Why, it's a den of thieves, he said, like Basilio,[7] I see nobody here but scoundrels.

The fact is that the stern abbé knew nothing about good society. But through his friends the Jansenists he did have very precise ideas about these men who worm their way into drawing rooms only through their extreme suppleness in the service of all parties or through an ill-gotten fortune. For several minutes that evening he answered Julien's eager questions out of the fullness of his heart, then stopped short, in despair at having nothing but evil to report about everyone, and charging it to himself as a sin. Being short of temper, a Jansenist, and a believer in Christian charity, his life in society was a perpetual struggle.

—What a frightful expression on that Abbé Pirard! said Mlle. de La Mole, as Julien returned toward the sofa.

Julien was irked, but she was perfectly right. M. Pirard was, beyond any doubt, the most honest man in the room, but his blotched face, distorted by the torturing of his conscience, rendered him

7. In Rossini's *Barber of Seville* (as, of course in Beaumarchais' original play), Basilio is a sour-faced music master and a hypocrite.

perfectly hideous at the moment. Trust to appearances after this!
thought Julien; it's precisely when Abbé Pirard in the delicacy of
his conscience is reproaching himself for some peccadillo that he
puts on an atrocious expression; while that little Napier, who is
known to everyone as a spy, carries about an expression of perfect,
tranquil happiness. Abbé Pirard had, however, made great concessions to the occasion; he had hired a servant and was quite well
dressed.

Julien noted an unusual stir in the room; all eyes were turned
toward the door, and an abrupt silence fell. Footmen announced
the famous Baron de Tolly, who had come to public attention in
the recent elections. Julien moved forward and got a good look at
him. The baron was in charge of a certain constituency: he had had
the luminous idea of abolishing the little slips of paper on which
were recorded the votes of one of the parties. But, in order to keep
things perfectly fair, he replaced them with other little slips of
paper bearing a name that was altogether agreeable to him. This
decisive maneuver was noted by several electors, who had hastened
to present their kind regards to Baron de Tolly. The excellent fellow
was still pale with the excitement of this great affair. Evil-minded
people had even ventured to use the expression *the galleys*. M. de
La Mole received him coolly. The poor baron made his escape.

—If he's off so quickly, it must be to go visit M. Comte,[8] said
Comte Chalvet; there was laughter.

Amid the crowd of great noblemen, mostly silent, and the swarm
of intriguers, mostly disreputable but all clever fellows, who moved
through M. de La Mole's drawing room that evening (there was
talk of his getting a ministry), little Tanbeau was fighting his first
battles. If he had not yet gained much delicacy of insight, he made
up for it, as we shall see, by the energy of his talk.

—Why not send the man to jail for ten years? he was saying, as
Julien approached his circle. Reptiles must be kept in the cellar;
we must put them away where they'll die in the dark, otherwise
their poison spreads and becomes more dangerous. Why condemn
the fellow to a mere fine of a thousand crowns? He's poor, all right,
so much the better; but his party will pay for him. Much better to
give him a fine of five hundred francs and ten years in a dungeon
cell.

Good Lord! who's this monster they're talking about? thought
Julien, who was amazed at his colleague's vehement tone and jerky
gestures. The meager, pinched face of the academician's favorite
nephew was hideous at that instant. Julien soon learned that the
man they were talking about was the greatest poet of the age.[9]

8. M. Comte was a famous magician
of the day; Baron de Tolly is off for
his lessons in prestidigitation.

9. The "greatest poet of the age" (it
is a generous judgment) was P. J.
Béranger; see p. 202, note 4.

Ah, the monster! Julien exclaimed under his breath, and tears of sympathy came to his eyes. Ah, you little beggar, I'll get back at you for those words.

So these, he thought, are the lost souls of the party within which the marquis is one of the leaders. And that great man he was just slandering, how many decorations, how many sinecures couldn't he have had if he had sold himself, I don't say to the vulgar administration of M. de Nerval,[1] but to any one of these passably honest ministers whom we've seen succeeding him.

From a distance Abbé Pirard beckoned to Julien; M. de La Mole had just said a word to him. But by the time Julien, who at that moment was listening with lowered eyes to the groanings of a bishop, could at last work free and join his friend, he found himself forestalled by that abominable little Tanbeau. This little monster loathed the abbé as the source of Julien's special favor, and had come to pay him court.

When will death deliver us from that ancient mass of corruption? It was in these terms, of biblical directness, that the little man of letters was talking at the moment of the respectable Lord Holland.[2] His claim to fame was a thorough acquaintance with the biographies of living persons, and he had just been running quickly through the various men who might aspire to some influence under the new king of England.[3]

Abbé Pirard stepped into a neighboring room; Julien followed:

—The marquis doesn't like scribblers, let me warn you; it is his only antipathy. Know Latin and Greek if you can, the history of the Egyptians, the Persians, and so on, he will honor you and protect you as a man of learning. But don't venture to write a single page in French, and above all on serious matters above your station in life, or he'll call you a scribbler and take a dislike to you. Can it be that you've lived in a nobleman's house without learning that phrase of the Duc de Castries about d'Alembert and Rousseau: that ruck want to have opinions about everything and don't even have a thousand crowns of income.[4]

Everything comes out, thought Julien, it's just like the seminary here! He had written eight or ten rather outspoken pages; it was a sort of historical eulogy of the old surgeon-major, who, he said, had made a man of him. And that little notebook, said Julien to himself,

1. M. de Nerval who, more distinctly even than the other habitués of M. de La Mole's salon, is an eclectic figure, has been identified with the Comte de Villèle, who had once formed an ultra ministry, and with the Prince de Polignac, who had not, but who shared some of his other traits (see Chap. 23).
2. Lord Holland (1773–1840) was a staunch Whig in the House of Lords, indeed for a while almost the only Whig in the upper house. As such, he was an English "liberal," relatively friendly to Napoleon, the American cause, and so on.
3. George IV died on June 28, 1830, and was succeeded by William IV, third son of George III.
4. The phrase that Stendhal attributes here to the Duc de Castries he uses elsewhere and attributes to other people; it was more than likely his own.

has always been kept under lock and key! He went up to his room, burned his manuscript, and returned to the drawing room. The clever rascals had gone; there was nobody left but men with decorations.

Around the table, which the servants had carried in fully set, were seven or eight women, very noble, very pious, very affected, between thirty and thirty-five years old. The brilliant widow of the Maréchal de Fervaques entered, with apologies for her lateness. It was past midnight; she went to sit beside the marquise. Julien was deeply moved; she had the eyes and the expression of Mme. de Rênal.

The group around Mlle. de La Mole still held together. She and her friends were engaged in jeering at the unfortunate Comte de Thaler.[5] This was the only son of the famous Jew, known far and wide for the fortune he had made out of lending money to kings to make war on their people. The old man had just died, leaving his son an income of a hundred thousand crowns a month, and a name, alas! all too well known. Such an extraordinary position demanded either great simplicity of character or great power of will.

Unfortunately, the count was nothing but a good man encrusted with a multitude of affectations suggested to him by his parasites.

M. de Caylus declared that someone had convinced him he was determined to pay court to Mlle. de La Mole (she was in fact being courted by the Marquis de Croisenois, who stood to become a duke with an income of a hundred thousand florins).

—Don't accuse him of determination, Norbert said pityingly.

In fact, what poor Comte Thaler lacked most conspicuously was just this faculty of will. As far as this side of his character went, he could have been a very proper king. Continually taking advice from everyone, he did not have the courage to follow out any opinion to the end.

His face alone, Mlle. de La Mole used to say, would have been enough to keep her laughing for life. It was a curious mixture of anxiety and disappointment; but from time to time there passed across it visible gusts of self-importance combined with a sharp tone such as suits the richest man in France, especially when he is reasonably handsome and not yet thirty-six. He is timidly insolent, said M. de Croisenois. The Comte de Caylus, Norbert, and two or three other young men with moustaches bantered him to their hearts' content, without his ever suspecting it, and then sent him away as one o'clock struck:

—Are those your famous Arabian steeds that you keep waiting outside in this sort of weather? Norbert asked him.

5. The Comte de Thaler represents the Baron de Rothschild. In addition, the thaler or zahler was a widespread unit of German currency; to be called the Baron de Thaler is like being called the Duke of Dollar or Count Gotrocks.

—No, I have a new pair, much less expensive, replied M. de Thaler. The left horse cost me five thousand francs, the one on the right only a hundred louis; but I assure you, he's only harnessed up at night. The fact is, his trot is exactly like the other's.

Norbert's words made the count conscious that a man in his position ought to have a passion for horses, and that he should not allow his to get soaking wet. So he left, and the other gentlemen followed an instant after, still laughing at him.

That's it, thought Julien, as their laughter echoed up the stairwell, I've now seen the absolute opposite of my own position. I don't have an income of twenty louis a year, and I've been with a man whose income is twenty louis an hour, and people laughed at him. . . . It's a sight to cure one of envy.

Chapter 5

SENSIBILITY AND A GREAT LADY OF PIOUS DISPOSITION

An idea of some vitality has the air of an indiscretion there, people are so used to flat language. Unhappy the man who makes it up as he goes along!

—Faublas[6]

After several months of experiment, this is where Julien stood on the day when the steward of the house gave him his third quarter's wages. M. de La Mole had put him in charge of his properties in Brittany and Normandy. Julien made frequent trips to those districts. His main task was to carry on the correspondence pertaining to the famous lawsuit with the Abbé de Frilair. M. Pirard had given the case over to him.

From the brief notes the marquis scribbled on the margins of the many papers addressed to him, Julien composed letters, almost all of which were signed.

At the theological school, the professors complained that he did not apply himself, but considered him nonetheless one of their most distinguished pupils. These various tasks, accepted with all the energy of a repressed ambition, quickly robbed Julien of all the fresh coloring he had brought with him from the provinces. His pallor was a special merit in the eyes of the young seminarians his companions; he found them much less mean, much less likely to prostrate themselves before a coin, than the seminarians of Besançon; for their part, they thought him a consumptive. The marquis had given him a horse of his own.

Fearful of being recognized when he was out riding, Julien had told them that this exercise had been prescribed for him by doctors.

6. Faublas is not an author but a character in a novel, *Les Amours du* *Chevalier de Faublas* (1787–1790), by Louvet de Couvray.

The Abbé Pirard had taken him to visit various Jansenist societies. Julien was astonished; the idea of religion was indissolubly linked, in his mind, with that of hypocrisy and money making. He admired these pious, severe men who never gave a thought to the budget. Several of the Jansenists became friendly with him and gave him advice. A new world opened before him. He met among the Jansenists a Comte Altamira,[7] a man six feet tall, condemned to death in his own country for liberalism, and pious. This strange mixture of piety and love of liberty impressed him.

Julien's friendship with the young count had cooled. Norbert had felt that he retorted too sharply to the jests of some of his friends. Julien, having committed a couple of social blunders, had sworn never to say another word to Mlle. Mathilde. People were always perfectly polite to him in the Hotel de La Mole, but he felt himself in vague disgrace. His provincial common sense explained this change in the words of the proverb: *familiarity breeds contempt.*

Perhaps he saw a little more deeply into things than at first, or else the first enchantment produced by Parisian urbanity had passed.

As soon as work was finished, he fell prey to mortal boredom; this was the withering effect of that politeness, admirable in itself but so calculated, so carefully measured out according to one's social position, which is peculiar to high society. Any heart with a bit of feeling becomes aware of the artifice.

No doubt provincials are often guilty of a common or rough manner; but they show a little concern in their answers to you. In the Hotel de La Mole, Julien's self-esteem was never wounded; but often, at the end of the day, he was ready to weep. In the provinces, a waiter in a café will take an interest in you if some little incident occurs as you enter his café; but if this little incident involves anything painful to your self-esteem, even as he sympathizes with you, he will repeat ten times over the word that makes you wince. In Paris, they are considerate enough to turn aside in order to laugh at you, but you will always be a stranger.

We pass silently over a multitude of little episodes that would have subjected Julien to ridicule if he had not been in some sense beneath ridicule. An absurd sensitivity caused him to commit thousands of awkward errors. All his diversions were forms of precaution: he practiced with pistols every day, and he was one of the better students of the more famous fencing masters. As soon as he had a free moment, instead of spending it over a book as formerly, he ran to the stable and asked for the most vicious horses. When he went out with the riding master, he was almost always thrown.

---

7. The Comte Altamira is Stendhal's Neapolitan friend, Di Fiore, in masquerade. François Michel has expressed doubts about this identification in *Etudes Stendhaliennes* (Paris, 1958), pp. 44ff., but some underlying connection seems very probable.

The marquis found him convenient because of his hard work, his silence, and his intelligence; gradually he turned over to him for sorting out any business affair that was at all complicated. During the periods when his real ambitions left him some freedom, the marquis acted the part of a shrewd businessman; he was in a position to get inside information, and speculated boldly [on the market]. He bought houses and timber, but he was easily irked. He gave away hundreds of louis and went to court over hundreds of francs. Rich men with lofty ambitions treat business as a source of entertainment, not profit. The marquis needed a chief of staff who would reduce his financial affairs to a clear and easily intelligible order.

Mme. de La Mole, though of so dignified a character, sometimes made fun of Julien. The *unexpected*, deriving from personal sensitivity, is horrifying to great ladies; it's the absolute opposite of the conventional. Two or three times, the marquis took his part: If he is absurd in your drawing room, he is master in his own office. Julien, for his part, felt he had found the key to the character of the marquise. She condescended to be interested in everything as soon as the Baron de la Joumate was announced. He was a cold creature with a wooden face. He was short, thin, ugly, very well dressed, spent his life at the Castle, and as a general rule said absolutely nothing about anything. His mind was like that, too. Mme. de La Mole would have been overjoyed, for the first time in her life, if she could have got him as a husband for her daughter.

Chapter 6

LESSONS IN DICTION

> It is their lofty assignment to judge calmly of the little events which make up the daily lives of nations. Their wisdom must forestall the growth of great anger from tiny causes, or from events which the voice of rumor transfigures as it carries them abroad.
>
> —Gratius[8]

For a new arrival who, out of pride, never asked any questions, Julien did not fall into too many gross errors. One day, when he had been driven by a sudden shower into a café on the rue Saint-Honoré, a big man in a beaver-trimmed overcoat was struck by his

8. The quote from "Gratius" can scarcely be from Faliscus G., Roman author of a poem on hunting, or Ortwinus G., a contributor to the *Epistolae Obscurorum Virorum* controversy. It is no doubt an invention. In any event, Stendhal's editor Colomb supplied in the editions of 1846 and 1854 an alternate epigraph: "If fatuity is pardonable, it is in early youth, for then it is the exaggeration of a pleasant quality. It demands an air of love, gaiety, carelessness. But fatuity with self-importance; fatuity with a grave and important air! this excessive idiocy was reserved for the nineteenth century. And these are the people who propose to enchain *the hydra of revolutions!*" (Le Johannisberg, *Pamphlet*): Le Johannisberg was doubtless Metternich, whose family estates were in the wine-town of Johannisberg, and whose second publication (1794) was a pamphlet urging the necessity of arming populations against the French Revolutionary forces. Metternich's pamphlet doesn't contain the words quoted here, though it's to much the same effect; it corresponds even more strikingly with M. de La Mole's proposals for arming the peasantry, in II, 22.

gloomy gaze and began to stare back at him, exactly like Mlle. Amanda's lover, long before, at Besançon.

Julien had too often blamed himself for letting that first insult pass to endure this one. He demanded an explanation. The man in the overcoat retorted with filthy insults: everyone in the café surrounded them, and passersby crowded the doorway. With provincial caution, Julien carried a pair of little pistols; his hand clutched them in his pocket with a convulsive gesture. But he thought better of it, and confined himself to repeating steadily to his man: *Sir, your address? I despise you.*

The steadiness with which he attached himself to these six words ended by impressing the crowd.

Damn it, that fellow who goes on talking all by himself ought to come out with his address. When the man in the overcoat heard these words running through the crowd, he flung a half-dozen cards at Julien. Luckily, none of them struck his face; he had sworn to use his pistols only if he were touched. The man went off, not without turning back from time to time to shake his fist and shout insults.

Julien found himself bathed in sweat. So it's within the power of the lowest of men to enrage me like this! he said furiously. How can I get rid of this shameful excess of feeling?

He had to find a second, now; and he had no friend. Several acquaintances there had been; but all of them, regularly, after six weeks of acquaintance, dropped him. I'm antisocial, and now I must suffer for it, he thought. But at last he thought of looking up a former lieutenant of the Ninety-sixth, a poor devil named Liévin, with whom he often used to fence. Julien told him the full story.

—I'll be glad to act as your second, said Liévin, but on one condition: if you don't wound your man, you will fight with me on the spot.

—Agreed, said Julien [with a hearty handshake], and they went to look up M. C. de Beauvoisis at the address indicated on the cards, in the heart of the Faubourg Saint-Germain.[9]

It was seven in the morning. Only after he sent in his name did Julien think that this might very well be the young relative of Mme. de Rênal, who had given a letter of introduction to the singer Geronimo.[1]

Julien had handed to a big footman one of the cards flung at him the day before and one of his own.

He was kept waiting, with his second, fully three quarters of an

9. Then as now the Faubourg Saint-Germain was the fashionable district of Paris, where "good" families lived.
1. M. de Beauvoisis was introduced to us first as M. de Beauvaisis (Book I, Chap. 23). These petty carelessnesses on Stendhal's part may well be deliberate; compare the several different dates of Boniface de La Mole's execution and the number of Mme. de Rênal's children.

hour; at last they were ushered into a room of admirable elegance. They found there a tall young man dressed like a doll [in a white and rose dressing gown]; his features had the perfection and the vacancy of a Greek statue. His remarkably narrow head was crowned with a pyramid of fine blond hair. It had been dressed with immense care; not one hair was out of place. He had to finish his hairdo, thought the lieutenant of the Ninety-sixth, that was why this damned fop kept us waiting out there. His striped dressing gown, his morning trousers, everything down to his embroidered slippers was perfectly correct and marvelously sleek. His expression, nobly empty, announced a man of few and ordinary ideas: one whose ideal was to be agreeable, with a horror of the unexpected and of levity, with an abundance of solemnity.

Julien, to whom his lieutenant of the Ninety-sixth had explained that the man's making them wait so long after flinging those cards rudely in his face was a further insult, marched stiffly into M. de Beauvoisis' presence. He had planned to be insolent, but was also intent on showing good form.

He was so impressed with M. de Beauvoisis' gentle manners, with his affected, portentous, self-satisfied air, and with the wonderful elegance of his surroundings, that in an instant all thoughts of being insolent disappeared. It was not his man of the day before. His astonishment was so great at finding so distinguished a personage instead of the rude fellow he had met in the café that he could not say a word. He presented one of the cards that had been flung at him.

—That is my name, indeed, said the man of fashion, who was not very favorably impressed by Julien's black coat, worn at seven o'clock in the morning; but, upon my word, I don't understand the honor. . . .

His manner of pronouncing these words restored to Julien a bit of his ill humor.

—I have come to fight with you, sir, he said; and he quickly explained the whole affair.

M. Charles de Beauvoisis, having considered the matter more maturely, was reasonably content with the cut of Julien's black coat. It's by Staub, that's clear, he said, as he listened to the conversation; the vest is in good taste, the boots are all right; but, on the other hand, that black coat in the early morning hours! . . . It will be to provide a poorer target for the bullet, said the chevalier de Beauvoisis to himself.

As soon as he had satisfied himself on this score, he resumed his perfect politeness, and spoke to Julien almost as an equal. The discussion was lengthy, the matter was of some delicacy; but in the end,

Julien could not refuse the evidence. The well-bred young man before him bore no resemblance whatever to the rude personage who had insulted him the day before.

Julien felt immense reluctance to go away; he drew out the explanations. He was studying the complacency of the chevalier de Beauvoisis, for it was thus that the man referred to himself; he had been shocked that Julien called him simply Monsieur.

He admired his gravity, which sometimes mingled with a certain modest fatuity, but never adandoned him for an instant. He was astonished by a peculiar mannerism he had of moving his tongue about as he pronounced certain words. . . . But in none of that was there the slightest ground for picking a quarrel with him.

The youthful diplomat offered very gracefully to fight anyhow, but the ex-lieutenant of the Ninety-sixth, who had been sitting for an hour with his legs stretched out, his hands on his hips, and his arms akimbo, decided that his friend M. Sorel was not the man to pick a quarrel with someone simply because his visiting cards had been stolen.

Julien took his leave in the blackest of moods. The chevalier de Beauvoisis' carriage was waiting for him in the courtyard at the foot of the stairs; as he passed, Julien glanced up and recognized his man of the day before in the coachman.

To see him, drag him down from his high seat by the tails of his long coat, and set to lashing him with his own whip was the work of an instant. A pair of lackeys tried to defend their fellow-servant; Julien was struck several times: instantly, he drew one of his little pistols and fired at them; they fled. It was all the work of a minute.

The chevalier de Beauvoisis descended the stairs with the most amusing gravity, repeating in his lordly accent: What's this, what's this? He was obviously much intrigued, but his diplomatic dignity did not allow him to betray the slightest interest. When he learned what had happened, loftiness still disputed, in his features, with the mildly mocking coolness which should never be absent from a diplomatic countenance.

The lieutenant of the Ninety-sixth understood that M. de Beauvoisis really wanted to fight; being a diplomat himself, he also wanted to keep for his friend the advantage of the initiative. —This time, he cried, we certainly have grounds for a duel! —Indeed, I think so, replied the diplomat.

—That rascal has left my service, he told his servants; one of you must drive. The door of the carriage was opened, and the chevalier insisted that Julien and his second get in first. They went to look up a friend of M. de Beauvoisis, who knew of a secluded place. The conversation as they drove to it was first-rate. The only odd thing was the diplomat in his dressing gown.

Noble though they are, thought Julien, these gentlemen aren't such bores as the people who come to dinner at M. de La Mole's; and I see why, he added a moment later, they let themselves be indecent. They talked about various dancing girls whom the public had much appreciated in a ballet given the night before. The gentlemen made allusion to various spicy stories of which Julien and his second, the lieutenant of the Ninety-sixth, knew absolutely nothing. Julien was not such a fool as to pretend to be knowing in these matters; he frankly confessed ignorance. This frankness gratified the chevalier's friend; he repeated the stories in explicit detail, and told them very well.

One thing absolutely astounded Julien. A street altar which was being constructed in the middle of the road for the Corpus Christi procession held up the carriage for a moment. The gentlemen allowed themselves various pleasantries; as they told it, the priest in charge was the son of an archbishop. Never would anyone have dared to talk of such matters in the house of the Marquis de La Mole, who had hopes of becoming a duke.

The duel was over in a minute: Julien had a bullet in his arm, they bound it up for him with handkerchiefs soaked in brandy, and the chevalier de Beauvoisis asked Julien very politely to be allowed to return him to his residence, in the same carriage that had brought them. When Julien said he lived at the Hotel de La Mole, glances passed between the diplomat and his friend. Julien had a cab waiting, but he found the conversation of the gentlemen far more amusing than that of the honest lieutenant of the Ninety-sixth.

Good Lord! is that all a duel amounts to! Julien thought. What a piece of luck it was that I came across that coachman again! What a humiliation, if I had to swallow still another insult in a café! The amusing conversation had scarcely been interrupted. Julien now understood that diplomatic affectation is really good for something.

So boredom is not really inevitable, he said to himself, when people of good birth have a conversation! These people joke about the Corpus Christi procession, they venture to repeat scabrous stories, full of picturesque details. The only thing they lack completely is good political sense, and that deficiency is more than made up for by the charm of their style and the perfect correctness of their expressions. Julien felt a warm attraction for them. How happy I should be to see them often!

Scarcely had they separated when the chevalier de Beauvoisis hastened off in search of information; what he heard was not hopeful.

He was very curious to be acquainted with his man; could he, in decency, call on him? The little information he could glean was by no means encouraging.

—But this is really frightful! said he to his second. It's unthinkable that I should confess I fought a duel with an ordinary secretary of M. de La Mole's, and just because my coachman stole my visiting cards.

—It's perfectly clear the whole story leaves one wide open to ridicule.

That evening the chevalier de Beauvoisis and his second spread everywhere the story that this M. Sorel, a most agreeable young man for that matter, was the illegitimate son of one of the Marquis de La Mole's intimate friends. The tale passed easily. Once it was well established, the young diplomat and his friend were kind enough to pay several calls on Julien during the fortnight he was confined to his room. Julien confessed to them that he had never in his life been to the opera.

—But this is shocking, they told him, it's the only place anyone ever goes. Your first visit must be when they put on *Le Comte Ory*.[2]

At the opera the chevalier de Beauvoisis introduced Julien to the famous singer Geronimo, who was having a tremendous vogue that year.

Julien fairly paid court to the chevalier; his mixture of self-esteem, mysterious importance, and youthful fatuity enchanted him. For example, the chevalier stammered a bit, because he had the honor to converse frequently with a great gentleman who had that mannerism. Never before had Julien seen in a single person both the absurdities that amuse one and the perfection of manners that a poor provincial is bound to imitate.

He was seen at the opera with the chevalier de Beauvoisis; their friendship caused his name to be mentioned.

—Well, indeed, M. de La Mole, said to him one day, so now you're the illegitimate son of a rich gentleman in the Franche-Comté, who is my intimate friend?

The marquis cut off Julien's protests; he wanted to say that he had done nothing to give this rumor currency.

—M. de Beauvoisis didn't want it thought that he had fought with a carpenter's son.

—I know, I know, said M. de La Mole; and now it's up to me to give the story some weight, as I'm perfectly willing to do. But I have a favor to ask of you, which will cost no more than a modest half hour of your time: every opera evening, about eleven-thirty, go and stand in the vestibule when the people of fashion come out. I still notice in you from time to time the mannerisms of the provinces; you really must get rid of them; besides, it's not a bad idea to know, at least by sight, important persons to whom I may have to send you some day on assignments. Call at the office to identify yourself; they have your name on the subscription list.

2. Rossini's *Le Comte Ory* had its debut at the opera on August 20, 1828.

Chapter 7

AN ATTACK OF GOUT

And so I was promoted, not on my merits, but because my master had the gout.

—Bertolotti[3]

The reader is perhaps surprised at this free and almost friendly tone; we have neglected to note that for six weeks the marquis had been kept within doors by an attack of the gout.

Mlle. de La Mole and her mother had gone to Hyères to visit the mother of the marquise. Comte Norbert saw his father only for a few moments at a time; they were on perfectly good terms, but had nothing to say to one another. Reduced to Julien for companionship, M. de La Mole was astonished to find he had some ideas. He had him read newspapers aloud. Soon the young secretary was able to select the interesting passages. There was a new paper, which the marquis despised; he had sworn never to read it, and he talked about it every day. Julien laughed, [and marveled at the feebleness of power before an idea. The marquis' pettiness restored him to the self-possession he might have lost after several evenings of private conversation with so great a gentleman.] The marquis, growing impatient with the present day, asked Julien to read him some Livy; the translation, improvised from the Latin text, entertained him.

One day the marquis said, with that tone of excessive politeness which Julien often found irksome:

—Allow me, my dear Sorel, to make you a present of a blue suit: when you feel disposed to put it on and pay me a call, you will be, in my eyes, the younger brother of the Comte de Retz, that is to say the son of my friend the old duke.

Julien was not too clear about this transaction; that same evening he ventured a visit in his blue coat. The marquis treated him as an equal. Julien had a heart capable of understanding simple politeness, but he had no notion of the finer shadings. He would have sworn, before the marquis took this whim, that one could not possibly be treated by him with more deference. What a remarkable gift! Julien said to himself; when he rose to take his leave, the marquis apologized for not being able to see him to the door because of his gout.

A curious idea took possession of Julien: can he be making fun of me? he asked himself. He went to take counsel with the Abbé Pirard, who, less polite than the marquis, only whistled and changed the subject. Next morning, Julien appeared before the marquis dressed in black, with his portfolio and his letters to be signed. He

3. A. Bertolotti (1784–1860) was a Turinese poet, mostly given to political themes.

was received in the old manner. That night, when he resumed the blue suit, he met with a completely different tone, and one just as polite as on the evening before.

—Since you aren't too bored by these visits which you are kind enough to make to a poor old invalid, said the marquis, you might as well describe to him all the little incidents of your life, but frankly, and with no other purpose than to tell the story clearly and amusingly. For people must be amused, continued the marquis; that's the only real thing in life. A man can't save my life in battle every day of the year, or present me every day with a fresh million; but if I had Rivarol[4] here by my couch, he would relieve me every day of an hour's suffering and boredom. I knew him well at Hamburg, during the emigration.

And the marquis told Julien stories of Rivarol among the Hamburgers, who used to form little societies in order to work out the point of his witticisms.

Limited to the company of this little abbé, M. de La Mole tried to liven him up. He challenged Julien's pride. Since he was asked for the truth, Julien determined to give it, but suppressed two things: his fanatical admiration for a name that enraged the marquis and his own perfect unbelief, which hardly suited a future clergyman. His little affair with the chevalier de Beauvoisis came in handy at this juncture. The marquis laughed until he cried at the scene in the café on the rue Saint-Honoré, with the foul-mouthed coachman. It was a period of perfect understanding between patron and protegé.

M. de La Mole grew interested in this singular character. At first, he cultivated Julien's absurdities for his own entertainment; soon he grew more interested in correcting gently the false conceptions of this young man. All the other provincials who come to Paris admire whatever they see, thought the marquis; this one hates whatever he sees. They have too much affectation; he has too little, and so fools consider him foolish.

The attack of gout was prolonged by cold winter weather and lasted several months.

One becomes fond of a fine spaniel, the marquis told himself, why should I be so ashamed of my fondness for this young abbé? He is an original. I treat him like a son; well, where's the harm in that? This notion, if it lasts, will cost me a diamond worth five hundred louis in my will.

Once the marquis was aware of his protegé's firm character, he gave him a fresh business assignment every day.

Julien was distressed to notice that his noble employer would sometimes give him contradictory instructions on the same subject.

This could compromise him seriously. Julien no longer acted

4. Antoine Rivarol (1753–1801), witty and malicious writer and conversationalist of the *ancien régime*.

for the marquis without a notebook, in which he wrote down all the decisions and gave them to the marquis for initialing. Julien had hired a clerk who transcribed all the decisions regarding each particular transaction into a special book. In this book were also filed copies of all the letters.

At first this scheme seemed ridiculous and tiresome in the extreme. But inside two months the marquis became aware of its advantages. Julien suggested hiring a clerk with banking experience, who should establish a set of double-entry books on all the receipts from and expenditures for properties of which Julien had charge.

These steps so enlightened the marquis on the conduct of his own business affairs that, to his delight, he was soon able to undertake two or three new speculations without the help of his broker, who had been swindling him.

—Take three thousand francs for yourself, he said one day to his young agent.

—But, sir, my conduct may be blamed.

—What do you want, then? said the marquis crossly.

—I want you to be good enough to make up a deed, and write it into the register with your own hand; it will grant me the sum of three thousand francs. As a matter of fact, it was the Abbé Pirard who thought up this system of accounting. The marquis, looking as weary as the Marquis of Moncade when he listens to the accounts of his steward M. Poisson,[5] wrote out the deed.

That evening, when Julien put in an appearance wearing the blue suit, there was no talk of business. The kind consideration of the marquis was so flattering to our hero's self-esteem, always on edge, that before long, in spite of himself, he felt a sort of affection for this genial old gentleman. Not that Julien was particularly sensitive, as the word is used in Paris; but he was no monster, and since the death of the old surgeon-major, nobody had spoken so kindly to him. He realized with astonishment that the marquis was more careful of his self-esteem than he had ever found the old surgeon to be. He understood at last that the surgeon had been more proud of his decoration than the marquis of his blue ribbon. The father of the marquis had been a great nobleman too.

One day, after a morning conversation during which the black suit was worn and business was discussed, Julien was chatting with the marquis, who kept him for several hours, and then insisted on giving him some bank notes which his broker had just brought in from the stock exchange.

—I hope, Monsieur le marquis, not to be lacking in the profound respect I owe, if I beg you to allow me a word.

—Speak, my friend.

5. The reference is to L. J. C. Soulas d'Allainval's comedy, *L'Ecole des bourgeois* (1728).

—Will Monsieur le marquis be good enough to let me decline this gift? It is not offered to the man in the black suit, and it would immediately spoil the pleasant relation which you have been kind enough to establish with the man in the blue suit. He bowed most respectfully, and left the room without a backward glance.

This stroke of character amused the marquis. He spoke of it that evening to Abbé Pirard.

—And now I must make an admission to you, my dear abbé. I know about Julien's birth, and I authorize you not to keep secret this confidence of mine.

His behavior this morning was noble, thought the marquis, and now I am making him a member of the nobility.

Some time later, the marquis was at last able to leave his room.

—Go spend a couple of months at London, he told Julien. Special couriers and some other messengers will bring you the letters I receive, along with my notes on them. You can write out the answers and send them back to me, enclosing each letter with its own response. I have figured that the delay will be no more than five days.

As he took the mail coach down the road to Calais, Julien thought with amazement of the triviality of the business on which he was being dispatched.

We shall not dwell on the sentiments of hatred and almost of horror which he felt as he touched English soil. We have made clear his insane passion for Bonaparte. In every officer he saw a Sir Hudson Lowe, in every grandee a Lord Bathurst,[6] giving orders for the shameful treatment of St. Helena, and being rewarded for it with ten years in a ministry.

At London he at last made the acquaintance of the higher fatuity. He made friends with some young gentlemen from Russia, who initiated him.

—You're absolutely born for it, my dear Sorel, they all told him, you have by nature that cool expression, *a thousand miles from the sensation of the moment*, which we are all eager to acquire.

—You haven't understood our century, Prince Korasoff told him: *always do exactly the contrary of what people expect*. Upon my word, that's the only religion which is current nowadays. Don't be foolish, don't be affected, for then people will expect of you follies and affectations, and the commandment will not be fulfilled.

Julien covered himself with glory one day in the drawing room of the Duke of Fitz-Fulke,[7] who had invited him to dinner along with

6. Sir Hudson Lowe was commanding officer of St. Helena during Napoleon's confinement there, while Henry, third Earl of Bathurst, was secretary of war during the same period. Both men were the objects of bitter hatred on the part of Las Cases and the Napoleonic myth-makers.

7. The Duke of Fitz-Fulke probably gets his name from Byron's *Don Juan*, Canto XVI, where the Duchess of Fitz-Fulke is just starting to become important to the poem when it breaks off.

Prince Korasoff. They were kept waiting for an hour. The way in which Julien carried himself, amid the score of people who were waiting, is still cited as a model to young secretaries in the London embassies. His expression was inimitable.

In spite of [the jokes of] his friends the dandies, he wanted to make the acquaintance of the celebrated Philip Vane,[8] the only philosopher in England since Locke. He found him just rounding out his seventh year in prison. The aristocracy doesn't trifle with its enemies in this country, thought Julien; in addition, Vane is disgraced, abused, etc.

Julien found him in a merry mood; the rage of the aristocracy kept boredom at a distance. There, said Julien, as he left the prison, there is the only cheerful man I've seen in England.

The most useful idea, for tyrants, is the idea of God, Vane had said to him.

We pass in silence over the rest of the philosopher's system, as being *cynical*.

When he returned: —What amusing notion have you brought me back from England? M. de La Mole asked him. . . . There was a silence. —What notion did you pick up, amusing or not [, which shows something about the people]? said the marquis sharply.

—Item one, said Julien, the wisest Englishman is crazy for an hour every day; he is haunted by the demon of suicide, who is the national deity.

—Second, wit and genius are subject to a twenty-five percent discount when they disembark in England.

—Third, there's nothing in the world so beautiful, so admirable, so heartwarming, as the English landscape.

—Now it's my turn, said the marquis:

—First, what made you say at the Russian ambassador's ball that there are in France three hundred thousand young men of twenty-five who are passionately eager for a war? Do you think that is altogether polite to the crowned heads?[9]

—One never knows how to make small talk with great diplomats, Julien replied. They have a mania for starting serious discussions. If one limits oneself to the usual newspaper commonplaces, they think one a fool. If one indulges in something a little true and new, they are stunned, they don't know what to say, and the next morning at seven o'clock they let one know through the first secretary of the embassy that one has been indiscreet.

8. Philip Vane: Though partly ficti- tious, his name reminds us of the Vanes who played so large a part in the Puritan revolution. His sources have been studied by François Vermale in *Le Divan,* No. 266 (1948), pp. 325– 28, who finds that an original figure was Richard Carlile, a free-thinking disciple of Tom Paine, who suffered years of imprisonment as a result of his devotion to free speech (see *Dictionary of National Biography*).
9. The crowned heads were the assembled monarchs of Europe, united against Napoleon and assembled after his downfall to divide Europe among themselves.

—Not bad, said the marquis with a laugh. But apart from that, mister deep thinker, I'll wager you haven't discovered why you were sent to London.

—I beg your pardon, replied Julien; I was sent there to dine once a week with the royal ambassador, who is the most genteel of men.

—You went to earn the decoration which you see there, the marquis told him. I don't want you to give up your black suit, and I've grown accustomed to the more entertaining style I've adopted with the man in blue. Until further instructions, will you keep to this understanding: whenever I see this cross, you are the younger son of my friend the Duc de Retz, who, though he doesn't know it, has been pursuing a diplomatic career for the last six months. Please note, added the marquis, looking very serious, and cutting short all expressions of gratitude, note that I do not on any account want you to rise in the world. This is always a mistake, and a misfortune for the patron as well as for his favorite. When my lawsuits start to weary you, or you no longer suit me, I shall request a good living for you, like that of our friend Abbé Pirard, and *nothing else*, the marquis added drily.

The cross set Julien's pride at ease; he spoke up more freely. He was less apt to think himself insulted and made the butt of remarks, which though capable of rude interpretation, may unintentionally escape from anyone in the course of a vigorous conversation.

His cross was the occasion of an extraordinary visit; it was from M. le Baron de Valenod, who had come to Paris to thank the minister for his barony and to make his better acquaintance. He was going to be appointed mayor of Verrières after the dismissal of M. de Rênal.

Julien was shaken with silent laughter when M. de Valenod told him it had just been discovered that M. de Rênal was a Jacobin. As a matter of fact, in the new elections coming up, the new baron was to be the ministerial candidate, while in the district as a whole, which was naturally conservative, it was M. de Rênal who was being pushed by the liberals.[1]

In vain did Julien try to learn something about Mme. de Rênal; the baron seemed to recall their former rivalry, and was impenetrable. He ended by asking Julien to help secure his father's vote in the next election. Julien promised to write.

—You really ought to introduce me, M. le chevalier, to the Marquis de La Mole.

I really *should*, thought Julien; but a rascal like this one! . . .

—To tell you the truth, he replied, I'm much too small a person around the Hotel de La Mole to undertake introductions.

1. Liberals and reactionaries, though ostensible enemies, trade positions easily in the works of Stendhal; there is not really much to choose between them. As the Raversi-Mosca factions reverse positions almost without comment in the *Chartreuse,* so here with the Valenod-Rênal factions.

Julien told the whole story to the marquis; that evening, he told him not only of Valenod's pretensions but of his whole life and career since 1814.

—Not only, said M. de La Mole with great seriousness, not only will you introduce me tomorrow to the new baron, but I will invite him to dinner for the day after tomorrow. He will be one of our new prefects.

—In that case, Julien said coldly, I request the office of director of the poorhouse for my father.

—Absolutely, said the marquis, putting on his chaffing manner; I grant it, I was expecting a moral lecture. You are shaping up.

M. de Valenod informed Julien that the director of the lottery office at Verrières had just died: Julien found it a good joke to award his post to M. de Cholin, the ancient imbecile whose petition he had once picked up in the room occupied by M. de La Mole. The marquis laughed heartily at the petition which Julien repeated as he prepared for his signature the letter requesting this post from the minister of finance.

M. Cholin had barely been named when Julien learned that the post had been requested, by the deputies of the district, for M. Gros, the celebrated mathematician:[2] this large-spirited man, who himself had an income of only fourteen hundred francs, had been lending six hundred of them every year to the late holder of the post, to help him raise his family.

Julien was stunned at what he had done. [What are the dead man's family to do now? The thought wrung his heart.] It's nothing important, he told himself, there are plenty of other injustices which I will have to commit if I'm to be successful; and what's more, I'll have to conceal them under lofty, sentimental words. Poor M. Gros! He deserved the cross; I have it, and I must play along with the government that gave it to me.

Chapter 8

WHICH DECORATION CONFERS DISTINCTION?

> Your water does not refresh me, said the thirsty genie. —Yet it's the coolest well in the whole Diar Békir.
> —Pellico[3]

One day Julien was returning from the charming property of Villequier, along the banks of the Seine, an estate in which M. de La Mole took particular interest because, of all those he possessed, it was the only one that had belonged to the famous Boniface de La

2. M. Gros: See p. 114, note 2.
3. During the turbulent 1820's, Silvio Pellico, tragic poet and ardent liberal, suffered both a sentence of death and a long jail sentence for conspiracy—so that his name rightly stands at the head of this chapter.

Mole. At the hotel Julien found the marquise and her daughter, just back from Hyères.

Julien was a dandy now and understood the art of living in Paris. He behaved with perfect coolness toward Mlle. de La Mole. He seemed to remember nothing at all of the period when she was asking so gaily for details on his technique of falling [gracefully] off a horse.

Mlle. de La Mole found him taller and paler. Neither his figure nor his dress betrayed any longer the mark of the provincial; not so, however, with his conversation: this was still too serious, too positive. But despite all these reasonable qualities, thanks to his pride, it conveyed no hint of servility; one was simply aware that he still considered too many things to be important. But it was clear that he was a man to maintain his opinion.

—He lacks the light touch, but not intelligence, said Mlle. de La Mole to her father; and she teased him about the cross he had given to Julien. My brother has been requesting it for these eighteen months, and he is a La Mole! . . .

—True; but Julien is capable of the unexpected, and that has never occurred to the La Mole you mention.

The Duc de Retz was announced.

Mathilde was overcome with an irresistible urge to yawn; the sight of him somehow brought to mind all the antique gilt work and elderly visitors of her father's drawing room. She had a vision of the completely boring life she would be taking up again in Paris At Hyères she had missed Paris.

And yet I'm nineteen years old! she thought; it's the age of happiness, at least according to all these gilt-edged idiots. She glanced at eight or ten volumes of new poetry that had piled up on the drawing room table during her absence in Provence. She had the misfortune to be cleverer than Messieurs de Croisenois, de Caylus, de Luz, and her other friends. She could foresee everything they would tell her about the beautiful sky of Provence, poetry, the south, etc., etc.

Her lovely eyes, in which there was an expression of profound boredom, and, worse still, of despair that she would ever find pleasure, paused a moment upon Julien. At least, he was not exactly like the next comer.

—Monsieur Sorel, she said in that short, sharp, completely unfeminine voice which is customary among young women of the upper class, Monsieur Sorel, are you coming this evening to the ball of M. de Retz?

—Mademoiselle, I have not had the honor of an introduction to M. le duc. (One would have said that these words and this title scorched the lips of the lofty provincial.)

—He has asked my brother to bring you along; and if you came, you could tell me something about the estate at Villequier; they're talking of moving out there this spring. I would like to know if the house is livable, and if the district is as pretty as I'm told. There are so many undeserved reputations!

Julien made no answer.

—Come to the ball with my brother, she added in a dry tone.

Julien bowed with respect. So even in the course of a dance I must render accounts to all the members of the family. Don't they pay me to be their businessman? His black humor added: God knows if what I tell the daughter won't cross in some way the plans of the father, the brother, or the mother! It's absolutely like the court of a reigning prince. One is expected to be a complete non-entity, but not to give anyone the slightest cause for complaint.

How disagreeable that big girl is! he thought, as he watched Mlle. de La Mole leave the room in response to a call from her mother, who wanted to introduce her to a number of women friends. She exaggerates all the styles, her dress is falling from her shoulders . . . she is even paler than she was before her trip. . . . What colorless hair, she overdoes even blondness! You would say the light was shining through it. What arrogance in her way of greeting you, in her glance! She has the gestures of a queen!

Mlle. de La Mole had just summoned her brother back as he was leaving the drawing room.

Comte Norbert came up to Julien:

—My dear Sorel, he said, where would you like me to pick you up, about midnight, for M. de Retz's ball? He told me specifically to bring you along.

—I know very well to whom I owe such kindness, Julien replied, bowing to the ground.

His ill humor, finding nothing to quarrel with in the tone of politeness, and even of interest, which Norbert had assumed with him, discharged itself on the reply which he, Julien, had made to this well-intentioned speech. He found in it a touch of obsequiousness.

That evening as he came to the ball he was struck by the magnificence of the Hotel de Retz. The courtyard by which one entered was covered with an immense canvas awning painted scarlet and studded with gold stars: nothing could have been more elegant. Beneath this awning, the courtyard had been transformed into a grove of orange trees and of flowering laurel bushes. As pains had been taken to set the garden pots into the earth, the laurels and orange trees seemed to rise naturally from the ground. The carriage way had been sprinkled with sand.

The whole scene seemed extraordinary to our young man from the provinces. He had no idea of such magnificence; in an instant, his imagination caught fire and lifted him a thousand leagues from his ill humor. In the carriage as they came to the ball, Norbert had been gay, and he had been somber of mood; scarcely were they inside the courtyard when the roles were reversed.

Norbert was aware of nothing in all this magnificence but a few details that had not been seen to. He calculated the expense of everything, and since it added up to an impressive sum, Julien noted that he appeared jealous and promptly turned cross.

As for himself, he arrived in a state of enchanted admiration, and almost timid with emotion at the first of the rooms where they were dancing. There was a jam at the door of the second room, and the crowd was so dense that it was impossible to get through. The decoration of this second room represented the Alhambra of Granada.

—She's the belle of the ball, there's no doubt about it, said a moustached young man whose shoulder was firmly lodged in the middle of Julien's chest.

—Mlle. Fourmont, who has held the number one spot all winter, said his neighbor, sees now that it's second place for her: look at her sulking.

—Actually, she's piling on canvas in an effort to attract. Look, look at that gracious smile when she moves into the central position in that quadrille. Upon my word, that's as good as a play.

—Mlle. de La Mole has the air of being superior to the pleasure she gets from her triumph, of which she is perfectly conscious. You would say she was afraid of pleasing anyone who speaks to her.

—Very good! That's the art of attraction.

Julien made vain efforts to catch sight of this seductive creature; seven or eight men taller than he prevented him from seeing her.

—There is plenty of coquetry in that lofty reserve, said the young man with the moustache.

—And those big blue eyes which lower so slowly just at the point when one would say they were about to give her away, added his neighbor. My word, she's a shrewd one.

—Look how, alongside her, the fair Fourmont seems common, said a third.

—That air of reserve seems to say: What delights I could unfold for you, if you were the man who is worthy of me!

—And who could be worthy of the sublime Mathilde? said the first: a reigning prince, perhaps, handsome, clever, manly, a hero in battle, and twenty years old at the most.

—A natural son of the Russian emperor . . . to whom, on the occasion of this marriage, a kingdom would be granted; or simply the Comte de Thaler, with his air of a peasant dressed up for a holiday. . . .

The door was now cleared, Julien could pass through.

Since these shop-window dummies consider her so remarkable,

he thought, it's worth my while to study her. I can learn what constitutes perfection for this sort of creature.

As he was trying to catch her eye, Mathilde looked directly at him. Duty calls, said Julien to himself; but his ill humor was now only in his features. Curiosity drew him forward, with a pleasure that was quickly augmented by Mathilde's dress, cut very low off the shoulder, in a manner that did little for his self-possession. Her beauty is that of youth, he thought. Five or six young people, among whom Julien recognized those who had been talking around him in the doorway, were between them.

—You can tell me, sir, as you've been here all winter, she said to him, isn't this the finest ball of the season?

He made no answer.

—This Coulon quadrille is a wonderful dance, and the ladies all do it so well. The young men all turned to see who was the happy man from whom she was thus requiring an answer. She did not encourage their stares.

—You are a wise man, Monsieur Sorel, she went on, with more pronounced interest; you look upon all these balls and parties like a philosopher, like Jean-Jacques Rousseau. These absurdities surprise you without beguiling you.

A single word had just extinguished Julien's imagination and driven the last illusion from his heart. His mouth assumed the expression of a somewhat exaggerated scorn.

—In my opinion, Jean-Jacques Rousseau was nothing but a fool when he undertook to pass judgment on society; he understood it not at all, and brought to it the feelings of a flunkey who has risen above his station.

—He wrote the *Social Contract*, said Mathilde, in a tone of deep respect.

—Even as he preaches republicanism and the overthrow of royal titles, this upstart is drunk with delight if a duke changes the direction of his after-dinner walk in order to keep company with one of his friends.

—Ah, yes, the Duc de Luxembourg at Montmorency walks with a M. Coindet in the direction of Paris . . . , replied Mlle. de La Mole, with the joyous abandon of a first venture into pedantry.[4] She was delighted with her own erudition, much like the academician who first discovers the existence of King Feretrius.[5] Julien's eye remained keen and severe. Mathilde had had an instant of enthusiasm; the coldness of her partner was profoundly disconcerting. She was all

4. Rousseau describes this incident of his own servility in the *Confessions* (Book X, section 22).
5. King Feretrius is a local joke, an allusion to an inspector of schools under the Restoration who invented a king of Rome named Feretrius (the name is really one of the epithets of Jupiter: Jupiter Tonans, Jupiter Capitolinus, Jupiter Feretrius, etc.) and delivered a public lecture on him.

the more struck by it, since generally it was she who produced this sort of effect on other people.

At that moment, the Marquis de Croisenois crossed the room briskly toward Mlle. de La Mole. He paused for a moment within a few feet of her, unable to reach her because of the crowd. He looked at her, smiling across the obstacle. Beside him was the young Marquise de Rouvray, who was a cousin of Mathilde's. She was arm-in-arm with her husband; they had been married only a fortnight. The Marquis de Rouvray, who was also youthful, displayed all that inane affection that enthralls a man who has made a conventional marriage, arranged entirely by the family lawyers, and then finds he has a perfectly beautiful bride. M. de Rouvray would be a duke as soon as his aged uncle died.

While the Marquis de Croisenois, unable to penetrate the crowd, stood smiling at Mathilde, she allowed her wide blue eyes to pass slowly over him and his companions. What could be duller, she said to herself, than that whole set! There's Croisenois, who wants to marry me; he's kind, he's polite, he has manners just as good as M. de Rouvray's. If it weren't for the boredom they create, these gentry would be very nice indeed. He too will follow me around at balls with that fatuous, complacent expression. A year after we marry, my carriage, my horses, my wardrobe, my country house twenty leagues from Paris, everything will be as fine as possible, exactly what's needed to make a vulgarian like the Comtesse de Roiville burst with envy; and after that? . . .

Mathilde was bored with expectations. The Marquis de Croisenois managed to get near her, and spoke, but she was dreaming without listening. The sound of his talk confused in her mind with the murmur and rustle of the ball. Her eye mechanically followed Julien, who had moved away with a respectful but haughty and discontented expression. She noted in a corner, far from the swirling crowd, Comte Altamira, who was under sentence of death in his own country, as the reader already knows. Under Louis XIV, one of his ancestors had married a prince of Conti; memories of this connection gave him some protection from the police of the congregation.

So far as I can see, nothing but the death sentence gives a man real distinction, Mathilde thought; it is the only thing that can't be bought.

Ah! there's a piece of wit I've wasted on myself! What a shame it didn't occur when I could get some credit for it! Mathilde was too well bred to bring a prearranged witticism into her conversation; but she had too much vanity not to be pleased with herself. A look of cheerfulness replaced the boredom on her face. The Marquis de Croisenois, who was still talking, thought he must be making an impression, and chattered away even more glibly.

What could a faultfinder say against my little joke? said Mathilde to herself. I could answer the critic like this: the title of baron, of viscount can be bought; a cross, a decoration is given away; my brother has one; what did he do for it? There are all sorts of ways to promotion. Ten years in a garrison, or a relative who's minister of war, and one is a squadron commander, like Norbert. Piles of money? . . . that's still the hardest thing to get, therefore the best proof of real merit. That's queer! All the books say exactly the opposite. . . . Oh, well! to get money one simply marries Rothschild's daughter.

Seriously, my little joke has some truth in it. A death sentence is still the only thing that people haven't thought of asking for.

—Are you acquainted with Comte Altamira? she asked M. de Croisenois.

She had such an air of coming back to earth, and her question had so little relation to everything the poor marquis had been saying for the last five minutes, that his good humor was somewhat shaken. And yet he was a man of wit, and well known as such.

Mathilde is very strange, he thought; it's a disadvantage, but she'll give her husband such a distinguished social position! I can't imagine how the Marquis de La Mole manages it; he's on good terms with all the best people in every party; he can't possibly lose his position. And anyhow, this strangeness of Mathilde's may very well pass for genius. If one is well born and has plenty of money, genius is no cause for ridicule, and then, what distinction it brings! Besides, whenever she wants to, she brings into play such a mixture of wit and character and acuteness, which is the height of good breeding. . . . As it's hard to do two things at once, the marquis replied to Mathilde with a vacant expression, like a man reciting a lesson:

—Ah, yes, poor Altamira, who doesn't know him? And he told her the story of his conspiracy and how it had failed ridiculously, absurdly.

—Absurd indeed! said Mathilde, as if talking to herself, but he *did* something. I should like to see a man; bring me to him, she said to the marquis, who was deeply shocked.

Comte Altamira was one of the declared admirers of Mlle. de La Mole's lofty and almost impudent manner; according to him, she was one of the loveliest women in Paris.

—How beautiful she would be on a throne! he said to M. Croisenois; and let himself be brought into her presence without difficulty.

Society includes plenty of people who are eager to establish that the most ill-bred thing in the world is a conspiracy; it smells of Jacobins. And what is more disagreeable than a failed Jacobin?

Mathilde's glance mocked the liberalism of Altamira with a

glance at M. de Croisenois, but she listened to him with pleasure.

A conspirator at a ball makes a pretty contrast, she thought. She thought that this one, with his black moustaches, resembled the features of the lion in repose; but she quickly noted that his mind had but one consideration: *utility, admiration for the useful.*

Except for those things which might give his country a bicameral legislature, the young count found nothing worthy of his attention. He departed from Mathilde with pleasure, and she was the most attractive woman at the ball, because he had seen a Peruvian general come in.

Having given up all hope of Europe [as M. Metternich has arranged it], poor Altamira was reduced to hoping that when the states of South America became strong and stable, they might be able to return to Europe the liberty that Mirabeau sent them.[6]

A storm cloud of young persons with moustaches drew near Mathilde. She had clearly seen that Altamira was not attracted and felt piqued at his departure; she saw his eye sparkle as he talked to the Peruvian general. Mlle. de La Mole surveyed the young Frenchmen before her with that deep seriousness which none of her rivals was ever able to copy. Which one of them, she thought, could get himself sentenced to death, even if he were granted the most favorable opportunities?

Her extraordinary gaze flattered those of little perception, but disturbed the others. They feared the explosion of a wit to which it would be hard to render an answer.

Being well born gives a man a hundred qualities, the absence of which would offend me: that I can see in Julien's case, thought Mathilde; but it dries up those qualities in a man's soul which might get him condemned to death.

At that moment, someone nearby said: That Comte Altamira is the second son of the Prince of San Nazaro-Pimentel; it was a Pimentel who tried to rescue Conradin, beheaded in 1268. They are among the noblest families of Naples.[7]

There we are, said Mathilde to herself, that bears out my theory beautifully: Good birth destroys the strength of character without which a man can never get himself condemned to death! I am fated to think nothing but nonsense this evening. Well, since I'm just a woman like any other, I suppose I'd better dance. She yielded to the beseechings of the Marquis de Croisenois, who for the last hour had been imploring a dance. To forget her failures in philosophy, Mathilde chose to be perfectly alluring; M. de Croisenois was in ecstasy.

6. This page was composed on July 25, 1830, and was set into type on August 4 [Stendhal's note]. Stendhal is here claiming credit for prophetic foresight.

7. The history is authentic; its purpose is to suggest that the tragedy of Boniface de La Mole has been many times enacted, throughout Europe, from remote antiquity onwards.

But neither the dance nor her wish to please one of the handsomest men of the court, nothing could distract Mathilde. Nobody could have had a greater success. She was the queen of the ball; she realized it, but coldly.

What a wasted life I shall pass with a creature like Croisenois! she told herself, as he led her from the floor an hour later. . . . What can pleasure be for me, she added gloomily, if I can't find it, after a six months' absence, in a ball where I'm the envy of every woman in Paris? Here I am the center of admiration in a company that couldn't possibly be more elegant. There isn't a bourgeois in the assembly except perhaps for a couple of peers and one or two people like Julien. And so, she added with deepening melancholy, fate has given me all the advantages: rank, wealth, youth, everything, alas! except happiness.

My most dubious advantages are those that people have been telling me about all evening. Wit I suppose I have, for they're obviously all afraid of me. If they dare to start a serious discussion, after five minutes' talk they arrive, puffing and breathless, as if they were making some great discovery, at something I've been saying for the last hour. I am beautiful, I have that advantage for which Mme. de Stael would have sacrificed all the others, and yet the fact is I'm dying of boredom. Is there any reason why I should be less bored when I have changed my name for that of the Marquis de Croisenois?

But, my God! she added, close to tears, isn't he the perfect man? He's the masterpiece of modern education; you can't so much as look at him without his finding something pleasant, and maybe even witty, to say; he is brave. . . . But that Sorel is an odd one, she said to herself, and her look of gloom was replaced by one of anger. I told him I had something to tell him, and he did not even bother to come back!

Chapter 9

THE BALL

The luxury of formal dresses, the glitter of candles, perfumes: so many pretty arms and lovely shoulders; bouquets, lively airs by Rossini, paintings by Ciceri! My head's in a whirl!
—Uzeri's *Travels*[8]

—You are cross tonight, said the Marquise de La Mole; Let me warn you, that's not the way to act at a ball.

—I just have a headache, replied Mathilde scornfully, it's too hot in here.

8. Perhaps Stendhal had in mind the *Schweizer-Reise,* a collection of songs of folk inspiration by the Zurich composer J. M. Usteri (1763–1827); but the sentiments of this epigraph are more Stendhal than Zurich.

At that very moment, as if to confirm Mlle. de La Mole, old Baron de Tolly grew faint and slipped to the floor; he had to be carried out. There was talk of apoplexy; it was a disagreeable moment.

Mathilde paid no attention. It was one of her traits never to pay attention to old men or people who spoke on gloomy topics.

She danced to get away from the discussions of apoplexy, though indeed it wasn't really such, for a few days later the baron turned up again.

But M. Sorel is not coming back, she said to herself again when the dance was over. She was just casting about for him when she caught sight of him in another room. And what was astonishing, he seemed to have lost that tone of icy calm that was so natural to him; he no longer acted like an Englishman.

He's talking with Comte Altamira, my man with the death sentence, thought Mathilde. His glance is dark and angry; he acts like a prince in disguise; he looks more arrogant than ever.

Julien moved toward the place where she stood, still deep in talk with Altamira; she looked steadily at him, studying his features as if to discover somewhere among them those lofty qualities that can earn a man the honor of a death sentence.

As he was passing close to her:

—Yes, he said to Comte Altamira, Danton was really a man!

Good Lord, is he going to be another Danton, said Mathilde to herself; but he has a noble expression, and that Danton was so horribly ugly, I suppose he was a butcher.[9] Julien was still so close to her that she did not hesitate to call out to him; she was aware of, and proud of, asking an extraordinary question for a girl.

—Wasn't Danton a butcher? she asked him.

—Yes, certain people thought so, Julien replied with an expression of ill-concealed contempt, his eyes still ablaze from his conversation with Altamira; but, unhappily for these noble gentry, he was a lawyer at Méry-sur-Seine; which is to say, Mademoiselle, he added in a biting tone, he began life very much like several of the peers whom I see here. It is true that Danton had one immense disadvantage as far as the fair sex is concerned, he was extremely ugly.

These last words were said quickly, with an extraordinary air that was certainly far from courteous.

Julien waited a moment, his shoulders slightly forward, in an attitude of arrogant humility. He seemed to be saying: I am paid to answer your questions, and I live on my pay. He did not deign to

9. Georges-Jacques Danton (1759–94) was the audacious and agile Jacobin chiefly responsible for the defense of the Revolution during its first years. He did indeed have heavy, almost brutal, features.

look Mathilde in the eye. She, with her beautiful eyes opened extremely wide and fixed on his face, had the air of being his slave. At last, as the silence drew out, he looked toward her, as a servant looks toward his master to get orders from him. Although his eyes directly encountered those of Mathilde, still fixed on him with that strange expression, he turned away with a striking suddenness.

For him, who is really so handsome, to pay such tributes to ugliness! thought Mathilde, coming out of her reverie. And never a reflection on himself! He is not like Caylus or Croisenois. This Sorel has something of the look my father assumes when he acts out so impressively the role of Napoleon at a ball. She had quite forgotten Danton. No question about it, I'm bored this evening. She seized her brother's arm, and, much to his disgust, forced him to stroll with her through all the rooms. She wanted to follow that conversation of Julien's with the man who had been condemned to death.

The crowd was immense. But she succeeded in overtaking them just as Altamira, standing a few feet away from her, had turned toward a tray to take an ice. He was talking to Julien and half turned toward him, when he noted an arm in a braided coat stretched forth beside his to take another ice. The gold braid seemed to attract his particular notice; he turned completely about to see whose arm it was. At once his dark eyes, lofty and direct, took on a veiled expression of disdain.

—You see that man, he said in an undertone to Julien; he is the Prince of Araceli, ambassador from _____.[1] This morning he made an application for my extradition to your French foreign minister, M. de Nerval. Look, there he is over there, playing whist. M. de Nerval is rather inclined to honor the request, since my country turned back to you two or three conspirators in 1816. If I am put in the power of my king, I'll be hanged within twenty-four hours. And it will be one of these pretty gentlemen with moustaches here who will *get his hands on me.*

—The villains! Julien exclaimed, in a low voice.

Mathilde did not miss a syllable of their talk. Her boredom had disappeared.

—Not such villains, replied Comte Altamira. I spoke of my own case only to make the picture clear. Watch the Prince of Araceli; every five minutes he glances down at his Order of the Golden Fleece; he's never really recovered from the pleasure of seeing that knicknack on his chest. At bottom the poor man is nothing but an anachronism. A hundred years ago the Fleece was a distinguished decoration, but at that time it would have been far out of his reach. Today, so far as well-bred people are concerned, you have to be an

1. Araceli is the name of the church to the Virgin which stands atop the Roman capitol, but the circumstances of Altamira's nationality are carefully left ambiguous.

Araceli to be excited by it. He would have hanged a whole city to obtain it.

—Was that the price he paid for it? Julien asked anxiously.

—Not exactly, Altamira answered coolly; he perhaps had some thirty rich landowners of his district, who were alleged to be liberals, flung into the river.

—What a monster! said Julien again.

Mlle. de La Mole, leaning forward with the keenest concern, was so close to him that her beautiful hair almost fell across his shoulder.

—You are very young! replied Altamira. I told you that I had a married sister in Provence; she is still pretty, good, gentle, she is an excellent mother to her children, a person responsible in every way, pious but not bigoted.

What's this about? thought Mlle. de La Mole.

—She is happy, Comte Altamira went on, and she was happy in 1815. I was in hiding at that time, in her house near Antibes; well, when she learned of Marshal Ney's execution, she began to dance!

—Impossible! said Julien, horrified.

—It is the spirit of faction, replied Altamira. Genuine passion doesn't exist any more in the nineteenth century; that's why everyone is so bored in France. People perform the cruelest actions but without cruelty.

—So much the worse! said Julien; the least one can do, when committing a crime, is to enjoy it; that's the only good thing about crimes, and the only thing that even partially justifies them.

Mlle. de La Mole, quite forgetful of her dignity, had placed herself almost directly between Altamira and Julien. Her brother, whose arm she still held, being accustomed to obey her, stood looking around the room, and to keep himself in countenance pretended that he had been held up by the press of the crowd.

—You are right, said Altamira; we do everything without pleasure and then we forget about it, even when it's criminal. I can show you at this very ball perhaps ten men who will be known as murderers. They have forgotten it, and so has everyone else.[2]

A good many of these people are moved to tears if their dog hurts his paw. At Père-Lachaise, when their tombs are being decked with flowers as you say so merrily in Paris, someone declares that they united in their persons all the virtues of all the knights of old, and we hear stories about the great things done by one of their ancestors who lived under Henri IV. If, despite the good offices of the Prince of Araceli, I don't go to the gallows, and if I ever come to the enjoyment of my fortune in Paris, I will invite you to dinner with eight or ten assassins, all in high public esteem, and all without remorse.

2. "It is a malcontent who says this": Molière's note to *Tartufe* [This is Stendhal's note, pretending to disclaim a view for which he is really claiming the authority of Molière.]

You and I will be the only ones at that dinner without blood on
our hands, but I will be despised and almost hated, as a bloody
Jacobin monster, and you will merely be despised as a plebeian who
has pushed his way into good company.

—Nothing could be more true, said Mlle. de La Mole.

Altamira looked at her in amazement; Julien did not deign to
look at her at all.

—You recall that the revolution I found myself heading up,
Comte Altamira continued, failed simply because I refused to
cut off three heads and distribute to our followers seven or eight
millions which were kept in a safe to which I had the key. My
king, who today is all eagerness to have me hanged, and who before
the revolution was my intimate friend, would have given me the
grand cordon of his order if I had cut off those three heads and
handed out the money in those safes; for I would have been half successful anyhow, and my country would have had a constitution of
sorts. . . . But that's how the world goes, it's like a game of chess.

—But at that time, Julien said, his eyes ablaze, you didn't know
the game; nowadays. . . .

—I would cut off the heads, you mean to say, and I should not be
a Girondin,[3] as you gave me to understand the other day? . . . I will
give you an answer, said Altamira with a gloomy air, on the day
when you've killed a man in a duel; and yet that's a good deal less
ugly than having him butchered by an executioner.

—My word! said Julien, if you want the end you accept the
means; if, instead of being an atom, I had a little power, I would
have three men hanged to save the lives of four.

His eyes gave expression to the fire of an aroused conscience, and
scorn for the vapid judgments of society; they met those of Mlle.
de La Mole, by his side, and this scorn, far from altering to anything gracious and civil, seemed to grow fiercer.

She was profoundly shocked; but it was no longer in her power to
forget Julien; she moved scornfully away, taking her brother with
her.

I must take some punch and dance a lot, she told herself; I want
to take the best there is, and create an effect at all costs. Good, here
is that notorious insolent fellow, the Comte de Fervaques.[4] She accepted his invitation; they danced together. What's to be settled
now, she thought to herself, is which of us will be more insolent;
but, in order to cut him down properly, I'll have to make him talk.

3. The Girondins represented the
liberal, theoretical, idealistic wing of
the revolution—originally radical but
later pushed into a conservative posture, and finally crushed by the "Mon-
tagne." They included heroic but relatively ineffectual figures like Buzot,
Petiot, and the Rolands.

4. The Comte de Fervaques is never
clearly related to Mme. la Maréchale
de Fervaques; both seem to get their
name from a Marshal of France who
died in 1613.

Before long, what was left of the dance was a mere formality. Nobody wanted to miss any of Mathilde's stinging repartees. M. de Fervaques grew uneasy, and, being unable to find anything but elegant phrases instead of ideas, began to sulk; Mathilde, who was in an ill humor, dealt savagely with him, and made an enemy of him. She danced till dawn, and went home at last, in a horrible state of exhaustion. But in her carriage the little energy she retained was still devoted to making her gloomy and wretched. She had been despised by Julien, and could not scorn him in return.

Julien was supremely happy. Delighted, without being fully aware of it, by the music, the flowers, the beautiful women, the general elegance, and above all by his imagination, he dreamed of distinctions for himself and liberty for everyone.

—What a fine ball! said he to the count, it lacks nothing.

—It lacks thought, said Altamira.

And his features expressed that contempt which is all the more stinging because one can see that politeness is making an effort to conceal it.

—You are here, Monsieur le comte. And what's more, your thoughts are on a conspiracy.

—I am here because of my name. But your drawing rooms hate thinking people. Thought should never get beyond the stage of a vaudeville joke: at that stage it's rewarded. But a man who thinks, if he has energy or originality in his remarks, is quickly called a *cynic*. Isn't that the name that one of your judges bestowed upon Courier?[5] You put him in prison, and Béranger as well. Anything of intellectual value, among you, is denounced by the congregation to the criminal division of the police bureau. And good society applauds.

The truth is, your senile society values conformity above everything else. . . . You will never get beyond the stage of military bravery; you'll have Murats but never any Washingtons.[6] I see nothing in France but vanity. A man who talks spontaneously as he thinks falls easily into a bold sally, and the master of the house feels disgraced.

At these words, the count's carriage, which was bringing Julien home, stopped before the Hotel de La Mole. Julien was in love with his conspirator. Altamira had made him a fine compliment, evidently the fruit of deep conviction: You don't have the French frivolity, you understand the principle of *utility*. It happened that just two

5. Paul-Louis Courier, a personal friend of Stendhal's, was a bitter opponent of the nobility and the reaction until his murder in 1825. Because he was a Hellenist and rejoiced in the exercise of a mordant wit, a judge ventured to call him a *cynic* in Greek, in which the word "dog" is more apparent than in French or English; Courier riposted ferociously.
6. The contrast between Murat and Washington is between a fierce soldier and a steady, thoughtful patriot.

nights ago Julien had seen the tragedy of *Marino Faliero* by M. Casimir Delavigne.[7]

Isn't it true that Israel Bertuccio [, a mere carpenter in the arsenal,] had more character than all those Venetian noblemen? our resentful plebeian asked himself; and yet those nobles could prove their pedigrees back to the year 700, a century before Charlemagne, while the most authentic aristocrats at M. de Retz's ball tonight can't trace their blood lines back, by hook or by crook, any further than the thirteenth century. Well, among all those noblemen of Venice, whose greatness came only from their birth, [but whose characters were so faded and washy,] it is only Israel Bertuccio who is remembered.

A conspiracy cancels all the titles given by society's caprice. There a man takes immediately the rank which he earns by his manner of facing death. Even intelligence loses its authority. . . .

What would Danton be today, in this century of Valenods and Rênals? Not even a second-string royal prosecutor. . . .

What am I saying? He would have sold out to the congregation; he would be a minister, for after all even the great Danton was a robber. Mirabeau sold out too. Napoleon stole his millions in Italy, without which he would have been cut short by poverty, like Pichegru.[8] Only Lafayette was never a thief. Do you have to steal, do you have to sell out? Julien wondered. This question drew him up short. He spent the rest of the night reading the history of the Revolution.

Next day, as he worked over his letters in the library, he thought of nothing but his conversation with Comte Altamira.

So, in fact, he concluded after a long reverie, if the Spanish liberals[9] had compromised the people by a few crimes, they would not have been wiped out so easily. They were high-minded, babbling children . . . like me! Julien suddenly exclaimed, as if waking from sleep with a start.

What difficult thing have I done which entitles me to pass judgment on some poor devils, who did, after all, for once in their lives, take action, and with daring? I'm like a man who rises from the table and exclaims: Tomorrow I shall eat no dinner; but that will not prevent me from being just as lively and vigorous as I am today.

---

7. Casimir Delavigne's *Marino Faliero* was first represented in 1829; it created a stir by disregarding classic rules. Israel Bertuccio was the major actor in a plot to murder the Venetian aristocracy and proclaim Faliero prince of Venice.
8. Charles Pichegru (1761–1804) was a magnificent general for the French revolutionary armies until he sold out to the Bourbons in 1795.

9. The Spanish liberals enjoyed a brief period of disorderly and divided power from 1820 to 1823; it is part of Stendhal's understated casualness about politics that Altamira (who is identified only casually and in afterthought as a Spaniard) is shown associating in a drawing room with Norbert de La Mole, whose service in the Spanish campaigns must have been devoted to crushing liberals of all persuasions.

Who knows what people feel in the midst of a great action? [For after all, these things are not done in an instant, as one fires a pistol.] . . . These lofty thoughts were interrupted by the unexpected arrival of Mlle. de La Mole, who came into the library. He was so aroused by his admiration for the great qualities of Danton, Mirabeau, Carnot, who never knew when they were beaten, that though his glance rested on Mlle. de La Mole, it was without thinking of her, without greeting her, almost without seeing her. When at length his great staring eyes took note of her presence, the light died in them. Mlle. de La Mole noted the fact with bitterness.

In vain did she ask him for a volume of Vély's *History of France* which stood on the highest shelf and thus obliged Julien to fetch the longer of the two ladders. Julien carried in the ladder, sought out the book, and handed it to her, still without being able to think of her. As he carried the ladder away, in his haste he elbowed against one of the glass panes covering the shelves; a clatter of fragments on the floor finally awakened him. He hastened to make his apologies to Mlle. de La Mole; he tried to be polite, but he was polite and nothing more. Mathilde saw clearly that she had disturbed him, that rather than talk to her, he would have preferred to think of the topic which was occupying him when she came in. After a long, long look at him, she slowly walked away. Julien watched her as she went. He was pleased at the contrast between her present simple attire and the splendid luxuriance of the previous night. The difference in her expressions was almost as striking. This girl, who had been so haughty at the Duc de Retz's ball, had now almost the look of a suppliant. Really, Julien thought, that black dress shows off the beauty of her figure better than ever; but why is she in mourning?

If I ask anyone the reason for this mourning, it will turn out that I'm making a fool of myself again. Julien had quite recovered from his flights of enthusiasm. I must read over all the letters I've written this morning; Lord knows what sorts of blunders and oversights I'll find in them. As he was reading with fixed concentration the first of these letters, he heard close beside him the rustle of a silk dress; he looked up sharply; Mlle. de La Mole was two steps from his table and smiling. This second interruption angered Julien.

As for Mathilde, she had just been made to feel painfully that she counted for nothing in this young man's life; the smile was intended to mask her embarrassment, and it succeeded.

—Apparently you're thinking of something very interesting, Monsieur Sorel. Isn't it some curious anecdote about the conspiracy which brought Comte Altamira here to Paris? Tell me what it's about; I'm dying to know; I can keep it quiet, I swear! She was astonished by this sentence, even as she heard herself say it. So now she was begging from a subordinate! As her embarrassment increased, she added, in an attempt at lightness:

—What could turn you, who are usually so chilly, into an inspired creature, a kind of Michelangelo prophet?

This direct and impertinent questioning cut Julien to the quick, and revived all his folly.

—Did Danton do right to steal? he said to her harshly, and in a manner that became more and more wild. The revolutionaries of Piedmont and in Spain,[1] should they have compromised the people by committing crimes? Distributed, even to worthless people, all the posts in the army, all the decorations? Wouldn't the men who got these decorations have had a reason to fear the restoration of the king? Was it necessary to pillage the treasury at Turin? In short, mademoiselle, he said, approaching her with a terrible air, shouldn't a man who wants to drive ignorance and crime from the earth pass through it like a whirlwind and do evil blindly?

Mathilde was afraid; she could not sustain his gaze, and stepped back instinctively. For a moment she looked at him; then, ashamed of her fear, turned and left the library with a light step.

Chapter 10

QUEEN MARGUERITE

> Love! What act of folly is there in which you cannot make us take pleasure?
>
> —*Letters of a Portuguese Nun*[2]

Julien read over his letters. When the bell sounded for dinner: What a fool I must have seemed in the eyes of that Paris doll! he told himself; what idiocy to tell her what I was really thinking! And yet maybe not idiocy at all. On this occasion the truth was worthy of me.

Besides, why should she come around questioning me on my private beliefs? The questioning was rude on her side. It was a piece of ill breeding. My thoughts on Danton are no part of the service for which her father is paying me.

As he entered the dining room, Julien was distracted from his broody thoughts by the deep mourning worn by Mlle. de La Mole; it was the more striking since no other member of the family was in black.

1. Revolutionaries in Spain (1820–23) and Piedmont (1821) had failed to hold power in the recent past because of high-minded indifference to the cruel facts of politics.

2. The title is that of an epistolary novel by Diderot, but the sentiment is a universal platitude.

After dinner he found himself quite relieved of the transports of enthusiasm that had obsessed him all day. By good fortune the academician who knew Latin was at the dinner party. There is the man who will sneer at me less than anyone else if, as I suppose, my question about Mlle. de La Mole's mourning is a piece of stupidity.

Mathilde was looking at him with an odd expression. That's playing the coquette as women in this part of the world do it, Julien thought; it's just as Mme. de Rênal described it for me. I wasn't agreeable to her this morning; I didn't indulge her little whim for conversation. So now she thinks better of me. And no doubt the devil keeps a finger in the pot. Later, her arrogance and pride will find a way to get back at me. Let her do her worst. What a difference from the woman I have lost! What natural charm there! What simplicity! I knew her thoughts before she did herself; I saw them forming in her mind; within her heart my only opponent was her fear that her children might die; it was a sensible and natural affection, such that even I, who suffered from it, found it admirable. I've been a fool. My imaginings about Paris prevented me from appreciating that glorious woman.

What a difference, good God! And what do I find here? Vanity, dry and arrogant, every conceivable variety of self-approval, and nothing else.

They rose from the table. I can't let my academician get away, said Julien. As they strolled into the garden, he intercepted him, put on a meek, docile air, and sympathized with his fury against the success of *Hernani*.[3]

—If we still lived in the days when a *lettre de cachet*[4] was possible! . . . he said.

—Then, he would never have had the audacity! cried the academician, with a gesture worthy of Talma.[5]

While they were discussing a flower, Julien quoted several phrases from Virgil's *Georgics* and declared his opinion that Abbé Delille's poetry was unsurpassed.[6] In a word, he flattered the academician to the top of his bent. After which, putting on an air of complete indifference:

—I suppose, he said, that Mlle. de La Mole has received a legacy from some uncle and is in mourning for him.

3. Victor Hugo's *Hernani* was produced February 25, 1830, amid stormy scenes of protest and counterprotest. It constituted a manifesto of the romantic party in France, to which the academician is, naturally, violently hostile.
4. *lettre de cachet*: under the old regime, a letter that could be procured from the king ordering some particular person or persons to prison without trial.
5. F. J. Talma (1763–1826) was the foremost tragic actor of his day.
6. Abbé Delille: see p. 145, note 9. He was a most innocuous and insipid poetaster of the late eighteenth century, best known for a translation of Virgil's *Georgics*.

—Good heavens! said the academician, you're in the household and you don't know about her mania? Really, it's very strange that her mother allows such goings on; but, just between us two, strength of character isn't their long suit around this house. Mlle. Mathilde has enough character for everyone, and manages them all. Today is April thirtieth! And the academician paused, looking at Julien with a knowing smile. In response, Julien put on the most intelligent smile he could manage.

What sort of connection can there be between managing the rest of the family, wearing a black dress, and the thirtieth of April? he asked himself. I must be even stupider than I thought.

—I must confess . . . he said to the academician, and his eye continued to question him.

—Let's take a turn around the garden, said the academician, delighted at seeing an opening for a long and elaborate lecture. Tell me now, is it really possible that you don't know what happened on the 30th of April, 1574?[7]

—Where? Julien asked in astonishment.

—On the Place de Grève.

Julien was so astonished that even now he failed to understand. His curiosity, and the expectation of a tragic tale, gave his eyes that brightness which a storyteller so much loves to see in his listener. The academician, overjoyed to discover a virgin ear, recounted at length to Julien the story of how, on the 30th of April, 1574, the handsomest young fellow of his day, Boniface de La Mole, and Annibal de Coconasso, a gentleman of the Piedmont who was his friend, had been beheaded on the Place de Grève.[8] La Mole was the adored lover of Queen Marguerite of Navarre; and you must note, added the academician, that Mlle. de La Mole is named *Mathilde-Marguerite*. La Mole was both the favorite of the Duc d'Alençon and the close friend of the King of Navarre, later Henri IV, his mistress' husband. It was on Shrove Tuesday of this year 1574; the court was at Saint-Germain around poor King Charles IX, who lay at the very point of death. La Mole wanted to rescue the princes his friends, whom Queen Catherine de Medici was keeping as prisoners at the court. He brought two hundred horsemen directly under the walls of St. Germain, the Duc d'Alençon took fright, and La Mole went to the block.

7. Note that when Abbé Pirard was describing the household to Julien (Book II, Chap. 1), he described the execution of Boniface de La Mole as taking place April 26, 1574.

8. In fact, Joseph de Boniface, seigneur de La Mole, and Annibal Coconasso did lead an insurrectionary movement and were executed in the Place de Grève on April 30, 1574. It is a curious element in Stendhal's intricate weaving of the sixteenth century with the nineteenth (and perhaps this is still another meaning for the dichotomy of the title) that the early history is generally factual, the nineteenth-century action largely imaginary.

But what appeals to Mlle. Mathilde, as she told me herself seven or eight years ago when she was only twelve, for she has a head on her shoulders, such a head! . . . and the academician rolled his eyes to heaven. What really impressed her in this political tragedy was that Queen Marguerite of Navarre, who had concealed herself in a house on the Place de Grève, had the audacity to ask the executioner for her lover's head. And the following night, at the stroke of twelve, she took that head in her carriage and went to bury it with her own hands in a chapel standing at the foot of the hill of Montmartre.

—Is it possible? Julien exclaimed, enthralled.

—Mlle. Mathilde despises her brother because, as you can see, he pays no attention to any of this ancient history, and never wears mourning on April 30th. And ever since this famous execution, and in order to memorialize the close friendship of La Mole for Coconasso, and because Coconasso, like the Italian he was, had the name of Annibal, all the men in the family have that name. And what's more, added the academician, lowering his voice, this Coconasso was, on the say-so of Charles IX himself, one of the most brutal murderers of August 24, 1572.[9] But how can it be, my dear Sorel, that you, who are a regular resident of the house, haven't been told these things?

—Then that's the reason why Mlle. de La Mole, at dinner this evening, twice addressed her brother as Annibal. I thought I hadn't heard right.

—It was a reproach. Strange that the marquise puts up with these follies. . . . That great girl's husband is going to have his hands full!

This expression was followed by five or six satiric observations. The malignant pleasure that glittered in the academician's eyes shocked Julien. Here we are like a couple of servants busy slandering their masters, he thought. But nothing ought to surprise me that comes from this academic gentleman.

One day Julien had surprised him on his knees before the Marquise de La Mole; he was begging a post in the tobacco monopoly for a nephew he had somewhere in the provinces. That evening a little maid of Mlle. de La Mole's, who was making advances to Julien as Elisa had done before, reassured him that her mistress' mourning was by no means a trick for attracting attention. She really loved this La Mole, adored lover of the wittiest queen of her century, who had died in an effort to set his friends at liberty. And what friends they were! The first prince of the blood, and Henri IV.

Accustomed as he was to the perfect naturalness that shone through all the conduct of Mme. de Rênal, Julien saw nothing but

9. On this date, St. Bartholomew's day, Catherine de Medici instigated her son Charles IX to order the massacre of Huguenots throughout France.

affectation in all the women of Paris, and when he was even slightly touched with melancholy, he found nothing to say to them. Mlle. de La Mole was an exception.

Gradually he ceased to assume that hardness of heart underlay that sort of beauty which accompanies a noble demeanor. He had long conversations with Mlle. de La Mole, who sometimes after dinner used to stroll with him in the garden [when the spring weather was fine,] past the open windows of the drawing room. She told him one day that she was reading d'Aubigné's history, and Brantôme.[1] Quite a reading list, thought Julien; and her mother won't even allow her the novels of Walter Scott!

One day she told him, with that gleam of pleasure in her eyes which betokens sincere admiration, about the behavior of a young woman during Henri III's reign, about whom she had just been reading in the *Mémoires* of l'Etoile:[2] finding that her husband was unfaithful, she stabbed him.

Julien's self-esteem was flattered. A person surrounded with so much deference, and who according to the academician ran the whole house, condescended to talk with him on terms that might well resemble those of friendship.

But then he thought, No, I was mistaken; this isn't friendship; I am only an audience for a tragedy she wants to recite, it all rises from her need to talk. I pass in this family as a man of learning. So I shall go read Brantôme, d'Aubigné, l'Etoile. Then I can match some of the stories Mlle. de La Mole tells me. For I've got to get out of this role of the passive listener.

Gradually his conversations with this girl whose bearing was so impressive and at the same time so casual became more interesting. He forgot to play the depressing part of a resentful plebeian. He found her to be learned and even rational. Her judgments in the garden were quite different from those she expressed in the drawing room. Sometimes she showed in his company an enthusiasm and a frankness that were completely at variance with her usual manner, so haughty and cold.

—The wars of the League[3] were the heroic days of France, she told him one day, her eyes sparkling with delighted enthusiasm. In those days a man fought to obtain something specific he wanted, in order to make his party victorious, not just to get a foolish decora-

1. d'Aubigné and Brantôme: The former (1550–1630) was a historian, the latter (1527–1614) a storyteller of the heroic age. Both are extraordinarily frank and outspoken, as men and as writers; and both serve as authorities for the story that Boniface de La Mole was the lover of Marguerite of Navarre.
2. Pierre de l'Etoile (1546–1611) was a Parisian bourgeois who kept an immensely detailed diary for many years, not unlike Pepys's.
3. The League was a confederation of French Catholics toward the end of the sixteenth century. Henri IV had to fight and bargain with them to gain his throne and access to Paris.

tion, as in the days of your emperor. You must agree, there was less
self-glorification and pettiness then. I love that century.

—And Boniface de La Mole was the hero of the age, said he.

—At any rate he was loved as, very likely, it's a pleasure to be
loved. What woman alive today would not be too horrified to touch
the head of her decapitated lover?

Mme. de La Mole called her daughter. To be effective, hypocrisy
must conceal itself; and Julien, as we have seen, had half admitted
to Mlle. de La Mole his admiration for Napoleon.

That's the main advantage they have over us, thought Julien, left
alone in the garden. The history of their ancestors raises them far
above vulgar feelings, and they aren't required to be always thinking
about making a living! What wretchedness! he added bitterly; I'm
not even in a position to think about the real interests of life. [I'd
probably judge falsely of them, anyhow.] My life is nothing but a
long train of hypocrisies because I don't have a thousand francs'
income to buy my bread.

—What are you thinking of, sir? Mathilde asked him. [There was
a note of intimacy in her voice and she was out of breath from running to rejoin him.]

Julien was weary of his own self-contempt. Out of pride, he told
her frankly what he was thinking. He blushed deeply at talking of
his poverty to a person who was so rich. He tried to make very clear,
by his proud tone, that he was not asking for anything. Never had
he seemed so handsome to Mathilde; she saw in his face an expression of sensitivity and of frankness which he often lacked.

Less than a month later, Julien was strolling thoughtfully through
the garden of the Hotel de La Mole; but his face no longer had
the hard, philosophical arrogance that had been printed on it by
his continual sense of his own inferiority. He had just escorted
back to the door of the drawing room Mlle. de La Mole, who pretended to have hurt her foot while running with her brother.

She hung on my arm in the strangest way! Julien thought. Am I
a complete fool, or does she have some liking for me? She listens
to me so gently, even when I talk to her of all the sufferings of my
pride! She, who takes such a lofty tone with everybody else! They
would be really surprised in the drawing room if they saw her put on
that expression. It's perfectly clear, she takes this gentle, friendly
way with nobody else.

Julien made some effort not to exaggerate this odd friendship.
In his own mind he compared it to an armed truce. Every day when
they saw one another, before resuming the old intimate tone of the
day before, they almost asked one another: Well, shall we be friends
or enemies today? [The first sentences they exchanged counted for
nothing as far as content was concerned. On both sides they were

concerned with nothing but the forms.] Julien had understood that
to let himself be offended by this arrogant girl just once without
retaliation was to forfeit everything. If I have to quarrel with her,
isn't it better to do so from the first, in defense of my own legitimate
pride, rather than in resenting the various marks of scorn that
would certainly follow my first surrender of any part of my personal
dignity?

Several times, when she was in a bad humor, Mathilde tried to
assume with him the position of the great lady; she employed all
her diplomacy in these ventures, but Julien repelled them coarsely.

One day he interrupted her suddenly: Has Mademoiselle de La
Mole any instructions to give her father's secretary? he said to her.
He is bound to hear her orders and carry them out respectfully;
apart from that, he has not one single word to say to her. He is not
paid to communicate his thoughts to her.

This state of affairs, and the singular doubts that Julien was
fostering, dispelled the boredom which [during the first months]
he had always felt in that grandiose drawing room where people
were afraid of everything and where it was not respectable to joke
about anything.

It would be amusing if she fell in love with me. Whether she
loves me or not, Julien went on, I have as my intimate confidant a
girl of intelligence, before whom I can see that the whole household
is afraid, and more than anybody else, the Marquis de Croisenois.
That young man who is so polite, so gentle, so brave, and has all the
advantages of birth and fortune, just one of which would quickly
set my heart at ease! He's madly in love with her, [that is, so far as
such a thing is possible for a Parisian,] and they're to be married.
Think of all the letters M. de La Mole has had me write to the two
lawyers who are drawing up the contract! And I, who every morning
act out the part of a subordinate, with my pen in my hand, two
hours later, here in the garden, I triumph over that exceedingly
agreeable young man; for in fact her preference is striking, unmistakable. Perhaps she feels hatred for him as a future husband. She
is arrogant enough for that. Then her kindness for me is on the
basis of my being a confidential servant.

But no, either I am mad or she is making love to me; the more
chilly and respectful I show myself toward her, the more she seeks
me out. That might be a policy of hers, or an affectation; but I see
her eyes light up when I appear unexpectedly. Are Paris women
capable of that degree of deceit? Why should I care! Appearances
are on my side; let's make what we can of appearances. My God,
how beautiful she is! How fond I am of her big blue eyes, when
they come close and look up at me as they often do! What a difference between this spring and last year's, when I was living in

misery and keeping alive by sheer determination, in the midst of three hundred dirty, hateful hypocrites! I was almost as evil-minded as they were.

On days of black misgivings: This girl is playing a game with me, Julien used to think. She has a scheme with her brother to pull the wool over my eyes. But then she seems to despise her brother's lack of energy so heartily. He is brave, and that's it, she told me. [And even then, brave only when facing the swords of the Spaniards. In Paris everything frightens him, he sees everywhere a danger of being ridiculous.] He hasn't one thought that is bold enough to go against the fashion. It's always I who am obliged to come to his defense. A girl of nineteen! At that age can anyone devote every hour of the day to living up to the code of hypocrisy which one has laid down to follow?

On the other hand, when Mlle. de La Mole fixes her big blue eyes on me with a certain strange expression, Comte Norbert always turns away. That's very suspicious; shouldn't he get angry that his sister gives special treatment to one of the *domestics* about the house? For that's the word I once heard the Duc de Chaulnes use about me. And as he remembered that, rage wiped out every other sentiment. Is it just a fondness for the old-fashioned terms in that idiotic duke?

In any case, she's pretty! Julien went on, with the glare of a tiger. I'll have her, then I'll leave, and woe to the man who tries to get in my way!

This idea became Julien's sole concern; he could no longer think of anything else. His days passed like hours.

Every time he tried to involve himself with some serious business, [his thoughts drifted off into a profound reverie,] he dropped everything, and came back to his senses only a quarter of an hour later, his heart throbbing [with ambition], his head in a whirl, and with this idea uppermost in his mind: Does she love me?

Chapter 11

A GIRL'S EMPIRE

I admire her beauty, but I fear her wit.
—Mérimée

If Julien had spent as much time reflecting on events in the drawing room as he devoted to exaggerating Mathilde's beauty and waxing indignant against the natural arrogance of the family which she was forgetting for his sake, he might have understood the source of her power over everyone about her. As soon as anyone displeased Mlle. de La Mole, she was able to take her revenge with a sarcasm so deadly, so appropriate, so conventional in appearance, and so shrewdly aimed that the more one thought it over, the more deeply wounding it appeared. Over a period of time, such a phrase could become atrocious for the victim's self-esteem. As she valued not at all most of the things the rest of the family took seriously, they considered her cold and indifferent. Aristocratic drawing rooms are amusing to talk about in other social circles, but that's all. [Their complete vapidity, the interminable platitudes with which they encounter even hypocrisy, end by irking one with an excess of cloying sweetness.] Mere politeness counts for something only during the first days. That was Julien's experience; he was first enchanted, then appalled. Politeness, he told himself, is nothing but the absence of that anger which bad manners would create. Mathilde was often bored; perhaps she would have been bored anywhere. Then, sharpening an epigram became for her both a diversion and a real pleasure.

It was, no doubt, to have somewhat more amusing victims than her distinguished family, the academician, and the five or six other underlings who made up such a devoted following that she had encouraged the Marquis de Croisenois, the Comte de Caylus, and two or three other young men of the highest distinction. In her eyes they were nothing but new targets for epigrams.

With grief do we say it, for we are fond of Mathilde, but she had received letters from several of them, and had on occasion written replies. We hasten to declare that this character is a complete exception to the general rules and customs of the age. As a rule, lack of prudence is not a charge that can be leveled against the pupils of the noble Convent of the Sacred Heart.

One day the Marquis de Croisenois returned to Mathilde a moderately compromising letter she had written him the day before. He expected this token of supreme prudence would much advance his suit. But it was imprudence which Mathilde was aiming at in her letter writing. She loved to play with fire. For six weeks she refused to say a word to him.

She liked to get letters from young men; but in her opinion, they were all alike. It was always the same passion, as profound and melancholy as possible.

—They're always the same perfect gentle knights, ready to leave for Palestine, she told her cousin. Can you imagine anything more insipid? And this is the sort of letter I'm going to receive for the rest of my life! Letters like these must change about every twenty years, according to the trade that happens to be fashionable at the time. Maybe they were less colorless in the days of the Empire. Then all the young men in high society had done or seen actions in which there was something *really* great. My uncle, the Duc de N_____, was at Wagram.[4]

4. Near Vienna, Wagram was the scene of a smashing Napoleonic victory over the Austrians, July 5–6, 1809.

What brains do you need to hit somebody with a saber? And when anyone has done it, he always talks about it so much! said Mlle. de Sainte-Hérédité, Mathilde's cousin.

—Still, those stories are amusing. To have been in a *real* battle, a Napoleonic battle, where ten thousand soldiers were killed, that's proof of some courage. Exposure to danger livens the spirits, and saves one from the bog of boredom in which all my poor admirers seem to be sunk; and their boredom is contagious. Which one of them has the wit to do anything out of the ordinary? They seek my hand in marriage—a big operation! I'm rich and my father will do something for his son-in-law. Ah, I only wish he could find me one who's a bit amusing!

Mathilde's way of seeing things, which was sharp, lively, and picturesque, had an unfortunate effect on her speech, as can be seen. Often an expression of hers seemed positively painful to her more polite friends. If she had been less the rage, they might even have admitted that her speech had about it something a little too highly colored for feminine delicacy.

She, on her part, was altogether unfair to the handsome horsemen who populate the Bois de Boulogne. She looked to the future, not with terror, that would be too strong a term, but with a disgust not often felt at her age.

What could she want? Fortune, noble birth, intelligence, beauty (as everyone kept telling her and as she believed herself) had been piled on her by the hand of fate.

Such were the thoughts of the most envied heiress of the Faubourg Saint-Germain when she began to take pleasure in strolling with Julien. She was astonished at his pride; she admired the cleverness of this young commoner. He'll know how to make himself a bishop like Abbé Maury,[5] she thought.

Before long the vigor, sincere and by no means feigned, with which our hero opposed various of her ideas intrigued her; she thought of him; she described to her friend the most minute details of their conversations, and found that she could never succeed in representing them completely.

Suddenly an idea struck her: I must be in love, she said one day in a transport of incredible delight. I'm in love, I'm in love, it's clear! At my age, a girl who is young, beautiful, clever—where can she find sensations, if not in love? Whatever I do, I'll never feel anything like love for Croisenois, Caylus, or any of that lot. They're perfect, maybe too perfect; in a word, they bore me.

She reviewed in her mind all the descriptions of passion she had

5. Jean-Siffrein Maury (1746–1817) began life in a humble station, but through a combination of wit, bravery, eloquence, and ruthless ambition gained a cardinal's hat during the course of the Revolution.

read in *Manon Lescaut*, the *Nouvelle Héloïse*, the *Letters of a Portuguese Nun*, and so on, and so forth.[6] The only thing in question, naturally, was a grand passion; frivolous love was unworthy a girl of her age and station. She gave the name of love only to that heroic sentiment that existed in France during the days of Henri III and Bassompierre.[7] [Such a love as that never submitted basely before obstacles, it was not life's diversion, but a force capable of changing life altogether.] What a shame that I don't have a real court, like that of Catherine de Medici or Louis XIII! I feel I could rise to the heights of daring and nobility. What couldn't I accomplish with a king, who was also a man of feeling, like Louis XIII, at my feet! I would lead him into the Vendée,[8] which is what Baron de Tolly is always talking about, and from there he could regain his kingdom; then, no need of a constitution . . . and Julien would be my agent. In what way is he lacking? Only a reputation and a fortune. He could make a name for himself and acquire a fortune.

Croisenois has everything, and for the rest of his life he will never be anything but a duke, half liberal, half conservative, a creature of indecision, [of words not deeds,] always avoiding the extremes, and consequently *always falling into the second position.*

What splendid action can there be which is not *an extreme* at the moment when one undertakes it? Only after it's accomplished does it seem possible to people with ordinary minds. Yes, it's love with all its wonders, which must come to command my heart; I feel it in the fire that stirs within me. Fate owed me this favor, lest all its gifts be lavished on one person in vain. My new joys will be worthy of me. Each of my days will not pass, a frigid imitation of the one before. Already there is some splendor and boldness in my daring to love a man placed so far beneath me on the social scale. Let's see: will he continue to deserve me? At the first sign of weakness I find in him, I'll leave him. A girl of my station, and with the chivalric temper they say I have (it was her father's expression), shouldn't act the fool.

Isn't that the role I'd play if I were in love with the Marquis de Croisenois? I should have a new edition of my cousins' happiness, which I despise so heartily. I already know in advance everything that poor marquis is going to say to me, and everything I'll have to say in reply. What sort of love is it that makes you yawn? I might as well take up religion. I should have a contract to sign, like that

---

6. All these books have a vaguely lascivious and pornographic reputation.
7. Bassompierre (1579–1646) was a marshal and diplomat of France who confronted Richelieu and as a result spent a dozen years in jail. His *Mémoires* are of major historical and biographical interest.

8. The Vendée was the scene of a peasant counterrevolt (1793) against the Revolution and its accompanying wars. Centering in the west country and starting as a rural uprising, the revolt soon acquired enough aristocratic leadership and English support to require serious countermeasures.

of my younger cousin, over which all the noble relatives would wax
sentimental, unless of course they should get angry over a clause
slipped into the contract at the last minute by the lawyer for the
other side.

Chapter 12

WILL HE BE A DANTON?

> *The need for excitement,* that was the ruling passion of the lovely
> Marguerite de Valois, my aunt, who shortly married the king of Navarre,
> who reigns at present in France under the title of Henri IV. The need
> to gamble was a fundamental impulse of this pleasant princess; hence her
> quarrels and reconciliations with her brothers, which continued from the
> age of sixteen. But what has a girl got to gamble with? The most precious
> thing she owns: her reputation, the thing she must think about all her
> life long.
>
> —*Mémoires* of the Duc d'Angoulême, natural son of Charles IX

Between Julien and me there is no contract to be signed, no
lawyer [to arrange a settlement], everything is heroic, everything is
up to the free play of chance. Apart from nobility, which he does
not have, it is the love of Marguerite de Valois for young La Mole,
the most distinguished man of his day. Is it my fault if the young
people around the court today are so devoted to the *conventional*,
and pale at the mere idea of a very minor adventure the least bit out
of the ordinary? A short trip to Greece or Africa is for them the
height of audacity, and even then they'll go only in a crowd. As
soon as they see they stand alone, they become afraid, not of the
Bedouin's lance, but of ridicule, and that fear drives them wild.

My little Julien, on the other hand, much prefers to act alone.
Never, in this favored being, the slightest idea of seeking support
and help from other people! He despises other people, and that is
why I don't despise him.

If Julien, though still poor, happened to be noble, my love would
be nothing but a bit of vulgar stupidity, a fool's mistake; I should
not like that; it would have none of the qualities of a grand passion:
an immense difficulty to be surmounted, and the black uncertainty
of the outcome.

Mlle. de La Mole was so taken up with these fine reflections that
the next day, without being aware of what she was doing, she began
extolling Julien to the Marquis de Croisenois and to her brother.

—Better be careful of this young fellow who has so much energy,
exclaimed her brother; if the Revolution begins again, he'll have
us all guillotined.

She took care not to answer back, and began to tease her brother
and the Marquis de Croisenois about their fear of energy. At bottom,
it was nothing but fear of the unexpected, fear of being caught un-
prepared by something unforeseen. . . .

—Always and always, gentlemen, the same fear of ridicule, a monster that, unfortunately, perished in 1816.

Nothing is ridiculous, M. de La Mole used to say, in a country where there are two parties.[9]

His daughter had picked up this idea.

—And so, gentlemen, she told Julien's enemies, you will have been frightened all your lives, and later someone will tell you: *It wasn't a wolf at all, it was only his shadow.*[1]

Mathilde soon left them. What her brother had said filled her with horror; she was much disturbed by it; but the next morning, she was ready to interpret it as the highest possible praise.

In this age when all energy seems dead, his energy terrifies them. I shall tell him what my brother said; I can watch the answer he makes. But I will choose one of those moments when his eyes are alight; then he cannot lie to me.

—Could he become another Danton? she added, after a long, vague reverie. All right, let us suppose the Revolution has begun again. What parts could Croisenois and my brother play? The script was prepared long ago: Sublime resignation. They would be heroic sheep, permitting their throats to be cut without a peep of protest. Their only fear even in the act of death would still be that of displaying poor taste. My little Julien would blow out the brains of the Jacobin who came to arrest him, as long as he had the least hope of escape. He has no fear of bad taste, not he.

The last phrase rendered her thoughtful; it raised painful memories, and robbed her of all her boldness. It recalled various jests of Messieurs de Caylus, de Croisenois, de Luz, and her brother. These gentlemen all charged Julien with having a *priestly* air: humble and hypocritical.

—But, she suddenly resumed, her eye sparkling with joy, by the bitterness and the frequency of their attacks they prove in spite of themselves that he is the most distinguished man we have seen this winter. What matter if he has faults, absurdities even? He has greatness, and they are shocked by it, though otherwise so gentle and indulgent. He knows very well that he is poor, and that he has studied to become a priest; they are squadron commanders, and have no need to study; it's the easier way.

Despite all the disadvantage of his perpetual black coat and that priestly face which he has to put on, poor boy, if he is not to die of hunger, his merit terrifies them, that's evident. And the priestly

9. M. de La Mole's dictum seems to imply that where politics is a contest of popularity, with public opinion as the arbiter, absurdity is no drawback to an idea. Stendhal sketched, but never published, an essay to show that comedy has been impossible since the Revolution because there are now two publics, one crude, the other clever. A draft of it can be found amid the *Mélanges de littérature* of the Divan edition.
1. La Fontaine, "The Shepherd and his Flock," *Fables*, IX, 19.

face, as soon as we've been alone together for a few moments, he no longer wears it. And when these gentlemen make a remark which they consider clever and unexpected, isn't it always Julien at whom they glance? I've often noted it. And yet they know very well that he never ventures to address them except in answer to a question. It is only with me that he ventures to talk freely. He thinks I have a lofty spirit. He never answers their objections except as politeness demands it. He immediately turns respectful. With me he will talk for hours on end; he is not sure of his ideas if I offer the slightest objection to them. And besides, we haven't heard any gunshots all winter; the only way to attract attention has been by talk. Well, my father, who is a great man and bound to raise high the fortunes of our house, respects Julien. Everyone else hates him, but no one despises him except my mother's devout friends.

The Comte de Caylus had, or pretended to have, a great passion for horses; he passed his life in the stable and often ate lunch there. This devouring passion, combined with the habit of never laughing, earned him much consideration among his friends: he was the leader of the little circle.

As soon as they had convened next day behind Mme. de La Mole's sofa, Julien not being present, M. de Caylus, supported by Croisenois and by Norbert, launched a sharp attack on Mathilde's good opinion of Julien, without any preliminaries, almost at the first instant he caught sight of Mlle. de La Mole. She saw through the strategy from a mile off, and was delighted by it.

Here they all are, she thought, banded together against a man of genius who has not ten louis of his own and can answer them back only when he's spoken to. They are afraid of him in his little black coat. What would they do if he wore epaulets?

Never had she been more brilliant. After the first attack, she raked Caylus and his allies with sarcasms. When the drumfire of jests from these brilliant officers was extinguished:

—Let some country squire from the Franche-Comté come tomorrow, she told M. de Caylus, suppose he discovers that Julien is his natural son, gives him a name and a few thousand francs; in six weeks he will have moustaches like you gentlemen; in six months he'll be an officer of the hussars like you gentlemen. And then the greatness of his character will no longer be a joke. I can see you reduced, Mr. Duke-in-the-future, to that old, bad argument about the superiority of court nobility to provincial nobility. But what will you have left if I push matters to the limit, if I am mean enough to assign Julien, as father, a Spanish duke, prisoner of war at Besançon in Napoleon's time, who, from a scruple of conscience, recognizes his son on his deathbed?

All these suppositions of illegitimate birth were considered most ill bred by Messieurs de Caylus and Croisenois. But that was the only thing they saw in Mathilde's argument.

Though Norbert had been put down, his sister's meaning was so clear that he put on a grave look, which, it must be confessed, hardly suited his smiling, open features. He ventured to say a few words.

—Are you unwell, my dear? Mathilde replied with a small, serious expression. You must be really sick if you're answering jokes with moral lectures.

Moral lectures, from you! You must be getting ready to ask for a prefect's position.

Mathilde quickly dismissed from her mind the irritation of the Comte de Caylus, Norbert's ill humor, and the silent despair of M. de Croisenois. She had to reach a decision upon a fatal idea that had just taken possession of her.

Julien is quite open with me, she thought; at his age, in a position of inferiority, and miserable as he is by virtue of his terrible ambition, he needs a friend. I may perhaps be that friend; but I see no signs in him of love. Given the boldness of his character, he would certainly have told me of it.

This uncertainty, this inner dialogue, which from this moment on filled Mathilde's life, and within which she found new material for debate every time Julien spoke with her, completely banished those attacks of boredom to which previously she had been subject.

As the daughter of an intelligent man who might become a minister and return their estates to the clergy, Mlle. de La Mole had been subjected at the Convent of the Sacred Heart to the most outrageous flatteries. For such a misfortune as this there is no remedy. They had persuaded her that because of all her advantages of birth, fortune, etc., she ought to be happier than anybody else. This is the reason why princes are so bored and commit so many acts of folly.

Mathilde had never really escaped from the fatal influence of this notion. However intelligent one may be, there is no guarding at ten years old against the flattery of an entire convent, especially when it seems to be so well grounded.

From the moment of her decision that she loved Julien, she was no longer bored. Every day she congratulated herself on her decision to indulge in a great passion. It's a dangerous game, she thought; so much the better! A thousand times better!

Without a great passion, I was pining away from boredom during the best period of a girl's life, from sixteen to twenty. I had already wasted the best years of my life, with no other amusement than listening to the nonsense talked by my mother's friends—who, so I'm told, were by no means so strict in their behavior at Coblenz in 1792 as you would think to hear them talk today.

While Mathilde was still shaken by these immense uncertainties, Julien was unable to understand the long stares she kept directing at him. He found fresh coolness in the behavior of Comte Norbert and new arrogance in Messieurs de Caylus, de Luz, and de Croisenois. He was used to it. This sort of misfortune often befell him after an evening in which he had been more clever than befitted his social position. If it had not been for the special welcome which Mathilde granted him, and for the curiosity which the whole scene inspired in him, he would have found a way out of accompanying these brilliant young men with the moustaches when after dinner they escorted Mlle. de La Mole on a stroll around the garden.

It's true, I can't overlook it, Julien said to himself; Mlle. de La Mole keeps looking at me in a very odd way. But, even when her beautiful blue eyes seem to be gazing on me most openly and with least restraint, I always feel that they are studying me, coldly and even with malice. Can that possibly be love? What a difference from the way Mme. de Rênal used to look!

One evening after dinner, Julien had accompanied M. de La Mole to his study and was returning unexpectedly to the garden. As he approached the group around Mathilde incautiously he overheard several words spoken loudly. She was provoking her brother. Julien distinctly heard his own name repeated twice. He appeared; a profound silence at once descended on the group, and only weak efforts were made to break it. Mlle. de La Mole and her brother were too aroused to venture on any other topic of conversation. Messieurs de Caylus, de Croisenois, de Luz, and another one of their friends behaved toward Julien with icy coldness. He left.

Chapter 13

A PLOT

> Random words, accidental encounters turn into conclusive evidence in the mind of an imaginative man, if he has a bit of fire in his heart.
> —Schiller

Next day he again surprised Norbert and his sister deep in conversation about him. Just as the night before, a deathly silence followed his appearance. His suspicions knew no limits. Are these nice young people trying to make a fool of me? That would be much more probable, much more natural, than any pretended passion on Mlle. de La Mole's part for a poor devil of a secretary. Who knows if these people even have passions? Misleading other people is their long suit. They're jealous of my miserable little superiority of language. Jealousy, that's another one of their weaknesses. That explains everything. Mlle. de La Mole wants to convince me that I'm her special favorite, simply so she can make a spectacle of me for her intended.

This bitter suspicion completely altered Julien's moral posture. The notion of a plot found in his heart the first seed of a love it had no difficulty in exterminating. This love was founded on nothing but Mathilde's rare beauty, or rather on her queenly manners and admirable style of dress. In this respect, Julien was still an upstart. A pretty woman of high fashion is, we are told, the thing that most impresses a clever man of low birth when he first finds his way into the upper ranks of society. Certainly it was not Mathilde's character that had inspired Julien's dreaming for several days past. He had enough sense to realize that he knew nothing at all about her character. Whatever he had seen of it might be just a pretense.

For example, Mathilde would not have missed Sunday mass for anything in the world; in fact, she went to mass with her mother nearly every day. If some foolish fellow forgot himself in the drawing room of the Hotel de La Mole so far as to make a remote allusion to some joke against the real or supposed interests of either the throne or the altar, Mathilde would freeze on the instant into icy seriousness. Her glance, which had been so sparkling, would take on all the lofty impassivity of an old family portrait.

But Julien knew very well that she always kept in her room one or two of the most philosophical writings of Voltaire. He himself often borrowed several volumes of the handsomely printed and beautifully bound edition. By slightly separating each of the remaining volumes from its neighbor, he concealed the absence of the one he had borrowed, but before long he noticed that somebody else was reading Voltaire. He had recourse to a seminary trick; he placed snippets of horsehair across the volumes he thought might interest Mlle. de La Mole. They disappeared for weeks on end.

M. de La Mole, becoming irked with his bookseller who kept sending him all the mock *Mémoires*,[2] instructed Julien to buy anything new that seemed likely to have some life in it. But to keep the venom from spreading through the household, the secretary was told to place these books on some shelves in the marquis' own bedroom. Before long he was quite certain that these new books,

2. A man named Soulavie was particularly ingenious and prolific in fabricating fake memoirs pretending to be the work of Revolutionary figures; the Napoleonic wars and Empire produced a flock more.

whenever they were hostile to the interests of throne or altar, disappeared immediately. Certainly, it was not Norbert who was reading them.

Julien, exaggerating the incident, attributed to Mlle de La Mole the duplicity of Machiavelli. Her pretense to criminality was a charm in his eyes, almost the only moral charm she had for him. Boredom with hypocrisy and virtuous conversation drove him to this excess.

He excited his own imagination more than he was carried away by his love.

It was after he had lost himself in dreams about the grace of Mlle. de La Mole's figure, the excellence of her taste in dress, the whiteness of her hand, the beauty of her arms, the ease of all her movements that he found he was in love. Then, to complete the spell, he imagined her a Catherine de' Medici.[3] Nothing was too subtle or too wicked for the character he attributed to her. It was the ideal of the people like Maslon, Frilair, and Castanède, whom he had admired in his youth. In a word, it was for him the ideal of Paris.

Was ever a man so ridiculous before as to attribute profundity and criminality to the Parisian character?

It is possible that this trio has undertaken to make a fool of me, thought Julien. The reader has little sense of his character if he has not already envisaged the gloomy, cold expression which his features assumed in response to the glances of Mathilde. A bitter irony repelled, to her great astonishment, the friendly assurances on which Mlle. de La Mole ventured two or three times.

Stung by this sudden whim, the heart of this girl who was naturally cold, bored, and responsive to wit became as much aroused as it was in her nature to be. But there was a great deal of pride in Mathilde's character, and the birth of a sentiment that left all her happiness dependent on someone else was accompanied by a dark melancholy.

Julien had learned enough since his arrival in Paris to perceive that this was not the dusty melancholy of boredom. Instead of being eager, as she used to be, for parties, shows, and distractions of every sort, she avoided them.

Music performed by French singers bored Mathilde to death, and yet Julien, who made it his responsibility to appear every night at the end of the opera, noted that she had herself escorted there as often as possible. He thought he could discern that she had lost a little of that perfect control which used to be evident in all her

3. Catherine de' Medici was the wife of Henri II but became more famous as the mother of Henri III, whom she instigated to the St. Bartholomew's Day massacre of the Huguenots.

actions. She sometimes answered her friends with sarcasms that outraged them, so pointed and forceful were they. It seemed to him
that she had taken umbrage at the Marquis de Croisenois. That
young man must be furiously in love with money, Julien thought, if
he doesn't drop that girl cold, however rich she is! And for his own
part, furious at her insults to masculine dignity, he grew colder than
ever toward her. Often he went so far as to answer her back im-
politely.

Though determined not to be duped by Mathilde's marks of
interest, Julien found them so apparent on certain days, and now
that his eyes had begun to see so much more clearly, he thought
her so pretty, that sometimes he was embarrassed.

These young people with their experience of high society, he told
himself, are so subtle and tenacious that in the end they will overcome my inexperience; I must go away and put an end to all this.
The marquis had just made him responsible for a number of small
properties and houses which he owned in lower Languedoc.[4] A
visit became necessary: M. de La Mole authorized it reluctantly.
Except in matters of lofty ambition, Julien had become his second
self.

The game is over and they still haven't caught me, Julien said to
himself as he prepared to leave. Whether Mlle. de La Mole's
sarcasms against these gentlemen are sincere or just designed to
entrap me, I've had my fun with them.

If there is no conspiracy against the carpenter's son, Mlle. de
La Mole is a riddle, but she is so for the Marquis de Croisenois at
least as much as for me. Yesterday, for example, her ill humor was
perfectly genuine, and I had the pleasure of seeing her snub in
my favor a young man who is as noble and rich as I am plebeian
and poor. That was the finest of my victories; the thought of it will
keep me amused in my mail coach as it rolls across the plains of
Languedoc.

He had kept his departure a secret, but Mathilde knew even better
than he that he would be leaving Paris the next day, and for a long
time. She resorted to a wretched headache, which was intensified
by the stuffy atmosphere of the drawing room. For a long time she
walked about in the garden and plied her morbid shafts of wit so
vigorously in tormenting Norbert, the Marquis de Croisenois,
Caylus, de Luz, and several other young men who had dined at the
Hotel de La Mole that at last she drove them from the field. She
was watching Julien in a strange way.

The look may be a piece of make-believe, Julien thought, but
that quick breathing, that troubled expression! Bah! he told himself, who am I to judge of things like this? This is the most superb

4. Languedoc: the south of France, the Midi.

and subtle example of Parisian women. That quick breathing, which almost convinced me, she has doubtless copied from Léontine Fay,[5] whom she admires so much.

They had been left alone; the conversation languished. No! Julien has no feeling for me, Mathilde told herself in a moment of genuine unhappiness.

As he was taking his leave, she grasped his arm forcefully:

—You will receive a letter from me tonight, she said to him, in a voice so altered that it was scarcely recognizable.

Her altered speech had an immediate effect on Julien.

—My father, she went on, fully appreciates all the things you do for him. You *must* not leave tomorrow; find an excuse. And she ran from the garden.

Her figure was charming. No woman ever had a prettier foot; she ran with a grace that enchanted Julien; but would you ever guess what was his second thought after she was gone? He was offended at the imperious way she had pronounced that word *must*. Louis XV, too, lying on his deathbed, was deeply distressed by that word *must*, foolishly used by his chief physician, and yet Louis XV was no upstart.[6]

An hour later a footman delivered a letter to Julien; it was, quite simply, a declaration of love.

There's not too much affectation about the style, Julien thought, trying by means of literary observations to suppress the joy that was distorting his features and forcing him to laugh in spite of himself.

So it's happened, he suddenly exclaimed, the passion having proved too strong to be bottled up; I, poor peasant that I am, I have a declaration of love from a great lady!

As for my performance, it's not been too bad, he added, controlling his delight as much as possible. I've been able to sustain the dignity of my character. I never said I loved her. He began to study the shaping of the various letters; Mlle. de La Mole wrote a delicate little English script. He required some physical activity to distract him from a joy that had begun to verge on delirium.

"Your departure forces me to speak out. . . . It would be more than I could stand not to see you again."

A thought struck Julien like a sudden discovery, interrupting his careful examination of Mathilde's letter, and redoubling his joy. I am carrying the day over the Marquis de Croisenois, he exclaimed; I, who never talk except about serious things! And he is so hand-

5. Léontine Fay was the stage name of a light comic actress at the Gymnase who first took part in various frivolous plays of Scribe and later graduated to more solemn exercises of the tragic muse.

6. Louis XV, who was five years old when Louis XIV died, attained his legal majority at thirteen, and reigned until his death at the age of sixty-four, had every reason to feel insulted at a command, even from his doctor.

some! He has moustaches, an impressive uniform; and he's always able, at the proper moment, to come up with some observation which is witty and acute.

Julien had a moment of supreme pleasure; he was wandering at random through the garden, mad with happiness.

Later he went up to his office and asked to see the Marquis de La Mole, who, by good fortune, had not gone out. He easily demonstrated, by showing him various marked papers coming from Normandy, that business in connection with the Norman properties made it necessary to put off his departure for Languedoc.

—I'm glad you're not going, the marquis told him when they had finished their business talk, *I like to see you.* Julien took his leave; the expression upset him.

And now I am going to seduce his daughter! perhaps render impossible that marriage with the Marquis de Croisenois which makes his future rosy; if he isn't a duke himself, at least his daughter will have a *tabouret.*[7] The idea occurred to Julien that he might leave for Languedoc in spite of Mathilde's letter, in spite of all his explanations to the marquis. This ray of virtuous resolution disappeared almost at once.

I'm really a good one! he told himself; I'm a plebeian, but I must feel pity for a family of this rank! I'm the man whom the Duc de Chaulnes calls a domestic servant! How does the marquis add to his immense fortune? By selling securities when he hears around the court that there's likely to be some show of revolutionary opposition next day. And I, whom wretched fate placed in the lowest rank of society, I, who have been cursed with a noble heart and not a thousand francs of income, which is to say, not enough for my daily bread, *literally speaking not enough for my daily bread*; am I to turn down a pleasure that offers itself? A cooling spring which comes along to quench my thirst in the burning desert of mediocrity through which I have to struggle! My word, I'll be no such fool; every man for himself in this desert of selfishness they call life.

And he recalled various looks of disdain cast in his direction by Mme. de La Mole, and above all by *the ladies,* her friends.

The pleasure of triumphing over the Marquis de Croisenois occurred to him at this point, and completed the rout of lingering virtue.

How pleased I should be at his rage! Julien thought; how confidently, now, I could cross swords with him. And he sketched in the air a gesture of riposte. Before this, I would have been a fag,

7. Literally, a *tabouret* is a footstool; metaphorically it is the rank of duchess, since only duchesses had the right to take these seats around the queen's circle.

taking vulgar advantage of a bit of courage. After this letter, I am his equal.

Yes, he said to himself with infinite pleasure, rolling the words slowly in his mind, our merits have been weighed, the marquis' and mine, and the poor carpenter from the Jura takes the prize.

Good! he cried, that's the way in which I shall sign my reply. Never imagine, Mlle. de La Mole, that I am going to forget my social position. I will make you understand and feel that it is for the son of a carpenter that you are betraying a descendant of the famous Guy de Croisenois, who accompanied St. Louis on his crusade.

Julien could not contain his joy. He was obliged to go down to the garden again. His room, into which he had locked himself, seemed too narrow for him to breathe there.

I, a poor peasant from the Jura, he kept repeating to himself over and over, I who am condemned to wear forever this gloomy black costume! Alas! twenty years ago I would have worn a uniform, as they do! In those days a man like me was either killed or a *general at thirty-six!* The letter, which he was still clutching in his hand, gave him the bearing and gestures of a hero. Nowadays, it is true, by using that black coat, a man can have a hundred thousand francs in salary, and a blue ribbon, like the bishop of Beauvais.[8]

All right! said he to himself, laughing like Mephistopheles, I've got more brains than they do; I know how to choose the uniform of my century. And he felt his ambition redoubled, as well as his attachment to the ecclesiastical garb. How many cardinals born lower than I was have risen to power in the government! my countryman Granvelle, for example.[9]

Gradually Julien's agitation subsided; prudence came to the surface. He told himself, like his master Tartufe, whose role he knew by heart:

I'll trust these words, an honest artifice.
. . . .
But not believe in such beguiling speeches
Unless I have some proof from her I love
To validate what she's been talking of.
Tartufe, Act IV, scene v

8. Jean-Hyacinthe Feutrier, who became Bishop of Beauvais in 1825 at the age of forty, was responsible for several orders limiting the power of the Jesuits; when the ministry changed, August 8, 1829, he retired to Beauvais, having recently been made count, peer of France, and a pensionnaire to the tune of twelve thousand francs. But he did not enjoy his good fortune for long, as he died in 1830.

9. Antoine Perrenot de Granvelle was a sixteenth-century cleric, born in Besançon, whose learning and capacity for business made him one of the most trusted ministers of the Roman Emperor Charles V and of Philip II of Spain. He was made cardinal in 1561.

Tartufe too was ruined by a woman, and he was just as good a man as the next one. . . . My answer may be shown about . . . for which we'll find this remedy, he added, pronouncing his words very slowly and with an expression of contained ferocity; we will begin the reply by repeating the most striking expressions in the letter of the sublime Mathilde.

All right, but then four of M. de Croisenois' lackeys may jump on me and tear away the original.

No, for I go well armed, and they know very well that I have some practice in firing on lackeys.

Well, let's suppose one of them has a bit of spunk and attacks me. He's been promised a hundred napoleons. I kill him or wound him; that's just great, I've played right into their hands. They throw me into jail, with all the law on their side; I appear in police court, and they send me with all the forms of judicial correctness to keep company in Poissy with Messieurs Fontan and Magalon.[1] There I'm thrown into a dungeon with four hundred other beggars higgledy piggledy. . . . And I would take pity on these people! he cried, jumping furiously to his feet. Do they ever have any for the common people when they have us in their clutches? This outburst was the dying gasp of his gratitude toward M. de La Mole, which in spite of him had been tormenting him until then.

Let's go easy now, my fine gentlemen, I understand this little trick out of Machiavelli; Abbé Maslon or M. Castanède in the seminary couldn't have planned it better. You rob me of the letter which *incited* me, and then I become volume two in the story of Colonel Caron at Colmar.[2]

Just a moment, gentlemen, I'm going to send this all-important letter in a sealed parcel for Abbé Pirard to keep. He's an honest man, a Jansenist, and as such beyond the temptations of a budget. Yes, but he opens letters. . . . I'll have to send this one to Fouqué.

It must be admitted that Julien's expression was atrocious, his features hideous; it was the look of a criminal outlaw. It was an unhappy man at war with his whole society.

To arms! Julien cried. And he rushed at one bound down the steps and out of the house. Around the corner was a letter writer's booth; Julien entered, alarming the man. Copy this, he said, handing him Mlle. de La Mole's letter.

While the copyist was at work, he himself wrote to Fouqué, asking him to receive and keep a precious item in trust. But, he said,

1. Fontan and Magalon had edited a little satiric periodical, *The Album,* and were sent to jail by the Restoration government as a result of their attacks on it.

2. Colonel Caron was executed by firing squad at Colmar as a conspirator against the restored Bourbons. Stendhal thought of him as a typical victim of the reactionary terror.

stopping in the middle, the secret service agents in the post office will open my letter and return to you the one you're looking for; no, gentlemen. Off he went to buy an enormous Bible at a Protestant bookstore, cleverly concealed Mathilde's letter under the binding, had it wrapped, and sent off the package by the stagecoach, addressed to one of Fouqué's workmen whose name was completely unknown in Paris.

That done, he returned joyous and free to the Hotel de La Mole. *And now it's our turn!* he exclaimed, locking himself into his room and throwing off his jacket:

"Can it be, mademoiselle," he wrote to Mathilde, "is it Mlle. de La Mole who had Arsène, her father's servant, bring a much too alluring letter to a poor carpenter from the Jura, no doubt in order to take advantage of his simplicity. . . ." And he proceeded to transcribe the most outspoken sentences from the letter he had received.

His own letter would have been a credit to the diplomatic prudence of the chevalier de Beauvoisis. It was still only ten o'clock; Julien, drunk with joy and the sense of his own power, completely new sensations for a poor devil like him, went off to the Italian opera. He heard his friend Geronimo sing. Never had music so exalted him. He was a god.[3]

Chapter 14

REFLECTIONS OF A GIRL

What perplexities! How many sleepless nights! Good God! Will I expose myself to contempt? He will despise me himself. But he is leaving, he is going away.

—Alfred de Musset

Mathilde had not written without an inner struggle. Whatever the source of her original interest in Julien, it soon overrode the pride that, so long as she had been aware of her own character, had been her dominant trait. For the first time that cold and arrogant spirit was swept away by a feeling of passion. But though passion dominated pride, it was still true to the habits pride had formed. Two months of inner strife and novel sensations had, so to speak, reconstituted her whole moral nature.

Mathilde felt that happiness lay before her. This prospect, irresistible to courageous spirits when linked with superior intelligence,

3. *Esprit per. pré. gui II. A. 30* [Stendhal's note]. This mysterious footnote of Stendhal's has nothing to do with the novel, but relates to an incident that occurred while he was correcting the proofs. The message expands into "Esprit perd préfecture Guizot 11 August 1830." The minister Guizot denied Stendhal an administrative appointment after the July revolution because he did not trust men of wit; a few weeks later, however, Stendhal was named consul at Trieste.

struggled for a long time against her sense of dignity and of simple obligation. One day she entered her mother's room at seven in the morning, begging to be allowed to take refuge at Villequier. The marquise did not even deign to give her an answer, and told her to go back to bed. That was her last effort at vulgar prudence and at deference to conventional ideas.

The fear of doing "wrong" and violating the values held sacred by people like Caylus, de Luz, and Croisenois disturbed her not at all; such creatures didn't seem to be constructed to understand her; she might have asked their opinion if it had been a matter of buying a carriage or a property. Her real terror was that Julien might be displeased with her.

Perhaps he too has only the outer show of a superior man?

She abhorred want of character; it was her only objection to the handsome young men who flocked around her. The more graceful jokes they made about people who disregarded fashion, or followed it clumsily though obediently, the more they lost her consideration.

They were brave, and that was all. And even then, how were they brave? she asked herself: in duels, but duels nowadays are mere formalities. Everything is known beforehand, even the victim's dying words. Stretched out on the turf, with a hand on one's heart, one breathes a generous pardon for the adversary and a word for the fair creature, often imaginary—or else she goes dancing the day of your death, to ward off suspicion.

Men may face danger bravely at the head of a squadron all aglitter with steel; but danger that is solitary, strange, unexpected, and actually ugly?

Alas! thought Mathilde, it was in the court of Henri III that men showed themselves great by character as well as by birth! Ah, if Julien had seen action at Jarnac or at Moncontour,[4] I should have no doubts of him. In those days of power and prowess, Frenchmen were not mere puppets. The day of battle was almost the simplest of all.

Their life was not wrapped up like an Egyptian mummy in a coating always the same for everyone, always identical. Yes, she added, there was more real courage in walking home alone at eleven o'clock at night from the Hotel de Soissons, where Catherine de' Medici lived, than there is nowadays in a trip to Algiers.[5] A man's life was one continual train of dangers. Nowadays civilization [and policemen have] eliminated danger, and the unexpected never

4. Jarnac and Moncontour were two military victories won for Henri III by the Maréchale de Tavannes (1569).
5. The Hotel de Soissons, originally the Hotel de Nesle, was an immense, intricate structure, long since destroyed, but thronged in Catherine de' Medici's time (the sixteenth century) with men-at-arms, courtiers, and assorted quick-tempered ruffians. Algiers had just been captured by the French, July 4, 1830; like most of Stendhal's tiny, incidental details this one has a specific timeliness or applicability.

happens. If by chance it appears among our ideas, there are not epigrams enough to drive it away; if it appears in the form of action, no act of cowardice can properly express our terror. Whatever idiocy we do out of fear is excused. What a dull, degenerate century! What would Boniface de La Mole have said, if, raising his severed head from the tomb, he had seen seventeen of his descendants taken captive in 1793 like so many sheep, in order to be guillotined two days later? Death was certain but it would have been bad form to defend themselves and take a Jacobin or two with them. Ah, in the heroic days of France, in the age of Boniface de La Mole, Julien would have been the squadron commander, and my brother the young priest of conventional manners, with wisdom in his eyes and reason on his lips.

A few months before, Mathilde had been in despair that she would never meet anyone the least out of the common run. She had found some amusement in allowing herself to write to various young men of rank. This act of boldness, so unconventional and improper in a young girl, might well have dishonored her in the eyes of M. de Croisenois, her grandfather the Duc de Chaulnes, and the whole household, who, when they saw the proposed marriage broken off, would have wanted to know why. In those days, when she had written one of her letters, Mathilde could not sleep at night. But those letters were only answers.

Now she had had the audacity to confess herself in love. She was writing, and writing *first* (what a terrible word!) to a man in the lowest ranks of society.

This circumstance guaranteed, in case she were discovered, eternal disgrace. Which of the women who visited with her mother would have dared take her part? What polite formula could be handed to them which would soften the shock of society's fearful contempt?

And then talking was frightful, but writing was worse! *There are some things one doesn't put on paper*, Napoleon shouted when he heard of the surrender of Bailen.[6] And it was Julien himself who had told her of this expression, as if teaching her a lesson in advance!

But all this was still nothing; Mathilde's anguish had other sources. Forgetting the terrible effect on society, the ineffacable blot of shame as a result of betraying her class, Mathilde was writing to a being entirely different from people like Croisenois, de Luz, and Caylus.

The depth, the *unknown* quality of Julien's character would have

6. General Dupont surrendered Bailen to the Spanish on July 23, 1809; when Napoleon learned of the terms, which he thought humiliating since they involved an admission of various misdeeds, he was furious.

frightened her, even if she had been forming an ordinary relation with him. And she was going to take him for her lover, perhaps her master!

What won't he pretend to, if ever he is in a position of power over me? No matter! I can say like Medea: *Amid so many perils, still I have MYSELF*.[7]

Julien, she understood, had no veneration for blue blood. Worse still, it was possible that he felt no love for her!

In these last moments of fearful doubts, ideas of feminine pride rose to afflict her. Everything must be strange in the destiny of a girl like me, Mathilde cried with impatience. Thus the pride that had been taught her from the cradle became an adversary to her virtue. And at this moment, Julien's announced departure precipitated everything.

(Such characters are fortunately very rare indeed.)

That night, very late, Julien was spiteful enough to have an extremely heavy trunk carried down to the porter's room; to carry it, he summoned the footman who was paying court to Mlle. de La Mole's maid. This little device may be pointless, he thought, but if it succeeds, she will think I've left. He went to sleep much pleased with this bit of cleverness. Mathilde never closed an eye.

Next morning very early Julien left the house without being seen by anyone, but he came back before eight.

Hardly was he in the library when Mlle. de La Mole appeared in the doorway. He handed his answer to her. He thought it might be his duty to say a few words to her; nothing would have been easier, but Mlle. de La Mole refused to listen and disappeared. Julien was delighted at this turn; he had not known what to say.

If this whole thing isn't just a game worked out with Comte Norbert, it's clear that my cold looks have sparked the extraordinary affection that this high-born girl has persuaded herself she feels for me. I should be a good deal more stupid than the situation calls for if ever I let myself be attracted into some feeling for this big blond doll. This bit of logic left him more cold and calculating than he had ever been before in his life.

In the battle that is shaping up, he added, pride of birth will be like a high hill, forming a point of military vantage between us. That's where we have to maneuver. I made a mistake to stay in Paris; putting off my departure cheapens me and leaves me wide open if this is nothing but a game. What danger was there in going? I would have fooled them, if they had been trying to fool me. And if there's anything to her interest in me, I would have strengthened it a hundredfold.

7. Corneille, *Médée*, I, 5; inaccurate, as usual.

Mlle. de La Mole's letter had so roused Julien's vanity that he had forgotten, in his joy at what was happening, to think seriously of all the advantages of going away.

It was a fixed feature of his character to be very conscious of his own faults. This particular one annoyed him extremely, so that he almost forgot the incredible victory that had preceded this slight oversight. Then, about nine o'clock, Mlle. de La Mole appeared on the threshold of the library door, tossed him a letter, and fled.

It looks as if this is going to be an epistolary novel, he said, as he picked up this missive. The enemy makes a false move; I reply with coolness and virtue.

The letter demanded a decisive answer with a haughtiness that increased his inner glee. He gave himself the pleasure of mystifying for two pages the people who were trying to make a fool of him, and by way of another pleasantry he ended his reply by announcing that he had decided to leave next morning.

When his letter was finished: The garden can serve me as a way of delivering it, he thought, and went there. He looked up at the window of Mlle. de La Mole's room.

It was on the second floor, beside her mother's bedchamber, but there was a rather high mezzanine.

The second floor, in fact, was so high that Julien as he walked under the row of linden trees with his letter in his hand could not be seen from Mlle. de La Mole's window. The vault formed by the lindens, which had been carefully pruned to shape, screened him from view. But what have I done now! Julien told himself angrily. Another piece of folly! If they're trying to make a fool of me, I'm just playing the enemy's game if I let myself be seen walking around with a letter in my hand.

Norbert's room was directly above his sister's, and if Julien came out from under the vault formed by the trimmed lindens, the count and his friends would have been able to follow his every move.

Mlle. de La Mole appeared behind her window; he half showed her the letter; she bowed her head. Julien promptly returned to his own room at a run, and just happened to meet on the main staircase the fair Mathilde, who grasped his letter with perfect assurance and gay eyes.

What passion there was in the eyes of poor Mme. de Rênal, thought Julien, when even after six months of intimate relations she ventured to accept a letter from me! In her whole life, I daresay, she never once looked at me with a laugh in her eyes.

He did not formulate so clearly the rest of his judgment; was he ashamed of the futility of his present motives? But also, what a difference, his thought added, in the elegance of her morning dress, of her whole appearance! Looking at Mlle. de La Mole from a distance of thirty feet, a man of taste would be able to recognize at a glance her social rank. That's what one could call an explicit advantage.

Even as he jested, Julien avoided giving full expression to his thought; Mme. de Rênal had had no Marquis de Croisenois to sacrifice to him. As a rival he had had only that ignoble subprefect M. Charcot, who had himself called de Maugiron because there are no more real de Maugirons.

At five o'clock Julien received a third letter; it was tossed to him through the library door. Once more Mlle. de La Mole ran away. What a craze for writing she has! said he, with a laugh, when it would be so easy for us to talk! The enemy wants to have my letters, that is clear, and lots of them! He was in no hurry to open this one. More elegant phrases, he thought; but as he read it, he paled. It was only eight lines long.

"I must speak with you: I must speak with you tonight; be in the garden when one o'clock strikes. Take the gardener's long ladder from beside the well; place it next to my window and come up. There will be a full moon: no matter."

Chapter 15

IS IT A PLOT?

> Ah! what a painful interval between the first thoughts of a project and its execution! So many vain terrors! So many doubts! Life is at stake. Or rather, much more than life—honor!
> —Schiller

This is becoming serious, Julien thought . . . and altogether too obvious, he added, after a bit of thought. What! This fine young lady can talk to me in the library just as freely, God be praised, as she wants; to keep from being bothered with accounts, the marquis never comes there. What the deuce! M. de La Mole and Comte Norbert, the only people who ever come here, are out almost all day; nothing is easier than to see when they return to the house, and the sublime Mathilde, for whose hand a reigning prince would not be too noble, begs me to commit an act of abominable rashness!

It's perfectly clear, they're out to ruin me, or turn me to ridicule at least. First they tried to ruin me with the letters, but I was too shrewd for them; well, now they need an action as open as daylight. These pretty little gentlemen either think I'm dumb or think I'm conceited. What the devil! Under the brightest moonlight in the world, they want me to climb a ladder to a second-story window twenty-five feet from the ground! People will have time to see me even from the houses down the street. I'll be a fine sight on my ladder! Julien went up to his room and began to pack his trunk.

whistling as he went. He had decided to leave without even answering the note.

But this sensible decision gave him no peace of mind. If by chance, he suddenly thought as his trunk snapped shut, if Mathilde were sincere! Then I will have acted, in her eyes, the role of an accomplished coward. I have no distinction of birth, so I need great qualities, to be produced on demand without flattering promises, qualities thoroughly backed by eloquent actions. . . .

He was a quarter hour [striding up and down his room.] Why deny it? he said at last; I shall be a coward in her eyes. I shall lose not only the most brilliant woman in high society, as everyone kept telling me at the Duc de Retz's ball, but also the heavenly pleasure of seeing her sacrifice for me the Marquis de Croisenois, who is the son of a duke and will be a duke himself. A charming young man, who has all the qualities I lack: wit on demand, birth, fortune. . . .

The missed opportunity will haunt me all my life, not for her sake, there's no lack of mistresses!

> *But there's only one honor!*

as old Don Diego says,[8] and here, clearly and explicitly, I draw back from the first danger I encounter; for that duel with M. de Beauvoisis turned out to be a mere joke. Here everything is different. I may be shot dead by a concealed servant, but that's the least of it; I may be dishonored.

This is getting serious, my lad, he added, putting on a Gascon accent and a Gascon gaiety. It's a *pint of honnur*. A poor devil like me, dropped by fate in the lowest rank of society, will never get a chance like this again; adventures I may have, but not on this scale. . . .

For a long time he thought it over, now striding hastily up and down the room, now stopping short for a while. There stood in his room a splendid marble bust of Cardinal Richelieu,[9] toward which his eye involuntarily strayed. [Under the lamplight,] the bust seemed to look at him with a severe expression, as if reproaching him for lacking that audacity which ought to be so instinctive in the French character. In your day, O great man, would I have hesitated?

At the worst, Julien told himself at last, let's suppose the whole thing is a trap; it's a very ugly one, and very compromising for a young girl. They know I'm not the man to keep my mouth shut. So they will have to kill me. That was all right in 1574, in the days of Boniface de La Mole, but today's La Mole would never dare. These

8. Corneille, *Le Cid*, III, 6.
9. Cardinal Richelieu, who was diverted from a military career into the church by a mere accident, became during the early seventeenth century what Julien aspires to become in the early nineteenth, a figure of immense political and social power.

people are not what they used to be. Mlle. de La Mole is so much envied! Four hundred drawing rooms would echo to her shame the next day, and what pleasure would be found in it!

The servants joke together about the marked preference she shows for me, I know it, I've overheard them.

On the other hand, her letters! . . . They may suppose that I'll have them on me. When they catch me in her room, they'll take them. I'll have to deal with two, three, four men, how can I tell? But where can they find men for this job? Where in Paris can they find discreet agents for a job like this? They're afraid of the law. . . . By God, it will be Caylus, Croisenois, and de Luz themselves. That moment when they've caught me, and the idiotic figure I'll cut in their midst, will be the last reward of their plot. Beware the fate of Abelard,[1] master secretary!

By God, though, gentlemen! You'll carry away a few scratches from me; I'll strike at the face, like Caesar's soldiers at Pharsalia. . . .[2] As for the letters, I can get them into a safe place.

Julien made copies of the two last letters, hid them in a volume of the fine Voltaire in the library, and with his own hand carried the originals to the post office.

When he returned to the house: What sort of idiocy am I jumping into? he asked himself, in surprise and terror. He had been a quarter of an hour without looking squarely at the evening's proposed action.

But if I turn back, I'll despise myself forever! All my life long this action will be a matter of doubt for me, and in my case this sort of doubt is the most terrible of pains. Didn't I feel the same way about Amanda's lover? I believe I'd pardon myself more readily for an open crime; once I had confessed it, I should never think of it again.

How's this? I find myself, by some stroke of luck, in rivalry with a man bearing one of the finest names in France, and now I propose in all cheerfulness to declare myself his inferior! At bottom, it's cowardice not to go. That word decides it, Julien exclaimed, rising to his feet . . . and besides, she is really pretty.

If it isn't all a trap, what madness she's undertaking for my sake! . . . If it is a trap, by God, gentlemen, I can turn jest to earnest, and that's just what I'll do.

But if they pinion my arms as I enter the room; or they may have some clever contraption there, ready to catch me!

It's like a duel, said he, with a laugh, there's a parry for every thrust, so my fencing master says, but the good Lord, who wants to

---

1. Abelard was castrated by the father of Heloïse, the canon Fulbert.
2. Plutarch (*Life of Caesar*) tells how, at the battle of Pharsalia, Caesar, seeing that many of Pompey's troops were vain, good-looking Roman blades, ordered his own grim veterans to strike chiefly at their faces.

get it over with, manages things so that one of the two forgets to parry. And for that matter, I have here an answer for them: he drew his pocket pistols, and though they were already loaded, renewed the primings.

There were still many hours to wait; in order to be doing something, Julien wrote to Fouqué: "My friend, you must not open the enclosed letter except in case of accident, that is, if you hear that something strange has happened to me. Then, erase all the proper names from the manuscript I am sending you, and make eight copies of it, which you will send to the newspapers of Marseilles, Bordeaux, Lyon, Brussels, and so forth; ten days later, have the manuscript printed, and send the first copy to the Marquis de La Mole; then, two weeks after that, scatter the remaining copies at night through the streets of Verrières."

This brief apologetic memoir, arranged in the form of a story, was only to be opened by Fouqué in case of accident; Julien tried to phrase things in a fashion as little compromising as possible for Mlle. de La Mole, but he described his position very explicitly indeed.

Julien finished making up his package just as the dinner bell sounded; it made his heart beat rapidly. His imagination, caught up in the story he had just finished writing, was full of gloomy forebodings. He had pictures of himself seized by servants, throttled, carried down into a dungeon with a gag in his mouth. There a flunkey stood guard over him, and if the honor of the noble family demanded a tragic end to the story, nothing was easier than to finish it off with one of those poisons which leave no trace; then they would say he had died of an unfortunate illness and would carry his corpse back to his room.

Stirred by his own story like a playwright by his play, Julien was in real physical fear when he entered the dining room. He looked at all the servants in their full livery. He studied their faces. Which of them have been selected for tonight's expedition? he asked himself. In this family, memories of the court of Henri III are so strong, so often recalled, that if they think themselves insulted, they will react more decisively than other people of their rank. He looked at Mlle. de La Mole to read in her eyes her family's plans; she was pale, and he thought she had a thoroughly medieval appearance. Never had he seen such an air of grandeur about her; she was truly beautiful and impressive. He almost fell in love with her. *Pallida morte futura*,[3] he said to himself (Her pallor presages a great action).

In vain, after dinner, did he walk ostentatiously for a long time in the garden. Mlle. de La Mole did not appear. Being able to talk

3. The phrase is Virgil's, describing Dido: *Aeneid*, IV, 644.

with her would have relieved his heart, at that moment, of a great burden.

Why not admit it? he was afraid. As he had resolved to take action, he abandoned himself to this emotion without shame. Provided I find the necessary courage when action is needed, he told himself, who cares what I feel now? He went over to survey the situation and discover the weight of the ladder.

It's an implement, he told himself with a laugh, of which I'm destined to make use! here, as at Verrières. What a difference! There, he added with a sigh, I didn't have to mistrust the person for whose sake I was running risks. What a difference, too, in the danger!

I might have been killed in M. de Rênal's gardens, but without any risk of dishonor. It would have been easy enough to make my death inexplicable. Here, what abominable stories they'll tell in the drawing rooms of the Hotel de Chaulnes, the Hotel de Caylus, the Hotel de Retz, and so on, all over Paris. I shall be a monster to all posterity.

That is, for two or three years, he laughed, catching himself up. But the thought depressed him. And as for me, who will take my part? Supposing Fouqué prints my posthumous pamphlet; it will be only one more disgraceful act. What a picture! I'm taken into a house, and as a reward for the hospitality I receive there, for the kindness that is lavished on me, I publish a pamphlet on the things that happen there! I attack the honor of the women! Ah, better a thousand times to be duped!

It was an awful evening.

Chapter 16

ONE O'CLOCK IN THE MORNING

> It was a big garden, laid out only a few years ago, in perfect taste. But the trees had stood in the famous Pré-aux-Clercs, so renowned in the days of Henri III, and were more than a hundred years old. There was something pastoral about it.
>
> —Massinger[4]

He was about to countermand his instructions to Fouqué when the clock struck eleven. He rattled the key in the lock of his door loudly, as if he was locking himself in. Then he prowled like a wolf through the rest of the house to see what was happening, especially

---

4. Since Stendhal corrected various phrases of this epigraph in the Bucci copy, he evidently felt free to exercise an author's right over it. Massinger (whom he probably never read) was a wicked and hard-minded author, therefore good to cite.

[in the attic rooms] on the fourth floor, where the servants slept. Nothing unusual was to be seen. One of Mme. de La Mole's maids was having a party, and the servants were drinking punch very merrily. People who laugh like that, Julien thought, will not be taking part in any expeditions tonight; they would be more serious.

At last he stationed himself in a dark corner of the garden. If their plan is to keep the house servants out of it, they will get in the mercenaries who are going to attack me by way of the garden wall.

If M. de Croisenois keeps cool about all this, he is bound to find it less compromising for the young person he wants to marry if he has me caught before I get into her room.

He carried out a reconaissance patrol, after the military fashion, and very detailed. It's a matter of my own honor, he thought; if I fall into some ambush, it will be no excuse in my own eyes to say: I never thought of that.

The sky was infuriatingly clear. The moon had risen about eleven, and by twelve-thirty it shone full on the façade of the house facing the garden.

She is crazy, Julien said; as one o'clock struck, there was still light in the windows of Comte Norbert's room. In all his life Julien had never been so terrified; he saw nothing but the dangers of the undertaking, and felt not the slightest enthusiasm.

He went to take up the vast ladder, waited five minutes to give time for a counterorder, and at five minutes past the hour placed the ladder against Mathilde's casement. He climbed quietly, pistol in hand, astonished at not being assailed. As he rose to the level of the window, she opened it noiselessly:

—So here you are, sir, said Mathilde with deep emotion; I've been following your movements for the last hour.

Julien was much embarrassed; he did not know how to behave; he felt no love whatever. In his embarrassment he decided he must make a bold gesture; he tried to kiss Mathilde.

—Oh, come now! she said, and thrust him away.

Much relieved at this repulse, he proceeded to look around the room: the moon was so bright that the shadows it cast in Mlle. de La Mole's room were black. There could well be men hidden in those shadows without my seeing them, he thought.

—What's that you have in your coat pocket? Mathilde asked him, delighted at finding a subject of conversation. She was strangely distressed; all the sentiments of reserve and timidity, so natural to a girl of good family, had taken command again and were putting her to the torture.

—I have all sorts of weapons and pistols, Julien replied, no less happy at having something to say.

—We must lower that ladder, said Mathilde.

—It's enormous, and may break a pane of glass in the living room or the mezzanine.

—Mustn't break the glass, said Mathilde, trying to catch the tone of ordinary conversation; you ought to be able to get it down, I should think, by tying a rope to the top rung. I always keep plenty of ropes in my room.

And this is a woman in love! thought Julien, a woman bold enough to declare her love! Such coolness, such wariness in the arrangements, makes plain that I'm not victorious over M. de Croisenois, as I was fool enough to suppose; I'm merely his successor. But after all, what does it matter? It's not as if I loved her. I triumph over the marquis in this sense, that he'll be furious to have a successor, and particularly to have me for a successor. How arrogantly he looked at me last night in the café Tortoni,[5] when he pretended not to recognize me! And then what a sulky face he put on it when he couldn't avoid greeting me!

Julien had tied the rope to the top rung of the ladder and lowered it gently, leaning far out over the balcony to make sure it did not touch the windows. A good time to kill me, he thought, if there's anyone hidden in Mathilde's room; but perfect silence reigned everywhere.

The ladder touched the ground; Julien succeeded in burying it in a bed of exotic flowers which ran along the wall.

—What will my mother say, Mathilde remarked, when she sees her beautiful flowers all trampled down! . . . You must throw down the rope, she added, very coolly. If anyone saw it running up to the balcony, that might be a hard thing to explain.

—And how me gwine get way? said Julien, speaking playfully and assuming a Creole dialect. (One of the household maids had been born in Santo Domingo.)

—You, you go way by the door, said Mathilde, delighted with this notion.

—Ah! but this man is really worthy of all my love! she thought.

Julien had just dropped the rope into the garden; Mathilde clutched his arm. He thought he was being seized by an enemy, and turned sharply about, drawing a dagger. She thought she had heard a window being opened. They remained motionless, not even breathing. The moon shone full upon them. As there was no further sound, their anxiety faded.

Then embarrassment set in again, as thick as ever on both sides. Julien made sure the door was locked with all its bolts; he thought of looking under the bed, but was ashamed of doing so; they might

5. Tortoni opened his cafe in Paris on the Boulevard des Italiens in 1804 and grew rich selling there his delectable *biscuits* and other varieties of ice cream.

have been able to slip a servant or two underneath it. Finally the fear of future reproaches from his common sense overcame him, and he looked.

Mathilde had fallen into all the distress of extreme timidity. She felt a horror of her present position.

—What did you do with my letters? she finally asked.

What a good way to baffle those gentlemen, if they're spying around, and so avoid fighting with them! Julien thought.

—The first is hidden in a big Protestant Bible which yesterday's mail coach has carried far from here.

He spoke very distinctly as he explained these details, and in such a manner as to be heard clearly by anyone who might be hidden in the two great mahogany wardrobes he had not dared to inspect.

—The two others are at the post office and going the same way as the first.

—Good Lord! Why all these precautions? said Mathilde in amazement.

Why should I lie? thought Julien, and told her of all his suspicions.

—So that's the reason your letters were so cold! Mathilde exclaimed, with an expression more of madness than of affection.

Julien paid no attention to this subtlety; she had used the grammatical form of intimacy, and this singular pronoun made him lose his head—[at any rate, he rose in his own esteem,] and his suspicions evaporated. He ventured to embrace this girl who was so beautiful and whom he respected so much. Her rebuff was only half hearted.

He called upon his memory, as formerly at Besançon with Amanda Binet, and recited several of the finest passages from the *Nouvelle Heloïse*.

—You have a manly heart, she told him, without listening too carefully to his phrases; I wanted to prove your bravery, I must admit. Your first suspicions and then your determination prove you're even braver than I thought.

Throughout this speech Mathilde made a conscious effort to use the intimate form; she was obviously paying more attention to this novel grammatical form than to what she was saying. This use of endearments stripped of every sort of affectionate expression soon ceased to give Julien any pleasure at all; he was surprised at not feeling the least happiness; finally, in order to feel some, he had recourse to his reason. He saw himself much admired by this girl who was so proud and who never bestowed her praises unreservedly; and this line of reasoning led him finally to a happiness founded on self-approval.

True enough, this was not that spiritual delight he had sometimes found in the company of Mme. de Rênal. [My God, what a difference!] There was absolutely nothing tender in his sentiments at this first moment. He was happy over his gratified ambition, and Julien was nothing if not ambitious. He spoke further of the men whom he had suspected, and of the precautions he had contrived. As he talked, he was thinking of various ways to profit by his victory.

Mathilde was still much embarrassed, and had the air of one appalled at her own conduct; she seemed enchanted to find a new topic of conversation. They talked of ways to meet again. Julien reveled in the display of wit and bravery which this discussion made possible. They had to deal with extremely sharpsighted people: little Tanbeau was certainly a spy, but Mathilde and he were not wholly unskilled either.

What could be easier than to meet in the library, and there arrange everything?

—Without arousing suspicion, Julien said, I can appear anywhere in the house, practically in Mme. de La Mole's bedchamber. In fact, that room had to be passed through in order to reach her daughter's. If Mathilde thought he should always come by ladder, he would be overjoyed to expose himself to that little danger.

As she listened to him talk, Mathilde was shocked by his triumphant air. He is now my master! she told herself. Already she was assailed by remorse. Her reason stood in horror of the extraordinary folly she had just committed. Given the power, she would have wiped herself and Julien from the face of the earth. When the force of her will momentarily suppressed the voice of remorse, feelings of timidity and outraged modesty rendered her wretched in the extreme. She had never anticipated the frightful condition in which she found herself.

But I must talk to him, she told herself, that's in the rules, one talks to one's lover. And then, to fulfill her duty, and with a tenderness that expressed itself much more in the words she selected than in the tone with which she pronounced them, she described the various decisions she had reached regarding him in the last few days.

She had decided that if he ventured to climb up to her room with the gardener's ladder, as she had asked him to do, she would give herself to him. But never were such tender things said in a colder, more formal way. So far, their assignation had been ice cold. It was enough to render the very idea of love hateful. What a lesson in morality for a rash young woman! Is it worthwhile for her to ruin her future for a moment like this?

After prolonged uncertainties, which a superficial observer might have supposed to spring from implacable hatred—so hard is it for the feeling of respect which a woman bears toward herself to give way even before a powerful will—Mathilde ended by becoming his loving mistress.

To tell the truth, their transports were a bit *conscious*. Passionate love was still more a model for them to imitate than a reality.

Mlle. de La Mole supposed she was fulfilling a duty to herself and to her lover. The poor boy, she thought to herself, he's shown perfect bravery, he ought to be happy or else the fault lies in my want of character. But she would have been glad to ransom herself, at the cost of eternal misery, from the cruel necessity imposed upon her.

In spite of the frightful violence with which she repressed her feelings, she was in perfect command of her speech.

No regret, no reproach came from her lips to spoil this night, which seemed strange to Julien, rather than happy. What a difference, good God! from his last stay of twenty-four hours at Verrières! These fancy Paris fashions have found a way to spoil everything, even love, he said to himself, in an excess of injustice.

He was indulging in these reflections as he stood in one of the great mahogany wardrobes into which he had slipped at the first sounds coming from the next room, which was that of Mme. de La Mole. Mathilde went off with her mother to mass; the maids quickly left the room, and Julien easily escaped before they came back to finish their tasks.

He took a horse and sought out the loneliest parts of the forest of Meudon near Paris. He was far more surprised than happy. The happiness that came from time to time like a gleam of light in his soul was like that of a young second lieutenant who after some astounding action has just been promoted full colonel by the commanding general; he felt himself raised to an immense height. Everything that had been far above him yesterday was now at his level or even beneath him. Gradually Julien's happiness increased as it became more remote.

If there was nothing tender in his soul, the reason, however strange it may seem, was that Mathilde in all her dealings with him had been doing nothing but her duty. There was nothing unexpected for her in all the events of the night, except the misery and shame she had discovered instead of those divine raptures that novels talk about.

Was I mistaken, don't I love him at all? she asked herself.

Chapter 17

AN OLD SWORD

> I now mean to be serious;—it is time,
> Since laughter now-a-days is deem'd too serious;
> A jest at vice by virtue's called a crime.
> —*Don Juan,* canto XIII, stanza 1

At dinner she did not appear. That evening she came for an instant to the drawing room but never looked at Julien. This behavior seemed strange to him; but, he thought, I don't know the ways of these fine folk [except from their everyday behavior, which I've watched many times;] no doubt she'll give me some good reason for all this. Still, as he was tormented by the most unbearable curiosity, he studied Mathilde's features; and he could not deny that she had a dry, sharp expression. Evidently, it was not the same woman who, the night before, had or feigned to have transports of delight too extravagant to be true.

The next day, the day after, the same coldness on her part; she never looked at him, she never noticed his existence. Julien, victim to the keenest uneasiness, was far removed from the sense of triumph which had been all that stirred him on the first day. Could this by any chance, he asked himself, be a return to virtue? But that was a word too plebeian for the lofty Mathilde.

In the ordinary course of life, she hardly believes in religion at all, Julien thought; she likes it because it's useful to the interests of her caste.

But out of simple womanly delicacy, may she not be reproaching herself bitterly for the irreparable mistake she has committed? Julien thought he was her first lover.

But, he told himself at other moments, it must be admitted that there is nothing innocent, simple, or tender in any part of her being; [I've never seen her look more like a queen just stepped down from her throne.] Maybe she despises me? It would be just like her to reproach herself for what she's done for me, simply because of my humble birth.

While Julien, filled with ideas he had drawn from books and memories of Verrières, was pursuing the phantom of a mistress who should be naturally tender and give not a thought to her own existence as soon as she had made her lover happy, Mathilde's vanity was furiously inflamed against him.

As she had not been bored for two months now, she had lost her fear of boredom; thus without suspecting it in any way, Julien had lost his greatest advantage.

I have given myself a master! said Mlle. de La Mole, [walking about her room in great agitation.] She was suffering from black remorse. He's the soul of honor, well, maybe so; but if I strain his vanity, he'll take his revenge by making our relations known. [This is the malady of our century; not even the strangest follies are proof against boredom;] Julien was Mathilde's first lover, and in this relationship, which generally affords a few tender illusions even to the most withered souls, she was racked by thoughts of the utmost ferocity.

He holds immense power over me, since he reigns by terror and can punish me atrociously if I drive him to it. This idea alone was enough to make Mlle. de La Mole insult him, since courage was the first trait of her character. Nothing could provide her with any distraction and cure her of the boredom that was continually building up inside her, except the idea that she was playing, double or nothing, with her entire existence.

The third day, as Mlle. de La Mole persisted in not glancing at him, Julien followed her after dinner into the billiard room, obviously against her wishes.

—Well, sir, I suppose you think you have some special rights over me, she broke out with ill-concealed rage, since in opposition to my clearly declared desires, you keep trying to talk to me? [What sort of cruelty and treachery is this?] Do you realize that nobody else in the world would take such liberties?

Nothing could have been more amusing than the dialogue of these two young lovers; without fully realizing it, they felt for one another nothing but the keenest hatred. As neither one of them had a patient disposition, and as they were both trained in the manners of good society, they were not long in reaching the blunt conclusion that they were enemies for life.

—I swear to you eternal secrecy, said Julien; I should even add that I will never address another word to you, if it weren't that your reputation might suffer from too marked a change. He bowed coldly and left her.

Without too many pains he accomplished what he regarded as a duty; for he was far from realizing that he was deeply in love with Mlle. de La Mole. No doubt he hadn't been in love three days before when he was hiding in the mahogany wardrobe. But things changed quickly in his spirit as soon as he saw that he had quarreled with her forever.

His cruel memory set itself the task of retracing every slight detail of that night which in reality had left him so cold.

On the [second] night after their declaration of perpetual hatred, Julien nearly went mad when he found himself forced to confess that he was in love with Mlle. de La Mole.

Frightful struggles followed this discovery: all his feelings were uprooted.

A week later, instead of being arrogant with M. de Croisenois, he felt like falling on his neck and bursting into tears.

As he became accustomed to his misery, a gleam of common sense made itself felt; he decided to leave for the Languedoc, packed his trunk, and went to the post house.

He almost fainted when they told him at the booking office that by the merest chance there was a seat in the mail coach for Toulouse tomorrow. He took it and returned to the Hotel de La Mole to tell the marquis he was leaving.

M. de La Mole was out. More dead than alive, Julien went to wait for him in the library. What were his feelings when he found Mlle. de La Mole there!

When she saw him come in, she assumed an air of malignant hatred which it was impossible to misconstrue.

Carried away by his misery, stunned by surprise, Julien had the weakness to say, in the most tender and heartfelt tones: Then you don't love me any more?

—I am horrified at having given myself to the first comer, said Mathilde, weeping with fury at herself.

—*To the first comer!* cried Julien, and snatched from the wall an old sword of the Middle Ages which was kept in the library as a curiosity.

His grief, which he thought at its peak when he first spoke to Mlle. de La Mole, had been increased a hundredfold by the tears of shame which she shed. He would have been the happiest of men had it been in his power to kill her.

Just as he was drawing the sword, with some difficulty, from its ancient sheath, Mathilde, delighted at such a new sensation, advanced proudly toward him; her tears had dried.

A thought of the Marquis de La Mole, his benefactor, rose vividly in Julien's mind. I would be killing his daughter! he thought; what a horrible thing! He made a gesture as if to throw away the sword. Certainly, he thought, she will start laughing now at this melodramatic scene: this idea was responsible for restoring all his self-control. He looked carefully over the blade of the old sword, as carefully as if he were inspecting it for rust spots, then thrust it back in the sheath, and with the greatest tranquillity hung it on the gilt bronze nail where it usually rested.

This whole performance, very deliberate toward the end, lasted for a full minute; Mlle. de La Mole watched it in amazement. So I have been on the verge of being killed by my lover! she thought to herself.

The idea carried her back to the finest years of the age of Charles IX and Henri III.

She stood motionless before Julien [erect and taller than usual]; as he replaced the sword, she looked on him with eyes from which hatred no longer shone. It must be admitted that she was very desirable at that moment; certainly no woman ever looked less like a Paris doll (and this phrase summed up Julien's objections to the women of that part of the world).

I'm going to relapse into a certain fondness for him, Mathilde thought, and then right away he'll be sure he's my lord and master, especially if I give in right after speaking so sharply to him. She took flight.

My God! but she's beautiful, Julien said as he watched her run off: that's the creature who flung herself into my arms so frantically not a fortnight ago. . . . And those moments will never return! And it's all my fault! And at the time of such an extraordinary action, which concerned me so deeply, I was only half awake to it! I can't deny it, I was born with a terribly dull, uninteresting nature.

The marquis made his appearance; Julien hastened to tell him he was leaving.

—Where to? asked M. de La Mole.

—To Languedoc.

—No, indeed, if you'll be so kind, you are reserved for higher destinies; if you leave at all, it will be for the north . . . in fact, to put it in military terms, I confine you to barracks. You will oblige me by not being gone for more than two or three hours at a time; I may need you at any minute.

Julien bowed and retired without saying another word, leaving the marquis in a state of great astonishment; he was in no condition to speak, and locked himself into his room. There he was free to expatiate on the awful misery of his fate.

And so, he thought, I can't even go away! God knows how long the marquis will keep me here in Paris; good God! what's going to become of me? And not a friend to whom I can talk: Abbé Pirard wouldn't let me finish the first sentence, and Comte Altamira [to distract my mind] would try to involve me in some conspiracy.

And meanwhile, I am going mad, I can feel it, I'm going mad! Who can guide me, what's to become of me?

Chapter 18

BITTER MOMENTS

And she tells me all about it! She gives me all the details down to the most trifling! Her lovely eye, fixed on mine, reveals the love she feels for someone else!
—Schiller

In her delight, Mlle. de La Mole could think of nothing but the joy of having come within an inch of losing her life. She went so far as to say: he is worthy to be my master, since he came so close to killing me. How many pretty young gentlemen of good society would you have to melt down to get one such moment of passion?

I must admit, he did look handsome just then when he climbed on the chair to replace the sword in precisely the same position the interior decorator had found for it! After all, I was not so crazy to be in love with him.

At that moment if some suitable way of making up had presented itself, she would have seized it with pleasure. Julien, locked in his room, was prey to the most violent despair. In his madness, he thought of flinging himself at her feet. If, instead of hiding away in a hole in the wall, he had wandered out into the garden and the house, in such a way as to be ready for any opportunity, he might in a single instant have changed all his awful misery into the keenest happiness.

But the social poise which we reproach him for not having would have rendered impossible the sublime gesture of snatching the sword, which for that single moment made him appear so fine in Mlle. de La Mole's eyes. This caprice of looking favorably on Julien lasted for the rest of the day; Mathilde made for herself a charming picture of the brief instants during which she had loved him, and she recalled them regretfully.

In fact, she said, my passion for this poor boy only lasted, as he sees the matter, from one o'clock in the morning, when I saw him climb the ladder with all his pistols in his coat pockets, until nine o'clock of the same morning. It was a quarter hour later, while I was hearing mass at Sainte-Valère, that I began to think of how he would be my master, and that he might try to terrify me into obeying him.

After dinner, Mlle. de La Mole, far from avoiding Julien, talked to him and practically obliged him to accompany her to the garden; he obeyed. There was a new test for him to pass. Mathilde was yielding, without too many misgivings, to a love that was once more gaining ascendancy over her. She found it very pleasant to walk beside him, looking with curiosity at those hands which only this morning had seized a sword to kill her.

But after such an action, after everything that had passed between them, there was no longer any question of their picking up old conversational threads.

Gradually, Mathilde began to talk to him, confidentially and intimately, of the state of her heart. She found a particular delight in this sort of conversation; she proceeded to tell him of the various fleeting impulses she had felt first for M. de Croisenois, then for M. de Caylus. . . .

—What! for M. de Caylus too! exclaimed Julien; and in this expression was made manifest all the bitterness of a cast lover. Mathilde took it this way, and was by no means displeased.

She continued to torture Julien by describing to him in full detail all her former feelings, using the most vivid and particular language and speaking in tones of absolute, intimate sincerity. He saw that she was describing something immediately present to her. He was further stricken to see that as she talked she made new discoveries among her own feelings.

The misery of jealousy can go no further.

To suspect that one's rival is preferred is a bitter blow, already; but to hear in detail about the love that rival inspires in the woman one adores is beyond any doubt the peak of misfortune.

Oh what a punishment descended on Julien at that moment for his many gestures of pride at the expense of people like Caylus and Croisenois! With what an intense and intimate misery did he now dwell on their most trifling advantages! With what ardent and artless sincerity did he despise himself!

Mathilde seemed to him [a superhuman creature]; words are too weak to express the excess of his admiration. As he walked beside her, he kept glancing furtively at her hands, her arms, her queenly carriage. He was on the point of falling at her feet, crushed with love and misery, and crying: Mercy!

And this woman who is so beautiful, so superior to everything, who once loved me, doubtless will be in love with M. de Caylus before long!

Julien could not question Mlle. de La Mole's sincerity; the accents of truth were too apparent in everything she said. Lest anything whatever be lacking to his grief, there were moments when, as a result of dwelling on the sentiments she had once felt for M. de Croisenois, Mathilde began to talk of him as if she were in love with him still. Certainly, love spoke in her accent, Julien could sense it clearly.

Had his chest been poured full of molten lead, he would have suffered less pain. How could the poor boy guess, stretched as he was on this rack of torment, that it was precisely because she was talking to him that Mlle. de La Mole took such pleasure in running over the faded recollections of that love she had felt in the past for M. de Caylus or M. de Croisenois?

Words cannot express Julien's torments. He was listening to detailed accounts of the love she felt for others in the shade of those very lindens where, a few days before, he had been waiting for one o'clock to strike before going to her room. A human being cannot sustain pain of higher intensity than this. [Mathilde left the garden and dismissed Julien after nine-thirty only when she had been called three times by her mother. . . . The man I love now, how much better he is than those I was on the point of loving before! she thought, without being fully aware of what she meant.]

This type of savage intimacy lasted for a whole long week. Sometimes Mathilde seemed to seek him out, other times she did not avoid occasions for talking to him; and the subject of these conversations, to which they both returned with a kind of cruel delight, was always what she had felt for someone else; she told him about the letters she had written, she recollected the very expressions she had used, and repeated for his benefit entire sentences. As time passed, she seemed to be contemplating Julien with a kind of malignant joy. His misery was a source of keen enjoyment to her. [She saw in them her tyrant's weakness and so could permit herself to love him. The future tyrant's grief was a source of delight for her.]

It's clear that Julien had no experience of life; he had not even read novels; if he had been a bit less awkward, and merely said with some coolness to this girl whom he adored and who made such strange confessions to him: You agree, of course, that though I'm not the equal of any of these gentlemen, I am the one you love. . . .

She might have been happy to be found out; at least, the outcome would have depended on the grace with which Julien expressed this idea and his choice of an opportune moment. In any case, he might have emerged successfully and with advantage for himself, from a position which was threatening to become monotonous for Mathilde.

—So you no longer love me, and I adore you! Julien told her one day, in an access of love and grief. This was perhaps the most foolish thing he could possibly have said.

His speech destroyed instantly all the pleasure which Mlle. de La Mole found in talking to him about the state of her heart. She was beginning to feel some astonishment that after everything that had happened he did not take offense at her confessions; when he made this stupid speech, she had almost gone so far as to imagine that he no longer loved her. His natural pride has no doubt killed all love, she told herself. He is not the man to watch meekly while preference is given to people like Caylus, de Luz, and Croisenois, even though he admits they are so superior to himself. No, I shall never again see him at my feet.

In earlier days, in the simplicity of his grief, Julien often made eloquent panegyrics describing the brilliant qualities of these gentlemen; he went so far as to exaggerate. This subtlety had not escaped Mlle. de La Mole; she was surprised at it but could not guess the reason. In the depths of his frantic spirit, Julien, when he praised a rival whom he thought happy, was sympathizing with his joy.

His perfectly frank, but perfectly stupid, expression changed everything in an instant: Mathilde, confident of his love, despised him completely.

She was strolling with him at the moment of his unlucky expression; she left him at once, and her last glance expressed the most murderous contempt. Back in the drawing room, she never gave him another look for the rest of the evening. Next day this scorn was in full command of her heart; there was no further question of the impulse that, for the last week, had made her find so much pleasure in treating Julien as her most intimate friend; the very sight of him was odious to her. Before long, Mathilde's feeling reached the point of disgust; nothing could express the extraordinary contempt she felt when her eyes happened to fall on him.

Julien had understood nothing at all of what had been going on in Mathilde's heart for the past week, but contempt he understood. He had the good sense to appear in her presence as rarely as possible, and he never looked at her.

But it was not without mortal pangs that he deprived himself almost entirely of her company. He thought his misery was actually increased thereby. The courage of a man's heart can go no farther, he told himself. His life was spent at a little window in the attic of the house; the shutters were carefully closed, but through them he could at least see Mlle. de La Mole during the brief moments when she was in the garden.

What were his feelings when he saw her strolling after dinner with M. de Caylus, M. de Luz, or some other man for whom she admitted having formerly felt some erotic inclination?

Julien had no notion of such intense misery; he was on the point of screaming aloud; this hypocritical soul, to whom hypocrisy was almost second nature, was completely overwhelmed.

Every idea that did not pertain to Mlle. de La Mole became hateful to him; he was incapable of writing the simplest letters.

—You must be mad, the marquis told him one morning.

Julien, fearful of being found out, talked of being sick and managed to carry some conviction. Luckily for him, the marquis joked with him at dinner about his next trip: Mathilde grasped that it might well be a long one. For several days now, Julien had been avoiding her, and the brilliant young people, who had everything this pale, gloomy creature once loved by her did not, were incapable of drawing her out of her reverie.

An ordinary girl, she thought, would have selected the man of her choice from among these young men who attract every eye in a drawing room; but one of the traits of genius is not to drag its thought through the rut worn by vulgar minds.

As the companion of a man like Julien, who lacks only the fortune I possess, I shall continually attract attention, I'll never pass through life unperceived. Far from living in continual dread of a revolution, like my cousins, who for fear of popular dislike don't even dare to scold a postilion who drives them badly, I shall be sure of playing a role, and a great role, for the man I have chosen has character and boundless ambition. What does he lack? friends, money? I can provide them. But in her secret thoughts she considered Julien an inferior being, whose fortune one makes when and how one chooses and whose devotion is never even to be questioned.

Chapter 19

THE OPERA BUFFA

O how this spring of love resembleth
The uncertain glory of a summer day;
Which now shows all the beauty of the sun,
And by and by a cloud takes all away.
—Shakespeare[6]

Occupied with thoughts of the future and the singular role she hoped to play in it, Mathilde soon began to miss the dry metaphysical discussions she used to have with Julien. Wearied too by such lofty ideas, she missed the moments of happiness she had known with him; these last memories were not untouched by remorse; at times she was overcome by it.

But if one has a weakness, she told herself, it is very much up to a girl like me never to neglect her duties except for a man of merit. Never let it be said that his handsome moustaches or the graceful way he mounts a horse seduced me, but rather his profound thoughts on the future which awaits France, his ideas about a possible parallel between the events soon to burst upon us and the revolution of 1688 in England.[7] I have been seduced, she answered boldly back to her own remorse, I am nothing but a weak woman, but at least I wasn't deceived like a stuffed doll by exterior advantages. [What I loved in him was the breaking out of a great soul.]

If there should be a revolution, why shouldn't Julien play the part of Roland, and I that of Mme. Roland?[8] I much prefer that to the part of Mme. de Staël:[9] immoral behavior is going to be a great impediment in our century. Certainly no one will ever be able to reproach me with a second weakness; I should die of shame.

Not all Mathilde's meditations were so solemn, it must be admitted, as the thoughts we have just transcribed.

She watched Julien furtively, and found a delightful grace in his least actions.

No doubt, she told herself, I have succeeded in destroying every notion that he might have certain rights.

The air of grief and deep passion in which the poor boy spoke to me of his love, [spoke so naïvely in the garden about a week ago,] is proof of it. I must admit, it was very strange of me to be provoked

6. See Book I, epigraph to Chapter 17.
7. The English revolution of 1688 sent into permanent exile the House of Stuart, which Stendhal clearly identified with the Bourbons, and fully vindicated the democratic rights of English property owners.
8. Calm and noble as a queen, Mme. Roland was, with her husband, an intellectual leader of the Girondin party until 1793, when she was guillotined and he committed suicide. For Stendhal, she was a type of the sensitive and noble soul for whom he was writing.
9. Mme. de Staël, whose latest biography titles her, rather fulsomely, *Mistress to an Age,* had in prose, as in love, an enthusiastic, undiscriminating style which was Stendhal's abomination.

by words in which there shone so much respect, so much passion. Am I not his wife? What he said was perfectly natural, and, I must admit, it pleased me. Julien still loved me after those endless conversations in which I talked to him, and pretty cruelly I must admit, of nothing but the feelings of love which my boredom had encouraged toward those young fellows of whom he's now so jealous. Ah, if he only knew how little he has to fear from them! How faded and pale they seem to me, as if each one had been copied from the other!

As these thoughts strayed through her mind, Mathilde, [to keep herself in countenance with her watching mother,] began to trace at random a few lines in her album. One of the profiles as she finished it struck her with delight: it looked remarkably like Julien. It's the voice of heaven, one of the miracles of love, she cried in a transport, unconsciously I draw his portrait!

She fled to her room, locked herself in, [took some pastels,] and with a great deal of effort undertook seriously to make a portrait of Julien, but it was a failure; the profile penciled at random was a far better likeness; Mathilde was delighted with it; she saw in it conclusive evidence of a great passion.

She did not lay down her album until late, when the marquise summoned her to go to the Italian opera. She had only one idea, to catch sight of Julien and ask her mother to have him escort them.

But he was not to be seen; the ladies had only commonplace beings in their box. During the entire first act of the opera, Mathilde dreamed of the man she loved now with the keenest transports of passion; but during the second act a phrase about love, sung to a melody that was really worthy of Cimarosa, struck her to the heart. The heroine of the opera sang: You must punish me for the excessive adoration I feel for him, I love him far too much!

From the moment when she heard this sublime aria, everything in the world faded into nothingness for Mathilde. People talked to her; she made no answer; her mother scolded, she could barely bring herself to look at her. Her ecstasy rose to a point of exalted passion comparable to the most violent sentiments that Julien had felt for her over the past several days. The aria, a divinely graceful melody over which played the phrase that seemed to bear so strikingly on her position, occupied every instant in which she was not thinking directly of Julien. Thanks to her love of music, she was for that one evening what Mme. de Rênal always was when she thought of Julien. Doubtless the love born in the head is more witty than real love, but it experiences only instants of enthusiasm; it knows itself too well; it is always standing in judgment over itself; far from baffling thought, it is built only on a frame of thought.

When they were back home, Mathilde pretended, in spite of

everything Mme. de La Mole could say, that she had a fever, and spent a part of the night playing over the aria on her piano. She sang the words of the celebrated tune which had enchanted her:

> *Devo punirmi, devo punirmi,*
> *Se troppo amai,* etc.[1]

The outcome of this night of madness was that she supposed she had triumphed over her love. (This page will damage the unfortunate author in more than one way. Ice-cold souls will accuse him of indecency. It does no harm to the young ladies who glitter in the drawing rooms of Paris to suppose that one of them is capable of such mad impulses as degrade the character of Mathilde. Her character is entirely imaginary, and indeed imagined at a great distance from those social customs that, among all the ages of history, will assure such a distinguished rank for the civilization of the nineteenth century.

It is by no means prudence that is lacking in the young ladies who have been the ornaments of this winter's balls.

I don't think, either, that anyone can accuse them of undervaluing a brilliant fortune, horses, fine properties, and everything that assures an agreeable position in the world. Far from seeing nothing but boredom in these advantages, they generally desire them most constantly, and whatever passion their hearts hold is for these things.

Nor is love generally the path by which young men endowed with some talent like Julien hope to gain their fortune; they attach themselves immovably to a certain "crowd," and when the crowd arrives, all the good things of society pour down on them.[2] Woe to the man of education who belongs to no "crowd"; even his uncertain little successes will be held against him, and the higher virtue will condemn him even as it robs him. Look here, sir, a novel is a mirror moving along a highway. One minute you see it reflect the azure skies, next minute the mud and puddles of the road. And the man who carries the mirror in his pack will be accused by you of immorality! His mirror shows the mud and you accuse the mirror! Rather you should accuse the road in which the puddle lies, or, even better, the inspector of roads who lets the water collect and the puddle form.

1. *Devo punirmi:* I have been unable to locate this aria, or, consequently, the name of the opera responsible for Mathilde's conversion.
2. In October, 1829, Henri de Latouche published, largely against the growing romantic moment, an article, "On Literary Friendship," which laid a bitter lash to the literary cliques. *Le Globe,* too, led off on p. 1 of vol. 1, no. 1, with an attack on cliques—then itself promptly became the center of one. In short, the topic was a commonplace in the nineteenth as it is in the twentieth century.

Now that it's fully understood that a character like Mathilde's is impossible in our age, no less prudent than virtuous, I am less afraid of distressing the reader by describing further the follies of this attractive girl.)

All the following day she sought for occasions to prove that she had overcome her insane passion. Her great aim was to displease Julien in everything; but none of his actions escaped her notice.

Julien was too wretched and above all too agitated to see completely through such a complicated strategem of passion; still less could he see in it the element making for his advantage: he fell victim to it. Never, perhaps, had his misery been so extreme. His actions were so little under conscious control that if some gloomy philosopher had told him: "Think of making good use of circumstances favorable to you; in this sort of love-in-the-head which prevails at Paris, a single disposition can never last more than two days," he would not have understood it. But throughout his distractions Julien retained a sense of honor. His first duty was to be discreet; and so he understood it. To ask advice or tell the tale of his sufferings to the first comer would have been a happiness equal to that of the man who, while crossing a scorching desert, receives from heaven a glass of ice water. He recognized his danger; he was afraid if any curious person questioned him, he would reply only with a torrent of tears; he shut himself in his room.

He saw Mathilde walk for a long time in the garden; when finally she went in, he came down and went to a rose bush from which she had plucked a blossom.

The night was dark. He could give himself up to his griefs without fear of being seen. It was perfectly plain to him that Mlle. de La Mole was in love with one of those young officers with whom she had just been chatting so gaily. Once she had loved him, but she had recognized his unworthiness.

And in fact, I am not worth much! Julien said to himself, with full conviction; take me for what I am, I'm a dull fellow, very common, a great bore to other people, completely unbearable to myself. He was sick to death of all his good qualities, of all the things he had once loved with enthusiasm; and in this state of *inverse imagination* he undertook to criticize life imaginatively. It was the error of a superior man.

Several times the idea of suicide rose up before him; it was an idea full of charm, like a delicious resting place; it was the glass of ice water offered to the wretch wandering in the desert and dying of thirst and heat.

My death will even increase her contempt for me! he exclaimed. What a memory I'll leave behind!

Fallen into the absolute pit of misery, a human being has no recourse except courage. Julien had not the inspiration to say: Be bold; but as he watched Mathilde's window, he saw through the shutters that she put out her light. He recalled that charming room, which he had seen, alas! just once in his life. His imagination went no further.

One o'clock tolled. To hear the bell and say to himself: I shall climb the ladder, was the work of an instant.

It was the flash of genius; supporting reasons flooded in on him. I can't possibly be more miserable, he told himself. He ran to the ladder; the gardener had chained it down. With the hammer of one of his little pistols, which he broke in the process, Julien, whose strength at that moment was superhuman, twisted open one of the links of the chain holding the ladder; in a few instants it was free, and he placed it against Mathilde's window.

She will be furious; she will heap contempt on me, what matter? I will give her a kiss, one last kiss, go up to my room, and kill myself . . . ; my lips will touch her cheek before I die.

He flew up the ladder and rapped at the shutter; after a few moments Mathilde heard him; she wanted to open the shutter but the ladder was in the way. Julien clung to the iron latch used to hold the shutter open, risking a fall at every instant, gave a violent push at the ladder, and moved it over a bit. Mathilde was able to open the shutter.

He flung himself into the room, more dead than alive.

—It is you, my dear, she said, as she threw herself into his arms. . . .

Who could describe the extravagance of Julien's joy? Mathilde's was almost as great.

She talked against herself, she denounced herself to him.

—Punish me for my atrocious pride, she told him, straining him in her arms as if to throttle him; you are my master, I am your slave, I must beg your pardon on bended knees for having tried to revolt. She slipped out of his arms to fall at his feet. Yes, you are my master, she told him, still drunk with love and happiness; reign forever over me, punish savagely your slave whenever she tries to rebel.

At another moment, she leaped from his arms, lit a candle, and Julien had all he could do to prevent her from cutting off one whole side of her hair.

—I want to remind myself, she told him, that I am your servant: if ever I'm misled again by that horrible pride, show me this lock of hair and tell me: it's not a matter of love, it's not a matter of the sentiment your heart happens to hold at this instant, you have sworn to obey, now obey, on your honor.

But it is wiser to suppress the description of such wild felicity.

Julien's virtue was equal to his good fortune; I must go back down the ladder, he told Mathilde, when he saw daylight touching the distant chimneys on the far side of the garden. The sacrifice I am undertaking is worthy of you; I am depriving myself of a few more hours of the most astounding delight a human being can enjoy; it's a sacrifice I make to your reputation. If you know what I feel, you will understand the violence I am inflicting on myself. Will you always be for me what at this moment you are? Honor speaks, and that's enough. But you must know that since our first meeting, there has been suspicion, and not only of robbers. M. de La Mole has ordered a watch kept on the garden. M. de Croisenois is dogged by spies; they report what he does every night. . . .

—The poor fellow, cried Mathilde, with a burst of laughter. Her mother and a serving girl were awakened by it; suddenly they began calling to her through the door. Julien glanced at her, she turned pale as she scolded the maid and avoided saying a word to her mother.

—But if they open the window they can see the ladder! Julien said to her.

He clasped her once more in his arms, leaped onto the ladder, and slid rather than clambered down it; in an instant he was on the ground.

Three seconds later the ladder was under the linden trees, and Mathilde's honor was safe. Julien, returning to consciousness, found that he was bleeding and almost naked: he had cut himself in his wild descent.

An immense joy had restored the full energy of his character: had twenty men confronted him at that moment, to attack them singlehanded would have been only a pleasure the more. By good fortune, his military ardor was not put to the test. He replaced the ladder in its usual place; he put back the chain which fastened it; nor did he forget to come back and rub out the marks which the ladder had left in the border of exotic flowers under Mathilde's window.

As he was passing his hand, in the darkness, over the soft earth, to make sure that the prints were entirely obliterated, he felt something fall on his hands; it was one whole side of Mathilde's hair which she had cut off and was now throwing to him.

She was at the window.

—This is what your servant sends to you, she told him, speaking quite loudly, it is the mark of an eternal obedience. I surrender the right to exercise my own reason; you must be my master.

Julien, overcome, was on the point of picking up the ladder again and climbing back up to her. Reason finally prevailed.

To get back into the house from the garden was not easy. He succeeded in forcing the door of a cellar; then, once inside the house, he was obliged to force, with the utmost silence, the door of his own room. In his agitation, he had left behind in the little room he had just quitted so hurriedly everything, including the key which was in his coat pocket. Let's hope, he thought, that she remembers to hide all that fatal evidence!

At last, weariness won out over happiness, and as the sun rose he sank into a deep sleep.

The luncheon bell barely succeeded in waking him; he descended to the dining room. Shortly after, Mathilde appeared. Julien's pride had a moment of joy when he saw the love glowing in the eyes of this girl who was so beautiful and surrounded by so much deference; but soon his prudence had reason to feel affrighted.

Under pretext of inadequate time to prepare her coiffure, Mathilde had arranged her hair in such a way that Julien could see at a glance the extent of the sacrifice she had made for him when she cut it off the night before. If such lovely features could be spoiled in any way, Mathilde might seem to have done it; one whole side of her beautiful head of ash-blonde hair had been clipped to within half an inch of the scalp.

At lunch, Mathilde's whole behavior bore out this original act of rashness. It seemed she was trying to make everyone aware of her insane passion for Julien. Fortunately, on that day, M. de La Mole and his wife were much exercised over a list of promotions to the order of the blue ribbon, in which M. de Chaulnes had somehow not been included. Toward the end of the meal, it happened that Mathilde, in the course of talking to Julien, addressed him as *my master*. He blushed to the whites of his eyes.

Whether it was accidental, or part of a plan by Mme. de La Mole, Mathilde was not alone for an instant all day. But that evening, as they were passing from the dining room to the drawing room, she found a moment to tell Julien:

—[All my plans are upset.] Will you think this is only a pretext on my part? My mother has just decided that one of her maids will spend the night in my room.

The day passed in a flash. Julien was at the peak of happiness. Next day at seven A.M. he was at his post in the library; he hoped that Mlle. de La Mole would appear there; he had written her an interminable letter.

He did not see her until a good many hours later, at lunch. And this time her hair was done up with the greatest care; a marvelous art had been invoked to hide the place where the hair had been clipped. She glanced once or twice at Julien, but with a courteous and calm expression; there was no question now of calling him *my master*.

Julien gasped in astonishment. . . . Mathilde was blaming herself for practically everything she had done for him.

When she reflected on the matter at leisure, she decided that this was a being, if not altogether common, at least not sufficiently out of the ordinary to deserve all the strange follies she had ventured to commit for him. On the whole, she did not want to think of love; that day, she was tired of loving.

As for Julien, the reactions of his heart were those of a sixteen-year-old. He was assailed alternately by frightful doubt, amazement, and despair throughout that luncheon which seemed to last forever.

As soon as he could decently leave the table, he dashed rather than ran to the stable, saddled his horse for himself, and was off at a gallop; he was afraid of disgracing himself by some show of weakness. I must kill my feelings by physical exhaustion, he told himself, as he galloped through the woods of Meudon. What did I do, what did I say, to deserve such disgrace?

I must do nothing, I must say nothing today, he thought, as he came back to the house; I must be dead in the body as I am in the soul. Julien is no longer alive, it is his corpse that is still writhing.

Chapter 20

THE JAPANESE VASE

> At first his heart does not realize the full extent of his misery; he is more bothered than distressed. But as reason returns, he feels the depth of his misfortune. All the pleasures of life are ruined for him, he can feel nothing but the keen edges of despair tearing at him. But what good is it to talk of physical pain? What pain felt by the body alone is comparable to this one?
>
> —Jean Paul

The bell rang for dinner; Julien had just time to dress. He found in the drawing room Mathilde, who was imploring her brother and M. de Croisenois not to go and spend the evening with Mme. la Maréchale de Fervaques.

She could scarcely have been more alluring and attractive with them. After dinner Messieurs de Luz, de Caylus, and several of their friends put in an appearance. It seemed that Mlle. de La Mole had resumed, along with friendship for her brother, a cult of strict conventionality. Although the weather was delightful that evening, she insisted they must not go into the garden; she refused to leave the armchair where Mme. de La Mole was seated. The blue sofa was the center of the group, as in winter.

Mathilde was angry with the garden, or at least it seemed to her completely boring: it was linked with the memory of Julien.

Misery weakens the judgment. Our hero was fool enough to return to that little cane-bottom chair which formerly had been the scene of his brightest triumphs. Today nobody said a word to him; his presence passed as if unperceived, or even worse. Those of Mlle. de La Mole's friends who sat near him, at the end of the sofa, seemed to make a point of turning their backs on him, or at least so he thought.

It's like the fall of a favorite in a court, he thought. He wanted to study for a while the people who pretended thus to crush him with their disdain.

The uncle of M. de Luz had an important post in the king's service, from which it followed that this spruce young officer began his conversation with each successive arrival by bringing forth the following fascinating detail: his uncle had left about seven o'clock for Saint-Cloud and expected to spend the night there. This detail was introduced with many formulas of good fellowship, but it never failed to turn up.

Observing M. de Croisenois with the acid eye of the unhappy, Julien noted what an extraordinary consequence this decent and agreeable young man ascribed to occult influences. He carried it so far as to grow gloomy and sulky if he saw an event of any importance at all explained by a simple and natural cause. There's a touch of madness here, Julien thought. His character corresponds remarkably with that of the Emperor Alexander as it was described to me by Prince Korasoff. During the first year of his stay in Paris, poor Julien, who came straight from the seminary, was so dazzled by the graces of all these attractive young men, which were quite new to him, that he could only admire them. Only now was their real character starting to unfold before his eyes.

I am playing an undignified part here, he thought suddenly. The problem was how to leave his little cane chair in not too clumsy a manner. He wanted to invent; he demanded something new of an imagination fully engaged elsewhere. He was obliged to have recourse to memory, and his was, admittedly, not very fertile in resources of this sort; the poor fellow still had very little polish, so that when he rose to leave the drawing room, his clumsiness was complete and everyone noticed it. Misery was all too evident in his whole deportment. For three quarters of an hour he had been playing the role of a bothersome underling from whom people don't bother to conceal their opinion of him.

The critical attention he had been paying his rivals, however, prevented him from taking his misery too tragically; and, to sustain his pride, he had the memory of what had occurred the night before last. However many advantages they may have over me, he thought, as he wandered into the garden by himself, Mathilde has never been for any of them what twice in my life she deigned to be for me.

His wisdom went no further than that. He understood not at all the character of the singular person whom chance had rendered absolute mistress of all his happiness.

The following day he undertook to kill both his horse and himself with exhaustion. That evening he made no effort to approach the blue sofa to which Mathilde remained faithful. He noted that Comte Norbert did not even condescend to look at him when they met around the house. He must be doing some violence to his feelings, Julien thought, since by nature he is so polite.

For Julien, sleep would have been perfect happiness. Despite physical fatigue, memories that were all too seductive began to occupy his entire imagination. He did not have the wit to see that when he took those long horseback rides through the woods around Paris, acting only on himself and not at all on Mathilde's mind or heart, he was leaving up to chance the disposition of his own destiny.

It seemed to him that only one thing could bring perfect solace to his grief: that would be to talk to Mathilde. But then what would he dare to say to her?

This is what he was brooding over one morning about seven o'clock when suddenly he saw her enter the library.

—I know, sir, that you want to talk to me.

—Great God! Who told you that?

—I know it, what more do you want? If you are devoid of honor, you can ruin me, or at least try it; but this danger, which I don't think is real, will certainly not stop me from speaking my mind. I no longer love you, sir, my foolish imagination misled me. . . .

Under this terrible blow, frantic with love and misery, Julien tried to excuse himself. Nothing more ridiculous. Is there any excuse for failing to please? But reason was no longer in control of his behavior. A blind instinct drove him to put off the decision of his fate. It seemed to him that as long as he was talking all was not over. Mathilde did not hear his words; their very sound angered her; she could not imagine anyone having the audacity to interrupt her.

This morning she was being tormented equally by remorse springing from virtue and remorse springing from pride. She was practically crushed at the thought of having given rights over her person to a little abbé, the son of a peasant. It is very nearly, she told herself when exaggerating her grief, as if [, after dreaming of the lofty qualities and distinction of the man I loved,] I had to be ashamed of a weakness for one of the footmen.

With these bold, proud people, it is always just one step from self-hatred to fury against other people; when this step is taken, transports of rage give them keen pleasure.

In an instant, Mlle. de La Mole reached the stage of overwhelming Julien with marks of the most withering contempt. She was fearfully clever, and her cleverness was at its best in the art of torturing peoples' self-esteem and inflicting savage wounds.

For the first time in his life Julien found himself subjected to the working of a superior mind, aroused against him to the most violent hatred. Far from having the slightest idea of defending himself at this moment, [his agile imagination] turned at once to self-contempt. When he heard himself covered with a scorn so bitter and so skillfully directed to the destruction of every last good opinion he might have of himself, he thought that Mathilde must be right, and that she wasn't going far enough.

For her part, she felt a delicious pleasure in thus punishing herself and him for the adoration she had felt several days before.

She had no need to invent or to cultivate originality when she began heaping bitter words upon him with so much self-satisfaction. She had merely to repeat the things that had been said in her heart for the last week by the spokesman of the anti-love party.

Every word increased Julien's fearful misery a hundredfold. He tried to escape; Mlle. de La Mole gripped him imperiously by the arm.

—Be good enough to observe, he told her, that you are talking very loud; people can hear you in the next room.

—What do I care? replied Mlle. de La Mole arrogantly, who will ever dare to tell me he listened? I want to purge your puny little self-esteem forever of certain conceptions it may have formed on my account.

When Julien could leave the library, he was so stunned that he actually felt his grief less keenly. All right! so she doesn't love me any more, he kept saying to himself, speaking aloud as though explaining his position to himself. It seems she loved me for eight or ten days, and I shall love her all my life long.

Is it possible that she meant nothing to me, nothing at all, only a few days ago!

The pleasures of pride flooded through Mathilde's heart; so she had managed to break off forever! To triumph absolutely over so pronounced an inclination would surely render her perfectly happy. And so this little gentleman will understand, once and for all, that he doesn't have and will never have any power of command over me. She was so happy that at this moment she was really quite drained of love.

After so atrocious and humiliating a scene, anyone less impassioned than Julien would have found love impossible. Without abandoning for an instant her dignity, Mlle. de La Mole had flung at him certain of those disagreeable remarks that are so subtly calculated that they seem to be true even when one recollects them in a moment of calm.

The first conclusion that Julien drew on the spot from this amazing scene was that Mathilde's pride was limitless. He firmly believed that all was over between them, and yet, next day at luncheon, he was awkward and timid in her presence. That was a fault that could not have been found with him before. In little as in great things, he had usually known exactly what he should do, and wanted to do, then carried it out.

That day, after lunch, Mme. de La Mole requested a seditious and rather rare pamphlet that her parish priest had given her secretly that morning; as he picked it up from a side table, Julien knocked over an old vase of blue porcelain, the most hideous thing there could be.

Mme. de La Mole rose with a cry of distress and came over to inspect the shattered ruins of her favorite vase. It was an antique from Japan, she said; it came from my great aunt the Abbess of Chelles; it was a present given by the Dutch to the regent Duke of Orleans, who gave it to his daughter. . . .

Mathilde had followed her mother, rejoicing in the ruin of this blue vase, which had always seemed to her horribly ugly. Julien was silent and by no means overly disturbed; he glanced at Mlle. de La Mole, standing beside him.

—The vase, he said, is destroyed forever, and so it is with a feeling that once ruled in my heart; I beg you to accept my apologies for all the follies into which it led me; and he went out.

—Really! said Mme. de La Mole as he left, one would think this M. Sorel was proud and pleased at what he has just done.

The phrase struck Mathilde to the heart. It is true, she told herself, my mother guessed right, that is exactly how he feels. Only then did her joy in the scene she had played with him the day before come to an end. All right, everything is over, she told herself with apparent calm; what I have left is a great example; this sort of mistake is frightful, humiliating! It will guarantee my wisdom for the rest of my life.

Wasn't I telling the truth, Julien thought; why does the love I felt for that madwoman keep on tormenting me?

That love, far from dying away, as he had hoped, was making rapid strides. She is crazy, it's true, he told himself, but is she any less adorable for that? Is it possible for a girl to be more beautiful? Everything that the most elegant civilization can offer in the way of brilliant delight, isn't it all perfectly present in Mlle. de La Mole? Memories of bygone happiness took possession of Julien and rapidly undermined all the fortifications of reason.

Reason strives in vain against memories of this sort; its sternest efforts succeed only in augmenting the charm.

Twenty-four hours after breaking the antique Japanese vase, Julien was decidedly one of the unhappiest of mortals.

Chapter 21

THE SECRET NOTE

For everything I describe I've seen; and though I may have seen
incorrectly, I am certainly not deceiving you in my descriptions.
—From a letter to the author

The marquis summoned him; M. de La Mole seemed younger, his eye was sparkling.

—Let's have a word about your memory, he said to Julien, I hear that it's prodigious. Could you get four pages by heart and go and recite them in London? But without changing a word! . . .

The marquis was thumbing crossly through the pages of that morning's *Quotidienne* and trying vainly to conceal an air of great seriousness which Julien had never seen him assume, not even when they were talking about the lawsuit with Frilair.

Julien had enough social grace to feel that he ought to go along with the casual manner that was being displayed.

—Very likely this issue of the *Quotidienne* is not particularly amusing; but, if Monsieur le marquis will allow me, tomorrow morning I shall have the honor to recite the whole thing to him.

—What! even the ads?

—Precisely, and word for word.

—You give me your word? replied the marquis, looking suddenly grave.

—Indeed, sir, only the fear of not keeping it might disturb my memory.

—The fact is, I should have asked that question yesterday: I am not going to ask you for a vow never to repeat what you are about to hear; I know you too well to insult you that way. I have vouched for you, I am going to bring you into a room where some dozen people will be gathered; you will keep notes of what each one says.

Don't be upset, it won't be confused conversation, each one will speak in turn; I don't mean to say formally, the marquis added, resuming that light, clever tone that was his natural manner. While we talk, you will write down twenty pages or so; we will come back here and reduce those twenty pages to four. Those four pages are what you will repeat to me tomorrow morning instead of this whole issue of the *Quotidienne*. You will then leave at once; you will have to travel post like a young man traveling for pleasure. Your chief purpose will be to pass unnoticed by anyone. You will come into the presence of a great personage. There you will need more subtlety. It will be a matter of deceiving his whole retinue; for among his secretaries, among his servants, there are men in the pay of our enemies, who are on the lookout for our agents to intercept them.

You will have a meaningless letter of introduction.

When His Excellency first looks at you, you will pull out my watch, which I have here and will lend you for your trip. Take it now, while we think of it, and give me yours.

The duke himself will condescend to copy, from your dictation, the four pages you have learned by heart.

When that is done, but, mark my words, not a moment sooner, you may, if His Excellency questions you, tell him about the meeting you are going to attend.

It may keep you from feeling bored on your trip to know that between Paris and the minister's residence there are people who would like nothing better than to put a bullet into Abbé Sorel. Then his mission is over, and I foresee a long delay in our business; for, my dear fellow, how will we learn of your death? Your zeal will scarcely suffice to bring us the word.

Run along now, and buy yourself a complete outfit, the marquis resumed, speaking seriously. Dress after the fashion of a couple of years back. Tonight you must have a slightly scruffy look. When you travel, however, you will look as usual. That surprises you; you are suspicious enough to guess why? Yes, my friend, one of the venerable persons who will be delivering his opinion tonight is quite capable of sending dispatches, as a result of which you would be given opium at least one evening in some fine inn where you had asked for supper.

—It might be better, said Julien, to do another thirty leagues and not take the direct road. I am heading toward Rome, I suppose. . . .

The marquis assumed an air of lofty discontent which Julien had not seen in so marked a form since Bray-le-Haut.

—That's a matter of which you will learn, sir, when I think it appropriate to tell you. I don't like questions.

—This wasn't a question, Julien replied effusively; I swear, sir, I was just thinking out loud, I was trying to imagine the safest road.

—Yes, it's apparent your mind was wandering far away. Never forget that an ambassador, especially when he is of your age, must not seem to be forcing confidences.

Julien was greatly mortified; he was in the wrong. His self-esteem cast about for an excuse, and found none.

—You should understand, too, M. de La Mole went on, that people always appeal to their sincerity when they have done something foolish.

An hour later, Julien was in the marquis' waiting room, dressed as an underling in a castoff suit with a neckcloth of dubious whiteness, and something definitely menial about his whole appearance.

When he saw him, the marquis burst out laughing, and only then was Julien really returned to favor.

If this young man betrays me, thought M. de La Mole, whom

can I trust? And yet when action is called for, one must trust somebody. My son and his brilliant friends of that ilk have honesty and
loyalty enough for a hundred thousand; if it came to a battle, they
would perish on the steps of the throne, they know everything . . .
except what we need at this moment. Devil take me if I can think
of one of them who could learn four pages by heart and cover a
hundred leagues without being tracked down. Norbert might get
himself killed like his ancestors, and that's what a conscript can
do too. . . .

The marquis sank into a deep meditation: And even at getting
himself killed, he reflected with a sigh, perhaps this Sorel could do it
just as well as he. . . .

—Let's take the carriage, said the marquis, as if to banish an unwelcome thought.

—Sir, said Julien, while they were getting this costume ready for
me, I learned by heart the first page of today's *Quotidienne*.

The marquis took up the paper; Julien recited without missing a
single word. Good, thought the marquis, very much the diplomat
that evening; during all this time the young man is paying no attention to the streets through which we are driving.

They entered a large room of rather gloomy aspect, partly paneled
and partly hung in green velvet. In the middle of the room a hard-
faced footman had just finished setting up a big dinner table, which
he then converted to a work table by spreading over it an immense
green cloth spattered with ink blots, discarded from someone's office.

The master of the house was an enormous man whose name was
never mentioned; Julien thought he had the features and the
eloquence of a man preoccupied with his own digestion.

At a gesture from the marquis, Julien had taken his position at
the foot of the table. To give himself countenance, he began to trim
his pens. Out of the corner of his eye, he counted seven speakers,
but he could see nothing of them but their backs. Two of them
seemed to address M. de La Mole on a footing of equality, the others
seemed more or less deferential.

Another person arrived unannounced. This is odd, Julien thought,
they don't announce people in this house. Have they taken this precaution in my honor? Everyone rose to welcome the newcomer. He
wore the same extremely distinguished decoration as three other
people already in the room. They talked in undertones. To judge
the newcomer, Julien was forced to rely on what he could learn
from his features and his dress. He was short and thick-set, ruddy
in coloring, with a keen eye and no other expression on his face than
the ferocity of a wild boar.

Julien's attention was distracted abruptly by the arrival of a quite
different person. It was a tall man, very lean, wearing three or four
waistcoats. His expression was soothing, his comportment suave.

That's just the expression of the old bishop of Besançon, Julien thought. This man plainly belongs to the church; he doesn't look more than fifty or fifty-five, and no one could have a more paternal expression.

The young bishop of Agde appeared, looking very much astonished; as he glanced over those in attendance, his eye fell on Julien. He had not addressed a word to him since the ceremony of Bray-le-Haut. His look of surprise embarrassed and irked Julien. What the deuce! he said to himself, is knowing a man always going to be held against me? All these great gentlemen whom I've never laid eyes on before disturb me not at all, and a look from this young bishop turns me to ice! It can't be doubted, I'm a strange, unlucky fellow.

A small black-haired man entered noisily and began to talk as he crossed the threshold; he had a sallow complexion and a slightly distracted expression. As soon as this pitiless talker arrived, little groups began to shape up, apparently to escape the boredom of listening to him.

As the group around the fireplace broke up, they came closer to the foot of the table where Julien was placed. His expression became more and more embarrassed; for, in fact, whatever efforts he made, he could not help overhearing them, and however little experience he had, he could not help understanding the full importance of what was being openly discussed. And he understood too how important it was for the distinguished people around him to keep these matters secret.

Already, working as slowly as he could, Julien had sharpened a score of pens; before long this resource would fail him. He looked vainly for instructions from the eyes of M. de La Mole; the marquis had forgotten him.

What I am doing is silly, Julien thought, as he trimmed his pens; but these people who look so mediocre and are charged, either by others or by themselves, with such great interests must be extremely touchy. My unhappy expression has about it something questioning and disrespectful, which will surely irk them. And if I lower my eyes too far, it will look as if I am trying to keep account of their words.

His embarrassment was extreme; he was hearing some extraordinary things.

Chapter 22

THE DISCUSSION

> The rebublic—there is not one person today who would sacrifice his all to the public good; there are thousands and millions who know nothing but their pleasures, their vanity. A man is esteemed in Paris because of his carriage, not because of his conscience.
>
> —Napoleon, *Mémorial*

The footman burst in, saying: His Excellency, the Duke of _____.

—Hold your tongue, you fool, said the duke as he entered. He said it so well, and with so much dignity, that in spite of himself Julien thought that the sum of this great man's knowledge must be his talent for getting angry with footmen. Julien raised his eyes, then lowered them at once. He had estimated so exactly the capacity of the new arrival that he was afraid his glance might be thought an indiscretion.

The duke was a man of fifty, dressed like a dandy, and moving as if he had been wound up. He had a narrow head with a big nose, and a face that seemed to curve forward as if to come to a point; it would have been hard to appear more noble or more insignificant. His coming marked the start of the discussion.

Julien was startled out of his study of physiognomies by the voice of M. de La Mole. —Let me introduce to you Abbé Sorel, said the marquis; he is possessed of an astounding memory. Barely an hour after I told him of the mission that might be entrusted to him, he gave proof of his memory by learning verbatim the first page of the *Quotidienne*.

—Ah, the strange news about poor N_____, said the master of the house. He snatched up the paper, and, looking at Julien with a mocking eye, in an effort to look important, said to him: Well, begin, sir.

Silence fell; every eye was fixed on Julien; he recited so well that after twenty lines the duke said: —All right, that will do. The little man who looked like a boar sat down. He was to preside over the meeting, for as soon as he had sat down, he showed Julien a card table and gestured for him to place it alongside his seat. Julien established himself there with all his writing materials. He counted twelve persons seated around the green cloth.

—M. Sorel, said the duke, withdraw into the next room, we will send for you.

The master of the house grew uneasy: the shutters aren't locked, he said half audibly to his neighbor. —There's no good your trying to look out the window, he called foolishly to Julien. —Well, thought the latter, here I am caught up in a conspiracy, or maybe something worse. Fortunately, it's not one of the sort that lead to the Place de Grève. Even if there is a bit of danger, I owe this and a lot more to the marquis. I should be happy if I could atone in this way for all the distress my follies may some day cause him.

Even as he was thinking of his follies and his griefs, he was studying his surroundings to be sure of never forgetting them. Only then did he recall that he had never heard the marquis tell his footman the name of the street to which he was going, and that the marquis had called a public cab, as he never used to do.

Julien was left long to his own reflections. He was in a room hung in red velvet with wide gold fringe. On the side table stood a big ivory crucifix, and on the mantlepiece lay M. de Maistre's book *On the Pope*, with gilt edges and a magnificent binding. Julien opened it in order not to seem to be eavesdropping. From time to time loud voices were heard from the neighboring room. At last the door opened and he was summoned.

—Remember, gentlemen, said the chairman, from this moment on, we speak as in the presence of the Duc de _____. This gentleman, he added with a nod at Julien, is a young levite, devoted to our holy cause, who, thanks to his astonishing memory, will be able to repeat to the duke every last word we say.

The gentleman has the floor, he said, indicating the fatherly looking man who wore extra waistcoats. Julien felt it would have been more natural to call the man with the waistcoats by his name. He took paper and wrote copiously.

(Here the author would have liked to place a page full of dots. That'll be rather clumsy, says the publisher, and for a book as frivolous as this one, clumsiness is fatal.

—Politics, replies the author, is a millstone hung on the neck of literature: within six months it will drag it to the bottom. Politics in the midst of imaginative activity is like a pistol shot in the middle of a concert. The noise is shattering without being forceful. It doesn't harmonize with any of the other instruments. Half the readers will be mortally offended at this politics, and the other half, who have already found more exciting and immediate politics in their morning paper, will be bored. . . .

—If your characters don't talk politics, says the publisher, then they are no longer Frenchmen of 1830, and your book is no longer a mirror, as you claim. . . .)

Julien's transcript ran to twenty-six pages; here is a pallid extract of it; for it was necessary, as usual, to suppress absurdities, which otherwise would be so many and tedious as to be quite improbable (See the *Gazette des Tribunaux*).[3]

3. The *Gazette des Tribunaux* was a Paris journal, first established during the 1820's, reporting law cases from all over France; here Stendhal first en- countered the story of Antoine Berthet, germ of the *Rouge*. But he did not much admire its ordinary style.

The man with waistcoats and a fatherly expression (perhaps he was a bishop) smiled frequently, and then his eyes, between their quivering lids, took on a singular brilliance and an expression less indecisive than usual. This personage, who was asked to speak first in the presence of the duke (but what duke? Julien asked himself), and who seemed to take the role of attorney general, fell prey in Julien's opinion, to the uncertainty and indecisiveness which is the common failing of such officials. In the course of the discussion, the duke went so far as to rebuke him for this.

After a few phrases of morality and indulgent philosophy, the man in waistcoats said:

—Noble England, guided by a great man, the immortal Pitt, has spent forty billion francs to destroy the Revolution. If this gathering will permit me to express frankly an unhappy truth, England never really understood that with a man like Bonaparte, especially when one had nothing to put up against him but a collection of good intentions, the only decisive thing was personal measures. . . .[4]

—Ah! now we're back to praises of assassination! said the master of the house, looking uneasy.

—Spare us your sentimental homilies, cried the chairman angrily; his boar's eye glittered with a ferocious gleam. Go on, he said to the man in waistcoats. The cheeks and brow of the chairman were turning purple.

—Noble England, the speaker began again, is prostrate today because every Englishman, before buying his daily bread, is obliged to pay interest on the forty billion francs spent in defeating the Jacobins. She no longer has a Pitt. . . .

—She has the Duke of Wellington,[5] said a military personage, assuming a most imposing air.

—Silence, gentlemen, please, shouted the chairman; if we keep on arguing, there will be no point in our having sent for M. Sorel.

—We all know the gentleman has plenty of ideas, said the duke, looking angrily at the interrupter, who was a former general of Napoleon's. Julien saw this expression alluded to something personal and extremely offensive. Everyone smiled; the turncoat general seemed beside himself with fury.

4. "Personal measures" is a polite term for assassination. The conspiracy represented in these chapters of the *Rouge* undoubtedly corresponds largely to the reality of ultraconservative political circles during the years between Waterloo and 1830. There were conspiracies to bring in foreign aid against reviving French radicalism. But though Stendhal built on fact, and many of the conspirators have traits reminiscent of actual figures of the ultra party, the conspiracy itself is very much a matter of fantasy. To take only the most obvious instance: bishops and cardinals are described as taking part in it, a major aim is to restore wealth and influence to the church, yet the enemies who try to interfere with it are Jesuits and churchmen.

5. The Duke of Wellington was, after Waterloo, a sort of unofficial guardian of the peace of Europe; reactionaries everywhere kept in touch with him.

—Pitt is no more, gentlemen, the speaker resumed, with the discouraged look of one who despairs of making his listeners hear reason. Even if a new Pitt should arise in England, it's impossible to diddle a nation twice with the same tricks. . . .

—That's exactly why a victorious general, a Bonaparte, will never be seen again in France, shouted the military heckler.

Neither the chairman nor the duke ventured to show their anger at this juncture, though Julien thought he could see in their eyes that they would very much have liked to. They lowered their eyes, and the duke contented himself with sighing loudly enough to be heard by everyone.

But the speaker had taken umbrage.

—You're very anxious to see me finish, he said heatedly, dropping completely all that smiling politeness and oily language that Julien had thought was his natural way of expressing himself: you're anxious to see me finish; you don't appreciate the efforts I'm making not to offend anyone's ears, however long they happen to be. All right, gentlemen, I shall be brief.

And I will tell you in plain blunt words: England has not a penny left for the service of the good cause. Even if Pitt himself came back, with all his genius he would never succeed in deluding the petty English landlords, because they know that short campaign at Waterloo cost them, all by itself, a billion francs. Since you want plain words, added the speaker, growing more and more excited, I will give you one: *Help yourselves*, because England has not a guinea to give you, and when England doesn't pay, then Austria, Russia, and Prussia, which have only courage and no money, can fight no more than one or two campaigns against France.

It's possible to hope that the raw recruits raised by Jacobins will be beaten in the first campaign, maybe even in the second; but in the third, though to your partial eyes I may seem like a revolutionary, in the third, you'll have the soldiers of 1794, who were no longer the untrained peasants of 1792.[6]

Here interruptions broke out from three or four speakers at once.

—Sir, said the chairman to Julien, go into the next room and correct the first part of the transcript you've made. Julien left, much to his regret. The speaker had touched on a set of speculations that formed the usual topic of his own thinking.

They're afraid that I'll laugh at them, he thought. When they called him back, M. de La Mole was saying with a seriousness that, for Julien who knew him, seemed extremely droll:

6. Remembering the wars in which enthusiastic French Jacobins defended their revolution against all Europe during the early 1790's, the speaker assumes that royalist Europe will once more be united against revolutionary France.

. . . Yes, gentlemen, this is the unhappy nation of which, more than any other, it can be said:

Shall it be a god, a table, or a pot?

Let it be a god! was the poet's cry.[7] And you, gentlemen, are the ones to whom this word, so noble and profound, should most appeal. Act on your own, and a noble France will reappear, much as our ancestors formed her, and as we ourselves saw her before the death of Louis XVI.

The English, or at least their noble lords, loathe as much as we do the shameful Jacobin: without English financing, Austria, Russia, and Prussia can hardly fight more than two or three battles. Will that serve to bring about a successful occupation, such as M. de Richelieu[8] frittered away so stupidly in 1817? I don't think so.

Here there was an interruption, but it was repressed by a general murmur for silence. Its source once again was the former imperial general, who wanted the blue ribbon decoration and so was eager to be included among the writers of the secret note.

—*I* do not think so, M. de La Mole resumed, when the stir had subsided. He emphasized the "I" with an insolence that charmed Julien. That was a fine stroke, he told himself, even as his pen flew over the paper almost as fast as the marquis' words. With a single well-placed emphasis, M. de La Mole wiped from the slate all the turncoat's twenty campaigns.

—We cannot depend on foreigners alone, the marquis continued, in the most judicial of tones, for a new military occupation. All these young people who are now writing incendiary articles in the *Globe* will give you three or four thousand young captains, among whom there may be found a Kléber, a Hoche, a Jourdan, a Pichegru,[9] but less well intentioned.

—We didn't know how to give him his proper glory, said the chairman, we ought to have made him immortal.

There must, in a word, be two parties in France, M. de La Mole resumed, two parties, not merely in name, but two clear, sharply

7. "Shall it be a god, a table, or a pot?" La Fontaine, "The Sculptor and the Statue of Jupiter," *Fables*, IX, 6.
8. M. de Richelieu is not, of course, the cardinal but his namesake the duke (1766–1822), who at the congress of Aix-la-Chapelle obtained in 1818 the departure of foreign troops from French soil.
9. Kléber had been an architect, Hoche a private soldier, Jourdan a silk merchant, and Pichegru the son of a day laborer when the Revolution uncovered their military talents and made them generals and marshals of France. (But Pichegru sold out to the Bourbons—hence the chairman's melancholy reflection.) The *Globe* was a journal, liberal in its politics and romantic in its literary tastes, (and one of the first French journals to combine those stances, thereby giving French romanticism a decisive turn away from the conservative "Throne and Altar" views of German romanticism); Stendhal contributed to the *Globe,* and it was widely influential in the July revolution of 1830.

divided parties. Let us know who has to be crushed. On the one
hand, the journalists, the electors, public opinion; in a word, youth,
and everyone who admires it. While these people stupefy themselves
with empty words, we on our side have the definite advantage of
eating off the budget.

At this point, more interruptions.

—You, sir, said M. de La Mole, addressing the interrupter with
an admirable indolent ease, you don't eat off the budget, since that
word seems to shock you, no, you devour forty thousand francs
carried on the state budget and eighty thousand that you get from
the civil list.

All right, sir, since you force me to it, I'll take you boldly as an
example. Like your noble ancestors who followed St. Louis on the
crusade, in return for these hundred and twenty thousand francs,
you ought to show us at least a regiment, a company, or if that's
too much, just a half company, just fifty men, ready to fight and
devoted to the good cause, come life, come death. You have nothing
but footmen, who in case of a revolt would be a threat only to
yourself.

The throne, the altar, and the nobility may perish tomorrow, gentlemen, unless you can create in each district a force of five hundred
dedicated men; dedicated, I mean, not only with the gallantry of the
French but also with the tenacity of the Spanish.

Half of this troop should be composed of our sons, our nephews,
in a word, of true gentlemen. Each one of them will have by his
side not a cheeky little ribbon clerk who will show his true colors
in a minute if ever 1815 recurs but an honest peasant, simple and
straight as Cathelineau;[1] our gentleman will have indoctrinated him,
will be his foster brother if possible. Let each one of us sacrifice a
fifth part of his income to form this little troop of five hundred
dedicated men to a district. Then you can count on a foreign
occupation. Foreign soldiery will never enter our country even as far
as Dijon unless they are certain of finding five hundred friendly
soldiers in each district.

The crowned heads will never listen to you until you can report
twenty thousand gentlemen ready to take up arms to open for them
the gates of France. The service is hard, you say; gentlemen, this is
the price of our heads. Between a free press and our existence as
gentlemen it is war to the knife. Either you become businessmen,
peasants, or you take up your guns. Be weak, if you want, but don't
be stupid; open your eyes.

Form up your battalions, I say to you, in the words of the Jacobin
song; then there will appear some noble Gustavus-Adolphus, who,

---

1. Cathelineau was a peasant leader of the Vendée revolt, killed at the siege of
Nantes in 1793.

seeing the principle of monarchy in imminent danger, will march three hundred leagues beyond his own boundaries and do for you what Gustavus did for the Protestant princes. Will you always go on talking instead of acting? In fifty years nothing will be left in Europe but presidents of republics, not a single king. And with those four letters, K-I-N-G, away go the priests and the gentlemen. I see in the future nothing but *candidates* making up to slimy *majorities.*

There's no point in my reminding you that France does not have today a trusted general, known and loved by all; that the army is organized only in the interests of the throne and the altar; that it has lost all its old troopers while each one of the Prussian and Austrian regiments counts fifty noncoms who have been under fire.

Two hundred thousand young men of the middle class are passionately eager for war. . . .[2]

—No more of these unpleasant truths! The words came decisively from a grave personage, apparently a lofty ecclesiastic, for M. de La Mole smiled graciously instead of losing his temper—a point not lost upon Julien.

No more of these unpleasant truths. Let us sum up, gentlemen. The man who is about to have a gangrenous leg amputated has no business telling his surgeon: This diseased leg is perfectly sound. If you'll forgive the expression, gentlemen, the noble duke of ____ is our surgeon.

There's the key word at last, thought Julien; so I shall be posting toward the ____ tonight.

Chapter 23

THE CLERGY, LAND, AND LIBERTY

> The first law of every creature is self-preservation, to keep alive. You sow hemlock and expect to reap corn!
>
> —Machiavelli

The grave personage went on; it was clear that he was in the know; he expounded, with a gentle and moderate eloquence, wonderfully pleasing to Julien, the following grand truths:

1. England has not a guinea to give us; economy and Hume are in fashion there. Not even the *Saints* will contribute money, and Mr. Brougham will laugh in our faces.[3]

2. Julien's phrase (p. 223) is picked up here by M. de La Mole as a cry of warning to the reaction.
3. The *Saints* and Mr. Brougham are, in the ultra accounting, the nonconformists and a leading independent of liberal leanings. Their interest in economy and Hume, representing rationalism, skepticism, and self-interest, dooms any thought of a new crusade against Jacobinism.

2. Impossible to obtain more than two campaigns from the crowned heads of Europe without English gold; and against the middle classes two campaigns will not be enough.
3. Necessity of forming an armed party in France, failing which the monarchical principle in Europe cannot be roused even to venture those two campaigns.

The fourth point I venture to propose to you as evident is this:

Impossibility of forming an armed party in France without the clergy. I say this boldly because I am going to prove it to you, gentlemen. The clergy must have everything.

1. Because, going about their business day and night, under the guidance of highly able men established far from the center of the storm, three hundred leagues from your frontiers. . . .

—Ah, Rome! Rome! cried the master of the house.

—Yes, sir, *Rome,* the cardinal replied proudly. Whatever jokes, more or less clever, may have been customary when you were young, I will say flatly that in 1830, the clergy, guided by Rome, is the only body that speaks to the little man.

Fifty thousand priests repeat the same words on the exact day appointed by their leaders and the common people, who, after all, furnish the soldiers, will be more stirred by the voice of their priests than by all the little worms in the world. . . . (The directness of this remark aroused some murmurs.)

The clergy have a spirit superior to yours, resumed the cardinal, raising his voice; every step you have taken in the direction of this capital point, *having an armed party in France,* has been taken by us. Here various facts were cited. Who sent eighty thousand guns into the Vendée? . . . etc., etc.

As long as the clergy do not have their lands, their wooded lands, they have nothing.[4] The minute war breaks out, the minister of finance writes to his agents, there's no more money except for parish priests. At heart, the French have no religious faith, and they love war. So whoever gives them a war will be doubly popular, for making war is starving Jesuits, to use a vulgar expression; making war is delivering the French people, those monsters of pride, from the threat of foreign occupation.

The cardinal was heard with favor. . . . It is imperative, he said, that M. de Nerval resign from the ministry; his name angers people to no purpose.

At this, they all rose to their feet and began talking at once.

4. After the Restoration a concerted move to restore to the clergy their ancient domains of forest land was de- feated, but the issue remained alive, in the minds of the clergy particularly.

They'll send me out again, Julien thought; but even the prudent chairman had forgotten Julien's presence and existence.

All eyes were turned on a man whom Julien recognized. It was M. de Nerval, the first minister, whom he had seen before at the Duc de Retz's ball.

The disorder was at its height, as newspapers say when they talk about the Chamber of Deputies. After a long quarter hour, a measure of quiet was established.

Then M. de Nerval got up and put on an apostolic manner:

—I shall not for a moment pretend, said he in an unnatural voice, that I do not want to remain in the ministry.

It has been demonstrated, gentlemen, that my name multiplies the influence of the Jacobins by turning many of the moderates against us. I should, therefore, be happy to resign; for the Lord's ways are visible to only a few; but, he added, looking directly at the cardinal, I have a mission; heaven has said to me: Either you will forfeit your head on a scaffold or you will reestablish monarchy in France and reduce the chambers to what they were in the parliament of Louis XV, and that, gentlemen, *that I will do.*[5]

He stopped, sat down, and a great silence followed.

There's a good actor, thought Julien. As usual, he made the mistake of crediting people with too much intelligence. Agitated by the evening's lively controversy, and above all by the sincerity of the discussion, M. de Nerval for the moment actually believed in his mission. With a great deal of courage, he had little common sense.

Midnight struck during the silence that followed the fine phrase, *that I will do.* Julien felt that the clock's striking had something funereal and imposing about it. He was much moved.

Soon the discussion resumed, with increasing energy and above all with an incredible simplicity of mind. These people will have to have me poisoned, Julien thought at certain moments. How can they say such things in front of a plebeian?

Two o'clock struck, and they were still talking. The master of the house had long been asleep; M. de La Mole was obliged to ring for fresh candles. M. de Nerval the minister had left at quarter of two, but not until he had carefully studied Julien's features in a pocket mirror which the minister had with him. His departure seemed to leave everyone more at ease.

While the candles were being replaced, —God knows what that man is going to say to the king, the man in waistcoats whispered to his neighbor. He can make us all look foolish and spoil our game for the future.

5. The mystical religiosity evinced in this passage by "M. de Nerval" probably derives from a similar strain of feeling in the arch-reactionary Prince Jules de Polignac.

But you must admit he shows plenty of assurance, or you might even call it effrontery, in turning up here. Before he became a minister, he used to be one of the regulars; but the portfolio changes all that; it buries a man's private concerns; he ought to have realized that.

No sooner had the minister left than Bonaparte's general closed his eyes. Now he murmured something about his health, his wounds, glanced at his watch, and took his leave.

—I'll bet, said the man in waistcoats, that the general is running after the minister; he is going to make his excuses for being found here, and pretend that he is our leader.

When the heavy-eyed servants had finished replacing the candles:

—Let's reach some decisions now, gentlemen, said the chairman, let's not try to persuade one another any more. Let us try to decide the tenor of the note that in less than forty-eight hours will be reaching our friends abroad. There has been talk of ministers. Now that M. de Nerval is gone, we can say openly, What do we care for ministers? They will want what we want.

The cardinal indicated his approval with a thin smile.

—Nothing easier, it seems to me, than to summarize our position, said the young bishop of Agde, with the concentrated, collected passion of the most exalted fanaticism. He had been silent until now; after the first hour of discussion, his expression had changed, as Julien watched it, from an original gentle calm to fiery energy. Now he poured forth his soul like lava from Vesuvius.

—Between 1806 and 1814, England made only one mistake, said he, and that was not to act directly and personally against Napoleon. As soon as that man began creating dukes and chamberlains, as soon as he reestablished the throne, the mission that God gave him was over; the only thing to do was to destroy him. The Holy Scriptures teach us in more than one passage how to get rid of tyrants. (Here there were several citations in Latin.)

Today, gentlemen, it is not just a single man who must be destroyed, it is Paris. All France takes Paris as its model. What good will it do to arm your five hundred men per district? A dangerous project, and an endless one. Why involve all France in a matter that pertains only to Paris? Paris alone with its newspapers and its drawing rooms has done the harm; let the new Babylon perish.

Between the altar and Paris there is war to the death. This catastrophe is even to the worldly advantage of the throne. Why didn't Paris dare to breathe under Bonaparte? Ask the artillerymen of Saint-Roch. . . .[6]

6. Near the church of St. Roch by the Tuileries, Napoleon's artillerymen fired the "whiff of grapeshot" which brought the French Revolution to an end and established Napoleon as dictator (October 5, 1795).

It was not until three in the morning that Julien left with M. de La Mole.

The marquis was tired and disheartened. For the first time in his conversations with Julien there was a tone of appeal in his voice. He begged him on his word not to reveal the excesses of zeal, that was his expression, which he had just chanced to observe. Don't speak of it to our friend abroad unless he really insists on it in order to know something about our young hotheads. What do they care if the state is overthrown? They will be cardinals, and will take refuge in Rome, while we, in our country houses, are being massacred by the peasants.

The secret note the marquis drew up on the basis of Julien's big twenty-six page transcript was not ready until quarter of five.

—I am dead tired, said the marquis, and that's perfectly plain from the note itself, which is rather short on clarity toward the end; I'm more dissatisfied with it than with anything I ever did in my life. And now, my friend, he added, go get a few hours' rest, and just to keep anyone from kidnapping you, I'm going to lock you in your room.

The next day the marquis brought Julien to an isolated country house at some distance from Paris. His hosts there were some remarkable people, whom Julien supposed to be priests. They gave him a passport bearing a false name, but did at last reveal the destination of his journey, of which he had always pretended to be ignorant. He drove off alone in an open carriage.

The marquis had no misgivings about his memory since Julien had recited the secret note several times, but he was much afraid of his being waylaid.

—Be sure at all costs to look like a fop traveling to kill time, was his last friendly warning as he left the room. There may have been more than one false friend at our meeting last night.

The trip was rapid and very monotonous. Julien was scarcely out of the marquis' sight when he forgot the secret note and the mission and began to think of nothing but Mathilde's contempt.

At a village several leagues beyond Metz the master of the posting station came to inform him that no horses were to be had. It was ten o'clock at night; Julien, much put out, ordered supper. He strolled about before the door, and gradually, without seeming to do so, wandered toward the stable yard. No horses were to be seen.

Just the same, that man had a funny look about him, Julien said to himself; his ox-eye kept staring at me.

The reader will note that he was starting not to believe exactly everything that was told him. He thought about getting away after supper, and to learn something about the lie of the land, he left his room to go down and warm himself by the kitchen fire. He was overjoyed to find there Signor Geronimo, the celebrated singer.

Firmly planted in an armchair he had had shoved close to the fire, the Neapolitan was groaning aloud and talking more, all by himself, than the twenty gaping German peasants who stood around him.

—These people are going to ruin me, he called to Julien. I've promised to sing tomorrow at Mainz. Seven sovereign princes have gathered there to hear me. But let's go out for a breath of air, he added in a significant tone.

When he was a hundred feet down the road and out of earshot:

—Do you know what's going on? he asked Julien; this postmaster is a scoundrel. While strolling about, I gave twenty sous to a little blackguard who told me everything. There are more than a dozen horses in a stable at the other end of town. They're trying to hold up some courier.

—Oh, really? said Julien with an innocent air.

It wasn't enough to uncover the cheat, they had to get on with their journey; and this Geronimo and his friend were unable to do.

—Let's wait for daylight, said the singer at last, these people suspect us. Perhaps it's you or me that they're looking for. Tomorrow morning we'll order a good breakfast; while it's preparing, we'll go for a stroll, make our escape, hire some horses, and use them to get to the next post station.

—And how about your luggage? said Julien, who was thinking that perhaps Geronimo himself might be an agent sent to intercept him. There was nothing to do but eat supper and go to bed. Julien was still in his first sleep when he was awakened with a start by the voices of two men talking in his room without any effort at concealment.

He recognized the master of the post, who was carrying a dark lantern. The light shone on the trunk of Julien's carriage, which had been carried up to his room. Beside the postmaster was a man who was coolly ransacking the open trunk. Julien could make out only the cuffs of his coat, which were black and very close fitting.

It's a cassock, he said to himself, and reached quietly for the little pistols he had put under his pillow.

—Don't worry about his waking up, your reverence, said the postmaster. The wine they were served was some of that you prepared yourself.

—I find no trace of papers, replied the priest. Plenty of clean linen, perfumes, ointments, fripperies; it's a young fellow of good society, interested in his own pleasures. The messenger is probably the other fellow, who pretends to speak with an Italian accent.

The men turned toward Julien to rummage in the pockets of his traveling coat. He was greatly minded to kill them as thieves. His moral position would have been unassailable. He was sorely tempted. I'd be no better than a fool, he thought, I would be endangering my mission. The priest finished searching through his coat, and said: This is no diplomat. He turned away, and it was a good thing he did.

If he touches me in my bed, so much the worse for him, Julien was thinking; it's perfectly possible he'll be trying to stab me, and that I can't have.

The priest turned his head; Julien half opened his eyes; and what was his amazement to see Abbé Castanède! Actually, though the two men had lowered their voices a little, he had felt from the first that he recognized the speech of one. Julien was seized with a sudden impulse to purge the earth of one of its lowest scoundrels. . . .[7]

—But my mission! he reminded himself.

The priest and his acolyte went out. After a quarter of an hour Julien pretended to wake up. He shouted and woke the entire house.

—I've been poisoned! he cried. I'm in agonies! He needed a pretext for going to the aid of Geronimo. He found him half overcome by the dose of laudanum that had been in his wine.

Julien, fearing some trick of this sort, had eaten nothing but some chocolate brought from Paris. He could not succeed in rousing Geronimo enough to get him on the road.

—You could offer me the whole kingdom of Naples, said the singer, I still wouldn't give up the pleasure of going back to bed.

—But the seven sovereign princes!

—Let them wait.

Julien left by himself and arrived without further adventures at the residence of the great personage.[8] He wasted a whole morning asking vainly for a hearing. Luckily, about four o'clock the duke decided to go out for a stroll. Julien saw him leave the house on foot and had no hesitation about going up to him and begging for charity. When only a few feet away from the great personage, he drew forth the marquis de La Mole's watch and ostentatiously consulted it. *Follow me at a distance,* he was told without so much as a second glance.

A quarter of a league further on the duke turned abruptly into a little *Kaffeehaus.* It was in a room of this very inferior inn that

7. The irrationality of having a plot hatched by reactionaries and churchmen impeded by a conspiracy of churchmen and reactionaries needs no emphasizing.

8. According to Stendhal himself, the great person Julien encounters is at Mainz, and he is an ambassador; but he is vague enough to be now a duke, now a prince, and now a great statesman.

Julien had the honor of reciting his four pages to the duke. When he had finished, he was told: *Begin again and go more slowly.*

The prince took notes. *Go on foot to the next post. Leave your luggage and your carriage here. Go to Strasbourg any way you can, and on the twenty-second of this month* (it was now the tenth) *be in this Kaffeehaus at half past twelve noon. Wait half an hour before you leave here. Silence!*

These were the only words that Julien heard. They sufficed to raise him to a pitch of admiration. Now this, he thought, this is the way to handle great affairs; what would this great statesman say if he had heard those passionate babblers three days ago?

Julien put two days into reaching Strasbourg, where he supposed he would have nothing to do. He took the long way around. If that devil Abbé Castanède recognized me, he is not a man to be easily thrown off the scent. . . . And what pleasure it would be for him to make a fool of me and bring my whole mission to naught!

Fortunately, Abbé Castanède, chief of the congregation police along the northern frontier, had not recognized him. And the Jesuits of Strasbourg, though thoroughly zealous, never dreamed of setting a watch on Julien, who, with his cross and his blue greatcoat, had the look of a youthful soldier much attached to his own personal appearance.

Chapter 24

STRASBOURG

Fascination! you have all the energy of love, all its power to endure suffering. Only its enchanting pleasures, its sweet delights, are beyond your sphere. I could not say, when I saw her lying asleep: she is all mine, with her angelic beauty and her sweet frailties! There she is delivered into my power, just as heaven created her in its compassion to enchant the heart of man.
—Ode of Schiller

Compelled to spend a week in Strasbourg, Julien tried to divert himself with thoughts of military glory and patriotic devotion. Was he really in love? He could not tell; he knew only that within his tortured spirit Mathilde remained in full command of his happiness as of his imagination. He required the full energy of his character to maintain himself above the level of despair. To think of something unrelated to Mlle. de La Mole was beyond his power. In earlier days ambition and the simple triumphs of vanity had distracted him from the feelings that Mme. de Rênal aroused in him. Mathilde had absorbed everything; he found her everywhere in his future.

Wherever he looked, Julien saw in this future nothing but failure

The man who appeared at Verrières so bloated with presumption and pride had now fallen into a ridiculous extreme of modesty.

Three days before, he would joyfully have killed Abbé Castanède, and now at Strasbourg, if a child had picked a quarrel with him, he would have knuckled under. When he numbered over the adversaries and enemies he had had during his life, Julien found that invariably he himself had been in the wrong.

The fact was that he now had as an implacable enemy that brilliant imagination of his, which previously had been busy all the time painting the future with his splendid successes.

The absolute solitude of a traveler's life further reinforced the power of this somber imagination. What a treasure a friend would have been! But, Julien asked himself, is there a heart anywhere that beats for me? And even if I had a friend, doesn't honor impose perpetual silence on me?

He took horse and rode gloomily in the suburbs of Kehl; it is a town on the banks of the Rhine rendered immortal by Desaix and Gouvion Saint-Cyr.[9] A German peasant pointed out to him the little streams, the roads, and the islands in the Rhine which the courage of those great generals made known. Julien, as he held the reins with his left hand, unfolded with his right the superb map that adorns the *Mémoires* of Marshal Saint-Cyr. A merry hail caused him to lift his head.

It was Prince Korasoff, that London acquaintance, from whom Julien had acquired some months before the first principles of the higher fatuity. Faithful to this great art, Korasoff, who had been at Strasbourg since yesterday and at Kehl for an hour, who had never in his life read a line about the siege of 1796, set about explaining the whole thing to Julien. The German peasant looked at him in amazement; he knew just enough French to recognize the enormous blunders the prince was making. Julien's ideas were a thousand miles from those of the peasant; he was looking with astonishment at this handsome young man and admiring his poise in the saddle.

What a happy disposition! he said to himself. How well his trousers fit, how elegantly his hair is cut! Alas! if I had been like that, perhaps after loving me for three days she might not have taken such a dislike to me.

When the prince had finished his siege of Kehl: —You look like a Trappist monk, he told Julien, you're overdoing the principle of gravity I laid down for you in London. A gloomy air can never be good form; what you need is the air of boredom. If you're gloomy,

9. Desaix and Gouvion St. Cyr won a brilliant victory at Kehl in 1796 by an audacious crossing of the Rhine against heavy opposition.

there must be something you lack, something at which you haven't succeeded.

It is admitting your inferiority. But if you're bored, on the other hand, it's the person who has tried unsuccessfully to please you who is inferior. You must understand, my dear fellow, what a grave mistake you are making.

Julien flung a crown to the peasant who was listening to them, open-mouthed.

—Well done, said the prince, there was grace in that gesture, a noble disdain! Very good indeed! And he put his horse to the gallop. Julien followed him, full of stunned admiration.

Ah! if I had been like that she would not have preferred Croisenois before me! The more his reason was shocked by the prince's absurdities, the more he despised himself for not admiring them, and thought himself unfortunate not to have them in his own person. [That's the way to be, he told himself.] Self-loathing cannot be carried any further.

The prince, finding him decidedly gloomy: —Come along, now, my dear fellow, he told him as they rode back to Strasbourg, [you're very poor company,] have you lost all your money or are you in love with some little actress?

The Russians copy French customs, but always at a distance of fifty years. They are just now coming into the age of Louis XV.

These jests about love brought tears to Julien's eyes: Why not seek the advice of this friendly man? he asked himself suddenly.

—Very well, my dear fellow, he told the prince, as a matter of fact you're right; here I am at Strasbourg, head over heels in love, but unhappily. A charming woman who lives in one of the towns nearby has turned me out after three days of passion, and this change will be the death of me.

Using fictitious names, he described to the prince the actions and character of Mathilde.

—Say no more, said Korasoff; to give you confidence in your doctor, I cut short your confession. Either this young lady's husband is enormously rich or else she belongs to the most distinguished nobility. She must have something to be proud of.

Julien inclined his head; he no longer had strength to speak.

—Very well, said the prince, here are three medicines, all rather bitter, for you to take without delay:

1. See every day Mme. . . . what's her name?

—Mme. de Dubois.

—What a name! said the prince, with a shout of laughter; but I beg your pardon, for you it is sublime. Well, you must see Mme. de Dubois every day; and make a point of never seeming cold or out of sorts in her presence. Remember the great principle of your

century: always be the contrary of what people expect. Show yourself as the exact same person you were a week before you were
honored with her favors.

—Ah, I was at peace then, Julien cried in despair, I wanted to
arouse her pity. . . .

—The moth burned up in the candle, said the prince, the oldest
story in the world.

1. You will see her every day;

2. You will court another woman whom she knows, but without
the slightest appearance of passion, do you understand? I won't
conceal from you, your role is a hard one; you are acting a comedy,
and if anyone suspects you of acting, there's no hope for you.

—She is so clever, and I am so dull, Julien said sadly; there's no
hope for me.

—No, you're just more in love than I thought. Mme. de Dubois
is deeply devoted to herself, like all women who have been granted
either too much nobility or too much money. She has her eye on
herself instead of on you, hence she does not know you. During the
two or three periods when she felt impulses of love toward you, she
made a great effort of imagination, seeing you as her dream hero,
but not yourself as you really are. . . .

But what the devil, these are the mere rudiments, my dear Sorel,
are you just a schoolboy?

Damn it, look at this shop window; there's a perfectly charming
black cravat, it might have been made by John Anderson of Burling-
ton Street; do me the great favor of accepting it and throwing away
that ignoble bit of black string you have around your neck.

Now then, continued the prince, as they left the shop of the
best haberdasher in Strasbourg, what sort of friends has your Mme.
de Dubois? Good God! what a name! Don't get angry, my dear
Sorel, it's too much for me. . . . Where are you going to do your
courting?

—To the most prudish prude in the world, daughter of a stocking
merchant who has become immensely rich. She has lovely eyes, they
please me no end; there's no doubt she's of the very highest
rank in the district; but in the middle of all this splendor, she blushes
and loses all her poise if anyone happens to talk of commerce and
shops. And unhappily, her father was one of the best-known trades-
men in Strasbourg.

—So if one mentions *industry*, said the prince with a laugh, one
can be quite sure the dear creature is thinking of herself and not of
you. A divine weakness and extremely useful; it will prevent you
from ever seeming foolish in her fair eyes. Success is assured.

Julien was thinking of Mme. de Fervaques, the maréchale's
widow, who often visited the Hotel de La Mole. She was a beautiful

foreigner who had married the maréchal the year before he died. Her whole life seemed to have no other aim than to make people forget she was the daughter of *a man in trade,* and in order to be something in Paris she had appointed herself leader of the party of virtue.

Julien admired the prince with all his heart; what wouldn't he have given to be possessed of his absurdities! The conversation between the two friends was interminable; Korasoff was in ecstasies: never had a Frenchman listened to him for such a long time. I've finally succeeded, the prince said to himself joyously. I've made my presence felt, and given lessons to my own teachers!

—We're agreed, then, he repeated to Julien for the tenth time, not a shadow of passion when you talk to this young beauty, the daughter of a Strasbourg stocking merchant, in the presence of your Mme. de Dubois. On the other hand, burning passion every time you write her. Reading a well-written love letter is the greatest pleasure in life for a prude; it is a moment of relaxation. She isn't playing the comedy; she summons up the courage to listen to her heart; so give her two letters a day.

—Never, never, said Julien, desponding; I'd sooner let myself be pounded up in a mortar than compose three sentences; I'm a corpse, my dear fellow, you can't expect anything of me. Let me die in a ditch.

—And who said anything about composing sentences? I have in my traveling case six volumes of manuscript loveletters. There are some for every different sort of woman; I have a set for the loftiest virtue. Don't you remember that Kalisky made love, at Richmond Terrace—you know, a few leagues from London—to the prettiest Quakeress in all England?

Julien was less wretched when he left his friend at two o'clock in the morning.

Next day the prince summoned a copyist, and two days later Julien had fifty-three love letters, carefully numbered, and designed to cope with the noblest and gloomiest case of virtue.

—The reason there aren't fifty-four, said the prince, is that Kalisky was given the boot; but what do you care if you're ill treated by the stocking man's daughter, since your only intent is to play on the heart of Mme. de Dubois?

Every day they went out riding: the prince was madly devoted to Julien. Not knowing how else to give proof of his sudden affection, he ended by offering him the hand of one of his cousins, a rich heiress in Moscow. Once married, he added, my influence and the decoration you have there will make you a colonel in two years.

—But this decoration was not given by Napoleon, far from it.

—What matter? said the prince. Didn't he invent it? It is still the most distinguished, by a long shot, in all Europe.[1]

Julien was on the point of accepting; but his duty called him back to the great personage; as he parted from Korasoff, he promised to write. He picked up the answer to the secret note he had delivered and posted toward Paris; but he had hardly been alone for two days on end when the thought of leaving France and Mathilde seemed to him a torture far worse than death. I shan't marry the millions Korasoff offered me, he said, but I will take his advice. After all, the art of seduction is his main business; he has thought about nothing else for more than fifteen years, since he is now thirty. You can't say he's lacking in brains; he's clever and shrewd; enthusiasm and poetry are impossibilities, given his character; he's a conniver; all the more reason why he probably is not wrong.

It's a necessity; I will pay court to Mme. de Fervaques.

She will bore me a good deal, no doubt, but I can gaze into those lovely eyes that resemble so much another pair which loved me more than anything in the world.

She's a foreigner; that's a new sort of character to study.

I am mad, I am drowning, I must follow the advice of my friend and not trust my own instincts.

Chapter 25

THE MINISTRY OF VIRTUE

> But if I sample this pleasure with so much prudence and circumspection, it will no longer be a pleasure for me.
>
> —Lope de Vega

Scarcely was he back in Paris, no sooner had he left the study of the Marquis de La Mole, who seemed much disconcerted by the messages delivered to him, than our hero hastened to visit Comte Altamira. Besides his special quality of carrying a death sentence, this handsome foreigner rejoiced in a grave demeanor and was naturally devout; these two merits, and, above all, the count's lofty birth, were most agreeable to Mme. de Fervaques, and she saw him frequently.

Julien solemnly assured him that he was passionately in love.

—She is pure and lofty virtue incarnate, replied Altamira, she is only a little Jesuitical and emphatic. There are days when I understand every individual word she uses but make no sense out of what she is saying. She often gives me the impression that I don't know

---

1. The order instituted by Napoleon is clearly the Legion of Honor, which he established in 1802.

French as well as people say. This acquaintance will make your name known; it will give you standing in the world. But let's go and see Bustos, said Comte Altamira, who had a strong sense of order; he has paid court to Mme. la Maréchale.

Don Diego Bustos required a full-length explanation of the matter; meanwhile, he said not a word, like a lawyer in his office. He had a fat monkish face with black moustaches and an unmatchable solemnity; for the rest, a good revolutionary.[2]

—I understand, he told Julien at last. Has the Maréchale de Fervaques had lovers ar hasn't she? Have you, thus, some hope of success or don't you? There is the question. I must confess that for my own part I failed. Now that I am no longer nettled at it, I reason this way: the lady is often out of sorts, and, as I shall explain to you shortly, has a certain talent for spite.

I do not recognize in her that bilious temperament that is often a mark of genius, and which casts over all one's actions, as it were, a veneer of passion. On the contrary, it is because she is calm and phlegmatic like a Dutchwoman that she preserves her rare beauty and fresh complexion.

Julien was waxing impatient with the slow pace and unruffled calm of the Spaniard; from time to time, in spite of himself, he gave vent to various monosyllables.

—Do you want to hear what I have to say? Don Diego Bustos said to him solemnly.

—Please excuse the *furia francese*,[3] Julien replied; I'm all ears.

—The Maréchale de Fervaques is, then, much addicted to hate; she pursues implacably people whom she has never seen, lawyers, poor devils of writers who have composed songs like Collé—[4] do you know it?

> I have the woeful folly
> To be in love with Polly, etc.

And Julien had to listen to the whole thing. The Spaniard was much gratified to be singing in French.

Never was that divine song listened to with greater impatience. When it was over: —The maréchale, said Don Diego Bustos, brought ruin upon the author of that song:

> One day the lover at the inn . . .

Julien shuddered lest he sing the whole thing. But he contented himself with a critical analysis. As a matter of fact, it was an impious and almost indecent song.

2. The original reads, for "revolutionary," *carbonaro*, that is, an Italian republican conspirator.
3. Renaissance Italians, astonished at the French audacity in a charge, by contrast with the decorous mercenaries to whom they were accustomed, coined the term *furia francese*, that is French madness.
4. Charles Collé (1709–83) wrote a great number of popular songs while employed as a government clerk.

When the maréchale grew angry with that song, said Don Diego, I took occasion to remark that a lady of her station should not read all the trash that people publish. However widespread piety and gravity become, France will always have its tavern literature, I said. When Mme. de Fervaques had deprived the author, a poor devil on half pay, of a post worth eighteen hundred francs, I told her: Watch out, you have attacked this rhymester with your weapons; he may come back at you with his own: he'll make a song about virtue. No doubt the gilded drawing rooms will be on your side, but the people who like to laugh will repeat his epigrams. Do you know, my dear sir, what the maréchale replied to me? —In the service of the Lord, all Paris could turn out to see me tread the martyr's path; it would be a new spectacle in France. The vulgar would learn to respect the quality. It would be the most beautiful day of my life. And her eyes had never been more enchanting.

—She has lovely eyes, Julien exclaimed.

—I can see that you're in love. . . . Well, then, said Don Diego Bustos with great solemnity, she does not have the bilious constitution that conducts a woman to vengeance. If, nonetheless, she likes to hurt people, it must be because she is unhappy; I suspect an *inward grief*. May she not be a prude grown tired of her trade?

The Spaniard stared at him silently for a full minute.

—This, then, is the basic question, he added gravely, and from this consideration you may draw some hope. I thought about it a good deal during the two years that I professed myself her humble obedient servant. Your entire future as a man in love depends on this great problem: Is she a prude grown tired of her trade and malicious because she is miserable?

—Or else, said Altamira, starting at last from his profound silence, would it be what I have told you twenty times over? simply French vanity. It's the recollection of her father, the famous haberdasher, which brings such grief to her naturally gloomy, dry character. There could be only one happiness for her, to live in Toledo and be tormented by a confessor who would describe to her every day the gaping mouth of hell.

As Julien was taking his leave: —Altamira tells me you are one of us, Don Diego told him, more gravely than ever. One day you will help us regain our liberty, so I should like to be of help to you in this little diversion. It would be a good idea for you to know the maréchale's style; here are four letters of her writing.

—I shall have them copied, said Julien, and bring them back to you.

—And no one will ever hear from you a word of what we've been saying?

—Never, on my honor! cried Julien.

—Then, God be with you! added the Spaniard; and without another word he ushered out to the staircase Julien and Altamira.

This scene restored our hero's spirits somewhat; he was on the verge of smiling. And here's the devout Altamira, he said to himself, helping me in an adulterous enterprise.

During all of Don Diego Bustos' weighty conversation, Julien had been listening to the hours as they were sounded by the clock of the Hotel d'Aligre.

Dinnertime was at hand; he was about to see Mathilde again! He went home and dressed with great care.

First piece of foolishness, he told himself, as he was going downstairs; I must follow the prince's instructions to the letter.

He went back to his room and changed to a traveling costume of extreme simplicity.

Now, he said to himself, it's a matter of how to look at her. It was only five-thirty and they sat down to dinner at six. He had the notion of going down to the drawing room, which he found empty. [At the sight of the blue sofa, he fell to his knees and kissed the spot where Mathilde placed her arm, tears flowed, his cheeks were afire.] I must work off this absurd sensitivity, he told himself angrily; it will betray me. He picked up a newspaper to give himself countenance, and strolled three or four times from the drawing room into the garden and back.

It was only with great trepidation, and from the concealment afforded by a great oak, that he dared to raise his eyes to Mlle. de La Mole's window. It was shut tight; he was on the point of collapse, and stood for a long time, leaning against the oak; then, with wavering steps, he went over to look at the gardener's ladder.

The link of chain, which he had twisted open under circumstances very different, alas, from the present, had not been repaired. Carried away by an impulse of madness, Julien pressed it to his lips.

After straying back and forth for a long time between the drawing room and the garden, Julien found himself horribly tired; it was a first success which gave him great pleasure. My glances will be dull and won't give me away! Gradually the guests gathered in the drawing room; the door never opened without striking mortal anguish to Julien's heart.

They sat down to table. At last Mlle. de La Mole appeared, faithful to her rule of making people wait for her. She blushed deeply at the sight of Julien; she had not been told of his return. Following Prince Korasoff's advice, Julien looked at her hands; they were trembling. Though indescribably disturbed by this discovery, he was lucky enough to appear merely tired.

M. de La Mole sang his praises. The marquise spoke to him a moment later and was kind enough to observe his air of weariness.

Julien kept saying to himself at every instant: I must not look too often at Mlle. de La Mole, but neither must my eyes seem to avoid her. I must seem to be exactly what I was in reality a week before my misfortune. . . . He had reason to be satisfied with his performance, and remained in the drawing room after dinner. Attentive, for the first time, to the lady of the house, he bent all his efforts toward making the men of her group talk and keeping the conversation alive.

His politeness was rewarded: promptly at eight Mme. la Maréchale de Fervaques was announced. Julien left the room and reappeared shortly, dressed with the most meticulous care. Mme. de La Mole was infinitely obliged to him for this mark of respect, and undertook to show her pleasure by talking to Mme. de Fervaques of his journey. Julien placed himself beside the maréchale in such a way that his eyes could not be seen by Mathilde. So stationed, and taking care to follow all the rules of the art, he focused upon Mme. de Fervaques his most open-mouthed admiration. The first of the fifty-three letters given him by Prince Korasoff began with a tirade on this sentiment.

The maréchale declared she was going to the Opera Buffa. Julien hastened there too; he found the chevalier de Beauvoisis, who took him to a box occupied by gentlemen of the chamber, right alongside that of Mme. de Fervaques. Julien gazed at her continually. As he returned to the house, he told himself: I must keep a journal of the siege, otherwise I'll forget my various attacks. He forced himself to write two or three pages on this tedious topic, and thus succeeded, miracle of miracles! in hardly thinking of Mlle. de La Mole at all.

Mathilde had almost forgotten him while he was away. After all, he is only a common creature; his name will always remind me of the blackest blot on my life. I shall have to go back to those vulgar ideas of prudence and honor; when she forgets them, a woman has everything to lose. She showed herself disposed to allow the final steps to be taken in her arrangement with the Marquis de Croisenois, which had been so long in preparation. He was mad with joy; and he would have been amazed to learn that resignation was at the root of Mathilde's new attitude which was making him so proud.

All Mlle. de La Mole's ideas changed when she saw Julien. Actually, that man is my husband, she told herself; if I'm really sincere about returning to the paths of prudence, he is the man I ought to marry.

She was looking for importunities, an air of grieving on Julien's part; she was preparing her responses: for no doubt, when dinner was over, he would try to say a few words to her. Far from doing so, he remained planted in the drawing room; his glances never even turned toward the garden, Lord knows at what cost to his feelings! It's best to get the whole scene over with, thought Mlle. de La Mole; she strolled alone into the garden; Julien did not go. Mathilde walked past the drawing room windows; she saw him fully engaged in describing to Mme. de Fervaques those ancient ruined castles which crown the hilltops along the Rhine and give that landscape so much character. He was starting to draw with some fluency on that vein of sentimental and picturesque diction which, in certain quarters, is known as *wit*.

Prince Korasoff would have been proud indeed had he been at Paris: the evening took exactly the form he had predicted.

He would have approved, too, of Julien's conduct during the following days.

An intrigue within the backstairs cabinet was about to make available various blue-ribbon decorations; Mme. la Maréchale de Fervaques insisted that her uncle must be made a knight of the order. The Marquis de La Mole was putting forward for the same honor his father-in-law; they joined forces, and the maréchale came almost every day to the Hotel de La Mole. It was from her that Julien learned that the marquis was to be a minister: he had offered the ruling clique an extremely clever scheme for destroying the charter, without any protest, in three years' time.

Julien might hope for a bishopric if M. de La Mole got into the ministry; but in his eyes all these great projects were hidden as behind a veil. His imagination grasped them now only hazily and, so to speak, from a distance. The frightful misery that was making a maniac of him converted all the interests of life into ways of being with Mlle. de La Mole. He calculated that after five or six years of constant effort he might make her love him again.

This head, usually so cool, had, as we see, sunk into a state of complete irrationality. Of all the qualities that had once distinguished him, nothing remained but a little firmness. Mechanically faithful to the plan of conduct dictated by Prince Korasoff, every evening he placed himself beside the armchair of Mme. de Fervaques, but he found it impossible to scrape up a word to say to her.

The effort he was making to appear healed in the eyes of Mathilde absorbed all the energy of his soul; he sat beside the maréchale like an almost lifeless being; even his eyes, as happens to men under the most extreme suffering, had lost all their light.

As Mme. de La Mole's way of seeing things was always a feeble imitation of the opinions of her husband, who might make her a ⁀duchess, she spent several days praising Julien to the skies.

Chapter 26

MORAL LOVE

There also was of course in Adeline
    That calm patrician polish in the address,
Which ne'er can pass the equinoctial line
    Of any thing which Nature would express:
Just as a Mandarin finds nothing fine,
    At least his manner suffers not to guess
That anything he views can greatly please.
            —*Don Juan,* canto XIII, stanza 84

This whole family has a rather crazy way of looking at things, thought the maréchale; they are all mad for their little abbé, who does nothing but sit still and listen, though it's true, his eyes are not bad looking.

Julien, for his part, found in the manners of the maréchale an almost perfect specimen of that *patrician calm* which breathes an air of perfect politeness and especially the total impossibility of any keen emotion. Any spontaneous gesture, any lapse of complete self-control, would have scandalized Mme. de Fervaques almost as much as a failure of dignified condescension toward one's inferiors. The slightest sign of sensitivity would have been in her eyes a sort of *moral intoxication* of which one ought to be ashamed, since it undermines everything that a person of lofty rank owes to herself. Her greatest happiness was to talk about the king's latest hunting party; her favorite book was the *Mémoires du duc de Saint-Simon,*[5] especially the genealogical part.

Julien knew just what position in the drawing room, as the lights were arranged, was most suitable for Mme. de Fervaques' variety of beauty. He was always there waiting for her, but took great pains to adjust his chair so as not to notice Mathilde. Astonished at his persistence in avoiding her, she left the blue sofa one day and came to do her needlework at a little table near the maréchale's armchair. Julien saw her nearby from under the brim of Mme. de Fervaques's hat. Seeing [so near to him] those eyes in which his destiny was to be read, he was first terrified, then flung violently out of his ordinary apathy; he talked, and very well.

All his words were addressed to the maréchale, but his only end was to work on the mind of Mathilde. He grew so animated that Mme. de Fervaques found herself unable to understand what he was talking about.

That was a first merit. If Julien had had the notion of piling on a few sentences of German mysticity, lofty religiosity, and Jesuitism,

5. The *Mémoires* of Saint-Simon (1675–1755) are a standard authority for the first half of the eighteenth cen- tury and a work of great literary merit; but the genealogies are not, precisely, the liveliest part of it.

the maréchale would immediately have placed him in the ranks of the superior men called to redeem the century.

Since he displays such bad taste, Mlle. de La Mole told herself, as to talk so long and so animatedly to Mme. de Fervaques, I shall pay no further attention to him. And for the rest of the evening she kept her word, though only with an effort.

That night, after Mathilde picked up her mother's candlestick to accompany her to her bedroom, Mme. de La Mole stopped short on the stairway to deliver an absolute eulogy of Julien. Mathilde at this finally lost her temper; she was unable to fall asleep. Only one idea soothed her: the man I despise still seems like a person of great merit to the maréchale.

As for Julien, he had taken an action, he was less miserable; his eyes fell by accident on the Russia-leather briefcase in which Prince Korasoff had placed the fifty-three love letters that were his gift to Julien. At the foot of the first letter was a note: *Send number one a week after the first meeting.*

I'm already behind schedule, Julien exclaimed, for I've been seeing Mme. de Fervaques a long time now. At once he sat down to transcribe this first love letter; it was a homily on virtue and deadly dull; Julien was lucky enough to fall asleep over the second page of it.

Some hours later the rising sun came upon him with his head resting on the table. One of the most painful moments of his life was that in which each morning as he awoke he *returned* to the sense of his misery. On this day, he finished copying his letter almost with a laugh. Is it possible, he asked himself, that anywhere in the world there's a young man who writes this way? He counted a number of sentences that were nine lines long. Under the original he found a penciled note.

These letters are delivered by hand: on horseback, black necktie, blue greatcoat. Hand the letter to the porter with an air of contrition; deep melancholy in the gaze. If one catches sight of a chambermaid, wipe the eyes furtively. Say a few words to the maid.

All these instructions were faithfully carried out.

What I am doing is very bold, thought Julien, as he left the Hotel de Fervaques; but so much the worse for Korasoff. Venturing to write to a woman so notorious for virtue! I shall meet with the fiercest scorn from her, and nothing could amuse me more. At bottom, it's the only sort of comedy I can enjoy. Yes, it will be fun to cover with ridicule that odious creature whom I call *me*. If I trusted my own feelings, I would commit some crime simply to divert myself.

For the last month, the happiest moment in Julien's life had been that in which he returned his horse to the stable. Korasoff had expressly forbidden him to look, on any pretext whatever, at the mistress who had left him. But the gait of that horse which she recognized so well, the way in which Julien knocked with his whip at the stable door in order to summon a man, these things sometimes attracted Mathilde behind the curtain of her window. The muslin was so filmy that Julien could see through. By looking in a certain way from under the brim of his hat he could see Mathilde's figure without seeing her eyes. Consequently, he told himself, she cannot see my eyes, and this does not amount, in any way, to looking at her.[6]

That night Mme. de Fervaques behaved toward him exactly as if she had never received that philosophical-mystical-religious dissertation he had passed to her porter that morning with such a melancholy expression. The night before, accident had revealed to Julien the path to eloquence; he placed himself in such a way as to catch sight of Mathilde's eyes. She, for her part, left the blue sofa an instant after the maréchale arrived. To do this was to desert her regular set. M. de Croisenois seemed thunderstruck at this new caprice; his evident distress relieved Julien of the most atrocious part of his own suffering.

This unforeseen episode made him talk like an angel; and as complacency sometimes slips even into those hearts that act as temples to the most austere virtue: Mme. de La Mole is right, said the maréchale to herself as she stepped into her carriage, this young priest is really distinguished. It must have been that during the first days my presence intimidated him. Indeed, the general tone of this house is tinged with a good deal of levity; such virtue as I see needs help from old age and requires assistance from the cool hand of maturity. This young man must have made good note of the difference; he writes very well; but I greatly fear that request he made in his letter, that I should enlighten him with my counsels, is at bottom nothing better than a sentiment unaware of itself.

And yet, how many conversions have begun in this way! The thing that makes me augur well for this one is the difference between his style and that of the other young people whose letters I have had occasion to see. It is impossible not to be aware of the unction, the deep seriousness, and an abundant conviction in the prose of this young levite; surely he will inherit the soothing virtue of Massillon.[7]

6. Julien, glancing at Mlle. de La Mole without looking at her, is fulfilling a characteristic ambition of the voyeuristic Stendhal hero—seeing without being seen. Compare Fabrizio in his tower making love to Clelia Conti through an immense wooden screen (*Chartreuse*, Chap. 29).

7. J. B. Massillon (1663–1742); his doctrinal liberality and persuasive eloquence made him popular with the philosophic skeptics of the later eighteenth century as a model of what a preacher in the pathetic strain should be.

Chapter 27

THE BEST JOBS IN THE CHURCH

Services! talents! merit! bah! join a clique.
—*Télémaque*[8]

Thus the concept *bishop* was for the first time joined to the image of Julien in the mind of a woman who sooner or later would be handing out the best jobs in the church of France. To have gained this ground would have meant little to Julien; at the moment his mind was incapable of any idea apart from his immediate grief: everything augmented it; for example, the very sight of his room had become intolerable. When he returned at night with his candle, every stick of furniture, every little ornament, seemed to have a voice in which to announce fresh details of his misery.

But on this particular day it was with more vivacity than he had felt in a long time that he urged himself: Back to our slave labor; let's hope the second letter is as boring as the first.

It was more so. What he was copying seemed so ridiculous that he began to copy it line for line without giving a thought to the sense.

It's even more emphatic, he told himself, than the official phrases in the treaty of Munster which my instructor in diplomacy made me copy out in London.

Only then did he recall the letters from Mme. de Fervaques, the originals of which he had forgotten to return to the solemn Spaniard, Don Diego Bustos. He pulled them out; and really, they were almost as wishy-washy as those of the young gentleman from Russia. Vagueness could go no further. The letters said everything and nothing. It's the Aeolian harp of style, Julien thought. Amid the loftiest reflections on the void, death, the infinite, and so forth, I see nothing solid except an abominable fear of ridicule.

The monologue we have just abridged was repeated for two weeks on end. Dozing off while copying a sort of commentary on the Apocalypse, carrying a letter the next day with a melancholy air, returning the horse to the stable while hoping to catch a glimpse of Mathilde's dress, working, putting in an appearance at the opera when Mme. de Fervaques did not visit the Hotel de La Mole—such were the monotonous incidents of Julien's life. It was a little more interesting when Mme. de Fervaques did come visiting; for then he could catch a glimpse of Mathilde's eyes from under the brim of the maréchale's hat, and wax eloquent. His picturesque sentimental phrases began to take on more striking and at the same time more elegant contours.

8. *Télémaque* is Fénélon's treatise on education and government, written for the guidance of the Duke of Burgundy and published in 1699.

He knew very well that what he was saying was absurd in the eyes of Mathilde, but he wanted to impress her with his elegance of diction. The more I say what is false, the more I'm bound to please her, Julien thought; and so, with abominable boldness, he began to exaggerate certain aspects of nature. He very quickly sensed that, to avoid seeming vulgar in the eyes of the maréchale, the most essential thing was to shun completely any simple or reasonable ideas. He continued to work on these principles, or cut short his amplifications, as he read success or indifference in the eyes of the two great ladies whom he was trying to please.

On the whole, his life was less frightful than when his days were passed in inaction.

But, he told himself one evening, here I am transcribing the fifteenth of these abominable disquisitions; the first fourteen have been faithfully delivered to the maréchale's doorman. Before long I shall have had the honor of filling every pigeonhole in her desk. And yet she treats me exactly as if I were not writing at all! Where will this whole thing wind up? Will my constancy finish by boring her as much as it does me? It's perfectly clear, that Russian, Korasoff's friend, who was in love with the fair Quakeress of Richmond, must have been a terrible fellow; they don't come any more deadly than that one.

Like all mediocre creatures who become involved by accident in the maneuvers of a great general, Julien understood nothing of the strategic assault launched by the young Russian against the heart of his severe Englishwoman. The first forty letters were intended merely to beg her pardon for his boldness in writing. It was necessary to induce this sweet creature, who perhaps was bored to tears, to form the habit of receiving letters perhaps a little bit less insipid than her everyday life.

One day Julien received a letter; he recognized the crest of Mme. de Fervaques and broke the seal with more eagerness than he would have supposed possible a few days before: it was nothing but an invitation to dinner.

He hastened to consult Prince Korasoff's instructions. Unfortunately, the young Russian had tried to cultivate a light tone, like Dorat,[9] just where he should have been simple and intelligible; Julien could not make out what moral position he should occupy at the maréchale's dinner party.

The drawing room was of the utmost magnificence, gilded like Diana's gallery at the Tuileries, with oil paintings in the panels. There were various white spots on the surface of the paintings. Julien learned later that the subjects had seemed improper to the

9. Claude Dorat (1734–80) was a French man of letters legendary for his awkwardness in handling peoples' feelings; he managed to provoke *all* the factions.

lady of the house, who had therefore had the paintings corrected. A *moral age!* was his thought.

In this drawing room he caught sight of three of the persons who had taken part in preparing the secret note. One of them, the Right Reverend Bishop of _____, the maréchale's uncle, was in charge of giving out benefices, and, as people said, could refuse his niece nothing. What giant steps I've taken, Julien thought with a melancholy smile, and how little difference it makes to me! Here I am dining with the famous Bishop of _____.

The dinner was mediocre and the conversation irksome. It's like the table of contents in a bad book, Julien thought. All the greatest topics of human thought are paraded proudly before you. Listen for three minutes, and you'll be asking which is worse, the emphasis of the speaker or his abominable ignorance.

The reader has no doubt forgotten that little man of letters named Tanbeau, the nephew of the academician and a future professor himself, who seemed employed expressly to poison with his snide slanders the drawing room of the Hotel de La Mole.

It was from this little man that Julien got the first notion that Mme. de Fervaques, while not replying to his letters, might well view with indulgence the sentiment that gave rise to them. M. Tanbeau's black spirit was torn to shreds when he thought of Julien's success; but since, on the other hand, a man of merit cannot be in two places at once any better than a fool, if Sorel becomes the sublime maréchale's lover, the future professor told himself, she'll put him in some snug berth in the church, and I'll be rid of him at the Hotel de La Mole.

Abbé Pirard also directed at Julien various long sermons on the topic of his success at the Hotel de Fervaques. There was a bit of *sectarian jealousy* between the austere Jansenist and the Jesuitical drawing room, reactionary[1] and monarchical, of the virtuous maréchale.

Chapter 28

MANON LESCAUT

> But once he was thoroughly convinced of the stupidity of that ass of a prior, he got along with him rather well by calling black anything that was white and white what was black.   —Lichtenberg[2]

The Russian instructions prescribed imperiously that one must never contradict to her face the person to whom one was writing. One must never abandon, under any pretext whatever, the role of

---

1. The French original is *régénérateur* —that is, revivalist, or reconstitutive, intent on regenerating the French Roman Catholic Church.

2. Georg Christoph Lichtenberg (1742–99), though primarily a physicist, was also a satiric writer of considerable acerbity and acuteness.

the ecstatic admirer; all the letters took this as their point of departure.

One evening at the opera, in Mme. de Fervaques's box, Julien praised to the skies the ballet of *Manon Lescaut*.[3] His only reason for talking this way was that he considered it contemptible.

The maréchale declared that this ballet was much inferior to Abbé Prévost's novel.

How's this! thought Julien, amazed and amused, a lady of such extraordinary virtue praising a novel! Mme. de Fervaques gave vent, two or three times a week, to her deepest scorn for those scribblers who make use of their shabby writings to corrupt a younger generation already all too prone, alas! to the errors of the senses.

Amid this class of immoral and dangerous works, continued the maréchale, *Manon Lescaut* occupies, as people tell me, one of the first places. The frailties and well-deserved sufferings of a profoundly criminal heart are depicted there, so people tell me, with a veracity that has some depth; yet this did not prevent your Bonaparte from remarking, at St. Helena, that it was a novel written for lackeys.

This expression restored to Julien all his spiritual energy. People have been trying to traduce me to the maréchale; they have told her of my enthusiasm for Napoleon. This story has irked her to the point where she has yielded to the temptation of talking about it. The discovery amused him all evening long, and rendered him amusing. As he was taking leave of the maréchale in the lobby of the opera:

—Remember, sir, she told him, people may not love Bonaparte when they love me; at best, one may accept him as a fatal necessity imposed by providence. In any case, the man had not a soul flexible enough to appreciate masterworks in the arts.

When they love me! Julien repeated silently; either that means nothing or it means everything. These are some of the secrets of language that will be forever hidden from us poor provincials. And he thought a great deal about Mme. de Rênal as he copied out an immense letter destined for the maréchale.

—How does it happen, she asked him next day with an air of indifference that he thought rather forced, that you speak to me of *London* and of *Richmond* in a letter you apparently wrote yesterday evening after leaving the opera?

Julien was much embarrassed; he had been copying line by line without thinking of what he was writing, and evidently had forgotten to substitute for the names *London* and *Richmond* in the original those of *Paris* and *Saint-Cloud*. He began two or three phrases, but was unable to finish any of them; he felt himself on the verge of bursting into peals of helpless laughter. Finally, as he cast about for words, he fell upon this idea: —Exalted by the discussion of the most sublime, the most lofty ideas of which the human soul is capable, my own spirit, as I wrote to you, must have suffered a momentary oblivion.

I am producing an impression, he told himself, so I can spare myself the boredom of the rest of the evening. He left the Hotel de Fervaques at a run. That evening, as he looked over the original of the letter he had copied the night before, he quickly found the fatal passage in which the young Russian spoke of London and Richmond. Julien was quite amazed to find that this letter was nearly tender.

It was the contrast between the apparent levity of his talk and the sublime profundity and almost apocalyptic spirit of his letters that had distinguished him. Above all, the length of his sentences pleased the maréchale; none of that swift, dashing style brought into favor by Voltaire, that immoral man! Although our hero made every effort conceivable to banish every sort of good sense from his conversation, it still retained an antimonarchical and irreligious flavor which Mme. de Fervaques had observed. Surrounded by persons of impeccable morality but who often didn't have an idea in an evening, this lady was profoundly impressed by anything resembling a novelty; but at the same time she thought it incumbent on her to be shocked by it. She called the failing, *retaining the imprint of the age's frivolity. . . .*

But such drawing rooms are worth observing only when one has a favor to solicit. No doubt the reader shares all Julien's boredom at this life without interest that he was forced to lead. These are the flatlands of our journey.

During the entire period occupied in Julien's life by the Fervaques episode, Mlle. de La Mole had to make constant efforts not to think of him. Her soul was the scene of a violent struggle; sometimes she was pleased to think she despised that gloomy young man; but in spite of herself, she was enchanted by his conversation. What amazed her more than anything was his perfect insincerity; he never said a single word to the maréchale that was not a lie or at least an abominable distortion of his point of view, which Mathilde knew perfectly well on practically all topics. This Machiavellianism impressed her. What subtlety! she said to herself; what a difference from those emphatic fools or the common cheats, like M. Tanbeau, who make use of the same language!

All the same, Julien had some frightful days. It was by way of fulfilling the most painful of his duties that he showed up every evening in the drawing room of the maréchale. His efforts to play a role ended by draining all his spiritual vitality. Very often as he crossed the immense courtyard of the Hotel de Fervaques at night, it was only by force of character and by dint of logic that he kept himself from sinking into abject despair.

I overcame despair in the seminary, he kept telling himself: and yet what a horrible future faced me then! Whether I made my fortune or failed of it, in either case I would be obliged to pass my whole life in intimate companionship with the most contemptible and disgusting creatures under heaven. Yet the following spring, just eleven short months later, I was probably the happiest young man of my age in the whole world.

But very often these fine reasonings proved ineffectual against hideous reality. Every day he saw Mathilde at lunch and dinner. From the numerous letters dictated by M. de La Mole, he gathered that she was on the point of marrying M. de Croisenois. Already that pleasant young man had begun to appear twice a day at the Hotel de La Mole: the jealous eye of a cast lover did not overlook one of his actions.

When he thought he noted that Mlle. de La Mole was treating her fiancé well, Julien as he returned to his room could not keep from looking lovingly toward his pistols.

Ah! how much wiser I would be, he said to himself, to remove the marks from my linen and go off into some lonely forest twenty leagues from Paris to put an end to this execrable life! As a stranger in that part of the world, my death would go unremarked for a fortnight, and who would think of me after a fortnight!

This was very good thinking. But next day a glimpse of Mathilde's arm, seen for an instant between her sleeve and her glove, was enough to plunge our young philosopher into some bitter memories which nonetheless renewed his attachment to life. All right, then, he told himself at that point, I'll follow out this Russian politics to the bitter end. How will it finish?

As far as the maréchale is concerned, when I've finished transcribing these fifty-three letters, I will never write any others.

As for Mathilde, either these six weeks of painful play acting will do nothing to alter her anger or they'll earn me an instant of reconciliation. Great God! I should die of joy! and he was unable to complete his thought.

When, after a long reverie, he succeeded in resuming the use of his reason: Well, then, said he, I might have a single day of happiness, after which she would resume her rigors—which are quite justified, alas, by my meager powers to please her; and then I should have no further resources; I should be ruined, lost forever. . . .

Given her character, what guarantee can she give me? My inadequate abilities, alas, are responsible for everything. My manners will have no distinction, my way of talking will be heavy and monotonous. Good God! why am I myself?

Chapter 29

BOREDOM

To sacrifice oneself to one's passions, well, maybe; but to passions one does not feel! Oh, the sad nineteenth century!

—Girodet[4]

Having begun by reading Julien's long letters without any pleasure, Mme. de Fervaques was beginning to be concerned with them; but one thought reduced her to despair: What a shame that M. Sorel was not really a priest! One might then admit him to a sort of intimacy; but with that decoration and that thoroughly middle-class jacket, one is exposed to ugly questions, and how to answer them? She did not complete her thought: some malicious friend may suppose, and even spread the story, that this is a little cousin from the provinces, a relative of my father's, a button salesman decorated by the National Guard.

Until the day she met Julien, the greatest pleasure in Mme. de Fervaques's life had been to write the title *maréchale* alongside her name. Afterwards, her upstart's vanity, uneasy and quick to take offense, had to struggle with a new interest.

It would be so easy, said the maréchale, for me to have him created a grand vicar in some diocese near Paris! But just plain M. Sorel, and what's worse a mere secretary to M. de La Mole! It is very distressing.

For the first time this soul *which was afraid of everything* was stirred by an interest alien to its social pretentions and claims of superiority. Her ancient porter remarked that when he brought a letter from that handsome young man who always looked so sad, that distracted, discontented air which the marquise was always careful to assume when one of her servants was present, was sure to disappear.

Boredom with a way of life wholly devoted to creating a public impression, and which did not have at the heart of it even any real enjoyment of this sort of success, had become intolerable since she began to think of Julien; the chambermaids were often exempt from ill treatment for a whole day because she had passed an hour, the evening before, in the company of this extraordinary young man. His growing credit withstood the assaults of several anonymous letters, extremely well composed. In vain did little Tanbeau supply Messieurs de Luz, Croisenois, and Caylus with two or three truly ingenious calumnies, which these gentlemen took pleasure in spread-

4. Girodet (1767–1824) was essentially a painter of mediocre merits, but tried to work in literature as well— where his talents were rather less than mediocre.

ing about without taking too much care to find out if they were true or not. The maréchale, whose spirit was not made to stand up against such vulgar tactics, talked over her misgivings with Mathilde, and was always consoled.

One day when she had asked three times if there were any letters, Mme. de Fervaques decided abruptly to write an answer to Julien. It was a triumph for boredom. With the second letter, the maréchale was almost brought up short by the disagreeableness of writing, with her own hand, such a plebeian address as: *To M. Sorel, at the Marquis de La Mole's.*

That evening she told Julien in the driest of tones: —You must bring me some envelopes on which your address is written.

So now I'm formally established as lover-flunkey, thought Julien, and as he made his bow he amused himself by grimacing like Arsène, the marquis' elderly valet.

That evening he brought the envelopes, and next day very early he received a third letter: he read five or six lines of it at the beginning and two or three toward the end. It amounted to four pages in a tiny, cramped script.

Gradually she fell into the gratifying habit of writing nearly every day. Julien replied with faithful transcripts of the Russian letters, and such is the advantage of the emphatic style that Mme. de Fervaques was in no way surprised at the lack of connection between letters and answers.

How deeply her pride would have been wounded if little Tanbeau, who had appointed himself spy in ordinary upon Julien's daily activities, could have reported to her that all these letters, with their seals unbroken, were flung pell-mell into Julien's desk drawer.

One morning the porter brought up to the library a letter for him from the maréchale; Mathilde encountered the man, and saw the address in Julien's handwriting. She entered the library as the porter left; the letter was still on the edge of the table; Julien, deeply involved with his writing, had not stuffed it into the drawer.

—This is something I will not endure, cried Mathilde, snatching up the letter; you have forgotten me completely, yes, me, and I am your wife. Your behavior is appalling, sir!

At these words her pride, overwhelmed by the frightful unconventionality of her behavior, choked her; she burst into tears and for an instant seemed to Julien to be struggling for breath.

Amazed and bewildered, Julien could not clearly sort out all the admirable and joyful elements of the scene. He helped Mathilde to a chair; she practically abandoned herself in his arms.

The first instant in which he became aware of this gesture was one of extreme joy. His second thought was for Korasoff: a single word and I lose everything.

His arms stiffened, so painful was the effort demanded of him by his political strategy. I must not even allow myself to embrace this yielding and delicate body or she will despise me and mistreat me. What a horrible character!

And even as he cursed Mathilde's character, he loved her for it a hundred times more than before; he felt that he was holding in his arms a queen.

Julien's impenetrable coolness multiplied the miseries of wounded pride that were flaying Mlle. de La Mole's spirit. She was far from having enough self-possession to read in his eyes what he was really feeling for her at that moment. She could not bring herself even to look at him; she was afraid of encountering an expression of scorn.

Seated on the library sofa, motionless and with her head turned away from Julien, she was a victim of the keenest anguish that love and pride can inflict upon a human soul. What a ghastly step she had just taken!

It was left for me, wretch that I am, to make the most indelicate advances and then have them repulsed! And repulsed by whom? she added, her pride inflamed by suffering, repulsed by one of my father's servants!

—This is something I will not endure, she cried aloud.

And, leaping furiously to her feet, she flung open the drawer of Julien's desk which stood a few feet away. She stopped as if frozen in horror when she saw there eight or ten unopened letters, similar in every way to the one the porter had just brought up. In all the addresses she recognized Julien's handwriting, more or less disguised.

—And so, she cried, beside herself with fury, not only are you intimate with her but you despise her. You, a man of no position at all, despising the Maréchale de Fervaques!

—Oh, forgive me, my dear, she added, flinging herself at his feet, despise me if you will, but love me, I can no longer live without your love. And she fell in a dead faint.

So there she is, that proud beauty, at my feet! thought Julien.

Chapter 30

A BOX AT THE ITALIAN OPERA

> As the blackest sky
> Foretells the heaviest tempest.
> —*Don Juan*, Canto 1, stanza 73

Amidst all these emotional upheavals, Julien was more astonished than happy. Mathilde's insults clearly showed him how wise the Russian policy had been. *Say little, do little*, that's my only salvation.

He raised Mathilde and without a word set her on the sofa again. Gradually she gave way to tears.

To give herself countenance, she picked up the letters of Mme. de Fervaques and slowly unsealed them. She started perceptibly on recognizing the maréchale's hand. She turned over the pages of these letters without reading them; most of them were six pages long.

— Tell me this at least, said Mathilde slowly, in the most supplicating manner but without even daring to look at Julien. You know very well that I am proud; it's the misfortune of my position in life, and, I'll admit it, of my character. So Mme. de Fervaques has taken your heart from me. . . . Has she made for you all the sacrifices into which passion betrayed me?

A gloomy silence was Julien's only response. By what right, he was thinking, does she think she can ask me for confidences unworthy of an honest man?

Mathilde tried to read the letters, but her eyes filled with tears and she could not.

She had been wretched for the past month, but her lofty spirit was far from admitting any such feeling. Only accident had brought about this outburst. For an instant, love and jealousy had overcome pride. She was seated on the sofa close beside him. Her hair and her alabaster throat were before his eyes. For a moment he forgot everything he owed himself; he passed his arm around her waist and strained her to him.

She turned her head slowly toward him: he was staggered at the extremity of grief he read in her eyes; he could scarcely recognize them as belonging to her.

Julien felt his powers slipping away, so deadly painful was the act of courage he required of himself.

In a minute those eyes will express nothing but icy disdain, Julien told himself, if I let myself be carried away by the joy of loving her. Meanwhile, in a strangled voice and with words she had barely the strength to form, she kept repeating to him her repentance for a line of conduct that she said had been dictated by her excessive pride.

—I have some pride myself, Julien said to her in a hardly distinguishable voice; his face gave evidence of complete physical exhaustion.

Mathilde turned sharply toward him. To hear his voice was a joy she had almost given up hoping for. At that moment she was aware of her own pride only as a quality to be cursed; she craved to find some extraordinary, incredible form of behavior to show how much she adored him and detested herself.

—It is probably because of this pride of mine, Julien went on, that you granted me for a moment your favor; it is certainly because of this firm and manly courage that you respect me now. I may be in love with the maréchale. . . .

Mathilde shuddered; her eyes assumed a strange look. She was about to hear her fate pronounced. This gesture did not escape Julien; he felt his courage weakening.

Ah! he thought, listening to the sound of the empty words being pronounced by his own mouth as he might have listened to an alien noise; if only I could cover those pale cheeks with kisses, without your knowing it!

—I may be in love with the maréchale, he went on, his voice growing weaker at each word; but certainly her interest in me has given no conclusive proof of itself. . . .

Mathilde looked directly at him: he met her gaze, at least he hoped his expression had not betrayed him. He felt himself suffused with love down to the inmost recesses of his being. Never had he adored her to this point; he was almost as mad as Mathilde. If she could have found in her own character enough coolness and courage to maneuver, he would have fallen at her feet, renouncing all idle play acting. He had just enough strength to keep on talking. Ah, Korasoff! his inner mind cried out, why aren't you here! How I need a word from you to control my conduct! And meanwhile his voice went on saying:

—Even in the absence of any other sentiment, gratitude would amply suffice to attach me to the maréchale; she has shown me great indulgence; she consoled me when I was in disgrace. . . . I may, perchance, not place unconditional confidence in certain signs that are extremely flattering, no doubt about it, but which may also prove of brief duration.

—Ah! Great God! cried Mathilde.

—Very well, then! What guarantee will you give me? Julien replied, in a quick, firm tone that seemed to cast aside in an instant the prudent forms of diplomacy. What guarantee, what god will assure me that the position you now seem inclined to restore me to will last more than two days?

—The excess of my love and of my misery if you don't love me any more, she said to him, seizing his hands and turning toward him.

Her sudden turning threw slightly aside her scarf; Julien had a glimpse of her delicate shoulders. Her hair, in some disorder, recalled to him an exquisite memory. . . .

He was about to break down. A single ill-timed word, he told himself, and I shall have to start again down that long track of despair-filled days. Mme. de Rênal always found reasons to do what her heart dictated; this high-society girl lets her heart be moved only when she has found proofs based upon good logic that it ought to be moved.

He grasped this truth in the flicker of an eyelash, and in the same instant regained his courage.

He freed his hands, which Mathilde had been pressing in her own, and with a deep bow stepped away from her. Human courage can do no more. He then busied himself gathering up the letters from Mme. de Fervaques which were scattered about the sofa, and it was with an air of almost excessive politeness, particularly cruel at that moment, that he added:

—Mademoiselle de La Mole will be kind enough to allow me to think things over. He turned swiftly away and left the library; she heard him closing all the doors, one after one, behind him.

The monster, he's not upset at all, she said to herself. . . .

But what am I saying, monster! He is sensible, careful, kind; I am the one who has done more wrong than can be imagined.

This outlook on things persisted. Mathilde was almost happy that day, for she was completely in love; you would have said her heart had never been lashed by pride—and such pride!

She shuddered with horror that evening in the drawing room when a footman announced Mme. de Fervaques; the man's voice seemed full of menace. She could not stand to look at the maréchale, and shortly left the room. Julien, not much emboldened by the day's painful victory and fearful of betraying himself through his glances, had not dined at the Hotel de La Mole.

His love and his happiness increased rapidly as the battle itself receded into the distance; he was now at the stage of finding fault with his own conduct. How could I have resisted her, he asked himself? Suppose she never loves me again! An instant can completely alter that disdainful spirit, and I confess I've treated her wretchedly.

That evening he felt it was absolutely necessary for him to be present at the Italian opera, in the box of Mme. de Fervaques. She had invited him directly; Mathilde would not fail to take note either of his presence or of an absence which would be rude. Though fully convinced by this logic, he simply did not have the strength at the beginning of the evening to plunge into society. By talking he would destroy half his happiness.

Ten o'clock struck; it was absolutely necessary that he make an appearance.

Fortunately he found the maréchale's box filled with women, and was relegated to a seat near the door where he was quite concealed by their hats. As a result of this position, he was spared an absurdity; the divine accents of Caroline's despair in the *Matrimonio segreto*[5]

5. Cimarosa's *Matrimonio segreto* (on a text of George Colman the elder and David Garrick) was always for Sten- dhal the archetypal opera, the voice of true passion set to music.

caused him to burst into tears. Mme. de Fervaques noticed these
tears; they provided such a contrast with the masculine firmness of
his ordinary expression that even the spirit of this great lady, long
immersed in the most corrosive acids of upstart ambition, was
touched by it. The little that was left in her of a woman's heart
stirred her to speak. She wanted to hear the sound of his voice at
that moment.

—Have you seen the de La Mole ladies? she asked him. They are
in the third tier. Immediately Julien rose to lean forward, supporting
himself rudely enough on the railing of the box: he saw Mathilde;
her eyes were bright with tears.

And yet it is not their day at the opera, Julien thought; what a
rush they must have had!

Mathilde had persuaded her mother to come to the Italian opera,
in spite of the inconvenient location of the box which a friend of
the family had hastened to offer them. She wanted to see if Julien
would be spending the evening with the maréchale.

Chapter 31

MAKING HER AFRAID

And so that's the supreme achievement of your civilization! You have
converted love into an ordinary concern.
—Barnave[6]

Julien hurried to Mme. de La Mole's box. His glance fell at once
on the tear-drenched eyes of Mathilde; she was weeping uncon-
trollably; there was nobody present of any particular importance,
only the lady who had lent the box and some men of her acquaintance. Mathilde placed her hand on Julien's; she seemed to have
forgotten to be afraid of her mother. Almost choked by her sobs,
she could say nothing but the single word: *guarantees!*

I must be sure not to say anything to her, Julien thought; he was
deeply stirred himself, and tried to cover his eyes as well as he could
with his hand, on the pretext of avoiding the glare from the lusters
that lit the third tier of boxes. If I say anything, she can no longer
be in doubt about the intensity of my feeling; my voice will betray
me, and the whole struggle will be lost again.

His inner conflict was far more painful than it had been that
morning; his spirit had had time to mobilize itself. He was afraid of
seeing Mathilde relapse into wounded vanity. Drunk with love and
pleasure, he took an oath not to speak to her.

In my opinion, this was one of the finest traits of his character;
a man capable of imposing such restraint on his own impulses may
go far, *si fata sinant*.[7]

6. On Barnave, see p. 4, note 1.　　　7. if the fates allow.

Mlle. de La Mole insisted on their taking Julien home. Fortunately, it was raining heavily. But the marquise had him seated opposite her, talked to him constantly, and prevented his saying a word to her daughter. One might have thought the marquise was standing guard over Julien's happiness. No longer afraid of destroying everything by the excess of his emotion, he yielded himself up to it with delight.

Dare I report that when he returned to his room Julien fell on his knees and covered with kisses the love letters given him by Prince Korasoff?

Oh, great man that you are! he cried in his madness; what don't I owe to you?

Gradually some coolness returned to him. He compared himself to a general who has just half won a great battle. The advantage is positive, it is immense, he told himself; but what will happen tomorrow? An instant can ruin everything.

On a passionate impulse, he opened the *Mémoires dictated at Saint Helena* by Napoleon[8] and for two long hours forced himself to read them; nothing in fact was reading except his eyes, but, no matter, he held himself to the task. During this singular exercise, his head and heart, rising to the level of everything great and grand, were unconsciously at work. This heart is very different from Mme. de Rênal's, he told himself, but he went no further.

Make her afraid, he cried suddenly, flinging the book away. The enemy will obey me only if I make him afraid, then he won't dare to despise me.

He strode about his little room, delirious with joy. In point of fact, this happiness derived from pride more than from love.

Make her afraid! he repeated proudly, and he had reason to be proud. Even in her happiest moments, Mme. de Rênal was always uncertain whether my love was equal to hers. Here, it is a demon with which I am wrestling, and it must be *beaten.*

He knew perfectly well that Mathilde would be in the library next morning at eight o'clock; he did not make his appearance until nine, aflame with love, but with his head in strict control of his heart. Probably not a single minute passed without his repeating to himself: Keep her always occupied with this one great doubt: Does he love me? Her brilliant position, the flatteries of all her friends, incline her *a little too much* to self-assurance.

He found her calm, pale, sitting on the sofa but apparently quite incapable of making a single movement. She held forth her hand:

—My dear, I have offended you, it is true; perhaps you are angry with me? . . .

8. Napoleon's *Mémoires dictated at Saint Helena* are probably those dictated to the Marquis de Montholon and published by him in 1821, 1823, and so on.

Julien had not expected such a simple tone. He was on the point of giving way.

—You ask for guarantees, my dear, she added, after a silence she had hoped he would break; that's only fair. Elope with me then, we'll go to London. . . . I shall be ruined forever, disgraced. . . . She had the courage to withdraw her hand from Julien's in order to cover her eyes. All the sentiments of reserve and female virtue had returned to her mind. . . . All right, then; disgrace me, she said with a sigh, it is *a guarantee.*

Yesterday I was happy because I was strong enough to be strict with myself, Julien thought. After a short period of silence, he had gained enough control over his heart to say, in an icy tone:

—Once we're on the road to London, once you're disgraced (to use your own expression), who can promise that you will still love me? that my presence in the mail coach will not seem irksome to you? I'm not a monster; the fact that I disgraced you in public opinion will be only one more misery for me. It's not your position in the world that stands in my way; it is, unhappily, your character. Can you answer for yourself that after a week you will still love me?

(Ah! let her love me for a week, just one week, said Julien silently to himself, and I shall die of joy. What do I care about the future, or about my life? And this divine happiness may begin this very minute if I choose; it depends only on me!)

Mathilde saw him deep in thought.

—So I am completely unworthy of you, she said to him, taking his hand.

Julien kissed her, but at that very moment the iron hand of duty clutched his heart. If she sees how much I adore her, I have lost her. And as he stepped back, he resumed all the dignity that befits a man.

On that day and on those that followed, he was able to conceal the immensity of his joy; there were moments in which he refused himself even the pleasure of holding her in his arms.

At other times, the delirium of happiness swept away all counsels of prudence.

It was beside a trellis of honeysuckle, which served to hide the ladder in the garden, that he used to post himself in order to watch the distant shutters of Mathilde's window, and deplore her fickle disposition. An immense oak grew nearby, and its trunk prevented his being seen by the curious.

As he strolled with Mathilde past this very spot which reminded him so vividly of his terrible sorrows, the contrast between past despair and present felicity was too much for his character; tears flooded his eyes, and as he lifted to his lips the hand of his mistress, he exclaimed: —Here I used to live with thoughts of you; from here I watched that shutter; I waited hours on end for the happy moment when I would see this hand open it. . . .

His weakness was abject. He described to her, in those true colors which it is impossible to invent, the extremities of his former despair. Short bursts of passionate emotion made plain the present bliss that had replaced that fearful suffering. . . .

Good God! what am I doing? Julien thought, returning to his senses abruptly. I am destroying the whole thing.

In the extremity of his alarm, he thought he could already read in Mlle. de La Mole's eyes the signs of diminishing love. It was an illusion; but Julien's face underwent a sudden change, and was overcome by deathly pallor. His eyes darkened in an instant, and an expression of arrogance tinged with malice succeeded that of the most sincere and unrestrained love.

—What's the matter, my dear? Mathilde asked him with tender concern.

—I am lying, Julien said, and I am lying to you. I blame myself for doing it, and God knows I respect you enough not to lie to you. You love me, you are devoted to me, and I have no need to make fancy phrases in order to please you.

—Good God! Then they were only fancy phrases, all those wonderful things you've just been saying to me?

—And I blame myself bitterly for them, my dear. I made them up long ago for a woman who was in love with me and a bore. . . . It's a defect in my character, I confess it to you, forgive me.

Bitter tears poured down Mathilde's cheeks.

—As soon as some trifle upsets me, Julien went on, and I am compelled to think of things for a moment, my wretched memory, which I could curse at this instant, offers me a way out, and I abuse it.

—Then I must have done something, without knowing it, which displeased you? said Mathilde, with charming simplicity.

—One day I recall, when you were passing by this honeysuckle, you plucked a flower, M. de Luz took it from you, and you let him have it. I was standing close by.

—M. de Luz? impossible! said Mathilde, with the lofty expression so natural to her: I never do things like that.

—I am quite sure of it, Julien replied quickly.

—All right! It is true, my dear, said Mathilde, lowering her eyes sadly. She was absolutely positive that it was many months since she had allowed M. de Luz any such liberty.

Julien glanced at her with indescribable tenderness: No, he told himself, her love for me has not grown *less*.

She playfully reproached him that evening with his love for Mme. de Fervaques: a *bourgeois* in love with a *parvenue!* Hearts of that sort are perhaps the only ones that my Julien cannot intoxicate. She had turned you into a real dandy, she said, as she played with his hair.

During the time when he thought himself in disgrace with Mathilde, Julien had become one of the best-dressed men in Paris. But he had one extra advantage over most men of this sort; once he was dressed, he never gave his appearance another thought.

One thing irked Mathilde; Julien continued to copy out the Russian letters and send them to the maréchale.

Chapter 32

THE TIGER

Alas! Why these things and not others?
—Beaumarchais

An English traveler tells how he lived on intimate terms with a tiger; he had reared it and used to pet it, but he always kept a loaded pistol on the table.

Julien never abandoned himself to the full sense of his joy except at times when Mathilde could not read the expression of it in his eyes. He carried out with exactitude the duty of every so often saying to her something disagreeable.

When Mathilde's sweetness, which he noted with amazement, and the full measure of her devotion were on the point of depriving him of all self-control, he found the courage to leave her abruptly.

For the first time, Mathilde was in love.

Life, which for her had always struggled past at a snail's pace, now flew by.

But as, all the same, her pride required some outlet, she wanted to expose herself boldly to all the dangers which her love might entail. It was Julien who showed prudence; and it was only when some danger was involved that she stood out against his will; but, though submissive and almost humble with him, she showed herself all the more haughty toward anyone in the household who came near her, whether relatives or servants.

At night in the drawing room, she singled out Julien from among sixty guests and held long, private conversations with him.

One day little Tanbeau sat down alongside them; she asked him to go to the library and get her the volume of Smollett describing the revolution of 1688; and as he hesitated: —You needn't hurry back, she added with an expression of insulting arrogance which brought balm to Julien's soul.

—Did you see how that little monster looked at us? she asked him.

—His uncle has done ten or twelve years' service in this drawing room, otherwise I should have had him thrown out this minute.

Her conduct toward Messieurs de Croisenois, de Luz, etc., though perfectly polite as far as formalities went, was in reality scarcely less provoking. Mathilde bitterly regretted all the confessions she had formerly made to Julien, and all the more since she did not dare admit to him that she had much exaggerated the almost wholly innocent marks of interest she had shown in these gentlemen.

Despite her best resolutions, feminine pride prevented her every day from saying to Julien: It was because I was talking to *you* that I took such pleasure in describing my weakness when I didn't withdraw my hand after M. de Croisenois, placing his hand beside mine on a marble table, managed to stroke it a trifle.

Nowadays hardly any of these gentlemen spoke to her for a moment without her finding some question on which to consult Julien; this was a pretext for keeping him by her side.

She found that she was pregnant, and told Julien joyously.

—Now do you have any doubts of me? Isn't this a guarantee? I am your wife forever.

This announcement struck Julien with profound astonishment. He was on the point of forgetting the first principles of his conduct. How to be deliberately cold and disagreeable to this poor girl who is ruining herself for my sake? If she looked in the least unwell, even though on that day reason was making heard its terrible voice, he no longer had the courage to address to her one of those brutal remarks that were so indispensable, as experience had shown him, to the continuance of their love.

—I want to write a note to my father, Mathilde told him one day; he has been more than a father to me, he has been a friend: as such, I should think it unworthy of you and me to try to deceive him, even for a moment.

—Good God! What are you going to do? Julien asked, in disquiet.

—My duty, she replied, her eyes glittering with joy.

She sensed that she was being more magnanimous than her lover.

—But he will dismiss me from the house in disgrace!

—That's his privilege, we must respect it. I shall give you my arm, and we will go out the front door together, in the full light of day.

Julien, staggered by this turn, begged her to wait a week.

—I cannot, she told him; honor calls, I have seen my duty, I must do it, and right away.

—Very well! I order you to wait. Your honor is safe; I am your husband. Both our conditions are going to be changed by this drastic step. I too have my rights. Today is Tuesday; next Tuesday is the Duc de Retz's party; that evening, when M. de La Mole comes home, the porter will hand him the fatal letter. . . . He has been thinking of nothing but making you a duchess, I'm sure of that; imagine how angry he will be!

—Do you mean: imagine what revenge he'll take?

—I may feel sorrow for my benefactor, and distress at harming him; but I am not, and never will be, afraid of any man.

Mathilde submitted. Since she announced her new state to Julien, this was the first time that he had spoken to her with authority; never had he been so much in love with her. The tender part of his soul seized gladly on this pretext of Mathilde's condition to free him of the obligation of addressing brutal words to her. The idea of confession to M. de La Mole distressed him greatly. Would he be separated from Mathilde? And, however sad she felt to see him go, once he had been gone a month, would she ever think of him again?

He felt almost as much horror at the prospect of the blame the marquis would heap on him, and with justice.

That night he admitted to Mathilde the latter cause of distress, and then, quite carried away by his love, he admitted also to the first.

She changed color.

—Is that really true, she asked him, that six months away from me would make you unhappy?

—Immensely so, he replied; it's the only prospect in the world I view with terror.

Mathilde was overjoyed. Julien had played his part so carefully that he had actually succeeded in making her think she was more in love than he.

The fatal Tuesday soon came around. When he returned home at midnight, the marquis found a letter addressed to him personally and confidentially, to be opened only when he was alone and unobserved.

My Father,

Every social bond between us is broken, all that is left is the bond of nature. After my husband, you are and always will be the dearest person in my life. My eyes fill with tears as I think of the pain I am causing you, but to prevent my shame from becoming public, to give you time to think and act, I could delay no longer the confession I owe you. If your generosity, which has always been excessive in my regard, can bring itself to grant me a small pension, I will go and settle wherever you say, in Switzerland, for example, with my husband. His name is so obscure that nobody will recognize your daughter in Mme. Sorel, daughter-in-law of a carpenter in Verrières. There is the name which I have found it so hard to write. I fear your anger against Julien, which seems so justified. I shall never be a duchess, dear father; but I knew it when I fell in love with him; for it was I who fell in love with him first, I who seduced him. From you and from our ancestors I inherit a spirit too proud to be attracted to anything that is or seems vulgar. I tried in vain, hoping to please you, to be interested in M. de Croisenois. Why had you placed genuine merit before my eyes? You told me yourself, when I came back from Hyères, This young Sorel is the only person who amuses me. The poor boy is as much distressed as I, if that be possible, to think of the grief this letter will cause you. I cannot prevent your being angry, as a father; but love me still as a friend.

Julien respected me. If he talked to me, sometimes, it was simply out of his profound gratitude to you: for the natural pride of his character leads him to reply only officially to people placed so far above him in rank. He has a strong inner sense of the differences of social position. I was the one, I must admit it with a blush to my dearest friend and will never admit it to anyone else, I was the one who one day in the garden took him by the arm.

After twenty-four hours, what reason will you have to be angry with him? My fault cannot be undone. If you insist, you will receive through me his assurances of profound respect for you and of grief at being the object of your displeasure. You will never see him again; but I shall go and join him wherever he chooses. It is his right, it is my duty, he is the father of my child. If your kindness will grant us six thousand francs on which to live, I will accept them with gratitude: if not, Julien plans to set up at Besançon as a teacher of Latin and literature. However low the rank at which he begins, I am sure he will rise. With him, I have no fear of obscurity. If there is a revolution, I am sure he will have a leading role in it. Could you say as much for any of the others who have sought my hand? They have fine estates! That doesn't seem to me sufficient grounds for admiration. Even under the present regime, my Julien would hold a lofty position if he had a million and were protected by my father. . . .

Mathilde, who knew that the marquis was a man of immediate impulses, had written eight pages.

—What's to be done? Julien said to himself, [as he paced the garden at midnight,] while M. de La Mole read the letter; where do (1) my duty and (2) my interest lie? My debt to him is immense: without his help, I should have been a subordinate rascal, and not even enough of a rascal to keep from being hated and persecuted by the others. He made me a man of the world. From now on my *necessary* rascalities will be (1) fewer, (2) less ignoble. That's better than if he had given me a million. I am in his debt for this decoration and the semblance of diplomatic services, which lift me out of the ruck.

If he were to take pen in hand to prescribe my conduct, what would he write?

Julien was suddenly interrupted by M. de La Mole's elderly valet.

—The marquis wants to see you this minute, whether you're dressed or not.

As he walked beside Julien, the valet added in an undertone:

—Be careful, the marquis is in a rage.

Chapter 33

THE HELL OF WEAKNESS

By cutting this diamond a clumsy jeweler deprived it of several of its brightest lusters. In the Middle Ages—what am I saying?—even under Richelieu, the Frenchman had *strength of desire*.

—Mirabeau

Julien found the marquis furious: perhaps for the first time in his life this great gentleman was in bad taste; he covered Julien with every insult that came to his tongue. Our hero was astonished, angered, but his feeling of gratitude was not altered. How many fine projects, long cherished in the back of his mind, must be collapsing within the poor man at this moment! But I owe him at least an answer; my silence will increase his anger. The response was furnished by the role of Tartufe.

—*I am no angel.* . . . I have served you well, you have paid me generously. . . . I was grateful, but I am twenty-two years old. . . . In this household there was nobody to understand my thoughts except you and that attractive person. . . .

—Monster! shouted the marquis. Attractive! attractive! The day you found her attractive you should have left.

—I tried to; that was the time I asked if I might go to the Languedoc.

Tired of pacing the room in a rage, the marquis, subdued by grief, flung himself into a chair; Julien overheard him saying, under his breath: —This is not really a vicious man.

—No, toward you I am not, Julien cried, and fell to his knees. But he was much ashamed of this gesture and quickly arose.

The marquis was quite out of his mind. When he saw this gesture, he again began to pour on Julien atrocious insults, worthy of a hackney coachman. The novelty of his oaths was perhaps a distraction.

—What! My daughter will be called Mme. Sorel! The devil! My daughter will not be a duchess! Whenever these two ideas appeared distinctly before him, the marquis was in agony, and the impulses of his mind were altogether beyond his control. Julien began to fear a beating.

In his lucid intervals, as the marquis began to get used to his distress, he reproached Julien in perfectly reasonable terms:

—You should have left, sir, he told him. . . . It was your duty to go away. . . . You are the meanest of men. . .

Julien went to the table and wrote:

For a long time my life has been unbearable; I am putting an end to it. I beg Monsieur le marquis to accept, with the expression of my boundless gratitude, my apologies for the embarrassment that my death within his house may cause.

—Will Monsieur le marquis be good enough to peruse this note. . . . Kill me, said Julien, or have me killed by your valet. It is one o'clock; I am going to walk in the garden by the wall at the far end.

—Go to the devil, the marquis shouted after him as he left.

I understand, Julien thought; he would not be sorry to see me spare his valet responsibility for my death. . . . Let him kill me, fair enough, it's a satisfaction I can offer him. . . . But, deuce take it, I am fond of life. . . . I have a duty to my son.

This idea, which was just forming clearly for the first time in his imagination, took full possession of him after the first few minutes of his stroll, which were devoted to the sense of danger.

His new concern made of him a prudent man. I need some advice on how to behave with this fiery man. He is beyond reason, he is capable of anything. Fouqué is too far away; besides he would never understand the impulses of a heart like the marquis'.

Comte Altamira. . . . Can I be sure he will keep it quiet forever? My request for advice must not be an outward action, or do anything to complicate my position. Alas! There's nobody left for me but that gloomy Abbé Pirard. . . . His spirit has been shriveled up by Jansenism. . . . A rascally Jesuit would know more of the world and suit my need better. . . . M. Pirard is capable of beating me the minute I tell what I've done.

The genius of Tartufe came to Julien's rescue: All right, I will go and make confession to him. That was the last decision he took in the garden, after walking about there for two long hours. He no longer thought he might be surprised by a gunshot; sleep was overtaking him.

Next day very early Julien was several leagues from Paris, knocking at the door of the stern Jansenist. He found, to his surprise, that his confession met with no great astonishment.

—Perhaps I too am to blame in part, said the abbé, more in sorrow than anger. I thought I could detect something of this affair. My affection for you, you little rascal, kept me from warning the father. . . .

—What will he do? Julien asked directly.

(At this moment he loved the abbé, and a quarrel would have been very painful to him.)

I see three possibilities, Julien went on: first, M. de La Mole may have me put to death; and he described the suicide note he had left in the marquis' possession; second, he may have me shot by Comte Norbert, who would challenge me to a duel.

—You would accept? said the abbé, leaping furiously to his feet.

—You aren't letting me finish. Certainly I should never fire on the son of my benefactor.

Third, he may send me away. If he told me: Go to Edinburgh, or Go to New York, I would obey. Then they can conceal the position of Mlle. de La Mole; but I shall never allow them to destroy my son.

—That's the first expedient, never fear, that that corrupt man will think of. . . .

At Paris, Mathilde was in despair. She had seen her father about seven o'clock. He had showed her Julien's letter, and she was fearful that he might have thought it the noble thing to end his own life: And without my permission! she said to herself with an anguish that rose out of anger.

—If he is dead, I shall die, she told her father. You will have been the cause of his death. . . . Perhaps you will be glad of it. . . . But I swear by his ghost, the first thing I shall do is to put on mourning, and declare myself publicly *Mme. veuve Sorel*; I shall send out the usual cards, you may be sure of that. . . . You will not find me weak or cowardly.

Her love reached the point of madness. For his part, M. de La Mole was dumbfounded.

He began to look upon events a little more rationally. At lunch Mathilde did not appear. The marquis was delivered of an immense burden, and flattered too, when he saw that she had said nothing to her mother.

[Toward mid-day Julien returned. The clatter of his horse's hoofs resounded through the court.] Julien dismounted. Mathilde had him summoned and flung herself into his arms, almost under the eyes of her maid. Julien was not too grateful for these transports; he had emerged very diplomatic and calculating from his long talk with Abbé Pirard. His imagination was depressed by the calculation of possibilities. Mathilde, with tears in her eyes, told him that she had seen his suicide note.

—My father may reconsider; you must do me a favor and leave right away for Villequier. Take horse again and leave the house before they have finished eating.

As Julien never altered his look of chilly surprise, she burst into tears.

—Let me manage our affairs, she cried passionately, clasping him in her arms. You know very well that it's not my decision to separate us. You must write as to my maid, disguising your hand in the address; as for me, I shall write volumes. Farewell! Be off!

Her last words wounded Julien's feelings, but he left nonetheless. It's in the stars, he thought, even in their best moments these people can find the trick of hurting me.

[M. de La Mole did not have enough determination to play the usual heavy father.] Mathilde maintained a solid defense against all her father's *prudent* plans. She would undertake negotiations on no other basis than this: She would be Mme. Sorel, and would live in poverty with her husband in Switzerland, or with her father in Paris. The idea of a clandestine confinement she dismissed altogether.

—That would be the beginning for me of possible calumny and disgrace. Two months after our marriage, I shall take a trip with my husband, and it will be easy for us to pretend that my child was born at the proper time.

Though he met it at first with transports of rage, her firmness ended by shaking the position of the marquis.

In a moment of tenderness: —Look, he said to his daughter, here is a paper conveying ten thousand florins a year; send it to your Julien and tell him to put it immediately where I can never call it back.

To *obey* Mathilde, whose love for giving orders was well known to him, Julien had made a useless journey of forty leagues: he was at Villequier, going over the tenants' accounts; this generous act of the marquis occasioned his return. He went to beg asylum with the Abbé Pirard, who during his absence had become Mathilde's most useful ally. Every time he was questioned by the marquis, he demonstrated that any step other than open marriage would be a sin in the eyes of God.

—And, by good fortune, added the abbé, worldly wisdom is here in agreement with religion. Given the fiery character of Mlle. de La Mole, could one count for a moment on her keeping any secret she had not imposed on herself? If you don't consent to the open course of a public marriage, society will concern itself much longer with this strange misalliance. Everything must be declared openly at one time, without the slightest mystery either in appearance or reality.

—It is true, said the marquis thoughtfully. If we follow your plan, talk of this marriage three days after it has taken place will be considered the chatter of a man who has no ideas. We might well profit by some great move of the government against Jacobins to slip unnoticed into the aftermath.

Two or three friends of M. de La Mole agreed with Abbé Pirard. The great obstacle, as they saw it, was Mathilde's obstinate nature. But after all these fine arguments, the spirit of the marquis could not bring itself to abandon hope of a *tabouret*[9] for his daughter.

His memory and his imagination were filled with tricks and devices of all sorts which had still been possible in his youth. Yielding to necessity and respecting the law seemed to him absurd and

9. On *tabouret*, see p. 261, note 7.

dishonorable recourses for a man of his rank. He was paying dearly now for those enchanting dreams in which, for the past ten years, he had been indulging concerning the future of his beloved daughter.

Who could have guessed? he asked himself. A girl of such lofty character, of so distinguished a mind, and prouder even than I am of the name she bears! Whose hand had been sought of me, previously, by all the most illustrious blood in France!

We must give up prudence! The age was created to bring everything into confusion! We are on the march toward chaos!

Chapter 34

A MAN OF SPIRIT

> The prefect riding down the road on his horse said to himself: Why shouldn't I be a minister, president of the council, duke? This is how I would carry on the war. . . . And so we'll throw all these radicals into irons. . . .
>
> —*The Globe*

No argument is strong enough to destroy the empire built up by ten years of agreeable reverie. The marquis realized it was unreasonable to be angry, but could not bring himself to grant a pardon. If that Julien would only meet with a fatal accident, he sometimes said to himself. . . . Thus it was that this wounded imagination found some relief in pursuing absurd phantasms. They paralyzed all the Abbé Pirard's sensible thoughts. A month passed in this way without a step being taken in the negotiations.

In this family affair, as in political affairs, the marquis had some brilliant insights over which he grew enthusiastic for three days. Then a course of conduct no longer pleased him because it was supported by good reasons; rather, the reasons pleased him insofar as they supported his favorite plan. During those three days he worked with all the fervent enthusiasm of a poet to bring matters to a certain stage; the next day he no longer gave them a thought.

At first Julien was disconcerted by the marquis' delays; but after several weeks he began to see that M. de La Mole had no fixed plan at all for managing this affair.

Mme. de La Mole and the whole household supposed that Julien was traveling in the provinces to look after the marquis' estates; he was actually hiding in Abbé Pirard's parsonage and saw Mathilde almost every day; she went every morning to spend an hour with her father, but they were often weeks on end without talking of the topic that occupied both their thoughts.

—I don't want to know where that man is, the marquis said to her one day; send him this letter. Mathilde read:

The estates in Languedoc bring in 20,600 francs. I give 10,600 francs to my daughter and 10,000 francs to M. Julien Sorel. That is, I give the estates themselves. Tell the notary to draw up two separate deeds of gift and to bring them tomorrow; after which, no further relations between us. Ah, sir, is this what I should have expected?

The Marquis de La Mole.

—Thank you very much, said Mathilde gaily. We shall settle at the Chateau d'Aiguillon, between Agen and Marmande.[1] They say it's a district as beautiful as Italy.

This gift was a great surprise to Julien. He was no longer the cold, severe man we have come to know. The destiny of his son was already absorbing all his thoughts. This unexpected fortune, which seemed very substantial to so poor a man, made him ambitious. He now saw himself possessed, between his wife's income and his own, of 36,000 florins per year. As for Mathilde, all her feelings were wrapped up in admiration for her husband, for that was the title her pride bestowed on Julien. Her great, her only, ambition was to have her marriage recognized. She passed her days in exaggerating the immense prudence she had displayed in joining her fate with that of a superior man. Personal merit was all the rage in her brain.

Their almost constant separation, the multiplicity of their business concerns, and the little time they had to talk of love put the crowning touches on the good effects wrought by Julien's wise policies in the past.

Mathilde at last grew impatient at seeing so little of the man with whom she had succeeded in really falling in love.

In a moment of anger she wrote to her father, and began her letter like Othello:[2]

"That I have preferred Julien above any of the pleasures that society offered to the daughter of the Marquis de La Mole, my choice of him shows clearly enough. The pleasures of status and of petty vanity are meaningless to me. It is now six weeks that I have been living in separation from my husband. That is enough to serve as evidence of my respect for you. Before next Thursday I shall leave my father's house. Your generosity has made us rich. Nobody knows my secret but the respectable Abbé Pirard. I shall go to him; he will marry us, and an hour after the ceremony we shall be off for Languedoc, never to reappear in Paris except on your orders. But what hurts me most is that all this will give rise to

1. The chateau of Aiguillon, which actually stood halfway between Agen and Marmande at the junction of the Lot and Garonne rivers, was an enormous eighteenth-century structure, begun by Armand-Désiré, the last duke of Aiguillon, but never completed because of the Revolution, and standing stripped and desolate after the expropriation.
2. like Othello: Actually, like Desdemona (I, 3).

nasty stories at my expense and at yours. It is possible that the
epigrams of a silly public may oblige our good Norbert to pick a
quarrel with Julien. Under these circumstances, I know him, I can
have no control of him. We should rouse in his character the
rebellious plebeian. I beg you on bended knee, my dear father!
Come and be present at my marriage in M. Pirard's church next
Thursday. The point of the ugly stories will be blunted, the life of
your only son, and the life of my husband will be made safe," etc.,
etc.

This letter cast the marquis into a strange predicament. Finally
he had now to *make up his mind*. All his little habits, all his old
friends, had lost their influence.

Under these strange circumstances his fundamental character,
which had been established by the events of his youth, resumed its
sway. The miseries of the emigration had formed him into a man of
imagination. After he had enjoyed for two years an immense fortune
and the highest distinction at court, 1790 had flung him into all
the miseries of exile. This hard school had quite transformed the
mind of a man who was just twenty-two. At heart, he was far from
being dominated by his present possessions; he merely camped out
in the midst of them. But this very imagination, which had preserved his mind from the gangrene of gold, had left him prey to an
insane passion for seeing his daughter possessed of a fancy title.

During the six weeks just passed, the marquis, as if driven by a
momentary caprice, had undertaken to make Julien rich; poverty
seemed to him ignoble, shameful to himself, M. de La Mole, impossible for his daughter's husband; he flung down the money.
Next day, his imagination taking another tack, it seemed to him that
Julien must hear the mute language of this financial generosity,
change his name, disappear to America, write to Mathilde that he
was dead to her. M. de La Mole imagined this letter already written;
he was tracing in his mind's eye its effect on his daughter's character. . . .

The day on which he was roused from these youthful dreams by
Mathilde's *real* letter, after having thought for a long time of killing
Julien or bringing about his disappearance, he was dreaming of
making him a brilliant fortune. He was conferring on him the name
of one of his properties; and why should he not pass on to him his
own position in the peerage? The Duc de Chaulnes, his father-in-
law, had spoken several times, since his only son had been killed in
Spain, of wanting to pass on his title to Norbert. . . .

There's no denying Julien has a singular aptitude for business,
boldness, perhaps even *brilliance*, thought the marquis. . . . But at
the root of his character is something terrifying. It's the impression
he produces on everyone, so there must be something real in it (the

harder this real point was to grasp, the more it terrified the imaginative spirit of the old marquis).

My daughter expressed it very shrewdly the other day (in a letter we have suppressed): "Julien has no connections with any set or any coterie." He has not built up any support against me, he hasn't the slightest resource if I abandon him. . . . But is that ignorance of the present state of society? . . . Two or three times I told him: There is no real, no profitable campaign, except that waged in the drawing rooms. . . .

No, he doesn't have the wily, cautious spirit of a conniver who never wastes a minute or misses a main chance. . . . He is not a character after the style of Louis XI.[3] On the other hand, I see in him the most ungenerous maxims. . . . And at that point I lose him. . . . Does he repeat those maxims to himself in order to use them as a *dike* against his passions?

In any case, one consideration prevails: he cannot stand contempt, and I have him there.

He has not the religion of high birth; it is perfectly true, he does not respect us on instinct. . . . That's a fault; but after all, the usual seminarian is impatient only when he lacks pleasure and money. He is very different; he cannot endure contempt at any price.

Under pressure from his daughter's letter, M. de La Mole saw the necessity of making up his mind: —Well, this is the great question: did Julien have the audacity to make love to my daughter simply because he knows I love her better than all the world, and that I have an income of a hundred thousand crowns?

Mathilde protests to the contrary. . . . No, Julien, my boy, that's one point on which I don't want to be under any illusions.

Was it authentic, spontaneous love? Or just a vulgar greed to raise himself to a good position? Mathilde saw very clearly from the first that this suspicion could ruin him in my good opinion, that was why she made that confession: that it was she who first thought of love. . . .

A girl of such lofty character forgetting herself so far as to make physical advances! . . . Catching him by the arm in the garden one evening, what a horror! As if she didn't have a hundred less indecent ways of letting him know that she favored him.

Excusing yourself is accusing yourself; I don't trust Mathilde. . . . On that day, the reflections of the marquis were more conclusive than usual. But habit carried the day. He resolved to gain time and write to his daughter. For they were writing letters, during this period, from one part of the house to the other. M. de La Mole was afraid of entering into a discussion with Mathilde in which he

3. Unscrupulous, suspicious, cunning, cruel, and dishonest are some of the adjectives that have been applied to Louis XI (1423–83).

would have to stand up against her. He was afraid of ending every-thing by a too-sudden concession.

Letter

Take care to commit no new follies; here is a commission as lieutenant of hussars for M. le chevalier Julien Sorel de La Vernaye. You see what I am doing for him. Don't contradict me, don't ask any questions. Let him leave in twenty-four hours and report to Strasbourg where his regiment is quartered. Here is a draft on my banker; I expect to be obeyed.

Mathilde's love and joy knew no bounds; she sought to profit by her victory, and replied at once:

M. de La Vernaye would be at your feet, overcome with gratitude, if he knew everything you have been kind enough to do for him. But in the midst of this generosity, my father has forgotten me; the honor of your daughter is in danger. One indiscretion may create a blot that would last forever: an income of twenty thou-sand crowns would not efface it. I shall send the commission to M. de La Vernaye only if you give me your word that in the course of the next month my marriage will be celebrated in public at Villequier. Soon after that period, which I implore you not to exceed, your daughter will not be able to appear in public except with the name of Mme. de La Vernaye. Let me thank you, dearest papa, for having saved me from that name of Sorel, etc., etc.

The reply was unexpected:

Obey, or I withdraw everything. Take care, foolish girl. I do not yet know what your Julien is, and you know even less than I do. Let him be off to Strasbourg, and walk the straight and narrow path. I shall make known my will in two weeks.

The firmness of this reply astounded Mathilde. *I do not know Julien;* that expression threw her into a reverie that presently led to the most enchanting suppositions; but she thought they were true. My Julien's mind has not donned the mean little *uniform* of the drawing rooms, and my father doesn't believe in his superiority precisely because of the quality that proves it. . . .

Still, if I don't give way to this whim of his, we may well come to a public scene; a scandal will lower my position in the world and perhaps render me less attractive to Julien. After the scandal . . . poverty for ten years; and the madness of choosing a husband on the score of merit can be rescued from ridicule only by the most brilliant opulence. If I live at a distance from my father, at his age he may forget me. . . . Norbert will marry a woman who is agreeable and clever: Louis XIV was beguiled in his old age by the Duchess of Burgundy. . . .

She decided to obey, but was careful not to show her father's letter to Julien; his wild nature might rush him into some act of folly.

That evening, when she told Julien he was a lieutenant of hussars, his joy knew no bounds. It can be estimated from the ambition of his whole life, and from the passion he was now feeling for his new son. The change of name struck him with wonder.

Now at last, he thought, the novel of my career is over, and the credit is all mine. I was able to make myself loved by that monster of pride, he thought, glancing at Mathilde; her father cannot live without her nor she without me.

Chapter 35

WHIRLWIND

My God, give me mediocrity!
—Mirabeau

He was absorbed in thought; he only half responded to the lively tenderness she showed him. He remained silent and somber. Never had he seemed so great, so adorable in the eyes of Mathilde. She was afraid of some subtle quirk of his pride that might turn up to overthrow the whole situation.

Nearly every morning she saw Abbé Pirard entering the house. Through his intervention might not Julien have learned something about her father's intentions? Might not the marquis himself, in a momentary whim, have written to him? After so great a happiness, how to account for Julien's severe air? She did not dare ask him.

She *did not dare!* she, Mathilde! From that moment, her feeling for Julien contained something vague, unaccountable, almost terrifying. That arid soul felt everything in passion that is possible for a person raised amid the excess of civilization which Paris admires.

Next morning very early Julien was at Abbé Pirard's parsonage. Post horses arrived in the court drawing a tattered chaise rented from the nearest stage house.

—This sort of rig is no longer suitable, said the stern abbé crossly. Here are twenty thousand francs which M. de La Mole bestows upon you; he requires you to spend them within the year, but with as few absurdities as possible. (In such an immense sum given to such a young man the priest saw nothing but an occasion for sin.)

The marquis adds: M. Julien de la Vernaye will have received this money from his father, whom it is useless to identify in any other way. M. de La Vernaye will perhaps find it appropriate to make a gift to M. Sorel, a carpenter at Verrières, who took care of him as an infant. . . . I myself will take care of this part of the business, added the abbé; I have finally convinced M. de La Mole to compromise with that Abbé de Frilair who is such a Jesuit. His position is definitely too strong for us. Implicit recognition of your high birth by that man who governs Besançon will be one of the tacit conditions of the compromise.

Julien could no longer master his transports; he embraced the abbé; he saw himself recognized.

—Pshaw! said M. Pirard, thrusting him away; what means all this worldly vanity? . . . As for Sorel and his sons, I shall offer them, in my name, an annual pension of five hundred francs apiece, which will be paid to them during my good pleasure.

Julien was already cool and correct again. He expressed his thanks, but in very vague terms which committed him to nothing. Is it actually possible, he asked himself, that I might be the natural son of some aristocrat exiled among our mountains by the terrible Napoleon? At every instant this idea appeared less improbable to him. . . . My hate for my father would be a proof. . . . I would no longer be a monster!

A few days after this monologue, the fifteenth regiment of hussars, one of the most distinguished in the army, was drawn up on parade in the public square of Strasbourg. M. le chevalier de La Vernaye bestrode the finest horse in Alsace, which had cost him six thousand francs. He had been accepted as lieutenant, without ever having been sublieutenant except on the rosters of a regiment he had never heard of.

His impassive air, his stern and almost savage glance, his pallor, his unruffled coolness earned him a reputation from the day he arrived. Before long, his perfectly measured courtesy, and his skill with pistol and sword, which he made known without too much affectation, tempered any tendency to make public jokes at his expense. After five or six days of hesitation, public opinion in the regiment declared in his favor. This young man has everything, said the older officers chaffingly, except youth.

From Strasbourg, Julien wrote to M. Chélan, former priest of Verrières, who was now verging on the last stages of old age:

> You will have learned with a joy of which I make no question about the events which have persuaded my family to make me rich. Here are five hundred francs, which I should like you to distribute quietly, without any mention of my name, to those poor folk who are in need, as I once was myself, and whom you are doubtless helping now as you once helped me.

Julien was wild with ambition, not vanity; still, he devoted a great deal of attention to his outward appearance. His horses, his uniforms, the liveries of his servants were maintained with a smartness that would have done credit to the style of an English gentleman. Though only a lieutenant, promoted by favor and with just two days' service, he was already calculating that to be a commander in chief by thirty at the latest, like all the other great generals, he would have to be more than a lieutenant at twenty-three. He thought of nothing but glory and his son.

It was in the midst of these transports of unbridled ambition that he was surprised by a young servant from the Hotel de La Mole, who arrived bearing a letter.

All is lost, (Mathilde wrote him); come as quickly as possible, give up everything, desert if need be. As soon as you get here, wait for me in a cab by the little garden gate, Number _____, rue de _____. I will come out and talk with you; perhaps I will be able to get you into the garden. All is lost, and I fear beyond redemption; you may count on me, you will find me steadfast and devoted in adversity. I love you.

Within a few minutes Julien obtained leave of the colonel and left Strasbourg at a gallop; but the frightful doubts gnawing at him did not allow him to continue this mode of travel any further than Metz. He leaped into a chaise, and with almost unbelievable rapidity reached the meeting place near the little garden gate of the Hotel de La Mole. The door opened and at once Mathilde, forgetting all restraint, flung herself into his arms. By good fortune it was five o'clock in the morning and the street was still empty.

—All is lost; my father, fearing my tears, left Thursday night. Where did he go? Nobody knows. Here is his letter; read it. And she got into the cab with Julien.

I could forgive everything except the plan of seducing you because you are rich. That, you unhappy child, is the awful truth. I give you my word of honor that I will never consent to your marriage with that man. I grant him ten thousand florins income if he will live abroad, outside the frontiers of France, or better still in America. Read the letter I received in reply to a request for information about him. The rascal told me himself to write to Mme. de Rênal. Never will I read a line from you about that man. I am horrified at Paris, at you. I implore you to cloak what must shortly happen in the greatest secrecy. Give up *honestly* this vile fellow and you will regain a father.

—Where is the letter from Mme. de Rênal? Julien asked coldly.
—I have it here. I didn't want to show it to you until you were prepared.

Letter

The obligations I feel toward the sacred cause of religion and morality oblige me, sir, to take the painful step of addressing myself to you; an unfailing rule requires me at this point to do harm to my neighbor, but only to avoid a greater scandal. The grief I feel must yield to a sense of duty. It is only too true, sir, the conduct of the person you ask about may have seemed inexplicable to you or even honorable. It may have seemed appropriate to conceal or disguise part of the truth, worldly wisdom as well as religion would require it. But this conduct, about which you wish to know the whole truth, has actually been extremely blameworthy, and more so than I can tell you. Born poor and greedy, this man has tried by means of the most consummate hypocrisy, and by the seduction of a weak and wretched woman, to find himself a position and rise in the world. It is part of my painful duty to add that I am forced to believe M. J_____ has no religious principles. In all conscience I am obliged to think that his way to rise in a household is to try to seduce the woman who is most influential there. Cloaking himself under the guise of disinterestedness and phrases from novels, he makes it his great and only end to gain control over the master of the house and his fortune. He leaves behind him a trail of misery and eternal regrets, etc., etc., etc.

This letter, which was extremely long and half blurred by tears, was indeed in the hand of Mme. de Rênal; it was even written with more than her usual care.

—I cannot blame M. de La Mole, Julien said, when he had finished it; he is perfectly right and proper. What father would want to give his beloved daughter to such a man! Farewell!

Julien leaped out of the cab and ran to his chaise, which was waiting for him at the end of the street. Mathilde, whom he seemed to have forgotten, took a few steps after him; but the stares of the shopkeepers who were looking out their doors and to whom she was known, forced her to return hastily into the garden.

Julien had left for Verrières.[4] On this swift journey he was unable to write to Mathilde, as he had intended to do; his hand formed nothing on the paper but illegible scrawls.

He reached Verrières Sunday morning. He went to the shop of a gunsmith, who overwhelmed him with compliments on his new fortune. It was the talk of the town.

Julien had great difficulty in making him understand he wanted a pair of pistols. At his request the gunsmith loaded the pistols.

Three bells sounded; this is a signal well known in the villages of France; following the various peals of the particular day, it announces the immediate beginning of the mass.

Julien entered the new church of Verrières. All the lofty windows of the church were draped in crimson curtains. Julien found himself standing a few paces behind Mme. de Rênal's bench. It seemed to

4. When he sets out to punish Mme. de Rênal, Julien is imitating not only Antoine Berthet but (evidently by anticipation) Hector Berlioz, who, when he was abandoned by his fiancée Camille Moke in February, 1831, set out to assassinate her. But he changed his mind *en route*. See Berlioz's *Mémoires* and Stendhal's *Marginalia* (in the Divan edition), II, 140.

him that she was praying fervently. The sight of this woman whom he had loved deeply made Julien's arm tremble so violently that at first he could not carry out his plan. I cannot do it, he told himself; physically, I cannot do it.

At that moment the young cleric who was serving the mass rang the bell for the *elevation*. Mme. de Rênal bowed her head, which for a moment was almost entirely hidden in the folds of her shawl. Julien no longer recognized her so clearly; he fired his first pistol at her and missed; he fired again, she fell.

Chapter 36

PAINFUL PARTICULARS

> Look for no weakness on my part. I took my revenge. I have merited death, and here I am. Pray for my soul.
> —Schiller

Julien stood motionless, unseeing. When he returned to himself a little, he saw the crowd of worshippers rushing out of the church; the priest had left the altar. Julien began to follow, at a walk, various women who were shrieking as they ran. One woman who wanted to get away faster than the others gave him a rude shove; he fell. His feet were tangled in a chair overturned by the mob; as he got up, he felt himself clutched by the collar; it was a policeman in full uniform, who was arresting him. Mechanically Julien reached for his little pistols, but a second policeman pinioned his arms.

He was led to jail. They took him to a room, handcuffed him, and left him alone; the door was closed on him and double locked; the whole thing was done very quickly, and he was quite unaware of it.

—Well, that finishes it, he said aloud as he returned to himself. . . . Yes, in a couple of weeks, the guillotine . . . or else kill myself between now and then.

His reasoning went no further; he felt a pain in his head as if it were being violently compressed. He looked around to see if somebody was holding onto him. After a few minutes he sank into a deep sleep.

Mme. de Rênal was not fatally wounded. The first bullet had passed through her hat; the second was fired just as she turned around. The bullet struck her in the shoulder, glanced off her shoulder blade and fractured it, and then, rather surprisingly, went on to strike a Gothic pillar from which it broke off a big splinter of stone.

When, after a long and painful dressing of the wound, the solemn-faced surgeon told Mme. de Rênal: I will answer for your life as for my own, she was deeply afflicted.

For a long time she had sincerely wanted to be dead. The letter that had been required of her by her present confessor, and which she had written to M. de La Mole, was a final blow to the poor woman, weakened already by excessive grief. Her grief was in fact the absence of Julien; she called it *remorse*. Her spiritual director, a young ecclesiastic newly arrived from Dijon, full of virtue and fervor, made no mistake about that.

To die in this way, but not by my own hand, cannot be a sin, thought Mme. de Rênal. God will perhaps pardon me for rejoicing in my own death. She did not dare to add: And to die by Julien's hand is the height of bliss.

Hardly was she rid of the surgeon and of the crowd of her friends who had come to see her than she sent for Elisa, her maid.

—The jailer, she said, blushing deeply, is a cruel man. No doubt he will mistreat him, thinking thereby to do something pleasing to me. . . . The idea is unbearable to me. Can't you go, as if on your own account, and give the jailer this little package containing a few louis? You must tell him that religion forbids his mistreating him. . . . It's particularly important that he shouldn't mention this gift of money.

It was to the circumstances we have just described that Julien owed the unusual humanity of the Verrières jail keeper; he was still that M. Noiroud, the perfect government man, whom we saw thrown into such a spasm of fright by the sight of M. Appert.

An examining magistrate appeared at the prison.

—I have taken life in a premeditated act, Julien told him; I bought the pistols and had them loaded at the shop of So-and-So, the gunsmith. Article 1342 of the penal code is perfectly clear, I deserve to die and I'm expecting to.[5]

The judge, amazed at this frank response, tried to multiply questions in order to make the accused *contradict himself* in his answers.

—But don't you see, said Julien with a smile, I am making myself out just as guilty as you could want? Be off with you, sir, you are not going to lose the prey you're hunting after. You will have the pleasure of condemning me. And now spare me your presence.

I have one more tiresome job to do, thought Julien; I must write Mlle. de La Mole.

I have my revenge, (he told her.) Unfortunately, my name will appear in the newspapers, I cannot escape from this world *incognito* [and for this I beg your pardon]. In two months I shall be dead. My vengeance was savage, like my grief at being separated from you. From this moment on, I forbid myself to write or speak your name. Never speak of me, not even to my son: silence is the only way to do me honor. For the ordinary run of

5. Article 1342 of the penal code is an impressive particularity; but the code of 1810 had only 484 articles.

men I shall be a vulgar murderer. . . . Allow me to speak truth at this supreme moment of my life: you will forget me. This great catastrophe, about which I advise you never to say a word to a human being, will have exhausted for several years everything I recognize as romantic and overadventurous in your character. You were made to live with the heroes of the Middle Ages; summon up for this occasion their firmness of character. Let what is going to happen happen, in secret and without compromising you. You will assume a pseudonym and have no confidant. If you absolutely require the help of a friend, I bequeath you Abbé Pirard.

Do not talk to anyone else, particularly not to people of your own class like de Luz, Caylus.

A year after my death, marry M. de Croisenois; I beg you to do this, I order you as your husband [I will have no argument on the point]. Don't write to me at all, I shall not reply. Though far less malicious than Iago, as it seems to me, I am going to say like him: *From this time forth I never will speak word.*[6]

No one will see me write or speak; you will have had my last words along with my last devotions.   J.S.

For the first time after he had sent off this letter, Julien, returning slightly to himself, became extremely unhappy. Each of ambition's promises had to be ripped in turn from his heart by this great thought: *I am going to die.* [*I must die.*] Death in itself was not *horrible* in his eyes. All his life had been nothing but one long preparation for misfortune, and he had certainly not overlooked that which passes for one of the greatest of them all.

What the deuce! he told himself, if in sixty days I had to fight a duel with a man who was an expert fencer, would I be weak enough to think of it continually, would I carry terror about in my soul?

He passed more than an hour trying to understand himself from this angle.

When he had seen straight into his soul, and the truth stood before his eyes as sharply outlined as one of the pillars of his prison, he thought of remorse.

Why should I feel any? I have been insulted in atrocious fashion; I have killed, I have deserved death myself, but that's all. I die after settling my score with humanity. I leave behind no unfulfilled obligation, I owe nothing to anybody; the only thing shameful about my death is the instrument of it: that alone, to be sure, is ample cause of shame in the eyes of the Verrières middle class; but, intellectually considered, what could be more contemptible? I still have one way to acquire distinction in their eyes: that would be to scatter gold pieces among the people on my way to the scaffold. My

6. *Othello,* V, 2.

memory, linked with the idea of gold, will glitter forever in their minds.

After this chain of thought, which when he had contemplated it for a moment seemed perfectly clear: I have nothing more to do on this earth, said Julien, and fell fast asleep.

About nine that evening, the jailer waked him to bring him some soup.

—What are they saying in Verrières?

—Monsieur Julien, the oath I swore on the crucifix in the king's court the day I took office obliges me to silence.

He was silent, but stayed in the room. The sight of this vulgar hypocrisy amused Julien. Let's keep him waiting a long time, he thought, for the five francs he wants as the price of selling his conscience to me.

When the jailer saw the meal finishing without any effort at bribery:

—The friendship I bear you, Monsieur Julien, he said with an air of false sweetness, obliges me to speak; although they do say that this is against the interests of justice because it may help you to set up your defense. . . . Monsieur Julien, who is a good fellow, will be happy to learn that Mme. de Rênal is feeling better.

—What! She isn't dead! Julien exclaimed, [jumping up from the table] in his excitement.

—What! you didn't know about that! said the jailer, with a stupid expression that quickly changed to one of joyful greed. It would only be right if Monsieur made a contribution to the surgeon, who, in all law and justice, shouldn't have talked. But to give Monsieur pleasure, I went to his house and he told me everything. . . .

—In a word, the wound isn't fatal, Julien said, turning upon him impatiently; will you answer for that with your life?

The jailer, a giant six feet tall, was afraid, and backed toward the door. Julien saw he was on the wrong tack, sat down again, and tossed a napoleon to M. Noiroud.

As this man's story proved to Julien that Mme. de Rênal's wound was not fatal, he felt the impulse to weep gaining on him.

—Go now, he said sharply.

The jailer obeyed. Hardly was the door closed: —Great God! She is not dead! Julien cried out; and he fell to his knees, weeping passionately.

At this supreme moment he was a believer. What matter the priestly hypocrisies? Can they do anything to diminish the truth and sublimity of the idea of God?

Only then did Julien begin to repent of the crime he had committed. By a coincidence that saved him from despair, only at that moment was he relieved of the state of physical irritation and half madness in which he had been sunk since he left Paris for Verrières.

His tears sprang from a generous feeling; he had not the slightest doubt about the sentence that awaited him.

And so she will live! he thought. . . . She will live to forgive me and to love me. . . .

It was late the next morning when the jailer waked him.

—You must have a first-rate heart, Monsieur Julien, the fellow said to him. Twice I came and didn't want to wake you. Here are two bottles of excellent wine sent by M. Maslon, our priest.

—How's that? Is that rascal still here? Julien asked.

—Yes, sir, replied the jailer, lowering his voice, but you mustn't talk so loud; that could harm your case.

Julien laughed heartily.

—At the point I've reached, my friend, you are the only one who can harm me if you stop being gentle and humane. . . . You will be well paid, said Julien, interrupting himself and resuming his imperious air. This air was immediately reinforced by the gift of a small coin.

M. Noiroud told all over again and in the greatest detail everything he had learned about Mme. de Rênal, but he said not a word about the visit of Mlle. Elisa.

The man was as humble and submissive as possible. An idea flashed through Julien's head: This species of misshapen giant may earn as much as three or four hundred francs, for his jail is not much occupied; I can guarantee him ten thousand francs if he wants to escape into Switzerland with me. . . . The hard thing will be to persuade him of my good faith. The idea of a long colloquy to be held with such a vile creature filled Julien with disgust; he thought of something else.

That evening there was no longer time. A mail coach came to take him away at midnight. He was much pleased with the policemen who were his traveling companions. Next morning, when he reached the prison at Besançon, they were kind enough to give him a room on the upper story of a Gothic tower. He estimated the architecture to date from the beginning of the fourteenth century; he admired its grace and sharp delicacy. Through a narrow interval between two walls on the far side of a deep courtyard there was a glimpse of a magnificent view.

Next day there was an interrogation, after which for several days they left him alone. His spirit was calm. He found nothing in his case that was not perfectly simple: I tried to kill, I ought to be killed.

His thought never moved beyond this logic. The trial, the bother of appearing in public, the defense, he considered all those matters trivial nuisances, boring ceremonies which there would be plenty of time to think about on the day itself. The moment of death

hardly concerned him any more: I'll think of that after the trial.
Life was by no means boring to him; he was considering everything
under a new aspect. Ambition was dead in him. He rarely thought
of Mlle. de La Mole. Remorse agitated him a good deal and often
brought before him the image of Mme. de Rênal, especially during
the silence of the nights, broken in this lofty tower only by the cry
of the screech-owl![7]

He thanked heaven that he had not wounded her mortally.
Astonishing thing! he said to himself; I thought that by her letter
to M. de La Mole she had destroyed forever my future happiness;
now, less than two weeks from the date of that letter, I never give
a thought to the things that used to occupy me completely. . . . Two
or three thousand florins a year to live peacefully in a little mountain town like Vergy. . . . I was happy then. . . . I didn't know how
happy I was!

At other moments he leaped from his seat. If I had wounded
Mme. de Rênal fatally, I should have killed myself. . . . I must be
sure of that to keep from feeling horrified at myself.

Kill myself! There's the big question, he thought. These judges
with their formalities who are so avid for the blood of the poor
accused, who would hang the best citizen in the town to get a
decoration for themselves. . . . I should be out of their power, free
from their insults in bad French, which the district newspapers
will describe as eloquence. . . .

I may still live five or six weeks, more or less. . . . Kill myself! My
word, no, he told himself, a few days later, Napoleon went on
living. . . .

Besides, life is pleasant for me here; I'm getting a good rest; I
have nothing to bother about, he added with a laugh, and began
to make a list of the books he wanted to have sent from Paris.

Chapter 37

A DUNGEON

The tomb of a friend.
—Sterne

He heard a great racket in the corridor; it was not the usual hour
for visiting his cell; the owl flew away screaming, the door opened,
and the venerable priest M. Chélan, trembling and leaning on a
cane, flung himself into Julien's arms.

7. The bird in Julien's tower is actually called an *orfraie* or "osprey." The ornithologically-oriented reader may wonder what the large marine fish-hawk he knows under the name of "osprey" is doing nesting in the prison-tower at Besançon. French *orfraie*, however, is often confused with "effraie" or screech-owl, the cry of which is supposed to terrify (*effrayer*) people because it is a premonition of death. Julien's bird has to be a screech-owl.

—Ah! Great God! Is it possible, my child. . . . Monster! I should say.

And the good old man could not add another word. Julien was afraid he would collapse; he was obliged to lead him to a seat. Time's hand had born heavily on this man, once so energetic. To Julien he seemed only the ghost of his former self.

When he had caught his breath: —Only the day before yesterday I got your letter from Strasbourg, with your five hundred francs for the poor of Verrières; it was delivered to me in the mountains at Liveru, where I have gone to live with my nephew Jean. Yesterday, I learned of the catastrophe. . . . Oh God! Is it possible! And the old man wept no more; he seemed to be stunned beyond all thought, and added mechanically: You will need your five hundred francs, I have brought them to you.

—I need to see you, Father! Julien cried with emotion. I have more money than I need.

But he could not get a coherent answer. From time to time M. Chélan shed a few tears, which trickled silently down his cheeks; then he looked at Julien, and was stunned to see him take his hands and raise them to his lips. His features which had once been so lively and expressed with such energy the loftiest sentiments were sunk in a kind of apathy. Before long a sort of peasant came to look up the old man. —He must not tire himself out by talking too much, he said to Julien, who understood that this was the nephew. The visit left Julien plunged in deep unhappiness, too deep for tears. Everything seemed to him sad beyond consolation; he felt his heart turn to ice in his bosom.

This moment was the bitterest he had experienced since his crime. He had just seen death, and in all its ugliness. All his illusions about spiritual grandeur and generosity had been dissipated like a cloud before a windstorm.

His frightful situation lasted several hours. A case of moral poisoning requires physical remedies, specifically a bottle of champagne. Julien would have thought himself a coward if he had sought comfort there. Toward the end of a horrible day which he had spent entirely in pacing up and down his narrow cell: What a fool I am! he exclaimed. If I expected to die like everyone else, the sight of that poor old man might well have made me completely miserable; but a quick death in the flower of my youth is just what will save me from that wretched decrepitude.

Whatever his reasonings, Julien found himself softened, like any other faint hearted fellow, and consequently despondent as a result of this visit.

There was nothing left in him of the rough and grandiose, nothing of Roman virtue; death seemed to him a more elevated matter, less easy to undergo.

Let this be my thermometer, he said. Tonight I am ten degrees below the courage which will lead me to the level of the guillotine. This morning I was brave. And for all that, what does it matter? provided I have it at the crucial moment. The notion of a thermometer amused him and ended by distracting his thoughts.

Next day when he woke up he was ashamed of his conduct the day before. My happiness, my peace of mind are at stake. He almost decided to write the district attorney and ask that nobody be allowed to visit him. And Fouqué? he thought. Suppose he undertakes a trip to Besançon, how upset he would be!

It was perhaps two months since he had given a thought to Fouqué. I was a great fool at Strasbourg; my thoughts never reached beyond my coat collar. The memory of Fouqué preoccupied his mind and left him in a more tender mood. He paced up and down agitatedly. Here I am a full twenty degrees below the death temperature. . . . If this weakness gets any worse, it will be better to kill myself. What a pleasure for the Abbé Maslons and Valenods if I die like a cur!

Fouqué came; this simple, honest fellow was haggard with grief. His only idea, if he had any at all, was to sell everything he owned in order to bribe the jailer and get Julien away. He talked to him for a long time of the escape of M. de Lavalette.[8]

—You're upsetting me, my dear fellow, Julien told him; M. de Lavalette was innocent, I am guilty. Without meaning to, you are making me think of the difference. . . .

But, is it true! The devil! Would you really sell everything you own? said Julien, returning to his old role of the suspicious observer.

Fouqué, overjoyed to see his friend at last responsive to his ruling passion, described to him in great detail, practically down to the last hundred francs, what he could realize on each one of his properties.

What a superb gesture on the part of a little provincial landowner, Julien thought. How many savings, how many petty economies which would make me blush if I saw them being practiced, he is ready to sacrifice for me! One of those handsome young men I used to see about the Hotel de La Mole reading *René*[9] might not have had any of these absurdities; but, except for a few who are very young, who have inherited their money and so have no idea of its value, which one of those fine Parisians would be capable of such a sacrifice?

8. After Waterloo, Comte Antoine de Lavalette was condemned to the guillotine. The day before the execution his wife made her way into the prison, changed clothes with her husband, and thus enabled him to escape (December 20, 1815).

9. Stendhal had a particular grudge against Chateaubriand, whose style was too flowery for his taste; the reference here mocks romantic young men who cultivate generous and pathetic sentiments in novels (*René*) but nowhere else.

All of Fouqué's mispronunciations, all his vulgar manners disappeared; Julien flung himself into his arms. Never did the provinces, when compared with Paris, receive a more handsome tribute. Fouqué, overjoyed at the momentary enthusiasm he read in his friend's eyes, mistook it for agreement to the escape.

This glimpse of the *sublime* restored to Julien all the energy that the specter of M. Chélan had dissipated. He was still very young; but in my opinion, he was a fine plant. Instead of treading the common path from softness to cunning, like most men, advancing years would have given him easy access to a fund of generous feeling; he would have overcome his morbid mistrust. . . . But what is the point of these vain suppositions?

The interrogations became more frequent despite the best efforts of Julien, whose answers all tended to cut the business short: —I have killed, or at least tried to kill, and with premeditation, he repeated every day. But the judge was a stickler for the formalities. Julien's statements in no way cut short the interrogations; they punctured the judge's self-importance. Julien did not know they wanted to move him into a frightful dungeon, and that it was thanks only to the efforts of Fouqué that they left him in his pleasant room a hundred and eighty steps above the ground.[1]

Abbé de Frilair was one of several influential men who dealt with Fouqué for their fire wood. The honest merchant managed to get himself in touch with the all-powerful grand vicar. To his inexpressible delight, M. de Frilair told him that, impressed by Julien's good qualities and by the services he had formerly rendered at the seminary, he intended to intervene with the judges. Fouqué glimpsed a half hope of saving his friend, and as he left the presence, bowing to the ground, he begged the grand vicar to expend on masses for the acquittal of the accused the sum of ten louis.

Fouqué was strangely in error here. M. de Frilair was by no means a Valenod. He refused, and even undertook to make the honest peasant see he would do much better to keep his money in his own pocket. Seeing that it was impossible to be clear without indiscretion, he advised him to give the sum in charities for the poor prisoners, who in fact lacked everything.

This Julien is a strange bird, his behavior is inexplicable, thought M. de Frilair, and for me nothing should be inexplicable. . . . Perhaps we can make a martyr out of him. . . . In any event, I shall get the *inside story* of this matter, and may even find a way to put some fear into that Mme. de Rênal, who has no respect for us, and really loathes me. . . . Perhaps I can even find in this business a way

1. Julien's prison, like Fabrizio's in *Chartreuse,* is a dungeon high atop a tower, an exalted seed bed of the soul.

of producing a spectacular reconciliation with M. de La Mole, who has a weakness for this little seminarian.

The compromise in the matter of the suit had been signed some weeks before, and Abbé Pirard had left Besançon, where he dropped a few words about the mystery surrounding Julien's birth, on the very day when the unfortunate young man was firing on Mme. de Rênal in the church of Verrières.

Julien saw only one more disagreeable episode standing between him and death: that was the visit of his father. He talked with Fouqué about writing to the attorney general for permission to be spared this visit. His horror at the thought of seeing his father, and at such a moment, profoundly shocked the honest middle-class mind of the wood seller.

He thought he could see why so many people hated his friend so violently. Out of respect for the unfortunate, he concealed his feelings.

—In any case, he said coldly, an order for solitary confinement would not apply to your father.

Chapter 38

AN INFLUENTIAL MAN

But there are so many mysteries in her deportment, and such elegance in her appearance! Who can she be?
—Schiller

The cell doors swung open very early next day. Julien woke with a start.

—Oh, Good Lord! he thought, here comes my father. What a disagreeable scene!

At the same instant a woman dressed as a peasant flung herself into his arms [and clung convulsively to him]. It was Mlle. de La Mole.

—Wretch, it was only from your letter that I learned where you were. What you call your crime, and which was only a noble act of vengeance that shows me the full loftiness of your spirit, this I learned of only in Verrières. . . .

Despite his prejudices against Mlle. de La Mole, to which in any case he had not yet admitted distinctly, Julien found her very beautiful. How could he not recognize in this style of speech and action a noble, disinterested sentiment, far beyond any of which a petty, vulgar soul would have been capable? He felt he was still the lover of a queen, [he yielded to the spell,] and after a few moments it was with a rare nobility of speech and thought that he said to her:

—The future was very clearly before my eyes. After my death, I married you off to M. de Croisenois, who would be marrying a widow. The noble if somewhat romantic soul of this lovely widow, frighted and turned back to the values of common prudence by an episode of singular tragic moment for her life, would easily have appreciated the genuine merits of the young marquis. You would soon have resigned yourself to what constitutes happiness for everyone else in the world: esteem, money, social position. . . . But, my dear Mathilde, your coming to Besançon, if ever it gets out, will be a mortal blow to M. de La Mole, and for that I should never forgive myself. I've already caused him so much sorrow! The academician will say he nourished a viper in his bosom.

—I confess, I didn't expect from you quite so much cold reason or quite so much concern for the future, said Mlle. de La Mole, half angry. My maid, who is quite as prudent as you, took a passport under her name, and it was as Mme. Michelet that I traveled here.

—And Mme. Michelet found it easy to gain access to me?

—Ah! You are still the superior man, the man of my choice! First I offered a hundred francs to a secretary of the judge, who had declared it was quite impossible for me to be admitted to the jail. But once he had the money, this honest fellow made me wait, raised objections, I thought he was out to rob me. . . . She paused.

—Well? said Julien.

—Don't be angry, my little Julien, she said, kissing him, I was obliged to give my real name to this secretary; he had thought I was a little Paris shop girl in love with the handsome Julien. . . . Those were actually his words. I swore to him that I was your wife and I have permission now to visit you every day.

Her folly is now complete, Julien thought; there was nothing I could do to prevent it. After all, M. de La Mole is such a great man that public opinion will be able to find excuses for the young colonel who marries this charming widow. My death, which is close at hand, will cover everything; and he yielded with delight to Mathilde's love; it was madness, grandeur of spirit, everything that was most strange. She seriously proposed to kill herself with him.

After these first transports, and when she had fully savored the pleasure of seeing Julien again, a lively curiosity invaded her spirit. She examined her lover carefully, and found him far above what she had imagined. Boniface de La Mole seemed reborn in him, but in an even more heroic mold.

Mathilde visited the leading lawyers of the district and offended them by offering money too crudely; but in the end they took the case.

She speedily reached the conclusion that in any controversial business of high importance everything at Besançon depended on Abbé de Frilair.

Under the unknown name of Mme. Michelet, she at first found insurmountable difficulties in reaching the all-powerful head of the congregation. But rumors of a beautiful young dressmaker who was madly in love and had come from Paris to Besançon to bring comfort to young Abbé Julien Sorel began to spread through the town.

Alone and on foot, Mathilde passed through the streets of Besançon; she hoped to escape recognition. In any event, she calculated it might not harm her cause to produce a strong impression on the people. Her madness even envisaged fomenting a revolt in order to save Julien as he walked to the scaffold. Mlle. de La Mole thought she was dressed simply and suitably for a woman in mourning; in fact, her dress made her the center of all eyes.

Everyone in Besançon took note of it when, after a week of pleading, she obtained an audience with M. de Frilair.

Courageous though she was, the notion of an influential leader of the congregation and the concept of profound, prudent rascality were so linked in her mind that she trembled as she rang the doorbell of the bishop's palace. She could scarcely walk when she had to climb the staircase leading to the apartment of the first grand vicar. The emptiness of the episcopal palace chilled her spirit. I may sit in an armchair, it will clutch my arms, I will be gone. Where can my maid ask after me? The police chief will take great care to do nothing. . . . I am all alone in this big town!

Her first glance around the apartment set Mlle. de La Mole's mind at rest. First, it was a footman in really elegant livery who showed her in. The room in which she was asked to wait displayed a sensitive and delicate luxury, quite different from crude magnificence, and such as one finds only in the best houses of Paris. As soon as she saw M. de Frilair approaching her with a fatherly air all ideas of foul play disappeared. She did not even find on his handsome features the imprint of a virtue, energetic and perhaps a bit savage, which is so antipathetic to good company in Paris. The half smile on the face of the priest who controlled everything in Besançon announced a man of good society, a knowing prelate, a clever administrator. Mathilde thought she was in Paris.

M. de Frilair needed only a few minutes to get Mathilde to admit that she was the daughter of his powerful adversary, the Marquis de La Mole.

—In fact, I am not Mme. Michelet at all, she said, resuming her usual lofty demeanor, and this admission does not much distress me, for I've come to consult you, sir, concerning the possibility of bringing about the escape of M. de La Vernaye. In the first place, he is guilty of nothing worse than a stupid blunder; the woman at whom he shot is perfectly well. In the second place, to corrupt the subordinates, I can put down, on the spot, fifty thousand francs and promise twice as much. Finally, my gratitude and that of my family will consider nothing impossible for the person who saves M. de La Vernaye.

M. de Frilair seemed surprised at that name. Mathilde showed him letters from the minister of war addressed to M. Julien Sorel de La Vernaye.

—You see, sir, my father had undertaken to make his fortune. [It is perfectly simple.] I married him in secret; my father wanted him to be a senior officer before making known this marriage, which is a little out of the way for a La Mole.

Mathilde noted that the expression of kindness and gentle gaiety vanished at once as soon as M. de Frilair began to learn something of importance. Subtlety mingled with profound duplicity began to appear on his face.

The abbé was doubtful; he reread the official documents slowly.

What can I get for myself from these odd confidences? he asked himself. Here I am, all of a sudden, in close relations with a friend of the celebrate Maréchale de Fervaques, all-powerful niece of my lord the Bishop of _____, through whom one becomes a bishop in France.

Things that I regarded as hidden in the future now turn up unexpectedly to hand. This may lead me to the great goal of all my ambition.

At first Mathilde was terrified by the sudden changes of expression on the part of this influential man with whom she found herself alone in a lonely chamber. But, what the deuce! she told herself shortly, wouldn't the worst thing have been to make no impression at all on the icy egotism of a priest already glutted on power and pleasure?

Dazzled by this rapid road to the episcopacy that had opened unexpectedly before his eyes, M. de Frilair dropped his guard for a moment. Mlle. de La Mole saw him almost at her feet, avid with ambition to the point of a nervous tremor.

It's getting clearer, she thought; nothing will be impossible here for a friend of Mme. de Fervaques. In spite of a twinge of still-painful jealousy, she had the courage to explain that Julien was the good friend of the maréchale, and at her house met nearly every day with my lord the Bishop of _____.

—If you were to draw by lot four or five times in a row a list of thirty-six jurors selected from the notable residents of this district, said the grand vicar, with the sour gaze of an ambitious man and giving great weight to each of his words, I should think myself very unfortunate if in each list I did not have eight or ten friends, and the most intelligent of the lot. Almost always I will have the majority, more than the majority needed to condemn; you see, mademoiselle, with what ease I can get an acquittal. . . .

The abbé stopped suddenly, as if astounded by the sound of his own words; he was admitting to things that are never uttered before the profane.

But he in turn dumbfounded Mathilde when he told her that what astonished and interested Besançon society more than anything else in the strange history of Julien was that he had once inspired a great passion in Mme. de Rênal, and that he had long returned it. M. de Frilair could not fail to note the extreme distress that his story produced.

I have my revenge! thought he. At last, here is a way of managing this very decided young person; I thought I would never find one. Her distinguished and independent air added in his eyes to the charm of the rare beauty which he now saw almost suppliant before him. He regained all his self-possession, and did not hesitate to twist the knife in the wound.

—I should not be surprised after all, he told her in a jesting way, if we should learn that jealousy impelled M. Sorel to fire a pistol twice at this woman whom once he loved so dearly. She cannot have lived without her diversions, and for some time now she had been seeing a good deal of a certain Abbé Marquinot in Dijon, some sort of Jansenist without any morals like the rest of that lot.

With great pleasure M. de Frilair tortured at his leisure the heart of this pretty girl, whose weakness he had discovered.

—I ask you, he said, fixing his burning eyes on Mathilde, why should M. Sorel have selected the church, if it was not because, precisely at that moment, his rival was celebrating mass there? Everyone concedes immense resources of wit and even more of prudence to the lucky man you have favored with your interest. What would have been simpler than to conceal himself in the gardens of M. de Rénal's house, with which he is so familiar? There, with the almost perfect assurance of being neither seen, nor captured, nor suspected, he could have killed the woman of whom he was jealous.

This reasoning, so just on the surface, succeeded in driving Mathilde out of her mind. Her soul was lofty, but saturated with that dry prudence which passes in the great world as the essence of the human heart; she was not made to understand the pleasure that lies in defying all prudence, and which can be so keen for an impassioned spirit. In the upper classes of Parisian society, where Mathilde had lived, passion only rarely dispenses with prudence, and it is only the people who live on the fifth story who jump out of the window.

At last Abbé de Frilair was sure of his conquest. He gave Mathilde to understand (doubtless he was lying) that he could influence any way he chose the district attorney, who would present the case against Julien.

After the names of the thirty-six jurors had been chosen by lot, he would make a direct and personal intervention with at least thirty of them.

If Mathilde had not seemed so pretty to M. de Frilair, he would not have been so clear and explicit until the fifth or sixth interview.

Chapter 39

SCHEMING

> Castres, 1676 (March 31) — He that endeavored to kill his sister in our house had before killed a man, and it had cost his father five hundred *écus* to get him off; by their secret distributions gaining the favor of the counselors.
>
> —Locke, *Journey through France*[2]

As she left the episcopal palace, Mathilde, without a moment's hesitation, dispatched a messenger to Mme. de Fervaques; fear of compromising herself did not restrain her an instant. She implored her rival to obtain a letter to M. de Frilair written entirely in the hand of my lord the Bishop of _____. She went so far as to beg her to come to Besançon herself. This was a heroic step on the part of a spirit both jealous and proud.

Following Fouqué's advice, she was prudent enough not to mention her actions to Julien. Her presence troubled him enough without that. A more honest man as death approached than he had ever been in life, he was experiencing remorse not only for M. de La Mole but also for Mathilde.

How can this be! he said to himself, I find there are times when, in her presence, I am absent-minded, or even bored. She is ruining herself for me, and that is how I repay her! Am I really an evil person? This question would not have concerned him much when he was ambitious; at that time, to fail in life was the only cause of shame he recognized.

His moral disquiet in the presence of Mathilde was the more striking because at that moment he was inspiring her to the most extraordinary and insane passions. She talked of nothing but the extravagant sacrifices she wanted to make in order to save him.

Exalted by a sentiment of which she was proud, and which trampled all her pride underfoot, she wanted to let not a moment of her life pass without filling it with some amazing action. The

2. From Peter King's *Life of John Locke, with extracts from his Corre-* *spondence, Journals, and Commonplace Books,* dated March 31, 1676.

strangest projects, the most perilous for herself, occupied her long conversations with Julien. The jailers, well paid, let her have her own way in the prison. Mathilde's ideas were not confined to sacrificing her reputation; little did she care about making her condition known to the whole of society. Falling to her knees before the king's careening carriage to beg a pardon for Julien, attracting the prince's attention at the risk of being crushed a thousand times over, these were the least of the dreams in which this exalted and courageous imagination indulged. Through her friends at court, she knew she could gain access to the reserved portions of the park at St. Cloud.[3]

Julien found himself scarcely worthy of all this devotion; to tell the truth, he was getting tired of heroics. He would have been responsive to a simple, a naïve and almost timid approach, whereas Mathilde's lofty soul always had to be conscious of a public and *other people*.

Amid all her anguish, all her fears for the life of this lover whom she did not want to outlive, Julien sensed in her a secret need to amaze the public with the splendor of her love and the sublimity of her projects.

Julien was irked to find that he was not touched at all by this excess of heroism. What would he have thought if he had known of all the follies with which Mathilde overwhelmed the devoted, but essentially reasonable and limited mind of the good Fouqué?

The latter was not too sure what to find fault with in Mathilde's devotion; for he too would have sacrificed his fortune and exposed his life to the greatest dangers to save Julien. He was dumbfounded at the quantity of money that Mathilde threw about. During the first days the sums disposed of in this way awed Fouqué, who had a provincial's reverence for money.

At last he discovered that Mlle. de La Mole's projects altered from day to day, and discovered, to his great relief, a word to describe this character that exhausted him: she was *changeable*. From this epithet to that of *wrongheaded,* the worst thing they can call you in the provinces, it's only a short step.

It is very strange, thought Julien one day, as Mathilde was leaving the prison, that such passionate feelings, of which I am the object, should leave me so unmoved! And only two months ago I adored her! I have read somewhere that the approach of death makes us lose interest in everything; but it is frightful to feel oneself ungrateful and to be unable to change. Am I an egotist, then? On this score he addressed to himself the bitterest reproaches.

3. the park at St. Cloud: see p. 202, note 5.

Ambition was dead within his heart; another passion rose from its ashes; he called it remorse for having tried to kill Mme. de Rênal.

As a matter of fact, he was madly in love with her. He found an extraordinary happiness when, in absolute solitude and without any fear of interruption, he could devote himself entirely to memories of the happy days he had once spent at Verrières or Vergy. The slightest incidents of that time that had slipped so rapidly from him retained an irresistible freshness and charm. He never thought of his success at Paris; he was bored by it.

These feelings, which grew in intensity from day to day, did not pass altogether unperceived by the jealous Mathilde. She saw very clearly that she must struggle against his love of solitude. Sometimes she spoke the name of Mme. de Rênal out of sheer terror. She saw Julien shudder. From then on her passion knew no measure or bounds.

If he dies, I shall die after him, she said with all the sincerity conceivable. What would the drawing rooms of Paris say upon seeing a girl of my rank adore to that point a lover condemned to death? To find feelings like that you must go back to the heroic days; it was love of this sort that animated hearts in the days of Charles IX and Henri III.

Amid the wildest transports, when she held Julien's head against her heart: Can it be! she said to herself with horror, is this precious head doomed to fall! Very well, she added, inflamed with heroic feelings that were not altogether unpleasant, my lips which are now pressed against his dear hair will be ice cold no more than twenty-four hours later.

Thoughts of these moments of heroism and of their fearful pleasures locked her in overpowering constraint. The idea of suicide, so potent in itself and hitherto so remote from her lofty spirit, made headway and soon came to reign over her with absolute sway. No, the blood of my ancestors has not grown tepid in its descent to me, Mathilde told herself proudly.

—I have a favor to ask of you, her lover told her one day: put your child out to nurse at Verrières; Mme. de Rênal will keep an eye on the nurse.

—What you said to me just then was really cruel. . . . And Mathilde grew pale.

—You are right, I beg your pardon a thousand times over, cried Julien, roused from his reverie, and clasping her in his arms.

Having dried her tears, he returned to his train of thought, but more subtly. He had given the conversation a tone of philosophic melancholy. He spoke of that future which would so soon be closed off for him.

—You must agree, my darling, that the passions are only an accident in life, but this accident happens only when superior people meet. . . . The death of my son would gratify the pride of your family, and that's what the flunkies will guess about it. Neglect will be the lot of this child of misery and shame. . . . I hope someday, at a time I don't want to determine, but which nonetheless I am bold enough to foresee, you will heed my dying wish: You will marry M. le Marquis de Croisenois.

—How can that be, a woman in disgrace!

—Disgrace has no power over a name like yours. You will be a widow and the widow of a madman, that's all. I will go further: since my crime did not have money for a motive, it will not be thought dishonorable. Perhaps by that time some philosophic legislator will have extracted from his prejudiced contemporaries abolition of the death penalty. Then some friendly voice will bring up an example: Look, Mlle. de La Mole's first husband was a madman, but not a really evil man, not a villain. It was absurd to cut off his head. . . . Then my memory will by no means be odious; at least after a certain period of time. . . . Your position in the world, your fortune, and, allow me to say, your genius will entitle M. de Croisenois, if he becomes your husband, to a role in society he could never attain on his own. He has nothing but birth and bravery, and these qualities all by themselves, which made a man of accomplishments in 1729, are an anachronism a century later, and only breed pretensions. Other things are needed to place a man at the head of the youth of France.

You will bring the support of a firm and enterprising character to any political party you direct your husband into. You could become a successor to the Chevreuses and Longuevilles of the Fronde. . . .[4] But by then, my darling, the celestial fire that glows in you at this minute will have cooled a little.

Allow me to say, he added, after a great many other preparatory phrases, that in fifteen years you will regard the love you have borne me as an excusable folly, perhaps, but still a folly. . . .

He stopped suddenly and sank into deep thought. He found himself once more face to face with that idea which so distressed Mathilde: in fifteen years, Mme. de Rênal will adore my son, and you will have forgotten him.

4. The Fronde was a civil war fomented in France by factions of disgruntled landlords from 1648 to 1652; it centered about the great Prince of Condé and his family, among whom two of the most passionate and influential figures were his sister the Duchess of Longueville, and Mme. de Chevreuse.

Chapter 40

TRANQUILLITY

It is because I was foolish then that I am wise today. O philosopher who sees nothing but the fleeting moment, how short is your vision! Your eye was not made to follow the underground working of the passions.
—W. Goethe

This discussion was cut short by an interrogation, followed by a conference with the lawyer for the defense. These were the only completely disagreeable moments in an existence marked by perfect resignation and tender reflections.

—It is a case of murder and premeditated murder, Julien said to the judge and to the lawyer as well. I am sorry, gentlemen, he added with a smile; but this reduces your task to a very trivial matter.

After all, Julien said when he had succeeded in escaping from these two creatures, I must be brave, and braver, it seems, than these two men. They regard as the supreme misfortune, as the monarch of terrors, this duel with a built-in unhappy ending, which I shall only have to think about seriously on the day itself.

The fact is, I have known worse misfortune, continued Julien, playing the philosopher for his own amusement. I suffered far more on my first journey to Strasbourg when I thought I had been abandoned by Mathilde. . . . And to think that I yearned then so passionately for this perfect intimacy which today leaves me absolutely cold! . . . Actually, I am more happy alone than when I have that lovely girl to share my solitude. . . .

The lawyer, a man of rules and formalities, thought he was crazy and supposed, like the general public, that it was jealousy that had put the pistol in his hand. One day he ventured to intimate to Julien that this allegation, whether true or false, would make an excellent line of defense. But the accused became on the instant a man of incisive passion.

—As you value your life, sir, cried Julien, beside himself, take care never to put forward that abominable lie. For a moment the prudent lawyer feared for his life.

He was preparing his brief because the decisive moment was rapidly approaching. Besançon and the whole district around had talked of nothing but this notorious trial. Julien was wholly ignorant of this circumstance; he had asked never to be told this sort of thing.

On that day, when Mathilde and Fouqué tried to tell him of certain public rumors very suitable, in their opinion, to raise his hopes, Julien stopped them at the first word.

—Leave me my ideal life. Your little tricks and details from real life, all more or less irritating to me, would drag me out of heaven.

One dies as one can; I want to think about death only in my own personal way. What do *other people* matter? My relations with *other people* are going to be severed abruptly. For heaven's sake, don't talk to me of those people any more: it's quite enough if I have to play the swine before the judge and the lawyer.

As a matter of fact, he told himself, it seems that my fate is to die in a dream. An obscure creature like myself, who is sure to be forgotten in two weeks' time, would be a complete fool to play out the comedy. . . .

Still, it is strange that I have learned the art of enjoying life only since I have seen the end of it so close to me.

He passed these last days walking about the narrow terrace atop his tower, smoking some excellent cigars Mathilde had had brought from Holland by a courier; he never suspected that his appearance was awaited each day by every telescope in town. His thoughts were at Vergy. He never talked about Mme. de Rênal with Fouqué, but two or three times his friend told him that she was recovering rapidly, and the phrase reverberated in his heart.

While Julien's soul was almost always wandering through the world of ideas, Mathilde, still occupied with real things, as befits an aristocratic spirit, had been able to advance the direct correspondence between Mme. de Fervaques and M. de Frilair to such a point that already the glorious word *bishopric* had been pronounced.

The venerable prelate whose care was the distribution of benefices added in a postscript to a letter to his niece: *That poor Sorel is merely a thoughtless fellow; I hope they will soon restore him to us.*

At the sight of these words, M. de Frilair was almost beside himself. He had no doubt of being able to save Julien.

—Without that Jacobin law that requires the drawing up of an immense list of jurors, and which has no other real purpose than to take away all influence from well-born people, he told Mathilde the night before the drawing of lots for the thirty-six jurors of the assize, I would have answered for the verdict. I was responsible, after all, for the acquittal of Curé N _____.

It was a great pleasure for M. de Frilair to discover next day, among the names drawn from the urn, those of five members of the congregation from Besançon, and among the people from outside the town the names of Messieurs Valenod, de Moirod, de Cholin. —To start with, I'll answer for those eight jurors, he told Mathilde. The five first are merely *machines*. Valenod is my creature, Moirod owes his whole existence to me, de Cholin is an imbecile who's afraid of everything.

The newspaper spread throughout the district the names of the jurors, and Mme. de Rênal, to the indescribable horror of her husband, expressed a desire to go to Besançon. The only thing M. de

Rênal could obtain of her was a promise not to leave her bed, lest she have to undergo the annoyance of appearing as a witness.

—You don't understand my position, said the former mayor of Verrières, I am now a liberal of the *defection*,[5] as people say; no doubt that scoundrel Valenod and M. de Frilair will easily get the attorney general and the judges to do anything that can be disagreeable to me.

Mme. de Rênal yielded without protest to the orders of her husband. If I appeared at the assize court, she told herself, it would seem that I was asking for vengeance.

In spite of all the promises of prudence she had made to her confessor and her husband, she had scarcely arrived in Besançon before she wrote, in her own hand, to each one of the thirty-six jurors:

"I shall not be present the day of the trial, sir, because my appearance might cast an unfavorable light on the case of M. Sorel. I desire only one thing in the world, and that passionately, his acquittal. You must have no doubt on this score, the frightful idea that because of me an innocent man has gone to his death will poison the rest of my life, and no doubt shorten it. How could you sentence him to death while I am still alive? No, there can be no doubt, society has no right to take life, above all from a man like Julien Sorel. Everyone at Verrières has seen him suffer short periods of distraction. This poor young man has influential enemies; but even among his enemies (and how numerous they are!) who is there who will call into question his admirable talents, his deep learning? It is not just an ordinary person whom you are called upon to judge, sir. During almost eighteen months we knew him to be pious, well-behaved, dutiful; but two or three times every year he suffered attacks of melancholy which verged on distraction. The whole town of Verrières, all our neighbors at Vergy where we pass the summer months, my whole family, even the subprefect himself, will bear witness to his exemplary piety; he knows by heart the entire Holy Bible. Would an impious person ever have applied himself whole years on end to learn the sacred scriptures? My sons will have the honor to bring this letter to you; they are mere children. Be good enough to question them, sir, they will tell you everything about this poor young man that is needed to convince you of the barbarity of condemning him. Far from revenging me, you would be dealing me a death stroke.

"What can his enemies advance in answer to the following fact? The wound resulting from one of those seizures which my

5. A liberal of the *defection* was one created during the 1827 elections by the defection of certain groups from the rightist coalition. M. de Rênal wants it understood that he is the most wishy-washy liberal that can possibly be.

children themselves remarked in their tutor is so far from dangerous that less than two months later it has allowed me to come
post from Verrières to Besançon. If I learn, sir, that you hesitate
ever so little to rescue from the barbarity of our laws a person
whose guilt is so slight, I shall rise from my bed, where only the
orders of my husband have kept me, to throw myself at your feet.

"Remember, sir, that premeditation has not been charged, and
you will have no occasion to reproach yourself with the blood
of an innocent being," etc., etc.

Chapter 41

THE TRIAL

The country will long recall that celebrated trial. Interest in the accused reached the point of agitation; it was because his crime was astonishing, though not atrocious. Even if it had been, the young man was
so handsome! His lofty destiny, so quickly come to grief, increased the
general sentiment of tenderness. Will they condemn him? was what
women asked the men of their acquaintance, and they grew visibly pale
as they waited for the reply.

—Sainte-Beuve

At last the day dawned so dreaded by Mme. de Rênal and by
Mathilde.

The strange look of the town multiplied their terror, and distressed even the solid soul of Fouqué. The whole province had
flocked to Besançon to watch the outcome of this romantic trial.

For the last several days there had been no room at the inns. The
president of the assize court had been besieged with requests for
tickets; all the ladies in town wanted to be present at the trial;
Julien's portrait was peddled in the streets, etc., etc.

Mathilde had been holding in reserve for this supreme moment
a letter written from beginning to end in the hand of my lord the
Bishop of _____. This prelate, who directed the destinies of the
church of France and who created bishops, deigned to request
Julien's acquittal. The night before the trial, Mathilde brought this
letter to the all-powerful grand vicar.

At the end of the interview, as she left the room in a flood of
tears: —I can answer for the verdict of the jury, M. de Frilair told
her, emerging at last from his diplomatic reserve and seeming almost
moved himself. Among the twelve persons charged with deciding
if your protégé's guilt is proved, and particularly if there was premeditation, I count six devoted friends of my fortune, and I have
given them to understand that it all depends on them to raise me
to the episcopate. Baron Valenod, whom I made mayor of Verrières,
carries in his pocket two of his subordinates, Messieurs de Moirod
and de Cholin. Actually, the drawing of lots has given us two quite
wrongheaded jurors; but though ultraliberals, they are faithful to

my commands on big issues, and I have asked them to vote with M. Valenod. I have learned that a sixth juror, a manufacturer who is immensely rich and always talks the liberal line, has secret hopes of getting a contract from the ministry of war, and no doubt he will not want to displease me. He has been told that M. Valenod has my last word.

—And who is this M. Valenod? Mathilde asked uneasily.

—If you knew him, you would have no doubt of the outcome. He is a loud talker, impudent, gross, made to be a captain among fools. 1814 saw him in the pit of misery, and I am going to make a prefect out of him. He is capable of beating the other jurors if they don't vote as he would have them.

Mathilde was somewhat comforted.

Another discussion awaited her that evening. Not to prolong a disagreeable scene which he felt could lead to only one conclusion, Julien had resolved to stand mute.

—My lawyer will talk, that's quite enough, he told Mathilde. I am going to be exposed long enough as a spectacle before all my enemies. These provincials were shocked by that rapid rise to fortune which I owe to you, and, believe me, there is not one of them that does not crave my conviction, though of course he'll blubber like a fool when I'm led to my death.

—They want to see you humiliated, it's perfectly true, replied Mathilde, but I don't believe they are all that cruel. My coming to Besançon and the spectacle of my grief have won the sympathy of the women; your handsome face will do the rest. If you say a word to the judges, the whole audience will be yours, etc., etc.

Next day at nine when Julien came down from his cell to enter the great hall of the district courthouse, the police had great difficulty holding back the immense crowd that had gathered in the yard. Julien had slept well, he was very calm, and had no feeling other than philosophic pity for this crowd of envious folk which, without any cruel intent, was about to applaud his sentencing to death. He was quite surprised when, having been held back for more than a quarter of an hour amid the crowd, he saw that his presence aroused in the public only warmth and compassion. He heard not a single disagreeable word. These provincials are less nasty than I thought, he told himself.

As they entered the trial room, he was struck by the elegant architecture. It was in pure Gothic style, with clusters of pretty little columns cut from stone with the most perfect workmanship. He might have been in England.

But soon his attention was caught by twelve or fifteen pretty women who were seated directly opposite the bench for the accused and filled three galleries above the judges and the jury. As he turned toward the public, he saw that the circular gallery which overhung the ground floor was filled with women: most were young and seemed to him quite pretty; their eyes were shining and filled with interest. Throughout the rest of the room, the crowd was immense; people were beating at the doors to get in, and the guards could not keep them quiet.

When all the eyes that were searching for Julien became aware of his presence as he sat down on the slightly raised bench reserved for the accused, he was met with a murmur of surprise and tender interest.

On that day you would have said he was not yet twenty; he was dressed very simply, but with perfect grace; his hair and brow were charming; Mathilde had insisted on presiding in person at his toilet. Julien's pallor was extreme. Scarcely was he seated on his bench than he heard from all sides: God! How young he is! . . . But he's only a boy. . . . He's much better looking than his portrait.

—Prisoner, said the policeman seated on his right, do you see those six ladies in the balcony up there? The policeman pointed to a little box jutting out above the amphitheater in which the jury were placed. That is the wife of the prefect, continued the policeman, alongside her is Mme. la Marquise de M_____. She is much attracted to you; I heard her talking to the examining judge. And there is Mme. Derville. . . .

—Mme. Derville! Julien exclaimed, and a deep blush rose to his face. When she leaves, he thought, she will write to Mme de Rênal. He did not know that Mme. de Rênal herself was in Besançon.

The witnesses were heard. [That took several hours.] At the first words of the indictment pronounced by the district attorney, two of the ladies in the little balcony opposite Julien burst into tears. Mme. Derville is not so soft, Julien thought. But he noted that she was very flushed.

The district attorney waxed pathetic in bad French on the barbarity of the crime committed; Julien noted that Mme. Derville's neighbors seemed most disapproving. Several jurors, apparently acquainted with these ladies, spoke to them and seemed to reassure them. That's very likely a good sign, Julien thought.

Until then he had felt within himself nothing but the purest contempt for all the people present at the trial. The district attorney's tepid eloquence increased his sense of disgust. But gradually Julien's frozen soul thawed a little under the marks of interest directed toward him.

He was satisfied with his lawyer's firm expression. No fine phrases, he whispered to him, as he was about to begin.

—All that emphasis cribbed out of Bossuet which they piled up against you has helped your cause, said the lawyer. And in fact, he had hardly been talking five minutes when all the women had their handkerchiefs out. The lawyer, taking fresh courage, addressed some extremely strong remarks to the jury. Julien shuddered; he felt he was on the point of shedding tears himself. Good God! What will my enemies say?

He was about to yield to the tender sentiment that was gaining on him when fortunately his eye met an insolent glance from the Baron de Valenod.

The eyes of that hound are all aglitter, he said to himself; what a triumph for that low beast! If my crime led to nothing but this, I would have to hate it. God knows what he will say about me to Mme. de Rênal [during the long winter evenings]!

This idea replaced all others. Soon after, Julien was brought back to himself by marks of public approval. The lawyer had finished his speech for the defense. Julien remembered it was the customary thing to shake his hand. The time had passed quickly.

Refreshments were furnished for the lawyer and the prisoner. Only then was Julien struck by an odd circumstance: none of the women had left the room for dinner.

—Upon my word, I'm starving, said the lawyer; how about you?

—Me too, said Julien.

—Look, there's the prefect's wife having her lunch too, said the lawyer, pointing up at the little balcony. Keep your chin up, it's going all right. The trial resumed.

As the presiding judge was summing up, midnight struck. The judge was obliged to stop; amid the silence of universal anxiety, the resonance of the great bell filled the whole room.

And so I begin the last day of my life, Julien thought. Soon he felt himself filled with the idea of duty. Hitherto he had dominated his own softer sentiments and preserved his determination not to speak; but when the presiding judge asked if he had anything to say, he rose. He saw before him the eyes of Mme. Derville, which under the lights seemed particularly brilliant. Has she been weeping, by any chance? he thought.

"Gentlemen of the jury: My horror of contempt, which I thought I could stand until the hour of my death, compels me to break silence. Gentlemen, I have not the honor to belong to your social class, you see in me a peasant in open revolt against his humble station.

"I ask no favors of you, Julien went on, his voice hardening. I have no illusions, death awaits me: I have deserved it. I have attempted to cut short the life of a woman most worthy of respect, most worthy of devotion. Mme. de Rênal had been like a mother to me. My crime is atrocious, and it was *premeditated*. I have therefore deserved the death sentence, gentlemen of the jury. But even if I were less guilty than I am, I see before me men who, without ever considering whether my youth merits some pity, are determined to punish in me and discourage forever a certain class of young men

—those who, born to a lower social order, and buried by poverty, are lucky enough to get a good education and bold enough to mingle with what the arrogant rich call good society.

"There is my crime, gentlemen, and it will be punished all the more severely because, in reality, I am not being judged by my peers. I do not see in the seats of the jury a single rich peasant, only outraged *bourgeois*. . . ."

For twenty minutes Julien talked in this vein; he said everything that was in his heart; the district attorney, who hoped to win the favor of the aristocracy, kept squirming on his seat; but in spite of the somewhat abstract turn Julien had imposed on the discussion, all the women were dissolved in tears. Mme. Derville herself had her handkerchief at her eyes. Before he finished, Julien returned to the matter of premeditation, to his regret, his respect, and to the unbounded filial adoration which in happier days he had felt for Mme. de Rênal. . . . Mme. Derville gave a little cry and fainted.

One o'clock was tolling as the jurors retired to their room. No woman had left her seat; several men had tears in their eyes. At first the spectators talked animatedly; but gradually, as the jury's decision was delayed, fatigue began to impose a measure of calm on the assembly. It was a solemn moment; the lamps were growing dim. Julien, though exhausted, heard various discussions going on around him as to whether the delay was a good sign or a bad one. He noted with pleasure that people's wishes were generally favorable to him; still the jury did not come back and still not a single woman left the hall.

As two o'clock sounded, a great commotion was heard. The little door of the jury room opened. M. le Baron de Valenod marched in, solemn and theatrical, followed by the other jurors. He coughed, then declared that on their souls and consciences the jury declared unanimously that Julien Sorel was guilty of murder, and murder with premeditation: this finding carried with it the death penalty, and it was pronounced a moment later. Julien glanced at his watch, with a thought for M. de Lavalette;[6] it was just two-fifteen. Today is Friday, he thought.

Yes, but this is a happy day for Valenod, who is pronouncing sentence on me. . . . I am too closely watched for Mathilde to be able to save me, as Mme. de Lavalette did. . . . And so, in three days at this same time, I shall know what to think about *the great perhaps*.

At that moment, he heard a cry and was recalled to things of this world. The women around him began to sob; he saw that all eyes were turned toward a little box hidden behind the capital of a Gothic pillar. He learned later that Mathilde had been hidden there. As the cry was not renewed, everyone turned back to stare

6. See p. 370, note 8.

at Julien, whom the police were trying to shoulder through the crowd.

Let's try to give no occasion for laughter to that villain Valenod, Julien thought. What a wheedling, oily look he had when he pronounced a sentence that carries with it the death penalty! whereas that poor presiding judge, even though he's a judge and has been one for many years, had a tear in his eye when he sentenced me. What a pleasure for Valenod to get his revenge here for our old rivalry over Mme. de Rênal! . . . So I shall never see her again! It's all over. . . . A last farewell is impossible between us, I sense it. . . . How happy I would have been to tell her what horror I feel of my crime!

Only these words: I feel I have been rightly convicted.

Chapter 42

When they returned Julien to jail, they put him in the death cell. Though ordinarily aware of the slightest circumstances, he did not even notice that they had not returned him to his former room. He was thinking of what he would say to Mme. de Rênal if he were happy enough to see her before the final moment. He thought that she might interrupt him, and was trying to show in his very first words the depth of his repentance. After such an action, how ever to persuade her that she is the only one I love? After all, I did try to kill her, out of ambition or out of love of Mathilde.

As he went to bed, he found his sheets were of coarse linen. His eyes were opened. Ah! I'm in the death house, he thought, sentence has been passed on me. Quite right.

Comte Altamira told me that the night before he died, Danton said in his great voice: It's a funny thing, the verb guillotine can't be conjugated in all its tenses. One can very well say, I will be guillotined, you will be guillotined, but it's impossible to say: I have been guillotined.

Why not, Julien thought, if there is an after life? . . . My word, if I find the God of the Christians, it's all up with me: he's a despot and, as such, full of vengeful ideas; his Bible talks of nothing but frightful punishments. I never liked him; I never could believe that anyone sincerely loved him. He is merciless (and he recalled several scriptural passages). He will punish me in some abominable way. . . .

But if I should find the God of Fénelon![7] He is capable of saying to me: much will be pardoned you, my child, because you have felt much love. . . .

7. Fénelon, like Massillon, was a priest of the late seventeenth and early eighteenth century whose invocation of sincere feeling and relative doctrinal toleration appealed to the *philosophes* of the later eighteenth century (and so to Stendhal) as a model of Christian piety.

Have I felt much love? Ah! I loved Mme. de Rênal, but I behaved terribly toward her. There, as everywhere else, I left simple,
modest merit in the lurch to run after what was flashy. . . .

But then, what a prospect! . . . Colonel in the hussars, if we
had a war; secretary of a legation in peacetime; afterwards, ambassador . . . for I would have picked up the business quickly . . . and,
as long as I'm not a mere fool, the son-in-law of M. de La Mole
surely need fear no rival. All my blunders would have been forgiven
or rather imputed to me as merits. A man of merit, and enjoying
the good life to the full in Vienna or London. . . .

—No, not exactly, sir, guillotining in three days' time.

Julien laughed aloud at this sally of his wit. It's really true, he
thought, man does have two spirits within him. Who the devil
thought up that malicious expression?

All right, yes, my friend, guillotining within three days, he answered his interrupter. M. de Cholin will rent a window, splitting
the price with Abbé Maslon. Well, when they fall to haggling over
the price of the window, which one of these worthy gentlemen will
cheat the other?

This passage from Rotrou's *Wenceslas*[8] came suddenly to mind.

> Ladislas: . . . My soul is all prepared.
> The King, *father of Ladislas:* So is the scaffold; just bring your
> head to it.

A fine answer! he thought, and fell asleep. Someone woke him up
in the morning by shaking him violently.

—What, already? said Julien, opening a haggard eye. He thought
he was in the hands of the executioner.

It was Mathilde. Fortunately, she did not understand. His awareness of this fact brought back all his self-possession. He found
Mathilde altered as by a six-months' illness: she was actually un-
recognizable.

—That unspeakable Frilair betrayed me, she told him, wringing
her hands; she could hardly speak for rage.

—Wasn't I fine yesterday when I began to talk? Julien replied.
I was improvising, and for the first time in my life! It's true, there's
also reason to fear it was the last.

At this point Julien was playing on the character of Mathilde
with all the self-possession of a skilled pianist at the keyboard. . . .
I lack the advantage of distinguished birth, it's true, he added, but
the glorious soul of Mathilde has raised her lover to her own level.
Do you suppose that Boniface de La Mole behaved any better
before his judges?

Mathilde on this day was unaffectedly tender, like any poor shop

---

8. *Wenceslas,* acted in 1647 and printed the year following, is considered the best
of Rotrou's many plays.

girl in a garret; but she was unable to extract from him any simpler speech. Without knowing what he was doing, he was paying her back for the torments she had often inflicted on him.

No man knows the sources of the Nile, Julien thought to himself; man's eye has not been privileged to see the king of rivers in the state of a simple brooklet: similarly, no human eye will ever see Julien weak, primarily because he isn't. But my heart is easily touched; the most ordinary word, if spoken with a genuine accent, can soften my voice and cause my tears to flow. How often the hard-hearted people have despised me for this failing! They thought I was begging pardon: that is what I will not endure.

They say the thought of his wife distressed Danton at the foot of the scaffold; but Danton had infused strength into a nation of coxcombs, and prevented the enemy from getting into Paris. . . . I alone know what I might have done. . . . For the others, I am at most nothing but a PERHAPS.

If Mme. de Rênal were here in my cell instead of Mathilde, could I answer for my own behavior? The excess of my despair and repentance might have been interpreted by the Valenods and the aristocrats of the district as ignoble terror of death; they are so proud, those feeble spirits whom their financial position places out of the reach of temptation! When they had just condemned me to death, Messieurs de Moirod and de Cholin might well have said: See what it means to be born a carpenter's son! You may become learned, you may become shrewd, but the heart! . . . the heart can't be trained. Even with this poor Mathilde, who is weeping now, or rather who can weep no more, he thought, looking at her red eyes . . . and he took her in his arms: the sight of authentic grief made him forget his syllogism. . . . Probably she has wept all night long, he thought; but one day, how ashamed she will be to think of this! She will picture herself as having been led astray in her early youth by the vulgar judgments of a plebeian. . . . Croisenois is weak enough to marry her, and, good Lord, for him that's the right thing to do. She'll make him play a role,

> by that right
> That a strong spirit, fixed in its designs,
> Holds over fools and their ignoble minds.[9]

Now there's an oddity: since I was condemned to death, all the poetry I ever knew in my life comes back in my memory. It must be a mark of decadence. . . .

Mathilde was saying to him, in a dying tone: He's there in the next room. He finally paid attention to what she was saying. Her

9. The verses are cited approximately, as is customary with Stendhal, from Voltaire's *Mahomet* (II, 5).

voice is weak, he thought, but all her imperious character is still to be heard. She is lowering her voice to keep from losing her temper.

—And who is it, out there? he asked her gently.

—The lawyer, with an appeal for you to sign.

—I shall not appeal.

—What's that! You're not going to appeal, she cried, leaping to her feet, her eyes blazing with rage, and why is that, if you please?

—Because, at this moment, I feel I have the courage to die without provoking too much laughter at my expense. And who knows if after two months spent in this soggy hole I'll be as well prepared? I can foresee interviews with priests, conversations with my father. . . . Nothing in the world could be more unpleasant. Let me die.

This unexpected perversity roused all the haughty part of Mathilde's character. She had been unable to see Abbé de Frilair before the visiting hours of the Besançon prison; her full fury fell on Julien. She adored him, and for a long quarter of an hour she raged against his character, and expressed her bitter regret at ever having loved him, while he reflected that this was indeed the proud spirit which had heaped such coals of burning fire on his head in the library of the Hotel de La Mole.

—For the honor of your family, he told her, providence should have formed you a man.

But as for me, he thought, I'd be a pretty fool to live two months longer in this disgusting hole, the butt of every disgraceful, humiliating tale the patricians can think up,[1] and having as my only consolation the diatribes of this crazy woman. . . . All right, day after tomorrow I fight a duel with a man known far and wide for his composure and his remarkable skill. . . . It's a most remarkable thing, whispered his Mephistopheles side, that man never misses his thrust.

All right, so be it, enough is enough (Mathilde continued to wax eloquent). No, by God, he said to himself, I shall never appeal.

This resolution taken, he returned to his thoughts. . . . The courier, making his rounds, will bring the newspaper at six, as he usually does; at eight, after M. de Rênal has read it, Elisa, walking on tiptoe, will come and leave it on her bed. Later, she will wake up: suddenly, as she reads it, she will grow disturbed; her delicate hand will tremble; she will read as far as these words. . . . *At five minutes past ten he had ceased to live.*

She will shed bitter tears, I know her; it does not matter that I tried to kill her, all will be forgotten. And the person whose life I tried to take will be the only one to weep sincerely for my death.

Ah! there is an antithesis! he thought, and for the full quarter

1. It is a Jacobin speaking [Stendhal's note].

of an hour during which Mathilde continued to play out her scene, he thought only of Mme. de Rênal. In spite of himself, and though he made frequent answers to what Mathilde was saying, he could not distract his thoughts from memories of the bedroom at Verrières. He saw the Besançon newspaper lying on the orange taffeta counterpane. He saw a white hand clutch at it with a convulsive gesture; he saw Mme. de Rênal weeping. . . . He followed the course of each tear down that charming face.

Mlle. de La Mole, unable to get anything out of Julien, summoned the lawyer. By good fortune it was a former captain of the army of Italy of 1796, where he had been a comrade of Manuel.[2]

For form's sake, he opposed the condemned man's resolution. Julien, wanting to treat him with respect, laid out all his reasons.

My word, one may think as you do, M. Félix Vaneau concluded; that was the lawyer's name. But you have three free days in which to appeal, and it is my duty to come back every day. If sometime in the next two months a volcano opened up under the prison, you would be saved. You may even die of a sickness, he said with a glance at Julien.

Julien shook his hand. —I'm grateful to you, you are a good man. I'll think it over.

And when Mathilde finally took herself off with the lawyer, he felt much more affection for the lawyer than for her.

Chapter 43

An hour later when he was in a deep sleep, he was awakened by tears which he felt trickling on his hand.

Ah! it's Mathilde again, he thought, still half asleep. Here she comes, true to her theory, attacking my decision with her tender sentiments. Bored by the prospect of another scene in the pathetic vein, he did not open his eyes. The verses about Belphégor in flight from his wife came into his mind.[3]

He heard an unusual sob; he opened his eyes, it was Mme. de Rênal.

—Ah! So I can see you again before I die, or is it an illusion? he cried, flinging himself at her feet.

But forgive me, madame, I am nothing but a murderer in your eyes, he said at once, returning to himself.

—Sir. . . . I have come to beg you to appeal; I know you don't want to. . . . Her tears choked her; she could say no more.

2. Jacques Antoine Manuel (1775–1827) was first a soldier of the Revolution, then a brilliant liberal orator whose inflexible courage under the Restoration roused Stendhal's warm admiration.

3. "Belphégor" is a story by La Fontaine imitated from one by Machiavelli, with the irksomeness of marriage as its central theme.

—Only if you forgive me.

—If you want me to forgive you, she told him, rising to her feet and throwing herself into his arms, appeal immediately against your death sentence.

Julien covered her with kisses.

—Will you come to see me every day during those two months?

—I swear it. Every day, unless my husband forbids me.

—I'll sign! cried Julien. What! You forgive me! Is it possible!

He seized her in his arms; he was out of his mind. She gave a little cry.

—It's nothing, she told him, you hurt me.

—Your shoulder, Julien cried, and burst into tears. He stepped back slightly and covered her hand with burning kisses. Who would ever have thought it the last time I saw you in your room at Verrières?

—Who would ever have thought I would write that terrible letter to M. de La Mole?

—You must know that I've always loved you, I never loved anyone but you.

—Is it possible! cried Mme. de Rênal, in equal ecstasy. She bent over Julien, who was at her knees, and for a long time they wept in silence.

Such a moment Julien had never known at any other period of his life.

Long afterwards, when they could talk again:

—And this young Mme. Michelet, said Mme. de Rênal, or rather this Mlle. de La Mole; for I am starting actually to believe this strange story!

—It's true only superficially, Julien replied. She is my wife but she is not my mistress.

And, interrupting one another a hundred times over, they succeeded with great difficulty in telling each other the things they had not known. The letter written to M. de La Mole had been the work of the young priest who was Mme. de Rênal's confessor, and she had copied it out.

—What a horrible thing religion made me do, she told him; and even so, I softened the most frightful passages of that letter. . . .

Julien's transports of joy proved how fully he forgave her. Never had he been so delirious with love.

—And yet I think myself a religious woman, Mme. de Rênal told him in the course of their conversation. I believe sincerely in God; I believe just as sincerely, and indeed it has been proved to me, that the crime I am committing is frightful, and as soon as I see you, even after you have fired a pistol twice at me. . . . And here, despite her protests, Julien covered her with kisses.

—Let me alone, she went on, I want to make this clear to you,

before I forget. . . . As soon as I see you, all my duties fade from
sight, I am nothing except love for you, or rather the word "love"
is too feeble. I feel for you what I should feel only for God: a mixture of respect, love, devotion. . . . In fact, I don't really know what
I feel for you. You could tell me to cut the jailer's throat, and the
crime would be done before I realized what it was. Explain that to
me quite clearly before I leave you, I want to see clearly into my
heart; for in two months we must be separated. Or, by the way,
need we be separated? she asked him with a smile.

—I withdraw my word, Julien cried, springing to his feet; I shall
not appeal against the death sentence if by poison, knife, pistol,
gas,[4] or any other manner you try to end your life or put it in
danger.

Mme. de Rênal's features altered abruptly; passionate affection
gave way to a dreamy expression.

—Suppose we should die right way? she said at last.

—Who knows what's to be found in the other world? Julien replied; perhaps tortures, perhaps nothing at all. Can't we pass two
months together in a delectable way? Two months, that's a good
many days. I shall never have been so happy before!

—You will never have been so happy!

—Never, Julien repeated, and I am speaking to you as I do to myself. May God keep me from exaggeration.

—To speak that way is to command me, she said with a sad,
timid smile.

—Very well. You swear, by the love you bear me, to make no
attempt on your own life, by any means, whether direct or indirect. . . . You must suppose, he added, that you are required to live
for my son, whom Mathilde will abandon to the care of lackeys as
soon as she is Marquise de Croisenois.

—I swear, she replied coldly, but I must take away with me your
appeal, written and signed in your own hand. I shall go myself to
the district attorney.

—Be careful, you will compromise yourself.

—After my act in coming publicly to visit your prison cell, she
said with an air of deep affliction, I shall be the subject of stories
forever, in Besançon and throughout the Franche-Comté. I am beyond the pale of prudence, of modesty. . . . I am a woman lost to
honor; it is true, I did it for you. . . .

Her voice was so sad that Julien kissed her with a pleasure that was
quite new to him. It was no longer the intoxication of love, but
rather a profound gratitude. He had just perceived, for the first time,
the full extent of the sacrifice she was making for him.

Some charitable soul evidently informed M. de Rênal of the long

4. The original French was *charbon*, "charcoal," where I have translated "gas";
the principle is asphyxiation.

visits his wife was making to Julien's prison cell; for, at the end of three days, he sent his carriage for her with explicit orders to return immediately to Verrières.

This bitter separation began the day badly for Julien. Two or three hours later, they told him that a certain priest, much given to intrigue but for all that incapable of getting along with the Besançon Jesuits, had set up in the street outside the prison gate since early morning. It was raining heavily, and there the man was, playing the martyr. Julien was already touchy; this piece of idiocy disturbed him deeply.

Already this morning he had once refused a visit from this priest, but the man had it in his head to confess Julien and make a name for himself among the girls of Besançon by retailing all the confidences he would pretend to have received.

He declared loudly that he would pass day and night before the prison gate; —God has sent me to touch the heart of this new apostate. . . . And the mob, always eager for a scene, began to gather.

—Yes, my brothers, he told them, I shall pass the day here, the night, every single day, and every single night from now on. The Holy Ghost has communed with me, I have a mission from on high; I am he who is chosen to save the soul of young Sorel. Join with me in prayer, etc., etc.

Julien had a horror of scandal and of anything that could draw public attention to him. He thought for a moment of seizing this occasion to get out of the world incognito; but he had some hope of seeing Mme. de Rênal again, and he was frantically in love.

The prison gate opened onto one of the busiest streets. The idea of this filthy priest gathering a crowd and making a scandal tortured his soul. —And, no doubt, every minute of the day he is repeating my name! This moment was more painful than death.

He called two or three times, at one-hour intervals, a turnkey who was his friend, asking him to go see if the priest was still at the prison gate.

—Sir, he's kneeling in the mud, was always the turnkey's answer; he's praying aloud, and reciting litanies for your soul. . . . What gall! Julien thought. And at that moment he actually heard a distant grumble; it was the crowd responding to the litany. To complete his frustration, he saw the turnkey himself begin to move his lips as he repeated the Latin words. —They're beginning to say, added the turnkey, that you must have a pretty hard heart if you refuse the help of this holy man.

—Oh, my native land! how barbarous you still are! Julien exclaimed, overcome by rage. And he continued his thought, without being aware of the turnkey's presence.

—What this man wants is an article in the newspapers, and he's bound to get it.

Oh, cursed provincials! At Paris I wouldn't have to put up with all these vexations. The frauds they have there aren't so crude.

—Let the saintly priest come in, he said at last to the turnkey, and the sweat stood out on his forehead. The turnkey made the sign of the cross and went off joyfully.

The saintly priest turned out to be horribly ugly, and even more dirty. The cold rain outside increased the darkness and dampness of the cell. The priest tried to kiss Julien, and began to wax pathetic as he talked to him. The basest hypocrisy was all too apparent; in all his life Julien had never been so enraged.

A quarter hour after the priest came Julien found himself a complete coward. For the first time death seemed horrible to him. He thought of the state of putrefaction in which his body would be two days after the execution, etc., etc.

He was about to give himself away by some sign of weakness, or else fling himself on the priest and strangle him with his chain, when he got the idea of asking the holy man to go say a good forty-franc mass for him that very day.

As it was nearly noon, the priest took himself off.

Chapter 44

As soon as he had left, Julien began to weep, and he wept at the thought of dying. After a while he realized that if Mme. de Rênal had been at Besançon he could have admitted his weakness to her. . . .

Just as he was feeling most regret at the absence of this woman whom he adored, he heard Mathilde's footstep.

The worst thing about a prison, he thought, is that you can't shut your door. Everything Mathilde said rubbed him the wrong way.

She told him that on the day of the trial, M. Valenod, having in pocket his appointment as prefect, had ventured to defy M. de Frilair and indulge himself in the pleasure of condemning Julien to death.

—"What came over your friend," M. de Frilair said to me just now, "to whip up and then attack the petty vanity of that *bourgeois aristocracy?* Why did he have to talk of *caste?* He pointed out to them what they ought to do in their own political interests: those boobies could never think it out for themselves, they were ready to weep. The interest of their caste came along and clouded their eyes to the real horror of condemning a man to death. It's very clear that M. Sorel is a novice in business matters. If we don't succeed in saving him through an appeal for mercy, his death will be a kind of *suicide.* . . ."

Mathilde, of course, did not mention to Julien something she herself did not yet suspect: that Abbé de Frilair, seeing Julien was doomed, thought it might serve his ambition to put himself in the way of becoming his successor.

Almost beside himself with repressed anger and frustration: —Go have a mass said for me, he told Mathilde, and let me have a minute's peace. Mathilde, who was already very jealous over Mme. de Rênal's visits, and who had just heard of her departure, understood the cause of Julien's anger, and burst into tears.

Her grief was genuine; Julien saw that it was, and was all the more angered by it. He was in absolute need of solitude, and how was he to get any?

Finally, Mathilde, after trying all the arguments she knew to soften him, left him alone, but just at that moment Fouqué appeared.

—I really must be alone, he said to that faithful friend. . . . And as he saw him hesitate: I am writing a paper in support of my appeal . . . and besides . . . do me a favor, and never talk to me about death. If I need any special services on the day itself, let me be the one to raise the subject.

When Julien had finally got himself some solitude, he found he was more crushed and cowardly than before. The little strength left to his enfeebled spirit had gone into concealing his condition from Mlle. de La Mole and from Fouqué.

Toward evening a consoling idea occurred to him:

If this morning, at the moment when death seemed so horrible to me, I had been called to execution, *the public eye would have been my spur to glory;* perhaps my step might have been a trifle heavy, like that of a timid fop entering a drawing room. And a few clairvoyant people, if there are any such in the provinces, might have been able to guess my weakness . . . but nobody *would have seen it.*

He felt himself delivered from a part of his grief. He made a tune and hummed it to himself: I am a coward this very minute, but nobody will ever know it.

An even more disagreeable event lay in wait for him next day. For a long time his father had been threatening to visit; next morning, before Julien was awake, the white-haired carpenter appeared in his cell.

Julien felt weak; he was expecting the most disagreeable tirades. To complete his sense of dread, he was prey that morning to remorse for not loving his father.

Chance has placed us near one another on the earth, he told himself, while the turnkey was setting the cell a bit to rights, and we've done one another almost all the harm we could. Here he's come at the moment of my death to give me the final kick.

As soon as they were alone together the old man's vituperation began.

Julien could not hold back his tears. What shameful weakness! he said to himself, in a rage. He will go all around the town talking about my lack of courage; what a triumph for the Valenods and all those stupid hypocrites who hold power in Verrières. They are the big men in France, they have in their fists all the social advantages. But until now I could always tell myself: they're piling up the honors, it's true, but I have nobility in my heart.

And now here's a witness they will all believe, and who will assure all Verrières, even exaggerating the facts, that I was fearful in the face of death! I shall be showed up as a coward in this test that everyone can understand!

Julien was close to despair. He did not know how to get rid of his father. And to feign well enough to deceive this shrewd old man was at this point quite beyond his power.

His mind ran quickly over the possible expedients.

—*I have some money saved up!* he exclaimed suddenly.

This inspired phrase immediately changed the expression on the old man's face, and Julien's position.

—What do you suppose I should do with it? Julien continued more calmly: the effect he had produced had freed him of all sense of inferiority.

The old carpenter was aflame with impatience to lay his hands on this money, a part of which it seemed that Julien wanted to bequeath to his brothers. He talked for a long time and with much animation. Julien was in a position to tease him.

—Well, the Lord has inspired me to make my will. I will give a thousand francs to each of my brothers, and the remainder to you.

—All right, said the old man, that remainder is my due; but since the Lord has touched your heart, if you want to die like a good Christian, you ought to pay your debts. There is still the whole expense of your feeding and your education which I laid down, and which you never think of. . . .

That's paternal affection for you! thought Julien, with desolation in his heart, when at last he was alone. Shortly the jailer appeared.

—Sir, after a visit from the family, I always bring my guests a bottle of good champagne. It's a bit dear, six francs a bottle, but it does the heart good.

—Bring three glasses, Julien said to him with boyish enthusiasm, and bring in two of the prisoners I hear walking about the corridor.

The jailer brought him two galley slaves condemned as second offenders and preparing for another term in the hulks. They were a pair of merry scoundrels, really quite remarkable for their cunning, courage, and self-possession.

—If you give me twenty francs, one of them told Julien, I'll tell you my whole life story. It's a real hairy tale.

—But you'll lie to me? said Julien.

—Not me, said he; here's my pal, would like to have my twenty francs; he'll peach on me if I lie to you.

His story was abominable. It showed a bold heart in which only one passion survived, that for money.

After they had left, Julien was no longer the same man. All his wrath against himself had evaporated. The savage grief, embittered by a sense of pusillanimity, to which he had been prey since Mme. de Rênal's departure, had turned into melancholy.

Had I been a little less the dupe of circumstance, he told himself, I would have seen that the drawing rooms of Paris are filled with honest folk like my father, or else clever rascals like these jailbirds. They are right, the men in the drawing room never wake up in the morning with this thought gnawing into their minds: How am I going to eat today? And yet they boast of how honest they are! And when they're called for jury duty, they are proud to condemn a man who stole a silver spoon because he felt he was dying of hunger.

But if there's a court, if it's a question of getting or losing a portfolio, then my honest men in the drawing room fall into crimes exactly like those my two jailbirds committed for lack of bread. . . .

There is no *law of nature*: the phrase is nothing but a bit of antiquated nonsense worthy of the district attorney who hunted me down the other day, and whose ancestor grew rich on one of Louis XIV's confiscations. There is no *right* except when there's a law to prevent one's doing such and such a thing on pain of punishment. Before the law, there's nothing *natural* except the strength of the lion, or the need of the creature that is hungry or cold, *need* in a word. . . . No, the people who stand well with the world are simply sneak thieves lucky enough not to have been caught in the act. The prosecutor whom society unleashes against me grew rich on disgraceful practices. . . . I attempted a murder, I am rightly condemned, but except for this one action, the Valenod who condemned me is a hundred times more harmful to society.

All right, Julien added sadly but without anger, my father for all his avarice is better than that lot. He never loved me. I have just filled his measure to overflowing, and disgraced him by coming to a shameful end. That fear of being left penniless, that exaggerated view of human wickedness which we call *avarice*, makes him see an immense source of consolation and security in a sum of three or four hundred louis, which I may actually leave him. One Sunday after dinner he will show off his wealth to all the envious spirits of

Verrières. And his glance will be saying to them, At this price, which one of you would not be delighted to have a son guillotined?

This philosophy might be true, but it was of a nature to make a man eager for death. Thus passed five long days. Toward Mathilde he was polite and gentle; he saw she was prey to the most furious jealousy. One evening Julien thought seriously of committing suicide. His soul was exhausted by the long misery into which Mme. de Rênal's departure had plunged it. Nothing gave him any pleasure, either in real life or in his imagination. Lack of exercise was starting to affect his health and give him the exalted, feeble temper of a young German student. He was losing that masculine haughtiness which rejects with a vigorous oath certain unconventional notions by which the souls of men in misery are assailed.

I have loved truth. . . . Where is it? Everywhere hypocrisy, or at least charlatanism, even among the most virtuous, even among the greatest; and his looks twisted to an expression of disgust. . . . No, a man cannot have any faith in men.

Mme. de _____, making a collection for her poor orphans, told me that some prince or other had just given ten louis; it was a lie. But what am I saying? Napoleon on Saint-Helena! . . . Pure charlatanism, a proclamation in favor of the King of Rome.[5]

Good God! if a man like that can sink to charlatanism, and just at the time when his troubles should be holding him strictly to duty, what can you expect from the rest of the species? . . .

Where is truth? In religion. . . . Yes, he added, with the bitter smile of the most intense scorn, in the mouths of the Maslons, Frilairs, Castanèdes. . . . Perhaps under real Christianity, when the priests would not be paid any more than the apostles were? . . . But St. Paul was paid with the pleasure of giving orders, of talking, of making himself talked about. . . .

Ah! if there were a true religion. . . . Fool that I am! I see a Gothic cathedral, ancient stained glass; my heart in its weakness forms from those windows a picture of the priest. . . . My soul would understand him, my soul has need of him. . . . I find nothing but a fop with greasy hair . . . a chevalier de Beauvoisis without the pleasing exterior.

But a real priest, a Massillon, a Fénelon . . . Massillon consecrated Dubois.[6] The *Mémoires* of Saint-Simon have spoiled Fénelon

5. When Napoleon abdicated the second time (June 22, 1815), he did so in favor of his son, known generally as the King of Rome. But this son, who was just four years old at the time, was never allowed to advance beyond the rank of a minor Bavarian dukedom and barely survived to the age of twenty-one.

6. Saint-Simon has a good many sharp things to say about Massillon's part in the consecration of Abbé (later Cardinal) Guillaume Dubois, a slippery fellow whose ecclesiastical careerism occasioned much scandal.

for me;[7] but still, a real priest. . . . Then the sensitive souls would have a meeting place in the world. . . . We would not be so isolated. . . . The good priest would tell us about God. But what God? Not that in the Bible, a petty despot, cruel and thirsting for revenge . . . but the God of Voltaire, just, kind, infinite. . . .

He was agitated by recollections of that Bible which he knew by heart. . . . But how, whenever *two or three are gathered together,* can we believe in that great name of *God,* after the fearful abuse our priests have imposed on it?

To live alone, in isolation! . . . What torture! . . .

I am becoming silly and unfair, Julien told himself, striking his brow. I am isolated here in this dungeon; but I have not *lived in isolation* on the earth; I had the powerful idea of *duty.* The duty I assigned myself, whether wrong or right . . . has been like the trunk of a solid tree, on which I supported myself during the storm; I wavered, I was shaken. After all, I was only a man. . . . But I was not carried away.

It is the damp air of this dungeon that makes me think of isolation. . . .

And why be hypocritical still, even as I curse hypocrisy? It's neither death, nor the dungeon, nor the damp air, it's the absence of Mme. de Rênal that is crushing me. If I were at Verrières, and in order to see her had to spend weeks on end hidden in the cellar of her house, should I complain of that?

The influence of my contemporaries is stronger than I am, he said aloud, and with a bitter laugh. Talking in solitude to myself, only two steps away from death, I am still a hypocrite. . . . O nineteenth century!

. . . A hunter fires his gun in a forest, his victim falls, he rushes forward to seize it. His boot strikes an ant hill two feet high, destroys the ant house, and scatters ants and ant eggs all around. . . . The most philosophical of the ants will never be able to understand that black, enormous, terrifying body: the hunter's boot that burst into their house with unbelievable rapidity, preceded by a terrifying blast and a flare of reddish flame. . . .

. . . And so death, life, and eternity, things perfectly simple for anyone who has organs vast enough to form a conception of them. . . .

A momentary little fly is born at nine o'clock one morning of a long summer's day, he dies at five that evening; how could he possibly understand the word *night?*

Give him five hours of existence more, he will see and understand what night is.

So with me; I shall be dead at twenty-three. Give me five years more of life, to be spent with Mme. de Rênal.

And he began to laugh like Mephistopheles. What lunacy to be thinking about these great problems!

First, I am a hypocrite, just as if there were someone here to hear me.

Second, I am forgetting to live and love, when I have so few days left to live. . . . Alas! Mme. de Rênal is not here; perhaps her husband won't let her come back to Besançon and disgrace herself any further.

That is what isolates me, and not the absence of a God who is just, good, all powerful, who is not malignant, not hungry for vengeance.

Ah! if He existed. . . . Alas! I should fall at His feet. I have deserved death, I should tell him; but, great God, good God, kind God, give me back the woman I love!

It was very late by now. After an hour or two of peaceful sleep, Fouqué came.

Julien felt himself strong and resolute, like a man who has seen clearly into his own soul.

Chapter 45

—I cannot play such a mean trick on poor Abbé Chas-Bernard as to summon him, he told Fouqué; he would not be able to eat his dinner for three days afterward. But try to find me a Jansenist, friendly to M. Pirard, and beyond the reach of intrigue.

Fouqué had been waiting impatiently for this overture. Julien carried out respectably all the observances required by public opinion in the provinces. Thanks to Abbé de Frilair, and in spite of his bad choice of a confessor, Julien in his cell was under the protection of the congregation; with more suppleness of spirit, he might have escaped altogether. But the bad air of the dungeon was producing its effect; his reason was fading. He was all the happier when Mme. de Rênal came back.

—My first duty is to you, she said, kissing him; I have fled from Verrières. . . .

In her presence, Julien was not subject to petty pride; he described all his weaknesses. She was kind and gracious toward him.

That evening as soon as she had left the prison, she summoned to her aunt's house that priest who had attached himself to Julien as to a victim; since he wanted nothing more than to make himself a name among the young ladies of the better classes in Besançon, Mme. de Rênal easily persuaded him to go off and offer a novena at the abbey of Bray-le-Haut.

Words cannot describe the excess and madness of Julien's devotion.

Through bribery, and the use or abuse of her aunt's reputation, a woman famous for her piety and her wealth, Mme. de Rênal gained permission to see him twice a day.

When she heard of this, Mathilde's jealousy rose to the level of insanity. M. de Frilair had admitted to her that all his power would not avail to overturn the decorums and get her permission to see her lover more than once a day. Mathilde had Mme. de Rênal followed, so as to be informed of her slightest actions. M. de Frilair exhausted all the resources of a most ingenious mind trying to prove that Julien was unworthy of her.

Amidst all these torments, she only loved him the more, and almost every day she made a horrible scene in his cell.

Julien wanted at all costs to behave honorably until the end toward this poor girl whom he had so strangely compromised; but at every moment the boundless love he felt for Mme. de Rênal carried him away. When he could not succeed in persuading Mathilde, by various bad reasons, that her rival's visits were quite innocent:

—Well, the end of the drama is very close now, he told himself; that must be my excuse if I cannot put up a better front.

Mlle. de La Mole learned that the Marquis de Croisenois was dead. M. de Thaler, that man who was so rich, had indulged himself in various disagreeable remarks on the disappearance of Mathilde; M. de Croisenois paid a call to ask him to withdraw them: M. de Thaler showed him various anonymous letters addressed to him, and full of details so skillfully woven together that the poor marquis could not possibly fail to see the truth.

M. de Thaler then permitted himself some jests that were quite devoid of subtlety; M. de Croisenois insisted on such sweeping apologies that the millionaire preferred a duel. Stupidity was triumphant; and one of the men most deserving of love in all Paris was dead at the age of twenty-four.

This death produced a strange and morbid effect on Julien's weakened spirit.

—Poor Croisenois, he told Mathilde, he acted the part of a perfectly reasonable, perfectly honest man, in our regard; he should really have hated me ever since you behaved so imprudently in your mother's drawing room, and should have picked a quarrel with me; for the hatred that grows out of scorn is generally insatiable. . . .

The death of M. de Croisenois changed all Julien's ideas about the future of Mathilde; he devoted several days to proving to her that she ought to accept the hand of M. de Luz. He's a timid man, not too Jesuitical, he told her, and no doubt he intends to get onto the ladder. His ambition is more limited and more steady than that of poor Croisenois, and there's no dukedom in the family, thus he will raise no objections to marrying the widow of Julien Sorel.

—And a widow who despises great passions, Mathilde replied coldly; for she will have lived long enough to see her lover prefer, after only six months, another woman, and what's more, a woman who was the source of all their troubles.

—That's not fair; Mme. de Rênal's visits will provide some remarkable arguments for the Paris lawyer who presents my appeal for clemency; he will describe the murderer being honored by the special care of his victim. That may make an effect, you may see me become the subject of some melodrama, etc., etc.

A raging jealousy, quite helpless to take vengeful action, a long-standing hopeless grief (for even supposing Julien freed, how could she hope to regain his heart?), the shame and sorrow of loving this faithless lover more than ever, all had cast Mlle. de La Mole into a gloomy silence from which neither the eager concern of M. de Frilair nor the rude frankness of Fouqué could rouse her.

As for Julien, except for the moments usurped by Mathilde's presence, he was living on love and almost without a thought for the future. By a strange effect of this passion when it is at its height and perfectly sincere, Mme. de Rênal almost shared in his indifference and gentle gaiety.

—In the old days, Julien told her, when I could have been so happy during our walks through the forest at Vergy, smoldering ambition dragged my soul away into imaginary lands. When I should have been pressing to my heart this lovely form that was so close to my lips, I was stolen away from you by the future; my mind was on the endless struggles I would have to endure in order to build a colossal fortune. . . . No, I should have died without ever knowing happiness if you had not come to see me in this prison.

Two incidents arose to disturb this peaceful existence. Julien's confessor, Jansenist though he was, was not beyond reach of a Jesuit intrigue, and without knowing it became their agent.

One day he turned up saying that unless Julien wished to fall into the frightful sin of suicide, he would have to take all the steps necessary to gain clemency. Since, now, the clergy had a great deal of influence in the ministry of justice at Paris, an easy means of enlisting their support appeared: he would have to undergo a sensational conversion. . . .

—Sensational! Julien repeated. Ah! so I've caught you at it too, Father, you want to act in a play like any missionary. . . .

—Your age, the Jansenist resumed solemnly, the interesting features providence has bestowed on you, the motive of your crime which still remains inexplicable, the heroic struggles that Mlle. de La Mole has undertaken on your behalf, in a word, everything, including the astounding friendship your victim continues to show for you, everything has conspired to make you the hero of all the young ladies in Besançon. They have forgotten everything for you, even politics. . . .

Your conversion would strike them to the heart and leave a profound impression there. You can be of the greatest service to the cause of religion, and am I to palter over the frivolous objection that on a similar occasion the Jesuits would follow the same policy? In that case, they would be able to do harm even in this particular situation which is beyond reach of their rapacity! Perish the thought. . . . The tears shed over your conversion will wash away the corrosive effect of ten editions of the impious works of Voltaire.

—And what will be left for me, Julien asked coldly, if I despise myself? I have been ambitious, but I have no intention of blaming myself for that; I was acting in those days according to the code of the times. Now I am living from day to day. But it seems to me that I should make myself very miserable indeed if I took part in some cowardly scheme. . . .

The other incident that affected Julien far differently arose from Mme. de Rênal. Some intriguing friend or other had succeeded in persuading this naïve, timid soul that it was her duty to rush off to Saint-Cloud and fall on her knees before the king, Charles X.[8]

She had resigned herself to a separation from Julien, and after that effort, the unpleasantness of making a public spectacle of herself, which at other times would have seemed worse than death, was nothing to her eyes.

—I shall go to the king, I shall tell him frankly that you are my lover: the life of a man, especially a man such as Julien, overrides all other considerations. I shall say that it was jealousy that led you to attempt my life. There are many instances of poor young men rescued under these circumstances by the humanity of the jury, or that of the king. . . .

—I will refuse to see you, I will ask that you be barred from the prison, Julien cried, and I vow that the next day I will kill myself in despair if you do not swear that you will do nothing to make us both a public spectacle. This idea of going to Paris isn't your own. Tell me the name of that conniving female who suggested it to you. . . .

Let us be happy during the few days remaining to us of this short life. Let us conceal our existence; my crime is only too apparent. Mlle. de La Mole has immense influence at Paris; you must believe she is doing everything that is humanly possible. Here in the provinces I have against me all the rich and influential people. Your action would embitter even further those rich and particularly moderate men for whom life is such an easy affair. . . . Let us give no

8. For the first time in the book Stendhal mentions the monarch who reigned over France until his abdication, July 30, 1830.

cause for laughter to the Maslons, Valenods, and a thousand people who are worth more than they are.

The bad air of the prison cell was becoming insupportable to Julien. Fortunately on the day set for his execution a bright sun was shining upon the earth, and Julien was in the vein of courage. To walk in the open air was for him a delicious experience, as treading the solid ground is for a sailor who has been long at sea. There now, things are going very well, he told himself, I shall have no lack of courage.

Never had that head been so poetic as at the moment when it was about to fall. The sweetest moments he had ever known in the woods at Vergy came crowding back into his mind, and with immense vividness.

Everything proceeded simply, decently, and without the slightest affectation on his part.

Two days before he had told Fouqué:

—As for emotion, I can't quite answer; this dungeon is so ugly and damp it gives me feverish moments in which I don't recognize myself; but fear is another matter, I shall never be seen to grow pale.

He had made arrangements in advance that on the last day Fouqué should take away Mathilde and Mme. de Rênal.

—Put them in the same coach, he told him. Keep the post horses at a steady gallop. Either they will fall in one another's arms or they will fall into mortal hatred. In either case, the poor women will be somewhat distracted from their terrible grief.

Julien had forced from Mme. de Rênal an oath that she would live to look after Mathilde's son.

—Who knows? Perhaps we retain some consciousness after death, he said one day to Fouqué. I should like to rest, since rest is the word, in that little cave atop the big mountain that overlooks Verrières. I've told how several times when I spent the night in that cave and looked out over the richest provinces of France, my heart was afire with ambition: that was my passion in those days. . . . Well, that cave is precious to me, and nobody can deny that it's located in a spot that a philosopher's heart might envy. . . . You know these good congregationists in Besançon can coin money out of anything; go about it the right way, and they'll sell you my mortal remains. . . .

Fouqué was successful in this morbid transaction. He was spending the night alone in his room beside the body of his friend, when, to his great surprise, he saw Mathilde enter. Only a few hours before he had left her ten leagues from Besançon. Her eyes were wild.

—I want to see him, she said.

Fouqué was afraid to speak or rise. He pointed at a blue greatcoat on the floor; it covered everything that remained of Julien.

She fell to her knees. The memory of Boniface de La Mole and Marguerite of Navarre no doubt gave her superhuman courage. Her trembling fingers opened the coat. Fouqué turned his eyes away.

He heard Mathilde stride swiftly about the room. She was lighting a number of candles. When Fouqué had the strength to look, she had placed in front of her, on a little marble table, the head of Julien, and was kissing its brow. . . .

Mathilde followed her lover to the tomb he had selected. A great number of priests accompanied the bier, and, unknown to all, alone in her draped carriage, she carried on her knees the head of the man she had loved so much.

Arriving thus near the peak of one of the highest mountains in the Jura in the middle of the night, in that little cave magnificently lighted by innumerable candles, twenty priests celebrated the service for the dead. All the inhabitants of the little mountain villages through which the procession had passed followed it, drawn by the oddity of this strange ceremony.

Mathilde appeared among them, swathed in black, and after the service ordered several thousand five-franc coins to be distributed among them.

Left alone with Fouqué, she insisted on burying with her own hands the head of her lover. Fouqué almost went mad with grief at the sight.

By Mathilde's orders, this savage grotto was adorned with marbles sculptured at great expense in Italy.

Mme. de Rênal was true to her word. She never tried in any way to take her own life; but three days after Julien, she died in the act of embracing her children.

The End

The great disadvantage to the reign of public opinion, which does indeed achieve *freedom,* is that it meddles in matters where it does not belong, for example: private life. Hence the gloom of America and England. To avoid laying a finger on private life, the author has invented a little town, V*errières,* and when he had need of a bishop, a jury, a court of assizes, put the whole thing in Besançon, where he has never been.

Backgrounds and Sources

ROBERT M. ADAMS

France in 1830: The Facts of Life

When he subtitled his novel "a chronicle of 1830," Stendhal was perpetrating a paradox which time has robbed of most of its point. A "chronicle" is supposed to record events of an age long past; Stendhal was proposing a historical novel about the present, a costume drama in modern dress. But the "modernity" of his novel has aged almost as much as its historical perspective; 1830 is, for us, not much less remote than Mathilde's heroic age of Henry III and Charles IX. So it has seemed appropriate to include a little section to explain some of the peculiar institutions appearing in the *Rouge* which would have been obvious to a contemporary reader but which are now rather exotic. "France in 1830" is an effort to summarize basic information about the money-values used in the *Rouge*, the ecclesiastical structures and parties of the day, the political and legal frameworks surrounding the story.

Money and Measures

French money of 1830 was calculated according to a system of perfect Gallic lucidity complicated by quite a bit of Gallic complexity. The basic unit is the franc, equal in English currency to about one shilling thruppence, or in American currency of that age to a little less than twenty cents. There are a hundred sous in a franc, so a sou is worth very little indeed—less than a fifth of a cent. So far, so good. But with the livre (translated *florin* in this text), things get complicated. Like the English guinea, the French *livre* or florin is not a physical coin but a measure of value; and it is particularly confusing because it is worth sometimes a bit more than a franc, sometimes a bit less. Like the English guinea, again, the florin (livre) is a more dignified measure than the franc, and is always used in estimating incomes. Six livres make an écu (translated "crown" in this text). By the decrees of August 18 and September 12, 1810, the value of this six-livre écu (or six-florin crown, as we shall translate it) was set at 5.8 francs. So a crown of six florins, or 5.8 francs, is roughly equivalent to an American dollar of that age, or ten dollars of this present one (1968). The next largest coin is a napoleon, worth twenty francs; and the largest coin in circulation is the louis, worth twenty-five francs. Because they are not much mentioned, I have not translated "napoleons" or "louis," although a good equivalent might be found in "eagles" and "double eagles." The whole thing can be put in tabular form, as here:

100 sous (untranslated) make
1 franc (untranslated), which makes
about 1 livre (translated *florin*); 6 florins make
1 écu (translated *crown*); about 4 crowns make
1 napoleon (untranslated); a napoleon and a crown make
1 louis (untranslated).

Except for the complicating livre, this is all neat enough, but it must be applied to the novel with some caution. The smallest sum mentioned in the book is the twenty sous Julien pays for a dinner that would normally cost fifty (I, 24). If we transpose mechanically, on the basis of a franc being worth twenty American cents, Julien will be paying four cents for a dinner that would normally cost ten. We are in the provinces, of course, and people tell us that money used to be worth much more than it is today, but four cents is a very cheap dinner. Still, things are evidently very reasonable in the provinces; Fouqué bribes his way into the seminary with ten francs, literally two American dollars (I, 26), and Julien contemptuously tosses a napoleon (literally, four dollars) to his jailer (II, 36). Champagne in jail is rather dear at six francs ($1.20) a bottle (II, 44). To get contemporary (1968) equivalents, we had better try multiplying by about ten. That would make Julien's dinner cost about forty cents instead of a dollar; it would make his starting salary with M. de Rênal (I, 5) somewhere in the neighborhood of seventy dollars a month—plus, of course, room, board, and a clothing allowance. On the other hand, when he goes to work for M. de La Mole, his starting salary is a hundred louis (II, 1), i.e., 2,500 francs (or five hundred 1830 dollars, which we guess equal five thousand 1968 dollars). He may later rise to eight thousand francs (sixteen hundred dollars of 1830 money or sixteen thousand dollars of 1968 money); this latter sum is about the income of the ordinary hanger-on in M. de La Mole's salon. But the Baron de Thaler, who is the richest man in the book, has an income of a hundred thousand crowns a month, or a little less than a million and a half dollars a year, calculated literally in 1830 dollars. If we multiplied these figures by our standard ten, we should be defying credibility, even when dealing with a Rothschild. Similarly, when they have made their settlement with M. de La Mole, Julien and Mathilde can count on an income of 36,000 florins (livres) a year; literally transposed into American money of 1830, this is about nine thousand dollars—but if, to get a contemporary equivalent, we multiplied by ten, we should come out with ninety thousand dollars, which is grotesque opulence, and throws the whole latter part of the book out of balance. So mathematical calculations do not work out very well. It is apparent that Stendhal, in this matter of money, is given to exaggerating the extremes. His rich are immensely rich, his poor are poor to the point of squalor, and the contrast between them is a theme of his art.

The major measure of distance in the *Rouge* which requires definition is the lieue, or league, which is ordinarily about two and three quarters English miles. In all these contexts it is useful to know that though the metric system was adopted in France in 1799, the old systems persisted until officially outlawed in 1837.

The Church

The church within which Julien Sorel undertakes to make his career is, of course, Roman and Catholic, but it is also French and nineteenth-century. History has thus imposed upon it certain special characteristics, which are taken for granted in the novel without explanation. Far in the background of history, their origins lost in the mists of medieval custom, are certain ill-formulated, much disputed, but very important privileges, the so-called "Gallican liberties." Their general tendency was to give the French church and the French laity special immunities from the upper hierarchy of the church, especially the pope. For example, papal bulls could not be published without prior consent of the French state. Or again, wherever the law of the land was alleged to be broken, secular courts took cognizance and control of ecclesiastical affairs. This is why there is never any question of trying Julien in an ecclesiastical court. Further, Julien is never worried about the inquisition, and though he is an ecclesiastic of sorts, he makes no scruple of reading books, like those of Voltaire, which were on the *Index Librorum Prohibitorum*. The Gallican liberties protect Frenchmen against the inquisition, and deny any standing to the *Index*. Against the extremes of papal authority, as exercised in Spain or pre-reformation Germany, the French bishops, kings, and nobility have always asserted their special French freedoms. Indeed, there was a time when Louis XIV, while carrying out what amounted to a holy war against the Huguenots (after the revocation of the edict of Nantes, in 1685), was simultaneously invading the papal enclave at Avignon because Innocent XI had presumed to veto some of the king's privileged nominations to bishoprics. The long history of struggle over these special national liberties, and in opposition to the papal theories of ultramontanism (i.e., beyond-the-mountainism, the creed of absolute papal supremacy), perhaps helps to explain the instinctive hostility to Rome so apparent in the political discussions (II, 23) that even the Marquis de La Mole gives voice to it.

The obverse of limited papal power in the French church is strong secular influence. This was a matter of both formal administrative policy and of pervasive informal control. As a matter of policy, all administrations, whether revolutionary or reactionary, sought during the nineteenth century to make the priesthood an arm of secular government. Falcoz the old Bonapartist recalls with nostalgia Napoleon's success in this direction (II, 1), and the cardinal urges his fellow reactionaries to be less recalcitrant about restoring their independent incomes to the clergy (II, 23), on the persuasive grounds that they cannot do good service against the state while dependent on it for their pay. More significant even than these indications of high policy is the immediate power of M. de La Mole to dispose of good benefices to M. Pirard and of bishoprics to his nephew, as well as the power of the maréchale de Fervaques to assign good ecclesiastical offices as she will. Julien's fate in the church is determined not by churchmen but by laymen, and laywomen, of influence. He looks not to Rome for promotion, but to Paris, to the Faubourg Saint-Germain.

During the eighteenth century, the church had offered a convenient haven for younger sons of well-to-do families, who, sheltering under the equivocal title of *abbé*, found it feasible to serve Christ without altogether, and in every respect, permanently abandoning Mammon. A church on such easy terms with the *ancien régime* was inevitably involved in its downfall. The Revolution, though not overtly anticlerical in its early stages, became more so as it gained momentum. Priests were persecuted, deprived, and guillotined, church properties pillaged, church structures mutilated, church services forbidden. It was not till Napoleon, in his later, imperial phase, decided that a church might be useful to sanction his legitimacy and adorn his court that, through the Concordat of 1801, the Church of France was re-established as the national church.

But what sort of church was the restored church of France to be, especially under the Bourbons, who were no less eager than Napoleon to keep control of it, but far more deeply indebted to the reactionaries, both lay and clerical, on whom their position depended? The church of Julien Sorel is represented as torn between two competing tendencies or factions—the Jesuits, supple, subtle, insinuating agents of international reaction, and the austere, conscience-ridden Jansenists. The influence of both groups is exaggerated, in Stendhal's portrayal, and their opposing characteristics are overstated; but the Jesuits had, in the factual world of 1815–30, more historical reality than the Jansenists. Technically speaking, the Society of Jesus had been banished from France in 1764 and suppressed by Clement XIV in 1773; but Jesuits continued to function, though in secret and under different names, until in 1814, Pius, newly liberated from harsh, humiliating bondage to Napoleon and determined to fortify himself against all liberalism, restored their constitution. Under the Bourbons, they were allowed some free-doms, were active in organizing "congregations," perhaps under-took the sort of espionage attributed in the novel to M. Castanède, but pretty surely exercised only in very rare instances the sort of despotic power attributed by the book to M. de Frilair. They were bitterly hated by the populace and so great a political liability, even for a reactionary government, that an insensitive bigot like Charles X was forced to deny them the right to teach. Yet they did exist up to 1830, and in significant numbers, did wield influence, and were powerful in the general ways, though not perhaps to the degree, that the book indicates.

Quite otherwise with the Jansenists, as Mme. Marill Albérès points out (see Bibliography). The great period of their society had been the middle of the seventeenth century, when their great seminary at Port-Royal and the extraordinary genius of their convert Pascal brought them widespread recognition. They were, in those days, very much men of the iron stamp of Abbé Pirard in the novel, men whose devotion to the direct intuitions of the individual conscience seemed to bring them close to Protestantism. But persecution at the hands of the aging Louis XIV drove many of the ablest Jan-senists from the land, the bull *Unigenitus* (1713) declared a hun-dred and one of their propositions heretical, and by the third decade of the eighteenth century, Jansenism was in general decay and disrepair. In its decadence, the movement was afflicted with messianic delusions and visionary pretensions. Jansenists performed public "miracles," threw themselves into inspired fits or "con-vulsions", and cultivated persecution and derision after the tradi-tional manner of vulgar fanatics. No doubt Jansenist habits of feeling and thought persisted into the nineteenth century; M. Pirard is not an actual anachronism; but as a vital idea, Jansenism was pretty well spent. M. Léon Séché, the gossippy, diffuse historian of the last Jansenists (Paris, 1891, three volumes) describes scattered bands of Illuminists and a few remnants of great houses with Jan-senist traditions; but a figure like M. Pirard and an ambience like that into which he brings Julien are evidently more of the seven-teenth than the nineteenth century.

In fact, by a curious reversal much too complicated for Stendhal to have recorded in his novel, the newest and most vigorous move-ment to redeem the French church from its subservience to political bondage was being prepared in 1830 by the ultramontane Abbé de Lamennais. His version of popular Catholicism, promulgated in the newspaper *L'Avenir* (The Future), proclaimed the independence of the church from all secular authorities whatever; it led him ultimately into heresy, out of the church, and into an alliance with Blanqui's socialists, whose help Lamennais hoped to enlist in building a Heavenly City on earth, a Catholic communist utopia without any secular powers at all. But this takes us far beyond *Le Rouge et le Noir*. For the understanding of that novel it is enough to note that the two semi-secret, semi-conspiratorial religious orders portrayed as in bitter rivalry within the church had deep roots in history, less deep roots in contemporary reality, and served Stendhal chiefly to darken still further the "black" half of his canvas.

Politics

All nineteenth-century European politics is dominated by the immense, enigmatic figure of Napoleon. His importance to Stendhal's novel needs no emphasizing. All his admirers within the book recognize the need to defend him; all his enemies are capable of seeing something in him to admire. What to accept and what to reject of the Napoleonic heritage was particularly the problem of the restored Bourbons. They could not undo the massive economic changes wrought under Napoleon, could not wipe from the books the *Code Napoléon* (i.e., unified statute of laws), could not abolish the Legion of Honor, could not undo the Bank of France, liquidate the Napoleonic aristocracy (Proust's Duchesse de Guermantes is still sniffing about one of the breed, the Duc d'Iena, that his family was "named after a bridge"), or restore the church to anything like its old powers. In order to be asked back at all, Louis XVIII had to grant the nation a *Charte* or written constitution guaranteeing various economic and political rights. The Bourbons were thus committed, however insincerely (and on the part of Charles X with active, open loathing) to a constitutional monarchy of sorts. What they then tried to create around these original compromises was a regime centering like the old regime on court and church, drawing support from the now somewhat homogenized aristocracy, supported internally by hangers-on and careerists, and really dependent for its continuing existence on foreign intervention or the threat of it. The degeneracy of this regime is Stendhal's constant theme. If Paris salons are deserts of boredom in 1830, it is because nobody dares to say an original word there; whereas, fifty years before, the intellectual life of all Europe flowed through them, because genuine aristocrats are afraid of no idea, however audacious. If the marquis de La Mole invites baron de Valenod to dinner, instead of having a lackey show him the door, it is because his sort is now necessary to govern France. If the reactionaries, gathered to draft a secret note (II, 22, 23), can think of nothing to propose but more foreign intervention, more support from Rome, and more ferocious repression of internal dissent, it is because the regime as a whole is bankrupt.

Among the political institutions inherited by the reactionary regime from its revolutionary predecessor, that requiring most explanation is probably the system of prefects and subprefects. These were men, appointed by the central government and relatively well paid, broadly responsible within their districts for the execution of government policy, and for representing the needs of their districts to the central government. They had considerable power over the local legislative bodies (*conseils généraux*), as well as over local officials such as mayors, municipal councils, and policemen. On the other hand, the institution of a parliament with two chambers (peers and deputies) was an innovation of Louis XVIII, copied by him from the English Lords and Commons, which he had learned to admire during the hard years of emigration. Government by "Charte" and "Two Chambers" always strikes Stendhal's characters as a bit of a novelty.

Ultras (reactionaries) and liberals are the two terms of Stendhal's political world as Jesuits and Jansenists are the terms of his religious world; but because his perspective on nineteenth-century politics was so remote (it's doubtful whether he believed in "politics" at all, in any sense distinct from "character"), the differences between liberal and ultra are not very great. Liberals become ultras without inordinate difficulty; ultras become liberals by arrangement. It is a war of words, nothing more. Politics in depth, on the other hand, revolutionary politics, is always lurking behind the smokescreen of verbal politics. The assurance of a revolution to come is a fixed element in the world of the *Rouge*; everyone counts on it, and calculates character in terms of it. This may be an *idée fixe* of Stendhal's or simply a natural conclusion drawn from watching Bourbons try to govern.

The Law

About Julien's encounter with the law in the latter part of the *Rouge*, all the reader need know is that it is technically accurate. Julien is charged with murder though he has not in fact killed Mme. de Rênal; the *Code Napoléon* of 1811 made no difference between a crime accomplished and a crime unsuccessful for reasons outside the criminal's control. As in all Continental countries, Julien's crime is subject to secret pre-trial investigation, and he undergoes preliminary questioning without benefit of counsel; the chief agent in these investigations is a *juge d'instruction*, who combines, in a way Anglo-Saxons would find odd, the functions of policeman (defender of the public order) and judge (arbiter of the accused's guilt or innocence). The case is presented by a *procureur général*, who is close enough to an American district attorney, though he is not simply a local official but represents the national administration as well. The assize court before which Julien is tried sits routinely every three months in the capital of every department; it handles only serious cases (*crimes*, as distinguished from *délits* and *contraventions*) and is the only French court routinely using the jury system. A panel of thirty-six is convoked, twelve are chosen, and a simple majority suffices for decision.

ROBERT M. ADAMS

Stendhal's Use of Names

Unless, like Henry James, a novelist systematically loads the names of his characters with pointed characteristics, it is apt to be a pretty sterile game to shuffle the fractured syllables in search of occult allusions. But Stendhal, in the *Rouge* as in the *Chartreuse*, was writing about two collapsed and almost identified eras; one way to bring them together was to use names familiar from the earlier period in contexts supplied by the later one. In addition, Stendhal was not always above the temptation to build a character's name out of words descriptive of his character—distorting them a little, in the process, of course, to avoid the effect of a placard. The following partial and provisional list of names in the *Rouge* is intended merely to suggest some of his ingenuities in the evocation of overtones:

Julien may be derived either from Julie, the heroine of *La Nouvelle Héloïse* or from Julian the Apostate, a late Roman emperor who fought fiercely against Christianity.

Sorel may be derived either from Agnes Sorel, the mistress of Charles VII (1422–1450), or from Charles Sorel, author of the *Histoire comique de Francion* (1623).

Louise de Rênal may owe her first name to Louise de Warens, Rousseau's beloved "maman;" her last name carries overtones of kidneys and foxes.

Mathilde de La Mole no doubt gets her first name from Matilda Viscontini Dembowska of Milan, with whom Beyle was woefully in love during the late 'teens and early 'twenties; she may also draw an overtone from Matilda of Tuscany, twelfth-century Italian countess and a redoubtable lady of action.

M. de la Vernaye, Julien's acquired title, may derive from Richard Varney, villain of Scott's *Kenilworth*, a blackhearted seducer of the heiress Amy Robsart; or, perhaps better, from Jacques La Verne,

Sieur d'Athée and Mayor of Dijon, beheaded October 29, 1594, in consequence of a plot to surrender the city to Henri Quatre; some curious tales are told of his head, like Julien Sorel's, taking a separate path to the grave.

Abbé de Frilair surely gets his name from *frileux*, meaning, essentially, "cold," but with a slang sense of "cowardly," plus, perhaps, an extra fillip of connotation from *fripon*, rascal, thief.

Verrières implies a town under glass, or perhaps with many panes of glass, the inhabitants of which should be careful about throwing stones.

Abbé Castanède sounds Spanish and inquisitional; there were several Spanish writers of memoirs named Castaneda in the sixteenth century.

The Duc de Chaulnes bears a title famous in the seventeenth century which gradually dwindled during the eighteenth and was extinct at the time of Stendhal's writing.

Mlle. Fourmont, Mathilde's rival at the ball, bears a name reminiscent of Hélène Fourment, wife of Peter Paul Rubens.

The Duc de Retz takes his name from the Cardinal de Retz (1614–1679), whose vigorous and sharply characterized *Mémoires* formed some of Stendhal's favorite reading; as a reluctant churchman, whose real talent was for politics and warfare, he provides a reverberation for Julien.

Mme. la Maréchale de Fervaques is evidently the widow of the Maréchal de Fervaques, who distinguished himself in the Wars of the League and died in 1613.

The Baron de la Joumate, Mme. de la Mole's candidate for her daughter's hand, gets his name from a property near Grenoble once owned by Cherubin Beyle, which Stendhal once thought of adding to his own fake title for extra gentility—"Baron Stendhal de la Jomate."

Noiroud and Moirod, from words meaning "swarthy" and "mottled," contaminate one another with a sense of vague, black baseness.

Falcoz*, Gros*, Chazel, Sainclair, Derville, Rubempré*, Geronimo, Thaler, and Chélan* all involve direct or indirect biographical references to Stendhal's acquaintance; see the appropriate footnotes, and, for the names marked with asterisks, Martineau's *Petit Dictionnaire Stendhalien.*

[The Trial of Antoine Berthet] †

Criminal Proceedings

SESSION OF THE CRIMINAL COURT OF ISÈRE (GRENOBLE)
(SPECIAL REPORT)
PROSECUTION OF MURDER COMMITTED BY A SEMINARIAN IN
A CHURCH.

It was on December 15th that the arguments in this extraordinary case began. The lengthy preparation necessarily entailed in giving a complete account of these arguments as it will appear in the *Gazette des Tribunaux* will explain and justify a delay of several days. The depositions of witnesses, the replies of the accused, his explanations of the motives of his crime, of the passions by which his soul was consumed, will offer to the speculations of the moralist a multitude of very interesting details, which are still unknown and which we ought not to sacrifice to unwarranted haste.

Never had the entrances to the Criminal Court been beset by a greater multitude. They jammed the doors of the chamber, access to which was allowed only to people provided with tickets. Love and jealousy were to be discussed there, and the most splendid of ladies had hastened to be present.

The accused is presented and immediately all eyes turn on him with eager curiosity.

There appears a young man of less than average height, slender, and of delicate complexion; a white handkerchief tied beneath his chin and knotted above his head recalls the shot which was intended to take his life, and which had the cruel effect of leaving two bullets,

† From *La Gazette des Tribunaux,* December 28 and 31, 1827, and February 29, 1828. When Stendhal experienced the "idea of Julien" during the night of October 25–26, 1829, and set about writing a first draft of *Le Rouge et le Noir,* he had before him two models for a provincial crime of passion. In the little village of Bagnéres in the Pyrenees, a woodworker named Lafargue had recently murdered his mistress and had been condemned (21 March, 1829) to five years in jail. Stendhal was much interested in this story and drew upon it for an essay, inserted bodily in the *Promenades dans Rome,* then just going to the printer, the point of which was that vital passion was still to be found in France. M. Claude Liprandi has written an extended account of this crime and trial, as they worked on Stendhal's imagination; and there seems no doubt that he was most taken by the criminal's capacity for heroic energy. But there are also striking parallels between the *Rouge* and another crime of passion which took place just a year or two before in Stendhal's native town. Antoine Berthet, a seminarian from the little town of Brangues near Grenoble, was perhaps a less colorful character than Lafargue, but the pattern of his career, the nature of his crime, and his final fate come very close to Julien Sorel's. Stendhal read about the matter in the recently founded *Gazette des Tribunaux,* a journal reporting notable trials at law from all corners of France; we excerpt from the *Gazette's* somewhat puffy journalese the narrative of Antoine Berthet's trial.

only one of which could be extracted, between the lower jawbone and the neck. Yet his dress and hair are meticulous; his face is expressive; his pallor contrasts with the great dark eyes which bear the marks of fatigue and sickness. He lets them wander over the business going forward around him; some bewilderment is apparent in his gaze.

During the reading of the charges and the presentation of the case by the District Attorney, M. Guernon-Ranville, Berthet remains immobile. The following facts are learned:

Antoine Berthet, present age twenty-five, was born of poor but honest artisans; his father is a blacksmith in the village of Brangues. A delicate constitution hardly fit for physical toil, an intelligence superior to his position, a precociously evident taste for higher studies attracted the favorable interest of several persons; their benevolence, more enthusiastic than enlightened, proposed to remove young Berthet from the modest condition in which the accident of birth had placed him and make him a member of the clergy. The pastor of Brangues adopted him as a favorite child, taught him his first lessons, and thanks to his kindness, Berthet entered the junior seminary at Grenoble in 1818. In 1822 a serious illness forced him to discontinue his studies. He was taken in by the pastor, whose solicitude successfully made up for the poverty of his parents. At the urgent solicitation of this sponsor, he was taken into the home of M. M⸺, who entrusted to him the education of his children; thus grim fate paved the way for him to become the scourge of that family. Did Mme. M⸺, a pleasant and intelligent woman, then aged thirty-six and of an impeccable reputation, think that she could without risk lavish tokens of kindness on a young man of twenty whose delicate health required special attentions? Did a precocious depravity in Berthet cause him to mistake the nature of these attentions? Whatever the case, before the year was out M. M⸺ had to think of terminating the stay of the young seminarian in his house.

Berthet entered the junior seminary at Belley to continue his studies there. He remained there two years, and returned to Brangues to spend the holiday of 1825.

He was unable to return to that institution. He then managed to be admitted to the advanced seminary in Grenoble; but after remaining there a month, having been judged by his superiors unworthy of the office to which he aspired, he was dismissed without hope of returning. His father, angered, banished him from his presence. In the end he could find shelter only with his married sister in Brangues.

Were these rejections the consequence of the discovery of weak principles and serious faults in his conduct? Did Berthet consider himself the victim of a secret persecution by M. M____, whom he had offended? Some letters which he wrote at that time to Mme. M____ contain virulent reproaches and calumnies. In spite of that, M. M____ made some efforts on behalf of the former tutor of his children.

Berthet succeeded in placing himself as a tutor again with M. de C____. He had then given up the church; but after a year M. de C____ dismissed him for reasons which are not clear and which appear to involve another intrigue.

He again considered the career which had been the aim of all his efforts, the priesthood. But his appeals and the appeals that he had others make to the officials of the seminaries at Belley, Lyons, and Grenoble were futile. He was accepted nowhere. Then he was seized with despair.

While these efforts were in process, he attributed their failure to the M____ family. The pleas and reproaches which filled the letters that he continued to send to Mme. M____ became terrifying threats. Sinister remarks are found there: *I want to kill her*, he said in a fit of sullen melancholy. He wrote to the pastor at Brangues, his first benefactor's successor: *When I appear beneath the steeple of the parish church, they will know why*. These bizarre methods produced a partial effect. M. M____ actively set about reopening the door of some seminary for him; but he failed at Grenoble; he likewise failed at Belley, where he travelled expressly with the pastor of Brangues. All he could manage was to find a place for Berthet with M. Trolliet, a notary in Morestel connected with the M____ family, by concealing the reasons for his dissatisfaction. But Berthet, in his frustrated ambition, was disgusted, according to his disdainful remark, at the thought of being forever nothing more than *a village schoolmaster with a two-hundred-franc salary*. He did not cease sending a stream of threatening letters; he declared to several persons his intention to kill Mme. M____ and then take his own life. Unfortunately, its very heinousness made the atrocious project seem improbable; yet it was on the point of fulfillment!

It was during the month of June just past that Berthet entered the Trolliet household. About July 15 he goes to Lyons to purchase some pistols; from there he writes to Mme. M____ a letter full of new threats; it concludes with these words: *Your triumph will be like Haman's, short-lived*. Back in Morestel, he practices with the pistols; one of his two weapons is misfiring; after considering having it repaired, he replaces it with another pistol, which he takes from the room of M. Trolliet, who is away at the time.

On Sunday, July 22, very early in the morning, Berthet loads his two pistols with a double charge, puts them beneath his coat, and leaves for Brangues. He arrives at the home of his sister, who makes him eat a light meal. At the hour for the parish mass, he goes to the church and places himself about three paces from Mme. M_____'s pew. He soon sees her arrive accompanied by her two children, one of whom had been his pupil. There he waits, unmoving . . . until the moment when the priest is distributing communion. "Neither the countenance of his benefactress," said the District Attorney, "nor the sanctity of the place, nor the celebration of the most sublime mystery of a religion to whose service Berthet was to have dedicated himself, nothing can move that soul devoted to the demon of destruction. His eye fixed on his victim, a stranger to the religious feeling being expressed all around him, he awaits with diabolic patience the moment when the elevation of the host will give him the chance to fire two safe shots. This moment arrives, and when all hearts rise up to God present on the altar, when Mme. M_____, bowed low, is perhaps mingling with her fervent prayers the name of the ingrate who had made himself her cruelest enemy, two shots in rapid succession ring out. The horrified congregation see Berthet and Mme. M_____ fall almost simultaneously; the latter's first impulse, anticipating a further crime, is to protect her two terrified children with her own body. The mingled blood of the murderer and of his victim gush as far as the sanctuary steps."

"Such," continues the District Attorney, "is the crime that leads Berthet into these precincts. We could have foregone calling witnesses, gentlemen of the jury, and built our case upon facts which have been admitted by the accused himself; but we have acted in deference to that philanthropic maxim that a man cannot be condemned on the strength of his own admissions alone. Your task, like ours, will be confined to the primary matter of confirming the admissions of the accused through these testimonies.

"But another matter of high importance will arouse all our solicitude, will invite your consideration. A crime so atrocious as this would only be the result of a dreadful madness, if it had not been explained by one of those violent passions whose fatal power you have daily had opportunity to study. We ought therefore to consider in what moral perspective it was conceived and executed; if in the actions which preceded and prepared for the crime, if, in the very act, the accused did not perhaps cease to enjoy the full use of his reason, as much, at least, as can exist in a man disturbed by a violent passion.

"An adulterous love affair, the scorn growing out of it, the conviction that Mme. M_____ was by no means unconnected with his humiliations and the obstacles excluding him from the career to which he had dared to aspire, and a thirst for vengeance—such were, in the pattern of indictment, the causes of this fierce hatred, this frantic despair, resulting in murder, sacrilege, suicide.

"The quite extraordinary horror of the crime would suffice to capture your attention; but your concern, gentlemen of the jury, will be more strongly exercised by the need not to pronounce a sentence of death except insofar as you have become overwhelmingly convinced that the act was voluntary, and the result of lengthy premeditation."

The court next hears the witnesses.

Four persons are summoned to verify the material circumstances, so to speak, of the event of July 22; three of them state that Berthet remained standing, without kneeling, during the whole mass up to the communion; his bearing and the expression on his face were calm; suddenly he was seen drawing a pistol from under his clothing and firing it at Mme. M_____.

M. Morin, surgeon and deputy-mayor of Brangues, rushed down from the gallery at the sound of the explosion, and immediately another report was heard. In the midst of the terrible confusion which reigned in the church, he saw only Berthet, his face horribly stained by the blood which gushed from his wound and ran from his mouth. He hastened to lead him away and apply an emergency dressing; but soon he was sought to return to attend a second victim; it was Mme. M_____, mortally wounded; she had been taken home, unconscious and completely paralyzed. Revived with the greatest difficulty, she was very reluctant to consent to the extraction of the bullet; but after that painful operation, the surgeon noticed that there remained a second bullet which had penetrated the epigastrium and which also had to be removed.

Berthet identifies the pistols shown him. With a total absence of emotion he indicates the larger as the one he used against Mme. M_____.

His Honor, the judge: What motive can have driven you to to this crime?

Berthet: Two passions which have tormented me for four years, love and jealousy.

The District Attorney concentrates, in making the case for premeditation, on fixing the period of the crime's conception: "Accused," he says, "I warn you that your answers to the questionings you have undergone up to the present are not recognized; you could have been mistaken, or wanted to be mistaken; it does not matter: your defense has remained uncommitted; therefore I ask you when you conceived the plan of killing Mme. M_____?"

Berthet, after hesitating, traces his decision back to the trip that he made to Lyons to purchase the pistols; "But," he adds, "up until the last moment I was not sure that I would do it; I wavered constantly between the idea of killing myself alone and that of including Mme. M_____ in my destruction." He acknowledges that he had loaded the pistols in Morestel just before leaving for Brangues.

District Attorney: What thoughts, what moral considerations passed through your mind during the trip from Morestel to Brangues; and up to the moment when you fired on Mme. M——? Prisoner, we do not want to trick you; I am going to tell you the purpose of the question that I ask you: might you not have been somewhat deranged during the period of time I have mentioned?

Berthet: I was so beside myself that I could scarcely recognize a route which I had taken many times; I nearly missed finding a bridge along the way, my vision was so confused! As I stood behind Mme. M——'s pew, so close to her, my thoughts were wild and full of incoherencies; I did not know where I was; I confused the past and the present; my very existence seemed an illusion to me; at certain moments I thought of nothing but suicide; but finally, I saw in my imagination Mme. M—— giving herself to another; then I was seized by a jealous rage, I was no longer in control of myself and I aimed my pistol at Mme. M——; but until then I had been so indisposed to act on my fatal resolution that, when I saw Mme. M—— enter the church with another lady and whisper to her after having noticed me, as if she were thinking of withdrawing, I felt quite clearly that if she had taken this course, I would have turned the two pistols on myself alone, if necessary; but her evil destiny and mine determined that she should remain. . . .

District Attorney: Did you feel remorse for what you had done?

Berthet: My first thought was to demand urgent news of Mme. M——'s condition. I would gladly have given what remained of my life to be certain that she was not mortally wounded.

M. Morin states that in fact Berthet manifested some regret for his action; nevertheless, he enjoyed full use of his reason and remained quite calm.

Criminal Court of Isère (Grenoble)

(SPECIAL REPORT)

PROSECUTION OF MURDER COMMITTED BY A SEMINARIAN IN A CHURCH.

(CONCLUSION)

Mme. Marigny, friend of Mme. M—— since childhood, had come to the church with her on the fatal day. She fainted at the moment of the explosion; recovering consciousness, her first impulse was to run to the aid of Mme. M——; she found her completely

426 • *The Trial of Antoine Berthet*

paralyzed; when she undressed her, the blood spurted from the wound with such force that she was completely covered by it.

"A month before," said Mme. Marigny, "I received a letter from M. Berthet; knowing that I took an interest in him as I did in many others, he begged me to do something on his behalf. He complained of *the fatality which was intent on pursuing him,* and ended with vague remarks through which he seemed to warn of a homicide and a suicide. I had the occasion to tell Mme. M⎯⎯ of this letter; she told me that she was all too sure that it was she that M. Berthet meant. Mme. M⎯⎯ told me of the threats to which she had been long subjected by that young man."

"Four or five days afterwards, M. Berthet came to my home and told me that he was going to Lyons; I asked him if he had hopes of finding a job in that city. 'No', he replied, 'I am going there to buy some pistols to kill Mme. M⎯⎯ and kill myself after. I had intended to kill her last Sunday, on Corpus Christi day, with a piece of iron that I had sharpened; but now I am determined.' This horrifying admission upset me terribly. —What, do you mean to kill her, I cried out! —Yes, he said, she has done me nothing but harm. —But, M. Berthet, instead of committing two tragic wrongs, as you seem to have decided to do, you ought at least to commit only one and kill yourself alone."

District Attorney: The advice was bad.

Mme. Marigny: I was in such a state of confusion, sir, that I was visibly exhausted by it; for M. Berthet, in leaving me, apologized for having come to tell me such a thing; he asked me not to mention it to Mme. M⎯⎯; but I hastened to inform her of it.

Berthet confirms all these facts and adds that if he did not carry out the plan he had conceived on Corpus Christi day, it was because he had meanwhile learned that they were doing something for him.

District Attorney, in a forceful tone: That explanation is an overwhelming indictment against you. Thus it was a position that was the object of all your threats; it was a position that you were demanding with pistol and dagger! You consented to let Mme. M⎯⎯ live after Corpus Christi only because you had been given hopes that they would find a job for you! That is cowardly, cruel behavior.

The hearing of the witnesses concluded, the session is recessed, to be resumed with the pleas of counsel.

The District Attorney speaks in support of the charge. The material fact is admitted; as for the free and considered will which directed the crime, the speaker bases it on Berthet's calm, unruffled patience in the church at Brangues. The premeditation seems to him obvious from the threats made in advance, the confidences imparted to Mme. Marigny by the accused, the preparations for the murder. As for Berthet's excuses, he refutes them one after another. "Before ordinary judges," says this officer of the court, "we would successfully maintain that one can not accept any extenuations except those recognized as such by the law; before you, gentlemen of the jury, we must use another kind of language. You need account only to God for the influences on your decision; you will have to decide if the accused is guilty, and this word applies to the morality as much as to the material fact; we have therefore had to resist everything that might qualify the morality of the act in your eyes."

The defense's turn having arrived, Berthet rises and reads a long account written in an elegant, natural style, in which, going into minute details and excusing himself for portraying Mme. M——— as the corrupter of his youth on the grounds of his dangerous situation, he tells how through a series of caresses and insinuations she apparently lost her own innocence and guided all too skilfully his long-blind, ignorant simplicity toward a goal which he should have foreseen. This account, painful to those who had taken an interest in Berthet, and read coldly, gave proof that if it was necessary to admit the jealousy of love as one of the inciting motives of the crime, a second, no less powerful motive existed in the soul of the accused, the frustrated pride of ambition and egotism. This young man, endowed by nature with physical advantages and an excellent mind, made too much of by those around him, misled by his very successes, had in imagination created for himself a brilliant future all the more glorious in that it would not be based on his own talents. The son of the Brangues blacksmith saw in the distance a horizon which was perhaps limitless. Then, suddenly, one and the same cause betrays and annihilates his hopes; everything goes wrong at once; humiliating rebuffs everywhere replace benevolence and favors. Then, weary of life, despair makes him resolve to end it and impels him at the same time to include in his destruction the woman who was the first to launch him on his fatal course. Such a story could not help but inspire general interest.

"What a picture we have before us," said M. Massonnet, his defender: "in Berthet's heart was innocence; he outstripped his rivals through his talents; from the bosom of the school a great citizen might perhaps have risen; and now you see him as good as destroyed before you. . . . He seems lost to society."

"Perhaps if I could have obeyed his wishes, I would not have come to defend him at all. Life is not at all what he desires; what does life without honor mean to him? Life . . . he has half lost it; a fatal bullet is there, awaiting his last sigh. Berthet himself condemned himself to death. . . . Your condemnation would only aid his futile efforts to destroy an unbearable life. But no, Berthet, I must defend you; your wish to die serves as proof in the eyes of men that you still deserve to live; in the eyes of heaven that you are not ready to die."

"This case, gentlemen of the jury, is of a kind rare in the annals of the Criminal Courts; it is not by means of the cold words of the law, *all who are guilty of murder shall be punished by death*, that one ought to evaluate an action which can have no judges except conscience, humanity, a heart which feels. I intend to prove that love caused the death; that love is often a madness, that the will of the accused was not his own when he became simultaneously a suicide and a homicide."

"Of course, it will be necessary to reveal details which will make my task painful, as they will make yours painful, gentlemen of the jury; but it is quite necessary to show you how the storm gathered, the tempest which dragged this luckless young man into the abyss. Why should we not portray for the judges, as a true defense requires, the spectacle of love, when every day unnecessary and even incestuous loves fill our tragic dramas with horror for the vain pleasure of audiences? Will what is permitted in order to arouse the frivolous curiosity of men be forbidden when it is intended to save them from the scaffold?"

The able defender portrays Berthet at the mercy of his fatal passion; he describes all the periods up to the moment when, a prey to the delirium of jealousy, he goes to seek out and slay his victim even in the temple of that God which she herself had chosen as judge and witness when she swore before his image never to be forsworn.

M. Massonnet then maintains the proposition that the murder was committed without real intent: "There are two kinds of madness," he says, "the madness of those whose faculties are forever impaired, the madness of those whose faculties are only momentarily overshadowed by a great passion. These madnesses differ only in duration. The lawmaker cannot impose any penal responsibility on men who are afflicted by one or the other; like blind men without guides on an unknown road, the misfortunes that they cause are *accidents*, and never *crimes*. . . . The luckless Berthet is a distressing example of those overwhelming aberrations of love. Ah, gentlemen of the jury, if at this moment I should question those members of the tender sex who have entered these precincts to lament the misfortunes of the passion which they know so well how to inspire; if I appealed to their emotions, they would join their voice with ours to recommend to you the doctrines that love justifies, that human law could not condemn."

After M. Massonnet's speech and the judge's summary, the jurors begin their deliberations. Some time later, they reappear, and from the grave expressions which can be seen on their faces, the terrible sentence of death is foreseen. Berthet is declared guilty of wilful murder with premeditation. The accused is presented and the Court pronounces the fatal decision, which he hears without the slightest show of emotion.

The day after next, Berthet has the presiding judge of the criminal court come to his place of imprisonment and makes some important revelations. There, he puts in his hand a written declaration in which he expresses his regret for the scheme of defamation into which the exigencies of his defense drew him during the trial. He declares that the jealousy which consumed him had made him think that Mme. M_____ had been at fault; he concludes by begging *pardon for a young man who was misled by a passion and by emotions which she had never shared. It is*, he adds, *without hope of leniency that I speak.*

Actually, he had as yet made no appeal against his sentence; but since that time he has appealed for a reversal of the decision and sent a request for pardon to the king. "He asks to live," he says, "only in order not to dishonor a humble but honest family by dying on the scaffold."

[Execution of the Seminarian Berthet]

It was at 11 a.m. on February 23 that Berthet suffered his punishment in the Place d'Armes in Grenoble. An immense throng, composed chiefly of women of all ages, crowded the street through which he was to pass. The sympathy which his infamous defense had alienated revived at that supreme moment; one could see in this unfortunate young man, who had escaped the death of despair only to achieve death at the scaffold, neither an ordinary murderer nor a villain; it was rather a victim of his passions, dragged to his ruin by a fatal conjunction of circumstances, who evoked wonder and pity rather than terror. The space of time which had elapsed since his condemnation had given rise to a general belief that his petition for pardon would be followed by a commutation of the sentence; and that clemency, sought by the District Attorney, would have satisfied the public's expectations. M. Appert, member of the society for the improvement of prisons, visiting, some time ago, the prison in Grenoble, saw Berthet, and promised to take up his cause. On his return to Paris, he made some efforts which remained fruitless; he finally wrote him a letter which, as far as anyone knows, must have left him little hope. Thus, the evening before, Berthet said to one of those prison women who constantly turned up at his side: *I have a premonition that tomorrow will be my last day!* The answer could only be silence; it was known that his peti-

tion for pardon had just been rejected. All the consolations of religion were lavished on him; he had asked for them, and received
them calmly; the exhortations of the priest at one moment brought
tears to his eyes.

He was seen leaving the prison, attended by two priests, one of
whom supported him with one hand and with the other held out a
crucifix to him. Extremely emaciated, pale, his beard long, and his
face wan, he bent over the crucifix and appeared to recite prayers
in an undertone, but with a movement of the lips so rapid that one
might have attributed it to the convulsive agitation of delirium as
much as to fervor. Thus he reached the foot of the scaffold. There,
however, he seemed to regard the terrible apparatus without fear.
He turned back toward the two priests who had rendered him a sad
last duty, and embraced them; then, recovering his steadfastness,
he climbed up alone; the executioner had preceded him. On the
scaffold, he genuflected and seemed to collect himself and pray. A
moment later he rose and assumed the position himself. . . . A kind
of involuntary cry, wrung from the emotion of the throng, announced that all was finished.

"BLAISE DURAND": The Geology of Morals†

Paris, July 28, 1822

*Concerning granite and deposits of calcium or of vegetable detritus:
an essay in Moral Geology,* by Blaise Durand.

Here are some granite rocks. Vegetable detritus has filled in the
shaded areas, 2,2.

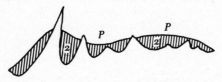

The area P,P looks like a level plain to unskilled eyes.

One must know how to distinguish granite from fill.

Granite is the natural character of a man, his habitual way of
seeking happiness. Character is like the features, one starts to
notice it at the age of two or three, it's perfectly apparent at sixteen
or seventeen, it manifests its full force at twenty-six or thirty.

The fill, 2,2, is what politeness, the way of the world, and prudence do to a character.

† This little joke essay-letter, written
by Stendhal under one of his innumerable pseudonyms long before any of
the fiction, presents a notion about
human character which, if applied to
Julien Sorel, would yield some interesting conclusions.

A young man mistakes the space P,P for a plain. He does not see that, as soon as the man must do something he considers important, he will follow the contour of the *granite* in his character. Thus, on important occasions, space P,P is very far from being a plain.

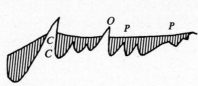

A second use to be made of this cross-section of a mountain is to help us judge of our own character.

For good or for evil, our character is like our body, that we recognize at the age of sixteen, when we start to reflect on things. *Handsome, ugly,* or *mediocre,* you must take it as it comes; only the wise man knows how to make the best of it.

Once we know what our character is, we can prepare ourselves *for the good and* the evil which are predicted in books describing such characters. For example:

Violent character,

Phlegmatic,

Tender and melancholy, like J.-J. Rousseau.

A young man of sixteen, judging his own character by his actions, might fall into the error of supposing space P,P to be a plain, and thus fail to recognize that there's a precipice at C,C.

Cassio, for example, getting drunk in the tragedy they're giving tomorrow at the theatre of Porte-Saint-Martin, fails to look ahead and see that there's a precipice in his own character at C,C.

The lithograph in the *Mirror,* today, the 28th, shows the granitic character of Voltaire, coming to a point as at O, abruptly rising out of his ordinary politeness and the even simpler manners of his society. Receiving a call from Lekain, instead of asking what news his visitor brings, he gives him the cue for his role. A love of lasting glory was at the root of Voltaire's character.

This, my dear sir, is your second lesson in the lore of the human heart.

I shall be much obliged to you for the return of this paper; put it in an envelope and leave it at my door on Thursday.

I have the honor of being, &c.,

Blaise Durand

STENDHAL: [Too Rough A Style]†

Fortunately, the magnificent panorama from a window of the college next to the Latin Room, which I discovered *all by myself*, and where I used to go for solitary meditations, overcame the profound disgust which rose up in me at the phrases of my father and of the priests his friends.

Thus it was that, so many years later, the numerous and pretentious phrases of MM. Chateaubriand and Salvandy[1] made me write *Le Rouge et le Noir* in too rough a style. A great stupidity, for in twenty years who will give a thought to the hypocritical jumbles produced by these gentry? As for myself, I've bought a ticket in a lottery, the grand prize of which amounts to this: being read in 1935.

† An ugly episode in the police gazette, a boyish essay on the mechanics of human personality; these are two ingredients which entered into the writing of the *Rouge*. And the style—that laconic, almost contemptuous, abruptness in the handling of gigantic chords? Stendhal associates it (in *The Life of Henry Brulard*) with a remembered landscape, as seen from the Ecole Centrale in Grenoble, and with a sense of bitter scorn for the men inhabiting it.
1. Narcisse-Achille Salvandy (1795–1856) described himself as a stylistic imitator of Chateaubriand; Stendhal's linkage of them is a deliberate denigration of Chateaubriand.

Criticism

Essays in Criticism

ERICH AUERBACH

In the Hôtel de La Mole†

Julien Sorel, the hero of Stendhal's novel *Le Rouge et le Noir* (1830), an ambitious and passionate young man, son of an uneducated petty bourgeois from the Franche-Comté, is conducted by a series of circumstances from the seminary at Besançon, where he has been studying theology, to Paris and the position of secretary to a gentleman of rank, the Marquis de La Mole, whose confidence he gains. Mathilde, the marquis's daughter, is a girl of nineteen, witty, spoiled, imaginative, and so arrogant that her own position and circle begin to bore her. The dawning of her passion for her father's *domestique* is one of Stendhal's masterpieces and has been greatly admired. One of the preparatory scenes, in which her interest in Julien begins to awaken, is the following, from Book II, chapter 4:

> Un matin que l'abbé travaillait avec Julien, dans la bibliothèque du marquis, à l'éternel procès de Frilair:
>
> —Monsieur, dit Julien tout à coup, dîner tous les jours avec madame la marquise, est-ce un de mes devoirs, ou est-ce une bonté que l'on a pour moi?
>
> —C'est un honneur insigne! reprit l'abbé, scandalisé. Jamais M. N. . . l'académicien, qui, depuis quinze ans, fait une cour assidue, n'a pu l'obtenir pour son neveu M. Tanbeau.
>
> —C'est pour moi, monsieur, la partie la plus pénible de mon emploi. Je m'ennuyais moins au séminaire. Je vois bâiller quelque-

† From *Mimesis: the Representation of Reality in Western Literature* by Erich Auerbach, translated by Willard R. Trask, pp. 454–466. Reprinted by permission of Princeton University Press, 1953.

Professor Auerbach's epochal *Mimesis* uses a series of texts selected over a period of three thousand years, studying them closely to reveal the differing conceptions of reality they represent and imply through such elements as the syntactic linking of generals and particulars, abstractions and specifics. A crucial instance of a new and apparently random realism, which wholly fractures the old idea of arbitrarily divided levels of style, is provided by the chapter on Stendhal and Balzac, from which we reproduce the first half. This is a major crux in Auerbach's book; in his terms, Stendhal and Balzac represent a turning point in the representation of reality, a turn which his book exemplifies as well as defines. His instances seem to be chosen at random; yet they illustrate fundamental principles of conflict and growth, even as Stendhal, with a girl, an abbé, and a young man in a library, suggests an entire complex of social forces in post-Napoleonic Europe.

fois jusqu'à mademoiselle de La Mole, qui pourtant doit être
accoutumée à l'amabilité des amis de la maison. J'ai peur de m'en-
dormir. De grâce, obtenez-moi la permission d'aller dîner à quar-
ante sous dans quelque auberge obscure.

L'abbé, véritable parvenu, était fort sensible à l'honneur de
dîner avec un grand seigneur. Pendant qu'il s'efforçait de faire
comprendre ce sentiment par Julien, un bruit léger leur fit tourner
la tête. Julien vit mademoiselle de La Mole qui écoutait. Il rougit.
Elle était venue chercher un livre et avait tout entendu; elle prit
quelque considération pour Julien. Celui-là n'est pas né à genoux,
pensa-t-elle, comme ce vieil abbé. Dieu! qu'il est laid.

A dîner, Julien n'osait pas regarder mademoiselle de La Mole,
mais elle eut la bonté de lui adresser la parole. Ce jour-là, on at-
tendait beaucoup de monde, elle l'engagea à rester. . . .

(One morning while the Abbé was with Julien in the Marquis's
library, working on the interminable Frilair suit:

"Monsieur," said Julien suddenly, "is dining with Madame la
Marquise every day one of my duties, or is it a favor to me?"

"It is an extraordinary honor!" the Abbé corrected him, scandalized. "Monsieur N., the academician, who has been paying
court here assiduously for fifteen years, was never able to manage
it for his nephew, Monsieur Tanbeau."

"For me, Monsieur, it is the most painful part of my position.
Nothing at the seminary bored me so much. I even see Mademoiselle de la Mole yawning sometimes, yet she must be well inured
to the amiabilities of the guests of this house. I am in dread of
falling asleep. Do me the favor of getting me permission to eat
a forty-sou dinner at some inn."

The Abbé, a true parvenu, was extremely conscious of the
honor of dining with a noble lord. While he was trying to in-
culcate this sentiment into Julien, a slight sound made them turn.
Julien saw Mademoiselle de la Mole listening. He blushed. She
had come for a book and had heard everything; she began to feel
a certain esteem for Julien. He was not born on his knees, like that
old Abbé, she thought. God, how ugly he is!

At dinner Julien did not dare to look at Mademoiselle de la
Mole, but she condescended to speak to him. A number of guests
were expected that day, she asked him to stay. . . .)

The scene, as I said, is designed to prepare for a passionate and extremely tragic love intrigue. Its function and its psychological value
we shall not here discuss; they lie outside of our subject. What interests us in the scene is this: it would be almost incomprehensible
without a most accurate and detailed knowledge of the political
situation, the social stratification, and the economic circumstances
of a perfectly definite historical moment, namely, that in which
France found itself just before the July Revolution; accordingly, the

novel bears the subtitle, *Chronique de 1830.* Even the boredom which reigns in the dining room and salon of this noble house is no ordinary boredom. It does not arise from the fortuitous personal dullness of the people who are brought together there; among them there are highly educated, witty, and sometimes important people, and the master of the house is intelligent and amiable. Rather, we are confronted, in their boredom, by a phenomenon politically and ideologically characteristic of the Restoration period. In the seventeenth century, and even more in the eighteenth, the corresponding salons were anything but boring. But the inadequately implemented attempt which the Bourbon regime made to restore conditions long since made obsolete by events, creates, among its adherents in the official and ruling classes, an atmosphere of pure convention, of limitation, of constraint and lack of freedom, against which the intelligence and good will of the persons involved are powerless. In these salons the things which interest everyone—the political and religious problems of the present, and consequently most of the subjects of its literature or of that of the very recent past—could not be discussed, or at best could be discussed only in official phrases so mendacious that a man of taste and tact would rather avoid them. How different from the intellectual daring of the famous eighteenth-century salons, which, to be sure, did not dream of the dangers to their own existence which they were unleashing! Now the dangers are known, and life is governed by the fear that the catastrophe of 1793 might be repeated. As these people are conscious that they no longer themselves believe in the thing they represent, and that they are bound to be defeated in any public argument, they choose to talk of nothing but the weather, music, and court gossip. In addition, they are obliged to accept as allies snobbish and corrupt people from among the newly-rich bourgeoisie, who, with the unashamed baseness of their ambition and with their fear for their ill-gotten wealth, completely vitiate the atmosphere of society. So much for the pervading boredom.

But Julien's reaction, too, and the very fact that he and the former director of his seminary, the Abbé Pirard, are present at all in the house of the Marquis de la Mole, are only to be understood in terms of the actual historical moment. Julien's passionate and imaginative nature has from his earliest youth been filled with enthusiasm for the great ideas of the Revolution and of Rousseau, for the great events of the Napoleonic period; from his earliest youth he has felt nothing but loathing and scorn for the piddling hypocrisy and the petty lying corruption of the classes in power since Napoleon's fall. He is too imaginative, too ambitious, and too fond of power, to be satisfied with a mediocre life within the bourgeoisie, such as his friend Fouqué proposes to him. Having observed that a man of petty-bourgeois origin can attain to a situation of command only through the all-powerful Church, he has consciously and deliberately become a hypocrite; and his great talents would assure him a brilliant intellectual career, were not his real personal and political feelings, the direct passionateness of his nature, prone to burst forth at decisive moments. One such moment of self-betrayal we have in the passage before us, when Julien confides his feelings in the Marquise's salon to the Abbé Pirard, his former teacher and protector; for the intellectual freedom to which it testifies is unthinkable without an admixture of intellectual arrogance and a sense of inner superiority hardly becoming in a young ecclesiastic and protégé of the house. (In this particular instance his frankness does him no harm; the Abbé Pirard is his friend, and upon Mathilde, who happens to overhear him, his words make an entirely different impression from that which he must expect and fear.) The Abbé is here described as a true parvenu, who knows how highly the honor of sitting at a great man's table should be esteemed and hence disapproves of Julien's remarks; as another motive for the Abbé's disapproval Stendhal could have cited the fact that uncritical submission to the evil of this world, in full consciousness that it is evil, is a typical attitude for strict Jansenists; and the Abbé Pirard is a Jansenist. We know from the previous part of the novel that as director of the seminary at Besançon he had had to endure much persecution and much chicanery on account of his Jansenism and his strict piety which no intrigues could touch; for the clergy of the province were under the influence of the Jesuits. When the Marquis de la Mole's most powerful opponent, the Abbé de Frilair, a vicar-general to the bishop, had brought a suit against him, the Marquis had made the Abbé Pirard his confidant and had thus learned to value his intelligence and uprightness; so that finally, to free him from his untenable position at Besançon, the Marquis had procured him a benefice in Paris and somewhat later had taken the Abbé's favorite pupil, Julien Sorel, into his household as private secretary.

The characters, attitudes, and relationships of the dramatis personae, then, are very closely connected with contemporary historical circumstances; contemporary political and social conditions are woven into the action in a manner more detailed and more real than had been exhibited in any earlier novel, and indeed in any works of literary art except those expressly purporting to be politico-satirical tracts. So logically and systematically to situate the tragically conceived life of a man of low social position (as here that of Julien Sorel) within the most concrete kind of contemporary history and to develop it therefrom—this is an entirely new and highly significant phenomenon. The other circles in which Julien Sorel moves— his father's family, the house of the mayor of Verrières, M. de Rênal, the seminary at Besançon—are sociologically defined in conformity with the historical moment with the same penetration as is the La Mole household; and not one of the minor characters—the old priest Chélan, for example, or the director of the *dépôt de mendicité* [poorhouse], Valenod—would be conceivable outside the particular historical situation of the Restoration period, in the manner in which they are set before us. The same laying of a contemporary foundation for events is to be found in Stendhal's other novels—still incomplete and too narrowly circumscribed in *Armance*, but fully developed in the later works: in the *Chartreuse de Parme* (which, however, since its setting is a place not yet greatly affected by modern development, sometimes gives the effect of being a historical novel), as also in *Lucien Leuwen*, a novel of the Louis Philippe period, which Stendhal left unfinished. In the latter, indeed, in the form in which it has come down to us, the element of current history and politics is too heavily emphasized: it is not always wholly integrated into the course of the action and is set forth in far too great detail in proportion to the principal theme; but perhaps in a final revision Stendhal would have achieved an organic articulation of the whole. Finally, his autobiographical works, despite the capricious and erratic "egotism" of their style and manner, are likewise far more closely, essentially, and concretely connected with the politics, sociology, and economics of the period than are, for example, the corresponding works of Rousseau or Goethe; one feels that the great events of contemporary history affected Stendhal much more directly than they did the other two; Rousseau did not live to see them, and Goethe had managed to keep aloof from them.

To have stated this is also to have stated what circumstance it was which, at that particular moment and in a man of that particular period, gave rise to modern tragic realism based on the contemporary; it was the first of the great movements of modern times in which large masses of men consciously took part—the French Revolution with all the consequent convulsions which spread from it over Europe. From the Reformation movement, which was no less powerful and which aroused the masses no less, it is distinguished by the much faster tempo of its spread, its mass effects, and the changes which it produced in practical daily life within a comparatively extensive territory; for the progress then achieved in transportation and communication, together with the spread of elementary education resulting from the trends of the Revolution itself, made it possible to mobilize the people far more rapidly and in a far more unified direction; everyone was reached by the same ideas and events far more quickly, more consciously, and more uniformly. For Europe there began that process of temporal concentration, both of historical events themselves and of everyone's knowledge of them, which has since made tremendous progress and which not only permits us to prophesy a unification of human life throughout the world but has in a certain sense already achieved it. Such a development abrogates or renders powerless the entire social structure of orders and categories previously held valid; the tempo of the changes demands a perpetual and extremely difficult effort toward inner adaptation and produces intense concomitant crises. He who would account to himself for his real life and his place in human society is obliged to do so upon a far wider practical foundation and in a far larger context than before, and to be continually conscious that the social base upon which he lives is not constant for a moment but is perpetually changing through convulsions of the most various kinds.

We may ask ourselves how it came about that modern consciousness of reality began to find literary form for the first time precisely in Henri Beyle of Grenoble. Beyle-Stendhal was a man of keen intelligence, quick and alive, mentally independent and courageous, but not quite a great figure. His ideas are often forceful and inspired, but they are erratic, arbitrarily advanced, and, despite all their show of boldness, lacking in inward certainty and continuity. There is something unsettled about his whole nature: his fluctuation between realistic candor in general and silly mystification in particulars, between cold self-control, rapturous abandonment to sensual pleasures, and insecure and sometimes sentimental vaingloriousness, is not always easy to put up with; his literary style is very impressive and unmistakably original, but it is short-winded, not uniformly successful, and only seldom wholly takes possession of and fixes the subject. But, such as he was, he offered himself to the moment; circumstances seized him, tossed him about, and laid upon him a unique and unexpected destiny; they formed him so that he was compelled to come to terms with reality in a way which no one had done before him.

When the Revolution broke out Stendhal was a boy of six; when he left his native city of Grenoble and his reactionary, solidly bourgeois family, who though glumly sulking at the new situation were still very wealthy, and went to Paris, he was sixteen. He arrived there immediately after Napoleon's *coup d'état*; one of his relatives, Pierre Daru, was an influential adherent of the First Consul; after some hesitations and interruptions, Stendhal made a brilliant career in the Napoleonic administration. He saw Europe on Napoleon's expeditions; he grew to be a man, and indeed an extremely elegant man of the world; he also became, it appears, a useful administrative official and a reliable, cold-blooded organizer who did not lose his calm even in danger. When Napoleon's fall threw Stendhal out of the saddle, he was in his thirty-second year. The first, active, successful, and brilliant part of his career was over. Thenceforth he has no profession and no place claims him. He can go where he pleases, so long as he has money enough and so long as the suspicious officials of the post-Napoleonic period have no objection to his sojourns. But his financial circumstances gradually become worse; in 1821 he is exiled from Milan, where he had first settled down, by Metternich's police; he goes to Paris, and there he lives for another nine years, without a profession, alone, and with very slender means. After the July Revolution his friends get him a post in the diplomatic service; since the Austrians refuse him an exequatur for Trieste, he has to go as consul to the little port of Cività Vecchia; it is a dreary place to live, and there are those who try to get him into trouble if he prolongs his visits to Rome unduly; to be sure, he is allowed to spend a few years in Paris on leave—so long, that is, as one of his protectors is Minister of Foreign Affairs. Finally he falls seriously ill in Cività Vecchia and is given another leave in Paris; he dies there in 1842, smitten by apoplexy in the street, not yet sixty. This is the second half of his life; during this period, he acquires the reputation of being a witty, eccentric, politically and morally unreliable man; during this period, he begins to write. He writes first on music, on Italy and Italian art, on love; it is not until he is forty-three and is in Paris during the first flowering of the Romantic movement (to which he contributed in his way) that he publishes his first novel.

From this sketch of his life it should appear that he first reached the point of accounting for himself, and the point of realistic writing, when he was seeking a haven in his "storm-tossed boat," and discovered that, for his boat, there was no fit and safe haven; when, though in no sense weary or discouraged, yet already a man of forty, whose early and successful career lay far behind him, alone and comparatively poor, he became aware, with all the sting of that knowledge, that he belonged nowhere. For the first time, the social world around him became a problem; his feeling that he was different from other men, until now borne easily and proudly, doubtless now first became the predominant concern of his consciousness and finally the recurring theme of his literary activity. Stendhal's realistic writing grew out of his discomfort in the post-Napoleonic world and his consciousness that he did not belong to it and had no place in it. Discomfort in the given world and inability to become part of it is, to be sure, characteristic of Rousseauvian romanticism and it is probable that Stendhal had something of that even in his youth; there is something of it in his congenital disposition, and the course of his youth can only have strengthened such tendencies, which, so to speak, harmonized with the tenor of life of his generation; on the other hand, he did not write his recollections of his youth, the *Vie de Henry Brulard*, until he was in his thirties [actually, his fifties: R.M.A.], and we must allow for the possibility that, from the viewpoint of his later development, from the viewpoint of 1832, he overstressed such motifs of individualistic isolation. It is, in any case, certain that the motifs and expressions of his isolation and his problematic relation to society are wholly different from the corresponding phenomena in Rousseau and his early romantic disciples.

Stendhal, in contrast to Rousseau, had a bent for practical affairs and the requisite ability; he aspired to sensual enjoyment of life as given; he did not withdraw from practical reality from the outset, did not entirely condemn it from the outset—instead he attempted, and successfully at first, to master it. Material success and material enjoyments were desirable to him; he admires energy and the ability to master life, and even his cherished dreams (the silence of happiness) are more sensual, more concrete, more dependent upon human society and human creations (Cimarosa, Mozart, Shakespeare, Italian art) than those of the *Promeneur Solitaire.* Not until success and pleasure began to slip away from him, not until practical circumstances threatened to cut the ground from under his feet, did the society of his time become a problem and a subject to him. Rousseau did not find himself at home in the social world he encountered, which did not appreciably change during his lifetime; he rose in it without thereby becoming happier or more reconciled to it, while it appeared to remain unchanged. Stendhal lived while one earthquake after another shook the foundations of society; one of the earthquakes jarred him out of the everyday course of life prescribed for men of his station, flung him, like many of his contemporaries, into previously inconceivable adventures, events, responsibilities, tests of himself, and experiences of freedom and power; another flung him back into a new everyday which he thought more boring, more stupid, and less attractive than the old; the most interesting thing about it was that it too gave no promise of enduring; new upheavals were in the air, and indeed broke out here and there even though not with the power of the first.

Because Stendhal's interest arose out of the experiences of his own life, it was held not by the structure of a possible society but by the changes in the society actually given. Temporal perspective is a factor of which he never loses sight, the concept of incessantly changing forms and manners of life dominates his thoughts—the more so as it holds a hope for him: In 1880 or 1930 I shall find readers who understand me! I will cite a few examples. When he speaks of La Bruyère's wit (*Henry Brulard,* chapter 30), it is apparent to him that this type of formative endeavor of the intellect has lost in validity since 1789:

"Wit, so delicious for one who relishes it, does not last long. As a peach goes bad in a few days, so wit goes bad in a couple of centuries, even quicker if there is a revolution in the mutual relations of the different social classes."

The *Souvenirs d'égotisme* contain an abundance of observations (for the most part truly prophetic) based on temporal perspective. He foresees (chapter 7, near the end) that "at the time when this chatter is read" it will have become a commonplace to make the ruling classes responsible for the crimes of thieves and murderers; he fears, at the beginning of chapter 9, that all his bold utterances, which he dares put forth only with fear and trembling, will have become platitudes ten years after his death, if heaven grants him a decent allowance of life, say eighty or ninety years; in the next chapter he speaks of one of his friends who pays an unusually high price for the favors of an "honest working-class woman," and adds in explanation: "five hundred francs in 1832, that amounts to a thousand in 1872"—that is, forty years after the time at which he is writing and thirty after his death.

It would be possible to quote many more passages of the same general import. But it is unnecessary, for the element of time-perspective is apparent everywhere in the presentation itself. In his realistic writings, Stendhal everywhere deals with the reality which presents itself to him: "I take at random whatever turns up in my path," he says not far from the passage just quoted: in his effort to understand men, he does not pick and choose among them; this method, as Montaigne knew, is the best for eliminating the arbitrariness of one's own constructions, and for surrendering oneself to reality as given. But the reality which he encountered was so constituted that, without permanent reference to the immense changes of the immediate past and without a premonitory searching after the imminent changes of the future, one could not represent it; all the human figures and all the human events in his work appear upon a ground politically and socially disturbed. To bring the significance of this graphically before us, we have but to compare him with the best-known realistic writers of the pre-Revolutionary eighteenth century: with Lesage or the Abbé Prévost, with the preeminent Henry Fielding or with Goldsmith; we have but to consider how much more accurately and profoundly he enters into given contemporary reality than Voltaire, Rousseau, and the youthful realistic work of Schiller, and upon how much broader a basis than Saint-Simon, whom, though in the very incomplete edition then available, he read assiduously. Insofar as the serious realism of modern times cannot represent man otherwise than as embedded in a total reality, political, social, and economic, which is concrete and constantly evolving—as is the case today in any novel or film— Stendhal is its founder.

However, the attitude from which Stendhal apprehends the world of event and attempts to reproduce it with all its interconnections is as yet hardly influenced by Historism—which, though it penetrated into France in his time, had little effect upon him. For that very reason we have referred in the last few pages to time-perspective and to a constant consciousness of changes and cataclysms, but not to a comprehension of evolutions. It is not too easy to describe Stendhal's inner attitude toward social phenomena. It is his aim to seize their every nuance; he most accurately represents the particular structure of any given milieu, he has no preconceived rationalistic system concerning the general factors which determine social life, nor any pattern-concept of how the ideal society ought to look; but in particulars his representation of events is oriented, wholly in the spirit of classic ethical psychology, upon an "analysis of the human heart," not upon discovery or premonitions of historical forces; we find rationalistic, empirical, sensual motifs in him, but hardly those of romantic Historism. Absolutism, religion and the Church, the privileges of rank, he regards very much as would an average protagonist of the Enlightenment, that is as a web of superstition, deceit, and intrigue; in general, artfully contrived intrigue (together with passion) plays a decisive role in his plot construction, while the historical forces which are the basis of it hardly appear. Naturally all this can be explained by his political viewpoint, which was democratic-republican; this alone sufficed to render him immune to romantic Historism; besides which the emphatic manner of such writers as Chateaubriand displeased him in the extreme. On the other hand, he treats even the classes of society which, according to his views, should be closest to him, extremely critically and without a trace of the emotional values which romanticism attached to the word people. The practically active bourgeoisie with its respectable money-making, inspires him with unconquerable boredom, he shudders at the "republican virtue" of the United States, and despite his ostensible lack of sentimentality he regrets the fall of the social culture of the *ancien régime.* "My word, there's no more wit," he writes in chapter 30 of *Henri Brulard,* "everyone is saving all his energy for a job which will give him standing in the world." No longer is birth or intelligence or the self-cultivation of the *honnête homme* the deciding factor—it is ability in some profession. This is no world in which Stendhal-Dominique can live and breathe. Of course, like his heroes, he too can work and work efficiently, when that is what is called for. But how can one take anything like practical professional work

seriously in the long run! Love, music, passion, intrigue, heroism—
these are the things that make life worthwhile. . . .

Stendhal is an aristocratic son of the big bourgeoisie of the old
regime, he will and can be no nineteenth-century bourgeois. He says
so himself time and again: "My views were Republican even in my
youth but my family handed down their aristocratic instincts to me"
(*Brulard*, ch. 14); "since the Revolution theater audiences have
become stupid" (*Brulard*, ch. 22); "I was a liberal myself (in 1821),
and yet I found the liberals outrageously stupid" (*Souvenirs d'égotisme*, ch. 6); "to converse with a fat provincial tradesman makes me
dull and unhappy all day" (*Egotisme*, ch. 7 and *passim*)—these
and similar remarks, which sometimes also refer to his physical
constitution ("Nature gave me the delicate nerves and sensitive skin
of a woman," *Brulard*, ch. 32), occur plentifully. Sometimes he has
pronounced accesses of socialism: in 1811, he writes, "energy was to
be found only in the class which is struggling to satisfy real needs"
(*Brulard*, ch. 2). But he finds the smell and the noise of the masses
unendurable, and in his books, outspokenly realistic though they are
in other respects, we find no "people," either in the romantic "folk"
sense or in the socialist sense—only petty bourgeois, and occasional
accessory figures such as soldiers, domestic servants, and coffee-house
mademoiselles. Finally, he sees the individual man far less as the
product of his historical situation and as taking part in it, than as an
atom within it; a man seems to have been thrown almost by chance
into the milieu in which he lives; it is a resistance with which he
can deal more or less successfully, not really a culture-medium with
which he is organically connected. In addition, Stendhal's conception of mankind is on the whole preponderantly materialistic and
sensualistic; an excellent illustration of this occurs in *Henry Brulard*
(ch. 26): "What I call the character of a man is his habitual manner of undertaking the pursuit of happiness, or to put it in clearer
but less definite terms, *the sum of his moral habits*." But in Stendhal,
happiness, even though highly organized human beings can find it
only in the mind, in art, passion, or fame, always has a far more
sensory and earthy coloring than in the romanticists. His aversion to
philistine efficiency, to the type of bourgeois that was coming into
existence, could be romantic too. But a romantic would hardly con-
clude a passage on his distaste for money-making with the words:
"I have had the rare pleasure of doing throughout my life pretty
much what it pleased me to do" (*Brulard*, ch. 32). His conception
of wit and of freedom is still entirely that of the pre-Revolutionary
eighteenth century, although it is only with effort and a little spas-
modically that he succeeds in realizing it in his own person. For
freedom he has to pay the price of poverty and loneliness and his wit

easily becomes paradox, bitter and wounding: "a gaiety which terrifies" (*Brulard*, ch. 6). His wit no longer has the self-assurance of the
Voltaire period; he manages neither his social life nor that particularly important part of it, his sexual relations, with the easy
mastery of a gentleman of rank of the old regime; he even goes so
far as to say that he cultivated wit only to conceal his passion for a
woman whom he did not possess—"that fear, a thousand times repeated, was actually the controlling principle of my life for ten
years" (*Égotisme*, ch. 1). Such traits make him appear a man born
too late who tries in vain to realize the form of life of a past period;
other elements of his character, the merciless objectivity of his
realistic power, his courageous assertion of his personality against
the triviality of the rising middle-of-the-roads, and much more, show
him as the forerunner of certain later intellectual modes and forms
of life; but he always feels and experiences the reality of his period
as a resistance. That very thing makes his realism (though it proceeded, if at all, to only a very slight degree from a loving genetic
comprehension of evolutions—that is, from the historistic attitude)
so energetic and so closely connected with his own existence: the
realism of this "fractious horse" is a product of his fight for self-asser-
tion. And this explains the fact that the stylistic level of his great
realistic novels is much closer to the old great and heroic concept
of tragedy than is that of most later realists—Julien Sorel is much
more a "hero" than the characters of Balzac, to say nothing of
Flaubert.

HENRI MARTINEAU

[The Ending of the *Red and Black*] †

Stendhal put too much skill, too much mastery, into the description of Julien's homicidal act, and into that return to passionate
adoration of his victim which is the logical crown of his behavior,
not to have been, at bottom, very well satisfied with himself.

† From Henri Martineau, *L'Oeuvre de
Stendhal* (Paris, 1945), pp. 343–51.
Reprinted with permission of his daughter, Mme. M. M. Cahen-Martineau.
    M. Henri Martineau, for many years
the dean of Stendhal scholars, describes
in his *Oeuvre de Stendhal* how the author used to declare that nobody could
say anything worse about the ending
of his novel than he was ready to say
himself. But, M. Martineau argues, this
phrase of Stendhal's was merely authorial modesty; in reality, Stendhal
knew very well that the ending of the
novel was psychologically and artistically right; and M. Martineau pro-
ceeds to rap over the knuckles those
temerarious critics who had taken
Stendhal at his word and ventured unfavorable statements about the ending
of the *Rouge*.

And yet, I am not unaware this conclusion has appeared to some readers "rather strange, and in fact a little more contrived than is really legitimate."

These are the words of Emile Faguet, following upon his assertion that Stendhal is not intelligent. He pretends to show, further, that the pistol shot fired by Julien at Mme. de Rênal in the presence of an entire congregation was no more in the character of Julien Sorel than in the logic of events.

Julien, as Faguet sees him, once he has taken the decision to seek revenge and begun to race like a madman down the road to Verrières, seems to have forgotten that he is still in control of the situation. No doubt the Marquis de La Mole has just expressed a desire to break all relations with him, but this great gentleman has already had to put up with disappointments quite as grievous as those revealed to him by the letter from the chatelaine of Verrières. Did he really stand in need of this last witness to suspect that Julien Sorel might be a vulgar seducer of women? Once his new access of anger has died down, will it not become apparent to him that only marriage can save his daughter's honor? Only think of what he has already done, despite his rage, for his future son-in-law, by obtaining for him a title and a lieutenancy in the hussars!

Thus Julien need only wait a few hours, a few days at most: the formal *veto* rather childishly imposed on projects already far advanced will be withdrawn. But just here Julien, "the flawless man of ambition, of terrifying assurance and unshaken will" (these are the expressions of M. Faguet himself) loses his head and rushes off furiously to murder the woman who has denounced him and thus broken his career. Rather than a crime, what he commits on this occasion is an act of foolishness.

Such, in its main lines, is the argument of Faguet. It seems to be considered completely conclusive by a great many people who, following the lead given by the author of *Politicians and Moralists*, have taken the pains to write a great many pages along these lines.

Certainly, the practical men who see in the hero of the *Red and Black* a prudent and calculating spirit will never forgive him for shattering, in a single instinctive gesture, the structure he has so painstakingly built up. The fact is, they treat Julien Sorel as a vulgar type of man-on-the-make, and want to see in him merely a success-chaser. That's their basic mistake. If you make that mistake, it's perfectly apparent you will never understand how a person who had meticulously managed his career, and was just about to pluck the fruits of his long and patient hypocrisy, could suddenly become foolish or passionate enough to sacrifice everything to a momentary fury.

But can it be conceded that Julien Sorel is an artful dodger? Certainly not: throughout the book he is continually behaving awkwardly, against his own interests, and passion always prevails, in his soul, over calculation.

He devotes himself to hypocrisy simply because he has seen that it rules the world and imposes on credulous people by concealing all the worst weaknesses behind its smiling mask. But he himself is by no means, properly speaking, a hypocrite. He is a man of impulse, an extremely intelligent man of impulse who has come to understand the dangers of frankness in social life and who attempts to repress all his own impulses of loyalty, to throttle all the bold, wild impulses of youth which spring up so easily within him each time he forgets to stand guard over himself. He applies himself to *tartufery*, and because he is industrious as well as a keen observer, doesn't do too badly at it. But for all that he's a novice at the trade, and is far indeed from having the practiced manner and thick hide of Molière's Tartufe, with whom people have been all too ready, following Albert Thibaudet's lead, to identify him. His wrath will therefore break forth in outbursts more violent even than those of Orgon's false friend, when he sees himself stripped of his mask.

Neither a man of ambition nor a Tartufe, Julien is a young man whose social style is nearly always clumsy, to make use of Stendhal's own word. He is above all a plebeian in revolt, driven far less by the thought of immediate advantage to be gained than by a sense of outraged dignity and pride. And besides, he is absolutely deprived of any moral sense at all, and that is what shocked Faguet so much, and with good reason.

There's no cause for surprise, then, if this young man who is perfectly spontaneous and just as capable of evil as of good decides in an access of rage to take revenge on Mme. de Rênal. He is all the more furious with her because at the bottom of his heart he has never ceased to cherish her. He brings against her all the resentments generated by a great love which has been betrayed. Is anything more needed to turn him to crime?

It is, therefore, a mark of singular timidity or of extraordinary inattention to the characters of the novel if one excuses Stendhal for the ending of his novel by saying that he didn't invent it, he merely reproduced accurately the details he had read in the *Gazette des Tribunaux*. And isn't it also a way of diminishing Stendhal's personal contribution when one sees in the crime of Julien Sorel nothing but a mechanical copy of Antoine Berthet's?

The intransigent critics add that the pistol shot fired in reality by Berthet is not in the logic of Julien Sorel's character, at least the character of that prudent, calculating, and clever Julien whom they say the author substituted for the feeble little seminarian who served him as a model. This objection blurs somewhat with that misunderstanding of Julien's true and individual nature which we have already pointed out. And if one asked these subtle logicians what grounds they had for thinking Mme. Michoud's murder by Antoine Berthet derived logically from the character of that ludicrous being, they would obviously have no answer but this: the murder must have been in his character since he committed it.

The argument is pitiful, but it's all-purpose and will apply equally well to the impulsive act of any criminal not rigidly conditioned to his crime, any criminal of occasion, as it were.

One will be just as near to right if one says Julien Sorel had to murder Mme. de Rênal because of the psychological genius of Stendhal, who couldn't possibly cause his characters to behave contrary to their nature. Or, on the other hand, one can try an experiment: one could consider the story of Berthet up to the point where he was driven out of the Cordon household; one could recount the story of Julien Sorel up to the moment when Mathilde, in an access of nerves, sent the fatal courier to Strasbourg. And one would then ask which of these two men is more likely to arm himself and seek vengeance in blood? Will it be the weak Berthet, cowardly and sullen, or Julien Sorel, ravaged by his emotions, arrogant, and always a bit reckless?

Stendhal, who knew very well when he wrote the first words of his book what end his hero must meet, multiplied during the course of his story examples of his hero's often rather savage energy, an energy always under pressure which escapes every now and then in a puff of steam. He, who worked out resolutely the fundamentals of every character in his drama, who unhesitatingly created new characters and important episodes when he needed them, does anybody suppose he felt himself obliged to follow in every last detail the conclusion of the story at Brangues, simply because that random incident had served as his point of departure?

The novelist retained that conclusion, we can be sure, not just because it was symbolic and suggested vividly the defeat of a whole generation's frantic aspirations, but above all because, given the ardent nature of Julien Sorel, always ready to pass from dreamy meditation to sudden acts, everything predisposed him toward a crime of passion.

Beyle has noted somewhere, à propos of the *Learned Ladies,* the extent to which this comedy is "solidly grounded on the medical principles of the temperaments." These same principles the impenitent disciple of Helvetius and Cabanis himself used as the support of all the characters in his novels.

Over and over again Julien Sorel, in the violence of his rages, has been seen on the point of killing himself. And the day on which

Mathilde de La Mole spoke these insolent words to him, "I am horrified at having given myself to the first comer," don't we see him snatch up an old sword which happens to lie within his reach? Never was he closer than on that day to committing a crime of blood, and killing Mathilde, whom he always loved as much for reasons of class hatred as for genuine tenderness. All that held him back was the feeling which invariably had command over his soul: fear of ridicule. Another trait, this, which Stendhal could have discovered in his own character.

Perhaps it seems appropriate now to explain the rapidity with which Stendhal recounted this last episode as due to his embarrassment at its inadequacy? Not knowing how to explain and describe Julien Sorel's madness, Stendhal—so these curious critics declare— devoted just a page or two to him, and then shoved him offstage. "Stendhal has deprived us of several decisive days in the life of his hero. We may be allowed to see in this swiftness less a trait of character than an artifice, we were going to say a bit of trickery." That is what M. Henri Rambaud has been bold enough to say in his discussion of the question; and we in turn are amazed that this critic should be so ignorant of the principles of morbid psychology. The brevity of Stendhal's account, far from seeming a consequence of embarrassment, seems to us to provide new proof of his genius. No man ever had fewer preconceived theories; he never sought anything but the truth. He felt spontaneously that Julien Sorel, who is such a reasoner, even a logic-chopper, who always ferrets out his reasons for acting by means of a passionate inner meditation, would have to make up his mind suddenly under the impulsion of a powerful emotion and that he would commit his crime driven unconsciously by an irresistible compulsion. The observer who has a little insight into the instinctive and often contradictory impulses of the human heart, the reader who has paid some attention to the stories of everyday crimes of passion, could bring generous understanding to the study of this simple, classic case.

Charles Du Bos is, I believe, one of the first critics to insist on the state of somnambulism into which "we are plunged by certain impulses of inward enthusiasm." He has rightly remarked that Julien found himself in such a state for the first time after a scene with Mathilde, and that he was drawn out of it only by the shattering of a pane of glass in the library, when the splinters of broken glass falling on the parquet flooring at last aroused him.[1]

1. Another fine example of a hallucinated person in a state of full activity will be provided later by the account of Fabrice del Dongo's escape in the *Chartreuse de Parme*.

This might be, we shall hear from those critics who don't really want to understand, if it were simply a question of an instinctive reaction, a kind of unconscious reflex. But between the initial impulse and the moment when Mme. de Rênal falls to the church-pavement, several days elapse, and Julien, ordinarily so much master of himself, has had twenty different occasions to recover his self-control—supposing always that he is a creature of flesh and blood, and not the mechanical puppet which the stupidity of his final act obliges us to see in him.

But thinking this way is entangling oneself perversely in an intricate closed system, while ignoring all the most elementary discoveries of psychiatry. One must have read nothing at all on the subject of unpremeditated murder, one must never have had the slightest glimmer of the mental mechanism common in one important class of hallucinated criminals.

There is a class of criminals, among which we may number Julien Sorel, who act only under the constraint of an obsession, and for whom no other consideration has any significance until their crime is accomplished. Very clearly, Julien has become another being the instant he has read Mme. de Rênal's letter: Mathilde is close to him, and yet in his eyes she has ceased to exist.

When he thinks, a little later, of writing, "his hand formed nothing on the paper but illegible scrawls." When he enters the shop of the Verrières gunsmith, he has "great difficulty in making him understand he wanted a pair of pistols." All these points accumulating within three consecutive paragraphs show clearly enough that we no longer have to do with a normal person, but with a man who is seriously sick. Stendhal has the great merit of having divined this by instinct at a time when medical scholarship had not yet described the process or isolated the laws of this phenomenon. And so it is not by any means embarrassment which caused him to reduce his account to a minimum, but a concern for the truth: he clearly understood that Julien had suddenly become incapable of registering anything at all: he scarcely notices the most commonplace impressions of the outside world, the ordinary mill of associated ideas no longer turns within him. Since making up his mind to act, he no longer reasons; he does nothing but pursue an image. In prey to a sort of hypnosis, he marches toward his chosen end without any chance of being distracted from it by anything in the world. Time and space no longer have meaning for him: fifteen minutes and a week are exactly the same thing. And so he has seen nothing, heard nothing, thought nothing during his whole long journey from the moment when fury started him off till the moment when he roused himself from the deep sleep into which he fell after his arrest.

We no longer have before us the talky Julien who used to plague himself with a series of interminable questions as to whether he should or shouldn't capture the hand of Mme. de Rênal, as to whether he should or shouldn't mount a ladder by moonlight to Mathilde's bedroom. The time of these endless oscillations is over: Julien reflected, Julien asked himself, Julien reminded himself. . . . There is no more need for these great soliloquies: henceforth we have nothing but the silence of a lucid hypnosis.

All the great novelists have been perfectly conscious of this point when they have had to deal with types like Julien, and the brothers Tharaud have made excellent use of certain particularities of this hypnotic state in their account of Ravaillac. I need only allude here to the copious literature one might assemble on this topic, in France as well as abroad, and most particularly among the Russians.

I do not by any means think, however, that Beyle got out of any books the idea of annihilating all thought in Julien Sorel as soon as he resolved to commit his crime. He must have composed his story on instinct, because he sensed that only in this way would the sequence of events seem comprehensible. But less than a year after his book appeared, he heard in Rome (no doubt in the Villa Medici, where he spent much time) a little tale which must have struck him vividly, first because it had as its hero one of his compatriots, and then because it strengthened his thesis. He made a note of it on the margin of his novel, on the very page where Julien is shown leaving Paris for Verrières. It concerned Hector Berlioz, who later described the incident in his *Mémoires;* Louis Royer was the first to decipher Stendhal's note, and to see, like Stendhal himself, what reinforcement his story received from this true incident. Berlioz had left Rome the first of April, 1831, in order to get some word about his fiancée, Camille Moke, who had ceased to write to him. Stopped by sickness at Florence, he received a letter from the girl's mother which advised him that she was going to marry Pleyel. Immediately Berlioz resolved to go kill the two women and then commit suicide. He bought a costume with which to disguise himself as a woman, concealed his pistols in his luggage, and left Florence. But at Pietrasanta he lost his disguise. He bought another disguise at Genoa and left for Nice. There he *woke up*. He abandoned his project for revenge and went back to Rome. Thus Berlioz, just like Julien, acted under the influence of a kind of hypnotic spell.

Stendhal had intuited this mechanism, and faithful to his ideal of imitating nature, he was bound to limit himself to the dryest possible analysis of the event itself. From the instant in which, after reading the letter from Mme. de Rênal which Mathilde gives him, Julien takes his implacable resolution, forty lines serve to describe everything that happens till the second pistol shot that wounds Mme. de Rênal. If three days have passed since Julien left Paris, or five, what does it matter? And the reason is not, we cannot say it too often, that Stendhal considered Julien's feelings during this period of three or five days uninteresting, or hard to describe; that is not why he suppressed them, but because Julien was actually feeling nothing at all. His thought, ordinarily so active, has been annihilated, he gallops holding before his eyes a single image to be reached, a single act to be performed.

Only after his hero has carried out this act will Stendhal abandon his almost telegraphic style and resume the ordinary course of a narration interspersed with remarks, hesitations, and the secret thoughts of his characters. "Well, that finishes it, he said aloud as he returned to himself. . . ." There is a clear notation of the precise instant when the sleepwalking comes to an end. The young hero falls immediately into a heavy natural slumber, the natural consequence of the exhaustion caused by his nervous tension. When he wakes up, we find the Julien we knew before. The machinery of reflection has started to function again. Julien will be making monologues uninterruptedly till the very foot of the scaffold.

One might discourse at length on the necessity of this conclusion, which terminates more harmoniously than a successful accomplishment of his ambition the story of Julien Sorel's life, and provides the only realistic terminus for the struggle between the individual and society. But I have been less concerned with showing the fatality of the crime than its logical mechanism* * *

JEAN PRÉVOST

[Stendhal's Creativity] †

I. The fullness of the apprenticeship: duality of invention. II. How Beyle's memories blend with outside sources. III. Sorel: a Berthet tempered by Napoleon. M. de La Mole and Destutt de Tracy. V. Métilde, not a model, but a source of emotion. VI. Improvisation, a prerequisite of the unforeseen and of counterpoint. VII. Fixing the roots and the presentation of characters from within. VIII. Through whose eyes do we see the action? A duality necessary for perspective. IX. Transitions from one point of view to another,

† From Jean Prévost, *La Création chez Stendhal* (Paris, 1951), pp. 239–53, 264–72. Reprinted by permission of Mercure de France.

Prévost's book was published posthumously; he had been killed in 1944, fighting against the Nazis. It is the book of a talented poet and a rarely gifted critic, delicate in its perceptions, frank and vigorous in its dialectic.

the total transparence of the book. [X. "Counterpoint" and satirical descriptions. XI. Chapters of diversion and of repose. XII. Description of places replaced by a preliminary episode. XIII. The passing of time; its unequal rhythm. XIV. Analysis always as swift as the action. XV. Emotion prolonged by a resonance or suppressed by an unexpected narration. XVI. Interior monologue: brevity and verisimilitude. XVII. Dialogue with comments: swiftness of the commentary. XVIII. Secondary characters seen in cruder outline.] XIX. Doubling of characters; how this relationship is genuine. XX. Confidantes: assenting or opposed. XXI. The effects of the *negative* or of the inner void. XXII. The double ending of the *Rouge*. XXIII. The style: brevity and impetus, sureness of the vocabulary.[1]

I

At the time when he undertakes the *Rouge*, Stendhal has just completed the prodigious program of preparations that he had planned at the end of his adolescence, when he was writing his *Filosofia Nova*. He had explored as a critic and a philosopher, always with pen in hand, the moralists and the dramatic poets of his country, and those of Italy. He had prepared a stock-in-trade of personal experiences superior to what he had hoped for: instead of the bank, it was the Napoleonic government that had shown him the inner workings of human societies. He had prepared his sensibility by studies in the fine arts, again more fully than he had been able to plan in advance. With his essays on Italy, he had begun the study of comparative customs; with his book on *Love*, he renewed the study of one of the principal passions. This vast theoretical shaping perhaps neglected the essential duty, which is, as he will later state it, "to write every day, whether inspired or not." But since 1814, curiosity and poverty have served him well: he translates, adapts, or creates on the average two pages a day.

He says of the perfect dandy that once his dress is arranged he thinks no more about it. He has the same fortune in literature: the better he knows his trade, the less he thinks about the formulas and difficulties of the craft. The exigencies of the book trade and the need to sell quickly forced him to promptness. After thirty years of intense work, he is entitled to improvise; he knows how to portray with the first stroke, with one single stroke. He has slowly created that tool of swift prose which is himself: his most perfect style has become his natural voice. Originality is no longer an end that he intends to achieve: it is in him.

1. Sections X–XVIII have been omitted from this translation of M. Prévost's chapter. The brief phrases above will give some notion of their contents. [*Editor*]

We do not know of a first draft of the *Rouge*. But a note by
Stendhal in the margin of a copy of *Promenades dans Rome* dates
the idea back in 1828: "Night of 25th–26th of October, Marseilles,
I think, the conception of Julien, since called *Red and Black*."
Messrs. Martineau and de Marsan debate the exact date, which
they are tempted to alter, the first to 1829, the second to 1827. At
any rate Stendhal's first imaginative work on this novel is anterior
to *Promenades dans Rome* and *Vanina Vanini*; after this work of
erudition and ideas, he must have mounted a new assault on the
old materials; at the very least, the invention took place at two
times, as in all the rest of his works.

II

Many sources have been found, from the portrait of the seminarian Berthet to the flight of Mlle. de Neuville and the author's
intrigue with Giulia Rinieri. Our essential purpose is not to look
for sources but to study the way they are used and the workmanship
of the author. We bring new elements to this study of sources; it
is undertaken not for pleasure or the value of our trifling discoveries.
We think we can show that a source is never single, even for one
page: always an objective idea, in order to revive and fructify in the
author's imagination, must fall in with an old personal memory: the
fact used deliberately requires a pre-existing emotion which gives it
its interest and its life.

Why, in the case of the Laffargue trial as in the Berthet trial, was
Stendhal so moved by the man who had just killed his mistress?
And what is the origin of the scenes of tenderness which follow the
murder? The Berthet trial did not supply them.

When still very young, while he was reading Tasso, Beyle had
found that the most beautiful scene possible would be "Tancred
baptizing Clorinda, his mistress, whom he had just killed." Ten
years later, writing the *History of Painting*, he again proposed this
subject to young painters. He thought at first of suggesting it to
Guérin; and it is precisely a painting by Guérin, his *Dido*, "a
charming sketch," that evokes an epigraph for the *Rouge* concerning Mme. de Rênal. Doubtless without the author's knowledge, this memory from Tasso, newly imagined by him as a plastic
image, helps him to transmute a murder into a moving, heroic
scene. The common aspects of the love between Julien and Mme.
de Rênal, such as the astonishment of the young boy before the
closet of fineries, his apprenticeship in a multitude of practical little
details of life, the page where Mme. de Rênal is really seen by
nineteen-year-old eyes, sprang naturally from memories that Beyle
had kept of his affair with Mme. Rebuffel, when he himself was
nineteen years old. On the other hand, the extreme timidity, the

decisions made far in advance for very petty "battles" are the imaginary fulfillment of Beyle's love for the Countess Daru. One or two traits of Pauline and the confidante, Mme. Derville, whose name is not even invented, will have contributed, not to the affair, but to the conversation and the charm of Mme. de Rênal. Each of these distant figures was able to give the author the degree of admiration or the pitch of tenderness that he needed at the very moment.

As for Julien, he has been seen from the outset as a transformation of Antoine Berthet and a physically idealised and morally heightened Beyle. Beyle's youthful writings provide us with much more precise information:

In Marseilles at the end of 1805 and the beginning of 1806, young Beyle undergoes a crisis: first, love of glory and self-examination, then ambition.

"It is an immense advantage to have a good memory. I have, I think, a very good one. Crozet calls Beyle the man with the terrifying memory" (December 12, 1805). This memory will be imparted to Julien.

One of the rare psychological anachronisms of the *Rouge* gives Julien, from the beginning of his tutorship, an ideological habit of mind less natural to him than to Beyle. On December 12, 1805, Beyle had said: "I sympathized with a character, I felt myself to be him, and from that moment I anticipated his successes." Similarly, but in clearer language, Julien will say in Chapter 8: "From now on I must rely only on those parts of my character that I've thoroughly tested."

There was a day in the life of young Beyle when he thought himself not only a Julien Sorel, but an Antoine Berthet:

I then resumed my reading, but I was no longer attentive, I was imagining the happiness I would feel if I were an auditor in the State Council or anything else . . . I should have been the happiest of men through love; but now that passion seems to me totally quenched, and little by little I am developing a frantic and almost furious ambition. I am ashamed to think of it: I stooped to the most shameful actions that I know. To portray an ambitious man, one must assume that he sacrifices everything to his passion; well, I am ashamed to say, Saturday night I was like that. (I thought about marrying my elderly neighbor in order to have the favor of her brothers for myself.) I felt myself capable of the greatest crimes and the greatest infamies. I no longer stuck at anything, my passion consumed me, its lashing drove me on, I died of rage at doing nothing at the very hour when, for my advancement, I would have been delighted to beat Mélanie, whom I was with.

That very month provides a much less complete but much more vigorous prototype for Valenod than the Michel who will later serve as model: it is Blanchet de Voiron: "How crude Blanchet is, all his impulses are quite obvious."

"His small eyes gleamed and gave some expression to his face, which is really that of a hospital steward, of a low knave, cutting down the rations of the poor sick people and having the cruelty necessary for that" (20 January). This Valenod (who on that day paid court to Beyle as the real Valenod does the day when he invites Julien to dinner) also spoke to him of his children's education. Here is the *felt* model; Michel is the coldly imitated model.

It is natural that to portray Julien's youth and his provincial life, Stendhal resorted to memories of his own life at twenty-two. It is also normal that, having arrived in Paris with his hero, he furnishes him, for the episodes of his youth, with memories of more recent date.

III

It is easy to idealize a physical picture of oneself: the model of physical beauty is everywhere. It is just as easy to idealize morally, to impart noble sentiments, feelings of heroism: pretty deeds are the plague of bad novels. It is a little more difficult to give a fictional hero more wit than one possesses oneself: one must make him hit off-hand on comments and ideas that the author chooses at leisure from among the successes of the year or the best remarks of his circle.

On the other hand, to give a hero real style, grandeur in little things, more energy than one possesses oneself, is a problem. It requires, in fact, that the reader submit to a domination, an instinctive enthusiasm that only tone can create.

If one wishes to follow step by step the reports, the letters, the declarations of the seminarian Berthet, he will see outlined a character quite opposite to that of Julien: a querulous child, quickly seduced, quickly forgotten, a weakling who demands to be helped in the name of his weakness, who wavers, infatuated, between blackmail and the ecclesiastical vocation, who thinks of suicide as much as of crime, and whose faith remains his sole refuge during the trial. Berthet is a pretext. Where is the model, the source of vigor?

Without any doubt, it is from a reading of the *Mémorial de Sainte-Hélène* that Stendhal drew this surplus of power—just as he made Julien draw on it under our very eyes. There the style of the hero takes on its grand air, as Stendhal's style gains anew in fire and abruptness. The pace of the *Rouge*, that gallop of a black horse, draws from the *Mémorial* the means to be superior to the *Mémorial*.

The exciting influence, the power of those discourses of great men written down by witnesses, arises from our attributing to the man of genius all that is great in them, and to the witness all that lapses into the mediocre; we think we choose according to the genius, and at the same time, we choose according to our desire to admire, heeding ourselves: this kind of book pushes each reader in his own direction.

IV

A model for M. de La Mole has been vainly sought in royalist society. Stendhal did not know royalist circles well. But M. de La Mole is an intelligent royalist, who discusses politics only in the "secret-note" scene (where, moreover, his temperament hardly figures). The author feels a sympathy, an admiration, even a tenderness for him which saves this political enemy from all caricature, increasing the dignity and human value of the book.

This is because the little man with the witty look who seems at first strange to Julien, whose manners date from before the Revolution, is copied not from a royalist, but from a liberal and a friend of Stendhal—a real pre-Revolutionary nobleman, the Comte de Tracy, "a short, remarkably well-made man of singular and elegant figure. His manners are perfect when he is not dominated by an abominable black humor. . . . He is an old Don Juan. . . . His conversation was entirely of acute, elegant insights. . . ."

All these characteristics apply perfectly to M. de La Mole, as does the ill-disposition toward Napoleon. This portrait from the *Souvenirs d'Egotisme* even raises the objection: "But the philosophy?" Since, according to Stendhal, M. de Tracy's conversation in no way resembled his writings, it was not difficult to forget this philosophy in order to give him, in a novel, a role as a great, sympathetic nobleman. As for the character of Mathilde de La Mole, it was thought to have been discovered quite complete when scholars found in the letters of Stendhal and Mérimée an account of the escapade of the young patrician, Méry. M. Luigi Foscolo Benedetto, minutely recounting the history of Giulia Rinieri, her declarations to Stendhal, and an amorous intrigue in which Stendhal's strategems finally succeeded, has without doubt shown us the real stimulus that made Stendhal describe Julien's fortunate maneuver and final success.

V

But what seems certain to us, in spite of M. Jules Marsan's conflicting opinion, is that Beyle's love for Métilde Dembowska contributed greatly to the story of Julien and Mathilde. There is, of course, no resemblance between Métilde and Mathilde, but let us repeat: the *sources of emotion* and the *model* are different things. All of Julien's misfortunes, his dreams when he is rebuffed, his dreams in the presence of Mathilde when he dares not approach her, have nothing to do with the person of Métilde or of Mathilde; it is a drama which takes place entirely in the hero's soul, and which is not occasioned by the woman with whom he is in love.

Nor was it the story of the seminarian Berthet that furnished those long monologues of unhappy passion. In 1830, life had taken its revenge on Beyle—the last blow being his love for Giulia. It would still have been too painful for him to transpose from close up this sad memory; several years later, in his *Souvenirs d'Egotisme*, he still did not dare to deal with it frankly. The imaginary requital, that dream of satisfaction which follows the pain of defeat and marks the beginning of recovery from it, is one of the strongest stimulants to the creative imagination. It is in this way, as imaginary revenge, that one must view the transposition from Stendhal to Julien, to Julien's beauty, his slimness. The immediate memories keep their secret and lacerating intensity because they are lodged among the raptures of imaginary revenge.

The art of using oneself in a book does not proceed without difficulty, without anxiety, without ruses, from the moment that violent emotions are involved. The cry of triumph at the end of II, 29: "So there she is, that proud beauty, at my feet," is necessary for the author's soul to render his memory and his dream at its most pointed —the brief and famous fragment: "Ah," he thought, listening to the sound of the empty words being pronounced by his own mouth as he might have listened to an alien noise; "if only I could cover those pale cheeks with kisses, without your knowing it!"

The danger in the search for personal sources (especially when they are incompletely known) is to imply a *roman à clef*. To the contrary, it is only on rare occasions that the autobiographical element is intended, deliberately introduced. For Stendhal, for many others, the novel builds on an external, objective given. It is fed and quickened, almost extemporaneously, by personal memories and feelings. The less the author thinks about them, the more immediate the memories. It is useless to suppose that introduction of memories is unconscious. That word, applied to aesthetic creation, is pretentious and misleading. It is enough that it be spontaneous and improvised to explain, in the *Rouge*, that fusion of alien elements, those totally inward words, formed of desire and dream.

VI

The richest substance of the *Rouge* is formed of Julien's meditations. Such a novel cannot be composed very far in advance; one cannot foresee how the current page is going to influence the following page, nor how the chapter which is going to follow will change something in the chapter (merely glimpsed) which must follow it.

Certain events: the introduction into the home of a rich provincial, the arrival at the seminary, the introduction to the home of a nobleman, the attempt at murder, an execution, serve as guides and landmarks, nothing more. A succession of meditations like Julien's, which beget each other, which react abruptly to all the events of life, can be imagined only in the very order in which it is portrayed, and at the same moment. But the absence of a detailed plan does not mean that the author does not arrange, that he does not obey precise personal rules.

What Stendhal had sought rather clumsily in *Armance* was a *rhythm* or an intersection of plot and portrayal of customs. He was too much in doubt, at that time, about the real nature of the book for the fusion to be harmonious. But experience aided the author. This time (in the course of a chapter, or at the moment of moving from one chapter to another) a more assured demand for variety and the problem of creating fresh interest, make him change the tone.

First an exposition which rather strongly evokes the setting and the hero for author and reader. Then a *counterpoint*, a regular intersection of the principal plot with the episodes which portray customs and relieve the plot; changes of scene each time the plot (which must always progress) has reached a maximum of intensity, each time interest is in danger of waning; a double, contrasting ending: the greatest triumph, immediately followed by the worst catastrophe.

VII

Stendhal does not launch out *in medias res* and does not hurl us into the middle of the plot. We have already seen this in *Rome, Naples et Florence*, the first of his books whose plan is his own: he begins as a tourist. Abrupt beginnings are excellent for tragedies, for epics, for historical novels: the characters, the setting are known in advance; they have, through their names alone, quite enough reality to gain the reader's interest. Comedy too is rather well adapted to these beginnings in the full tide of action: the actor suffices, even if the characters deviate slightly from nature, from the first speech onwards. On the other hand, all the great novelists are concerned to weave a reality slowly, to weave a plausible substance out of very simple facts blended with commonly accepted historical or geographical realities. This sum of plausible details gains the reader's confidence and at the same time places the novel. It is the equivalent, for the novel, of the *captatio benevolentiae* of ancient rhetoric. The beginning of *Robinson Crusoe*, that of *Tom Jones*, the prodigious preliminary descriptions of Balzac are examples of these preparations, which distinguish the art of the novel from dramatic art and the art of the fable.

The novel has recognized another kind of verisimilitude, which came to it from oral narratives and the descriptions of lawyers. It is a matter of the author's being able to answer the question: "But how do you know that?"

Robinson Crusoe and *Gil Blas* are presented as memoirs, *Manon Lescaut* as a confidence offered to a witness; others, especially the English novels, are "defenses," "apologies," imitated from judicial defenses; such is the case with Diderot's *La Religieuse* and Defoe's *Moll Flanders*. Others are given out as the publication of the contents of private archives or strongboxes: *Adolphe* is an "anecdote found among the papers of an unknown man," as are the *Pickwick Papers*. The epistolary novel, such as *La Nouvelle Héloise* or *Les Liaisons Dangereuses*, is the subterfuge that has succeeded best. Letters were a very vital genre. Dramatic art was the chief literary genre which influenced the others. Now, the epistolary novel, with its differentiated, divided, or rather discontinuous dialogue, like the acts of a play where an actor talks to his confidant, remains very close to the dramatic genre.

This kind of care for verisimilitude has disappeared from the modern novel; an author feels free to describe a man's death, or what happened to a character who was alone and made no confidences. The truth of a narrative seems aesthetic or moral to us. Attempts to counterfeit reality in writings no longer deceive anyone and add nothing to the work.

The *Rouge* breaks completely with the tradition of supporting proofs. Julien's, Mme. de Rênal's, and Mathilde's interior monologues cannot be known by another person. The characters' thoughts, instead of being guessed through suppositions, after the manner of Tacitus, are offered directly to the reader. Instead of having us witness the actions of the characters in order to work back from actions to motives, we encounter, *with all the characters* (and not only with the protagonist) the natural order from thoughts to acts.

The author never pretends not to know, no matter what it may be. The *Rouge* is a novel without shadows, but not without perspectives.

No one had ever gone so far along this path. Thus it was necessary to take certain precautions. The author, in the opening lines of the book, vouches for Verrières and M. de Rênal. Then, to recount Julien's childhood, he remains within the bounds of what a memorialist or an advocate is able to say.

In the course of his affair with Mme. de Rênal, Julien still thinks only simple thoughts, especially designs for himself. These designs are finer and of vaster scope than those of the seminarian Berthet (the first model for Julien, taken, as we know, from the *Gazette des Tribunaux*), but quite as lifelike. Mme. de Rênal's divine simplicity also allows the interior of her soul to be seen completely by her confidante, Mme. Derville, or by her lover. The scene of M. de Rênal's anger, in which this character, still almost a stranger to the reader, is seen from within for the first time, is the great audacity of the first part.

That audacity will be exceeded by far in the Parisian section of the *Rouge* by the characters' interior monologues, by the musings that unfold within them even as they speak. These monologues display that kind of thought of which almost everyone is unaware in himself, for one cannot think passionately and see oneself thinking at the same time. But one can *recognize* these movements of the heart in a novel.

Abandonment of "judicial" verisimilitude; lightness and swiftness of the narrative; conquest of a new domain and a new shade of truth; this victory of a new technique over the classic practices is rich in consequences which extend beyond the craft.

VIII

The epistolary novel, the novel written in the form of memoirs, the novel told as if by a witness, all resolve from the outset, by the laws of their form, the question of knowing *who is narrating*, through whose eyes the reader is supposed to see the events.

It is a custom which was little by little established in the French novel to prefer two or three points of view on the same fact. In the epistolary novel (as in the theater, in the confidences of the first act), each correspondent has his own manner of presenting events. The author, assuming the role of witness and narrating as a witness, shows the hero's thoughts about events, but corrects them from time to time against his own judgments. Finally, even in real or fictional memoirs, we require the author, instructed by the consequences of his actions, by the course of his life, and cooled by the remoteness of time, to revise his old judgments from time to time; he contrasts his folly with his wisdom. St. Augustine, in his *Confessions*, uses this dividing of the author in a constant, moving manner. In France, it is often by temperament that the author divides himself and offers us two different views of his own story. Just as objects do not take on depth except through the vision of two eyes, or mountains stand out in relief except when the traveller sees them from several different points of view, so a narrative, to give pause to the reader's judgment without appearing inconsistent, requires that the author provide us, at each significant occasion, with two or more views of the scene and the character. It is in this respect, as well as several other peculiarities, that the novel differs from the tale. The tale is one-eyed. An admirer of Balzac and Stendhal will be amazed to see that Flaubert, for example, almost never intervenes, but presents events only in accordance with the immediate reactions of the characters. Thus he causes the mind the fatigue, the bewilderment, the imperfect understanding caused the eyes by objects viewed too closely; it makes the reader's judgment squint. *Salammbô*, the masterpiece of Flaubertism, if not of Flaubert, is a tale.

On the other hand, it is not easy to present multiple judgments of one fact. The author risks boring, repeating himself. He takes the chance above all that these two opposed points of view regarding the same fact cannot be reconciled in the reader's mind.

In this part of the art of narrative, so little studied and so important, the *Rouge* is a masterpiece which has never been surpassed.

IX

When Julien is onstage, it is through his eyes that we see events; it is from the inside of the character that we follow his thoughts. We have just seen how the author progressively introduces us into the mind of his hero.

The direct monologues occupy only a few lines; the transition between the monologues and the rest of the narrative is made through brief passages of indirect discourse. This indirect discourse also serves to lead us from Julien's thought to that of the author. These transitions are so swift and so well contrived that the reader does not notice any change; he does not have to make the effort of accommodation necessary in an epistolary novel to pass from one letter to another.

Yet the distinctness remains complete. We never take the author's point of view for Julien's. When the author chaffs or criticizes, we are in no danger of confusion. When he approves, a special (and yet natural) form of style must lift us to a place well above the narrative, up to the level of objective judgment.

But it also happens that we may follow one particular scene by finding ourselves placed inside Mme. de Rênal, another from inside M. de Rênal. In the second, much more audacious, part, it will happen, in the course of a dialogue, that the author shows us both the interior of Julien's thoughts and the interior of Mathilde's thoughts (far different from their words).

If we could see these interior thoughts equally well, our point of view would be divided. Julien will thus be shown more amply. As for Mathilde, her thoughts are at first a matter of conjecture based on her attitude—then she is explained in a briefer comment.

We note, finally, that among the secondary characters only sev-

eral reveal to us, for an instant, the depths of their thoughts: Abbé
Pirard, sometimes M. de La Mole, for a moment Prince Korasoff.
These are only parentheses, the asides of comedy, or such brief sum-
maries that we have not time to establish sympathy with the character; we see through him, but we do not feel with him. These characters are important at such a moment only *because of the place*
they occupy; it is from that place that we glimpse them and the
action.

It is only with Julien that the author suggests we sympathize.
Those whom we never see from within—a Valenod, for example, or
a Croisenois—have no interior to reveal to us. In short, we see events
through Julien's eyes, and the author grants us the strange power
of placing ourselves above even Julien as soon as we must see things
from higher up, and of looking at the other characters as if they
were transparent. The novel's plot, rich in surprises, holds no enigmas. We are continually invited to understand; the reader is present
everywhere and sees everything, like a God.

This celebration of intelligence, effected through such a new
technique, was profoundly opposed to the romantic tradition, to
the romantic mode. A novel was not, it now appeared, a problem to
be unravelled in the conclusion. How is one to distinguish moral
sympathy from that intellectual sympathy one is forced to feel for
Julien by seeing the novel through his eyes? This novelty of interior
discourse at the center of the narrative must have strongly influenced the incomprehension, the moral outrage of the contemporary
reader. The heroes of Mérimée (who found the *Rouge* too harsh)
were even blacker than Julien, but the author kept them at a distance; he did not invite the reader to see the world through their
eyes.

XIX

Secondary characters and simple supernumeraries tend to be presented in pairs.

One feature more or less, changing an already familiar portrait,
gives another face. Of nearly the same age and occupation, Abbé
Chélan and Abbé Pirard are the same man. We find, as their counterparts, the Jesuit pair Maslon and Castanède. A touch of dark,
the words "contemptible upstart," a circle of jailers added to M.
de Rênal make Valenod. Beauvoisis and Korasoff, perfect coxcombs, but agreeable and capable of liking a man of merit, are the
same man, except for a stammer and a difference of nationality.

Certain characters have a *double*, a supernumerary who resembles
them and whom the reader catches sight of behind them, creating
overtones: Bustos behind Altamira, the duc de Chaulnes behind
M. de La Mole, M. de Luz behind M. de Croisenois—and even a

chambermaid of the de La Moles', who woos Julien as Elisa did at M. de Rênal's.

This process is not only a trick of the trade which an author permits himself in order to build several puppets from the same pattern. It corresponds, we think, to a law of the human mind.

We tend to form analogies in order to aid our memory; our memories control the similarities. Real history, when it is abridged or simplified, organizes around pairs of names which are almost always mentioned together. To limit ourselves to the period when Stendhal lived: Chamfort and Rivarol, Hoche and Marceau, Robespierre and Saint-Just, Bara and Viala, later Talleyrand and Fouché are linked two by two, one with the other, in the handbooks. Each of these names, often without logical reason, brings up the other. The story-tellers too, obeying the laws of their own memories, and finding a means of fixing a greater number of characters in their listeners' minds, naturally bring forward their characters two by two —sometimes equal, more often one behind the other. The *Iliad* shows us Patroclus behind Achilles, the two Ajaxes together, Agamemnon and Menelaus, Phoenix behind Ulysses, Aenèas behind Hector; among the women there are Briseis and Chryseis. Virgil follows suit by giving Dido a sister and by making the faithful Achates follow Aeneas. To return to the nineteenth century, and to the novel, the pairs or parallel characters are one of Balzac's laws of composition. There is just one single difference, age, between Desplein and Bianchon; a single difference, social level, between de Marsay and de Trailles. Only one, race, between Florine and Coralie, between "Europe" and "Asia." Stendhal did not give in too much to this natural tendency, which aids the creator so well in making his creations multiply: he created out of the mould only supernumerary figures.

Among those secondary types, who derive from classical comedy more than the novel's important characters do, we must place the confidantes, male and female; Fouqué and Mme. Derville have no other role. When Julien is in Paris, we are in danger of lacking a casual confidant: then enters the academician, an indiscreet confidant. In serious matters, Abbé Pirard (relegated in this second part to the rank of a supernumerary) takes up this same role again, but with more subtlety.

Thus the interior monologue does not completely eliminate the confidant. Yet the novel, differing in this from the theater, has no technical need for that reply which allows the protagonist to catch his breath and direct his gestures somewhere else than at the audience. This "business" is not at all a routine procedure, but an imitation of nature. Is Mme. de Rênal, for example, a woman to reason with herself?

She is one of those spontaneous beings who achieve consciousness of their own feelings only in answering questions, through confession. Fouqué is necessary to Julien, who soliloquizes, as the only *resistance* to his ideas or his dreams that he is forced to respect. Abbé Pirard will play this same role of the *confidant in opposition*.

XXI

The creation of characters seen from within and the art of setting down in the margins of the dialogue material to illuminate that dialogue permitted Stendhal a new kind of effect that one might call negative.

The peak of an effect is sometimes obtained by abandoning all the means which aim at that effect. Antiquity gave an example of this kind of pursuit in the fine arts: the painter, having to portray the sacrifice of Iphigenia, painted Agamemnon with his head in his cloak, because he was able to express more in this one figure than in all the others. More simple is the device used by singers who, having reached their highest or longest note, keep their mouths open without emitting any sound to give the audience the impression of an effect which is beyond human means. And sometimes the painter, drawing out a line in dark chiaroscuro, produces an effect of remoteness and mystery which color and a sharp outline could not give.

In a novel like the *Rouge*, this sort of effect corresponds to a human truth: *passions, having reached their peak, reverse their effects:* the more they agitate the person, the more immobile he seems; the more he is tormented, the more indifferent he appears. The classics recognize this truth, but they have no means of improving on it. They do say that a character (or the narrator himself) *remains numb*. But an actor in the theater can not appear paralyzed, mute. One would simply think that he had forgotten his part. And in tales, where all we know about the characters depends on dialogue, how can this muteness be expressed, this inner void be seen?

Stendhal, whose reader identifies with Mme. de Rênal or with Julien, suddenly breaks that impulse and that connection with the audience. That fully illuminated being in the midst of our mind, the author suddenly moves him into a shadowy region. Meanwhile his narrative evokes either awkward attitudes which weakly contrast with what we were thinking, or mysterious actions. The swift commentary, where he is at his best, can again contrast actions and words.

Three scenes especially show this art of negative effects. The farewell of Mme. de Rênal and Julien, so perfectly cold and indifferent, in which she says only a few insignificant words, troubles and disconcerts the reader. A lyrical piece is necessary to free us

through pity and at the same time explain the mystery: ". . . the icy kisses of this living corpse. . . ." These lines, perhaps Stendhal's most beautiful, were necessary to compensate for that cruel moment of entry into the shadow.

At the moment when his strategem has succeeded, Julien's replies, with which his victory over Mathilde begins, contrast the coldness and triviality of his words with the violence of his passion, which is expressed at each moment in concealed asides. The negative effect of the "hardly distinguishable voice" (p. 339) is at each moment balanced by the interior song of triumph.

Finally Julien, so entirely clear in our minds up to this point, enters through his crime into a total obscurity; he is no longer anything but a restless form; even inside the hero, there no longer remains anything. Here again, the psychological, or rather pathological, truth of this obscuring of the consciousness is confirmed by doctors of the mind (and in each of us by the memory of our rages). The effect of this brief madness terrifies the reader. Yet criticism has hardly done more with this portion than object to it; criticism is guided by the conventions of the fifth act. Moreover, in Stendhal's time and among his friends, the story of Berthet the seminarian foreshadowed what Julien was going to do. For the modern reader, the basic fact of the *Rouge* is so famous that that blind course seems tailor-made, too easy, a simple slope gliding toward the dénouement. It does not give us the explanations that the hero of a stage-tragedy, in Julien's position, would declaim to us.

XXII

Critical opposition to this chapter has perhaps still other, more general, causes. Like almost all of Stendhal's works, the *Rouge* concludes twice. Having reached the peak of his ambitions, Julien rightly says: "The novel of my career is over." From this moment on the reader, who was following the author step by step, sees him begin to gallop; he no longer finds much except a dry summary of the hero's life. Stendhal created great difficulties for himself by placing Julien in a garrison and a new career: it would have been necessary, for the fourth time, to describe an environment, and a new group of supernumeraries who would take no part in the action.

At this moment, Julien Sorel, Stendhal's dream and creation, had to take Antoine Berthet's course. Determined to follow the general outline of the action as he had found it in the *Gazette des Tribunaux*, the author was wise to preserve that tragic conclusion: a real success for Julien would undoubtedly have debased the book. But suddenly Antoine Berthet sweeps up Julien Sorel: that moment of the killer's moral void, which is clinically true, facilitates the

transition and the crime. Berthet recounted, as well as he was able, the state of aberration and void which he was in when he hastened toward the murder in Brangues. This truth fulfills the same function as a convenient evasion. And without doubt the author did not trouble himself enough in rendering the murder realistically *because this murder was real*.

Here is the danger of the real in the novel: one does not take enough care to vindicate it, and aesthetic truth is not judicial truth.

The author hastens through these swift passages toward the final heights of his work. It is only in prison that we see Julien above ambition, above even his ambitious love for Mathilde, and at Mme. de Rênal's level. He no longer strains toward the future. Stendhal can at last impart to him that freedom of dream and judgment, that noble part of his own character which was formed after 1815, the part which until then Julien had lacked.

Julien the murderer is better than at the time of his greatness; through the imminence of death *he is Stendhal's age*, for he has reached the age when one gives himself over to his memories. It is through the pleasure of mingling intimately with his hero for the last time and judging him from within that the final chapters of the novel are revived and prolonged.

XXIII

We have seen Stendhal's style develop in the course of the apprentice years and the many difficulties of the beginnings. Very certainly, the finest portions of the *Mémorial de Sainte-Hélène*, which so obviously influenced Julien's character, exerted influence on his chronicler as well. The impetus with which his style moves forward adds a new force to the qualities already acquired. All his new resources for illuminating the characters' interior life, for animating their dialogues with actions and thoughts, for rendering even their silences significant, need a controlling quality to be put into play: conciseness in the movement.

A certain conciseness is within the scope of all critical minds. La Rochefoucauld, La Bruyère, and Vauvenargues furnish excellent examples. It reduces to the art of correcting oneself, of suppressing from a written sentence everything that is not essential. But a sentence thus condensed loses all naturalness; one feels that thought is not formed this way. Animation disappears along with naturalness.

Through years of daily practice, through thinking over again what others had written and what he himself had written, Stendhal succeeded in being brief even as he invented. He passes judgment, he sets an action in motion with three words unexpectedly blurted out and assuming a part of their force from the unexpectedness of the formulation. One recognizes the man who, analyzing Corneille,

found that the most beautiful verses, once translated, should produce *a prose defective through the excess of ellipses.*

No internal divisions of the sentence, none of those symmetries which place the balancing point in the middle. The essential word is at the end: "All good reasoning offends." "All his pleasures lay in wariness." When it is necessary to recount at length a fact or a thought, the incisive phrase, the flash which simultaneously illuminates the thought and the movement of mood, is thrown at the end of the paragraph or chapter; it gives an extreme intensity to all that precedes it.

Julien, who thinks it is crazy to climb the ladder to Mathilde's room, sums up: "I'll be a fine sight on my ladder." Or when he despairs: "Why am I myself?"

The reader will recall Beaumarchais' famous remark which reproaches the universe: "Why these things and not others?" Stendhal turns this remark back against the self; he suppresses the second part of the sentence while preserving the same substance and the same force in the thought.

Is there need to defend Stendhal's style against certain inaccuracies for which he has been reproached? They prove at least that he sometimes devises a new word to expresse a new shade of meaning. Some have been inclined to see in the word "antisympathy" a simple mistake for "antipathy." Antipathy is merely a feeling of hostility for someone. Antisympathy is a hostile response to a sympathy which was seeking expression.

Stendhal's language is of an almost infallible exactness when it is a matter of nouns and verbs. The adjectives are more commonplace, and in using them the author does not transcend the habits of conversation. For example, the frequency of the word "frightful" has been noted. The epithets stand out only in the position of the attributive adjective, at the end of the sentence. (Often he establishes a relation according to the unusual locution: "There were . . . between . . . and . . ." which is a geometer's and legal man's turn of phrase.) But is not the adjective always proof of a pursuit which comes too late? Better chosen, more numerous, they would distract the reader from what is essential in the sentence and would hinder the movement.

Let us repeat again, this improvisation without garrulity is the fruit of twenty-five years of effort. For each of these pages, one could quote Whistler's comment on one of his paintings: "I did it in a quarter of an hour, with the experience of my whole life."

The corrections that the author later made in his interleaved copies *have no significance for the study of his style.* The majority of them are slight changes of conception. Thus, in Abbé Pirard's letter to Julien, it must not be a *leaf of a tree* which falls at Julien's feet, for the mail censor would also have dropped the leaf: better *a blot of ink in the middle of the thirteenth word.* Other corrections, almost purely objective, concerning a repeated word, etc., are those which a secretary or a careful printing foreman can make—like those which in his lifetime Stendhal left to Crozet or Mareste, and which he entrusted Colomb to make for him after his death.

It is odd that Stendhal should later have judged the style of the *Rouge* "too abrupt." He undoubtedly found himself more tender and closer to the verge of music than he had been in painting Julien. And the judgments of his friends, whose injustice cries out to us, perhaps made him regret having gone to the extreme of his own manner. Yet it seems to us that in judging his own books, whenever he does not undergo an alien influence, whenever he does not think about the works to come, he gives his approval to what is strongest in him: "Very well done, the seminary scenes." He has experienced the memory of the *Rouge.* That work changed him as a writer; perhaps he sometimes kept a lingering rancor toward it. But with an eye to fresh creation, not second thoughts.

GEORGES POULET

Stendhal and Time†

At Smolensk on August 24, 1812, that is, less than two weeks from the battle of the Moskva river, Stendhal writes this to a friend:

How man changes! That thirst to see things that I used to have is totally slaked; since I have seen Milan and Italy, everything I see disgusts me by its crudeness. . . . I have had a little pleasure only by making a person who feels music as I do the mass play for me on a little, out-of-tune piano. *Ambition is no longer anything to me*; the handsomest decoration would not seem a compensation for the muck in which I have sunk.

At precisely this moment when we choose to discover Stendhal, we catch sight of him close upon thirty, nearly at the mid-point of his existence, but lacking any bond with his existence, at the heart of the stupendous imperial epic, but bored and disgusted by the imperial epic, incapable of establishing contact either outwardly,

† Georges Poulet, "Stendhal and Time," in the *Revue Internationale de Philosophie*, XVI (1962), pp. 395–412. Reprinted by permission of the author and publisher.

Professor Poulet's essay may be seen as carrying forward the series of linked essays which he published, in 1949, under the title of *Etudes dans le temps humain* (translated by Elliott Coleman and published by the Johns Hopkins Press in 1956 as *Studies in Human Time*).

or with the past, or with the future. Such, it seems, is the experience of the ambitious man who renounces ambition. If at first, as he notes, ambition is now no longer anything to him, it therefore no longer produces in him the effect that it produced in his previous life. To renounce the emotion which had governed one's desires, his actions, his conduct of life is to renounce any connection of the moment in which one lives with all the antecedent moments, whose essence and driving power have been composed precisely of that sentiment. And it is also to renounce foreseeing the following moments, which, until then, had been almost the exclusive object and almost the posterior limit of thought. In short, the person who renounces the life of ambition gives up consciousness of his life in the form of the past as in the form of the future. And, suddenly, his life becomes a life without past or future. It is a life reduced to the present, a merely momentary life.

Is this to say that at that instant Stendhal finds himself completing an act of renunciation comparable to the great religious or spiritual conversions, which we know often take place in a moment of breaking with the past and founding a new existence? Obviously not. That would be to mistake grossly the meaning of a moment that, for Stendhal, has no importance other than to reveal a separation from the past which has undoubtedly been long since completed, and a disinterest in the future which has gradually replaced calculations and plans. No, what Stendhal asserts in all simplicity, in his letter of August 24, 1812, is the repulsion he now feels at making of the present moment a corridor for an ambitious being to a future determined by that ambition. Hence, a great indifference not only for the two directions of time, but for the conjunctions of the present itself. Stendhal's present is unbound. It floats free. Stendhal does not know what to make of it. If the surrounding reality disgusts him, that is because it bores him. Witness and participant in one of the greatest military adventures ever, on the eve of one of the great battles of history, Stendhal finds the present empty, exactly as Lucien Leuwen does in the garrison at Nancy. He feels the need to fill it by having music played and dreaming of Italy. "I picture," he writes in the same letter, "the heights that my soul inhabits—(composing works, listening to Cimarosa, making love to Angela in a beautiful climate)—as enchanting hills." A distant and bashful lover, pathetic victim of a mania for music, Stendhal fashions as he can a moment of absolutely disinterested enjoyment for himself in the midst of ugliness and mud.

How different from the young Julien Sorel Stendhal here reveals himself to be, not the Julien Sorel of the catastrophe, but the Julien of the novel's beginning and of the course of the narrative.

Here is how Julien himself describes himself to Mme. de Rênal, as he was at that time:

> In the old days . . . when I could have been so happy during our walks through the forest at Vergy, smoldering ambition dragged my soul away into imaginary lands. When I should have been pressing to my heart this lovely form that was so close to my lips, I was stolen away from you by the future; my mind was on the endless struggles I would have to endure in order to build a colossal fortune. . . .

And Julien adds: "I would have died without ever knowing happiness. . . ."

To confess that one is incapable of knowing happiness is therefore to admit, at the same time and for the same reason, that one is incapable of relishing the present moment. Awareness of the present and awareness of happiness are invariably mingled in Stendhal's thought. When the Stendhalian personage feels happy, it is because he feels himself coinciding with the moment in which he is living. This is what is done naturally, not by Julien, but by the woman to whom he at first thinks himself so superior because of his refusal to be happy, Mme. de Rênal: ". . . all the subtleties of her happiness were new to her. No gloomy truths could freeze her spirit, not even the specter of the future."

But in Julien, constantly driven to transcend the moment and project himself into the future, there is sometimes a sort of slackening, of relaxation, the awareness of a fleeting happiness glimpsed, so to speak, inadvertently: "At times when his ambition was forgotten, Julien admired with ecstasy Mme. de Rênal's very hats and dresses. He never tired of their perfume."

Thus Stendhal lets us sense in this person, who is straining toward the future and as little disposed as possible to enjoy the pleasures of the tangible moment, a contradictory disposition, which at first will be revealed only accidentally, at long intervals, in moments which he indicts as moments of weakness, and yet which announce an overturning, a total reversal of the person's spiritual orientation, in consequence of which what was exceptional will become natural, and what was the norm will disappear forever. For if we now go to the end of the book, that is to say to the period of imprisonment, of final meditations and last loves, we see a calmed, simple, spontaneous, happy Julien appearing in the old Julien's place, a Julien capable of accepting the moment just as it is and of savoring its inestimable richness. Now, if Julien has undergone such a complete metamorphosis, it is because he has finally and definitively renounced ambition and the future. This transformation though it leads to happiness, is nonetheless painful:

"Each of ambition's promises had to be ripped in turn from his heart by this great thought: *I am going to die.*"

It is thus in the consciousness of his imminent death, that is to say in the certainty of now being without a future, of having no other existence than that of the immediate moment, that Julien finds the strength to renounce precisely that ambition which had been the principle of his life. Killing off his own ambition, living his own death through anticipation, he enjoys all the better what remains to him of present life: " . . . he was living on love, and *almost without a thought for the future.*"

Nothing is more striking than the total agreement of Julien's mood on the eve of his execution and Stendhal's mood during the Russian campaign. Each one of them feels free of the care of foreseeing the future. From the moment they decide to live for the moment only, a new kind of existence begins for them, which is a life without past or future, a life always in the present moment, a life which is lived from day to day. That is the very expression Stendhal uses to describe it. It is that very one that Montaigne had already used: "I live each day as it comes; my plans extend no further." Before the extraordinary metamorphosis that makes him, several days before his execution, a being worthy of Stendhal (and of Montaigne), Julien Sorel had been described exactly as someone who "was not far from giving up on all his efforts, all his schemes, and living from day to day. . . . " Then he was told: " . . . you have by nature that cool expression, a thousand miles from the sensation of the moment. . . . "[1] At the last moment, on the other hand, Julien will say of himself: "I have been ambitious, but I have no intention of blaming myself for that; I was acting in those days according to the code of the times. *Now I am living from day to day.*" Once again, these are the very words Stendhal uses about himself: "I have always lived and I still live from *day to day* and without thinking at all about what I will do tomorrow."

* * *

To live from day to day, to renounce the future and one's ambition, is thus to give up all plans, and, in general, even the plan to live. Life is now without design, without plan, without premeditated intentions. It is improvised as it goes on.

No more of the itinerary carefully marked in advance by one who makes up a program for himself, but an advance without design which gives itself over to and puts its faith in unexpected encounters. It is like a journey without a specific destination, one of those journeys such as Stendhal liked to describe in *Rome, Naples,*

1. For the reason behind the apparent confusion in this passage, see p. 68 of the text, note 7, and p. 222.

and Florence, in *Promenades dans Rome,* in the *Memoirs of a Tourist:*

> This morning, the sky heavy with clouds allowed us to roam the streets of Rome, without being exposed to a burning and dangerous sun. The ladies who accompany us in our travels wanted to see the Forum again, *without plan or knowledge, and following only the impulse of the moment.*

Now, of the journeys that one can make, there is none more fascinating or more unpredictable than mental journeys, the kind of trips we are stimulated to make by the books that we compose. Stendhal writes them exactly as one strolls, that is with neither plan nor expertise: "Making the design in advance freezes me," he writes in the margin of the rough draft of his *Lucien Leuwen.* And he makes this interesting general remark:

> What keeps women, when they set up as authors, from achieving the sublime, except very rarely, what gives their most trivial notes grace, is that they never dare to be more than half frank: to be frank for them would be like appearing in public without a shawl. Nothing is more frequent than for a man to write entirely at the dictation of his imagination, and *without knowing where he will go.*

But to go forward without knowing where one is going is not for Stendhal a way of writing, it is a way of living, and even the only good way: "In those parts of life where I feel my strength," he comments, "I am inclined not to make decisions in advance." All good Stendhalian characters behave in the same way: "I obey, said Lucien, ideas which come to me suddenly and which I can not foresee a minute beforehand. . . . " Of all Stendhal's characters, Lucien, really, is the one who has most confidence in his powers, who least mistrusts himself and the world. He is always ready to welcome the gifts of fate, whether good or bad. In this, he is the very opposite of Julien Sorel, the person who is always mistrustful. Now, to be mistrustful is to be aware of one's lack of strength, of one's concealed weakness. "It is in the things in which I am weak," writes Stendhal, "that I have never made enough resolutions in advance." The notorious resolutions made by Julien (in a moment I must take that hand, I must squeeze it . . .) are thus not evidences of energy, but confessions of weakness. The person who calculates the future is the one who, in the depths of himself, does not find the resources necessary to face blithely the unpredictability of the present moment.

On the other hand, the strong person is the one who follows his soul's impulse, and the stronger that impulse, the more intense his reaction. Instead of a calculated future, which the considered acts of a Valmont predetermine and bring into being, we find an unforeseen future which suddenly appears and immediately excites a lightning response. Therefore with Stendhal there is no future that has been predicted and effected through the will of man; nor is there any inevitable fate of which man would discover himself to be the predestined prisoner, and against which he would retain no recourse except submission, as in the novels of Balzac and even of Flaubert. There is only a moment, always surprising in the suddenness of its appearance as in the newness of its context; a moment without causal relationship to what preceded, unexpected, without preparation, and to which the mind is immediately forced to improvise, as well as it can, a response; in short, a moment in which is revealed the conjunction of chance with a mind that immediately masters, interprets, and adapts it: "I take *as it comes* what fate places in my path." "Between Julien and me there is no contract to be signed, no lawyer, everything is heroic, everything is up to the free play of *chance*." At the court of Henry III, Mathilde de La Mole says to herself, "a man's life was one continual train of *dangers*."

He was enraptured, he no longer reasoned, he was at the peak of happiness. It was one of those fleeting instants which *chance* sometimes grants as compensation for so much evil, to souls made to feel strongly.

A fleeting moment in which one feels strongly, that is what Stendhalian temporality reduces to. Events spill out one after another in the very midst of consciousness; and sometimes, luck aiding, if the soul has the necessary quickness, the talent for improvising, and the boldness required to choose such a line of conduct, a marvellous adjustment is established instantaneously between the whims of fortune and the passionate vigor of the mind.

That is true everywhere, but more especially, thinks Stendhal, in that favored land where the human plant is more vigorous than anywhere else, that is, Italy: "The pleasure of Italy is to be left to the inspiration of the moment." " . . . Italy, where the transport of immediate sensation and the strength of character which results from it are not rare. . . . " " . . . Italy, the land of sensation. . . ."

While the *Red and Black* is the novel of ambition, that is of anticipatory, uneasy thought directed exclusively toward the future, ignoring the immediate sensation and thus consummating its own unhappiness, *The Charterhouse of Parma* is a novel of movement in the midst of which souls abandon themselves unhesitatingly to the emotion which possesses them, with the result that they are wonderfully fitted to "revel in the present moment." Fabrizio is an obvious example of this. But more than any other character in this work, or indeed in any of Stendhal's other novels, Gina Sanseverina embodies this type:

> Her beauty is the least of her charms; where else to find this ever-honest soul that never acts with prudence, that abandons itself entirely to the feeling of the moment, that asks only to be enraptured by some new object?

Mosca does not speak differently of the woman he loves: "I know Gina, she is a woman given to the first impulse; her conduct is unpredictable, even for her."

Unpredictable, whimsical, obedient to all the suggestions of the immediate moment and abandoning herself to it with a total lack of reserve, such is Gina Sanseverina. She is the very incarnation of that impassioned sensuality of which, for Stendhal, Italy is the mother country. Nothing more delightful than a person like the duchess. Yet, in the long run, her conduct is not without singular drawbacks, if not for her, at least for those who are close to her. Her lover, Count Mosca, reflects on it: "Always at the instant of action there comes to her a new idea which she follows enthusiastically, as being the best in the world, and which spoils everything."

In fact, how many times in the course of the narrative does one not see the impulsive duchess ruin her lover's prudent arrangements through her sudden enthusiasms? But there is something else. The duchess Sanseverina is not only irrational and fantastically capricious, she is, as Stendhal says, "the slave of the present sensation."

Slave! The impulsive being is therefore not a free being, he is on the contrary a being tyrannized by the emotion to which he is subject. On this point, Stendhal reiterates the most explicit assertions: the Italians, he says, are "a passionate people, *slaves* of the sensation of the moment."—"A young Italian, rich, twenty-five years old, when he has lost all his shyness, is the *slave* of the present sensation. He is entirely filled by it."

But it is especially, in Stendhal's view, the southern Italian, the Neapolitan, who falls most completely under the yoke of sensation: " . . . the immediate sensation, this *tyrant* of the southern man."—"The immediate sensation is everything for the Neapolitan."

Slave of the instantaneous, but of an instantaneousness which varies unceasingly and which never has time to give roots or depths to emotion, the Neapolitan has passions, but these are volatile passions. Lacking anything deep, his sensual experience is without intensity. He is not a truly passionate being, a powerful soul: "Properly speaking, the majority of Neapolitans do not have profound passions, but obey blindly the sensation of the moment." "The great and profound passions dwell in Rome. . . . As for the Neapolitan, he is the slave of the sensation of the moment."

Heedless, brisk, shallow, always distracted from himself and from the past caprice by some new whim, what is Lucien Leuwen, before he meets Mme. de Chasteller, if not a kind of Paris Neapolitan? The immediate sensation is always welcome to him. It has the virtue of relieving his boredom. ("Boredom is a spiritual disease," said Stendhal. "What is its basis? The absence of sensations which are vivid enough to engage us.") Thanks to sensation, therefore, Lucien escapes the boredom that lies in wait for him. But he escapes it only for the moment when he feels, and he must incessantly find new sensations to escape that unbearable condition, which for him is the absence of all sensation. It is true that the appearance of Mme. de Chasteller will change all that. For Lucien, she will miraculously become the source of an existence which constantly renews its own interest. But this is because Mme. de Chasteller will change her lover from a dilettante and amateur of sensations to a passionate lover. There is thus something besides "the moment's sensation." There is one's capacity to seize the moment to demonstrate his passion with vehemence. The truly passionate being is not simply "the slave of his sensation"; this is the expression of an emotion which is impossible to distinguish from the one who feels it. The passionate being does not feel and live under the control of a power which is independent of him. He really *is* his emotion. How could he struggle against it or dissociate himself from it, since the feeling that he has of himself can only be united with the energy which enflames and arouses him. In whatever direction it carries him, whether toward crime or amorous ecstasy, the energy in him is never anything but the ardent manifestation of his own self.

Thus, for Stendhal, the feeling of the impassioned self, as it is revealed to the very one who in the vital moment experiences it, is never limited merely to a simple passive awarness. The moment in which one feels is also the moment in which one acts: "No pleasure without action," said Stendhal. There is no emotion which does not surge up in an instant, and which does not immediately charge that instant with energy, to carry off the being who feels it in a movement through which the emotion finally is transformed irresistibly into action:

In almost all the emotions of life, the generous soul sees the possibility of an action of which the common soul has no conception. At the very instant in which the possibility of that action becomes apparent to the generous soul, it is in its own interest to perform it.

This remark of Stendhal's, moreover, repeats an idea of Helvetius: "It is contrary to the nature of man, it is impossible for him not to do what he thinks must lead him to happiness the moment he is given the opportunity."

It is easy to recognize here the doctrine of "enlightened self-interest." Stendhal indeed gives it a shade of meaning different from that which the utilitarian philosophers gave it. For him, it is a question, in fact, of an immediate choice by the person, a choice through which, so to speak, the person unhesitatingly opts for his self, for his happiness. To choose oneself, and, in choosing oneself, to choose happiness, such is the essential option, the one which the mind makes instantaneously, instinctively, without debating. Here, action is a true imperative.

We see it distinctly in this passage from the novel *Armance:*

> Since I have begun to see my *duty* [the heroine of the novel thinks], not to follow it immediately, blindly, without debate, is to behave like a common soul, is to be unworthy of Octave.

One recalls many examples of these duties and of these instantaneous choices in Stendhal. The example of Julien Sorel in the cafe in Besançon, when one of Mlle. Amanda's suitors approaches the counter and seems to look at Julien in a certain way: "Immediately," says Stendhal, "[his] imagination, always running to extremes, was filled with ideas of a duel."

Another example occurs when Fabrizio in Geneva, on his return from Waterloo, also gets caught up in a quarrel with someone who has looked askance at him:

> "In that quarrel," says Stendhal, "Fabrizio's first impulse was totally sixteenth-century: instead of proposing a duel to the Genevan, he drew his dagger and leaped at him to stab him with it. In that moment of passion, Fabrizio forgot all that he had learned about the rules of honor and reverted to instinct, or to be more precise, to the memories of early infancy."

A moment of passion which is at the same time, without transition and without any possible differentiation, a moment of action. Surprise, indignation, rage, desire for vengeance, and the act which must fulfill the desire, all take place in a single moment without duration. Thus is confirmed in Fabrizio "that passionate manner of feeling which reigned in Italy around 1559 [and which] called for actions and not words." Fabrizio, one knows, is only a character transposed from the history of the Farnese of the sixteenth century. And cannot one say the same of Lamiel, the most intensely, the most dangerously impassioned character that one finds in Stendhal's novels? She, the lover of an incendiary and a thief, according to whom "a soul of any worth should act and not speak"?

Yet Stendhal understands perfectly the dangerously exaggerated nature of his thesis. To present a morality according to which the person ought to yield without reflection to the most intense emotions at the very instant when he feels them is to push the cult of energy to the absurd, and, what is worse, to the point of catastrophe. Moreover, no one knows better than Stendhal with what fatal ease the passions veer, what lamentable turns they can take, when, in the presence of certain actions which he thinks affront or injure him, the passionate person suddenly sees his capacity to love changed into hatred and his sentiment into resentment.

In other words, Stendhal has vigorously insisted, the passionate person is only too likely to metamorphose into a maliciously and calamitously vindictive creature. Italy, the land of vigorous souls, is also the land of hateful and melancholy people: "There one finds the driving force of great men," says Stendhal, "but it is misdirected."

It is true that, for other reasons the details of which would take too long to discuss here, Paris and the French provinces can also have the power to change the passionate person deplorably: "I am convinced that in Paris," writes Stendhal, "I would be full of hate, that is, unhappy." And, speaking of his childhood in Grenoble: "I was malicious, gloomy, irrational, in a word, a *slave* . . . in the worst sense of the word."

Thus, as there is the slave of the momentary, fugitive sensation, there is the slave of perverted passion. Is it not the spectacle of this sort of slavery that we witness when, toward the end of *The Charterhouse,* we see the duchess, until then so exquisitely spontaneous, change disposition, become absorbed in the sense of injuries endured, and finally undertake the murder of the man who had wronged her? The intensity, the thoughtless entirety with which the passionate person yields to the emotion which occasion excites or modifies, is not, therefore, without grave dangers. And not the least of these dangers, in Stendhal's view, is that it diverts the person from his essential duty, which is to seize happiness the instant it is offered.

But how to seize this happiness which arises and vanishes in the fleeting moment? No longer to bind one's energies, no longer to strain oneself, but, on the contrary, to relax, to discover a wonderful suppleness which permits one to embrace immediately the opportunity that instinct offers.

Here once again Stendhal is very close to Montaigne. From the moment they realize that everything precious in human experience lies in the instant, both organize the person's every resource to succeed in snaring that infinitely, exclusively important prey, the instant. And for this, they strive to achieve the greatest possible flexibility of mind and heart. The instant, and the happiness it permits, can be snared only through the person's adaptation to precisely that which the instant itself offers or designates. The moment of happiness can be possessed only through a kind of abandonment of the person to that moment itself: "To say precisely what the momentary degree of intoxication allows. . . . To say to her [my mistress] what I shall find best at the moment . . . to tell her each moment what I think and feel, my eyes fixed on her soul. . . . "

Such, it seems, is the policy of happiness finally adopted by Stendhal: to say quite honestly what comes to mind; to follow the impulse of his soul. And thus to achieve, not each time (that would be too glorious), but from time to time, say "once or twice a year," one of "those moments of ecstasy when the whole soul is happiness."

The texts so frequently cited by Stendhal critics are all familiar now. They deal indiscriminately with Henri Beyle himself and the privileged characters in whom are embodied his dreams of happiness. One recalls the beginning of the *Notebook of the Resolute Will:* "I am as happy as possible, at three o'clock in the afternoon, a beautiful sunshine after rain, discovering the lovely thoughts that document the notebook of the resolute will."

There we have a "moment of happiness" experienced by Stendhal himself.

But how many others are reserved for his characters! "In her whole lifetime, a completely pleasant experience had never struck Mme. de Rênal so profoundly. . . . " "Julien experienced an exquisite moment. . . . " "Never had Lucien encountered a sensation that in the least approached the one which excited him. It is for one of these rare moments that it is worth living." "This moment was the most beautiful of Fabrizio's life. . . . " "It would be difficult to portray the transports of happiness that Lamiel felt at the moment her stage-coach left for Paris."

These texts are remarkably similar. Let us note that it is in each case a matter of *moments* and not of *states.* These moments indicate the intensity of the emotion in the one who lives them, and also the intensity of the consciousness which registers them. There is nothing gayer, nothing more vivid, but also nothing more lucid than Stendhal's rural picnic with [Mélanie] Louason, at which they have, he says, "lunched at our leisure, while *feeling our happiness keenly.*"

Such is, it seems, the essential condition. For there to be a moment of happiness, the person must abandon himself to it with all the spontaneous intensity of his powers of feeling; but it is necessary too that nothing be lost by the consciousness of that palpable ecstasy; there is no real moment of happiness without awareness of the small details of that happiness: "A passionate pleasure flooded my soul and wearied it; my spirit strove not to let any shade of happiness and sensuality escape."

To inventory happiness! Such then is the device extolled by Stendhal for taking greatest advantage of the present moment. From the time when he adopts it, he applies it unceasingly with, it must be admitted, rather variable success. For the application of this method of existing runs afoul of frequently insurmountable obstacles.

First, to analyze in too minute detail the happiness that one feels is to consider it dryly, to remain cold. In a very fine essay on "Literature and Sensation," Jean-Pierre Richard has clearly shown the ravages of a mind which attempts to be merely perceptive. It perceives everything, but no longer feels anything. It is admirably equipped to note, analyze, compare, and record the shadings of happiness, but at the same time, through its very action, through its withering action, it makes happiness vanish. To perceive is almost to render oneself incapable of feeling. But the reverse is equally true. To feel, at least to feel too intensely what one feels, is to render oneself incapable of perceiving: "A man in an ecstasy of passion," says Stendhal, "does not discriminate among the subtleties. . . . " Then what does he distinguish? Nothing at all. Stendhal merely summarizes here his own experience: "I had no wit at all; I was too agitated." "The slightest thing moves me, brings tears to my eyes, sensation constantly prevails over perception. . . ."

Finally, speaking of his mistress, of the emotions that she excites in him, and of his vain attempts to seduce her:

Here perhaps is the reason which keeps me from advancing my cause with her; I love her so much that, when she says something to me, she gives me such pleasure, that besides my no longer being capable of perception and being all sensation, even if I should have the strength to perceive, I would probably not have the power to interrupt her to speak myself. . . .

And Stendhal adds, rather gloomily: "Here perhaps is why real lovers do not possess their beloved beauties."

Here also, perhaps, is why the person who is content to submit to what he feels no longer feels anything. Literally, he loses his head; and, in losing his head, he loses at the same time the opportunity of enjoying his happiness.

What, then, to do? Since to feel and to perceive what one feels are two equally necessary things, can one make arrangements to feel first and then perceive, which seems a very simple and, more- over, a very frequent practice?

In fact, Stendhal points out, "weak eyesight is dazzled by a flash of lightning during the night; that flash agitates and enraptures it so much, it feels it so strongly, that it has no time (no presence of mind) to consider its direction or the number of its zigzags."

Conclusion: to perceive what we feel (and to exploit it), let us give ourselves the time we lack. Let us establish some distance be- tween the sensation and the perception. This is what everyone does, and what Stendhal tries to do:

> The day when one is moved is not the day during which one best notices the beauties and the flaws.

> As I was going out [as he was going out from his mistress's house where, once again, Stendhal had remained as mute as a carp] as I was going out, a stupendous number of tender and witty things occurred to me. When I am more *perception* and less *sensation*, I shall be able to say them to her.

What Stendhal practices, then, is a staircase wit, a retrospective wit, the wit for which one somehow divides the moment in two; in a first part one feels, one submits, one becomes confused, one is given the opportunity to say or do something; and then, in a second part, one discovers what he must say or do; one tardily and, so to speak, retrospectively improves on the occasion.

But without taking into account that in behaving thus one is always too late and that the perceptive-inventive activity thus ap- pears as futile as it is ineffectual, such a practice has the fatal fault of splitting the moment apart and making of it, so to speak, two moments which are not even consecutive. Undoubtedly, it is necessary not to cling further to the moment, to rise, as Doctor Sansfin wishes, "above the sensation of the moment," but still it must be done in such a way that the movement of the mind does not separate it irremediably from the tiny nugget of palpable dura- tion which it is intended to illuminate, from which it is to extract and increase the possibilities of enjoyment. No, the ideal is not to destroy the instant by placing the essential elements which must work together for its triumph and its delight at two disconnected points in duration, but rather, on the contrary, to reinforce and perfect the instant by taking care that sensation and perception, its two indispensable components, meet and join together in it, yet without, as we have seen, causing mutual paralysis. Since the overly vivid sensation tends to confuse the perception, and since an exces-

sively dry perception tends to kill sensation, there is only one possible solution: that which consists in tempering the disturbing
liveliness of the sensation and in mitigating the withering rigor of
the perceptive function. Then a proper balance is established
within the moment itself. The favorable alliance of lucid thought
and the tenderest emotion gives the immediate moment its perfection. It is this which Stendhal observes, for example, on Feb. 25,
1805, a glorious day when he succeeded, without spoiling it, in
"minutely analyzing his own way of feeling." "There, without
doubt," he cries, "is the most beautiful day of my life. . . . Never
have I shown more ability. My perception was precisely what was
necessary to direct the sensation, and no more."

An intelligence nimble enough to notice all the gradations of the
soul's vibration on the wing, so to speak, a vibration restrained
enough for the soul not to be dazzled by its own pleasure, is this
not the double function of the spirit that music requires? For music
is at once sensation and perception:

> What is most beautiful in music is indisputably a recitative
> spoken with the technique of Madame Grassini and the soul
> of Madame Pasta. The *pauses* and other embellishments which
> the impassioned soul of the singer devises, admirably portray
> (or, to speak the truth, *reproduce in your soul*) those little
> moments of delightful serenity which one encounters in real
> passions. During those brief instants, the soul of the passionate
> person considers in minute detail the pleasures and the pains
> that his spirit's step forward has just shown him.

An exquisite blend of serenity and ardor, of activity and passivity,
of spontaneity and calculation, of intelligence and tenderness, such
then is the marvellously happy result of the moments in which one
is neither rigid with the tension of effortful perception, nor blinded
by the dazzle of exploding sensibility. This is happiness, the only
possible happiness. It exists only in brief moments and in moments
as rare as they are brief: "Once or twice a year one has moments of
ecstasy in which the entire soul is happiness. . . . " These ecstasies,
in accordance with the nature of man, cannot endure."

The search for happiness is not, therefore, fruitless. However, one
cannot say that it is abundantly productive. In his game-basket the
hunter brings back several pieces of game, but he carries his prizes
easily and he can just as easily count their number: a handful of
happy moments. These constitute a very small number of exceptional experiences, noble and delightful successes achieved by the
person here and there in the course of his life, but they do not constitute a life. One can enumerate them, one can (sometimes)
remember them, one can, as Stendhal often tries to do, go from

one to another in thought. One can try to compare them. One can wonder, for example, if Adèle, leaning heavily on the arm which supports her occasions a more delightful moment than the braised spinach on which one dined on another day in the country. But these moments which one recalls (but how often imperfectly and in what a profoundly unsatisfying way)—there is one thing, in any case, that one can never make them do. One can not connect one with another, prolong one into another, make a current of life pass along the space of time which separates them. No one is less equipped to construct a duration for himself than Stendhal; no one is less gifted for experimenting with the feeling of time. Condemned to live—and to relive—the moments of his existence in isolation, Stendhal is neither capable nor even desirous of transforming these moments into a person's continuous time. No, his profound ideal, the hope which was constantly being disappointed and constantly being reborn in his mind, would be to bestow on each of these marvellous moments a kind of independent and particular eternity. The dream would be to preserve each of these moments fresh and available, ready to be relived in the mind at will. To use endlessly, in no matter what new instant, the several instants worth repeating, that is what Stendhal wants, and what, through an infinity of different processes, he tries to do. *Henry Brulard*, the *Memoirs of Egotism*, all the autobiographical works bear witness to this. But so do the entire range of novels, arranged each time so that the plot, the events, the setting and characters, all are laid out around several moments which are moments of happiness. The happy moment in which Julien, mounting the scaffold, remembers other happy moments passed in the woods of Vergy with Mme. de Rênal on his arm, the happy moment in which Fabrizio in prison discovers the charming proximity of Clelia Conti in "a celestial solitude" from which one discovers a horizon that reaches from Treviso to Mount Viso. The happy moment when, in the presence of Lucien, enamored of Mme. de Chasteller, certain Bohemian horns at the Green Hunter "play in a delightful manner a sweet, simple, rather slow music, while a ray of sunlight, obliquely piercing the depths of greenery, thus quickens the moving half-shadow of the great forest." In none of these episodes does the moment mesh with the rest of the whole, form with them that continuous totality of the complete life which, for example, the characters of Flaubert, Tolstoy, Thomas Hardy, Roger Martin du Gard almost always give us. One would say of these latter that they always carry the entire weight of their past (and even of their future destiny) on their shoulders. Now, it works in quite the opposite way for Stendhal's characters. Never living in anything but moments, they are always free of what does not belong to those moments. Is this to say that they lack an essential dimension, a certain density which is a density of duration? Possibly. But as we have been able to see from the examples just cited, the Stendhalian moments are not destitute of dimensions appropriate to them. The happy moment reserved to Julien is doubly exalted by the profundity of the reminiscences and the immediate prospect of death. The music of the Green Hunter rises in a place which the play of light in the undergrowth enlarges. Finally, what vast expansion is achieved at the moment when Fabrizio discovers Clelia, when he sees her against a background formed by all the outspread Alps!

Strictly speaking, the Stendhal novel has thus no duration. But in the several moments without duration that he presents to us, he offers us as compensation, to complete our happiness and that of the person who is placed in the very confined limits of these brief moments, a revelation of *space*.

"A lover," said Stendhal, "sees the woman he loves in the horizon of all the countries he travels."

JEAN-PIERRE RICHARD

Knowing and Feeling in Stendhal†

III

The world is fixed, drained under a scrutiny: it is the eye which, having separated and isolated things, reigns thereafter over this lifeless people, this soulless wasteland. And not satisfied with having killed everything outside the soul, this tyranny is now going to assail the soul itself. In order that his own undertaking actually turn back on himself, Stendhal need only feel that he himself becomes the object, and no longer the subject, of the analytic vision, and that instead of turning outward from him, the all-powerful gaze turns in upon him. For the process to which he has subjected things can as easily be inflicted on him by others. He in turn feels himself observed, tried, judged; he feels his liberty reduced to a definition,

† From Jean-Pierre Richard, "Connaissance et tendresse chez Stendhal," *Littérature et Sensation* (Paris, 1954), pp. 47–54, 100–116.

Following in the footsteps of Georges Poulet—whose predecessors are to be found in philosophy as well as among literary critics—much modern French criticism devotes its energies to laying bare the structure of an author's imaginative world, its characteristic assumptions as to time, space, perception, reflection, relatedness or lack of relation, value or absence of value. Jean-Pierre Richard's big essay on Stendhal, from which we reproduce sections III and V (both in part) and VI (entire) is such a study. The interested reader will find parts I and II translated in Victor Brombert's little anthology of critical texts on Stendhal (Prentice-Hall, 1962).

to an essence. Then a conflicting terror comes to blend with the joy of knowing, a terror every impulse of which pushes him toward flight, withdrawal, and the protection of his secret. One can account for several of the most typically Stendhalian attitudes by this fundamental desire to escape definitions, to mislead the witnesses and the judges.

He will be able to elude this immobilizing gaze by various methods, the mask,[1] for example, or flight. He refutes this idea to which others want to reduce him by opposing to it another idea, or by refusing to admit any idea, through hypocrisy or through modesty. Moreover, Stendhal has no choice between these two postures: because he is a man, he acknowledges his inability to practise or even to understand modesty. On the contrary, he sees in it the primary attraction and the great privilege of the woman, a mysterious mechanism before whose delicacy the most discerning analyst confesses his incapacity. Its evasive subtlety, he writes, results uniquely "from combinations of sensations which cannot exist in men, and, often from refinements not grounded in nature." Modesty would then be, and here Stendhal follows Helvetius, a delightful fruit of civilization. In any case a man can discuss it only by "hearsay." He can only record and submit to the charm of "those often incomprehensible customs, daughters of modesty."[2] But they are necessary to him if he is to feel himself charmed; he does not like women who are too transparent, tires quickly for example, of that Louason in whom he had once been so proud to be able to read at sight. In Mme. de Chasteller, on the contrary, it is the obscurity, the unpredictability, the shrinking withdrawals of an incessantly startled delicacy that Lucien Leuwen adores; and Lucien's feelings here merely reproduce those of Stendhal himself for Métilde. For the charm of modesty is primarily that of the incomprehensible.[3]

Modesty misleads. It is a "custom of lying," an instinctive and pliant falsehood. Hypocrisy, on the other hand, consists in a constantly sustained effort never to betray a lie which has been settled on before any act, and which orders all one's conduct into a systematic defense against the scrutinies that probe it. It does not retreat or attack, but wants to erect an unbreachable wall between

1. On these subjects one must read J. Starobinski's noteworthy article on "The Pseudonymous Stendhal," in *Les Temps Modernes*, 1950. [Later reprinted in *L'Oeil vivant* (Paris, 1961).]
2. *On Love*, I, 120.
3. The lover ought neither to see nor understand the beloved woman: he must respect her mystery. In the *Privileges of April 10, 1840*, Stendhal bestows on his "privileged man" a universal gift of second sight, but this gift stops short at the threshold of love:
"Twenty times a year, the privileged man will be able to guess the thoughts of all people twenty paces in front of him. One hundred times a year, he will be able to see what the person he desires is doing at that moment; *this is with the complete exception of the woman he loves best*." *Mélanges intimes*, I, 205.

the soul and the world. Yet insofar as the individual clings in the midst of it to a false definition of self, hypocrisy imprisons him in precisely that dessicated world which he wants to escape. For the false definition defines the being, or at least governs his movements more rigorously than could all the gazes leveled at him. Just as vanity does, the false definition transforms being into spectacle, forces it to live onstage: but while vanity unselfconsciously directs him only toward others, hypocrisy in addition makes him his own spectacle. Through hypocrisy he sees himself acting and controlling his slightest movements. The enemy of everything spontaneous, hypocrisy thus stifles and constricts; it enslaves, in the worst sense of the word. All his experiences as a child had shown Stendhal that it was a false remedy, a remedy worse than the disease, since while ostensibly concealing him from others, it only forced him to submit further to the judgment of the world, and in addition subjected him to that judge who is more pitiless than any other observer: himself. Let us not forget that for Stendhal Julien Sorel is a pitiable and unfortunate hero.

Thus Stendhal most often adopted a third posture: neither modest withdrawal nor hypocritical defense, but scandalous offensive. For him, provocation was inverted modesty. Smug vulgarity, self-dramatization, cynical coarseness, no longer is anyone deceived by this art of "Stendhalizing" which nevertheless succeeded in keeping a whole century of right-thinking men at a distance from him. Perhaps Stendhal's friends feel so much fondness for him only for having been obliged to win over their real Stendhal from so many false Stendhals. Their loving curiosity must undergo a whole series of initiations, overcome a whole course of obstacles, and discover all the key-words, the "open sesames" which will permit them to penetrate to the heart of a work which so many precautions still protect. The mystification in this case does not arise, as it does later in Baudelaire or the Surrealists, from a more inclusive purpose, from an aesthetic of astonishment or a morality of incongruity: the shocking uproar serves him only by concealing his inner truth. Going even further, he discovered that that very truth could become his best refuge, provided it appeared excessive, incredible. Such is *egotism*, at once a means of knowing the self and concealing it, of rejoicing in the self and baffling others. Sincerity appears here openly, but appears a little too crudely to seem really sincere. Valéry himself was caught in this subtle snare: one must love Stendhal very much to understand that his parading of the natural enables him to hide his true character, and sincerity serves to protect his freedom.

Only in secret does this freedom dare to assert itself: curtains lowered, shutters closed, keys turned in the lock, Julien can draw from beneath his mattress the portrait of Napoleon and continue the forbidden reading of the *Mémorial*. This protective mattress we shall encounter again at every moment of Stendhal's life. The constant disguises, punning riddles, enigmas, anagrams, and pseudonyms which today are still the torture and joy of the exegetes are simply literary counterparts of the mattress. And this is no simple game of hide-and-seek. For if there is one character who taints the Stendhalian universe, who infects all honest relationships in it, it is the spy. Stendhal sees him everywhere, puts him on the heels of all his heroes. Eternally hunted and spied upon, Julien, Lucien, and Fabrizio know they are watched, but do not know who is watching them. The power of the spy really derives from his seeing without being seen: hidden in shadow, he observes and gains possession of his victim while the victim cannot even attempt to protect himself. The supreme spy is thus the one who loses himself in a crowd, disappears in a collective identity. We know that for Stendhal this faceless spy, this anonymous professional in ambush and secrecy, was the *priest*. The *Congregation* seemed to him a kind of universal eye, plumbing the secrecy of lives through its temporal organization and probing the interior of the soul by means of confession. Disguised, dispersed, numberless, present everywhere and nowhere, the Jesuits stretch a net of unerring surveillance over Europe. Consider for example the fantastic scene where, in an Alsatian inn, the Abbé Castanède and his acolytes shine a dark-lantern on the face of Julien as he feigns sleep: how can one fail to see in that prying light a perfectly clear symbol of the moral rape that is confession? For the confessional looks on and condemns; the priest is a watcher and a thief. And Stendhal's atheism has discovered several prodigious ways to express this obsession, for example this remark by the Abbé Chas-Bernard to Julien on the day when both are in the midst of decorating the cathedral of Besançon: "Keep an eye on the confessionals; that's where the robbers' girlfriends hang out to spy on us the moment our backs are turned."[4] Words like these do not simply derive from anticlerical satire; they reveal at a stroke the hidden anguish of a conscience. For if Stendhal attributes the responsibility for his mistrust to the religious and police regimes under which his heroes and he were condemned to live, it certainly seems that such an obsession far exceeds the natural repugnance of generous minds for unjust power. It expresses much more directly an essential fear of others, and the unconquerable dread of feeling on one's life an alien gaze which judges and denies. Thus Ranuccio Ernesto lies flat on his stomach every night to look under his bed for highly unlikely assassins: choked by fear, and by shame for his fear, he is for us an exemplary victim of that obsession with the gaze that in varying degrees possesses all Stendhal's creations.

4. *Red and Black*, p. 154

Darkness alone can protect one against the gaze; and thus we understand why night occupies such an important place in Stendhal's geography of happiness. Night permits the fearful or strained soul to abandon its modesty or to ease its posture: it is night that in its darkness assumes the place of hypocrisy or modesty, and allows the hero to become truly himself. In the night at Vergy Julien forgets to play the role of Julien: "Julien gave no further thought to his black ambition or to his projects, so difficult to carry out. For the first time in his life he was carried away by the power of beauty."[5] Carried away, that is, swept beyond the self, lifted by "transports of affection and wild gaiety" far from the parched image of himself to which he would always like to reduce himself. Freed by the night, because protected by it.

And it is again the night which hides Fabrizio on the shore of Lago Maggiore from the eyes of the police who pursue him:

> Sitting on his isolated rock, no longer having to keep watch against the police, sheltered by the dark night and the vast silence, he felt gentle tears welling up in his eyes, and he found there, at little cost, the happiest moments he had tasted in a long time.[6]

This protection is also granted to Mme. de Chasteller, during her walk in the woods of the Green Hunter with Lucien, in that summer evening steeped in Mozartian echoes, "one of those bewitching evenings which can be numbered among the greatest enemies of the heart's indifference. . . . " "The night which fell completely," writes Stendhal, "allowed her to stop fearing observation."[7] It is then that she lets slip that silent half-avowal which will appear so horrible to her once back in the light of chandeliers and of day. Thus the night frees some from their roles, others from their mistrust or timidity. On all it bestows, in its great sober silence, rest and respite from tension. One must then know how to be silent. "Don't speak a word . . . ," says Mme. de Chasteller to Lucien: creating a new form of relationship, words, which assert, define, give form to the formless, would require resumption of the mortal duel, the game of sham and ostentation in which hearts are exhausted and destroyed. One must shelter in the greatest depth of shadow, flee even the glimmer of stars or "the indiscretion of a sky too deep and too light." For the Stendhal hero there is no real night except that which he spends crouched in the heart of a forest, hidden beneath great outspread branches which cloak and nurture his intimacy.

In those tranquil summer nights which surround without constricting, and whose darkness, tremulous as lake water, seems to

5. *Red and Black*, pp. 52–53.   7. *Lucien Leuwen*, II, 40.
6. *Chartreuse de Parme*, I, 270.

offer the soul some sort of opaque and gentle fluid medium in which to let its reverie drift, feelings come to lose all precise content. The reverie which seizes the being opens it so fully to all the emanations of the night that it creates in the consciousness a kind of pleasing void in which each sensation reverberates delightfully. Thus Julien:

> Lost in a vague, delightful dream, wholly foreign to his character, gently pressing that hand which seemed to him perfectly beautiful, he only half heard the rustling of the linden tree in the light night wind and the distant barking of dogs by the mill on the Doubs.[8]

It is a pause in which life sprawls out, and where the Stendhalian sentence abandons its habitual dryness in order to linger on a magnificent effect of indefinitely remote distance. Stendhal's nights are thus filled with grating little sensations, leaves pattering in the rain, waves breaking on a beach, the barking of dogs in the distance, which, fixing the external attention, allow profound abstraction. This appears nowhere better than in that page of the *Rouge* where Julien, alone in the cathedral of Besançon, dark and sweet-smelling as the wood of Vergy (and where he will soon actually see as in an ultimate hallucination the veiled spectre of Mme. de Rênal) hears the great bell ring and begins to muse. Stendhal entertains himself, a bit heavy-handedly perhaps, by juxtaposing the reflections that this sound would have inspired in the perfect ideological hero with the hazy reverie in which Julien loses himself:

> The solemn tolling of the bell should have caused Julien to think only of the work being done by twenty men at fifty centimes apiece and assisted perhaps by fifteen or twenty of the faithful. He should have calculated the wear and tear on the ropes or on the beams, should have considered the dangers from the bell itself, which falls every two centuries. . . .[9]

Instead of that:

> The silence, the perfect solitude, the coolness of the long nave rendered Julien's reverie all the sweeter. . . . His soul had almost escaped its mortal envelope, which continued to stroll slowly up

8. *Red and Black*, p. 53. In 1838, Stendhal considers creating a character, *Robert,* who would be his complete opposite, a kind of anti-Stendhal. "Set my imagination the task of portraying the absence of imagination. Ask myself: what would I feel in his position? And make him feel the opposite." "Kissing the prettiest of women, he sees only what the most unfeeling groom could not deny, that is to say . . . the value of her ear-pendants. Owing no pleasure to his imagination, Robert is greatly concerned with the comfort of his armchair, the excellence of his dinner, the coziness of his apartment, etc. . . ." He succeeds in life because "his opera glass is never clouded by the breath of imagination." He is pure gaze, because he cannot conceive that things can be known except by looking: "The impassioned soul, the young Jean-Jacques, clings to the predictions of his imagination, Robert values only what he sees." (*Mélanges de Littérature,* I, 235.)
9. *Red and Black,* p. 155.

the north aisle, over which it was to watch. . . . his eye looked without seeing.[1]

Instead of dissolving into an intellectual interpretation, the sensation serves only to tie the being to its "envelope." Last point of its contact with the actual, it prevents the consciousness from losing itself completely by continuing to make it feel its existence. I am here because I feel, but elsewhere since I feel myself scarcely feeling. To learn to look without seeing, to look in order not to see, such is without doubt the last word of wisdom for the sensitive hero, and for all those who like him put their sensations at the service of their reverie.

V

The semi-failure of the *Rouge* made Stendhal realize that the understanding could approach an isolated idea only with difficulty. Contemporaries of Lamartine and Chateaubriand had difficulty understanding this novelist who wrote like Montesquieu or Laclos. Rereading his novel in 1831, he admits to himself:

> The style too blunt, too abrupt. . . . It lacks the smooth development that J. J. has in the *Confessions*. Dominique's horror of the long, turgid sentences of the wits of 1830 drives him to the blunt, the abrupt, the staccato, the harsh.

Then, realizing that the content of a sentence is not limited to its explicit meaning, but extends also into its prolongation by the reader's musing, he sees the necessity "*of adding words to help the imagination* reconstruct the idea."[2] Therefore he now is concerned to fill the gaps and to establish bridges between the work and the reader. Again, in 1841, after the *Charterhouse*, he notes: "I find many words to change for the sake of mellowness," words "which appeal more to the heart."[3] And elsewhere: "I give balance, serenity, close attention to style. I think that this style exhausts the attention as would a French translation of Tacitus. It must be made fluent for an accomplished woman of thirty, and even amusing if possible."[4] Thus the writer invites the reader to examine his sentence, to survey it as it unfolds, to participate in its rhythm and its development: literature attempts primarily to work a charm, to lead the captivated reader "by the hand."

In a chapter significantly titled, "On the law of continuity," Helvetius himself had emphasized the usefulness of preparation in art.[5] Stendhal is eager to profit by these precepts. From now on,

1. *Red and Black*, p. 155.
2. *Marginalia*, II, 136.
3. *Marginalia*, III, 182.
4. *Marginalia*, III, 378.
5. Cf. Helvetius (*On Man*, Book II, section 8, ch. 16)
"Idea, image, feeling; in a book, everything must be prepared for and led up to. . . .

I take as an example a rapid succession of real and varied scenes. In general, such a succession is pleasing insofar as it stimulates in us vivid sensations. However, to produce this effect, one must skillfully prepare for it. I love to pass with Isis or the heifer Io from those scorched climates of the torrid zone to those caverns,

the sentence will no longer progress in a series of shocks, but will glide in an imperceptible movement. It is intended to convince, to establish communication even more than to surprise. For all literature is an attempt at seduction; it wants that reader for whom it sets its snares not simply to attend to, but to participate in, the argument or the adventure. It demands and must compel his complicity. It is then that it draws on the charming power of poetry or eloquence and unfolds the "second meaning" of rhythmic or tonal harmony which, expanding or enveloping the logical meaning, succeeds in convincing. "A turn of phrase," Stendhal remarks, "is often an idea." The harmony and linkage of sentences thus give style the same additional dimension that shading or slight variations in tone give to painting and music. Words, too, plumb the sentence and invite excursions of the imagination.

"That thing, imperceptible beyond all others, that one might call, with Charles du Bos, the atmosphere in which a style is steeped," one now feels circulating between the sentences. Thanks to this atmosphere the narrative begins to breathe. Behind the extraordinary swiftness of event is outlined the perspective of all that the writer omits, but the existence of which one senses, and the invisible richness of which supports the bold density of line. Stendhal kept on perfecting this *art of aeration* from novel to novel. In *Armance*, a novel of suffocation and sterility, consciousness is closed in upon its impotence. The conflict between two hostile self-esteems occurs entirely in the rarefied atmosphere of a drawing-room; the sentence itself contracts and strains, knotted up by pride and impediments. The *Rouge* gasps. It is the novel of a runner who has not caught his breath. Julien is not, like Octave, the victim of a lack of oxygen, of asphyxiation by scruple; he is choked and shrivelled by ambition, and diminishes himself because he wants to go too fast. But what freshness in the gusts of air that he sometimes stops to breathe, which swell his chest and give him, and at the same time the style, the ease and harmony of happiness! For Lucien Leuwen happiness is easy. Observation holds level, but rarely obtrudes, as if sentences and characters were strolling with such nonchalance in the invisible background and the hidden style, that we could no longer perceive any but the extremes of their postur-

---

those boulders of ice which the sun strikes with an oblique light. But the contrast of these images will not stimulate lively impressions in me if the poet, in proclaiming the might and jealousy of Juno, has not already prepared me for the sudden change of scene. . . .

Let us go on from feeling to ideas: Have I a new idea to present to the public? That truth, almost always too difficult for the generality of men, is at first understood only by the smallest number of them. [One thinks here of the "happy few."] If I want that idea to impress them generally, I must prepare their minds for this truth in advance; I must raise their minds little by little and finally show it to them from a clear and precise point of view."

ings. *Lucien Leuwen* was undoubtedly the easiest and most successful of Stendhal's creations, that in which his memories flowed most
unaffectedly. But one cannot help thinking that very ease detracted
from the density of the novel, relieved slightly the tension of his
hand, and slackened that striving of the imagination to toughen
reverie without which any novel remains a pretty collection of
memories. The *Charterhouse* remains the miracle: an amazing
narrative whose supple development is as taut as a passion, in which
all the observations seem to remain this side of a prodigiously rich
truth which they only circumspectly suggest, in which one has the
impression that everything is said, but also that everything remains
to be said. The slightest nuance here opens up a world of insights,
of abrupt precipices which the movement of the narrative immediately closes over. In the discontinuity, the brittleness, of this style,
one must now see a means of opening windows in the wall of the
sentence, of aerating the density of the thought, and of projecting
through the opacity of expression a light rather like that which the
rays of the setting sun send through the shadows of the forest of
the Green Hunter, and which, piercing "through the depths of
greenery . . . seem to quicken that impressive darkness of the great
forests."[6] Through an analogous effect silence animates the style;
allowing effects of linguistic chiaroscuro, it no longer separates sentences, but gives them life: it is the resonant form of the atmosphere.

The style itself, then, confirms the powers of the law of continuity. "We believe," writes Stendhal, "that tenderness needs to
be guided, prepared for. . . . For it never appears except in the bosom
of profound confidence. . . . "[7] Continuity of style serves to calm
and to bring back to safety the reader who is tossed to and fro by
the accidents of the adventure. Fénelon, whom the young Stendhal
considered a great artist in words, succeeded in this aim by covering
any angularities with a kind of oily liquid. Rhetoric cloaks the
truth. "Fénelon who loves simplicity so much says that a man of
parts does not like the bare story. He wants to adorn it, ornament
it with embellishments, curl its hair. Something to imitate."[8] And
without doubt the modern reader of the *Télémaque* considers
Fénelon sometimes a bit too artificial. But to Stendhal's ears what
sweetness

> in that train of simple and perfectly linked sentences, in the
> propriety of that author who does not use certain ellipses, made
> familiar by the writers of the eighteenth century, whether because
> they were not invented in his time or because he preferred to be
> a bit longer, and charm the ear by the roundness of his sen-
> tence.[9]

6. Lucien Leuwen, II, 36.
7. *Mélanges de littérature* III, 100.
8. *Mélanges de littérature*, III, 94.
9. *Mélanges de littérature*, III, 94.

Thus he succeeded in rendering nature in her "infinite variety," the literary counterpart of the "continuous variety" of Correggio. Jean-Jacques, on the other hand, using in literature a process analogous to that of general tone in painting, "gives everything a coloring." His sentences demand a constantly sustained sympathy:

> Rousseau's style is periodic, harmonious, and tends to produce a constantly strong impression; it has no moments of repose, of chiaroscuro. . . . Thus we believe that the style of Jean-Jacques is eminently suitable to excite sympathy, because, since it takes an interest in everything, our sympathy is always engaged. If you escape one of the grasps of sympathy, there are others ready to seize you.[1]

The beautiful style exerts a constant compulsion.

But here one must beware of a possible error: the persuasive power of a beautiful sentence is not equal, as the law of analytic examination would have it, to the sum of the convictions created by each of the elements of which the sentence is composed. The meaning of the combination exceeds the total of the meanings of the components of that combination. And this is true for psychology as it is for rhetoric. Examining those sympathetic "grasps" which compel constant engagement in a sentence by Rousseau, Stendhal realizes that the charm does not depend (as it does in the case of Fénelon, for example) on the perfect linking of various elements of the sentence, which leaves no opportunity for inattention, but that it arises from the sustained congruity of an element external to the sentence, and that that element must be called Rousseau's soul, or the soul of his style. This also is why Stendhal, although so little the poet, keeps wondering what meaning poetry achieves and how it does so. For a beautiful poem presents to its reader the concrete mystery of a sounded or imaged remainder which resists all logical analysis, but which nevertheless constitutes its power and its meaning. "The form, here, is part of the thing,"[2] asserts Stendhal. It is, indeed, the form itself which gives meaning and value to the thing. Analogously, it is the dynamic and formal unity of the emotion which governs the apparently incoherent progression of sentences through which this emotion is transmitted, or of the attitudes through which it appears. Lucien's love for Mme. de Chasteller, for example, is not the simple sum of the emotions that these two characters feel, but their dialectical unity. Thus it is no longer by the detail, however significant it may be, that one will be able to judge or recognize an emotion:

> Judging by the confusion involved in the conversations of lovers, it would not be wise to draw over-hasty conclusions from an

1. *Mélanges de littérature*, III, 111.   2. *Filosofia Nova*, II, 58.

isolated detail of the talk. They reveal their precise emotions only in unexpected words. Then it is the cry of the heart. Besides, it is only *from the character of all the things said that one can draw inferences*.[3]

Thus knowledge of combinations replaces knowledge of details, one discovers the true through the study of character as a whole and of generalized form—no longer from particular and individual preciseness. At one of the most pathetic moments of his life, when Métilde was scrutinizing and analyzing him in order to disparage the details of his slightest actions (treating him as he treated his own heroes), Stendhal begged the right to be judged by the totality of his conduct:

> When a man is dominated by an extreme passion, no one thing he says or does in a particular instance proves anything about him; it is the whole of his life that testifies for him. Thus, Madame, though I should swear at your feet all day long that I love you or that I hate you, that should have no influence on the degree of belief that you think yourself able to accord me. *It is the totality of my life that should speak*.[4]

How better to proclaim the falseness of that analysis which would make the particulars eloquent, and in which Stendhal had once seen the instrument privileged to discover truth?

Henceforth, literary creation can be seen in this perspective as a means of harmonizing and transcending in an imaginative totality the various moments and episodes of experience in life. From this existence, half-spoiled, or at least given over to the mercy of events, the novel gathers up nostalgias, remolds memories, and directs them according to the continuity of an imagined fate. To irrational, disjointed life it gives back a relationship and a meaning, grants a lasting vindication. The novel is a revenge on life, not only (as is so often said) because it transformed Stendhal into a whole gallery of young and handsome heroes, but because it transformed his life into a series of adventures.

The novel is no longer only, according to the famous formula, a mirror traveling a highroad: it becomes that highroad itself, down the whole length of which men and landscapes offer the traveller a succession of reflections and spectacles which, completely unforeseen and accidental as they most often pretend to appear, are nonetheless governed by the very order of the journey. However dominated by chance it pretends to be, the Stendhal novel remains in fact a novel, that is to say, a composition in which a number of selected persons act out an exemplary fate. Seen from a certain distance and judged in its entirety, the line of Julien's or Fabrizio's life unfolds and completes itself in a perfect curve: not a false step,

3. *De l'Amour*, I, 110.   4. *Aux âmes sensibles*, 265.

not a deviation from the normal, each of their actions seems to belong fully to them and to be capable of belonging only to them, as if, at each moment and without the least effort, they were completely at one with themselves. Judith Gautier, who confided to Stendhal's genius the task of joining together the sparse fragments of her own improvisation, knew this well: "As for me, I write in spurts, and when I must harmonize all these flutterings, I accomplish nothing but phrase-mongering of the worst sort . . . ," she wrote to him. To harmonize his own flutterings without grandiloquence, to transform a bundle of moments into "the totality of a life," such was in fact the great achievement of Stendhal.

VI

Real and imagined, explicit and implicit, determined and indeterminate, speech and silence, between these opposite poles the psychology of Stendhal has appeared to us traversed by a reciprocating movement whose amplitude only the fine arts, music, painting, or literature can limit, a back-and-forth which only they sometimes succeed in immobilizing. However, these balancings always result from a compromise: in order to mix and to adapt to each other, the hostile elements must each sacrifice something of themselves. How much more exciting it would be to find a method, not of balancing the two rival forces, but of satisfying one by means of the other in the unity of a single triumphant movement! Stendhal believes that *love* can effect this miracle.

And primarily because love, according to the remark of one of his favorite authors, is a *mania*. Beginning with a real object, and by a series of steps which recall rather precisely the obsessions of madness, it constructs a world of phantoms. "From the moment that he is in love, the wisest of men no longer sees any object as it is. . . . He no longer attributes anything to chance; he loses his sense of the probable. A thing he only imagines comes to exist for its effect on his happiness.[5] The imaginary alone exists, and reality no longer carries any weight except as it contributes to the constructions of the imagination. Here Stendhal very faithfully follows his masters the ideologues. He explains this derangement by "a physical cause, a beginning of madness, an abundance of blood in the brain, a disturbance in the nerves and the cerebral center"[6] Before him, Cabanis had explained an analogous phenomenon by the oddity "peculiar to the melancholic temperament," in whom decisions are "full of hesitation and reservation, and the will seems to achieve its end only circuitously. . . ." From that moment on, desire no longer seeks to fulfill itself, but folds back upon itself to feed on the illusions that it has already formed:

5. *De l'Amour*, II, 242.   6. *De l'Amour*, I, 65.

Thus the appetites or the desires of the melancholic will take on
the character of passion rather than that of need, often even the
true aim will seem totally lost from sight. . . . In the case of the
melancholic . . . it is the seminal humor alone which imparts a
new essence to the impressions, to the determinations, to the impulses; it is the humor which creates in the heart of the cerebral
organ those astonishing forms, too often used *to pursue phantoms,
to systematize visions.*[7]

Maine de Biran explains the power of these phantoms over the mind
and their progressive detachment from reality by the force that habit
has given them. The sensibility soon needs them as it would a necessary stimulant, and no longer cares to make any external reality
correspond to them:

Concentrated in the sphere of the very means of excitation, the
person clings to them each day with more strength and obstinacy,
calls on them incessantly, and neither can nor wants to be diverted
from them. These phantoms, inherent in the thought whose idols
(*idola mentis*) they become, seem to be for the organ of thought
what habitual artificial irritants are for the organs of sensation;
the same necessity, the same uneasiness, the same need to exaggerate some impressions to which habit has exclusively tied a
consciousness of existence which tends incessantly to revive itself.[8]

And in Stendhal too the imagination plunges the lover "into a
world of realities *modeled after his desires.*"[9] It draws him into "bewitching reveries of crystallization." But this immersion in the imaginary requires a real point of departure; this "modeling" is done on
concrete stuff. The crystals, says Stendhal, cover the branch of
Salzburg so completely that:

As soon as the crystallizations have taken effect, indifferent eyes
no longer recognize the branch of the tree.
For, 1) It is adorned with perfections or with diamonds which
     they do not see;
   2) It is adorned with perfections which are not such for
     them.[1]

But beneath the camouflage the branch itself remains. It is the
branch which provides the cluster of diamonds with its underlying
frame and its solidity. No one, to be sure, can recognize it any longer,
but it continues, faithful in spite of oblivion, to uphold the whole
structure of crystal. At the heart of love it is thus the real, and not
emptiness, that one finds. These "idols" or these phantoms are not

7. *Traité du Physique et du Moral de l'Homme,* ed Reisse, p. 287.
8. Maine de Biran, *Influence de l'habi-* tude, p. 149.
9. *De l'Amour,* II, 156.
1. *De l'Amour,* II, 39.

born simply of the excitement of a mind whose vain desires they would come to gratify: love in Stendhal is an idolatry of the true. It is the budding of the imaginary on the real starting with reality, it is a passing from one world to the other, or better, it is the creation of one world by the other.

Stendhal himself took care to emphasize all the distance which separates this concrete imagination, adhering completely to a truth which it transfigures without falsifying, from another imagination, that which chases after chimeras and which seeks primarily to flee a world in which it sees its worst enemy. It is to this latter form of imagination that the dreams of Fabrizio, in the first part of the *Charterhouse*, belong. "He was still too young," writes Stendhal; "in his moments of leisure, his soul was busy tasting rapturously the sensations produced by romantic circumstances that his imagination was always ready to supply to him." In short, he charges his daydreams with adorning, with concealing the ugliness of "this reality which still seemed insipid and vile to him;"[2] he asks his imagination to excite for him the charming sensations that will mask the melancholy triviality of his life. In this he succumbs to the temptation of the falsely fictional, to the ease of an illusory dream which, instead of elevating the real to its own level, hovers high above a world that it scorns. True imagination, as Fabrizio will later learn to recognize and use it, does not work without the preliminary acceptance of things. It is on this "flatness," this "vileness" that it constructs its most beautiful palaces. And it is when Fabrizo has learned that real, everyday life offers dreaming far greater riches and more numerous opportunities than any fictional existence, it is then, but only then, that Stendhal makes him the hero of a novel.

But if love rises from the real toward the imaginary, toward the transformation of the world, is it not true, inversely, that passion might become a source of knowledge, and that through it things might reappear, more pure, more precise than they appeared to the common or logical vision? From the heights of love, can one not descend again toward the earth?

Many of Stendhal's texts seem to deny the possibility of such a re-descent. They affirm that in love, as in a melody, "one surrenders blindly,"[3] "one does not know where he goes."[4] Love goes blindfolded or, if by chance it can see, its eyes are fixed on that single end that the desire of the lover assigns it:

> Love in these fleet moments fraught with itself
> Sees nothing, hears nothing but hope, its guide. . . .[5]

2. *Chartreuse de Parme*, I, 274. 4. *De l'Amour*, I, 162.
3. *Vie de Rossini*, II, 35. 5. *Filosofia Nova*, I, 59.

Blindness, deafness, maniacal obsession: it seems that passion is incapable of perceiving clearly that reality on which it erects its structure and on which it never ceases to rest.

And yet, if one reconsiders the metaphor of the branch of Salzburg, he will reflect that through the transparency of the crystals the wood remains visible, that perhaps the crystals even play the role of a sort of natural magnifying glass which allows the enlarged details of the wood to be seen more clearly. Similarly, at certain privileged moments, it seems that love suddenly removes its blindfold, and that its mocking blindness is followed by a sort of superior clarity which illuminates at a glance the innermost recesses, even the darkest recesses, of ourselves and of others. These sudden revelations cannot occur in the rapture or the ebullition of passion, in those "fleet instants" of which Stendhal spoke just now, and in which "one does not know where he goes." It is, on the contrary, at the moment when the torrent of passion moderates its course, when its agitated waters are decanted into memory or regret, in one of those stagnant reaches or pauses that the uneven rhythm of the emotional life gouges out between two periods of fever or exaltation, it is then that all the details of the felt passion slowly rise in disordered sheaves from the depths of the soul:

> The pauses and other embellishments that the impassioned soul of the singer invents admirably portray (or to speak precisely, *reproduce in your soul*), those little moments of delicious repose that one experiences in true passions. During these brief instants the soul of the impassioned being *counts over the pleasures or the pains* that the step forward taken by his mind has just shown him.[6]

The discontinuous progress of the passion allows the lover to take advantage of the "little moments of repose," to turn back and look over the route he has traveled. Like a mountain road whose every turning invites the traveler to search over a landscape which his progress never ceases to modify, love multiplies the perspectives from which the backward eye launches out toward those moments that have already been lived. But let us not believe that either thought or logical analysis uses these respites to reintroduce themselves furtively into the emotions. "Women's *imaginations* pore over such delicious moments at their leisure. . . ."[7] It is imagination, and not "cold reason," which is now charged with recognizing the true. And this is why the fine arts, not analysis, allow us, too late and through the play of their equivalences, to understand what we have *felt*:

6. *Promenades dans Rome*, I, 72.　　　7. *De l'Amour*, I, 48.

When, dreaming of some memory from our own life, and in some way still excited by the emotion of the past, we come suddenly to recognize the likeness of this emotion in some ballad that we know, we can affirm that it is beautiful. It seems to me that then there occurs a sort of verification of the resemblance between what the song expresses and what we have felt, *which causes us to see and taste more minutely the nuances unknown to us* until that moment. It is by this mechanism, if I am not mistaken, that music encourages and nourishes the reveries of the unhappy lover.[8]

Here then is emotion illuminating things (because it perceives them just as they are, or have been, from the inside) both in their inner being, and in their exactitude. "This degree of passion which makes one discover and feel the details"[9] it is of course difficult to maintain steadily; as it is difficult to *discover*, that is, to discriminate, and to *feel*, that is, to lose oneself in sensation, simultaneously. But Stendhal's attitude here is completely instinctive: and to believe in the possibility of such a paradoxical success, he has only to recall his own experiences in life.

But we are not forbidden to explain this victorious movement by means of the reflections made by young Stendhal as at twenty he read the works of Biran, and passed them on to us in his notebooks. We know that from Maine de Biran he borrows the essential distinction, to which he refers each time it is a matter of explaining the impossibility of recalling or describing happiness, between the *sensation*, or impression, which is pure passivity, and the *perception*, which assumes a certain activity, or at least a certain adaptive direction of the organs.

Biran, he notes, calls *sensation* that which one is aware of when he is passive in the process of impression. When one is active, that is to say when one distinguishes what one feels, and that by means of the propensities of the organ, he calls it *perception*.

and again:

To smell the odor of the rose is a passive faculty. The motor faculty is that which causes us to open our nostrils (to concentrate the attention of the organ the better to smell the rose).[1]

It is, above all, the effects of habit that permit the discrimination between sensation and perception; for if the first grows weak and languid through repetition, the second on the contrary gains in ease, skill, and precision from it. This distinction struck Stendhal forcefully and it is on it that he dwelt. ("Mere talk," he wrote, "up to the distinction of the effects of habit.")

8. *Vie de Rossini*, I, 87.   1. *Filosofia Nova*, II, 365.
9. *Promenades dans Rome*, I, 93.

And one easily guesses the reasons for this interest: it is to that second category of habits that the Stendhalian crystallization itself belongs. It too encloses the spirit in an intimacy which each day probes and clarifies further. Thanks to its creative power, the Stendhalian universe is perception, not sensation, activity not passivity. Here desire is directed toward an object which it is not content to invoke with vows, but which its movement eventually brings into being. It does not wait to be satisfied, but seeks fulfillment: "Reflection," he writes, "is the process of seeking distinctions (looking at something to understand the circumstances of it). Obstacles give rise to reflection."[2] Stendhal at this point is following Cabanis, Tracy, the first Biran, and all the ideologues who make consciousness arise from a resistance of external objects to the movement of the perceiver; he is thinking of the precise but melancholy view of the world that disenchanted hearts take. And in fact there is no doubt that the Stendhalian novel repeatedly guides its heroes to self-awareness by hurling them (if need be, making them break themselves) against an obstacle. It is through defeat that vigor is aroused in consciousness. But refusing to believe that the enchantment of passion necessarily forbids understanding, Stendhal adds: "Any passion whatever can also give rise to reflection without need of an obstacle. *Any desire whatever (the impelling force) can lead us to reflect.*"[3] Is not Stendhalian love precisely that impelling force, that simultaneous impulse to discover and achieve its object? If it remains true that from that time one cannot know and experience simultaneously, it does become possible, since love is made more of action than of impression, more of impetus than of waiting, to know and to love. The "natural" of Stendhal is nothing other than the facility and spontaneity with which emotion manages to translate itself into intelligence; but the speed of that translation would appear inconceivable if the emotion had not been permeated at its very origin by curiosity and intelligence, bent and straining toward the intellectual discovery of its object. It stirs up the being, orients and directs him toward the outside, excites in him a joyous ferment, a kind of impatience and healthy fever, a hope rather like musical sprightliness, and which, even as it speeds up the life of the heart, seems to multiply the powers of the mind. Such is Stendhalian freedom. "When he had no emotions," Stendhal writes of one of his characters, "he was mindless."[4] Thus there is no true and living intelligence except that brought forth by a complete stirring of the emotions. As "tears are the ultimate smile," understanding would thus be the ultimate tenderness; it would blossom at the end of the rapture or of the passion:

2. *Filosofia Nova*, II, 365.
3. *Filosofia Nova*, II, 365.

4. *Mélanges de littérature*, I, 85.

A head enlightened by a passion discovers in the things that that passion compelled him to consider many things which have been known only by heads obeying equally strong passions.[5]

It is the freemasonry of impassioned souls, and not the college of perfect ideologues, that will in the end find for itself the profound mastery of things. To those souls alone is it accorded to enjoy and to understand, to dream without falsifying, to recover the real beyond the imaginary, and, as Stendhal puts it in a magnificent phrase: "to enter the world through heaven."[6]

Here we are, it seems, arrived at the end of the journey. But before leaving Stendhal to his perpetual dialogue, we must warn of a possible misunderstanding, and strongly emphasize that in the end nobody has a right to see a conclusion; we must state quite precisely that these notes do not pretend, either dialectically or chronologically, to retrace a *route*. The Stendhalian experience is still today so rich in meaning and novelty only because of the resolute refusal it has always opposed to logical reconstruction, and even, as this essay has tried to show, to simple definition.

Let us therefore not believe that, beginning from a dry view of things, Stendhal had achieved a certain inner tenderness, then that he strove to attain to certain balances between these two forces and to realize one by beginning with the other: tenderness did not come to ripen in him from exhausted dryness like fruit on the withered petals of the flower. Of course, in proportion as he grew older and the future before him little by little diminished, his inspiration, more and more given over to the nostalgia of memories, seemed, work by work and year by year, to become increasingly tender. But let us bear in mind that after the *Charterhouse*, the wonderful symphony of love and tenderness, Stendhal takes *Lamiel* in hand, where, expressly intending to apply all the comic recipes that the young man of twenty thought he had invented, the man of fifty is pleased to sketch all the grimaces of the ridiculous and all the contortions of an unnatural energy. Tougher than the *Red and Black*, sharper than *Armance*, this great interrupted work, which marks a return to the most extreme and most deliberate dryness, breaks off Stendhal's literary destiny with an even more disturbing incompleteness. The harmonious curve ends in a brutal veering, and this ending forbids us even to attempt to guess what might have developed in the days to come.

Logically, the two impulses are not linked any more. Let us say rather that they illuminate each other, coexisting by causing each other to exist, as light creates shadow and shadow light. It must be acknowledged that the order in which these notes have been pre-

5. *Filosofia Nova*, II, 122.   6. *Filosofia Nova*, I, 16.

sented has been profoundly arbitrary, and that the very nature of the study precluded its being otherwise. In fact, it was a matter of sketching a horizontal stroke across certain inner regions where the traces of certain fundamental prejudices could be uncovered. The exploration could just as logically have been undertaken in the other direction. The essential thing was to find again in each moment the presence of certain abstract forms which appeared to us to govern living experience. Therefore it was much more important to emphasize the abstract terms in which certain problems of immediate experience were posed for him, than to go off in search of impossible solutions or of highly improbable reconciliations. One can also say, to speak in another language and to see things from the outside, that finding himself in the grip of two maladies, which are under certain aspects the maladies of the epoch, Stendhal wanted to oppose one to the other, but less to annihilate than to aggravate each of them, intending for example to "de-Rousseauize his judgment by reading Tracy," but on the other hand offering his hardened heroines, such as Mathilde de La Mole, the all-powerful and endearing resource of musical enthusiasm or romantic love. Health for Stendhal is made of this battle of diseases, and Stendhalian truth, far from lodging in a bland and prudent buffer zone, must always be sought in the impassioned combination of extremes and contradictions.

One last remark: Stendhal the man far exceeds all that can have been said or suggested of him in the preceding pages. His *scope*, to speak his language, outstrips all analysis: it outstrips even further analyses which, like this one, are intentionally limited to exploring certain very particular procedures. To speak of Stendhal is to condemn oneself each time to the impression that one has said nothing, that he has escaped you and that everything remains to be said. One must therefore be resigned and surrender to his unpredictable and marvelous upsurge.

RENÉ GIRARD

[Triangular Desire] †

According to literary historians Stendhal inherited most of his ideas from the *philosophes* or the *idéologues*.

If this were true, this novelist whom we consider so great would not have a thought of his own; for his whole life he would remain

† Chapter V of René Girard, *Mensonge romantique et vérité romanesque*, translated by Yvonne Freccero as *Deceit, Desire, and the Novel* (The Johns Hopkins Press, 1965), pp. 113–38.
Professor Girard's analysis of ro-

faithful to the thought of others. It is a hard legend to kill. It is popular both with those who would deny intelligence in the novel and with those who are trying to find a complete Stendhalian system and think they have found it in his early writing, that is, in the only more or less didactic texts ever written by Stendhal.

Their thoughts dwell longingly on a huge key which would open all the gates of his work. A whole bundle of such "keys" can be gathered from the childish *Letters to Pauline*, from the *Journal*, and from his *New Philosophy*. There is a loud rattle in the lock but the gates remain closed. No page of *The Red and the Black* will ever be explained by means of Cabanis or Destutt de Tracy. Except for occasional borrowings from the system of temperaments there is no trace of the theories of his youth in the novels of his maturity. Stendhal is one of the few thinkers of his time who won his independence from the giants of the preceding epoch. For this reason he can render homage as an equal to the gods of his youth. Most of his romantic contemporaries are incapable of doing as much; they look on the rationalist Pantheon with great condescension, but should it enter their head to reason we find ourselves back in the century of the Enlightenment. Their opinions are different and even antithetical but the intellectual frameworks have not changed.

Stendhal does not give up thinking the day he stops copying the thought of others; he begins to think for himself. If the writer had never changed his opinion on the great political and social problems, why did he declare, at the beginning of the *Life of Henry Brulard*, that he had at last decided on his point of view regarding the nobility? Nothing in the Stendhalian vision is more important than the nobility, yet this definitive point of view is never systematically set down. The real Stendhal had an aversion to didacticism. His original thought *is* the novel and only the novel, for the moment Stendhal escapes from his characters the ghost of the Other begins to haunt him again. Therefore everything has to be gathered from his novels. The non-novelistic texts sometimes contribute details but they should be handled with care.

Far from blindly trusting the past, Stendhal, even as early as *De l'Amour*, considers the problem of the *error* in Montesquieu and other great minds of the eighteenth century. The alleged disciple wonders why such keen observers as the *philosophes* should have

---

mantic lies and novelistic truths traces a political as well as a psychological and literary pattern through various romantic and post-romantic novelists. It is, essentially, the pattern of triangular desire, best illustrated by the mechanism of jealousy in which A supposes he desires something because he imagines B also desires it. B thus becomes a "mediator" of A's desire.

When his autonomous impulses are so contaminated by the thought of B that the rival need not even be present to inflame A's appetitive fantasies, we are confronted with what Professor Girard calls "inner mediation." It is his argument that Stendhal, like Dostoevsky and Proust, is an acute analyst of this unhealthy condition, in the body politic as well as within the psyche of his protagonists.

been so completely wrong in their visions of the future. At the end of *Memoirs of a Tourist* the theme of philosophical error is resumed and studied further. Stendhal finds nothing in Montesquieu to justify the condemnation of Louis-Philippe. The bourgeois king gave the French greater liberty and prosperity than ever before. The progress is real but it does not accord the people who benefit from it the increase of happiness foreseen by the theoreticians.

Stendhal's own duty is indicated to him by the mistakes of the *philosophes*. He must amend the conclusions of abstract intelligence by contact with experience. The intact Bastilles limited the vision of prerevolutionary thinkers. The Bastilles have fallen and the world is changing at a dizzying pace. Stendhal finds he is straddling several universes. He is observing the constitutional monarchy but he has not forgotten the *ancien régime;* he has visited England; and he keeps up with the constant stream of books dealing with the United States.

All the nations Stendhal is concerned with have embarked on the same adventure but they are moving at different speeds. The novelist is living in a veritable laboratory of historical and sociological observation. His novels are, in a sense, merely this same laboratory carried to the second degree. In them Stendhal brings together various elements which would remain isolated from each other even in the modern world. He confronts the provinces and Paris, aristocrats and bourgeois, France and Italy, and even the present and the past. Various experiments are carried out and they all have the same aim —they are all meant to answer the same fundamental question: "Why are men not happy in the modern world?"

This question is not original. Everybody, or almost everybody, was asking it in Stendhal's day. But few ask it sincerely, without having already decided a priori that one more or one less revolution is required. In his non-novelistic writings Stendhal often seems to request both at the same time. But these secondary texts should not be allowed to worry us too much. Stendhal's real answer is blended into his novels, scattered through them; it is diffuse, full of hesitations and modifications. Stendhal is as prudent in the novels as he can be assertive, when he is expressing his own "personal" opinion in the face of the opinion of others.

Why are men not happy in the modern world? Stendhal's answer cannot be expressed in the language of political parties or of the various "social sciences." It is nonsense to both bourgeois common sense and romantic "idealism." We are not happy, says Stendhal, because we are *vaniteux*.

Morality and psychology are not the only sources of this answer. Stendhalian vanity has a historical component which is essential and which we must now clarify. In order to do this, we must first set forth Stendhal's idea of nobility, which, he tells us in the *Life of Henry Brulard*, took a solid form rather late in his development.

In Stendhal's eyes, nobility belongs to the man whose desires come from within himself and who exerts every ounce of his energy to satisfy them. Nobility, in the spiritual sense of the term, is therefore exactly synonomous with passion. The noble being rises above others by the strength of his desire. There must originally be nobility in the spiritual sense for there to be nobility in the social sense. At a certain point in history both senses of the word "noble" coincided, at least theoretically. This coincidence is illustrated in *The Italian Chronicles*. In fourteenth- and fifteenth-century Italy the greatest passions were born and developed in the elite of society.

This relative accord between the social organization and natural hierarchy of men cannot last. The nobleman's becoming aware of it is, in a sense, sufficient to precipitate its dissolution. A comparison is necessary to discover that one is superior to others: comparison means bringing closer together, putting on the same level, and, to a certain extent, treating the things compared in the same way. The equality of man cannot be denied unless it is first posited, however briefly. The oscillation between pride and shame which defines metaphysical desire can already be found in this first comparison. The nobleman who makes the comparison becomes a little more noble in the social sense but a little less noble in the spiritual sense. He begins the reflection that will gradually cut him off from his own nobility and transform it into a mere possession mediated by the *look* of the commoner. The nobleman as an individual is thus the passionate being *par excellence*, but nobility as a class is devoted to vanity. The more nobility is transformed into a caste and becomes hereditary, the more it closes its ranks to the passionate being who might rise from the lower classes and the more serious the ontological sickness becomes. Henceforth the nobility will be leading constantly toward vanity the other classes dedicated to its imitation and will precede them along the fatal road of metaphysical desire.

Thus the nobility is the first class to become decadent, and the history of this decadence is identical with the inevitable evolution of metaphysical desire. The nobility is already eaten up with vanity when it rushes to Versailles, drawn by the lure of vain rewards. Louis XIV is not the demigod worshipped by the royalists, nor is he the oriental tyrant loathed by the Jacobins. He is a clever politician who distrusts the aristocracy and uses its vanity as a means of government, thereby hastening the decomposition of the noble soul. The aristocracy lets itself be drawn into sterile rivalries by the monarchy which reserves the right of arbitration. The Duc de Saint-Simon, perceptive but fascinated by the king, observes with quenchless rage this emasculation of the nobility. Saint-Simon, the historian of "impotent hatred," is one of Stendhal's and Proust's great teachers.

The absolute monarchy is one stage on the road to revolution and to the most modern forms of vanity. But it is only a stage. The vanity of the court presents a strong contrast with true nobility but it makes an equally strong contrast with the vanity of the bourgeois. At Versailles the slightest desires must be approved and permitted by a whim of the King. Existence at the court is a perpetual imitation of Louis XIV. The Sun King is the mediator for all who surround him, and this mediator remains separated from his faithful followers by an immense spiritual distance. The King cannot become the rival of his own subjects. M. de Montespan would suffer much more were his wife being unfaithful to him with an ordinary mortal. The theory of "divine right" provides a perfect definition of the particular type of *external mediation* which flourishes at Versailles and in the whole of France during the last two centuries of the monarchy.

What was the state of mind of a courtier of the *ancien régime*, or rather what was Stendhal's impression of it? Several secondary characters in his novels and the brief but suggestive remarks scattered through some twenty works provide us with a fairly precise answer to that question. The pain caused by vanity exists in the eighteenth century but it is not unbearable. It is still possible to enjoy oneself in the protective shade of the monarchy somewhat like children at the feet of their parents. Indeed a delicate pleasure is found in mocking the futile and rigorous rules of a perpetually idle existence. The great lord has a perfect ease and grace by knowing that he is nearer the sun than other human beings and thus a little less human than they, that he is illuminated by the divine rays. He always knows exactly what to say and what not to say, what to do and what not to do. He is not afraid of being ridiculed and he gladly laughs in ridicule of others. Anything which is the slightest bit different from the latest fashion at court is ridiculous in his eyes; thus everything outside Versailles and Paris is ridiculous. It is impossible to imagine a more favorable setting for the growth of a comic theater than this universe of courtiers. Not a single allusion is lost on this public which is not many but *one*. Diderot would have been astonished to discover that laughter in the theater disappears with the "tyrant!"

The revolution destroys only one thing—but that one thing is the most important of all though it seems trivial to barren minds—the divine right of kings. After the Restoration Louis, Charles, and Philippe ascend the throne; they cling to it and descend from it more or less precipitously; only fools pay any attention to these monotonous gymnastics. The monarchy no longer exists. Stendhal insists on this fact at some length in the last part of *Lucien Leuwen*. The ceremonies at Versailles cannot turn the head of a positive-minded banker. The real power is elsewhere. And this false king, Louis-Philippe, plays the stock exchange, making himself—the ultimate downfall!—the *rival* of his own subjects!

This last touch gives us the key to the situation. The courtier's external mediation is replaced by a system of internal mediation in which the pseudo-king himself takes part. The revolutionaries thought they would be destroying vanity when they destroyed the privileges of the noble. But vanity is like a virulent cancer that spreads in a more serious form throughout the body just when one thinks it has been removed. Who is there left to imitate after the "tyrant"? Henceforth men shall copy each other; idolatry of one person is replaced by hatred of a hundred thousand rivals. In Balzac's opinion, too, there is no other god but envy for the modern crowd whose greed is no longer stemmed and held within acceptable limits by the monarch. *Men will become gods for each other.* Young men of the nobility and of the middle class come to Paris to seek their fortune as courtiers once came to Versailles. They crowd into the garrets of the Latin Quarter as once they used to pile into the attics of Versailles. Democracy is one vast middle-class court where the courtiers are everywhere and the king is nowhere. Balzac, whose observations in all these matters frequently corroborate Stendhal's, has also described this phenomenon: "In the monarchy you have either courtiers or servants, whereas under a Charter you are served, flattered, and fawned on by free men." When speaking of the United States, Tocqueville too mentions the "esprit de cour" which reigns in the democracies. The sociologist's reflection throws a vivid light on the transition from external to internal mediation:

When all the privileges of birth and fortune have been destroyed so that all professions are open to everyone and it is possible to climb to the top by oneself, an immense and easy career seems available to men's ambitions, and they gladly imagine a great destiny for themselves. But they are mistaken, as daily experience proves to them. The very equality which enables each citizen to sustain great hopes makes all citizens equally weak. It limits their strength on all sides at the same time as it allows their desires to spread.

They have destroyed the annoying privileges of some of their fellow-men; they encounter the competition of everyone. The boundary has changed its shape rather than its position.

The constant opposition on the one hand of instincts which give birth to equality and on the other of the means provided to satisfy them, torments and tires souls. . . . However democratic the social state and political constitution of a nation may be, yet inevitably . . . each of its citizens will behold around him several aspects which dominate him, and it can be anticipated that he will obstinately fix his eyes in this one direction.

We find in Stendhal this "uneasiness" which Tocqueville attributes to democratic regimes. The vanity of the *ancien régime* was gay, unconcerned, and frivolous; the vanity of the nineteenth century is sad and suspicious; it has a terrible fear of ridicule. "Envy, jealousy, and impotent hatred" are the accompaniment of internal mediation. Stendhal declares that everything has changed in a country when even fools—always the most stable element—have changed. The fool of 1780 wanted to be witty; to make people laugh was his only ambition. The fool of 1825 wants to be serious and formal. He is set on appearing profound and easily succeeds, the novelist adds, because he is truly unhappy. Stendhal never tires of describing the effects of *la vanité triste* on the customs and psychology of the French. The aristocrats are most hard hit.

When one stops considering the serious results of the revolution, one of the first sights that strikes one's imagination is the present state of French society. I spent my youth among great lords who were very pleasant; today they are old, disagreeable reactionaries. At first I thought their peevish humor was an unfortunate effect of age, so I made the acquaintance of their children who will inherit great wealth and noble titles, in fact most of the privileges that men drawn together in society can confer on some among them; I found them sunk even deeper in despondency than their parents.

The transition from external to internal mediation constitutes the supreme phase in the decline of the nobility. Revolution and emigration completed what reflection had begun; the nobleman, physically separated from his privileges, is henceforth forced to see them for what they really are—*arbitrary*. Stendhal clearly understood that the revolution could not destroy the nobility by taking away its privileges. But the nobility could destroy itself by desiring that of which it had been deprived by the bourgeoisie, and by devoting itself to the ignoble sentiments of internal mediation. To realize that the privilege is arbitrary and to desire it anyhow is obviously the height of vanity. The noble thinks he is defending his nobility by fighting for its privileges against the other classes of a nation but he only succeeds in ruining it. He desires to recuperate his wealth as a bourgeois might and the envy of the bourgeoisie stimulates his desire and endows the pettiest of honorary trifles with immense value. Mediated by each other, henceforth the two classes will desire the same things in the same way. The Restoration duke who regains his titles and fortune, thanks to the millions granted to the *émigrés*, is little more than a bourgeois "who won in the lottery." The nobleman constantly grows nearer the bourgeois, even in the hatred he feels for him. They are all ignoble, Stendhal writes somewhat strongly in his letter to Balzac, *because they prize nobility*. . . .

Only their elegant manners and politeness, the results of long training, give the nobles a little distinction over the bourgeoisie, and even this will soon disappear. Double mediation is a melting-pot in which differences among classes and individuals gradually dissolve. It functions all the more efficiently because it does not even appear to affect diversity. In fact, the latter is even given a fresh though deceptive brilliance: the opposition of the Same to the Same, which flourishes everywhere, will hide itself for a long time to come behind traditional diversity, sheltering new conflicts behind the shadow of old ones and nourishing belief in the integral survival of the past.

Under the Restoration the nobility seems more alive than ever. Never have its privileges been more desired, nor its ancient families so eager to emphasize the barriers between themselves and the common people. Superficial observers are not aware that internal mediation is at work; they can only conceive uniformity as that of marbles in a bag or sheep in a meadow. They do not recognize the modern tendency to identity in passionate divisions, their own divisions. But the clash of cymbals is loudest when they fit each other exactly.

Because it is no longer distinct the aristocracy tries to distinguish itself, and it succeeds marvelously—but that does not make it any more noble. It is a fact, for instance, that under the constitutional monarchy the aristocracy is the stuffiest and most virtuous class in the nation. The frivolous and seductive nobleman of the Louis XV era has been replaced by the scowling and morose gentleman of the Restoration. This depressing character lives on his property, he works hard, goes to bed early, and worst of all, even manages to economize. What is the significance of such austere morals? Is it really a return to the "ancestral virtues"? This is what we are told constantly in the *bien-pensant* journals but there is no need to believe it. This gloomy, sour-tempered, and totally negative kind of wisdom is typically bourgeois. The aristocracy is trying to prove to the Others that it has "earned" its privileges; that is why it borrows its code of ethics from the class which is competing for those same privileges. Mediated by its bourgeois audience, the nobility copies the bourgeoisie without even realizing it. In *Memoirs of a Tourist* Stendhal remarks sardonically that the revolution has bequeathed to the French aristocracy the customs of democratic, protestant Geneva.

Thus their very hatred of the bourgeoisie makes them middle-class. And, since mediation is reciprocal, we must expect to find a bourgeois-gentleman to match the gentleman-bourgeois, we must anticipate a bourgeois comedy which is symmetrical and inverse to to aristocratic comedy. The courtiers may copy Rousseau's *vicaire savoyard* in order to capture the good opinion of the bourgeois, but the bourgeois will also play at being great lords to impress the aristocrats. The type of the bourgeois imitator reaches the height of comic perfection in the character of Baron Nerwinde in *Lamiel.* Nerwinde, the son of a general of the Empire, slavishly and laboriously copies a synthetic model, made up in equal parts of a *roué* of the *ancien régime* and a dandy from across the Channel. Nerwinde leads a tedious and boring existence, but its very disorder he has organized methodically. He goes bankrupt conscientiously while keeping very exact accounts. He does it all to make people forget— and to make himself forget—that he is the grandson of a hatter from Périgueux.

Double mediation flourishes everywhere; there is a "set to partners" in every figure of Stendhal's social ballet. Everything is reversed from its previous state. Stendhal's wit amuses us but it seems a little too geometric to be true. It is important to note that Tocqueville, who is a completely humorless observer, makes assertions parallel to Stendhal's. In *The Ancient Regime and the Revolution*, for instance, we find the paradox of an aristocracy that by its opposition to the middle class begins to resemble it, and that adopts all the virtues of which the middle class is trying to rid itself. He writes: "The most anti-democratic classes of the nation reveal most clearly to us the kind of morality it is reasonable to expect from a democracy."

When the aristocracy seems most alive is precisely when it is most dead. In an early edition of *Lamiel* Nerwinde is called D'Aubigné; this imitative dandy belonged to the aristocracy, not to the parvenu middle class: he was a descendant of Mme. de Maintenon. Otherwise his conduct was exactly the same as in the last version of the novel. No doubt Stendhal chose the parvenu bourgeois—the commoner—to play the comedy of the nobility because he felt that the comic effect would be more apparent and reliable, but this does not mean he was mistaken in the first version; it illustrates an essential aspect of the Stendhalian truth. In that case it was a nobleman by blood who played the comedy of nobility. With or without a coat-of-arms, one can "desire" nobility, under Louis-Philippe, only in the manner of Molière's *bourgeois gentilhomme*. One can only mime it, as passionately as M. Jourdain but less naïvely. It is this kind of mimicry which Stendhal is trying to reveal to us. The complexity of the task and the fragmentation of the public—which are, ultimately, one and the same phenomenon—make the theater unsuited to carrying out this literary function. Comic theater died with the monarchy and "gay vanity." A more flexible genre is needed to describe the infinite metamorphoses of *vanité triste* and reveal how void are its oppositions. This genre is the novel. Stendhal finally understood this; after long years of effort and failure, which transformed his soul, he gave up the theater. But he never renounced his ambition of becoming a great comic writer. All novelistic works have a tendency to the comic and Stendhal's are no exception. Flaubert excels himself in *Bouvard et Pécuchet*; Proust reaches his peak in the comic figure of the Baron Charlus; Stendhal sums up and completes his work in the great comic scenes of *Lamiel*.

The paradox of an aristocracy that becomes democratic through its very hatred of democracy is nowhere more striking than in political life. The tendency of the nobility to become bourgeois is clearly seen in its sympathy for the *ultra* party, a party devoted entirely to the defense of privilege; this party's conflict with Louis XVIII showed clearly that the monarchy was no longer the polar star of the nobility but a political instrument in the hands of the noble party. This noble party is oriented not toward the king but toward the rival bourgeoisie. The *ultra* ideology is merely the pure and simple reversal of revolutionary ideology. The theme throughout is *reaction* and reveals the negative slavery of internal mediation. Party rule is the natural political expression of this mediation; party platforms do not bring about political opposition—opposition brings about party platforms.

To understand how ignoble ultra-ism is, it must be compared with a form of thought which was anterior to the revolution and which, in its time, convinced a whole section of the nobility: the philosophy of the Enlightenment. Stendhal believes that this philosophy is the only one possible for nobility that intends to remain noble in the exercise of its thought. When a genuine aristocrat—and there were still a few during the last century of the monarchy—enters the territory of thought, he does not abandon his native virtues. He remains spontaneous even in his reflection. Unlike the ultras he does not expect the ideas he adopts to serve the interests of his class, any more than he would ask a challenger, in a truly heroic era, to present proof of nobility; the challenge alone would prove the nobility of the challenger, in the eyes of someone with self-respect. In the realm of thought rational evidence takes the place of the challenge. The nobleman accepts the challenge and judges everything in universal terms. He goes straight to the most general truths and applies them to all mankind. He does not acknowledge any exceptions, especially those from which he would profit. In Montesquieu, and in the best of the enlightened nobles of the eighteenth century, there is no distinction between the aristocratic and the liberal mind. Eighteenth-century rationalism is noble even in its illusions; it puts its trust in "human nature." It does not allow for the irrational in human relations, nor does it recognize metaphysical imitation, which frustrates the calculations of sound reflection. Montesquieu would have been less likeable had he foreseen the *vanité triste* of the nineteenth century.

Moreover, we soon realize that rationalism means the death of privilege. Truly noble reflection resigns itself to that death, just as the truly noble warrior is prepared to die on the battlefield. The nobility cannot reflect on itself and remain noble without destroying itself as a caste; and since the revolution forced the nobility to think about itself, its own extinction is the only choice left to it. The nobility can die nobly by the one and only political gesture worthy of it, the destruction of its own privileged existence—the night of August 4, 1789.[1] It dies meanly, in a bourgeois fashion, on the benches of some House of Lords, confronted by Valenods whom it ends up resembling through fighting with them over the spoils. This was the solution of the ultras.

First came the nobility; then followed the noble class; finally only a noble party is left. After the period when the two coincided, spiritual and social nobility now tend to exclude each other; henceforth the incompatibility of privilege with greatness of soul is so radical that it is patent even in the attempts to conceal it. Take for example the justification of privilege given by Dr. Du Périer, the intellectual jack-of-all-trades of the Nancy nobility:

A man is born a duke, a millionaire and a peer of France, it is not for him to consider whether his position conforms with virtue, or with the general good or with other fine ideas. His position is good; so he should do everything to maintain and improve it, or be despised generally as a coward and a fool.

Du Périer would like to convince us that the nineteenth-century nobleman is still living in a happy era, not yet affected by the "look" of the Other, still enjoying his privileges spontaneously. Yet the lie is so flagrant that Du Périer does not phrase it directly; he uses a negative periphrasis that suggests without affirming: "It is not for him to consider," etc. Despite this oratorical precaution, the "look" of the Other is too obsessive and Du Périer is forced to acknowledge it in the following sentence. But then he imagines a cynical point of honor to which this "look" forces the aristocrat to submit. If the privileged person does not hang on to his privilege, "he will be despised as a coward or a fool." Du Périer is once again lying. Aristo-

1. During the night the deputies of the aristocracy at the revolutionary *As-* *semblée constituante* voted the abolition of most feudal privileges.

crats are neither innocent nor cynical: they are merely *vaniteux*; they want privilege merely as parvenus. This is the horrible truth which must be hidden at all cost. They are ignoble *because they prize nobility.*

Since the Revolution no one can be privileged without knowing it. Stendhal's kind of hero is impossible in France. Stendhal likes to believe that he is still just possible in Italy. In that happy country, scarcely touched by the Revolution, reflection and concern with the Other have not yet completely poisoned enjoyment of the world and of oneself. A truly heroic soul is still compatible with the privileged circumstances which allow him free play. Fabrice del Dongo can be spontaneous and generous in the midst of an injustice from which he benefits.

First we see Fabrice flying to the aid of an emperor who embodies the spirit of the Revolution; a little later we find our hero, haughty, devout, and aristocratic, in the Italy of his childhood. Fabrice does not think for a minute he is "demeaning" himself when he challenges a simple soldier of the glorious imperial army to a duel. Yet he speaks harshly to the servant who risks his life for him. Still later, despite his devotion, he does not hesitate to join in the simoniac intrigues which will make him an archbishop of Parma. Fabrice is not a hypocrite, nor does he lack intelligence; he is merely lacking the historical foundations for the ability to reflect. The comparisons which a privileged young Frenchman would be forced to make never even enter his mind.

The French will never recover the innocence of a Fabrice for *it is not possible to move backward in the order of the passions.* Historic and psychic evolution are irreversible. Stendhal finds the Restoration revolting but not because he sees in it naïvely a "return to the *ancien régime.*" Such a return is unthinkable; moreover, Louis XVIII's Charter marks the first concrete step toward democracy "since 1792." The current interpretation of *The Red and the Black* therefore is inadmissible. The Jacobin novel described in the handbooks of literature does not exist. If Stendhal were writing for all those bourgeois who are temporarily cut off from lucrative careers by the temporary triumph of an absolutist and feudal party, his would be a very clumsy work. Traditional interpretations go counter to the most basic tenets of the author and disregard the *facts* of the novel, among which is the brilliant career of Julien. One might object that this career is broken by the reactionary and clerical *Congrégation.*[2] True, yet this same *Congrégation* a little later makes every effort to save the protégé of the Marquis de la Mole. Julien is not so much the victim of the ultras as of the wealthy and jealous bourgeois who will triumph in July, 1830. Moreover, we should not

2. A secret Catholic organization with great political influence.

look for any partisan lesson in Stendhal's masterpieces—to understand this novelist who is always talking politics we must free ourselves of political ways of thinking.

Julien has a brilliant career which he owes to M. de la Mole. In his article on *The Red and the Black* Stendhal describes the latter in these words: "His character as nobleman was not formed by the revolution of 1794." In other words, M. de la Mole retains some genuine nobility; he has not become middle-class through hatred of the middle class. His freedom of thought has not made him a democrat but it prevents him from being a reactionary in the worst sense of the word. M. de la Mole does not depend exclusively on excommunications, negations, and refusals; ultra-ism and the nobleman's reaction have not smothered all other sentiments in him. His wife and his friends judge men only by their birth, their fortune, and their political orthodoxy, and so would a Valenod in their place; but M. de la Mole is still capable of approving the rise of a talented commoner. He proves it with Julien Sorel. Only once does Stendhal find his character vulgar—when he loses his temper at the thought that his daughter, by marrying Julien, will never be a duchess.

Julien owes his success to that element under the new regime which has most truly survived from the *ancien régime*. This is a strange way for Stendhal to campaign against a return to the past; even if the novelist had shown the failure of the numerous young people who did not have the good fortune to meet their Marquis de la Mole, his novel would still not have proved anything against the *ancien régime*. In fact it is the Revolution which has increased the obstacles, since most people with status owe "their character of nobleman"—i.e., their implacable ultra-ism—to the Revolution.

Must then the obstacle in the way of these young people be called democratic? Is not this an empty subtlety, and even an untenable paradox? Surely it is only fair that the bourgeoisie should take over the controls since it is "the most energetic and active class in the nation." Is it not true that a little more "democracy" would smooth the way for the ambitious?

It is true; in any case, the stupidity of the ultras makes their downfall inevitable. But Stendhal looks further. The political elimination of the noble party cannot re-establish harmony and satisfy the desires that have been awakened. The political conflict which rages under the constitutional monarchy is considered the sequel of a great historic drama, the last thunderclaps of a storm that is moving away. The revolutionaries suppose they must clear the ground and make a fresh start; Stendhal is telling them that they have already started. Ancient historic appearances hide a new structure of human relations. The party struggle is rooted not in past inequality but in the present equality, no matter how imperfect it may be.

The historical justification of the internal struggles is scarcely more than a pretext now. Put aside the pretext and the true cause will appear. Ultra-ism will disappear like liberalism, but internal mediation remains; and internal mediation will never be lacking in excuses for maintaining the division into rival camps. Following religious society, civic society has become schismatic. To look forward optimistically to the democratic future under the pretext that the ultras, or their successors, are destined to disappear from the political scene is once again to put the object before the mediator and desire before envy. This error can be compared to that of the chronic sufferer from jealousy who always thinks his illness will be cured when the current rival is eliminated.

The last century of French history has proved Stendhal right. The party struggle is the only stable element in contemporary instability. Principles no longer cause rivalry; it is a metaphysical rivalry, which slips into contrary principles like mollusks that nature has not provided with shells and that install themselves in the first ones to come along, no matter what kind.

Proof of this can be furnished by the pair Rênal-Valenod. M. de Rênal abandons ultra-ism before the 1827 elections. He has himself entered as a candidate on the liberal ticket. Jean Prévost discovers in this sudden conversion proof that even Stendhal's secondary characters are capable of "surprising" the reader.[3] Prévost, usually so perspicacious, in this point has fallen victim to the pernicious myths of the "true to life" and "spontaneity" which plague literary criticism.

Julien smiles when he learns of the political about-face of his former patron—he knows very well that nothing has changed. Once more it is a question of playing a role opposite Valenod. The latter has gotten in the good graces of the *Congrégation*; he will therefore be the ultras' candidate. For M. de Rênal there is nothing left to do but turn toward those liberals who seemed so formidable to him a few years before. We meet the mayor of Verrières again in the last pages of the novel. He introduces himself pompously as a "liberal of the defection," but from his second sentence on he merely echoes Valenod. Submission to the Other is no less absolute when it assumes negative forms—a puppet is no less a puppet when the strings are crossed. With regard to the virtues of opposition Stendhal does not share in the optimism of a Hegel or of our contemporary "rebels."

The figure cut by the two businessmen of Verrières was not perfect so long as they both belonged to the same political party.

3. *La Création chez Stendhal* (Paris, 1955).

Double mediation demanded M. de Rênal's conversion to liberalism. There was a need for symmetry which had not yet been fulfilled. And that final *entrechat* was needed to bring to a proper end the ballet of Rênal-Valenod, which was being performed in a corner of the stage all through *The Red and the Black*.

Julien savors the "conversion" of M. de Rênal like a music lover who sees a melodic theme reappear under a new orchestral disguise. Most men are taken in by the disguises. Stendhal places a smile on Julien's lips so that his readers should not be deceived. He does not want us to be fooled: he wants to turn our attention away from the objects and fix it on the mediator; he wishes to reveal to us the genesis of desire, to teach us to distinguish true freedom from the negative slavery which caricatures it. If we take M. de Rênal's liberalism seriously we are destroying the very essence of *The Red and the Black* and reducing a work of genius to the proportions of a Victor Cousin or a Saint-Marc Girardin.

M. de Rênal's conversion is the first act of a political tragicomedy which excites the enthusiasm of naïve spectators throughout the nineteenth century. First the actors exchange threats, then they exchange roles. They leave the stage and return in a new costume. Behind this perpetually similar but different spectacle the same opposition continues to exist, becoming ever more empty and yet more ferocious. And internal mediation continues its underground work.

The political thinkers of our time are always seeking in Stendhal an echo of their own thoughts. They recreate a revolutionary Stendhal or a reactionary Stendhal according to their own passions. But the shroud is never large enough to cover the corpse. Aragon's Stendhal is no more satisfactory than that of Maurice Barrès or Charles Maurras. One line of the writer's own suffices to bring the weak ideological scaffoldings tumbling down into the void: "As regards extreme parties," we read in the preface to *Lucien Leuwen,* "it is always those we have seen most recently which seem the most ridiculous."

The youthful Stendhal most certainly leaned toward the republicans. The mature Stendhal is not lacking in sympathy for the incorruptible Catos who, deaf to Louis-Philippe's objurgations, refuse to grow rich and are preparing in the shadows a new revolution. But we must not confuse with political affiliation this very particular feeling of sympathy. The problem is discussed at length in *Lucien Leuwen* and the position of the later Stendhal—the Stendhal who carries most weight—is in no way ambiguous.

We must seek among the austere republicans whatever is left of nobility in the political arena. Only these republicans still hope for the destruction of all forms of vanity. They retain the eighteenth-century illusion concerning the excellence of human nature. They have understood neither the revolution nor *vanité triste*. They do not realize that the most beautiful fruits of ideological thought will always be spoiled by the worm of irrationality. These men of integrity do not have the *philosophes'* excuse of living *before* the Revolution; thus they are much less intelligent than Montesquieu, and they are much less amusing. If their hands were free, they would create a regime identical with that which flourishes under republican, protestant puritanism in the state of New York. Individual rights would be respected; prosperity would be assured, but the last refinements of aristocratic existence would disappear; vanity would take an even baser form than under the constitutional monarchy. Stendhal concludes that it is less distressing to flatter a Talleyrand or even a minister of Louis-Philippe's than to pay court "to one's shoemaker."

Stendhal is an atheist in politics, a fact hard to believe either in his day or in ours. Despite the levity of its manifestations this atheism is not a frivolous skepticism but a profound conviction. Stendhal does not evade problems; his point of view is the outcome of a whole life of meditation. But it is a point of view which will never be understood by party-minded people nor by many other people who unconsciously are influenced by the party spirit. An ambiguous homage is paid to the novelist's thought, which secretly denies its coherence. It is considered "impulsive" and "disconcerting." It is full of "whims" and "paradoxes." The unfortunate writer is lucky if "a double heritage, both aristocratic and popular" is not invoked which would tear him apart. Let us leave to Mérimée the image of a Stendhal dominated by the spirit of contradiction and we shall understand perhaps that Stendhal is accusing *us* and our time of self-contradiction.

As usual, if we are to have a better understanding of the novelist's thought, we should compare it with a later work which will amply justify its perspectives and will make even its more daring aspects seem banal, merely by revealing a more advanced stage of metaphysical desire. In Stendhal's case, we must ask Flaubert to provide us with a key. Although Emma Bovary's desire still belongs to the area of external mediation, Flaubert's universe as a whole, and especially the urban life of *The Sentimental Education*, are the result of an internal mediation which is even more extreme than that of Stendhal. Flaubert's mediation exaggerates the characteristics of Stendhalian mediation and draws a caricature of it that is much easier for us to figure out than the original.

The environment of *The Sentimental Education* is the same as that of *The Red and the Black*. Again the provinces and Paris are opposed to one another, but it is clear that the center of gravity has moved toward Paris, the capital of desire, which increasingly polarizes the vital forces of the nation. Relationships between people remain the same and enable us to measure the progress of internal mediation. M. de La Mole has been replaced by M. Dambreuse, a "liberal" who owes his character of rapacious big banker as much to 1830 as to 1794. Mathilde is succeeded by the venal Mme. Dambreuse. Julien Sorel is followed by a whole crowd of young men who come, like him, to "conquer" the capital. They are less talented but more greedy. Chances of success are not wanting but everybody wants the most "conspicuous" position, and the front row can never be stretched far since it owes its position purely to the inevitably limited attention of the crowd. The number of those who are called increases constantly but the number of the elect does not. Flaubert's ambitious man never attains the object of his desires. He knows neither the real misery nor the real despair caused by possession and disillusionment. His horizon never grows wider. He is doomed to bitterness, malice, and petty rivalries. Flaubert's novel confirms Stendhal's dire predictions on the future of the bourgeois.

The opposition between the ambitious younger men and those who are successful grows ever more bitter although there are no more ultras. The intellectual basis of the oppositions is even more ridiculous and unstable than in Stendhal. If there is a victor in this bourgeois *cursus honorum* described in *The Sentimental Education* then it is Martinon, the most insipid of the characters and the biggest schemer, who corresponds, though he is even duller witted, to little Tanbeau of *The Red and the Black*. The democratic court which has replaced that of the monarchy grows larger, more anonymous, and more unjust. Unfit for true freedom, Flaubert's characters are always attracted by what attracts their fellow men. They can desire only what the Others desire. The priority of rivalry over desire inevitably increases the amount of suffering caused by vanity.

Flaubert too is an atheist in politics. If we make allowance for the differences of time and temperament, his attitude is amazingly similar to that of Stendhal. This spiritual relationship becomes more apparent on reading Tocqueville: the sociologist, too, is immunized against partisan positions, and the best of his work almost succeeds in providing the systematic expression of an historical and political truth which often remains implicit in the great works of the two novelists.

The increasing equality—the approach of the mediator in our terms— does not give rise to harmony but to an even keener rivalry. Although this rivalry is the source of considerable material benefits, it also leads to even more considerable spiritual sufferings, for noth-

520 · René Girard

ing material can appease it. Equality which alleviates poverty is in itself good but it cannot satisfy even those who are keenest in demanding it; it only exasperates their desire. When he emphasizes the vicious circle in which the passion for equality is trapped, Tocqueville reveals an essential aspect of triangular desire. The ontological sickness, we know, always leads its victims toward the "solutions" that are most likely to aggravate it. The passion for equality is a madness unequalled except by the contrary and symmetrical passion for inequality, which is even more abstract and contributes even more directly to the unhappiness caused by freedom in those who are incapable of accepting it in a manly fashion. Rival ideologies merely reflect both the unhappiness and the incapability; thus they result from internal mediation—rival ideologies owe their power of persuasion only to the secret support the opposing factions lend each other. Fruits of the ontological scission, their duality reflects its unhuman geometry and in return they provide food for the devouring rivalry.

Stendhal, Flaubert, Tocqueville describe as "republican" or "democratic" an evolution which we today would call *totalitarian*. As the mediator comes nearer and the concrete differences between men grow smaller, abstract opposition plays an ever larger part in individual and collective existence. All the forces of being are gradually organized into twin structures whose opposition grows ever more exact. Thus every human force is braced in a struggle that is as relentless as it is senseless, since no concrete difference or positive value is involved. Totalitarianism is precisely this. The social and political aspects of this phenomenon cannot be distinguished from its personal and private aspects. Totalitarianism exists when all desires have been organized one by one into a general and permanent mobilization of being in the service of nothingness.

Balzac often treats very seriously the oppositions he sees around him; Stendhal and Flaubert, on the other hand, always point out their futility. In the work of these two authors, this double structure is embodied in "cerebral love," political struggles, petty rivalries among businessmen and the notables of the provinces. Starting from these particular areas, it is the truly schismatic tendency of romantic and modern society which in each case is demonstrated. But Stendhal and Flaubert did not foresee, and no doubt could not foresee, where this tendency would lead humanity. Double mediation has invaded the growing domain of collective existence and wormed its way into the more intimate depths of the individual soul, until finally it stretches beyond national boundaries and annexes countries, races, and continents, in the heart of a universe where technical progress is wiping away one by one the differences between men. Stendhal and Flaubert underestimated the extent to which triangular desire might expand, perhaps because they lived too early, or perhaps because they did not see clearly its metaphysical nature. Whatever the reason, they did not foresee the at once cataclysmic yet insignificant conflicts of the twentieth century. They perceived the grotesque element of the era which was about to begin but they did not suspect its tragedy.

F. W. J. HEMMINGS

The Dreamer†

Julien Sorel is one of those literary creations whose folly or perversity must be blamed on an abuse of literacy. Don Quixote and Emma Bovary are of the same kind: reading has turned their brains or corrupted their morals. In this Julien stands in contrast to Octave and Lucien, who are mathematicians, and to Fabrice, who is an ignoramus. Julien is a great lover of literature, addicted indifferently to Horace and Voltaire; one day perhaps some *stendhalien* will draw up a list of all the authors and books he can be shown to have studied. His reading during his boyhood is necessarily confined to the 'thirty or forty volumes' which an old army surgeon, his only childhood friend, bequeathed him on his death-bed. Among them are Rousseau's *Confessions* ('the only book his imagination had made use of in constructing a picture of the social world'), a copy of Napoleon's dispatches, and Las Cases's record of the Emperor's conversations at St. Helena, the famous *Memorial* published in 1822–3. 'He would have gone to the stake for these three works.'[1] It was the *Memorial* that his father knocked into the stream when he caught him reading at work.

There is an element of the fortuitous in Julien's choice of Napoleon as lodestar, since it hung on the chance that it should have been a veteran of Napoleon's armies who befriended him in his lonely boyhood and lent him books. It has been advanced more than once that, in making Julien a victim of the Napoleonic myth, Stendhal was using him to express a political attitude which, in 1830, it would have been unwise for the author to avow openly.[2] That he was a secret adherent of Bonaparte after Waterloo is a legend which seems to have been propagated by Beyle himself,

---

† From F. W. J. Hemmings, *Stendhal: A Study of his Novels* (Oxford, 1964), Chapter IV, "The Dreamer," pp. 111–131. Reprinted by permission of the Clarendon Press, Oxford.

1. *Le Rouge et le Noir*, i. 5.
2. Cf. M. David, *Stendhal*, p. 36; H. Jacoubet, *Variétés d'histoire littéraire*, p. 245; &c.

and is another instance of the delight he took in mystifying or shocking his friends. In his notorious *H.B.*, a brochure published seven years after Stendhal's death, Prosper Mérimée wrote: 'It was difficult to know what he thought of Napoleon. His almost invariable practice was to argue against whatever opinion was being advanced. Sometimes he spoke of him as a *parvenu* dazzled by false glitter, continually breaking the rules of logic. At other times he adopted a tone of admiration verging on idolatry. He was by turns as critical as Courier and as servile as Las Cases.'[3] His private papers, inaccessible to Mérimée, show Stendhal to have held consistently a perfectly coherent view: that Napoleon was a bene-factor of the nation until he betrayed the Revolution—until, in other words, he signed the concordat, had himself crowned emperor, and attempted to reconstitute court society. In addition, Stendhal was impressed by the tragic dignity of the lonely figure on St. Helena. So diluted an admiration is very different from Julien's passionate devotion to the memory of the Emperor. In fact, it was perhaps with the idea of suggesting how remote his own point of view was from Julien's, that Stendhal included, at the beginning of the second part of *Le Rouge et le Noir*, an apparently otiose dia-logue in the chapter entitled 'Country Pleasures". Julien is on his way to Paris to take up his duties under M. de La Mole. In the stage-coach he listens to a conversation between two travellers, one of whom (Saint-Giraud) is not merely Stendhal's mouthpiece but quite clearly Stendhal himself in almost every particular. 'I love music and painting,' he declares; 'a good book is a big event in my life; I shall soon be forty-four years old.' Stendhal was forty-seven in the year that *Le Rouge et le Noir* was published. It is not im-possible that when he wrote these pages he was giving Saint-Giraud his own age, or in other words that they antedate considerably the composition of the novel.[4] Saint-Giraud's jeremiad is very much in the key of certain laments Stendhal is known to have uttered in his forty-fourth year—in an article written for the *New Monthly Magazine*, 18 September 1826, and in two separate passages in the 1826 edition of *Rome, Naples et Florence*.[5] The gist is that a man who wants a quiet life, free from political embroilment, must give up the notion that anything of the sort can be found in the country. Your neighbours will not allow you to be a neutral: you have the choice of promising your vote to the Tories and enduring the in-numerable vexations the Whigs will be sure to put on you, or vice versa. In the end you will be driven to sell up and return to the capital, 'to get solitude and rural peace in the only place where they

3. *Portraits historiques et littéraires* (ed. P. Jourda), p. 157.
4. The discrepancy in ages is noted by Aragon (*Lumière de Stendhal*, pp. 52–53) who, however, omits to draw the conclusion that seems inescapable.
5. See C. Liprandi, 'Sur un épisode du *Rouge et Noir*: Les Plaisirs de la Cam-pagne', *Revue des sciences humaines*, fasc. 68 (1952), pp. 295–313.

can be found in France, a fourth-floor apartment off the Champs
Elysées'. And in the final analysis, who is responsible for this state
of affairs? continues Saint-Giraud heatedly. 'Your Emperor, may
the devil fly away with him' (his friend Falcoz, whom he is addressing, is a Bonapartist). 'Who drove me off my land? . . . The priests,
whom Napoleon recalled with his concordat . . . Would there be so
many arrogant gentry today, if your Bonaparte hadn't created barons
and counts? . . . ' The whole of this passage is strongly reminiscent
of the satiric dialogues for which Paul-Louis Courier was famous
at the time. The two speakers, Saint-Giraud and Falcoz, take no
further action in the novel and in fact never appear elsewhere than
in this chapter;[6] which gives additional force to the theory that the
passage was an unpremeditated intercalation, having been extracted
by Stendhal at a late stage from his unpublished papers. Its importance in the novel, once more, is that it underlines the divergence
between the author's feelings about Napoleon and the hero's. Julien
is a silent listener, intervening shyly only once, and then snubbed by
Saint-Giraud. The criticism of his idol that he is forced to hear
makes no impression on him. His first action on arriving in Paris is
to take a cab in spite of the lateness of the hour, and drive out to
view Joséphine's house at Malmaison.

'True passion', comments Stendhal here, 'never thinks of anything but itself.' Julien's devotion to Napoleon bears all the marks
of a private cult: is it not, in fact, his substitute for religion? To
divulge the mystery to the profane would be blasphemy; on one
occasion, before the story proper opens, he had been so indiscreet
as to betray in words his admiration for Napoleon, and to punish
himself had worn his arm in a sling for two months. Thereafter he
hides away to read the sacred books that retrace for him Napoleon's
life and exploits, and never lets the hallowed name cross his lips. He
has his relic: a portrait of the Emperor in a little black cardboard
box, with inscriptions on the back which testify to his devotion.
There is a tragi-comic incident (i. 9) concerned with this box.
Julien has hidden it in his mattress; he learns by chance that the
Mayor of Verrières (in accordance with the still simple country ways
of that time) is having the straw in all the mattresses renewed by
two servants under his personal supervision. Julien begs—almost
orders—Mme de Rênal to retrieve the portrait before her husband
arrives at his bed; this she goes to do, 'pale as if she were going to
her death', for she, of course, thinks the portrait is of Julien's
sweetheart.

A secret cult; a solitary one too. Bonapartism became a live issue
again in the late forties, after Stendhal's death; in the late twenties,
with Napoleon's only son a boy in his teens living under surveillance

6. Though Stendhal was careful to mention them by name in the first part of *Le
Rouge et le Noir* (i. 21, 23).

at Schönbrunn, it was a cause which had no predictable future. 'The delusion which led us', wrote Stendhal in 1825, 'to regard Buonaparte as the perfect model of a hero, as eminently useful to France, is now vanished, or holds its empire only over the minds of shopmen and country lieutenants on half-pay. What was in 1818 the nearly unanimous sentiment of all the strong and generous spirits of France is now fallen into a mere common place, condemned in good society.'[7] After the death of the old veteran who had communicated the faith to him, Julien never again encounters a fellow believer. It would be incredible that none existed, but, like him, they are silent. Only once, at Besançon, he overhears talk between two stonemasons working on the other side of the seminary wall, which shows the memory of 'the Other One' to be still alive among the common people. They regret his disappearance for roughly the same reasons as Julien: 'a mason got to be officer, got to be general; that happened once.'[8] His Bonapartism is one of the few real links connecting Julien with the proletariat from which he springs and which he claims to represent.

The example of Napoleon is a poison that works by over-stimulation: at once forcing his growth and blighting him inwardly. It is what turns him into the monster of single-minded egotism that he is, but it is also what makes him, ultimately, a tragic figure. The explanation of Julien's failure to achieve in the world that happiness groped after by each of Stendhal's heroes, is implicit in the words he uses in a candid moment to Mme de Rênal, though subsequently he retracts them nervously. 'Ah,' he exclaimed, 'Napoleon was really the man sent by God to the youth of France! Who can take his place? . . . Whatever becomes of us,' he added with a sigh, 'this fatal memory will prevent our ever being really happy!'[9] The point is not so much that, for a post-Napoleonic generation, the road to fortune is coloured black, not red (being the winding path of intrigue, hypocrisy, petty infamies, instead of the earlier royal road of virile, full-blooded valour); rather, it is that the incredible fulfillment of Napoleon's own ambitious dream has so dazzled the imaginative adolescent that he cannot conceive of happiness except in terms of the realization of some equally fabulous ambition. The proper gloss on Julien's melancholy outburst is a couple of sentences in Stendhal's *Promenades dans Rome*, the book which, as has been noted, immediately preceded *Le Rouge et le Noir*.

Because an artillery lieutenant became emperor, and tossed up to the social summits two or three hundred Frenchmen born to

7. *London Magazine*, new series, vol. ii, pp. 570–1.
8. *Le Rouge et le Noir*, i. 29. Cf. *Rome, Naples et Florence*, i. 63: "I spent two hours among the workers, listening to their conversation. At every instant, Napoleon was mingled with San Carlo. Both are adored." This was at Milan, however, not Besançon. [San Carlo Borromeo, sixteenth century saint and cardinal, was specially admired, in his own lifetime and since, by the Milanese: cf. Manzoni, *I promessi sposi*.]
9. *Le Rouge et le Noir*, i. 17.

live on thousand-franc incomes, a mad and necessarily wretched ambition seized every Frenchman. . . . In the presence of the greatest goods, a fatal bandage covers our eyes, we refuse to know them as such, and forget to enjoy them.[1]

The blindness or malady which Stendhal diagnosed here and which he illustrated in his novel as it affected a chosen representative of the Restoration period, was, as he saw it, a disorder widespread among his contemporaries even after 1830: Napoleon's shadow was a long one. When in 1837 Stendhal was writing up his tour of France, he was still acutely aware of the unlucky legacy of misguided ambition which Napoleon's career had bequeathed to the younger generation; but he was also, very possibly, thinking of *Le Rouge et le Noir* when he wrote, in the *Mémoires d'un touriste*, of

this wretched thirst after pleasure and a quick fortune, which is the folly of all young Frenchmen. Whichever way they look, they see an artillery lieutenant who becomes emperor, a postboy becoming king of Naples, a hatmaker becoming a marshal, the tutor of the village squire becoming a peer of France and a millionaire. . . . All these unhappy young Frenchmen are thus deluded by the glory of Napoleon and tormented by absurd desires. Instead of *inventing* their own destiny, they want to *copy* his; they would like to start all over again, in 1837, the age which began in 1792 with Carnot and Dumouriez.[2]

Murat, whom Napoleon created King of Naples in 1808, was an innkeeper's son. The hatter who became field-marshal is probably Jourdan, who had a drapery business at the time of the Revolution. The 'tutor of the village squire' sounds very like Julien Sorel, who might well have entered the peerage and become a millionaire if the guillotine had not abridged his career.

The vital criticism that Stendhal makes of his hero, implicitly in *Le Rouge et le Noir* and obliquely in this passage of a later work, is that he is living not his own life, but a modified *copy* of another's. He misses happiness, or all but misses it, through trying to live up to an alien ideal. Stendhal's language is existentialist in anticipation: Julien does not *invent* himself, he conforms to a borrowed model. He and Mathilde (who has a different model, placed in a more remote past, the queen of Navarre who was the mistress of one of her ancestors) are two of a piece: hence, initially, their secret sympathy, but, since each pursues incompatible dreams, hence too the secret rivalry which poisons their relations. Julien cannot be both Napoleon and Boniface de La Mole, nor Mathilde both Joséphine de Beauharnais and Marguerite de Navarre. Mme de Rênal, on the other hand, is always authentically herself; and hence is perpetually discovering herself, in love, in jealousy, in forgiveness, and finding true happiness or true horror in what she discovers. She is innocent, and she sins; she is the faithful wife, and deceives her husband, and repents, and returns to the fold, and transgresses again. 'There was no policy behind this conduct. She saw herself damned without pardon, and sought to hide her vision of hell by covering Julien with the most passionate caresses.'[3] She is not erratic, but she is no conformist, and she never acts a part. One cannot conceive, for example, that she should ever think of herself as a second Francesca da Rimini. She *invents* her destiny, outwardly humble but infinitely richer in spiritual content than that of the haughty aristocratic girl who temporarily supplants her.

To accuse Julien of folly for allowing his ambitious dream to come between himself and happiness is all very well; but it must not be overlooked that without this dream he would not have compelled Stendhal's interest or ours. Born in the eighteenth century, he might have furnished a duplicate of the amiable 'upstart peasant' Marivaux depicted in Jacob. Born when he was, on the morrow of the battle of Austerlitz, it is inevitable that he should resolve to 'die a thousand deaths rather than fail to make his fortune:'[4] His ambition is responsible for his exacerbated pride, his distrust of every man and every woman, his secretiveness and love of solitude, his prickly imperviousness to affection and his self-pity, his machiavellian dissimulation and patient cultivation of the difficult art of hypocrisy: everything in fact about him that made an earlier generation of critics regard *Le Rouge et le Noir* as a novel with a villain-hero.[5] But it is hard to hate this dreamer. His ambition is rooted in a chimerical fantasy, and for this he must be forgiven, where the coldly practical schemer would not be forgiven. Julien stands with Don Quixote, among the elect, on the other side of the bar from Maupassant's Bel-Ami with whom some mistakenly confuse him.

He is a man of infinite plans who owes his success to the fact that nearly all the plans he makes luckily miscarry. He plots in minute detail the seduction of Mme de Rênal, to the point of committing the grand design to paper. It avails him nothing: he owes his conquest to his youthful charm, to the impression he has already, quite unintentionally, made on her, to the compassion he arouses when, overcome by nervous exhaustion, he bursts into tears at her bedside; a piece of weakness that was certainly unpre-

3. *Le Rouge et le Noir,* i. 15.
4. Ibid., i. 5.
5. Blum instances Mérimée who referred to his 'atrocious qualities which disgust one', Vogüé who called him 'an evil soul', Caro who said he was 'the most infamous little roué in the world' (*Stendhal et le beylisme,* p. 93). Julien still succeeds occasionally in arousing virtuous indignation among schoolgirls who are required to read the book, and among certain others: thus, quite recently, in a curious essay entitled 'Julien Sorel ou le complexe de David', Jean Damien asserted: 'You may look in vain for a noble thought or a fine action to set down to his credit in the book of our morality' (*Stendhal Club,* no. 4 (1959), p. 310).

meditated when he formed the resolution to enter her room on a given night. At his theological college he thinks naïvely to win respect and favour by excelling at his studies; the result is the opposite of what he anticipated: he falls under suspicion of spiritual pride, for the Church requires other qualities than intellectual prowess in her parish priests. Chazel, a fellow seminarist who deliberately sows howlers in his Latin unseens, promises far better in the eyes of his superiors. At Paris, he never proposed to make Mathilde de La Mole fall in love with him; in fact, he kept her at arm's length; which is just why she fell in love with him. When later she turns against him, he commits one tactical error after another in vain attempts to win her back. He reconquers her only when he abandons the struggle to succeed by his own devices, places himself in the hands of a friend (Prince Korasoff), and humbly puts into operation a fool-proof plan devised by a friend of this friend, an acknowledged expert in the art of bringing recalcitrant beauties to heel.

Never was a young man so assured that he was shaping his own destiny, and so hugely mistaken. His errors arise invariably from what Stendhal calls his 'imagination', his 'wild imaginings', his 'imagination always darting to extremes'. This is what is responsible for his miscalculations at the seminary. 'Misled by the presumption natural to an imaginative man, he mistook his inward intentions for outward facts, and considered himself a consummate hypocrite.'[6] Imagination raises him at times to an unwarranted pitch of optimism, but it may also plunge him into equally unfounded despair, as when, thinking Mathilde's reaction against him to be due to his unworthiness, he lapses into a paroxysm of self-loathing. Stendhal calls this 'inverted imagination' and adds, in explanation: 'he undertook to criticize life imaginatively. It was the error of a superior man.'[7]

It had been Stendhal's error too, often enough. In showing his hero incapable of seeing situations steadily and dealing with them firmly he was drawing on the memory of the many mortifications his own over-lively imagination had brought on him. He too had elaborated pointless schemes for the reduction of one woman's virtue and been completely taken by surprise when another girl blurted out that she was in love with him.[8] The contradiction between Stendhal's unbridled imagination (he used to compare himself to a skittish horse[9]) and his pretentions to rational behaviour did not escape the more percipient of his friends. 'All his life,' wrote Mérimée, 'he was dominated by his imagination,

6. *Le Rouge et le Noir*, i. 26.
7. Ibid. ii. 19.
8. Alexandrine Daru in 1811, Giulia Rinieri in 1830.
9. 'Un cheval ombrageux', one that takes fright at shadows. Stendhal used the metaphor in letters to Pauline (1812) and Mme Curial (1824). *Correspondance*, iv. 20, and vi. 81.

and in everything he did, acted impulsively and enthusiastically. Nevertheless, he prided himself on behaving always in conformity with the dictates of reason. . . .[1] François Bigillion, one of his boy-hood companions of whom we may read in the *Vie de Henry Bru-lard*, warned him that he would be better guided by his level-headed friends than by his own unsteady temperament. 'For the sake of your own happiness, never act in accordance with your inclinations. Your imagination blinds you to reason.' Henri Gagnon, his grand-father, whose letters are peppered with good advice, likewise put him on his guard against this dangerous faculty. 'The sword wears out the scabbard, my boy; your ardent imagination makes you more unhappy than the circumstances in which you are placed would warrant.'[2] The two letters containing these remonstrances were both written to Beyle when he was at Marseilles, having settled there temporarily in pursuance of a peculiarly chimerical vision: that of making his fortune in an export-and-import business at a time when the Continental System was wreaking havoc with overseas trade.

Some eight years after *Le Rouge et le Noir* was published, Sten-dhal had the idea of writing a companion novel, the hero of which would be a young man anxious, like Julien, to make his way in the world, but differing from Julien in not being impeded by the visionary streak. He was to be a realist in the basest sense of the word. 'The passionate soul, the youthful Jean-Jacques, attaches himself to the intuitions of his imagination, Robert cares only about what he can see.' Robert was to be devoid of imagination; hence the curious title, *A-Imagination*, which Stendhal gave to the few pages he dictated of this work. His intentions, as stated in a pre-liminary note, confirm what has been advanced in respect of *Le Rouge et le Noir*.

> The author attempted, ten years ago, to create an honest and sensitive young man, he created him ambitious but at the same time full of imagination and illusion, in the person of Julien Sorel. He proposes to make Robert absolutely devoid of imagina-tion, save what will serve him to make his fortune; but he never diverts himself with imagining that fortune and its pleasures. Experience has already taught him that such imaginings never achieve reality; *we'll cross that bridge when we come to it*, he used to say; it was his favorite maxim.

Stendhal sums up his conception of this anti-hero in a single phrase: 'His opera glass was never clouded with the breath of his imagination.'[3]

The consequence is that Robert is a bigger rascal than any invented by the masters of the picaresque. He is ready to perform

1. Mérimée, op. cit., p. 155.
2. *Lettres à Stendhal . . . recueillies . . . par V. Del Litto*, i. 185; ii. 48.
3. *Mélanges de littérature*, i. 235–7.

whatever shabby service may be required of him provided he is well paid. He cuts out a viscount who is in love with a wealthy widow, and when challenged to a duel, proposes that the disappointed suitor should buy him off instead: 'Give me a hundred thousand francs, and I'll undertake to make her hate me.'[4] The subject was probably too unpleasant to be long pursued: the fragment that found its way on to paper consists mainly in scenarios.

The case of Robert is interesting because it suggests a correlation in Stendhal's judgment between moral depravity and the lack of imagination. Hence it is possible to maintain that Julien's imagination is the morally purifying element in him. The 'superiority' it confers on him is the superiority of the man whose mind, fixed as it is on some sublime and unattainable goal, is incapable of stooping to certain forms of meanness. For a poor peasant boy who knows well he will have to struggle for his bare livelihood, he is shown as extraordinarily unconcerned about questions of money: a minor implausibility essential if Stendhal was to adhere to the image he wanted to give of a hero raised above baseness by the power of the imagination. It is his father who argues for hours with M. de Rênal about his starting salary. He is given a rise which he neither wants nor expects; from something he said, his employer deduced he was tempted to take a better position elsewhere; in fact, when later Valenod offers him a salary of eight hundred francs, two hundred more than Rênal pays him, it never occurs to him to accept. When he leaves the mayor's household he prefers to borrow a small sum from his friend Fouqué rather than accept a gratuity from Mme de Rênal's husband. This is one respect in which Julien's sense of values is anything but distorted. In the De La Mole drawing-room, one evening, he sees the wealthy Baron de Thaler (in whom Stendhal is supposed to have portrayed one of the Rothschilds) mercilessly ragged by the same young dandies who would not dare to speak an uncivil word to the modest secretary living on his quarterly salary. 'It's enough to cure a man of envy', he reflects.[5] But Julien is the last man to need curing of that kind of envy. It is not merely that he is disinterested; he is what the world calls unworldly. He is, in short, a poet, in the sense that Stendhal judged himself to be one when he first arrived in Paris:

> I was not by any means tricky, clever, suspicious, capable of extracting myself from a twelve-penny bargain with an excess of subtlety and mistrust—like most of my comrades. . . . Amid the streets of Paris I was an impassioned dreamer, always looking up at the heavens and always on the point of being run down by a carriage.'[6]

4. Ibid. 250
5. *Le Rouge et le Nair*, ii. 4.

6. *Vie de Henri Brulard*, ii. 191. Cf. above, p. 49.

One of his teachers at the seminary takes Julien with him to assist in decorating the cathedral for the Corpus Christi celebrations. After the procession has left, priest and pupil remain to protect the rich hangings against thieves. The bells begin to toll in the almost empty cathedral. Julien is transported by the sound: 'His imagination rose from the earth.' The incident (i. 28) allows Stendhal to lead on to the following passage:

> The solemn tolling of the bell should have caused Julien to think only of the work being done by twenty men at fifty centimes apiece and assisted perhaps by fifteen or twenty of the faithful. He should have calculated the wear and tear on the ropes or on the beams, should have considered the dangers from the bell itself, which falls every two centuries, and should have worked out ways to lower the pay of the ringers, or to pay them with an indulgence, or some other favor that can be drawn from the church's stockpile without depleting her purse.
>
> Instead of these sensible calculations, Julien's soul, exalted by virile and capacious sounds, was wandering through imaginary space. Never will he make a good priest or a great administrator. Souls that can be so stirred are good, at most, to produce an artist.

Le Rouge et le Noir contains just enough such passages to indicate the silhouette of the authentic Julien, which social pressures and the drive to 'succeed' mask for most of the time. When Mme de Rênal and the children move from Verrières to their summer residence at Vergy, a different Julien, forgetful of the past and neglectful of the future, emerges briefly.

> After all that constraint and crafty managing, now that he was alone, far from the sight of men, and instinctively unafraid of Mme. de Rênal, he yielded to the sheer pleasure of existing, which is so vital at his age, and to the pleasures of the most beautiful mountains in the world.

When Mme Derville arrives on a visit, he treats her confidently as a friend who must share his love of nature, and takes her to the spot from which the best view can be had. Then there is a certain evening which Julien spends as usual in the open, seated between his mistress and Mme Derville under an enormous lime-tree, for coolness' sake.

> Julien gave no further thought to his black ambition or to his projects, so difficult to carry out. For the first time in his life he was carried away by the power of beauty. Lost in a vague delightful dream, wholly foreign to his character, gently pressing that hand which seemed to him perfectly beautiful, he only half heard the rustling of the linden tree in the light night wind and the distant barking of dogs by the mill on the Doubs.[7]

7. *Le Rouge et le Noir*, i. 8, 11.

But, adds Stendhal in the next sentence, 'this emotion was a pleasure, not a passion'. When he retires a little later to his room, it is to take up his book and pore once again over Napoleon's reminiscences. 'At the age of twenty, the idea of the world and the effect to be produced there is more important than anything else.'

The concluding chapters of *Le Rouge et le Noir*, on which we have not touched at all so far, show how in the end this 'passion' expires, leaving room for the reflowering, in memory and reality, of this 'pleasure':

> All the passions evaporate with age,
> One carrying off its vizard, the other its knife.

Julien, locked away, within a few weeks of execution, can let fall the vizard and let drop the knife.

No incident in the novel has incurred so much criticism and aroused so much speculation as Julien's attempt on Mme de Rênal's life which, although unsuccessful, ruins a career of unlimited promise and delivers him to the executioner. The situation which Stendhal has reached in chapter xxxv of the second part of *Le Rouge et le Noir* can be summarized in a few lines. Mathilde, discovering that she is with child by Julien, tells her father that they must marry. The Marquis de La Mole, another 'homme à imagination', had dreamed of seeing his daughter marry into a ducal family. His fury is boundless but he is obliged to yield to the realities of the situation; to make the match socially a little more acceptable, he has a minor title conferred on Julien, procures him a commission in the hussars, and settles an income on him. He delays giving his final consent only in order to complete his inquiries into Julien's character. These inquiries result in a letter from Mme de Rênal in which Julien is described as an ambitious young man who profits by his sexual attractions in order to enslave and dishonour whatever woman has most credit in the household in which he is serving.

M. de La Mole warns Mathilde he will never consent to her marriage with a man of this type. Julien, having been shown Mme de Rênal's letter, tells Mathilde her father's decision is perfectly understandable. Without another word he takes horse for Verrières, where he arrives on a Sunday morning. He purchases a pair of pistols and tells the gunsmith to load them for him; enters the church as mass is being celebrated; and sees Mme de Rênal a few pews away. He hesitates for so long as she is clearly visible. But when she lowers her head Julien fires once at the kneeling figure bathed in the red light which streams through the crimson awnings hung over the windows of the church. With the first shot he misses; he fires again and she falls.

Émile Faguet, at the beginning of this century, was apparently the first commentator to complain that this train of incidents was in total contradiction with the psychology of the various characters involved in them.[8] M. de La Mole ought to have reflected that little weight could be given to the denunciation of a jealous cast-off mistress. Mathilde, instead of sending Julien an agitated and despairing summons, ought to have waited for her father to come round to a more rational way of thinking. Julien, finally, ought to have seen that nothing was to be gained by assassinating his accuser. Whatever he may say or think, the Marquis is in no position to forbid or defer indefinitely his daughter's marriage to Julien.

Faguet suggests two reasons why Stendhal should have set plausibility at defiance here. In the first place, the fashion of the day required a melodramatic finish to a novel. There may be something in this, even though Stendhal had contented himself with an ending in a minor key for *Armance*. The successful novels—*Les Chouans, Notre-Dame de Paris, Indiana*—published in France about the same time as *Le Rouge et le Noir* were nothing if not sensational; and Stendhal was not indifferent to the claims of the contemporary romantic sensibility.[9] His concessions to this taste, however, though real, are seldom so conspicuous, and they must be looked for in rather subtler touches. To take but one instance, a careful reading of *Le Rouge et le Noir* allows one to detect traces of a kind of fate symbolism (admittedly more German than French in inspiration[1]) which might be held to represent a passing obeisance to romanticism. Has it ever been observed how, on three crucial occasions, the hero finds himself *in a church hung with red draperies* of one sort or another? When he enters the church at Verrières with intent to murder, 'all the lofty windows of the church were draped in crimson curtains'. The detail echoes an earlier incident which took place in the cathedral at Besançon, the gothic pillars of which, in celebration of the Corpus Christi holiday, were encased in 'a sort of red damask' rising to thirty feet; it was here, behind one of these red pillars, that Julien saw Mme de Rênal unexpectedly for the first time since he left Verrières. The shock of seeing him caused her to swoon away. Both these occasions are no doubt meant to recall the experience Julien had when he was on his way, for the first time, to the Rênals' house. On a whim, he entered the church —later to be the scene of his criminal attempt—and found it 'dark and deserted. Because of a festival, all the windows of the building

8. *Politiques et moralistes*, iii. 51–54.
9. Catalogues of the 'romantic' elements in *Le Rouge et le Noir* have been attempted by P. Bourget, *Nouvelles pages de critique et de doctrine*, i. 37; P. Jourda, 'Un centenaire romantique',

Revue des cours et conférences, vol. xxxii (1931), pp. 308–14; J.-B. Barrère, loc. cit. 453–4; &c.
1. Stendhal probably never read Kleist, but he did know, as we have seen, *Die Wahlverwandtschaften*.

had been covered with scarlet cloth. As a result, the sun struck through in shafts of brilliant light, creating an impressive and religious atmosphere.' Julien picks up a scrap of newspaper in the Rênal family pew. On one side are printed the words: '*Details of the execution and last moments of Louis Jenrel, executed at Besançon, on the* _____, and on the other the beginning of a sentence: '*The first step*. . . . ' Julien, on leaving the church, imagines he sees blood spilt on the floor. A closer inspection shows the illusion to have been created by drops of holy water which shine red in the red light which streams through the red curtains.[2] So discreet a use of omens and portents does not suffice to make *Le Rouge et le Noir* a *schicksalsroman*,[3] and perhaps, after all, bearing in mind Stendhal's literary preferences, it might be safer to trace such features to Shakespeare rather than to contemporary romantic literature. His admiration of *Macbeth* would have been strong enough to tempt him to this distant imitation.

Faguet's other suggestion is that Julien would not have been, as Stendhal wanted him to be, a second Laffargue, a man of 'energy', if he had not sooner or later tried to kill someone. Stendhal's conception of energy was a little more subtle than this: strength of character does not necessarily display itself in homicide. Nevertheless, the opinion that Stendhal's invention here was not altogether free received powerful reinforcement when the story of the seminarist of Brangues came to light. At the time Faguet was writing, Stendhal's incontrovertible use of this *cause célèbre* had not yet been fully established. Some of the most authoritative of his modern critics suppose that Stendhal's hand was in a sense forced by the necessity to dovetail Julien's career into the historical framework provided by Berthet's, even though Julien did not have Berthet's motives for murder or the character that might have led him to commit it.[4] Other apologists suppose Julien to have lapsed, at this point in the story, into a psychopathic condition, and are prepared to back up this theory with a wealth of clinical detail.[5]

In reality, it is unnecessary to suppose either that Stendhal was being clumsy or that Julien had taken leave of his senses. The incident, artistically desirable in that it provides a 'strong' climax, is

2. *Le Rouge et le Noir*, ii. 35; i. 28, 5.
3. For a more extended discussion of the point, see S. de Sacy, 'Le Miroir sur la grande route', *Mercure de France*, vol. cccvi (1949), pp. 64–80, and E. B. O. Borgerhoff, 'The Anagram in *Le Rouge et le Noir*', *Modern Language Notes*, vol. lxviii (1953), pp. 383–6.
4. L. Blum, op. cit. 86–88; J. Prévost, *Les Épicuriens français*, p. 95, and *La Création chez Stendhal*, p. 269; M. Bardèche, *Stendhal romancier*, p. 186;

F. O'Connor, *The Mirror in the Roadway*, pp. 53–54; &c.
5. H. Martineau, *L'Œuvre de Stendhal*, pp. 405–10; C. Liprandi, *Au cœur du 'Rouge'*, p. 241. The chief point in favour of this explanation is that Stendhal himself speaks of 'the state of physical irritation and half madness in which he had been sunk since he left Paris for Verrières' (*Le Rouge et le Noir*, ii. 36).

also well-founded psychologically and, if the phrase may be used, poetically true.

Well-founded psychologically, because Julien's violent reaction is perfectly explainable as that of a man of spirit who has been, to use an expressive contemporary word, 'smeared'. The question is not whether Mme de Rênal's accusation is true or false; the question is not even whether Mme de Rênal believes what she has written (it emerges later that she composed the letter at the prompting of her confessor). The point, as Julien sees it, is that, in everyone's eyes but his own, the picture that has been drawn of him corresponds a shade too closely to reality. It is undeniably true that, in the two households in which he served, he 'dishonoured the woman who had most credit'. His motives were not ignoble, or not as ignoble as the letter suggests; but who will believe him, when the motives attributed to him are so plausible? The essence of a 'smear' is that it presents a portion of the truth and adds a degrading lie which nothing in what is known of the truth contradicts. Whatever protestations he may now make, and however M. de La Mole may profess to accept these protestations, Julien could never be sure that, in his heart, the Marquis will not continue to believe that he had been forced to yield his daughter to a scheming adventurer. Like Octave in this, Julien cannot endure not to be esteemed by those he respects. M. de La Mole himself, baffled by the enigmas in Julien's character, is convinced of at least one thing: 'he cannot stand contempt . . . he cannot endure contempt, at any price.'[6]

With absolute logic, Julien chooses the only course which can efface this suspicion, because it is the very last course of action that would be expected of an ambitious schemer: committing murder in broad daylight and insisting, when interrogated, that the crime was premeditated. It is not an act of despair, for Julien has no reason to despair: he can still marry the Marquis's daughter and progress to the summits of society on which after all there is room for men with far more on their conscience than the seduction, for mercenary reasons, of their employer's daughter. It is not an act of despair, it is not even an act of vengeance, as he pretends to Mathilde. It is an act of self-justification. It cuts short his life, ruins his hopes, but ensures at least that no man will think him a wily scoundrel.[7]

The poetic truth of the episode lies in the opportunity it provided

6. *Le Rouge et le Noir*, ii. 34.
7. This interpretation was touched on, but not satisfactorily explored, by Mlle H. Bibas ('The double ending and the moral of the *Rouge*', *Revue d'histoire littéraire de la France*, vol. xlix (1949), pp. 21–36) and, before her, by J. Decour in his suggestive essay entitled simply 'Stendhal'; published clandestinely during the war, these pages were reprinted after the Liberation in *La Nef*, no. 3 (1944), pp. 8–16.

Stendhal to reveal in the end the authentic Julien, who had occasionally emerged in the early chapters, but who subsequently, in
the 'little world' of the seminary and in the 'great world' of Paris,
had drowned more and more deeply in a murk of artificiality. At
Besançon he was still an apprentice in the art of suppressing his
own personality. 'After several months of constant application,
Julien still had the look of a *thinker*. His way of moving his eyes
and opening his mouth did not declare a man of implicit faith,
ready to believe everything and endure everything, even martyrdom.'[8] But the more he committed himself to his ambition, the
easier he found it to act the parts required of him: the part of the
perfect secretary, the part of the intrepid horseman, the part of
the confidential agent. M. de La Mole asks him to post himself at
the door of the Opéra, at half past eleven every evening, to observe
the deportment of young men of fashion, and imitate them. He
forms a close friendship with a charming exquisite, the Chevalier
de Beauvoisis, and learns so well the art of foppishness that in
London, in the native land of dandyism, he eclipses all rivals.
Later, he acts for weeks on end the part of devoted admirer of a
pious prude in order to humiliate Mathilde and tame this notorious
shrew. Stendhal, it is true, professes to admire the 'courage' with
which Julien feigns indifference to his mistress and admiration for
Mme de Fervaques;[9] but is this not another instance of the 'double
irony', noted earlier, of the commentator who hides his deepest
meaning under a screen of deceptive transparency?

All through the second part of this novel, Julien is becoming
civilized; at the end of it, he is on the point of reaping civilization's
rewards. 'My adventure is over,' he exclaims the evening he learns
that he now ranks as a lieutenant of hussars; 'the novel of my
career is over, and the credit is all mine.'[1] He sacrifices all these
rewards by a single act of *energy*, making the most uncivilized, most
ungentlemanly gesture of shooting down the woman who had
impugned his honour, for all the world like a Corsican cut-throat.

He is recompensed by a serenity which he had never known
before, save in brief snatches in the garden at Vergy and in the
mountains above Verrières. His prison-cell is at the top of a tower,
with a 'superb view', and here, writes Stendhal (chapter xxxvi),
'his spirit was calm. . . . Life was by no means boring to him; he was
considering everything under a new aspect. Ambition was dead in
him. He rarely thought of Mlle. de La Mole';—instead, his mind
reverts with persistence to Mme de Rênal, 'especially during the
silence of the nights, broken in this lofty tower only by the cry of

8. *Le Rouge et le Noir*, i. 26. 1. Ibid. 34.
9. *Le Rouge et le Noir*, ii. 28, 30.

the screech-owl.' The cry of the screech-owl—an unusually evocative touch which is premonitory of the zone of poetry into which Stendhal is now moving.

> Astonishing thing! he said to himself; I thought that by her letter to M. de La Mole she had destroyed forever my future happiness; now, less than two weeks from the date of that letter, I never give a thought to the things that occupied me completely at that time. . . . Two or three thousand francs a year to live peacefully in a little mountain town like Vergy. . . . I was happy then. . . . I didn't know how happy I was!

Julien, by the proximity of death, is suddenly aged, as though a man's age depended not on the number of years lived but on the time left for him to live.

The happiness of the dreamer takes charge, with this difference, that formerly his dreams were of the future, and of clashes with men, triumphs over women, the battle of the sexes, and the war of the classes. Now he has done with *the others*. He shuts his ears to news of the outside world; cuts as short as he decently can his conferences with defending counsel; is impatient with his faithful friend Fouqué, who is pathetically plotting his escape from prison, and even more impatient with Mathilde. 'To tell the truth, he was getting tired of heroics.' He implores them not to trouble him:

> —Leave me my ideal life. Your little tricks and details from real life, all more or less irritating to me, would drag me out of heaven. . . . What do *other people* matter? My relations with *other people* are going to be severed abruptly. For heaven's sake, don't talk to me of those people any more. . . .
> As a matter of fact, he told himself, it seems that my fate is to die in a dream. . . .
> Still, it is strange that I have learned the art of enjoying life only since I have seen the end of it so close to me.[2]

He barely conceals from Mathilde the fact that his first love fills his thoughts. Before the trial he had been flooded by memories of incidents thought forgotten; Verrières and Vergy had completely displaced Paris in his thoughts, and he was truly happy only when, left in complete solitude, he was free to relive that more distant past. In the court room only the presence of Mme Derville has power to draw him out of his glacial indifference to the proceedings: he imagines she is there as Mme de Rênal's emissary. The following day, in the condemned cell, he is woken by Mathilde, frantic with grief and with the sense of failure. He is silent when she seeks, by entreaty, argument, and invective, to dissuade him

2. Ibid. ii, 39, 40.

from refusing to appeal against his sentence. He is not listening to her. Instead, his imagination shows him, in a vision of hallucinatory intensity, Mme de Rênal's bedroom in the house at Verrières, the local newspaper, with the story of his execution emblazed on its front page, as it lies on the orange counterpane, Mme de Rênal's hand crumpling its pages convulsively, the tears coursing down her face. . . .

The undeserved and crowning happiness is when Mme de Rênal, braving scandal and her husband's interdict, visits him in prison. Stendhal implies, in the few brief scenes in which he shows them together, something which a younger novelist than he could never have suggested, at any rate with such conviction: that the transcendent enchantment of love comes with the sharing of the past in recollection.

The other incidents in this culminating drama—Mathilde's intriguing, her furious and helpless jealousy, the attempted bribery of justice, Julien's appearance in court and deliberate taunting of the jurymen to ensure they should not acquit him—all these seem vaguely unreal, for we see everything with minds clouded by the powerful emanation of Julien's enraptured dream-state. Even his bitter animadversions against society, his anguished speculations on the after-life, seem less important than the granting of this unforeseen happiness. They do, however, succeed in making his death seem real, the finality absolute, even though, when he reaches the moment of death, Stendhal avails himself of his supreme resource: silence.

> Never had that head been so poetic as at the moment when it was about to fall. The sweetest moments he had ever known in the woods at Vergy came crowding back into his mind, and with immense vividness.
> Everything proceeded simply, decently, and without the slightest affectation on his part.[3]

The writer who was to narrate so scrupulously the gruesome tortures inflicted by her judges on Beatrice Cenci, says no more than this touching the execution of Julien Sorel.

He had not been allowed to refuse the consolations of religion, but had made it clear to the priest that he repented of nothing in his life. 'I have been ambitious, but I have no intention of blaming myself for that; I was acting in those days according to the code of the times.'[4] The words are addressed, on a deeper level, by Stendhal to the reader. If Julien was for most of his life misguided it is the ethos of his age that should be blamed. Napoleon is a symbol, a pretext, no more. The historical moment called for the kind of

3. *Le Rouge et le Noir*, ii. 45.   4. Ibid.

single-minded, resolute *arrivisme* that Julien did his best to display. One way or another, betrayal was inescapable: Julien's choice lay between betraying his soul through hardness and betraying his spirit through softness. Had he remained at Verrières, had he accepted the profitable partnership which Fouqué offered him in his timber business, he would perhaps have been happy, but he would not have been a hero; it is required of Aeneas that he leave Carthage and her queen, even though this Aeneas goes to found no new city. It would be naïve to write down *Le Rouge et le Noir* as a sermon on the folly of human ambitions; for things could not have been otherwise. But it is obviously far more than a piece of social satire; though it might not be altogether misplaced to speak of it as a piece of sublimated social history. Stendhal had perhaps something of the sort in mind when he gave his novel the sub-title *Chronicle of the Nineteenth Century*.

But any formula seems intolerably constricted. 'Every time you discuss Stendhal, you are left with the impression that you have said nothing at all, that he has eluded you, and that everything remains to be said. In the end you have to resign yourself and restore him to his unpredictable and miraculous utterance.'[5] *Le Rouge et le Noir* acts, in its own way, as Stendhal does in his larger fashion: the book, and the man, defy criticism, if criticism is the art of throwing a net of convincing approximations over the protean masterpiece or artist. It is not criticism merely to marvel. But in that case criticism is here powerless, for in the last resort there is nothing we can do but marvel at the sheer intellectual brilliance with which Stendhal has connected his several explosive themes in an ordered system, presented the complex totality lucidly and exhaustively, and irradiated the whole with that strange stark poetry which is peculiarly his own.

ROBERT M. ADAMS

Liking Julien Sorel

Should one *like* Julien Sorel? It seems rather a simple-minded question, at first glance, because it appears to involve that order of naïve, direct response which we voice most simply when we say that so-and-so is "a nice guy." And of course whether Julien Sorel is or is not "a nice guy" has little or nothing to do with the *Rouge*. As a matter of fact, the quality is probably irrelevant to prose fiction generally. Julien, like every other fictional character, is a creation

5. J. P. Richard, *Littérature et sensation*, p. 116.

of words on paper, not a person whom we can like or dislike on the intuitive, inchoate grounds of flesh-and-blood relationships; and novels stand or fall on more complex considerations than the like-ability of their heroes. But the words which create Julien have been arranged with some art to evoke impressions, awareness of specific qualities, with which judgments of sympathy or dislike are associated; and to ask when we like Julien and why may cast some light on the more general question of how an author manipulates his imagi-native creation, first in order to accumulate, and then perhaps to color and qualify, our sympathy-judgments. It is a bogus substitute for liking in which the literary artist deals, but precisely because it is bogus it may be worth talking about. The ebb and flow of a sensitive reader's response, the author's delicate management of his reader's fundamental impulse to get involved with a fictional character, promises to be a matter of some subtlety. A simple way to begin is to ask what Julien does to "earn" our sympathy in the course of the book which describes his career.

His pursuit of social success, for instance, is an ambivalent ac-tivity. When we see him making his way through a society of Rênals and Valenods, overcoming the boorish insensitivity of his fellow-seminarians, and outwitting Abbé Castanède, our natural sympathy goes out to him. He is sensitive, he is plucky, he is an underdog; overwhelmingly we see the world from his point of view, because he is more generous, sympathetic, and imaginative than the men against whom he is struggling. He spares a wince for a village dog, victim of a brutal accident, and so gains on a heart that M. de Rênal's brutal laugh had wounded. He senses the victimizing of the poor in M. Valenod's poorhouse, and inwardly protests against it. He stands outside the world of crafty, arranged greed which his fellow seminarians accept without question. In thinking of them, moreover, he gains strongly on the reader's sympathy by seeing around them, appreciating the pathetic reasons for a hardness of heart which is for him, at the moment, a source of anguish.

If largeness of sympathy draws us to Julien, coldness and delib-erate cruelty might be expected to alienate us, and they are cer-tainly evidenced in his dealings with Elisa. The calumny he loads on this inoffensive if inopportune girl, merely in order to escape from an awkward social situation, foreshadows the calumny he will heap on his own parents when, in order to rise in the world, he fosters the myth of his own illegitimate birth. Stendhal partially mitigates his hero's guilt by allowing us to observe, in Elisa's reac-tions, nothing more than a wounded pride which rapidly turns to malignant hostility.[1] But that the original calumny was Julien's, and

---

1. So far is the author from lending credence to Julien's impromptu charge of promiscuity with Valenod that when Elisa actually does meet and talk with Valenod (i., 19), the author invents a lawsuit expressly in order to provide an occasion for her meeting with him.

that it was gratuitous and unrepented, he does not allow us to
doubt. What then is the effect of this notably unheroic bit of char-
acter-assassination on the part of our hero? Curiously, it is not altogether negative. The reader wants to find in Julien a free, unstable
agent. Like Napoleon, though his fundamental aim is to be presumed good, he is to stun us by dealing good and evil blindly,
indiscriminately; given that he is a hero, he is the more "interesting"
as he reveals himself the more dangerous. And his struggle to rise is
the more authentic as it commits him to use not merely the nice
weapons, but tools as well of cruelty, calumny, malice, and hypocrisy.
Undeniably, his behavior toward Elisa is a toad to be swallowed;
the toads get bigger and more disgusting toward the end of the
book, and Julien's ambition is particularly unbearable as it comes to
be, more or less, successful. But we have had earlier glimpses that
his character provides tests to be passed. In the long tradition of
confidantes, Mme. Derville serves for Mme. de Rênal as the voice
of cool common sense. Julien in his manic, ambitious phase she
cannot endure; she does not trust him at all, and leaves Mme. de
Rênal's house when she can no longer protect her friend against
this shifty young adventurer. But when it is too late, in the court-
room scene, he sees her weeping, and at the end of his speech she
cries aloud and faints. It is as if she acted out, and personified, the
reader's own resistance to Julien—the essential inertia of which is
prudence, common sense. And the ambiguity of our feelings about
him extends down to the roots of his primary motivation, ambition,
which we see sometimes merely as cold careerism, sometimes as an
authentic revolt in the name of higher values, and in the end as a
tertium quid which is the more fascinating, the less assessable, as it
seems to develop out of so little in the first sixty-five chapters of
the novel.

In the first part of the book, Julien's ambition, as it is felt to be
escape from mere oafishness and directed against a society which
is continually offensive to us, accumulates sympathy for him. But
when his antagonist and victim is M. de La Mole, who has consistently behaved toward him as a kindly and generous father,
sympathy accrues for our hero more grudgingly. A great deal of his
charm, we realize, has come from the comedy of his innocence—
witness his belligerent dilemmas in the café at Besançon, or the
charade of his first duel. As his innocence wears off so does a good
deal of his puppy charm. He is more amusing by a long shot when
playing his solemn game of epistolary lovemaking with Mme. de
Fervaques than he is when tyrannizing over Mathilde de La Mole
after her resistance has been broken.

Most of what we think about Julien depends, of course, on our
judgment of his behavior with the two ladies; and here we come

up against the central paradox of the novel, that (like the ladies) we don't really think more highly of our hero the better he behaves. Quite the contrary. The worse he behaves, the more painful the sacrifices he requires of them, the more we are impressed by their determination to love him. Impervious to jealousy, untouched by his effort to murder her, Mme. de Rênal defies public scandal, leaves her husband and children, and comes to be with Julien in the hour of his anguish. Mathilde is in despair that he no longer loves her though she has sacrificed even more prodigally to her love of him. The revelation of Julien is not to be made directly, in the glare of open daylight, but only through the glow reflected on the faces of these devoted acolytes. As with Christ and Dionysus, the mystery of Julien is performed in the darkness of a prison-tomb, and his resurrection is celebrated in the presence of women. The cenacle of Julien allures its converts by withdrawing its mystery, etherealizing its cult: that is the work of the book's last important section.

Meanwhile we cannot quite dispose of the ladies, as mediators of the reader's sympathy for Julien, by saying that if they put up with him, there must be something there. It is clear, in the first place, that they represent two contrasting tests for the young man to pass. Mme. de Rênal, who is, as it were, a genius of generous and lofty sentiments, challenges Julien to open out of that shell of icy egotism in which his sense of social inferiority has encased him. As we first see him, a somewhat grotesque and boyish passion for Napoleon is the only mark he displays of a sensitive and passionate nature. Because his only experience of sincere talk has been with the old surgeon-major, his first sincerities with Mme. de Rênal consist of sickening descriptions of surgical operations. This mechanism is shrewdly and delightfully observed on Stendhal's part, but it evinces a narrowness of sympathy in Julien which is bound to distance the reader as it amuses him. The experience of Mme. de Rênal serves to fill out this lean, avid caricature of an emotional life and a social organism. Her sense that in loving Julien she is risking not only her own social status but the lives of her children and finally her own eternal salvation is bound to impress a reader, as it does Julien; but it also evokes from Julien qualities of understanding and response which give him human depth, complexity, and texture. The bundle of his responses in Chapter Nineteen is particularly interesting to consider in this light; he is by turns anguished, sympathetic, guilty, complacent, ashamed, tender, helpless. Faced with the full complexity and pain of an adulterous affair, he is shaken to the roots of a nature in which religion occupies a greater position than his conscious thoughts would ever concede it. And in these moments of violent stress and helplessness, he grows within the reader's mind as he could never do by acting like a social or ideological automaton. In a word, his failure of control is credited to his account more than a positive achievement would be.

Mlle. de La Mole provides a test not only different, but antithetically different, which brings less of Julien to the surface but compresses his emotional life into instants of great intensity. The "higher fatuity" which he practices so successfully upon her is but the parody of an ideology, the systematic application of a mechanical social method akin to the one we admired him (earlier in the novel) for giving up or surpassing. That it takes effect upon her only convinces us that there is more of the Parisian doll in her than she, in her "heroic" pose, ever imagines. For she is not only just snob enough to find her pleasure in being anti-snob (in her choice of Julien *against* Croisenois *et al.*); she is prompt to abase herself before one (and, we can't help suspecting, *any*one) who coldly and consistently disdains her. Julien at least has this saving grace, that in their grotesque comedy of arrogance and counter-arrogance he is a passionate hypocrite. But it is the surface of his hypocrisy that saves him in her eyes, whereas it is his half-buried, imperfectly dissembled vitality of feeling that gives him interest in ours. Her effect will inevitably be to reduce him to a cold and glossy manipulator. So far as their affair is concerned, she is an extremely simple mechanism for which he possesses (after Prince Korasoff) a complete instruction-sheet. And it is our feeling that she has almost achieved her end with him, that the wild emotional strains and passionate energies of Julien's life are being subdued to a bureaucracy of the emotions, that tones the novel toward its first, false, decorous conclusion. "The novel of my career is over," he thinks (II,34); like Napoleon, he has passed from insurrection and revolt through foreign conquests, and now is ready to settle into a staid administration, an orderly and well-administered empire. That Mathilde can think of nothing better to do with him is a score against her; that Julien is willing to settle for a big income, an empty job, and a flashy uniform is something against him, but nothing either new or large. He has been, all his life, a climber of social ladders, a jealous appetite avid to alter his circumstances but without any particular individual self to express or create. In this respect he exemplifies a persistent, if not very deep, quality of the Stendhalian spirit. In that curious personal document, the *Privilèges* of 10 April 1840, one feels this same restless, curious, and perhaps jealous quality of a mind which wants to creep into other bodies and accumulate other experiences, but doesn't have much capacity for inwardness. This limitation upon Julien's range of response would scarcely be worth dwelling upon if it did not illuminate the special achievement of the book's last ten chapters, the transcendence there performed.

But before we come to that last test of Julien's powers of self-transformation (and our powers of sympathetic response), let us pick up a few scattered, unsystematic elements from the book's first sections, such as control a reader's like or dislike of Julien. Elisa, as we have seen, is a minor character controlling one set of responses to Julien; Geronimo the basso is another. As he first appears, merry and talented, with a tale on his lips of youthful escapades in Naples, he radiates a sympathetic bonhomie to which Julien, Mme. de Rênal, and the children instinctively respond. The cold gloom of M. de Rênal's suspicious mood is suddenly dissipated; the mayor himself hardly shares in the new gaiety at all, but fades wordlessly from sight, and the little group pass a delightful evening together. Again, when he meets Geronimo on the road to Strasbourg, Julien finds him immediately cordial and frankly sympathetic; they share confidences, ally themselves instinctively against the odious innkeeper, reconnoiter the village together; and it is only in a last-minute subordinate clause, almost an afterthought, that we learn Julien has been suspecting Geronimo of being himself the spy-catcher he is trying to elude (II,23). It is a thought which has, of course, never crossed the reader's mind; and the oblique, belated angle from which this possibility enters the novel implies to the reader that Julien is far ahead of him in awareness, that the character's world is unexpectedly intricate, dangerous, and open to unsuspected possibilities. (Other instances of delay in imparting to the reader significant knowledge or suspicions which Julien has been harboring all along may be found in I,28 and 29, where we learn long after the fact that the seminarians perform military drill as part of their spiritual exercises; and that, despite Abbé Pirard's ferocious discipline, a secret society exists within the seminary, the operation of which he has discussed with his protégé.) The effect of this device is to render a reader perpetually suspicious of smooth surfaces in the novel and particularly in the hero, while at the same time feeling admiration for a mind more complex and controlled than one had supposed it. One likes Julien less but admires him more.

Through the greater part of the novel, Fouqué plays the role of an orthodox *fidus Achates* and confidant. In this character his action is a bit like that of Mme. de Rênal's children, an uncorrupted and incorruptible witness to Julien's magnetism. The generosity of his early offers, the final devotion of his attendance, point up the hero's special worth. Fouqué's own practical, uninteresting success in the lumber business underlines the adventurous quality of Julien's aspiration; and Julien trusts him implicitly as a recipient of dangerous documents, a safekeeper. But on more personal matters, Julien does not accord him very much trust. When he needs an excuse for declining a career in the lumber business, Julien accords his friend Fouqué a long lecture about the sacred vocation, a lecture which is completely hypocritical. And when Fouqué comes to visit his friend, and the conversation turns to Mme. de Rênal's new piety, Julien once more *manipulates* his friend's mind rather ruthlessly. Having momentary need of a distraction, he asks Fouqué abruptly for a copy of the liberal newspaper *Constitutionnel,* and diverts his attention from a potentially embarrassing topic by waving before him a rag of scandalous political heresy. It is a clever move, but not particularly friendly; it gives one to sense, rather too acutely, Julien's readiness to use his friends even if it means pulling them around by the nose.

And this is just what it does mean, more often than not, with his two ecclesiastical godparents, abbés Chélan and Pirard. He is a systematic and accomplished liar before both of them, deceiving Pirard as blithely about Amanda Binet as about Mathilde de La Mole, and Chélan about Elisa as about Mme. de Rênal—not to mention the ground-bass deception of both regarding his pretended ecclesiastical vocation. That his ecclesiastical superiors forgive him repeatedly, and are devoted to him even after the climactic disaster, may perhaps suggest that he is a lovable scapegrace; that the reader condones and conspires in their tolerance may be due to his predictable sense that ecclesiastical standards are painfully high. But there is another consideration for both the abbés, another comparison that forces itself on them: in Verrières as in the seminary, Julien is distinguished by intelligence; and the conspiracy of the intelligent against the clods is one in which readers are always ready to flatter themselves by taking part. Figures like Siéyès, de Pradt, Talleyrand, and above all Cardinal Richelieu lurk in Julien's background and occasionally advance directly into his line of vision (cf. II, 15), to suggest that one need not be a saint to be very useful indeed to the church. And perhaps abbé Pirard is anachronistically a Jansenist precisely to remind us that his rigorous honesty, however admirable, is a social anomaly in Restoration France.[2] The horizon of truth in the world around is lower than he sets it, by a long shot.

When all this is said, there is no getting around the fact that Julien in his relations with the agents of established society (even those most fond of him personally) is something of a *coquin,* a scoundrel. A reader is meant to sense this, and to sense that Julien's only authentic affinities are with the *déclassé*—with Altamira, Beauvoisis, and Korasoff, all aristocrats deprived for one reason or

2. Surely the Jansenist who in the novel's final pages proposes to Julien a low, Jesuitical trick exists in the novel mainly to remove a last resource of integrity from our hero, to cast doubt on a group which might otherwise seem immune from his general charge of moral unworthiness.

another of genuine aristocratic functions. In the actions of the novel, they are perfectly distinct from Croisenois, Caylus, de Luz, and the gilded youth of the La Mole salon; these two groups rarely cross paths, and when they do, they have nothing to say to one another. (Norbert, for instance, simply doesn't know what to make of Altamira.) But there is a spiritual difference as well, in the form of a deeper restlessness, a more violent cynicism among Julien's elected friends. Even Beauvoisis, the most fatuous of the lot, has a bored man's appetite for a duel and a cynical view of society as mostly façade. Altamira, who professes to be pious, helps Julien forward with what he understands to be an adulterous project, and Korasoff is a gay, impudent fop, a silly, likeable man. There is an emptiness behind them all, a spirit of mockery. Croisenois and his friends run in a pack; their wit is often mere malice and their emptiness simply that of conformity. But Altamira, Korasoff, and Beauvoisis are outside society in other ways; and their hollowness is so extreme, it is clearly deliberate, perhaps parodic. This again stimulates our sympathy for Julien; he belongs, as it were, to the *club-des-sans-club*, the outsiders' inner circle. Even Beauvoisis, the most conventional of the lot, earns from Julien this cachet that he is not boring; and the freedom of judgment that this verdict implies, even as it establishes Julien at the center of the novel, draws on our inbuilt hostility toward "artificial" social categories. For the sensitive novel-reader is by immediate implication from his position and his activity a republican, a free-thinker, and an enemy of established status. That is the reader at his best. In less conciliatory moods, he is a ravening anarchist who would gladly see the world consumed in fire if only the flames provided him with a momentary sensation. Whichever role the reader assumes, Julien, because he is a freer agent and capable of more radical instabilities than the novel's other characters, tends not only to engross our intimate sympathies himself, but to control our distribution of sympathy among the other characters.

One last incidental personage in the book has a special mediating influence on our judgment of Julien: this is of course the author. By an effort of consciousness, we know he is present throughout the book, inventing the dialogue and manipulating the figures; but for simplicity's sake, let us take a couple of passages where his presence is explicit and unmistakable. An interesting intervention occurs (I,8) just after Julien has committed his calumny against Elisa. Stendhal promptly takes over the scene in his own person, ostensibly discussing Julien's pretended devotion to an ecclesiastical career in the teeth of Abbé Chélan's cautious discouragements. And his intervention takes the form of a mock-panegyric on Julien:

Let us not think too poorly of Julien's future; he was inventing, with perfect correctness, the language of a sly and prudent hypocrisy. At his age, that's not bad. In the matter of tone and gestures, he lived among yokels, and so had never studied the great models. Later, circumstances permitted him to approach closer to fine gentlemen; no sooner had he done so than he was as skillful with gestures as with words.

The effect of these cold and measured generalizations is to divert the reader's generous indignation with Julien's sordid behavior into an indignation with society, which inevitably includes the reader's self. The author, with his broad view of society and of his own novel (he is careful to remind us unostentatiously how much more he knows about both than we do), stands as a reflector behind the figure of Julien; his polished surface turns wrath not only away but back upon that "way of the world" which, for the moment, is being invoked against the hero. "A gent just doesn't traduce a lady." "Well, Julien has just been following the models set before him (and you thought it was rather cute when Valenod plumed himself on rumors of his success with Mme. de Rênal); and later on, when he traduces other ladies in a more elegant style than this one, what will you care?" On the one hand, Beyle is lightening the character of Julien by darkening his own; but in addition, the passage is notable for the way it turns the reader's indignation against himself. He is, precisely, a "hypocrite lecteur," when he waxes indignant at an act of calumny, crudely performed but under pressure of necessity, while smiling at the same act when performed with witty malice and gratuitously.[3]

Another sort of intervention occurs in the course of Julien's dinner at M. Valenod's, (I,22), when, after the man has been silenced in his song, Julien is allowed to soliloquize his indignation. But the author will not give him this word unchecked:

> I confess that the weakness which Julien displays in this monologue gives me a poor opinion of him. He would be a worthy colleague of those conspirators in yellow gloves, who pretend to change the whole way of life of a great nation, but don't want to be responsible for inflicting the slightest scratch.

The last phrase here is of some importance: the French of it is "et ne veulent pas avoir à se reprocher la plus petite égratignure."

---

3. There is, in addition, a kind of indirect genuineness to Julien's duplicity, insofar as it reminds the reader of that passage in Rousseau's *Confessions* where his calumny about the innocent chambermaid Marion is explained—to the triumphant overthrow of the malignant reader, who of course wanted to see Jean-Jacques in as bad a light as possible. That chestnut is pulled out of the fire by means of psychology; Jean-Jacques, under pressure because of an accusation of theft, accused Marion because at bottom he liked her, and her name was already in his mind. Julien's accusation of Elisa takes on psychological interest, and so diminishes our moral indignation, when viewed in this context.

The point is not that the "conspirators in yellow gloves" mind inconvenience for themselves, but that they don't want to be responsible for hurting others. In the classic phrase, they want to make an omelet without breaking any eggs. Julien, of course, is in no position to make any omelets—nor, for that matter, is there any reason to doubt his readiness to crack eggs, Valenod particularly, when he has the power to do so. But he is just a pretext in the economy of this lecture; the weight of Stendhal's intervention falls against a rhetorical fraud perpetrated between a careless reader and an exaggerating character—perhaps most heavily of all on that most theatrical of pleas, that God not suffer such things to be. Thus Stendhal intervenes (1) to damp and qualify in the character rhetorical effects which are really his own, and which he retains, despite his own sarcasms, to widen the tonal range of the book; (2) to suggest Julien's moral independence of his creator, and his behavioral instability for better and for worse; and (3) to challenge the impressionistic estheticism with which the reader conditioned to novels approaches this one—to make him aware that it is a harder law than he is used to by which Julien is to be judged. And thus, by withdrawing his hero from varieties of verbal, and relatively facile, sympathy, Stendhal implies his own assurance that more delicate varieties are not beyond him.

But it is the end of the book that brings Julien into most intimate contact with the reader's mind, and here that Stendhal, by casting aside the old novelistic injunction to dramatize, succeeds in leading us into the presence of the mystery. M. Prévost has seen very clearly here the cessation of analysis and particular motivation; we do not know why Julien makes his provocative speech to the jury, or how we should reconcile his sense that he has been justly condemned with his later pretext (or is it more than a pretext?) that he is appealing for clemency. Some immense burden has been lifted from him by the murder attempt, the jail, or both—or perhaps simply by the resolution of that paradox which raises the man condemned to death above all snobbish competition. Which of these several notions should be invoked, we are not told. Finally, a major question about Julien's character, which has exercised the reader since the beginning of the book, disappears from the end of it—disappears, unanswered and unremarked, like the Cheshire Cat. After lurking uneasily in the wings of the reader's mind for better than four hundred pages, the charge that Julien is really an *interested* careerist, a vulgar adventurer, finally gets made in Mme. de Rênal's letter; but it is never answered or resolved, certainly not by Julien's blind pistol-shot nor by word or deed of anyone else. That element of the story is simply transcended. So that the reader, who is mobilized for redeeming demonstrations, is left with his demonstrations on his hands. Like the sources of the Nile (II,42), the root-motivations of Julien's character are to be hidden behind high mountain-ranges.

The rhetoric of Julien in jail is a free flow of thought, without formal structure, without prepared transitions; it is at a farther remove from the *Code Napoléon* than from the *Mémoires d'Outre-Tombe*, those eastern and western limits of Stendhal's prose rhythm. But the matter of his discourse is a general arraignment before what we must construe as a court of equity. The rules of evidence are not strict here, and the verdict is often no more than an implication; but the judgments run swiftly together. Isolated instances of vulgarity observed throughout the novel, summoned up in a phrase, converge into a panorama. By what mantic authority does this little peasant speak so carelessly, yet precisely? With almost impudent assurance, he asks whether he will find in the world after death the god of the Christians or the god of Fénelon (II,42). In an epithet, he has settled a century of controversy, unfrocked a bishop by making him an alternative to Christianity,[4] and taken sides with him against a thousand years of Christian tradition. From the single image of his father, overjoyed to have a son guillotined in return for a clear profit of three or four hundred louis, his view spreads to the honest folk in their parlors everywhere; he levels the jailbirds, to whom he talks, with the prosecutor who condemned him. In effect, he has risen beyond the purview of social morality, at Lear does in his great scene of mad justicing (IV,6), overturning all the machinery of reward and punishment. But what he rises to is an affirmation of his own spiritual worth, an individualism built on a reversal of Christ's promise that "where two or three are gathered together in my name, there am I in the midst of them" (Matt., xviii.20). Where two or three are gathered together, in Julien's world, hypocrisy is in the midst of them; the truly generous soul lives apart, sustained by his own idea of duty to himself, and warmed by the sympathy—perhaps—of the woman he loves. This sounds a little pretentious, but Julien's dismissal of his own sincerity as hypocrisy serves partly to take the curse off it. From the point of view of a novel-reader trained on passionate affirmations, his devotion to Mme. de Rênal provides a minimum of rendition and resolution needed to end his story on a satisfying note. But Julien has perhaps got out of range of his own story, as it relates to his ladies. When he bundles them off in the company of the sympathetic Fouqué, with the cool observation that whether they fight or weep,

4. Julien's opinion of Fénelon is perhaps less idiosyncratic, though even more interesting, than I have suggested here. It is a recurrent French judgment (see for example Maeterlinck, *Wisdom and Destiny*, par. 96) that Fénelon was rather a good human being than a Christian, more animated by human virtue than divine faith. Yet to make these two qualities antithetical is in itself (some might feel) to show a too limited, because too sharply defined, comprehension of both. It is to imply that goodness is somehow a less legitimate expression of faith than holiness —and the assumptions here invite a good deal of reflection.

it will probably be good for them, the implication is that he has more important business to perform. Here again we sense a masculine instinct of modesty at work; Julien's last acts are performed in solitude and, as it were, behind a veil, which neither readers nor characters are allowed to pierce. He gathers into a single knot his own duties to himself (rightly or wrongly conceived, as he had said), and completes them; it is of the essence of the effect that we should be left outside to admire precisely because we cannot altogether understand or sympathize. His last actions, like the mysterious cortége with which Mathilde conducts his corpse to the grave, are properly a source of wonder.

So on liking Julien Sorel: it turns out (not surprisingly) to be part of a rather complicated game, an *intrigue intérieur,* as Valéry called it, in which the author plays, now against, now into, the expectations of the average-sensual reader. Whatever can be predicated of that reader in the way of passive expectation, softness for rhetoric, innocence of intrigue, and conventional moral stances, Stendhal is ready to take advantage of. In some such sense as this, Vladimir Nabokov is surely right when he declares (in the novelist's own words) that Stendhal writes fiction for chambermaids, "romans de femme de chambre." Indeed, indeed, Stendhal exploits the booby reader; so, for that matter, does Nabokov. But, read carefully, with an awareness of the psychological games just under the surface, the *Rouge* is unlikely to leave anybody, even a *femme de chambre,* in the booby state. Speaking for the moment as a potential employer, I can imagine few books that would cause me more disquiet if I found one of my domestic employees looking into it and then glancing at me with a cold and speculative eye. Whether you like Julien Sorel, and for what parts of his behavior, depends, then, in some measure, on who you think you are and what conspiracies or complicities your imagination allows you to join, in the course of reading the book.

G. TOMASI di LAMPEDUSA

Notes on Stendhal: *Red and Black*[†]

Since it is idle to repeat once again that Stendhal is a genius as a poet, as an analyst of emotions, as an evoker of atmospheres, there is nothing left for me but to strive to examine the technical means employed by him to exploit those gifts. In art, of course, the pos-

[†] G. Tomasi di Lampedusa, "Notes sur Stendhal (Le Rouge et le Noir)," *Revue Stendhal-Club,* II, 156–63.

The author of *The Leopard* was an enthusiastic reader of Stendhal; he also read Jean Prévost. His thoughts on the

sibility of communicating is everything; in a novel, what is interesting is the manner of conveying time, of making the narrative concrete, of evoking the atmosphere, of manipulating the dialogue. . . .

[In the *Red and Black*] the manner of creating time is one of the most impressive in literature—that which will be used in the *Chartreuse* will not be inferior to it. There is not that slowing down that one finds in *War and Peace*; on the contrary, a constant acceleration. The duration of the actions *actually narrated* is *less* than the reading time, and from this arises the necessity of spurring on the work, which actually moves forward like the gallop of real horses. Stendhal must have had to sacrifice many things to this temporal necessity; we have lost several valuable and perhaps essential pages of introspection; but all is repaid by the magnificence of the rhythm. The entire work advances, straight and swift, like an arrow. And there is only a single "recapitulation."

Another major problem has been resolved in the best possible way: that of the narrator. I have already discussed elsewhere the scruples over their right to know their characters' emotions which worried the authors of the past. Some attempted to quiet these worries by recourse to the epistolary form; it tended to slow down the action and lead it astray. Others preferred the first-person narrative; it allows an extraordinary thoroughness, but relates only to the one person who speaks: *Adolphe* and *Dominique* are the best examples of this mode. Still others, like Proust, narrate in the first person, but attribute to themselves the ability to interpret others' thoughts as well; Proust was successful in this because he was a genius, but the method is hedged round with perils and absurdity.

Stendhal chose the shortest and most arrogant way, that which, to simplify, can be defined as the method of having the story narrated by God. Stendhal, playing the role of a god, knows the most intimate thoughts of each character, reveals them to the readers, with whom he shares his own omniscience, and leaves nothing obscure, unless he declines to express it in order to intensify emotion. At the beginning, the novel is in the indirect form. The sordid life of Verrières, the character of M. de Rênal, and the meanness of the interests which swarm around him are seen through a witness who, though not indifferent, is alien to the action. But when Julien comes onstage, the world is shown as it appears in his eyes. During the great anger scene, however, it is M. de Rênal who is the center and

---

Red and Black, published posthumously in the journal of Stendhal studies, present a novelist's special insights into the difficulties and accomplishments of his predecessor. Other 20th-century novelists who have drawn inspiration from the work of Stendhal include André Gide (*Les Caves du Vatican*), Roger Vailland (*La Loi*), Jean Giono (*Le Hussard sur le Toit*), and, curiously, John Braine (*Room at the Top*). Not many other novelists born in the eighteenth century could number as many, and as impressive, disciples.

the observer of the universe. In her turn, the simplicity of his wife is such that her thoughts are easily read by her friend and by her lover. In the second part, which takes place in Paris, the world is alternately perceived through Julien and through Mathilde. In one scene—Chapter 17 or 18, I think—we even pass in several lines from the viewpoint of one to that of the other, in a dialogue without peer in the past and still unequalled; a dialogue which bares these two souls, not with the help of spoken words, but by their thoughts reported as if in a commentary at the bottom of the page.

Moreover, there is not a character, however minor he may be, who does not for a moment become the center of observation; Abbé Pirard, M. de La Mole, and even Korasoff; and this is because, at that moment, each of them constitutes the channel through which the current of the action is passing.

Certain characters—Valenod, to cite him alone—are never seen from within; but this is because they are absolutely destitute of soul. They are only objects, never subjects. But they are very few.

The result of this almost incredibly subtle technique (in great part unconscious, moreover: "A man is always amazed at the cleverness of his own unconscious," as Freud said) is the complete fusion of the author, character, *and* reader. The latter is no longer a stranger who contemplates the action, but almost always one of the participants in the action itself.

This result is in large measure obtained by the method of the "interior monologue." This procedure, which was to be carried further by Proust, Joyce, and Virginia Woolf, is employed by Stendhal with a quite classical moderation indispensable to avoid slowing down the action while uncovering motives. That seems easy, but is not. The *Red and Black* is, above all, a lyrical effusion and a novel of psychological analysis, but also a picture of the age, and a book in which events follow upon each other at full speed. This last necessity really does not make itself felt in the works of the three authors mentioned several lines above. The necessity for action occasions a more sustained concentration of "interior monologues" than one finds in these authors, for whom the *means* had become the *end*. The action of *Ulysses*, for example, lasts twenty-four hours, and it is one of the simplest and most fluid of actions, but the reading takes at least five times as long in spite of the considerable efforts at concentration made by Joyce. But here it is a matter of verbal concentration; Stendhal's efforts achieve a substantial concentration of psychological moments. From each of them he has retained only the essential, subjecting it only in passing to the distillation of his style, which is one of the fastest-moving styles in the world. The "interior monologues" of the characters are extremely short, no more than several lines. One passes from these monologues to the rest of the narrative through several in-

552 · G. Tomasi di Lampedusa

direct sentences which in combination introduce, gradually and without any jolting, the different kinds of exposition.

Thus the reader is spared those shocks that he feels in passing from one letter to another in an epistolary novel, or, in a modern novel, from a ten-page monologue to direct action. He is aware of the change that the rhythm of expression has undergone only on a second reading, when he deliberately thinks of it. The narrative's fluidity remains intact.

But in the course of a novel, and especially when the psychological complication is intricate and the action swift, it is good to afford the reader some moments of respite. The reading is, of course, always more rapid than the writing of a novel, and even if the author has not for his part felt this necessity, he ought not to forget that the reader needs a rest. If the latter did not find an oasis in which to rest, he would close the book at the wrong time and reopen it only when the accumulated force had been dissipated. All the great authors of long works have granted these pauses: Homer, with his interpolated episodes; Dante always; Ariosto with his primitive technique of interrupting a narrative to occupy himself with other futilities destined to be cut off in their turn; Cervantes and Mme. de La Fayette interpolating secondary plots; Richardson and Thackeray themselves speaking in place of their characters. . . .

Stendhal too introduces pauses in the action; but these are pauses introduced in such a way that they are necessary to the action and not diversions. The feeling of respite is obtained through a simple change of tone. The Geronimo episode, the masterly interlude of life at the seminary—which, let it be remarked in passing, drew a cry of admiration from the author himself and moved him to note in the margin of his copy: "The seminary scenes: *very well done!*"—the Corpus Christi procession during which Julien's naive Machiavellianism seeks to discover the plots of Chas-Bernard who is, however, only a good old fool, the incident in the cafe in Besançon, the tailor who comes to measure Julien for his clothes, the characters of Beauvoisis and Korasoff and many more, are moments of necessary relaxation for the reader, but necessary also to the action and the portrayal of characters (these two ideas are only a single one for Stendhal). Thus the seminary will make Julien more perceptive, Chas-Bernard will help him in his career, Geronimo will serve as "guinea-pig" during his secret mission, Beauvoisis will help him to enter society on an equal social footing. These are not useless diversions, they are windows opening to refresh the atmosphere which, however, remains always the same.

Atmosphere, there we have it. Stendhal will not devote himself, like the director of a film, to those meticulous descriptions of buildings and furnishings from which Balzac was sometimes able to

obtain extraordinary poetic effects. Yet he does suggest these buildings and these furnishings, I really don't know how, in most cases.
When Julien enters Mme de Rênal's room after leaving the
seminary, the feeling of darkness, heat, enclosure, and unpleasant
odor is suggested; but how, I do not know. The oppressive luxury
of the La Mole mansion is evoked by five words at most: "vast
salons, gilded and melancholy." In fact, precisely those places
which are to be the scenes of essential episodes are not described;
they are suggested by a simple preliminary presentation. Later, when
the scene takes place there, the reader will be able to refer to the
picture he has already formed, and sometimes long since, without
having to submit to the double mental effort of sketching in his
imagination a setting at the very moment when he is seeing one
of the most complex scenes of the novel taking place.

In sum, the key scenes of the work never unfold in a place which
has not first become familiar. The church in Verrières, for example,
where Julien's crime will take place, has already been shown to us
at the beginning of the novel, with, in addition, a slight overtone of
the sinister. The end of Chapter 8 of the first part prepares us for
the following scene, that celebrated scene in which Julien, beneath
the linden tree, presses Mme. de Rênal's hand. In the La Mole
library, which is not described—but is it really not described?—
there is a certain little door hidden by books which takes on an
almost symbolic value. Episodes of secondary importance occur first,
episodes through which the reader will necessarily form a picture
of the place which will serve as setting for the stormy encounters of
Julien and Mathilde. The La Mole garden itself is evoked at the
very beginning in several conversations. In short, Stendhal, to create
settings, trusts largely to his reader's power of imagination, but
encourages that faculty through allusions which precede the moment
when that interior evocation will be most necessary. . . .

But only a slight portion of a conflict's setting is composed of
landscapes and buildings; primarily, a background is composed of
men, institutions, customs. These elements, which interested Stendhal most, are thus the most explicitly developed, yet always by
means of imperceptible and unemphasized strokes. And the meanness of the provincial atmosphere, the perpetual feeling of mistrust
at the seminary, the frivolity of certain worldly circles, as well as
the sense of intrigue that one feels in other circles, are expressed in
a manner so clear and so striking that additional examples are
superfluous.

The characters' dialogue in the *Red and Black* is managed with
a technique so subtle that it goes unnoticed. The flaw of so many
novels—and among them the greatest—has disappeared, that flaw
which consists in revealing the characters' souls through what they

say. Such verbal revelations we hardly ever find in real life; we understand people's characters through their actions, their looks, their faltering words, their clenched fists, their silences or their sudden loquacity, the flushing of their cheeks, the rhythm of their walk, almost never through their speeches, which are always modest or specious masks for the state of their soul. Stendhal understood this perfectly: *There is not one famous dialogue of his composition.* The principal characters are those whose words are least directly reported. When Julien refuses to marry Elisa, we are given only a summary of what he answered; when he himself asks M. de La Mole for permission to go away in order to flee his love, we know only the response of the old nobleman. Everywhere he can, Stendhal strives to avoid direct discourse; he prefers to report because that procedure offers to an author as expert as he is the opportunity to comment, *to qualify what has been said.*

Not only is the dialogue expressed in that masterly fashion which molds both the speeches and their psychological commentaries in one single context, but, as I have already said, it is especially underscored by the indications of gestures, postures, tone, all of which are necessary and all fraught with meaning. Chapters 8 and 9 of the second part are handled with a miraculous mastery in this respect. Other passages are too, particularly the conversations involving Julien, Altamira, and Don Diego Bustos. . . .

This overlong discussion of certain technical aspects of the *Red and Black* has certainly seemed tedious and may appear superfluous, but not to me. First of all because, in art, the "technique of execution" is everything, the artist being simply someone who knows how to express himself. Then because I have already spoken, quite insufficiently, of the principal themes of the *Red and Black*—which that technique throws so clearly into relief—and because what I have said about it is valid for his other works, and especially for the *Chartreuse*; and third, because one must attribute to this potent technique a great number of the negative moral judgments which have been passed on the novel.

Ever since its publication, many people have been indignant over the author's indifference to morality. When, fifty years later, Stendhal's reputation began to skyrocket towards its present glory, people continued to be scandalized by the apology for unscrupulous ambition and by the lack of "soul" which they persisted in seeing in this "monster" Julien Sorel. Not long ago I heard it said that in the *Red and Black* one glimpses the tail of the devil.

Perhaps I am accustomed to the sight of that malignant tail which I see wriggling in every corner of my field of vision; the fact is that I have never been excessively shocked while reading the *Red and Black*. Julien Sorel has always appeared to me to be a shabby, over-ambitious young man, too devoid of scruples, it is true, too inclined to push forward in the shelter of his mistresses' skirts, but after all, nothing worse than what we can notice among a number of our acquaintances. And then, compared to a Dorian Gray, to Lafcadio, to Morel, and even to Reverend Slope, he is positively a little angel. I see some "bad" in him, but not an exceptional malignity. He is an everyday fellow; unusual only in that in the midst of a weak generation, he represents energy. I will say more: I see in him something pathetic, and in his creator a tendency to attribute responsibility for his misdeeds to historical circumstance.

It is undeniable, nevertheless, that the impression of vigorous amorality which emanates from the character is too diffuse to be excessive. In my opinion, it is a question of a misunderstanding born of this singularly perfect technique.

There are thousands of good-for-nothings like Julien in life and scores of them in art. Yet he is one of the rare ones who has been portrayed with a technique which places before the reader's eyes that malignity which really does not exceed the commonplace. A flea, magnified a hundred times, seems a monster of the apocalypse; one can admire the microscopist, but the flea remains a rather innocuous insect. It is not a matter of a monster, but of a character monstrously alive, much more alive than those of flesh and bone that we meet every day and whose hand we shake—without cordiality, but also without horror. Stendhal's technique has succeeded in laying Julien bare to the reader, that same Julien who to the other characters still seems to have a great number of qualities and several virtues. All nudities which are not those of Praxiteles are disgusting. But without them one does not learn anatomy.

Another complaint is made against the *Red and Black;* it is more serious because it concerns art. Numerous readers, and not ordinary readers, are disconcerted by Julien's end, which they find psychologically unjustified, technically careless, and aesthetically unsuccessful. I do not understand this opinion.

In the novel, the crisis, from the arrival of Mme de Rênal's letter onward, seems to me to be the inevitable consequence of Julien's character and actions. Could it have been different? The conclusion seems to me to be the most important part and I have already striven to explain why. We find in it not only the logical resolution of the situation, but also the honesty of genius in Stendhal, who no longer feels any interest in Julien from the moment when he has been *discovered.* The author hastens to kill the character in order to be free of him. It is a dramatic and evocative conclusion unlike any other. If Stendhal did not trouble to explain himself, it ought, in my opinion, to be attributed to a double cause: the first is that he obviously was writing for the "happy few" gifted with intuition,

and not for those to whom explanations are necessary; the second is
that he did not need to explain, because the fact found its vindication in its being true. Berthet had committed his crime for Julien's
very reasons and under the same conditions. What was there to
explain?

The rather numerous pages which follow Julien's crime are very
strange: the world is no longer seen through Julien but through an
indifferent and melancholy X. Was Julien still able to feel, since he
was already dead for the author? His body alone was living, and
that is what the "foul atmosphere" of the prison rendered uncom-
fortable.

Julien is so completely dead that it is not said that he is
executed. His last moments are mentioned, his corpse is spoken of,
but there is not a word about his death. Here we have one of the
most characteristic examples of Stendhal's "elisions." Let us read
this passage. On the last day, Julien speaks to his friend Fouqué:
" . . . these good congregationists in Besançon can coin money (out
of anything;) go about it the right way, and they'll sell you my
mortal remains. . . .

"Fouqué was successful in this morbid transaction. He was spending the night alone in his room beside the body of his friend, when
to his great surprise. . . . "

The impulsive, energetic, handsome Julien speaks his last words
to tell his friend how he must go about buying back his body.

It is useless to explain the pathos of this situation to anyone who
does not have enough sensitivity to have felt it by himself.

ALAIN

[Love in Stendhal: Love in Voltaire]†

The heroes conduct their monologues more spaciously; whether
it is Mosca or Fabrizio, Julien or Lucien, the lover never flatters
himself; he talks to himself with blunt directness; he wants grandeur,
at least in the eyes of his beloved, as if the simple experience of love
opened up another world, in which the minutiae of politeness and
politics no longer matter. This idea hasn't been explored, to my
knowledge. The passions are generally depicted as if they were
maladies or errors; virtue consists in overcoming them, that is, in
not breaking the various rules of prudence and convention. But
Stendhalian love is the wellspring of the soul and the principle of all

† Alain, *Stendhal* (Presses Universi-
taires de France, 1959), pp. 61–65.
Emile-Auguste Chartier, who called
himself simply "Alain," after the
medieval poet whose last name was
also "Chartier," was a distinguished

virtue. Could one say this is a trait of Corneille? I don't want to miss the chance of citing here a youthful thought of our author's (*Pensées,* 11 October, 1805):

> It seems to me that, among those souls which have opened themselves to the public, none has experienced admiration in all its force and all its subtleties, like that of Corneille. Corneille's soul, loving admiration above all, gropes blindly to produce it. He is, in the highest degree, the poet of sublimity. . . . Studying my responses with the same attention when I read Racine, I should perhaps find that he was the poet of *anxiety,* as Corneille was the poet of *sublimity.*

Here I think I understand that Julien was not in love with Mathilde; he simply depended upon Mathilde as upon a force of nature, and awaited misfortune. But, on the other hand, with Mme. de Rênal he awaited happiness, and was not disappointed, for she gave him something to admire and not to fear. These are unexplored regions. Stendhal might thus be placed in the lineage of the indomitables, in the style of Louis XIII. Love, among these lofty souls, is absolutely guaranteed only by a sort of grandeur which excludes doubt and never fails to justify the faults of others by a fault of its own; its fidelity is proud and oath-bound. Racine, on these terms, is the painter of unhappiness. But the contrast is more natural between Stendhal and Voltaire, for they are of the same period, talk the same language, mock the same hypocrites. Love such as Stendhal cultivated simply does not exist in Voltaire. I should define Stendhalian love by its need for sublimity, or, if you will, by its need for admiration; and this leaves for the tender soul an immense freedom of self-mockery. Voltaire is more serious, in a sense which is not of the best; in fact, he knows very little of the truly serious, he is without a tincture of religion, a soul profoundly misanthropic. There is a bit of hatred in love of this sort; a man might well hope to be cured of this folly. Whereas the hero of Stendhal calls it a lovely folly, nourishes it with well-considered reflections which have as their object a discovery of the beloved woman's spiritual beauty and the study of her perfections. Thus it is that the branch at Salzburg, when it has lain a long time in the salt-mine, emerges bearing on each twig a glittering star; every little detail of nature is transformed into beauty. This way of understanding the famous comparison of crystallizations explains the matter properly. It is by no means a question here of an obsession one can't control, an obsession rooted in the mechanical part of the soul; quite the contrary, crystallization is desired and directed; it never ceases to make

popular philosopher and essayist of the period between the two wars; his little book on Stendhal appeared in 1935. It presents a characteristically lucid and succinct definition of love as it figures in Stendhal's novels.

for happiness. And its triumph is to create in reality the things it has believed.

"The principle of love in the French style," Stendhal writes in the *Promenades* (23 November, 1828), "is to attach oneself to whatever shows indifference, to follow what flees. But the appearance of coldness, and the doubt it engenders in the lover about the effect he has produced, make impossible for an Italian spirit that act of madness in which love begins, and which consists of covering with all conceivable perfections the image one has made for oneself of the being one is going to love. (A modern author has given the name of *crystallization* to this act of madness.)"

I don't suppose one could find in all Stendhal a more explicit statement. It is clear that crystallization is not called madness in the sense of superstitions, groundless fears, obsessions. The madness is voluntary, I might even call it heroic, and wonderfully happy. Fatalism is rejected here, under every form. The treatise *On Love* contains a number of anecdotes illustrating true love; for example, that young man who was struck dumb and remained so a long time, till the day when, his mistress telling him to speak, he spoke. This is an instance of purely voluntary and joyful obedience. And there is also that man named Salisbury who, when he left for the wars in France, swore to keep closed throughout the campaign one of his eyes, which his beloved had closed as a joke; and he kept his word. These legends make clear the idea. The lover worthy of that title is by no means a slave; on the contrary, he is lord and master of himself beyond all limits, and never ceases to give of himself out of his own free will; he is the opposite of a man sick with love, for sickness is weakness. And here on the other hand one must be strong in love, and invincible.

I don't think one can describe as "romantic" this fashion of loving; but one could call it "novelistic," because it places itself outside the social life, and seeks even to ignore it, taking refuge in a secret world full of unknown grandeurs. Stendhal talks somewhere of the happiness of loving "for example, myself, loving a woman of immense genius (on the order of Mme. Pietragrua), she loving me as I would love her. . . . " (*Pensées*, 31 July, 1804). One is well repaid for discovering such a genius; but in the first place one must want to see it, and then one must watch for signs from the eyes, the cheeks, the gestures, signs which are always uncertain as soon as one thinks they may be. It's clear, this is the cult of beauty, and that beauty has need of a cult. On the immense topic of Stendhal as an amateur of painting, I shall have the same things to say over again.

Angles of Vision

The odd shape of Stendhal's literary reputation, with a long period of oblivion followed by a sudden rebirth of interest in the late nineteenth century, has resulted in an immense amount of archaeological research into the originals of his characters, the careers of his acquaintances, the influence of his reading, the local significance of his allusions. That is one vast body of scholarship (far less likely to be dull, I think, than literary archaeology usually is), which our critical selections represent hardly at all. Again, Stendhal's political orientation has been the subject of much ardent discussion, with communists like M. Louis Aragon, proto-fascists like M. Maurice Bardèche, and underground-men (and -women) of various persuasions and colorings eager to claim him for their very own. These controversies too are only modestly represented in our selections. Psychoanalysts like Edmund Bergler have exercised their mantic art on Stendhal; believers and unbelievers have been at tug-of-war over his attitude toward religion, to the frequent detriment of their tempers and their prose styles. Almost as bewildering is the number of labels denoting literary "schools" which have been attached to him, however insecurely. He has been called a romantic, an anti-romantic, and a romantic anti-romantic; he figures largely in histories of literary "realism," yet there are many critics for whom the words "poetry" and "music" seem essential to an account of the distinctive Stendhal effect; and still others invoke the metaphor of "vaudeville." Still, literary categorizing is a whole area of work about Stendhal which in these critical selections it has seemed feasible to neglect.

Less portentous but often more illuminating is a class of comments made essentially by amateurs and outsiders—men who in the course of another argument entirely have turned to Stendhal as an instance making for their case, and seen in him a quality which formal literary scholarship might never have noticed. Paul Valéry, for example, in discussing the autobiographical element in Stendhal's fiction, falls upon a question much mooted in French criticism since Valéry raised it—the problem of literary bad faith. And this question, which is of supreme importance to Jean-Paul Sartre, the French philosopher seizes on, and pushes toward a questioning of literary writing as such. For Gide and Proust, on the other hand, a central question is stylistic; it is the peculiar quality of the Stendhal manner either to deny sweep and impetus to the novel by standing at the perpendicular to the narrative line, or else to rise above it into solitude and contemplation. The selections, though brief, show how acutely conscious these twentieth-century writers were of their nineteenth-century predecessor. On another level entirely, Paul Bourget, who was one of the most influential discoverers and popularizers of Stendhal in the 1890's, hails him as a nihilist born before his time; while Nietzsche, who had no use whatever for nihilists, also hails him as a precursor of a different sort, Finally, Ortega y Gasset, the Spanish philosopher, who added a twentieth-century book on love to the series which began with Stendhal's *De l'Amour*, pays tribute to his predecessor's insights; while Hippolyte Taine, who was one of the first to see in Stendhal a great psychologist, gives credit to the style which made his insights possible. Taine's essay has a special interest because of its date; for though it is not only trite but true that after Stendhal's death in 1842 his reputation suffered a decline, Taine's words of praise remind us that he was never without his admirers—even if their chief interest in Stendhal was as a club to beat romanticism and the allusive, highly-figured styles that grew out of it.*

PAUL VALÉRY†

Perhaps the increase in self-consciousness, the constant observation of one's self, may lead to self-discovery, to a diversity of identities? The spirit multiplies amid its possibilities, divides itself at every instant from what it just was, accepts what it just said, flies to the opposite position, turns back on itself, and studies the effect. I find in Stendhal the mobility, the fire, the quick reflexes, the elastic tone, and the honest cynicism of Diderot and Beaumarchais, those admirable comedians. Knowing oneself is nothing but anticipating oneself; anticipating oneself amounts to playing a role. Beyle's consciousness is a theater, and there is a great deal of the actor in this author. His work is full of phrases which play to the gallery. His prefaces address the audience from in front of the curtain, cock a knowing eye at the reader, make gestures of complicity with him, try to convince him that he's the least foolish fellow in the audience, that he's in on the secret of the farce, that he alone understands the finest of the fine points. "There's nobody here but you and me," they seem to say.

This has worked wonders for the posthumous career of Stendhal. He makes his reader proud to be one.

* * *

What is most striking in a page of Stendhal, what declares his immediate presence—what attracts or repels the spirit—is his *tone*. He possesses, and what's more, he affects, the most individual tone in all literature. This tone is so marked, it makes the man himself so present, that it excuses, in the eyes of the Stendhalians: (1) the negligence, the deliberate will to carelessness, the author's contempt for all formal qualities of style; and (2) numerous lootings and a good quantity of plagiarisms. In all criminal cases, the essential

* Unless otherwise indicated, all translations in this section are by the editor.
† Paul Valéry, "Stendhal," *Variété II* (Paris, Gallimard, 1930), pp. 85–86, 109–14. It should be pointed out that the authorized English translation of the works of Paul Valéry published in the United States vests exclusively in Bollingen Foundation; in England and the British Commonwealth, with Routledge & Kegan Paul Ltd. Their permission to publish Mr. Adams' translation of three pages from "Stendhal" is gratefully acknowledged.

thing for the accused is to render himself infinitely more interesting than his victims. What do we care for Beyle's victims? From other people's depressing possessions he constructs works which are read because he contributes to them a certain *tone.*

* * *

And how is this tone formed? I have perhaps already said: to be lively at whatever cost; to write as one talks when one is a man of wit, with allusions which can even be obscure, abrupt transitions, leaps, parentheses; to write almost as one talks to oneself; to maintain the sense of a free, gay conversation; to push sometimes as far as the stripped monologue; always and everywhere to avoid the poetic style, and to make clear that one is avoiding it, that one is marring the phrase-for-its-own-sake, which, by its rhythm and expansiveness would ring far too pure and too beautiful, rising to that sustained mode of speech which Stendhal mocks and loathes, in which he sees nothing but affectation, poses, and afterthoughts which are far from disinterested.

But it is a law of nature that the defence against one affectation is another.

This design, and these limitations which he imposes on himself, serve to make heard a genuine voice: his inner pretensions lead him to attempt the accumulation in a work of all the most expressive tokens of *sincerity.* His discovery in the matter of style was no doubt to dare to write according to his character, which he knew, and even imitated, to perfection.

I don't hate this tone that he made for himself. Sometimes it delights me, always it amuses me; but, it does so counter to the intent of the author, by the effect of comedy that so much sincerity and a trifle too much *life* inevitably produce in me. I accuse myself of finding his inflexions three or four times too sincere; I become conscious of the project of being oneself, of being true to the point of falsity. The truth one worships changes insensibly under the pen into the truth which is constructed in order to seem true. Truth and the desire for truth make up together an uneasy mixture within which a contradiction ferments, and from which there never fails to emerge a falsified product.

How can one fail to choose, out of the *truth* with which one works, the best aspects? How can one fail to underline, round out, color, clarify, strengthen—how can one not make the copy more disturbing, more intimate, or more brutal than the original? *In literature truth is inconceivable.* Sometimes by simplicity, sometimes by oddity, sometimes by excess precision, sometimes by negligence, sometimes by confessing to matters more or less shameful (but always *selected,* as well selected as possible)—always and by every means, whether it's a question of Pascal, Diderot, Rousseau, or Beyle, whether the nudity shown us is that of a sinner, a cynic, a moralist, or a libertine, it is inevitably lit up, colored, and qualified, according to all the rules of the mental theater. We know very well that a person disrobes only in order to produce certain effects. A great saint knew this principle very well when he undressed in the public square. Everything against common custom is against nature; it implies effort, consciousness of effort, intention, and thus artifice. A woman who strips naked is as if entering on a stage.

So there are two ways of falsifying: one, by the labor of embellishment; the other, by an effort to *enact the truth*.

The second instance is no doubt that which reveals the most implacable pretension. It implies also a certain despair of ever being able to arouse public interest by means of purely literary techniques. Eroticism is never far removed from truth-tellers.

Besides, the authors of Confessions, Souvenirs, or Intimate Journals are invariably dupes of their own wish to shock; and we are dupes of these dupes. One never sets out to exhibit oneself just as one really is; it's perfectly plain that a real person has nothing much to teach us about his reality. One writes the confessions of some other, more remarkable creature, more pure, more evil, more clever, more sensitive, or even more *itself* than reality allows—for the self has its degrees. The man who confesses, lies, running away from the real truth which is blank or shapeless and generally indistinct. But the confidential communication reaches always after glory, scandal, excuses, propaganda. . . .

JEAN-PAUL SARTRE†

Thus the essential structure of sincerity does not differ from that of bad faith, since the sincere man constitutes himself as what he is *in order not to be it*. This explains the truth recognized by all that one can fall into bad faith through being sincere. As Valéry pointed out, this is the case with Stendhal. Total, constant sincerity as a constant effort to adhere to oneself is by nature a constant effort to dissociate oneself from oneself. A person frees himself from himself by the very act by which he makes himself an object for himself. To draw up a perpetual inventory of what one is means constantly to redeny oneself and to take refuge in a sphere where one is no longer anything but a pure, free regard. The goal of bad faith, as we said, is to put oneself out of reach; it is an escape. Now we see that we must use the same terms to define sincerity. What does this mean?

In the final analysis the goal of sincerity and the goal of bad faith are not so different. To be sure, there is a sincerity which bears on

† Jean-Paul Sartre, *Being and Nothingness,* tr. Hazel E. Barnes (Philosophical Library, 1956), pp. 65–66.

the past and which does not concern us here; I am sincere if I confess *having had* this pleasure or that intention. We shall see that if this sincerity is possible, it is because in his fall into the past, the being of man is constituted as a being-in-itself. But here our concern is only with the sincerity which aims at itself in present immanence. What is its goal? To bring me to confess to myself what I am in order that I may finally coincide with my being; in a word, to cause myself to be, in the mode of the in-itself, what I am in the mode of "not being what I am." Its assumption is that fundamentally I am already, in the mode of the in-itself, what I have to be. Thus we find at the base of sincerity a continual game of mirror and reflection, a perpetual passage from the being which is what it is, to the being which is not what it is and inversely from the being which is not what it is to the being which is what it is.

ANDRÉ GIDE†

In Stendhal no phrase evokes the one after it or takes life from the preceding one. Each one stands perpendicular to the fact or idea. . . . Of all the instruments that have ever been used for sketching or writing Stendhal's traces the most delicate line.

MARCEL PROUST‡

Marcel, speaking anxiously to Albertine in an effort to distract her attention from perverse love-adventures to the Higher Things in Life:

"Do you remember the stonemasons in *Jude the Obscure*, in *The Well-Beloved*, the blocks of stone which the father hews out of the island coming in boats to be piled up in the son's studio where they are turned into statues; in *A Pair of Blue Eyes* the parallelism of the tombs, and also the parallel line of the vessel, and the railway coaches containing the lovers and the dead woman; the parallelism between *The Well-Beloved*, where the man is in love with three women, and *A Pair of Blue Eyes*, where the woman is in love with three men, and in short all those novels which can be laid one upon another like the vertically piled houses upon the rocky soil of the island. I cannot summarize the greatest writers like this in a moment's talk, but you would see in Stendhal a certain sense of altitude combining with the life of the spirit: the lofty place in which Julien

† André Gide, *Journal of "The Counterfeiters,"* tr. Justin O'Brien (New York, copyright 1951, © 1955 by Alfred A. Knopf), p. 382.
‡ Marcel Proust, "The Captive" (Vol. III of *Remembrance of Things Past*), tr. C. K. Scott-Moncrieff, pp. 514–15. Copyright 1929 and renewed 1957 by Random House, Inc. Reprinted by permission of Random House, Inc., George Scott-Moncrieff, and Chatto and Windus Ltd., London.

Sorel is imprisoned, the tower on the summit of which Fabrice is confined, the belfry in which the Abbé Blanès pores over his astrology, and from which Fabrice has such a magnificent bird's-eye view. You told me that you had seen some of Vermeer's pictures, you must have realized that they are always fragments of an identical world, that it is always, however great the genius with which they have been recreated, the same table, the same carpet, the same woman, the same novel and unique beauty, an enigma, at that epoch in which nothing resembles or explains it. . . . "

PAUL BOURGET†

. . . If I were writing criticism in the form of anecdotes, instead of a psychological study half social and half literary, which must proceed by general ideas and broad hypotheses, I could describe some strange conversations between established writers, where the citation of these little phrases, dry and rough as the formulas of the legal code, made up the whole substance of the discourse. One would say: "*M. de La Vernaye would be at your feet.* . . . " and the other would continue, "*overcome with gratitude.* . . . " The game was to find one's colleague in flagrant ignorance of a single one of the adjectives in the book. I give the fact for what it's worth. It is exceptional, but the exceptional happened, to my knowledge, a dozen times, and gives evidence of the intense seductiveness which the novel exerted.

*   *   *

To understand the conflagrations of the Commune and the terrifying recurrence in our soft civilization of primitive savageries, one must reread this book (*Red and Black*) and particularly the colloquy which Julien holds with himself in his cell as he is awaiting the day of his execution:

"There is no *law of nature*: the phrase is nothing but a bit of antiquated nonsense worthy of the district attorney who hunted me down the other day, and whose ancestor grew rich on one of Louis XIV's confiscations. There is no *right* except when there's a law to prevent one's doing such and such a thing on pain of punishment. Before the law, there's nothing *natural* except the strength of the lion, the need of the creature that is hungry or cold, *need* in a word. . . . "

Under the conventions with which our brain is loaded, under the principles of conduct that education fastens like a crust over our

† Paul Bourget, *Essais de Psychologie Contemporaine* (Paris, Lemerre, 1893), pp. 310, 320–323.

thought, under the hereditary prudence which reduces us to domesticated animals, here we see reappearing the primitive flesh-eater, savage and solitary, driven forward by the *struggle for life* like nature as a whole. You thought he was subdued, he was only asleep; you thought he had grown tame, he was only in chains. The chain breaks, the beast awakes, and you stand aghast to find that centuries of civilization have not suffocated a single one of the germs of yesterday's ferocity. . . .

"This philosophy," Stendhal wrote himself, commenting on Julien's last reflections, "this philosophy might be true, but it was of a nature to make a man eager for death." Do you see, at the very end of this work, the most complete that the author has left us, the break of the tragic dawn of pessimism? It rises, this dawn of blood and tears, and like the light of a new day gradually tints with red the loftiest spirits of our century, those who represent the peak of our achievement, those toward whom the eyes of tomorrow's man are raised—religiously. I have reached, in this series of psychological studies, the fifth of the personages I had proposed to analyze. I examined a poet, Baudelaire; a historian, M. Renan; a novelist, Gustave Flaubert; a philosopher, M. Taine; I have just examined one of those composite artists in whom the critic and the writer of imagination are closely joined together; and I have found, in these five Frenchmen of such tremendous worth, the same loathsome philosophy of the universal void. Sensual and depraved in the first, subtle and sublimated in the second, rational and enraged in the third, still rational but now resigned in the fourth, the philosophy recurs, as somber as ever but more courageous, in the author of *Red and Black*. This terrible nausea of the most splendid intelligences before life's vain efforts, can it be right? As man civilized himself, has he really done nothing but complicate his barbarism and refine his misery? I imagine that those of our contemporaries whom these problems concern are like myself, and in the face of this agonizing question they offer now an answer of despair, now an answer of hope and faith. And it is also an answer to buckle up one's soul, like Beyle, and oppose to the distresses of doubt the virile energy of the man who sees the black abyss of destiny, knows not what this abyss conceals from him—and who is not afraid!

FRIEDRICH NIETZSCHE†

As the opposite of the German inexperience and innocence *in voluptate psychologica* (which is not too remotely associated with the tediousness of German intercourse), and as the most successful

† Friedrich Nietzsche, *Beyond Good and Evil*, No, 254, tr. Helen Zimmern (New York, 1907).

expression of genuine French curiosity and inventive talent in the domain of delicate thrills, Henri Beyle may be noted: that remarkable anticipatory and forerunning man, who, with a Napoleonic *tempo*, traversed *his* Europe, in fact, several centuries of the European soul, as a surveyor and discoverer thereof:—it has required two generations to *overtake* him one way or other, to divine long afterward some of the riddles that perplexed and enraptured him— this strange Epicurean and man of interrogation, the last great psychologist of France.

JOSÉ ORTEGA Y GASSET[†]

Stendhal possessed a head full of theories; but he lacked the gifts of a theoretician. In this, as in other things, he resembles our Baroja,[1] who reacts in an abstract way to every human problem. Both, if regarded without necessary caution, present the picture of philosophers gone astray into literature. And, yet, they are exactly the opposite. To recognize this difference it is sufficient to note that both possess an abundant collection of theories. The genuine philosopher, on the other hand, does not have more than one. This is symptomatic of the essential difference between a true theoretical temperament and a merely apparent one.

The theoretician arrives at a philosophic conclusion due to an exasperated desire to concur with reality. With this end in mind, he takes infinite precautions, one of which is to maintain the multitude of his ideas in strict unity and cohesion. He is aware that what is real is remarkably singular. What terror Parmenides felt when he discovered this![2] In contrast to the real, our minds and our sensibilities are disjointed, contradictory, and multiform. In Stendhal and in Baroja, philosophic conclusions descend to mere language, to a literary genre which serves as an instrument for literary outburst. They think in terms of "for" and "against"—and this the thinker never does. In effect, they love and hate conceptually. Therefore, their theories are numerous. They swarm about like bacteria, disparate and antagonistic, each one engendered by the impression of the moment. In the manner of songs they tell a truth, not about things, but about the singer.

[†] José Ortega y Gasset, *On Love*, tr. Toby Talbot (Meridian Books), pp. 23–27. Copyright © 1957 by The World Publishing Company. Reprinted with permission of The World Publishing Company and Jonathan Cape, Ltd., London.

[1] Pío Baroja y Nessi (1872–1956), Spanish author of Basque extraction; voluminous, often violent author of many novels and essays, hard in style, intellectual in manner, nihilistic in content, and generally tinged with autobiographical elements.

[2] Parmenides of Elea (Greek philosopher of the sixth century B.C.) wrote a poem called "Nature" describing how, in an ecstatic vision, he was enabled to see the one immutable eternal substance of the world beneath its many shifting appearances.

I do not mean to insinuate any criticism by this. Neither Stendhal nor Baroja particularly aspired to be numbered among the philosophers; and if I have pointed out this indecisive aspect of their intellectual nature, it has been only for the delight of taking people as they are. They seem to be philosophers. *Tant pis!* But they aren't. *Tant mieux!*

Stendhal's case is, however, more difficult than that of Baroja, because there is one subject upon which he tried to theorize in complete seriousness. And it is, by coincidence, the same subject which Socrates, the patron of philosophers, thought to be his own specialty. *Ta erotika:* the question of love.

The study *De l'amour* is one of the most widely read of books. We arrive in the sitting-room of a marquise, an actress, or simply a cosmopolitan lady. We have to wait a few moments. The pictures —why are there inevitably pictures on the wall?—are the first to capture our attention. There is no escaping it; moreover, the pictures always produce in us the same impression of whim. The picture is what it is; but it could just as easily have been otherwise. We always miss that dramatic emotion of coming upon a necessary thing. Then comes the furniture, and with it some books. A book jacket. What does it say? *De l'amour*. It is like a work on diseases of the liver in a doctor's office. The marquise, the actress, the cosmopolitan lady, indefatigably long to be specialists in love; they want to become informed, just as someone who buys an automobile receives a complimentary manual on combustion engines.

The book makes delightful reading. Stendhal always tells a story, even when he is defining, reasoning, and theorizing. He is, for me, the best narrator there is, the supreme narrator before the Almighty. But is his famous theory defining love as a crystallization true? Why hasn't a thorough study been made of it? It has been toyed with, but no one has subjected it to an adequate analysis. Didn't it deserve the effort?

Note that, in sum, this theory defines love as an essential fiction. It is not that love sometimes makes mistakes, but that it is, essentially, a mistake. We fall in love when our imagination projects nonexistent perfections onto another person. One day the phantasmagoria vanishes, and with it love dies. This is worse than declaring, as of yesteryear, that love is blind. For Stendhal it is less than blind: it is imaginary. Not only does it not see what is real, but it supplants the real.

All anyone has to do is to study this theory on the surface to be able to situate it in time and space: it is a typical product of nineteenth-century Europe. It bears the characteristic features: idealism and pessimism. The theory of "crystallization" is idealistic because it makes the external object for which we live a mere projection of the individual. Since the Renaissance, the European leans toward this manner of explaining the world as a manifestation of the spirit. Up to the nineteenth century this idealism was relatively cheerful. The world which the individual projects about him is, in its own way, real, genuine, and meaningful. But the theory of "crystallization" is pessimistic. It tries to show that what we consider normal functions of our spirit are nothing more than special cases of abnormality. Thus, Taine wishes to convince us that normal perception is merely a continuous, connected hallucination. This is typical of the ideology of the past century. The normal is explained by the abnormal, the superior by the inferior. There is a strange persistence in the view that the Universe is an absolute *quid pro quo*, essentially nonsense. The moralist will try to insinuate that all altruism is masked egotism. Darwin will patiently describe the constructive service that death performs to life, and he will make the struggle for existence the prime vital force. Similarly, Karl Marx will place the class struggle at the root of history.

But the truth is so contrary to this harsh pessimism that it manages to slip in, unnoticed by the bitter thinker. So it is with the theory of "crystallization"; because finally one recognizes in it that a man loves only what is lovable, what is worthy of being loved. But not possessing it—so it seems—in reality, he is compelled to imagine it. These fantasized perfections are what elicit love. It is very easy to label fine things illusory. But whoever does this forgets to face the problem that then results. If these fine things do not exist, how did they come to our attention? If there are not sufficient real reasons in the woman for inspiring amorous exaltation, then at what nonexistent *ville d'eaux* could we have met the imaginary woman thus capable of exciting us?[3]

HIPPOLYTE TAINE[†]

In reality, suppression of style is perfection of style. When a reader no longer pays attention to phrases, but sees ideas in themselves, then the art has been perfected. A studied style which calls attention to itself is like a costume selected under the impulsion of folly or vanity. But a superior spirit is so fond of ideas, so eager to follow them out, so preoccupied with their truth and their linkage, that he refuses to be distracted for an instant by the need to choose elegant terms, to avoid consonantal repetition, to round off the periods. Such concerns betray the rhetorician, and one may well

3. If it weren't for the anachronism involved, one would think Señor Ortega was referring to "Last Year at Marienbad," the movie by Alain Robbe-Grillet and Alain Resnais, which was released in 1961; it deals with the haunted effort of a lover to verify an affair he thinks he must have had, in fantasy or in reality, at the *ville d'eaux* (spa, watering-place) of Marienbad.
† From Hippolyte Taine, "Stendhal," *Essais de critique et d'histoire* (Paris, 1866), pp. 55–59.

feel a grudge at Rousseau because he "often turned over a phrase in his head for three or four nights" the better to polish it. Deliberate negligence gives to Beyle's writing the charm of the natural. As you read him, you can imagine chatting with him. "Expecting to find an author," said Pascal, "one is astounded and delighted to encounter a man." Suppose yourself in a room with a few friends, men of intelligence; suppose you were obliged to describe for them an event in your life; affectation would be your chief aversion; lofty words and sounding antitheses would be the last thing you wanted. You would describe the thing as it was, without exaggeration, without display, without affectation. That's how Beyle tells a story. He writes as if oblivious to the presence of a public, without any wish to be applauded, face to face with the ideas which swarm about him, and which he feels compelled to "note down." Hence several unique qualities, with which various literary critics have reproached him, for example, barrenness of style, hatred of metaphor and figurative language. It is amusing to find Balzac declaring that "Beyle's weak point is his style,"—taking unquestioningly for granted that good taste consists of adding adornments to ideas. He himself thought he was enriching the language when, "in one of the most carefully wrought stories of his literary edifice," he began as follows:

> To what talent shall we one day owe the most moving elegy, the portrayal of sufferings undergone in silence by souls whose roots, in their youthful tenderness, encounter only hard pebbles in the domestic soil, whose first flowerings are ripped by hateful hands, whose flowers are frostbitten at the very moment of their opening?

He thought himself a great colorist because he invented ichthyological metaphors, and spoke of "the unknown abortions in which the offspring of genius sink to an arid grave." These extended images are like long scarlet robes trailing across the page, in which the idea gets entangled or disappears. Beyle in this respect is a complete classicist, or rather just a student of the ideologues and of common sense; for it must be stated flatly that the metaphoric style is the inexact style, that it is neither reasonable nor French. When your idea, for lack of reflection, remains imperfect and obscure so that you cannot bring it forth by itself, you gesture at something which it resembles; you leave the short, direct expression to fling yourself left and right into comparisons. Thus it is from impotence that you accumulate images; failing to outline your thought sharply the first time, you repeat it vaguely several times over, and the reader who wants to understand you must atone for your weakness or laziness by translating you to yourself, explaining to you what you wanted to say and didn't. The answer to those who claim that colors illumine is to say that in pure light there are no colors. Beyle is as sharp as the

570 · Hippolyte Taine

Greeks and our classics, pure spirits who brought scientific exactitude to the painting of moral qualities, and thanks to whom one can sometimes feel glad to be a man. Among these Beyle takes the first rank, in the same way and for the same reasons as Montesquieu and Voltaire; for, like them, he produces incisive words and piercing phrases which compel attention, burrow into the memory, and enforce belief. Such are those summary ideas contained in a strong image or a seeming paradox, all the more energetic as they are brief, and which cast an instant ray of light to the very depths of a situation or a character. Julien in the seminary finally understands the necessity of humble demeanor, lowered eyes, and the whole ecclesiastical comportment:

In the seminary, there's a way of eating a boiled egg which declares how far one has progressed down the saintly path. . . . What will I be doing all my life? he asked himself; I'll be selling the faithful a seat in heaven. How will that seat be made visible to them? by the difference between my exterior and that of a layman.

And elsewhere:

Public opinion is terrible in a land with a Charter. . . . I'm going to get my solitude and rural peace in the only place where they can be found in France, a fourth-floor apartment off the Champs Elysées.

Witticisms about Paris are charming and frequent. Here is one, for example:

True passion never thinks of anything but itself. This, it seems to me, is why the passions are so absurd in Paris, where your neighbor always pretends that people are thinking about him all the time. I shall not try to describe Julien's transports at Malmaison. He was in tears. What, you say? In spite of those ugly white walls, just put up that year, which cut the park into little pieces? Yes, sir: for Julien, as for posterity, there was no line to be drawn between Arcola, St. Helena, and Malmaison.

I completed the quotation to show how these powerful ideas arrive one on top of the other, like a volley. At the first reading, they escape notice, because they are everywhere, and never stand out. But on the second reading, they become more apparent, and as often as one re-reads, one discovers new ones. Beyle casts them into passages of transition, dialogues, little incidents; they are the *filling* of his book: you could call him a prodigal, who stuffs the cracks in his walls with bars of gold. And this witty style is never stiff, as that of Montesquieu occasionally is, nor clownish, as Voltaire's sometimes is; it is always easy and noble, never constrained or out of control; it is the work of an energy always under domination, and of an art which never gives itself away.

A Selected Bibliography

I. In English:
Brombert, Victor, ed. *Stendhal: A Collection of Essays* (Englewood Cliffs: 1962).
Clewes, Howard, *Stendhal, An Introduction to the Novelist* (London, 1950).
Green, F. C., *Stendhal* (Cambridge, England, 1939).
Giraud, Raymond, *The Unheroic Hero in the Novels of Stendhal, Balzac, and Flaubert* (New Brunswick, N.J., 1957), pp. 53–92.
Huneker, James, *Egoists* (London, 1909), pp. 1–65.
Levin, Harry, *Toward Stendhal* (Murray, Utah, 1945), revised and reprinted as part of *The Gates of Horn* (New York, 1963), pp. 84–149.
O'Connor, Frank, *The Mirror in the Roadway* (London, 1957), pp. 42–57.
Turnell, Martin, *The Novel in France* (London, 1950), pp. 123–208.
Selections from the *Diaries* and *Letters* of Stendhal have been translated into English, the former by Robert Sage (New York, 1954), the latter by Norman Cameron (New York, 1952); most of the novels and *De L'Amour* are available in several different translations.

II. Works of Stendhal in French:
Three novels (*Armance, La Chartreuse de Parme, Le Rouge et le Noir*) plus *La Vie de Henry Brulard* and *De l'Amour* are available in the Classiques Garnier edition. As the splendid set of *Oeuvres complètes* put out by Le Divan is somewhat cumbersome for a private library (seventy-two volumes), the most handy and handsome set for practical use is that of the Bibliothèque de la Pléiade (four volumes so far and more to come).

III. Biographies and Biographical Studies in French:
Arbelet, Paul, *La Jeunesse de Stendhal* (Paris, 1919), 2 vols.
Benedetto, Luigi Foscolo, *Indiscrétions sur Giulia* (Paris, 1934)
Del Litto, Vittorio, *La vie de Stendhal* (Paris, 1965) is less a formal biography than a *récit*, with many illustrations, documents, etc.
—————— *La vie intellectuelle de Stendhal* (Paris, 1962)
—————— *Lettres à Stendhal, 1803–1806* (Paris, 1943), two vols.
Dutourd, Jean, *L'Ame sensible* (Paris, 1959), tr. Robin Chancellor (New York, 1961). A reprinting of Mérimée's memorial essay on Stendhal, with extensive commentaries.
Martineau, Henri, *Petit dictionnaire Stendhalien* (Paris, 1948)
—————— *Le calendrier de Stendhal* (Paris, 1950)
—————— *Le coeur de Stendhal* (Paris, 1952–53), two vols.
—————— *Cent soixante quatorze lettres à Stendhal, 1810–1842* (Paris, 1947), two vols.
Michel, François, *Fichier de Stendhal* (Boston, 1964) is not a formal biography but an immense collection of detailed materials toward a critical biography.

IV. Critical Studies, Books
Albérès, Francine Marill, *Le naturel chez Stendhal* (Paris, 1956)
—————— *Stendhal et le sentiment religieux* (Paris, 1956)
Aragon, Louis, *La lumière de Stendhal* (Paris, 1954); shrewd despite a communist bias.
Bardèche, Maurice, *Stendhal romancier* (Paris, 1947); shrewd despite a fascist bias.
Blum, Léon, *Stendhal et le Beylisme* (Paris, 1914); the best literary work by a future prime minister since Disraeli's *Vivian Gray*.
Brombert, Victor, *Stendhal et la voie oblique* (New Haven: 1954); particularly acute in analyzing Stendhal's authorial interventions.
Faguet, Emile, *Politiques et moralistes du 19e siècle*, 3e série (Paris, 1903), pp. 1–64.
Le Breton, André, *Le Rouge et le Noir de Stendhal, étude et analyse* (Paris, 1934).
Liprandi, Claude, *Au coeur du Rouge: l'affaire Lafargue* (Lausanne, 1961)
Sainte-Beuve, C. A., *Causeries du lundi*, XI (Paris, 1854), 301–41; a work of spite.
Trompeo, P.-P., *Nell'Italia romantica sulle orme di Stendhal* (Roma, 1924)

572 · *Bibliography*

V. Critical Studies, Essays

Several series of *Soirées du Stendhal-Club* (1905, ed. C. Stryienski; 1908, ed. Stryienski and Arbelet; 1950, ed. Martineau and Michel) provide delightful browsing. *Le Divan,* a quarterly publication edited by Martineau was for many years a center for Stendhal studies; at its demise in 1958, following Martineau's, it was succeeded by *Stendhal Club.* These periodicals provide a rich and happy hunting ground for students. Highly miscellaneous, of course, they are rarely unrewarding for any long stretch of time.

VI. A few other important articles which have appeared in the last few years are listed here:

Amer, Henry, "Amour, prison, et temps chez Stendhal," *Nouvelle Revue Française,* (March, 1962), pp. 483–90.

Barrère, J. B., "Stendhal et le chinois," in *Revue des sciences humaines,* new series, 92 (1958), pp. 437–61.

Bauer, Roger, "Julie et Julien, ou le problème du bonheur chez J. J. Rousseau et Stendhal," *Romanische Forschungen,* Vol. 65 (1954), pp. 378–91.

Starobinski, Jean, "Stendhal pseudonyme," *L'Oeil vivant* (Gallimard, 1961)

VII. Bibliography

Professor F. W. J. Hemmings' admirable volume, titled simply *Stendhal* (Oxford, 1964), contains (pp. 212–27) a copious working bibliography, with references to still more exhaustive and detailed bibliographies.

NORTON CRITICAL EDITIONS